Otis Tufton Mason

Primitive Travel and Transportation

Otis Tufton Mason

Primitive Travel and Transportation

ISBN/EAN: 9783337189198

Printed in Europe, USA, Canada, Australia, Japan

Cover: Foto ©Andreas Hilbeck / pixelio.de

More available books at **www.hansebooks.com**

SMITHSONIAN INSTITUTION.

UNITED STATES NATIONAL MUSEUM.

——— ·— ——.

PRIMITIVE TRAVEL AND TRANSPORTATION

BY

OTIS TUFTON MASON,

Curator, Department of Ethnology, U. S. National Museum.

· ·

————

From the Report of the U. S. National Museum for 1894, pages 237–593, with plates 1–25 and figures 1–260.

————

WASHINGTON:
GOVERNMENT PRINTING OFFICE.
1896.

TABLE OF CONTENTS.

PRIMITIVE TRAVEL AND TRANSPORTATION.

By Otis Tufton Mason,

Curator, Department of Ethnology, U. S. National Museum.

GENERAL STATEMENT.

Invention has to do with the resources and forces of nature applied to human weal. In the earth, the waters, and the air, in the composite activity of the sun, in cosmic matter and powers little understood, are to be found the materials and servants by whose ministrations the cunning spirit of man effects those artificialities of life and culture which constitute the body of human industries, æsthetic arts, languages, social life, commerce, philosophies, and cults.

The complete account of the human species acquiring the resources of nature and dominating and understanding her forces is the history of culture.

The human species has approached, and in its best estate does now approach, the material resources of the earth under the impulse of five sets of motives, to wit:

(1) To explore, secure, and domesticate them.

(2) To change their form, to manufacture them.

(3) To move them and themselves artificially.

(4) To exchange, measure, and value them.

(5) To consume or to enjoy them.

The progress of the world started with these five primitive, fundamental activities. It is the purpose of the present publication to consider the third class, in their earliest forms and in relation to the others, so far as they are illustrated in the U. S. National Museum.

The manipulation of the material resources of nature involves in the second place the knowledge, the domestication, and the training of force or power, which may be thus set forth in its sources, epochs, and sciences.

Power of—	Epoch of—	Science.
1. Man	The hand	Anthropokinetics.
2. Beast	Domestication	Zookinetics.
3. Elastic springs	War and hunting	Elaterokinetics.
4. Fire	Mastery	Thermokinetics or pyrokinetics.
5. Wind	The sail	Anemokinetics.
6. Water	Rude machines	Hydrokinetics.
7. Steam	Machinery	Atmokinetics.
8. Chemism	Scientific industry	Chemykinetics.
9. Electricity	Ideal invention in speech light, and motion.	Electrokinetics.
10. Light	Cosmic invention	Photokinetics.

Among these sources of motion or motors it will be quickly noted that the first two derive their activity from animal muscle, the rest through some sort of device that takes the place of the human body. It will also be understood that for the purposes of invention the powers or forces may again be divided into two classes, the first being man power, the second class including all the rest enumerated. All artificial work goes back to man, all work is imitation of man's work, the primitive form of every moving device is the human body.[1]

Nature furnishes ready motive power in moving air and water. All other forms of mechanical motion, not excepting muscular power, require the application of heat, and this is obtained through combustion.

The mechanical nomenclature of all language is largely derived from the bodies of animals. Thus in English we have the head of a ship, river, lake, jetty, bolt, etc.; the brow of an incline; the crown of an arch; the toe of a pier; the foot of a wall; the forefoot, heel, ribs, waist, knees, skin, nose, and dead eyes of a ship; also turtlebacks and whalebacks; the jaws of a vice; the claws of a clutch; the teeth of wheels; necks, shoulders, eyes, nozzles, legs, ears, mouths, lips, cheeks, elbows, feathers, tongues, throats, and arms; caps, bonnets, collars, sleeves, saddles, gussets, paddles, fins, wings, crabs, horns, donkeys, monkeys, and dogs; flywheels, running nooses, crane necks, grasshopper engines, etc.[2]

The use of these natural forces and their application in the five great classes of industry above named gradually led invention to the discovering or devising of mechanical powers, to sacrifice time in order to overcome resistance too great for individual effort, to secure the cooperation of many persons or animals in one work, and to make effective the forces just mentioned in ways innumerable. The mechanical

---

[1] Cf. J. H. Cooper, Iconographic Encyclopedia, VI, p. 193, and the author's work on the "Origins of Invention," London, 1894.

[2] Cf. Jeremiah Head, Rep. Brit. Assoc., 1893, p. 862.

powers, in short, make possible the differentiation of employment and the organized cooperation which constitute a higher grade of industry.

The mechanical powers, as they are called, seem to have come into vogue in the following order:

(1) The weight, for hammers, traps, and pressure: later on for machinery.

(2) The elastic spring, in bows, traps, machines.

(3) Inclined and declined plane, in locomotion and transportation.

(4) The lever, of all kinds.

(5) The wedge, in riving and tightening.

(6) The sled, on snow or prepared tracks.

(7) The roller, for loads and in machine bearings.

(8) The wheel, in travel and carriage.

(9) Wheel and axle in many forms.

(10) Pulleys, with or without sheaves.

(11) Twisting, shrinking, and clamping devices.

(12) The screw.

It will be observed that for working with the forces enumerated, with or without the mechanical powers, tools and utensils are necessary in order to break, pierce, divide, unite, contain, move, and hold fast materials, and to make it possible for work to be done. In another publication the author will discuss the aboriginal American mechanic and his industries, so it is not necessary here to enlarge upon this intricate subject. Suffice it to say that not only every tool, but device for transportation and work, includes three distinct parts, to wit:

(1) The working part, which does the moving, breaking, battering, chipping, abrading, polishing, cutting, perforating, and so on. This portion of all appliances maintains a remarkably conservative plan of functioning. In the sled, for instance, or the sailing craft, the line and curve of runners or the strakes have undergone little change. The material and manipulation of the mechanical powers have changed amazingly, but no one can alter the modus operandi or the equation of any one of them.

(2) The manual part, or that connected with the human body or other prime mover that takes its place. The functioning part of a machine, to repeat, changes little, but the narrative of the harness of the motor or motive power constitutes the history of machinery. A very old-fashioned wagon differs from the latest freight train chiefly in the intricate engine and expensive track. The difference between a kaiak, with ribs of driftwood and skin of seal hide, and a cruiser, with ribs and skin of steel, is in the mode of pushing them through the water.

(3) The attachment or attaching devices of tools and machines. In the woman's knife the blade is wedged, glued, or tied into the handle. In the sled the dog and the sled are made one by hooks, toggles, frogs, etc. This subject of binding, uniting, attaching, detaching,

can not be overlooked in the study of travel and transportation. Its relation to progressive culture, to geography, and climate is most interesting. It will be seen in the progress of this study that environment, grades of culture, and tribal idiosyncrasies may be excellently differentiated thereby.

Again, with each art goes a series of devices which may be classed under the general name of receptacles, their only functions being to contain other perishable or precious or fragile things. The sewing woman has her housewife, the artisan his tool chest, and every one his pockets. In the travel and transportation arts these containers go by

a thousand names. The general term "package," however, has been adopted to include them all. The carrying trade has introduced an enormous variety of devices for packing and enriched the vocabulary with such words as barrel, box, pint, quart, peck, bushel, cask, bag, sack, crate, hamper, hogshead, and tierce. Furthermore, the conveniences of packing, as well as strength for transport, has reduced many of these words to standards of measure and fixed the metrics of carrying; such words as barrel, tub, firkin, and load have definite meanings of contents gauged by the carrier and now by law. These devices are sometimes permanent, but oftener thrown away at the end of the journey.

Among the inventions upon which ethnic and geographic traits are fastened the packages should be carefully studied. It is these that in the present enormous commerce are counterfeited for the purpose of gain and fraud. W. R. Carles represents a Korean peasant woman not only bearing a burden on the head, done up in somewhat local fashion, but she has under her left arm a number of eggs wrapped in straw and looking not unlike strings of sausage[1] (fig. 1).

Fig. 1.

KOREAN WOMAN TOTING MEAL AND CARRYING EGGS.

From a figure in Carles's "Life in Korea."

The modifications of all human phenomena that are the product of invention are far-reaching. They include changes—

(1) In the things invented or products of invention, commonly called inventions.

(2) In all the materials, processes, and apparatus involved.

(3) In the mental condition and powers of the inventor.

(4) In the rewards and benefits of the invention.

(5) In society, resulting from the invention.

---

[1] See figure on p. 63, "Life in Korea," New York, 1894, Macmillan & Co.

These changes have been very marked under the influence of travel and the carrying trade. A palace train does not resemble a savage woman's baby frame greatly, neither is a huge steamer like the sack on the back of a roustabout. The bustle of making and moving the former in each case is vastly greater. As for rewards, the savage woman gets nothing beyond a little easing of her load, and the rouster receives a few cents a day. The intellectual impulses in the beginning or copying stage and the ending or creative stage of an epoch-making invention differ in speed and momentum. And, as for the changes in society, nothing has contributed more to that end than beasts of burden and traction, ships and railroad trains.

Yet the old transportation survives everywhere and obtrudes itself into the new. The most costly steamer is compelled by law to carry for each passenger a little life-preserver as rude as that on which the Assyrian soldier floated himself across a stream, and trains must always have on board folk-appliances.

Among the negro population of Africa and in other savage communities carrying is a fine art. Fletcher and Kidder represent a woman bearing at the same time freight on her head and steadying it with the right hand, while she sustains her child on the lumbar region, wrapped in her shawl, and supported by the left hand.

All the changes of exploiting nature's resources, forces, and powers—of the art of inventing—have followed the laws of progress from—

(1) Naturism to greater and greater artificiality.
(2) Simplicity or monorganism to complexity or polyorganism.
(3) Clumsiness to delicacy and economy.
(4) Discomfort to comfort.
(5) Solitary work to cooperation.
(6) Individual weal to common weal.

All of these laws apply to each class of work in the Patent Office, and it will be seen there that the number of patents concerned with the working out of this scheme in traveling devices is very great.

From this point of view the climax of invention in any line of activity, individual or social, is the intentional and cooperative application of all knowledge to the production of new tools, machines, words, fine arts, social structures, and philosophies. This purposeful and systematic devising is the climax of the process. But in the beginning it was not so. Industries, fine arts, languages, social structures, and beliefs almost created themselves, but each had in its processes and results the germs and becomings of all future human achievements.

The relations of each element above mentioned in each class of notions to the earth as it is constituted rather than to the earth as a homogeneous unit can not be neglected. In no class of human activities is the careful study of geography more demanded. This is so true that if the clothing, shoes, pack, and appliances of a traveler or porter be laid before a student of this subject, he will be able to describe with tolerable accuracy the region or culture area, its temperature, weather, geographic features, and productions.[1]

Now every substance and thing before mentioned scarcely ever exists at first where it is needed or is used up where it is first taken. The same is true of what is made out of those, and what is made out of these secondary, tertiary, and further products, the result of each activity being the groundwork of another. None of them is wanted where it is produced. Hence the locomotive activity is a kind of middle trade in the most comprehensive and varied sense, a go-between and a carry-between for them all ad infinitum.

Hence the endless running to and fro of men and women, covering in a single day fifty times the distance from the sun and back again. The miner, the quarryman, the gem collector; the gleaner, the lumberman, and the farmer of every type; the hunter, the fisherman, and herdsman, all have to go and to haul all sorts of things to their work, before they deliver the goods to the manufacturer. After endless goings, carryings, and haulings about the establishment, the transportation has scarcely begun. The products must go away by land or by water, either to some other manufacturer to be further modified, or they must hie away to the centers of shipment; and thence, after having been lifted and lugged again and again, these products in new packages are ready for a journey to the seats of commerce; first of wholesale, then of retail. Now begin the little carryings of the endless procession of shoppers and porters. There would hardly seem to be anything else to do but to go and fetch.

The carrying industry not only acts as middleman between all other activities, but in its operations it absorbs a great deal of the life of the others. The mineral kingdom is the roadbed of water, snow, and earth over which locomotion passes. The inventor has not been idle in changing them for the historic evolution of the carrying art. The vegetable kingdom, in its forms of textile and timber, have always been indispensable to the mechanism of transportation. Animal products appear in receptacles, bone ware, rawhide lines, and a million kinds of leather bags. The building of baby cradles, carrying frames, wagons, boats, saddles, cars, not to mention clothing of special material and pattern for this industry, occupy thousands of men and women. Now in the primitive status the same person may in his life play many of these parts, or all the parts necessary. But these activities have to be performed by somebody always. It would be perfectly safe to say that every trade on earth did some specialized work for the traveler and common carrier.

The three kingdoms of nature have been man's teachers. The very conduct of the earth, the waters, the air has provoked him to movement and transporting. The powers of nature keep the solid earth on

[1] See Hahn's Map of Plant Industries, Petermann's Mittheilungen, Jan., 1892; Proc. Roy. Geog. Soc., XIV, p. 182.

the move, and the surface material, with all human beings, are impelled along. Every thing that floats in the water is an object lesson in locomotion. The winds drive the clouds, which go away never to return; it scatters the leaves, and brings the snow or the summer.

The living kingdoms are more instructive and suggestive. The beaver, the bird, the lamprey eel, the ant, and the bee are all industrious carriers. Their perseverance and strength amaze the modern engineer. In a certain sense they were the instructors of man in the arts of travel and transportation. There are those who emphasize these facts to the great disparagement of our species. But after all it is the genius of invention which appropriates, dominates, and utilizes the whole world. It is true that they can be taught a little discretion in such matters. Jeremiah Head tells us that the donkey at Carisbrooke

Fig. 2.

DONKEY CARRYING WATER JARS IN CRATE.

From a photograph in the U. S. National Museum, by Rev. E. F. X. Cleveland.

castle draws water from a deep well by a treadmill arrangement just as well as a man could do it. He watches the rope on the barrel till the full pail rises above the parapet of the well, then slacks back a little to allow it to be rested thereon, and only then leaves the drum and retreats to the stable.[1]

Bearing on the head had a different effect on the ceramic art from that of burden bearing on the back or on beasts (fig. 2). The former is illustrated in the modern pitcher, with handle on the side, with the bulge near the bottom to bring the center of gravity as low down as possible, with the bottom concave, and often fitted with an extra rim, the lineal descendant of the carrier's head pad. There are features of the pitcher which have been occasioned by other than carrying motives, but the forms had the origin here described.

[1] Rep. Brit. Assoc., 1893, p. 861.

All handles and rims have their original motive in the carrying activity, and these elements when made decorative are survivals from the utilitarian epoch of the thing. Doubtless, carrying devices in dugout stems, in pottery, and in hard textiles had as their natural prototypes objects which could be utilized with little modification. But it is also true that the genius of modification is the most marked human characteristic. The gourd with the receding bottom may be the prototype of the jar of the same form. It is also doubtless true that Sandwich Islanders selected the seeds of those gourds that had the most convenient carrying form, and these seeds were planted as a matter of course. After the same motive there are examples from various peoples of tying strings about gourds to give attachment to the carrying strap. This form is imitated in pottery and basketry after it had been worked out in gourd culture.

The illustration here given (pl. 1) is from a photograph in the U. S. National Museum, taken by Hillers, of the Geological Survey. The woman rests the water jar on the head, without the pad, and the concave bottom shows how at the behest of the woman's comfort the shape of the vessel has been modified. The dark band at the bottom is the boundary line of what would be the bottom ring of the sling if one were there.

Upon this artistic side the history of human movements over the earth and of the journeys which its productions have taken at the bidding and for the comfort of our species is like an enchanted dream. It is as though many ages back a naked man had started out in the world and was now returning clothed in all the earth's finest fabrics, the winds, the ocean currents, fire and lightning rowing his boat or drawing his chariot. Through what experiences this one man must have passed to be in himself the epitome of all pedestrians, riders, and carriers and to have used every vehicle and sailing craft that ever existed.

Traffic in its complexity and changes is also characterized by its noises. Surely the quiet peon urging his way along his lonely path is very different from the roar, the din, the rattle, the bells, the whistles one hears on Cortlandt street. The latter is a kind of Wagnerian symphony of transportation, in which discord heightens the harmony.

Primitive commerce and all the carrying and running involved in primeval arts connected with food, shelter, clothing, rest, enjoyment, news carrying, and war were accomplished on the heads or foreheads, shoulders or backs, or in the hands of men and women; and civilization, while it has invented many ways of burden bearing, finds also an endless variety of uses for the old methods. How many thousands of our fellow-creatures are still in this condition of mere beasts of burden! It is, for instance, only a few years since the invention of the passenger and freight elevator began to supplant that train of "hod carriers," who have been since the beginning of architecture bearing

EXPLANATION OF PLATE 1.

ZUÑI WOMAN CARRYING WATER.

The water jar among the Pueblo Indians performs a double function; namely, for carrying and for storage.

Carrying water on the head, and not on a beast or in a sling or canteen, requires the bottom of the jar to be either round and accompanied with a sustaining pad for the head and for the ground, or to be concave on the bottom, as in this plate. In most examples of Pueblo pottery the decorations are pictorial and symbolical.

Jars with concave bottoms are extremely rare in ancient American collections, but carrying with the headband is in vogue from Smith Sound to Patagonia. It is possible, therefore, that the method here figured is post-Columbian.

The woman is partly dressed for the occasion in blankets of her own handiwork in dark blue, red, and white wool, and adorned with a silver necklace made by a native jeweler. Her leggings are for out-of-door work. The sole of the moccasin has attached to it for the "upper" an entire deerskin, and as the old footing wears out, it is renewed at the sacrifice of the top, which constantly decreases in size. The upper is neatly doubled and wrapped about the limb. The carrying of water for all purposes was an unremitting task with the ancient cliff and mesa dwellers.

ZUÑI WOMAN CARRYING WATER.
From a photograph in the U. S. National Museum.

upward to its completion every wooden and brick structure in the world.

To get something like an adequate conception of the enormous amount of labor performed by human backs, calculate the weight of every earth-work, mound, fort, canal, embankment, wooden, brick, metal, and stone structure and fabrication on earth. These have all been carried many times and elevated by human muscle. In the light of this contemplation, Atlas, son of Heaven and Earth, supporting on his shoulders the pillars of the sky, is the apotheosis of the human son of toil, and the gaping wonder of archæologists over the hand-made structures of Thebes, Palenque, Carnac, and Salisbury Plain subsides to the level of a mathematical problem. Indeed, the great majority of earthworks, mounds, menhirs, cairns, cromlechs, dolmens, and megalithic structures now to be seen witnessed the exertions of no other artisan than the human carrier and mover.[1]

The traffic by land and by sea has grown tenfold since 1850. The carrying trade is at present one of the chief occupations of men, as may be seen by the numbers employed on railways and in seagoing shipping.

	Railways.	Shipping.	Total.
Europe	1,540,000	550,000	2,090,000
United States	874,000	60,000	934,000
Other countries	480,000	95,000	575,000
Total	2,894,000	705,000	3,599,000

The gross receipts of the carrying trade in which the above men are employed amount to about £650,000,000 sterling per annum.[2]

The incentives to going about and transportation are:

(1) The necessity of food and comfort, the daily round.

(2) The procurement of tools and materials necessary to the getting and preparing of the food and comforts of life, herding and droving.

(3) Fear and desire for quiet, individual and social.

(4) Love of conquest, the movements of hordes.

(5) Desire to see and know what is beyond, exploration and intelligence.

(6) Gold and other rare treasures, prospecting.

(7) Religious pilgrimage.

(8). Involuntary movements.

---

[1] For illustrations of women as beasts of burden, see the author's work, "Woman's Share in Primitive Culture," New York, 1894, chapter VI; Schoolcraft, History, etc., of the Indian tribes of the United States, VI, plate opposite p. 560; Wood, "Uncivilized Races," I, p. 330 et seq.; Lucien Carr, "Mounds of the Mississippi Valley," and Isaac McCoy, "Coal Carriers in the West Indies," for calculation of the time required to build an earth mound.

[2] Mulhall, Contemp. Rev., 1894, p. 820.

Between the gratification centers are often long, cheerless spaces to be crossed and to increase the journey.

In the satisfaction of these cravings the whole earth was occupied long ago by unlettered peoples. They walked most of the way; they swam and paddled in shallow waters; they followed the fishes, the birds, the mammals, the streams, the winds, the voices innumerable within them. No modern Crusoe has failed to see in the shore-sands the footprints of those fearless pedestrians and guideless sailors who in the darkness of human ignorance felt their way to nearly every corner of the world.

The great forests never supported large aboriginal populations. There is a continuous tract north of the St. Lawrence, in Quebec and Ontario, extending to Hudson Bay and Labrador, 1,700 miles in length from east to west and 1,000 miles from north to south. Another tract lies in Washington State and British Columbia. A third occupies the valley of the Amazon, embracing much of northern Brazil, eastern Peru, Bolivia, Ecuador, Colombia, and Guiana—a region 2,100 miles long by 1,300 wide. In Africa, in the valley of the Kongo, including the head waters of the Nile to the northeast and those of the Zambesi on the south, is a forest region not less than 3,000 miles from north to south and of vast width from east to west. In Siberia, from the plains of Obi to the valley of the Indigirka, embracing the valleys of the Yenisei, Olenek, Lena, and Yana, is a timber belt more than 1,000 miles from north to south and a length of 3,000 miles from east to west. In Yenisei, Lena, and Olenek are thousands of square miles where no human being has ever lived.[1] The same is true of arid regions. To keep the tribes of men in fraternal or inimical contact and to enable the progressive races to enjoy the fruits of the whole earth these uninhabitable regions had to be traversed. First they discouraged, then they demanded locomotion.

Bandelier says: "In every age gold has presented one of the strongest means of enticing men from their homes to remote lands, and of promoting trade between distant regions and the settlement of previously uninhabited districts."[2]

It has been previously intimated that one of the results of all inventions is the profound modification of society. In a special sense, society has had to adapt itself to the travel and traffic art. No two areas of the earth are alike in resources. Quite the contrary, all habitable places superabound in some requisite of human existence, some raw material, or spring, or good landing place, or sunny exposure, or source of power, or pasture land. The extreme variety of physiographic characteristics set agoing the activities we call traffic. Note that each

---

[1] From the Youth's Companion.

[2] "The Gilded Man," New York, 1893, D. Appleton & Co., mentions on page 1, the Argonauts, Hercules seeking the golden apples of the Hesperides, the settlement of the Phœnicians in Spain, and the journeys to Ophir.

little group or family has had its daily round of cares and then lain down to rest; the feet were tired as well as the hands. A day's journey for all this group combined is the family round of activity.

Note again, that this little group in the course of a year has a succession of seasons, and then the circle returns into itself. There is the hunting month, the fishing month, the planting month, the hoeing month, the berry month, and so on, till the year is exhausted. The amount of going, no matter where, of the whole group is the circle of annual activity.

In the third place, it is almost impossible for one of these little groups in its daily round and annual circle to be so shut off from the rest of mankind as not to come in contact with other groups beyond their territory, and they carry on war or trade with them, mutually invading and being invaded. The total of all contacts let us call the sphere of influence or of contact.

Again, there is an outside world, of which our group has heard, and in former years their ancestors moved in a part of it. Some of their own men have been there and relate marvelous stories on their return. The memory of the outside world is treasured up in story or myth or song, or acted in the tribal drama. They will tell in the southland of the place where there is neither sun nor trees and the people make their boats of sea-monsters' skins. Or perhaps there may be in western America the tale of a country where the trees are hollow.

At any rate, ethnologists do not know of a time when there was not a deal of moving about over the earth and going away from home and returning, or of getting into a great highway or gulf stream of travel. These journeyings became world encompassing at the close of the fifteenth century of our era. These movings may be called the streams of human commerce and acquaintance.

Finally, there is a heritage of experience and wisdom, a commerce of inventive thought, moving over the globe ever like the currents of the atmosphere. Temperatures, rainfalls, winds, hygienic conditions, depend upon the air currents. But here it is meant that there are thought movements into which and out of which our group may get themselves to modify or to crystallize their activities, their modes of travel and commerce especially. The social life of a people in its goings therefore includes—

(1) Their daily round of actions from bed to bed.

(2) Their annual circle of activities from year to year.

(3) The sphere of influence or outside relations.

(4) The streams of commerce, their contact with them.

(5) The currents of intellectual force, more or less continuous in time and place.

Mr. Ravenstein gives from Russian sources an interesting account of the manner in which the Orochons (Tungus stock) on the upper Amur spend their hunting year. In March they go on snowshoes over snow, into which, at that season, cloven-footed animals sink, and shoot elks, roe, and musk deer, wild deer and goats; the tent being fixed in valleys and defiles where the snow lies deepest. In April the ice on the rivers begin to move, and the huntsman, now turned fisherman, hastens to the small rivulets to net his fish. Those not required for immediate use are dried against the next month, which is one of the least plentiful in the year. In May they shoot deer and other game, which they have decoyed to certain spots by burning down the high grass in the valleys so that the young sprouts may attract the deer and goats. June supplies the hunter with antlers of the roe. These they sell at a high price to the Chinese for medicinal purposes. The Chinese merchants come north in this month, bringing tea, tobacco, salt, pow-der, lead, grain, butter, etc., so that a successful huntsman is then able to provide himself with necessaries for half the year. In July the natives spend a large part of the month catching fish, taken with nets or speared with harpoons. They are able also to spear the elk, which likes a water plant growing in the lakes. It comes down at night, wades into the water, and, while engaged tearing at the plant with its teeth, is killed by the huntsman. In August they catch birds, speared at night in the retired creeks and bays of the river and lakes. Their flesh, except that of the swan, is eaten, and the down is exchanged for ear and finger rings, bracelets, beads, and the like. Thus they spend the summer months, afterwards retiring again to the mountains for game. In the beginning of September they prepare for winter pursuits. The leaves are falling, and it is the season when the roebuck and the doe are courting. The natives avail themselves of this, and by cleverly imitat-ing the call of the doe on a wooden horn entice the buck near enough to shoot him. Generally speaking, this is the plentiful season of the year so far as flesh is concerned; but, should the hunters not be fortu-nate, they live upon service berries and bilberries, which they mix with reindeer milk. They also eat the nuts of the Manchu cedar and of the dwarf-like Cembra pine. The latter part of September and the beginning of October are again employed in fishing, for the fish then ascend the river to spawn. About the middle of October begins the hunting of fur-bearing animals, the most profitable of all game, and this goes on till the end of the year.[1] .

Speaking of the town of Leh in Kashmir as a center and exhibition ground of travel and traffic, Mrs. Bishop says that great caravans en route for Khotan, Yarkand, and Chinese Tibet arrived daily from Kash-mir, Panjab, and Afghanistan and stacked their goods in the place; the Lhasa traders opened shops for sale of brick tea and implements of worship; merchants from Amritsar, Cabul, Bokhara, and Yarkand opened bales of costly goods; mules, asses, horses, and yaks kicked and squealed and bellowed. There were mendicant monks, Indian fakirs, Moslem dervishes, Mecca pilgrims, itinerant musicians, and Buddhist

---

[1] Lansdell, "Through Siberia," Boston, 1882, pp. 509–510.

ballad howlers. Women with creels on their backs brought in lucerne. Ladakhis, Baltis, and Lahulis tended the beasts. Lhasa traders exchanged tea for Nubra and Baltistan dried apricots, Kashmir saffron, and rich stuffs from India. Yarkand merchants on big horses of Turkestan offer hemp for smoking in exchange for Russian stuff.[1]

Speaking of globe trotting, Vambery says: "We must mention the slender thread of correspondence maintained by single pilgrims or beggars from the most hidden parts of Turkestan with the remotest parts of Asia. Nothing is more interesting than these vagabonds, who leave their native nests without a farthing in their pockets to journey for thousands of miles in countries of which they previously hardly know the names, and among natives entirely different from their own in physiognomy, laws, and customs."[2]

For each one of these movements there is a center about which the activity revolves. At first it is a purely natural or supply center. Such a state of life could not long exist, so artificial centers take the place of natural ones. A spring of water and not the hunting or fishing ground attracts the group. In higher life the civic center is the climax of this process.

In the industrial world, as a whole, there are centers of supply or natural material regions and areas. These come to be, as every one knows, social centers of manufacture, of exchange, and even of consuming and enjoying. Transportation centers, distributing centers, crossroad centers of social structure and activity have always existed also. Now these civic centers grow more and more to be a reality, until the modern city has six zones, not circular in their outline but having social and economical boundaries, namely:

(1) The central nucleus or governing place and regulative body. The city hall, the citadel, the capitol, conveys the idea.

(2) The busy mart, where going is the duty. In point of fact everything is in motion there.

(3) The homes of the industrious, the thrifty, the well to do—in short, the residence zone. There is more travel there and going to and fro about it than one might first suspect.

(4) The slums, the aftermath of savagery, where a portion of society goes to seed, to ruin.

(5) The garden zone, where the waste of the city and proximity to market makes it possible to get the best soil effects with least effort and greatest profits.

(6) The farmer zone, in fact a zone of thrift, and outside of that a zone of unthrift, from which all natural supply, fertility, and resources are gradually exhausted and carried to the industrial center to be used up, and little or nothing comes back to it. It is as though the soil had moved into town and left away out on the confines a broad ring of no

[1] "Among the Tibetans," Chicago, 1894, p. 60.
[2] "Travel in Central Asia," New York, 1865, p. 459.

man's land. This is what every eye gazes on at each moment of the day. All moving feet and beasts, trains, and boats are engaged in constructing one of these civic rings. The small centers are only like our little group; the large centers, like London or New York, are world-embracing. They rule the world, their trade is with all mankind, their good people are cosmopolitan, their vices are those of the whole race from the birth of time; hundreds of smaller civic centers minister to them and are enriched by them, and the four corners of the earth concentrate their productions there.

The map of the world has undergone wonderful changes in this regard in historic times in the location of these centers of commercial circulation, and the kind of roads that radiate therefrom, as well as in the character of the forces and vehicles involved. It would be an absorbing study for one to trace these centers, and to note the changes in roads and vehicles, but the subject of this paper relates entirely to the primitive centers and routes before there was a wheel conveyance on earth.

Burden bearing, in addition to this general participation in the creation of artificial industrial centers and great civic groups, has created special phases of society. Legislation has had no small trouble in regulating the laws of travel and trade, of interstate and international commerce. Citizens who go abroad and who traffic have been the occasion of no end of diplomatic correspondence and even of war. Those engaged in travel and transportation have themselves always had their rules, societies, corporations, organized service, and trades unions. Savage no less than civilized men travel and trade by route and by rule.

The carrying activity and trade are most intimately associated with slavery. It is not time yet to say that it was thus allied more than with other arts, nor that it was most confined thereto. Looking at the movements of men and women, the porters, roustabouts, coal stokers, and carriers are even now the most abject and hardest worked of servants. The women and captives in America did the carrying as the peons do now. In Africa the backs of slaves are the vehicles of travelers and of merchandise. The southern and southeastern Asiatic is himself a beast of burden, and so has it always been.

The complete study of this topic is full of interest to the ethnologist as well as to the technologist. It has had its ethnic elaboration as well as its industrial evolution. No less does each tribe and people of the earth have its bodily structure, manufactures, art, speech, and social life than it has its own artificial conveyances and ways of getting about and carrying. To speak after the manner of the naturalist, the species of such inventions are tribal, national, and racial.

One can hardly fail to discover in a study of this sort how much its phases enter into the æsthetic arts and pleasures of mankind. Going for the sake of going, sailing in unknown waters, visiting new lands and gazing on new skies are now and always have been ruling motives in the wills of men. The landscape gardener constructs his varied effects about meandering roads and paths; the most stirring and costly music is martial; moving scenes of men and beasts and stately ships cover the painter's canvas and sculptor's slab; we ransack the earth for a new perfume or delicious fruit. Finally, mythology and the stories of all mysterious beings begin and end with recounting their works and travels. The sky is full of paths and trails. Charon's boat bears the souls of men abroad. The obsequies of the dead are a preparation for journeying barefooted. Atlas uplifts the world over on his broad neck and back. The Caryatides are the apotheosis of all patient women porters.

An American example of Atlas type is the stone chair of Guayaquil (fig. 3). A man on all fours supports a curved seat on his back. The whole is cut from a single block of stone.[1]

In Polynesian phrase: "As I hope to escape perdition, Whakatauroa is the basket wherein rests the pillar of the earth. Its strap is Rangiwha-kaokoa." · This saying is applied to the world. Its meaning is: If the basket had not

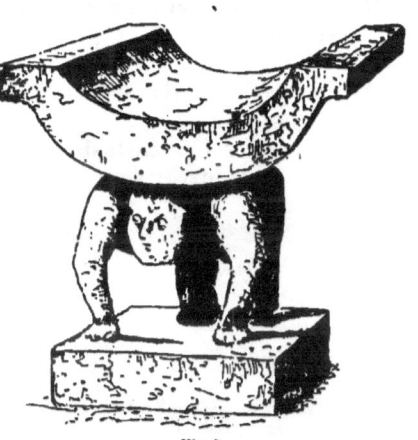

Fig. 3.

CHAIR OF SANDSTONE FROM GUAYAQUIL, PERU.

From a figure in Wiener's " Pérou et Bolivie."

been placed as a support for the pillar, the earth would have moved to and fro over the surface of the waters, and would have sunk therein; there would have been no resting place for the being called mau, or anything else, or for anything which lives. When the overwhelming earthquake comes, the pillar is there in the basket; however great the quaking, the pillar is firm. By means of the head strap the basket is able to carry the pillar: were it not for that, the end would not be attained. There are, however, other uses of the strap as well.[2]

The activities here treated embrace all that may be included in the word "locomotion," or essentially all traveling, carrying, or being carried. The words traveler, freight, and passenger make the group of industries sufficiently plain. All human inventions begin with natural objects little modified, so the locomotive activities have their rise in merely going or carrying and being carried without inter-

[1] Wiener, " Pérou et Bolivie," Paris, pp. 522-523.

[2] Hare Hongi, "Contest between Fire and Water." Journ. Polynesian Soc., III, No. 3, p. 156.

mediate apparatus. Furthermore, while the aboriginal mineralogist, botanist, and zoologist wander about at random and do not care ever to repeat the trail, this desultory and trackless wandering soon gives place to efforts to go over the same journey even upon the water. The uses of hands and head and shoulders, and especially the feet, for journeying and transporting, and all the inventions for making these convenient and cooperative, together with the fixing and preparing of ways to facilitate them, united constitute the industry of travel and transportation.

This subject naturally divides itself into land travel and water travel. But these two can not always be separated. In the present paper, however, attention will be given to the former, which may be thus classified:

(1) Going afoot, including the study of special costumes and appliances occasioned thereby.

(2) Man as a carrier and in drawing loads. This chapter will treat of the two aspects of carrying, namely, riding and freighting, and will consider the beginnings of harness, as applied to the human body.

Fig. 4.

MEN RIDING, LEADING, AND DRAGGING.

From a figure in Whymper's "Great Andes of the Equator."

(3) The domestication of animals for riding beasts, packing beasts, and for traction.

(4) The origin of the road, of trails, routes, conveniences on the road, foot bridges and the beginnings of engineering.

(5) Subsidiary activities, signals, food, time keeping, receptacles, trade, stimulants, slavery.

This study will be chiefly from an objective point of view, and will be largely based on the collections in the U. S. National Museum and such other material as may be helpful thereto.

Whymper gives a little figure which in a small space comprehends all that is included in this paper (fig. 4). In the rear, as he should be, is a man painfully bearing and dragging a number of poles—burden and draft beast in one. His load is a sled without snow, a cart without wheels, a travois in which the man is the dog. Ahead of him a man is walking and leading a pack mule. This is a step higher in culture, in the epoch of domestication and breeding. In the man's hand is a whip, which bears the same relation to the firebrand that industrialism does to militancy. In front a man, possibly Mr. Whymper, rides on a mule, representing the highest grade in culture of the era of biological force, of the hand and beast.[1]

---

[1] Whymper, "Great Andes of the Equator," New York, 1892, Scribner's Sons, p. 19.

TRAVELING ON FOOT.

In the exercise of the function of traveler, men use their inventive powers to render their traveling structures more effective in going faster, in going farther, in going to places inaccessible to them in a state of nature, in going in groups, and with greater ease and comfort, and in going for longer periods. One of the elements of progressive culture is the multiplication of the necessities of travel.

Bush says of the Giliaks. " We could not make them understand that all our supplies would be required for the journey, as they carry little while traveling." [1]

The first consideration in this study of man as a traveler and a burden bearer is his body as an instrument or apparatus to this end. Structurally this investigation includes—

(1) The skeleton, its versatility and strength.
(2) The muscular system.
(3) The vital parts in reference to these.

Functionally the student would have to regard the activities of—

(1) Walking, running, swimming, diving, etc.
(2) Lifting and carrying.
(3) Pulling and hauling.
(4) Pushing and forcing.

In the case of migratory birds and fishes, the habit is explained by saying that they have endowments of locomotion that fit and impel them to be going. In harmony with this instinct of going, this irresistible attraction, are the exigencies of desire and supply. The environment without and the nature within conspire.

It is reasonable to suppose that in the conduct of men, the actual possession of the whole earth, their capabilities, attributes, wants, inherited proclivities are coupled with structure specially adapted to the conduct. When the cosmopolitan structure of man is considered, the domination of the earth is the legitimate functioning of his wonderful organism.[2]

Professor Munro has said that, as the quadrupedal animals became more highly differentiated, it followed that the limbs became also modified, so as to make them suitable not only for locomotion in various circumstances, but also useful to the animal economy in other ways, as swimming, flying, climbing, grasping, etc. But no animal, with the exception of man, has ever succeeded in divesting the fore limbs altogether of their primary function.[3] What a profound fact is this in the industry here considered, both in getting about and carrying at the same time. The erect position provides the diversified requisites for the versatile walker and burden bearer in one person. Indeed, it may be said that the erect position was effected by and through the carrying art.

[1] "Reindeer, Dogs, and Snowshoes," New York, 1871, p. 125.
[2] Cf. Baker, "The Ascent of Man," American Anthropologist, Oct., 1890.
[3] Cf. Rep. Brit. Assoc., Nottingham, 1893, p. 886.

(1) In the very act of progressing and supporting a load the erect position achieves the maximum of result with the minimum of effort.

(2) The fore limbs are set free from walking, climbing, flying, swimming, and all sorts of leg work, so that they may have all their time to lift and carry, to push and pull, to move themselves and objects in directions innumerable.

(3) The freeing of the fore limbs has thus been accompanied by such structural modification of them that they may hold on, balance, grasp, a handle or rope, put a burden on the head, or shoulder (fig. 5) or back, hold it in place, act singly and independently at diametrically opposite functions, or cooperate in a diversity of actions to produce and vary motion or overcome resistance.

(4) The erect position and the modifications of structure involved make it possible for so feeble a creature as man to bear great loads on the head, shoulders, back of the neck, hips, knees, breast, and arms,

and to vary their position while himself in motion. Upon this point Professor Munro says that everybody knows how much labor can be saved by attention to the mere mechanical principles involved in their execution. In carrying a heavy load the great object is to adjust it so that its center of gravity may come as nearly as possible to the vertical axis of the body, as otherwise force is wasted in keeping the mass in equilibrium. The continued maintenance of this unique position necessitated the turning of an ordinary quadruped a quarter of a circle in the vertical plane to render the spine perpendicular or in line with the posterior limbs. The osseous walls of the pelvis were modified to take the additional strain. Special groups of muscles gave stability to the trunk and conferred upon the body its freedom and grace.

The lower limbs were placed wide apart at the pelvis; thigh and leg bones were lengthened and strengthened; the spinal column took on special curves; the skull was moved backward until it became nearly equipoised on the top of the vertebral column. The upper limbs became flail-like appendages, the shoulder blades receded to the posterior aspect of the trunk, having their axes at right angles to that of the spine. Further, like the haunch bones, they underwent certain modifications to afford points of attachment to the muscles required in the complex movements of the arms. The elbow joint became capable of movements of complete extension, flexion, pronation, supination, in which respects the upper limbs of man are differentiated from those of all other vertebrates.[1]

In his sinew-backed bow, made of driftwood and sinew cord, the Eskimo ingeniously converts a breaking strain of the fragile wood into a columnar strain thereon, wherein it is strongest and a tensile strain upon the sinew wherein it also is strongest. The erect position and the possibility of resting a load on vertical bones in a great variety of positions enables the carrier to get the greatest lifting result with the least danger to the body. So far this change to the erect position, with all that it implies, is just as serviceable to the exploitive, manufacturing, and consuming activities as with those that are here studied.

There is no end of encomium upon the human hand, and it does a great deal in lifting and carrying, but the especial organ of the travel and transportation industry is the foot.[2]

Upon this useful organ Dr. Munro may again be allowed to speak. It is in the distal extremity of the limbs that the most remarkable anatomical changes have to be noted. The foot is virtually a tripod, the heel and the ball of the great toe being the terminal ends of an arch, while the four outer digital columns group themselves together to form the third or steadying point. The three osseous prominences that form this tripod are each covered with a soft elastic pad, facilitating progression and acting as a buffer. Progression is performed by an enormously developed group of muscles, known as the calf of the leg. The walker is thereby enabled to use the heel and the ball of the great toe as successive fulcrums from which the forward spring is made, the action being greatly facilitated by that of the trunk muscles in simultaneously bending the body forward. The foot is thus a pillar for supporting the weight of the body and a lever for mechanically impelling it forward. Man possesses, moreover, the power to perform a variety of quick movements and to assume endless attitudes and positions. He can readily balance his body on one or both legs, can turn on his heels as if they were pivots, and can prostrate himself comfortably in a prone or a supine position. As the center of gravity of the whole body is nearly in line with the spinal axis, stable equilibrium is easily maintained by the lumbar muscles. This combination of structures and functions places man in a category by himself, and yet preserves the homologies common to all the vertebrates.[3]

The enormous multiplication of motions and methods of resistance, combining in one human body every variety of work ever done by animals, finds a correspondence in the increased size and complexity of

---

[1] Cf. R. Munro, Rep. Brit. Assoc., 1893, p. 887, for an elaborate treatment of this subject.

[2] Cf. J. Cross, "On the Mechanics and Motions of the Human Foot and Leg," Glasgow, 1819, and J. C. Plumer, "The Mechanical Affections of the Human Foot," Portland, 1850.

[3] Cf. R. Munro, Rep. Brit. Assoc., 1893, pp. 885-895.

brain and nervous tissue—the multiplication of nerve cells.   It is vain to speculate upon the priority of development in the brain or in the body as a versatile instrument of locomotion and work.   Wherever the remains of man have been found the characteristics of locomotion, of the erect position necessary to human work, are stamped thereon.   Man, then, the carrying animal, the beast of burden par excellence, the master of all other burden bearers in the world, is the groundwork and support of the entire carrying industry.

Jeremiah Head, in speaking of the mechanical principles of invention actually existing in the body of man and referring to some involving the carrying art, says that the human foot contains instances of the first and second and the fore arm of the third order of lever.   The patella is part of a pulley; there are hinges and ball-and-socket joints with lubricating arrangements; lungs are bellows, and the heart is a combination of force pumps; the wrist, ankle, and spinal vertebræ form universal joints; the nerves form a complete telegraph system with up-and-down lines and a central exchange; the circulation of blood is a double line of canals, in which the liquid and the boats move together, making the circuit twice a minute, distributing supplies wherever required, and taking up return loads without stopping; it is also a heat-distributing apparatus, establishing a general average, as engineers endeavor to do in building.[1]

Physiologists, in speaking of the functioning of the brain, sometimes overlook these wonderful facilities for blood supply and removal.   Compared with the smooth brain of the lower vertebrates, the brain of man is as New York City of to-day with Manhattan Island of the sixteenth century.

With accessories to his body, without aid of beast or physical power, man far outstrips all animal rivals.   A skater at Haarlem, in Holland, went 3.1 miles at the rate of 21 miles per hour.   One mile has been cycled in 1 minute, 54 seconds, and 900 miles have been made at 12.43 miles per hour, while Count Starhemberg's ride on horseback averaged only 5.45 miles per hour, and the horse died from the effort.   The modern railroad is virtually a surrender of man's legs to his brains and the harnessing of physical force.[2]

Under exceptional circumstances man has accomplished in walking matches over 8 miles in one hour, and an average of $2\frac{3}{4}$ miles per hour for one hundred and forty-one hours.   In running he has covered about $11\frac{1}{2}$ miles in an hour.   In water he has proved himself capable of swimming 100 yards at the rate of 3 miles per hour, and 22 miles at rather over 1 mile per hour, and he has remained under water $4\frac{1}{2}$ minutes.   He can easily climb the most rugged mountain path and descend the same.   He can swarm up a bare pole or a rope, and when trained

[1] Cf. Rep. Brit. Assoc., 1893, p. 862.
[2] Ibid., p. 864.   Locomotion in both air and water are also specially considered.

can perform most wonderful feats of strength and agility. He has shown himself able to jump as high as 6 feet 2⅞ inches from the ground, and over a horizontal distance of 23 feet 3 inches; and he has thrown a cricket ball 382½ feet.

The attitude and action of a man in throwing a stone or a cricket ball, where he exerts a considerable force at several feet from the ground, to which the reaction has to be transmitted and to which he is in no way fastened, are unequaled in any artificial machine. The similar but contrary action of pulling a rope horizontally, as in tug-of-war competitions, is equally remarkable. The living mechanism, although fitted for an external atmospheric pressure of about 15 pounds per square inch, has been able to ascend to a height of 7 miles and breathe air at a pressure of 3½ pounds per square inch. Divers have been down in the water 80 feet deep, entailing an extra pressure of 36 pounds per square inch.

Fasting operations are not less remarkable when we are comparing the human body as a piece of mechanism with those of artificial construction. For what artificial motor could continue its functions forty days and nights without fuel; or, if the material of which it was constructed were gradually consumed to maintain the flow of energy, could afterwards build itself up again to its original substance?

The marvel is not that the human bodily mechanism is capable of any one kind of action, but that in its various developments it can do all or any of them, and also carry a mind endowed with far wider powers than those of any other animal.

No animal burrows into the earth a greater depth than 8 feet, and then only in dry ground. By aid of the steam engine for pumping, for air compressing, ventilating, hauling, rock boring, electric lighting, etc., and by the utilization of explosives man has obtained complete mastery over the crust of the earth and its mineral contents down to the depths where, owing to the increase of temperature, the conditions of existence become difficult to maintain.[1]

As will appear, the physical man as a traveler and carrier takes on special ethnic peculiarities in this regard. The races of men do not walk alike, have not the same endurance in going, do not use the same part of the body in carrying and in locomotion artificially effected.

Now many of these differences are not racial, but physiographic. The burdens to be carried and the resistances to be overcome are different. There are varieties of elevation, climate, exposure, salubrity which modify the body. The apparatuses of riding and of burden bearing also have to conform to the nature of things. So we not only have types of burden bearers, but types of burden bearing and of burden utensils. The American aborigines were chief of the races in this regard. They had no riding beast and were compelled to walk.

---

[1] Cf. Harley, "On the Recuperative Bodily Power of Man," Journ. Anthrop. Inst., London, 1887, XVII, pp. 108–118.

Their helpful animals were the dog in the north and llama in the Andes; otherwise men and women had to work in traces and under great loads. The network of inland streams in both Americas developed also the boatman class.

The Africans of negro type, south of the Sahara, were also their own beasts of burden. Wherever the burden camel or ass appears it is a Hamitic introduction. In the chapter on burden bearing the special types of carrying will be shown. Carrying on the head, or toting, with the anatomical peculiarities that this implies, is common with the nappy haired tribes. The exigencies of food getting, of slave capture, of long reaches of uninhabitable country, of war made of the African a great walker and wanderer. This is manifest in the condition of the language problem.

The Polynesian is a boatman, a swimmer, and makes few foot journeys of any length. His carrying muscles are not developed and his rounded form is not suggestive of Atlas or Hercules. His paddling muscles are splendidly emphasized, and his agility with his hands is surprising. He has been the greatest of modern aboriginal travelers, the short distances that he could make afoot acting as an efficient impulse to the invention of seaworthy craft.

His cousin, the Malay, lives on larger islands, and, having no domestic animal, must necessarily be a more wiry pedestrian, a better carrier and pack animal. Indeed, there are two kinds of him, land Dyak and sea Dyak, physically different as any one would suppose. The land Dyak is a walker, and is on his feet constantly. Books of travel invariably represent him barefooted, with a long staff or spear and bearing on his back a load supported by a head band.

The Sinitic group are in the South great watermen, have only a little to do with cattle, much for elephants to do, and hence are not addicted to carrying as the Chinese are. But the Celestials and the Japanese have marvelous backs. Later on the Chinese carrying trade and methods shall be reviewed, but here let it suffice to say that the physical endowments of the Chinese coolie are not surpassed. China is in the hand and back epoch of culture. Pack beasts are common enough, but they do not enter into competition with the legitimate burden bearers.

The Hamito-Semitic stock have taken to riding and to pack beasts and are not specially modified in body for beasts of burden. Layard long ago said that the Arab has no wheelbarrow muscle, and he might have added that his muscles for a long walk are likewise defective. India is somewhat like farther India. The aboriginal peoples are largely water folk.

The long Piedmont of northern Asia is the home and special training ground of most of the beasts of burden—dog, reindeer, camel, horse, ass, ox. Upon these the people lay their loads or exact the duty of dragging their vehicles. Walkers are not rare, but professional carriers are so. It is not, therefore, to be expected that the bodies of the people should have been specially changed. In this region, however, the process of domestication is in its infancy, and under such circumstances always man has more than half of the walking and working to do.

Within the areas called civilized, where local movements give place to world movements, all ancient forms of going and carrying survive and the active pursuit of them becomes professional. Roustabouts and porters are there a class. Their backs, limbs, and whole anatomy are greatly modified by their trade.

Vambery mentions in his company from Teheran one Hadji Kurban, a peasant by birth, who as a knife grinder had traversed the whole of Asia, had been as far as Constantinople and Mecca, had visited on occasions Tibet and Calcutta, and twice the Khirghiz Steppes to Orenburg and Tagaarog.[1]

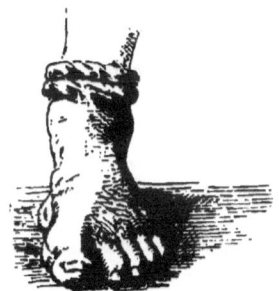

Fig. 6.

PERUVIAN ANKLE BANDS FOR TRAVELERS

From a figure in Wiener's "Pérou et Bolivie."

Bodily deformations result from the carrying art. Commencing with the cradle, the back of the heads of American Indian infants are said to be compressed by contact with the hard papoose frame in which they are carried. "Flattened or platycnemic tibias have often been mentioned as a pithecoid reversion and also as a racial trait. They are neither. Virchow has abundantly shown that they are produced in any race by the prolonged use of certain muscles, either in constant trotting, in prolonged squatting, in carrying burdens, or in the use of peculiar foot gear. The proof that it is acquired is that it is never found in the tibias of young children."[2]

The custom of belting the body and bandaging the legs (fig. 6) found so common in tropical America may have had its origin in the exigencies of travel or going about. Among the ignorant laborers in America,

[1]"Travels in Central Asia," New York, 1865, p. 42.

Brinton, Am. Anthropologist, Washington. 1894, p. 381. quoting Dr. Matthews, Mem. Nat. Acad. Sci., VI, p. 224.

especially among the negroes in the South, the opinion prevails that a
strip of eel skin about the leg has a beneficial effect in preventing
rheumatism, cramp, sprains, and the like. That this belief has a wide
dispersion may be supposed from the frequency of bands about the
ankles noted among primitive peoples. The ancient Peruvians wore
about the ankle bands of metal, cord, or textile.

With relation to the elements in which man travels the species may
be said to be terrestrial, aquatic, and semiaerial. Because he not only
progresses on the ground, but moves freely in and under the water
naturally and by his inventions, he also climbs into the air naturally
on trees, and by his machinery ascends above the flight of any bird.

SPECIAL COSTUME FOR TRAVEL.

The special costume for going away from home became more and
more differentiated with the extent of a journey of a day, with the
annual circle of activities, with the sphere of trade and influence, and
with the knowledge of those ever-widening currents of acquaintance
and intercourse which quickened the pace and lengthened the excursions of travel. All these were extremely limited at first, as they are
now limited among rustic and other folk, and consequently the traveling clothing little differed from that worn at home. The outfit of the
primitive traveler, though not to be compared with that of his modern
representative, was devised to meet his wants. It would include: (1)
Special costume for the body; (2) special protection for the head;
(3) protection for the eyes; (4) foot gear; (5) snowshoes; (6) creepers
for walking on ice; (7) stilts and other elevating devices; (8) staff and
scrip; (9) climbing devices. In this connection should be considered
runners and couriers of various kinds.

Costumes of most useful patterns were invented for those who go away
from home. It has often been asserted that men and women adorned
their bodies before they clothed them. As regards clothing for the
sake of clothing this may be true. But those who had to go away far
from the accustomed shelter must need to take temporary shelter with
them, and that is clothing. This useful apparatus must not be con-
founded with that artistic and ceremonial toggery which in association
with tattooing, cosmetics, and artificial deformation constitutes the costume of staying at home and is never seen on the road. Traveling costume was devised and perfected as culture widened. In the tropics,
prior to the art of plaiting blankets or mats and weaving cloth, nature's
textile, or bark cloth, was in vogue. The Africans used a very crude
variety of this fabric, and in tropical America similar cloth is employed
both for travelers' clothing and for the attachment of ornaments. The
Polynesians were most expert in beating from the inner bark of certain
trees a tough fabric which was protective and easily removed.

In addition to the bark cloth, in all three tropical areas, specially
good mat makers may be found.

The aborigines of the three areas also carried the notion of the personal journeying roof to the extent of inventing rain cloaks and umbrellas, which are no more than thatches to cover one man. The U. S. National Museum possesses examples from Japan and middle or Latin America.[1]

The temperate zone man found himself the possessor of a few textiles and used them economically in clothing, hemp, flax, cedar bark, cotton, and jute. But his land abounded in ruminants, whose dressed hides and whose hair enabled him to house his body for any journey. In America the tawed hides of buffalo, moose, caribou, deer, elk, and the pelts of buffalo, bear, and a great variety of carnivores and rodents were more than sufficient for the exigencies.[2]

The going away from home was by both men and women, and therefore the temperate region aborigines of North America were the best clad savages in the world. This is especially true of the hunter tribes, while the agricultural eastern tribes are represented by the old artists as quite devoid of clothing. The fragile and movable tents of the Plains Indians were supplemented by better garments more constantly worn.

The buckskin, fur, and woven fur clothing in America reaches from Mexico to the Eskimo border. In the corresponding area of Europe in earliest historic times similar dress was worn by the primitive Aryan tribes. It may be that the Piedmont hordes of northern Asia were once so arrayed, but since the earliest records garments of wool woven and felted have been in vogue. Quite frequently the pelts of lambs and other domestic animals constitute a survival from an earlier period.

The elevated regions of South America demand of the traveler artificial clothing and furnish him one of the best substances in the hair and the skins of the Auchenias. The spindle is a common object in all Peruvian collections, and all mummies are comfortably clad for their long journey.[3]

The Africans are good spinners and weavers of cotton and of palm fiber. For this operation they use looms only a few inches wide and sew together several widths of cloth, which they wrap around their bodies not only as a protection from the elements, but in its folds they carry both children and merchandise.

The coolies, in south China, usually have on nothing but a pair of loose trousers, tucked up above the knees. They have jackets, but rarely wear them while on the road. They have the body above the loins naked while at work just as men here go in their shirt sleeves. A straw hat and a pair of trousers or simple loin cloth is all the clothing most of them wear throughout the year. In the winter they put on thick jackets. This is on the testimony of Dr. R. N. Graves, for many years a missionary in China.

---

[1] Illustrated in the "Capitals of South America," by W. E. Curtis.
[2] Mason, "Aboriginal Skin Dressing." Rep. Smithsonian Inst. (U. S. Nat. Mus.), 1889 (1891), p. 553.
[3] Wiener, "Pérou et Bolivie."

The traveling Chinaman and Japanese thatch the head and the body against the rain with broad hats and abundant rain cloaks, as will be specially shown further on.

These two countries furnish the best examples of highest achievement in the industrial epoch of the hand. More men are professionally carrying burdens, the distances between artificial culture centers are longer, the tonnage carried on backs of human beings is vaster, and the outfit of the carrier is more differentiated.

The hyperborean man and woman go almost as naked in their hut or underground house as their congeners farther south. It is when they venture forth that they exhibit the highest invention in dress. It is possible though risky, for tropical or temperate region man to defy the elements, but the hyperborean man can not for one moment. So he constructs an air-tight nonconducting house of skin, whether of reindeer, bear, hair seal, bird, or marten. Herein he is as safe as in his home.

Omitting the inquiry how so many stocks of mankind, from North Cape to east Greenland came to be dressed substantially alike, it is true that they are dressed so harmoniously to the environment that the white man when he goes to live among them simply has to don their garb with few modifications.[1]

The body clothing of the Kamchatkan traveler includes: (1) The kuklander, long tunic of deerskin, double, reaching to the knees, with hood; (2) torbossas, long fur boots with fur socks inside; (3) malachis, fur bonnet or nightcap worn inside the hood; (4) archaniles, long tippets held in the teeth to protect the face. These with mittens and deerskin trousers complete the costume.[2]

Bush, at Ghijigha, speaks of his sleeping dress as follows: "My robe de nuit consisted of an immense fur kuklander of double thickness and extending to my ankles; a heavy spacious hood covered the head and was bordered with a thick fringe of wolf hair to keep the drifting snow out of my face while sleeping; fur sleeping socks, one of which was as large as a small-sized barrel. All else needed to complete my comfort was to throw my bearskin on the soft snow for a mattress."[3]

Among barbarous and semicivilized peoples travelers note some special form or attribute of dress, perhaps inexplicable at first but easily explained when the environment is known. The Yuma Indians put mud on their bodies at night or in the morning to keep out the chill, but as the sun advances it wears off and leaves the body naked. The Latin Americans and all other Latin peoples don the poncho, which may be now a shawl, now a rain protector, or it may be doubled

[1] On the making of the Eskimo garment, see Murdoch, Ninth Ann. Rep. Bureau of Ethnology.
[2] Bush, "Reindeer, Dogs, and Snowshoes," New York, 1871, p. 61.
[3] Ibid. p. 361.

up and carried against an emergency. The Semito-Hamitic girdle or sash, that may on occasion become a shawl, belongs to this general utility garment. The light shawl on the arm of the opera goer or evening visitor is a survival of this very old precautionary garment.

HEAD GEAR.

The second class of special costume demanded for the traveler chiefly was protection for the head. Not only is the head especially exposed and vulnerable, but it occupies an important place in the traveler's outfit. It is his watchtower from which he looks out on the track, his telegraph and telephone office into whose receiver the voices of nature whisper, his transmitter of messages to his fellows, his detective to advise and warn. The sun, the storm, the cold strike the head first and most, so aside from any idea of ornament dame nature has given to the negroid and other tropical peoples and to Arctic peoples an abundance of hair. The skin of the head has a remarkably adaptive power, suiting itself to enormous differences of temperature. But for cosmopolitan man these did not suffice, and before he had any notion of adorning his head he covered it to protect it.

Each culture region has its type of hat, each isothermal belt covers the head of the traveler conveniently. Elevation, temperature, rainfall, wind, natural materials all tell upon the head cover. There are also among travelers race hats, national hats, and guild hats. There are in the U. S. National Museum a large collection of hats from all parts of the world which enables the student to make some interesting comparisons in this regard.

Among the types of men the Australioid travel little and protect their heads less, either to keep them warm, to shade them, to shed the rain, or to defend the eyes. There is not an Australian hat in the U. S. National Museum.

In tropical Africa, both among the negroes and the Bantu, the head receives much adornment and no protection. The Africans are good braiders, however, and make excellent hats for others to wear. In America and other lands whither the African was borne as a slave, he disdains the hat and may be seen working bareheaded in the fields. But in Latin America, as is well known, the negro and the Indian united their blood and their arts to such an extent that some of the excellent hat making of that region must be accredited to the influence of the former.

The American aborigines of the tropics are divided into highlanders and lowlanders. The latter wear no hats; at least in pictures they appear unclothed as to the head, and the U. S. National Museum has no specimen. In the upland or montagnais of the tropics the Indian carriers appear constantly with skullcaps woven from paco wool. The natives that have become Latinized wear the sombrero, both of vegetable fiber and of wool.

The Polynesians or, more properly speaking, the Indo-Pacific races, Malay, Negroid, and Polynesians, go bareheaded. They are a maritime people largely, and ignore the hat as a protection in their canoe travel.

In the temperate regions there has been most land travel always and more demand for head covering, and yet there is great difference of opinion evidently as to what kind of hat to wear. The heaviest hats and turbans regardless of heat belong to the traveling races—the camel, mule, and horse riding stocks in America, in north Africa, and in western Asia as far east as the Mohammedan religions and mongoloid peoples extend.

The turban is also at home in India, and it is a perpetual wonder how in a land of so much heat the human head can stand such bundling. It is a fact that this head gear belongs to an alien and conquering race, that it now stands for caste and there is no telling what mankind are willing to suffer for pride and vanity. The native peoples of India are pictured as bareheaded. The climate renders the headdress unnecessary, and the noncaste people are not given to moving about.

As soon as one approaches the Sinitic area and the land of rattan and bamboo the turban gives place to the umbrella and the parasol and to hats akin to them. The widest and most varied head gear belongs to China, Korea, and Japan. The distinctions of rank, locality, and sect are drawn on the hat. With these, further than they are survivals from earlier industrial forms, there is nothing to do here. The traveling hat of all these regions and of farther India, so far as it is related to China, the traveler's and the Coolie's hat is an individual roof, a defense against sun and rain.

Says Bush:

I could not help admiring the taste displayed by many of these Giliaks whom we passed in the manufacture of their hats. They are made of birch bark, shaped like a low, broad cone, the outside covered with beautiful scroll-work figures cut from stained bark.[1]

In the temperate regions there has been most traveling, but, aside from fur, hat material is scarce. Above the temperate, in the boreal regions, men are compelled to draw in the awnings for rain and sun shedding, to substitute a wind and cold proof material, and to encase the head in the hat to keep out the cold. In other words, the boreal man wears a hood rather than a hat.

The distribution of the hood is as follows: (1) All Eskimo, of fur, attached to parka; (2) Athapascans, of buckskin, ornamented; (3) Koraks.

---

[1] "Reindeer, Dogs, and Snowshoes," New York, 1871, p. 99. Compare Tlingit painted and overlaid hat, Aleut visor hats covered with carved ivory, painted bands, and figures, and cast Greenland articles adorned with little figures, Albert P. Niblack, Rep. Smithsonian Inst. (U. S. Nat. Mus.), 1888; also G. Holm, "Ethnologisk Skizze," Copenhagen, 1887, pls. XXVIII-XI..

SUNPROOF AND TRAVELERS' HATS IN THE U. S. NATIONAL MUSEUM.

Museum number.	Specimen.	Locality.	By whom contributed.
5362	Hat, conical	China	J. Varden.
154249	Hat, palm leaf and rattan	Hoihow, China	Dr. Julius Neumann.
167190	Hat	Mongolia	W. W. Rockhill.
167188–167189	...do	Tibet	Do.
167191–167193	....do	...do	Do.
77061	Hat, coolie's	Korea	J. B. Bernadou.
77065	....do	...do	Do.
60236	Hat, rain	Southeast Alaska	J. J. McLean.
73840	Hat, grass	Alaska	T. Dix Bolles, U. S. N.
16267	Hat, woven straw or plaited	...do	W. H. Dall.
72447–72449	Hat, straw	...do	J. J. McLean.
20884–20885	Hat, Haida Indians	Queen Charlotte Island	J. G. Swan.
670	Hat, basket	Northwest Coast	George Gibbs.
1782	Hat, native	...do	Dr. Suckley.
2576	Hat, plaited straw	...do	Lieut. Wilkes, U. S. N.
2577	Hat, water-tight	...do	Do.
2581	....do	...do	Do.
2695	Hat, straw	...do	Do.
2719–2722	Hat	...do	Do.
671	Hat, basket	Strait of Fuca	George Gibbs.
1039	Hat, conical, Makah Indians	Neah Bay, Washington	J. G. Swan.

RAIN CLOAKS.

The rain cloak is a roof of thatch for the body. It is found in regions where there is much going about, much rain, and suitable material for its manufacture. In its manufacture or plan of structure will be found not only provision for turning rain from the wearer's body, but that other omnipresent thought in the minds of manufacturers which compels them to make things easy of transportation in the least compass. There is more time and cost expended in making a parasol or umbrella easy to carry than in making it sunproof or rainproof.

Museum number.	Specimen.	Locality.	By whom contributed.
447, 448	Japanese rain cloaks	Japan	Commodore Perry.
73062	Rain coat	North Formosa. China	Royal Gardens, Kew, England.
152534	Rain cloak	Kiungchow, China	Dr. Julius Neumann.
36186–36187	Waterproof shirt, intestine	C. East, Siberia	E. W. Nelson.
49101	....do	C. Prince of Wales	Do.
43337–43338	....do	Golovin Bay	Do.
38817	Waterproof dress, fishskin	Mission, Alaska	Do.
153733	Waterproof dress, intestine	St. Michaels, Alaska	J. H. Turner.
129816	....do	...do	Mrs. M. McL. Hazan.
129339	....do	...do	L. M. Turner.
43283	....do	Nushagak, Alaska	E. W. Nelson.
127671	....do	Fort Alexander, Alaska	J. W. Johnson.
127668	.... do	...do	Do.
56083	....do	Bristol Bay, Alaska	C. L. McKay.
55966	....do	...do	Do.

RAIN CLOAKS IN THE U. S. NATIONAL MUSEUM—Continued.

Museum number.	Specimen.	Locality.	By whom contributed
20919	Waterproof dress, intestine....	Unalashka, Aleutian Islands.	J. G. Swan.
8943	....do	.... do	A. H. Hoff, U. S. A.
68134	.....do	Hudson Bay	J. T. Brown.
10170	....do	Igloolik...............	C. F. Hall.
74450–74451	.....do	Ungava, Canada........	L. M. Turner.
36944	Waterproof cloak..............	Upernivik, Greenland ..	Governor Fenckner.
128870	Rain coat of rushes	Washington State	Charles Willoughby.
76930	Palm-leaf rain cloak...........	Mexico	New Orleans Exposition.
126583	Rain cloak, palm leaves........	Guadalajara, Mexico...	Dr. E. Palmer.
75954–75956	.....do	Indians of Central America.	Miles Rock.
131050	Rain cloak of feet..............	Eastern Tibet	W. W. Rockhill.

SUNSHADES AND UMBRELLAS.

The sunshade and umbrella are in effect hats. They do not exist in eastern Asia outside the bamboo area, the lightness and strength of

Fig. 7.

THE PRIMITIVE UMBRELLA IN GUATEMALA.

From a figure in "The Capitals of South America," by W. E. Curtis.

the material inviting to their creation. In tropical America they may be an innovation (fig. 7). But in antiquity gorgeous examples are part of the traveling conveniences of royal persons. In the sculptures of Egypt, Nineveh, and Persepolis umbrellas are frequently figured. In ancient Greece and Rome, in medieval Europe, they had reached the stage of art and effeminacy. Useful umbrellas were plentiful in London in the eighteenth century, and we read of common examples for coffee houses and parishes.[1]

[1] Cf. Gay, "Trivia," London, 1716; "Notes and Queries," London, series 5, VI, pp. 202, 313.

EAR PROTECTORS.

Museum number.	Specimen.	Locality.	By whom contributed.
175101	Ear protectors	Leh Ladakh	Dr. W. L. Abbott.
45088–45089	Face protectors, bearskin	Kings Island	E. W. Nelson.
38094	Ear flaps or protectors of fur	Kongig, Alaska	Do.
55981	Ear lapets	Bristol Bay, Alaska	Charles L. McKay.
76724	... do	Fort Alexander, Alaska	J. W Johnson

GLOVES AND MITTENS IN THE U. S. NATIONAL MUSEUM.

The defense of the hand is imperative in Arctic and boreal travel, hence, the glove is universal around the hyperborean region. The clothing of the hand is bound by the conditions of (1) temperature, (2) piercing wind, (3) material most handy and effectual, (4) the use to which the hand must be put on the journey of fishing, hunting, paddling, trap setting, dog driving, etc. Hence will be found the mitten with and without thumb, the glove with each finger distinct, and the glove with other dividing of the fingers. As the student moves from Eskimo to Athapascan tribes in America he passes from the fur mitten to the buckskin glove.

In an elaborative series the hand covering may be classified by material, by complexity of structure, and by function. The U. S. National Museum series divide themselves into mittens, divided mittens, and gloves. All of these may be further separated into haired and unhaired, the former into hair inside and hair outside. The gloves in the series have the fingers sewed on all around where they join the hand and are not continuous as in the modern examples. Among the Eskimos gloves are essential not only against cold, but also in handling the vicious dog.

In the Nelson collection (Nos. 1038, 5250) in the U. S. National Museum is a pair of gloves from the Kaviarigmut, south of St. Michaels. The three compartments of the left hand glove are characteristic of this region only. Unaleet name, aghe 'gäät, 'Malemut, ad the gäät.

Museum number.	Specimen.	Locality	By whom contributed.
129426	Gloves, knit	Norway	Mrs. E. S. Brinton.
128328	Gauntlets (one pair)	Persia	Charles Heap.
73108	Gloves, antelope skin	Tate Yama, Japan	P. L. Jouy.
150688	Mittens	Yezo, Japan	Romyn Hitchcock.
1439	Mittens, Chukchi	N. E. Asia	Commodore John Rodgers.
38454	Gloves, European model	Bering Straits	E. W. Nelson
48176, 48177	Gloves, embroidered	Siberia	Do.
153529	Mitts	North Siberia	Lieut. G. B. Harber, U. S. N.
64271	Gloves, beaded	Point Hope, Alaska	E. W. Nelson.
43322	Mittens, waterproof, very long	Golovina Bay, Alaska	Do.
43324	Gloves, deerskin	....do	Do.
43341	Gloves, seal pelt	....do	Do.
43342, 43343	Mitts, two pairs, seal pelts	....do	Do.

GLOVES AND MITTENS IN THE U. S. NATIONAL MUSEUM—Continued.

Museum number.	Specimen.	Locality.	By whom contributed.
48101	Gloves, deerskin, fine, long......	Kings Island, Alaska...	E. W. Nelson.
48381	Mittens, waterproof...............	....do	Do.
45084	Mittens, man's, seal skin........	Sledge Island, Alaska...	Do.
45085	Gloves, man's, seal skin..........	....do	Do.
45398	Mittens, man's, seal skin........	....do	Do.
48127	Mittens, seal skin, waterproof...	....do	Do.
48127	Mittens. waterproof..............	....do	Do.
43782	Gloves, seal skin..............	Cape Nome, Alaska.....	Do.
45286	Gloves, waterproof, seal skin....	....do	Do.
8783	Mittens, leather............,.....	Kusilvak, Eskimo......	W. H. Dall.
7584	Mittens, dogskin	St. Michaels	Do.
44350	Mittens, deerskin	Norton Bay, Alaska.....	Do.
572	Mittens, man's	Yukon River, Alaska...	B. R. Ross.
892	Mittens	Yukon, Alaska	R. Kennicott.
7592	Gloves, winter	Unalakleet	W. H. Dall.
7593, 7594	Gloves, summer	....do	Do.
7595	....do	....do	Do.
2017	Mittens	Yukon River, Alaska...	B. R. Ross.
8781	Mittens, fishskin and seal pelt...	....do	W. H. Dall.
10489	Mittens, dogskin.................	....do	J. T. Dyar.
38455	Gloves, embroidered	Anvik, Alaska.........	E. W. Nelson.
64280, 64287	Mittens, deerskin, fine..........	Yukon River, Alaska ..	Do.
24324	Gloves, deer pelt..............	Norton Sound..........	Do.
7600	Gloves, summer, deerskin.......	Mahlemuts, Alaska.....	W. H. Dall.
72842	Mittens, buckskin, embroidered	Alaska Indians........	Ivan Petroff.
21598	Mittens	Alaska	Dr. J. B. White.
730F6	Mittens, with strap to hang around the neck, ornamented with beads.	Bristol Bay, Alaska	C. L. McKay.
74433, 74434	Gloves, buckskin	Sitka, Alaska..........	J. J. McLean.
153759	Mittens	....do	J. H. Turner.
127335	Mittens, fishskin..............	Bristol Bay	I. Applegate.
55967	Mittens, fishskin.............	Bristol Bay, Alaska....	Charles L. McKay.
55968	Mittens, woven grass..........	....do	Do.
55970	Mittens, fishskin	....do	Do.
56066	Gloves	....do	Do.
56067	Mittens	....do	Do.
36207	Gloves, white fur on back......	Bering Straits	E. W. Nelson.
44145	Gloves, fingers sewed in, 2 pairs.	Kotzebue Sound	Do.
48135	....do	....do	Do.
89829	Gloves, deerskin (two pairs).....	Point Barrow, Alaska...	Lieut. P. H. Ray, U. S. N.
128398	Gloves, boy's...................	....do	E. P. Herendeen.
128400	Gloves, infant's.............,..	....do	Do.
153602	Mittens, winter.................	....do	John Murdoch.
64269	Mittens, old, bird skin..........	Diomede Island, Alaska.	E. W. Nelson.
90461	Mittens, fishskin................	Igiagik River....	William J. Fisher.
90462	Mittens, grass..................	....do	Do.
49115	Mittens, buckskin and quill	Tanana River..........	E. W. Nelson.
887	Mittens, woman's	Lower Mackenzie River.	R. Kennicott.
1716	Gloves, deerskin, man's.........	....do	R. MacFarlane.
1727	Mittens, bearskin, woman's.....	Mackenzie River	Do.
1728	Mittens, deerskin, man's.	....do	Do.
5131	Mittens, bearskin.............	....do	Do.
5132, 5133	Mittens, wolverine	....do	Do.
1337	Mittens, deerskin..............	Anderson River	C. P. Gaudet.

GLOVES AND MITTENS IN THE U. S. NATIONAL MUSEUM—Continued.

Museum number.	Specimen.	Locality.	By whom contributed.
1338	Mitten (one), Polar bearskin....	Anderson River........	C. P. Gaudet
1665	Gloves, bearskin.................	....do..............	R. MacFarlane.
1668	Mittens, fox skin	....do	Do.
1680, 1681	Gloves, deerskin.................	....do	Do
1682	Mittens, deerskin................	....do	Do.
1684	Mittens, fox and deer skin.......	....do	Do.
1701	Mittens, fox skin................	....do	Do.
1729, 1730	Mittens, deerskin................	....do ....'.....	Do.
2224, 2225	Gloves.......................	....do	Do.
7638	Gloves, white bearskin	Fort Anderson	Do.
7639–7641	Gloves, black and white wolverine	.....do	Do.
7643–7646	.....do......................	....do	Do.
7647	Gloves (odd), fur-lined..........	....do	Do.
11008	Gloves, chamois.................	Baffin Land............	Capt. C. F. Hall.
5212	Mittens	Repulse Bay...........	Do.
68118	Mits, sealskin	Hudson Bay............	Charles G. Osbourne.
68119	Gloves, fur	....do	Do.
14254	Mittens	Baffin Land............	Capt. C. F. Hall.
13137	Mittens, sealskin...............	Greenland	Frank Y. Commagère.
13136	Mittens, woolen	....do	Do.
37546	Gloves	....do	N. P. Scudder.
153519	Mittens	Labrador	Henry G. Bryant.
90071	Mittens, child's, beaded	....do	L. M. Turner.
90074	Mittens, long, sealskin	....do	Do.
90194, 90195	Mittens	.... do	Do.
90200	.....do......................	....do	Do.
90355	Mittens, toy..................	....do	Do.
74482, 74483	Gloves, skin.................	....do	Do.
74484	Gloves, white fur..............	....do	Do.
23741	Gloves	South Dakota	Paul Beckwith.
20794	.....do......................	Sitka, Alaska..........	J. G. Swan.
18911	Mittens, buckskin..............	Northwest coast........	Do.
131245	Gloves, embroidered, Colvilles ..		Dr. Geo. M. Kober, U. S. A.
12080	Mittens, Pai Ute Indians.......	Southern Utah	Maj. J. W. Powell.
14629	Mittens, fur, Pai Ute Indians....	.....do	Do.
14634	.....do......................	....do	Do.

TRAVELERS' STAVES.

The traveler is usually seen with some sort of stick or staff in his hand. This series of utensils find their artistic culmination in the modern costly cane and in many beautiful uses of the word in poetry. The magic staff and the crozier connect this class of objects with mythology, folklore, and ecclesiasticism. The uses of the walking stick are as follows: For staff on which to lean and as a weapon; the walking stick, in the hand of all carriers; climbing stick, or alpenstock; rest for load, often forked; steering for skees, frequently shod; help in rising, as among the Papago, etc.; protection, culminating in the crozier.

The frequency of the staff in the hands of Assyrian kings, shown on the ancient monuments, recalls the days when it was a necessity to every pedestrian, not only for support but for defense.

The staff of the Norwegian skee rider is a mere balancing pole, which may, and probably does, come by and by to be the alpenstock. Nansen, in his excellent chapter on the skee, to be noted further on, condemns the staff for the professional skee rider, and shows how the best prize riding is done without it. Practically, however, while on his journey across the inland ice, he is never seen without one in his hand.

The indispensable accompaniment of the Indian and rude peoples on snowshoes is the pole or staff. It exists in two forms, the shod and the unshod. At the bottom of the shod staff a little wheel about 6 inches in diameter is made of wood in Norway, but in Finland or northeastern Asia or in Alaska the wheel is a hoop of bone with four or more spokes of rawhide. Doubtless the snowshoe staff is of recent Asiatic introduction.

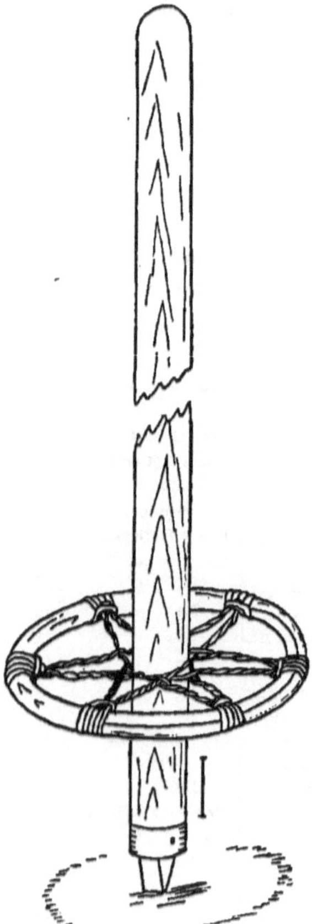

The snowshoe staff of the Lapps, Finns, and Norwegians (fig. 8) is a pole 8 feet or more long, shod at the bottom with a strip of antler or bone. A very few inches above this point or spud is a hoop about 6 inches in diameter, attached to the staff at right

Fig. 8.

FINLAND SKEE STAFF WITH SNOWSHOE
AT THE BOTTOM.

Cat. No. 161849, U. S. N. M. Collected by John M.
Crawford.

angles by rawhide strings radiating and forming a kind of snowshoe. Precisely this form is to be seen in Alaska but the Giliaks on the Amur attach a paddle to the upper end of the staff[1] (fig. 9).

Fig. 9.

THE SNOWSHOER'S STAFF
OF THE GILIAK.

From a figure in Schrenk's "Reisen
und Forschungen im Amur-
lande."

At Oudskoi, on the Okhotsk Sea, Bush figures natives on skees carrying in hand the pole with a little wheel stop near the bottom.[2]

[1] Schrenk, "Reisen und Forschungen im Amur-Lande," St. Petersburg, 1891, K. akad. Wissensch., III, p. 476.

[2] "Reindeer, Dogs, and Snowshoes," New York, 1871, p. 194.

Hooper speaks of a "long, thin staff of driftwood, shod at the foot with pointed ivory or seal's tooth, and furnished with a circular frame, generally of whalebone, sometimes 6 or 8 inches in diameter, attached to it 3 or 4 inches above the shoe; this frame is covered with a net work of hide cord, and its use is intended to prevent the staff going deep in the snow and so tripping him whose support it should.be. It is a valuable acquisition, particularly with snowshoes"[1] (fig. 10). There are in the U. S. National Museum examples from Finland, western Alaska, and Schrenk figures them from the Amur country.[2]

The only staff used by the young and vigorous at Point Barrow, according to Murdoch, is the shaft of the spear, when one is carried. The aged and feeble, however, support their steps with one or two staves about 5 feet long, often shod with bone or ivory. (The old man whom Franklin met on the Coppermine River walked with the help of two sticks.)[3]

The walking stick of the Carrier Indian of British Columbia, which he uses in winter, is precisely like that seen in the hands of the hyperboreans, with a little circular snowshoe fastened about the stock near the bottom. The Indian makes a novel use of his staff. Having a leather loop like the guard of a sword fastened at the top, he puts his left hand through it and lays his gun barrel on his hand for a rest. Father Morice figures a carrier kneeling and shooting with his gun thus sustained.[4]

Fig. 10.

SNOWSHOER'S STAFF OF THE CAPE NOME ESKIMO.

Cat. No. 45423, U. S. N. M. Collected by E. W. Nelson.

"Sometimes a man shall meet a lame man or an old Man with a Staffe; but generally a staff is a rare sight in the hand of the eldest, their Constitution is so strong. I have upon occasion travelled many a score, yea many a hundred mile amongst them without need of stick or staffe, for an appearance of danger amongst them."[5]

Many of the market people (of Ayacucho) come on foot from considerable distances, the women carrying their babies on their backs in bundles called ccepi, and the young men using a walking stick for support in passing up and down the wearisome ravines.[6]

[1] "Tents of the Tuski," London, 1853, Murray, p. 147.
[2] "Reisen und Forschungen im Amur-Lande," p. 476.
[3] Murdoch, Ninth Ann. Rep. Bureau of Ethnology, p. 352, quoting Franklin, "First Expedition," II, p. 180.
[4] Trans. Canadian Inst., 1894, IV, 155, figs. 144, 145.
[5] See Coll. R. I. Hist. Soc., I, p. 76, for paper by Roger Williams, "Key into the language of the Indians of New England."
[6] Markham, "Journey to Cuzco," London, 1856, p. 64.

TRAVELERS' STAVES IN THE U. S. NATIONAL MUSEUM.

Museum number.	Specimen.	Locality.	By whom contributed.
167689, 167890	Skee staves	Finland	Hon. J. W. Crawford.
45423–45425	Staves used for supporting travelers on ice	Cape Nome, Alaska	E. W. Nelson.
46297	Bottom of snow cane	Alaska	W. H. Dall.
14953	Staff	Aleutian Islands	W. H. Dall.
151695	Staff with knob, Kaffirs	Africa	British Museum.
165348	Cane, walking	....do	Carl Steckelmann.
165349	Staff, walking	....do	Do.
166114	....do	West Africa	Heli Chatelain.

The stilt and the stilted shoe scarcely enter into this study. The latter is more for lifting the feet out of a wet environment, or in some countries to elevate the bodies of persons of high degree. There is an endless variety of stilted shoes in the Mohammedan areas, in Persia and in Japan.

The stilt finds favor in certain parts of France, but here they serve chiefly to lift the shepherd to enable him to keep his eye on his flock. They are, in company with his staff, a kind of tripod watchtower or light-house.

The Popular Science Monthly records a race between pedestrians, stilt walkers, and horses from Bordeaux, France, over a course of 400 kilometers. The pedestrians dropped out at 235 kilometers. At the end of sixty-two hours the race was completed, the horse reaching the goal twenty-eight minutes ahead of the best stilt walker.[1]

One of the favorite amusements among these people (Washington Island, Marquesas,) says Langsdorff, is running on stilts over paved dancing places, children being thoroughly habituated to the exercise by the time they are 12 years old.[2]

Carved stilts of the Marquesas islanders, attached to bambo handles, beautifully etched, are in the Christy collection and the Munich Museum as well as in the U. S. National Museum.[3]

LOCOMOTION AND BURDEN BEARING IN THE AIR.

The serpent, having no limbs whatever, would seem at first sight to be terribly handicapped; yet, in the language of Professor Owen, "it can outclimb the monkey, outswim the fish, outleap the jerboa, and suddenly loosing the close coils of its crouching spiral, it can spring into the air and seize the bird on the wing." Here we have the spiral spring in nature before it was devised by man.

[1] Popular Science Monthly, New York, 1891, XLVI, p. 284; also Guyot-Daubes, "Stilts and Stilt Walking," ibid., XL, p. 467.

[2] Langsdorff, "Voyages," London, 1813, I, p. 169.

[3] Figured by Ratzel, "Völkerkunde," II, pp. 133–134.

Flying animals conform to this law of variety of gifts. Thus we have birds, like the penguin, which dive and swim, but can not fly; others, like the gannet, which dive, swim, fly, and walk; others, like the ostrich, which run, but neither fly nor swim, and numberless birds which fly well, but have only slight pedestrian powers.[1] Those who enjoy the contemplation of nature, as the tireless pedagogue of man, will find innumerable examples in this portion of the traveling art. Every kind of ascending and descending obtrudes itself on the human imagination as an example and a challenge.

It has been previously remarked in this paper that through the exercise of the faculty of invention locomotion in the three elements, to wit, on the land, in the water, and in the air can be prosecuted further, longer, and more effectually by man than by any other living beings whatever. Traveling about and moving of things require not only horizontal motion, but movement upward, and in primitive life this may be considered under the general head of climbing.

The inclined plane is the most simple of the mechanical powers. It exists everywhere in nature, and simply in following the lines of least resistance animals, especially the ruminants, have covered the earth in its elevated portions with a network of paths and trails which have been subsequently adopted by aboriginal peoples.

The whole subject of the inclined plane, in its relation to travel and transportation, would better be considered after the division of roads; and even devices like stairways, such as may be seen in various parts of the world cut in the highways in order to facilitate locomotion and to get over difficult places, would also better come under the same division.

The discouragement of travel is quite as great among the wealth of nature as amid its poverty; the magnificent forest, where there can be no track and where the traveler must cut and climb for himself, is just as tenantless as the dry and thirsty land where no water is. But there is a small class of devices or inventions for mounting trees and other objects which may be considered apart from the general topic of roads.

Nowadays the patent elevator carries freight and passengers to the tops of buildings over twenty stories high, but in the beginning men knew how to ascend trees by the simple use of hands and feet. To facilitate this operation, however, among very low savages will be found a small class of inventions which at once divides itself into two species; one leading to the perfection of the ladder, the other is attached to the human body, and renders more effective the grip of the hand and the feet in the ascent. This class finds its latest expression in the devices used by those engaged in laying and repairing telegraph wires at the top of the long poles. The loops on the savage man's feet are the spikes on

---

[1] Cf. Jeremiah Head, Rep. Brit. Assoc., 1893, pp. 860–873.

the climber's boots, and the coarse vine about the tree and the waist of the former answers to the broad strap used by the latter. The action is the same; the man's body is alternately shortened by drawing up the feet and lengthened by straightening the body.

The ladder was a common feature in ancient warfare. Besieging by escalade appears frequently in Assyrian sculpture in the works of Layard. In fact, the ladder is a carrying instrument, that may be easily carried in turn, a portable stairway, in which the maker's problem is to get an elevating device of the greatest efficiency combined with the least weight and inconvenience. It would lead too far away from the subject to consider now the topic of ladder and antiladder in ancient warfare.

All through the Malay area, for many purposes not necessary here to discuss, the houses are erected above ground, and are approached by ladders, which may be drawn up, and indeed are difficult to mount except by those who are accustomed to doing so.

Forrest, in his voyage, speaks of the ladder as a long, notched stick, made of the clove tree, and used by the Malays to ascend to their houses, which he declares to be usually built on posts above the ground.[1]

It will be remembered in this connection that aboriginally all the stone and adobe architecture of the southwestern States of the Union was conceived on the idea of the greatest possible use of the movable ladder (fig. 11), not only in ascending from the outside, but also in descending to the different apartments. A ladder of stout bamboos, to which cross steps are lashed, shored or braced with bamboos extending from vantage points to the ground, is shown in Le Tour du Monde.[2]

Fig. 11.

PRIMITIVE NOTCHED LADDER FROM TUSAYAN, ARIZONA.

From a figure in Mindeleff's "Study of Pueblo Architecture," Eighth Annual Report of the Bureau of Ethnology

Raffray figures a New Guinea house on trestlework, access to which is gained only by shinning up a group of five bare poles close together at the top on the doorsill and spread out a little below, where they rest on a small platform on top of short piles.[3]

All travelers among the Kamchadals and the Koraks speak of the ladder by which their underground dwellings are entered. It is a log with holes cut into it as steps. One is figured in Bush's work[4] as the stairway upon the light-house at Ghijigha at the northern end of

[1] Forrest, " Voyage to New Guinea and the Moluccas," p. 33; E. Best, Journ. Polynesian Soc., Wellington, 1892, I, p. 12; Ellis, " Polynesian Researches," London, 1859, I, p. 57.

[2] Vol. I, p. 9; also Wallace, " Malay Archipelago," New York, 1869, pp. 66, 207.

[3] Cf. Ratzel, " Völkerkunde," II, p. 269.

[4] " Reindeer, Dogs, and Snowshoes," New York, 1871, p. 352.

Okhotsk Sea. The handy use of the ladder is spoken of as a dextrous feat.

The Cosumnes of California ascend the piñon trees to the height of 30 or 40 feet by means of spliced poles long enough to reach the first limbs. The pole was held in place by Indians on the ground while an expert climber ascended and beat off the cones with a short pole.[1] This is not quite explicit. The splicing of poles is also known to the Amur people, who sometimes harpoon a seal 100 feet from shore by means of a spliced shaft.[2]

In the Eighth Annual Report of the Bureau of Ethnology, the architecture of all the Pueblos is elaborately worked out, and numerous examples will be seen of the manner in which these ladders are used by the inmates for ascending and descending.[3]

The ancient Mexicans, in mining, used a system of ladders not unlike those employed by the modern hod carriers in ascending to the top of a tall building, only they were of a much ruder sort. Mark Beaufoy, in speaking of these mines, says: "The carriers work their way to the surface by means of notched poles put across a part of the shaft in a zigzag fashion; and they then give their load to the breakers, who knock the ore into pieces exactly as if they were going to macadamize a road."

Squier, in speaking of the Mosquito Coast, describes a method of climbing the tree employed by the natives, but it is not certain that this method is aboriginal, since the population of the Mosquito Coast is extremely mixed. Here are his words:

Antonio had brought a kind of sack of coarse netting which he tied about his neck. He next cut a section of a tough vine and braided a hoop around one of the trees. Slipping this over his head and down to his waist he literally walked up the tree. Leaning back he planted his feet against the trunk, clinging to which first with one hand, and then with the other, he worked up the hoop, taking a step with every upward movement. In a minute he was 60 feet from the ground, leaning back and filling his sack with nuts. This done he swung his load over his shoulders, grasped the tree in his arms, let the hoop fall, and slid rapidly to the ground.[4]

Mercer describes the ladders made by the women of northern Yucatan for descending into the water caves as made of boughs, the rungs bound on with twigs. On a series of them he descended into the cave of Actun Chack.[5] A similar water cave at Caba Chen is entered by a staircase of one hundred stone steps.

Aeronautics seem to have been a very early study. The inquiry, "Birds can fly, and why can't I?" seems long ago to have entered ingenious minds. Archytas, of Tarentum, as far back as 400 B. C., is

---

[1] Cf. Mooney, Am. Anthropologist, 1890, p. 259.

[2] Schrenk, "Reisen und Forschungen im Amur-Lande," III.

[3] Eighth Ann. Rep. Bureau of Ethnology, fig. 46.

[4] Squier, "The Mosquito Coast," London, 1857, p. 62.

[5] H. C. Mercer, "The Hill Caves of Yucatan," Philadelphia, 1896, pp. 92, 140; Morelet, "Travels in Central America," New York, 1871, pp. 327, 420.

said to have made a bird that could fly. But up to the moment of this writing neither freight nor passengers have been carried through the air by the force of the wind or by any engine.

The balloon belongs to the epoch of chemistry, the eighth in the series of powers put to work by man (page 240). It was not until human ingenuity had succeeded in alienating and confining hydrogen that such a device as a balloon was thought of.[1]

Dr. Emil Schmidt figures a Comorin man climbing the palm tree to gather the palm wine. The essential parts of the apparatus are (1) the loop uniting the feet and giving a bearing against the tree, (2) the seat and its sling passing from the ends of the seat about the tree and inclosing the man. The climber rests alternately in the seat and on his feet as he hitches himself upward.[2]

In the U. S. National Museum is a model of "The palmyra climber and his implements," from Ceylon, acquired at the Chicago Exposition. A man with the apparatus attached to himself is mounting a palm-tree and gathering the sap.

The following list mentions all of the objects connected with this operation: (1) The knife and the basket; (2) the cocoanut-shell bottle which contains an oil for rubbing around the tree to prevent the ants from getting to the toddy pot; (3) the chaunam basket of the toddy drawer, containing lime to put into the pot to prevent fermentation; (4) the short club of the toddy drawers, used to beat the young tender spathe for preparing it; (5) the double stick used by toddy drawers for pressing the young tender spathe to facilitate the flow of sap; (6) the toddy drawer's basket; (7) the toddy pot; (8) the leather piece to protect the breast of the climber; (9) the leather piece to protect the ankles of the climber; (10) the foot brace used for the feet in climbing.

The parts of the palmyra are (1) young tender palmyra leaves; (2) green palmyra leaves; (3) dried palmyra leaves; (4) the bottom of a leafstalk encircling the tree; (5) the young spathe of a palmyra tree and toddy pot; (6) the tender fruit bunch of the palmyra on its first appearance; (7) the young fruit bunch of the palmyra half grown; (8) the amateur fruit bunch of the palmyra; (9) the full-grown unripe fruit bunch of the palmyra; (10) the fully ripe fruit bunches of the palmyra.

Ellis says of the Polynesian climbing that the cocoanut trees are often 60 or more feet high, with a tuft of leaves on top. Yet the natives gather the fruit with ease. A little boy strips off a piece of bark from a puran branch and fastens it around his feet, leaving a space of 4 or 5 inches between them, and then clasping the tree he vaults up its trunk with greater agility than a European could ascend a ladder to an equal

---

[1] Cavendish discovered hydrogen in 1766, and Montgolfier's first balloon was sent up in 1783.

[2] "Reise nach Südindien," Leipzig, 1894, p. 101.

elevation. When they gather a bunch at a time they lower them down with a rope.[1]

The Ætas or pigmy negritos of the Philippines are said by Gironiere to be prodigiously active in climbing trees, clasping the trunks with their hands and setting the soles of the feet against the trunk.[2]

The Marquesans climb the highest trees with incredible celerity, not with the knees pressed close to the trunk, but with the toes spread out. They will climb the steepest rocks with extreme facility; in running they are not equally expert.[3]

Lumholtz, in his work, "Among the Cannibals" (p. 89), speaks of the Australians climbing huge trees by means of the calamus (*Calamus australis*), native name Kamin. In a sketch the native Australian is represented as climbing a tree by means of a piece of vine, the function of which is simply to lengthen his arms so that he may grasp the trunk. He has no appliances upon his feet whatever, grasping the tree with his knees and toes for an instant, and before he has time to fall he throws the vine higher up where it catches upon the rough bark, and he is thus able to pull himself a little further along[4] (fig. 12). In the Malay and Indian areas the climber has a loop connecting his two ankles. This device is to increase the grasp of his

Fig. 12.
AUSTRALIAN TREE-CLIMBING DEVICE.

feet upon the tree and to form a ratchet in the rough bark, which device sustains the body of the climber until he can throw his loop higher up.

The Indians of southeast Alaska understood the process of climbing trees by means of a stout line made of twisted cedar bark fiber. In the Emmons collections in New York from that region are two specimens of the apparatus thus used.

Lieutenant G. T. Emmons, U. S. N., whose superb collections from the Tlingit area are without a parallel, sends to the U. S. National Museum a climbing device, which in its complexity reminds one of the palmyra climber of India. It is No. 168806, is 32 inches long, nearly

[1] Ellis, "Polynesian Researches," London, Bohn, i, p. 57.
[2] "Twenty Years in the Philippines," quoted by E. Best, Journ. Polynesian Soc., Wellington, 1892, i, p. 12.
[3] Langsdorff, "Voyages," London, 1813, i, p. 174.
[4] Also Standard Natural History, vii, p. 35.

6 inches wide, and 1¼ inches thick in its strongest part. It is made of
cedar, and this piece of wood has indeed a double function. The greater
part is like a swing board or boatswain's chair, having its upper side
chamfered for the rider, and the underside carved to represent his
totem. Holes are bored for this stout cedar rope, which is knotted at
one end and passes through the outer hole. The other end is rove
through the inner hole and has a long, loose end. Outside of this swing-
board arrangement is carved a portion which resembles a cleat and has
that function.

Lieutenant Emmons informs the writer that he has not seen this
apparatus at work, though he was very anxious to do so. It appears,
however, that the woodcutter or carver, as the case might be, sits upon
the seat, puts the rope around the tree and through the inner hole and

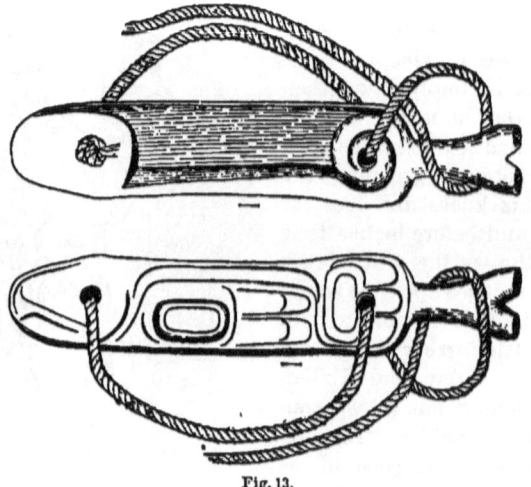

Fig. 13.

TREE-CLIMBING DEVICE OF THE TLINGIT INDIANS, SOUTHEASTERN ALASKA.

Cat. No. 168806, U. S. N. M.   Collected by Lieut. G. T. Emmons, U. S. N.

makes it fast, by one or more half hitches, to the cleat. He uses the
apparatus in climbing the tree in the same way it is employed in India,
and also uses it as a boatswain's chair in holding himself in position
while he is operating upon the trunk. This is the only example the
author has ever seen or heard of belonging to this class in America
(fig. 13).

Accompanying this specimen and probably independent of it is a
much smaller device yet quite as effective, as will be seen in the drawing. A number of long strips, or ribbons, of cedar bark are doubled
in two sets so that by their middles, for a foot or more, they are twisted
into a two-ply rope forming a stout loop, and this is wrapped with a
sennit of cedar bark so as to hold the loop in place. The ribbons are
then laid out edge to edge for the distance of 3 feet or more and used

as a warp across which, by open zigzag, a continuous line of twine weaving is carried from one end to the other. By this operation the ends are gathered in and wrapped with a three-ply braid. The remaining part of the ribbons are then split or shredded and twisted into a fine three-ply rope. The loop in this example serves the same purpose as

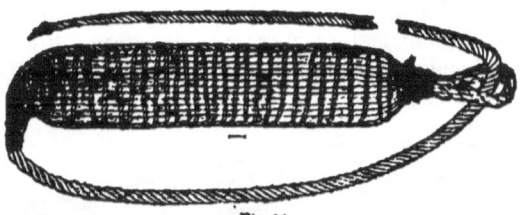

Fig. 14.

TREE-CLIMBING DEVICE OF CEDAR BARK USED BY THE TLINGIT INDIANS, ALASKA.

Cat. No. 168807, U. S. N. M.   Collected by Lieut. G. T. Emmons, U. S. N

the cleat in the other. The broad band is the boatswain's chair and the finely twisted rope passes around the tree through the loop and is made fast by half hitches. The purpose of this seems to be the same, although Lieutenant Emmons had not the good fortune to see this example at work (fig. 14).

CLIMBING APPARATUS IN THE U. S. NATIONAL MUSEUM.

Museum number.	Specimen.	Locality.	By whom contributed.
151338	Climbing ropes...................	San Thomé, East Africa.	Heli Chatelain.
152626	Tree climber.....................	Southwest Africa.......	Carl Steckelmann.
165352	Climber, Lukoze.................	Mayumba, Africa.......	Do.
168806	Climbing implements............	Tlingit, Alaska..........	Lieut. G. T. Emmons, U. S. N.
168807	Climbing implements, cedar bark..	......do	Do.

SNOW GOGGLES.

After the long arctic winter comes the trying season of the morning, when the low sun shining over the glassy ice nearly blinds the hunter and compels him to utilize his inventive faculty to the utmost. There are two lines of patents, as we might call them, for protecting the eyes under the circumstances—the visor and the goggles or eyeshade with slits. In the U. S. National Museum the visor reaches its climax in the highly ornamented kaiak hat of the Aleutian seal and otter hunter and its counterpart, worn by the Giliaks on the Amur, but these belong to water travel.

There is in the U. S. National Museum (Cat. No. 68141) a pair of snow goggles obtained by the U. S. Fish Commission from one of the crew of the whaling brig *George and Mary*. The collector affirms that such objects are used not only by the Eskimo but by United States and Hudson Bay whalemen to shield the eyes from the glare of the sun. The example here referred to (fig. 15) is made of polished spruce. The eye cavities and the nose groove are of standard eastern type. The eye slits, however, are extremely regular, and the whole apparatus was certainly made with steel tools and goods polishers. There is not a shadow of a visor on this example. The head band consists of a strip of red flannel and loops of braided sinew, the last named being the only really aboriginal feature about the specimen. (Cat. No. 68141, U. S. N. M., 4¼ inches in length, collected for the U. S. Fish Commission by J. Temple Brown.)

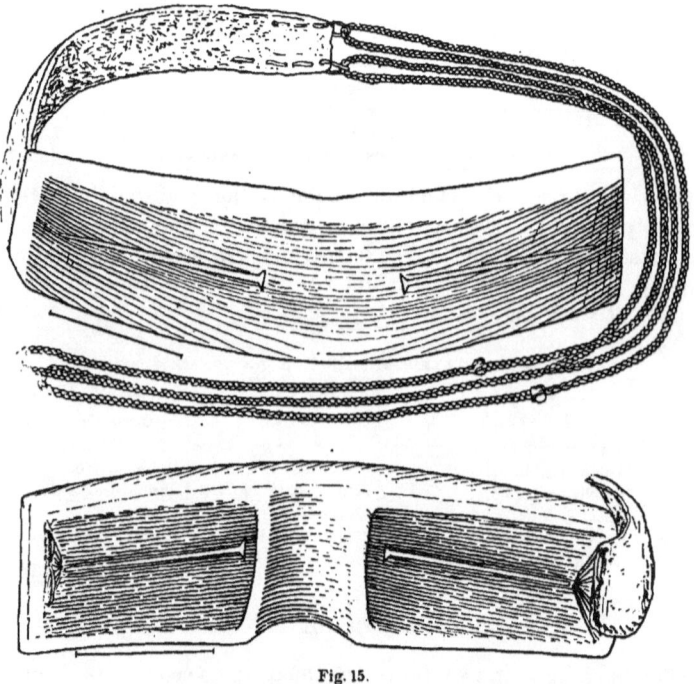

Fig. 15.

SNOW GOGGLES WORN BY HUDSON BAY ESKIMO.

Cat No. 68141 U S N M   Collected by J Temple Brown.

Ravenstein mentions opthalmia, from the action of the snow, as a dire affliction among the Goldi, terminating at an advanced age in blindness.[1]

The visor is also a common defense for the eyes on land, and in this capacity attains its most elaborate development in medieval armor. It has been previously said that in hot countries, where there are at least twelve hours of sunset or shadow every day, most peoples take no pains to shade the eyes. The fez, the turban, and the bare head are in vogue. The Laplander, however, wears a far-projecting visor on

---

[1] Cf. "Russians on the Amur," London, 1861, p. 97.

his cap. So does the Russian and so do most Asiatics. The rim of the thousand and one styles of hat made in straw and palm leaf is partly visor for the eyes, partly sunshade, and partly umbrella, but always the utensil of the traveler. The essential part of the snow goggles, however, is the provision for the eyes immediately. In a great many masks throughout the world there are little holes, narrow slits, and openings, through which the actor may peep. In the same manner the goggles will be found divided into those in which the eye peers out through a slit or slits and those in which it looks out through elliptical holes. These slits and holes are in various structural relations with the visor, giving rise to many local types of apparatus for the same function. The climax of the invention in cultured areas is the goggle with colored glasses. Among the Tibetans the glare of the sun is shut off by means of a silken network, of which the universal veil in civilization is a refinement. It will be seen also that the Eskimo has somewhere caught the notion of our modern wire screen over the eyes of persons suffering with inflammation of this organ, only he substitutes tubes of wood for the wire gauze and smoked glass for the refined colored glass. Beginning with the purely aboriginal device there is in the U. S. National Museum collection a complete series, showing the insinuation of civilized ideas into the savage mind.

The almost universal custom is to blacken the inside of the goggles to further exclude the glare and strong reflection. Where this is not done the dark color of old wood renders it unnecessary. Some of the specimens in the Museum are smoked, many are rubbed with graphite, others are painted black. There is no lack of modern appliances, since the Eskimo have been under the discipline of the white man from two to nine centuries.

Bonvalot figures a petty chief in the western borders of Tibet wearing snow goggles over his eyes.[1] From this point the apparatus may be traced eastward, and it will be convenient to examine first the Asiatic specimens and after that the Eskimo types, in order to note the flourishing of varietal changes under stress of material, of climate, of ethnic genius, and of outside influences.

On the tundras of northeastern Siberia the sun of spring, reflecting from the glassy surface of the melting snow, almost blinds the Korak drivers of the dog sledges. They can not wear the smoked goggles and watch their teams, so they wear strips of tin perforated with small holes or having long, narrow slits cut through them, while others are of wood, shaped so as to fit the upper part of the face, through which are cut narrow slits, one for each eye.[2]

Hooper states that no kind of snow goggles or spectacles are used by the Tuski to protect the eyes from the glare of the snow in springtime, for the people suffer dreadfully from snow-blindness and ophthalmia.

[1] "Across Tibet," New York, 1892, Cassell, p. 233.
[2] Cf. Bush, "Reindeer, Dogs, and Snowshoes," New York, 1891, p. 349.

To relieve this the skin on the temples is perforated and a kind of seton is inserted.[1] The snow goggles and the visor are both known in that locality, so the reason for not wearing them is to be sought in the demands of the daily life in spring.

To the dress of the men (Chukchi), says Nordenskiöld, there belongs a screen for the eyes, which is often beautifully ornamented with beads and silver mounting. This screen is worn especially in spring as a protection from the strong sunlight reflected from the snow plains.[2] At this season of the year snow-blindness is very common, but notwithstanding this, snow spectacles of the kind which the Eskimo and even the Samoyeds use are unknown there. The various kinds of goggles used by the Eskimo have been explained; but Nordenskiöld describes neither those of the Chukchi nor those of the Samoyeds.

Parry relates that the affection of the eyes, known by the name of snow-blindness, is extremely frequent among these people (Central Eskimo). With them it scarcely ever goes beyond painful irritation, while among strangers inflammation is sometimes the consequence. I have not seen them use any other remedy besides the exclusion of light; but as a preventive a wooden eye screen is worn, very simple in its construction, consisting of a curved piece of wood 6 or 7 inches long and 10 or 12 lines broad. It is tied over the eyes like a pair of spectacles, being adapted to the forehead and nose and hollowed out to favor the motion of the eyelids. A few rays of light only are admitted through a narrow slit an inch long, cut opposite to each eye. This contrivance is more simple and quite as efficient as the more heavy one possessed by some who have been fortunate enough to acquire wood for the purpose. This is merely the former instrument, complicated by the addition of a horizontal plate projecting 3 or 4 inches from its upper rim like the peak of a jockey's cap. In Hudson Strait the latter is common, and the former in Greenland, where also we are told they wear with advantage the simple horizontal peak alone.[3] It will be noted that Parry here refers to the simple visor, the simple goggles, and a mixed type in which the two are combined.

As with other classes of technical apparatus, so with the goggles or slit eye shade, there are excellent opportunities of studying the relations of invention and environment among the divisions of the selfsame people. For the purposes of comparison the same regions may be marked off as were observed with the "throwing sticks,"[4] to wit, Greenland, Labrador, Cumberland Gulf and Baffin Land, Mackenzie River district, Point Barrow, Kotzebue Sound, Bering Strait and vicinity, Norton Sound, Yukon River, Nunivak, Bristol Bay, Alaskan Peninsula and Kadiak, and other localities.

[1] Hooper, "Tents of the Tuski," London, 1853, p. 185.
[2] Nordenskiöld: "Voyage of the Vega," New York, 1882, p. 473.
[3] Parry, "Second Voyage," London, 1824, p. 547.
[4] Mason, "Throwing Sticks in the U. S. National Museum," Rep. Smithsonian Inst. (U. S. Nat. Mus.) 1884 (1885), p. 279.

The U. S. National Museum possesses three examples of snow goggles from East Greenland, numbers 16 938–'40. Number 168938 is a large, plain eye shade of wood, like the front of a sailor's cap. Number 168939 is a hooded eye shade made by attaching a deep curtain of wood to the border of a visor. The example here mentioned is decorated with a large number of strips of ivory pegged on in shape of the plumules on a feather. Number 168940 is a pair of tray-shaped goggles whittled out with a metal knife. The eyes are bulging as in fig. 31. All these specimens were collected by Captain G. Holm, of the Royal Danish Navy, and given to the U. S. National Museum by the Ethnological Museum of Copenhagen. In pl. XX of Holm's "Ethnologisk Skizze" will be seen a cap made of unborn seal skin and one of fox skin, and each of these has a visor, the former of rawhide, the latter of wood. Beneath these are two snow goggles, one of the Bristol Bay type having a thick, hollow visor with an elongated, rectangular wide slit in front and a notch for the nose. The other has two lenticular openings for eye slits, a nose carved in relief between the eyes, and a nose slit on the lower margin. These examples have slight relation with the Central Eskimo type in which goggles and visor are combined [1]

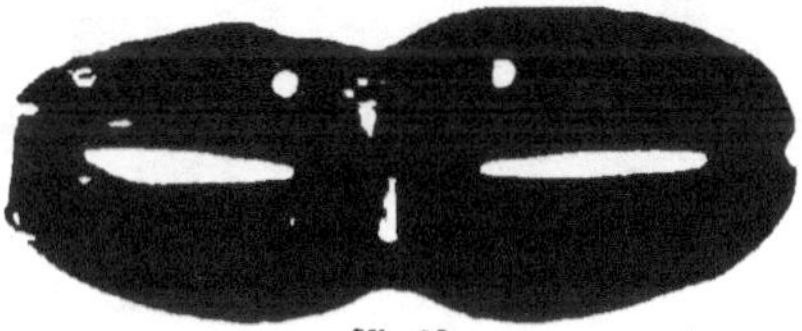

Fig. 16.

ESKIMO SNOW GOGGLES OF IVORY, FROM CUMBERLAND SOUND.

In the Museum für Völkerkunde, Berlin.

From a figure in "The Central Eskimo," by Boas, Sixth Annual Report of the Bureau of Ethnology.

F. Nansen figures an old man at Cape Bille, East Greenland, wearing snow goggles, a simple block of wood with one long slit.[2] The Kaiak hat of this old man, consisting of a wooden ring, should also be noted.

In Holm's pl. XXXVI are two visors beautifully ornamented with little flat ivory figures common to East Greenland. His figure 3 is a hood for the face fitting against the forehead, projecting like a visor from which descends perpendicularly, a wooden curtain covered with ivory ornaments. This curtained visor is unique so far as the U. S. National Museum is concerned. If in any other museum exist like forms from other areas it will be interesting to know the fact.

Of somewhat similar type to Holm's tray-shaped snow goggles is an ivory specimen found by Boas in Idjorituaqtuin, Cumberland Sound (fig. 16). It is in the Museum für Völkerkunde, Berlin, and has the appearance of being very old. It is suggestive of light and neatly finished specimens from Sledge Island southward, but there is no intimation of a visor. Attention is called, however, to the two holes bored above the eye slits in precisely the spots where on the Bean specimen from Cape Lisburne two holes are utilized in fastening on a visor. Nordenskiöld's Port Clarence specimen seems to have holes for the

[1] G. Holm, "Ethnologisk Skizze," Copenhagen, 1887, pl. XX.
[2] "Across Greenland," London, 1890, 1, p. 361.

added visor in the same spot. But the little openings may have served as ventilators.

The examples of snow goggles from Fury and Hecla Strait in the U. S. National Museum are such as have been worn by white men or explorers. The one here figured was worn by Captain Hall in his Arctic explorations. It is sharply angular in outline, as if made by machinery from a block of wood 2 inches thick. Especial attention is called to the deep excavations for the eyes, which are separated by an equally

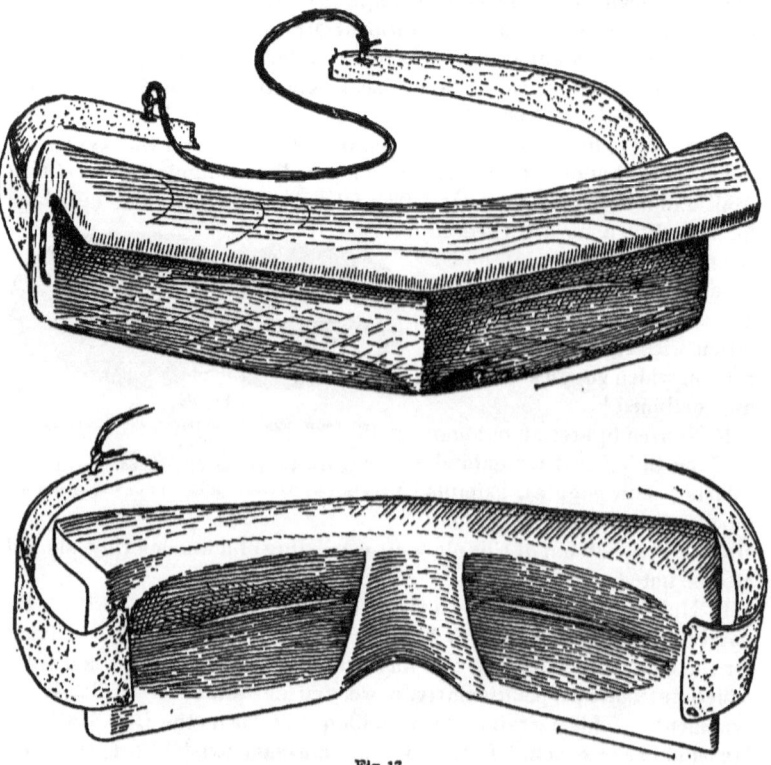

Fig. 17.

SNOW GOGGLES USED BY THE ESKIMO OF FURY AND HECLA STRAIT.

Cat. No. 10200, U. S. N. M.   Collected by Capt. C. F. Hall.

deep transverse cut for the nose. The eye slits are, therefore, entirely distinct in front and in the rear.

In front, a visor projects squarely an inch over the eye slits, and is flat on top. The goggles are fastened on the head by a band of soft hide attached at the ends by means of sinew threads, sewed through holes in the wood. To further cut off the light, the eye cavities are rubbed with some black substance.

The specimen here figured (fig. 17) measures 5¾ inches in length, and is to be seen among the relics of the Hall expedition.

This angular form constitutes a type peculiar to the central region, where for centuries whalers have congregated, and through their trade as well as their mechanical assistance, profoundly modified the native arts. Similar to the specimens figured, are No. 10292, collected by Captain Hall, Nos. 29976–77–78, gathered in Cumberland Gulf by Mintzer, and also, though much ruder and newer looking, Nos. 90176 to 90188, from Ungava, north of Labrador, collected by Mr. Lucien M. Turner.

Captain Hall's collection also contains a specimen of the same general type carved from oak, but there is no information concerning the

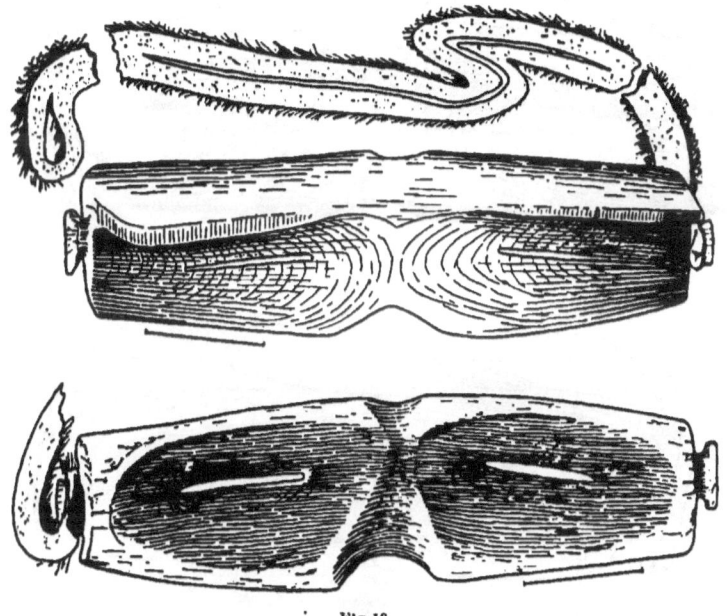

Fig. 18.

SNOW GOGGLES USED BY THE ESKIMO OF UNGAVA, NORTHERN LABRADOR.

Cat. No. 90188, U. S. N. M. Collected by Lucien M. Turner.

carver. The wood is from a whale ship. The visor in this example is not flat on top as the other, but slopes downward right and left from the middle.[1] (Cat. No. 10292, U. S. N. M. Length, 5½ inches; height, 2¼ inches. Collected in Frobisher Bay.) Franz Boas says that the natives of Cumberland Gulf always use snow goggles in spring to protect them from snow-blindness. In describing them he calls the visor-goggle type here figured the modern variety.

Lucien M. Turner brought home from Ungava several specimens of snow goggles similar to those shown in fig. 18. (Cat. No. 90188, U. S. N. M.)

[1] Cf. Parry, "Second Voyage," p. 547 and plate opposite p. 548, fig. 4, and plate opposite p. 14; Sixth Ann. Rep. Bureau of Ethnology, p. 575, fig. 529, p. 576.

The noticeable characteristics of this example are the short and wide eye slits and the shape of the visor, which is straight along its front border, making it quite shelving at its outer end and little projecting over the nose. There are buttons or knobs at the ends of the goggle for the strap of seal hide which is split along the middle so that one-half may pass above the occiput and the other half beneath it. These characteristics of the split headband and the buttons will be found elsewhere.

Somewhat similar to this example with little or no visor or projec-

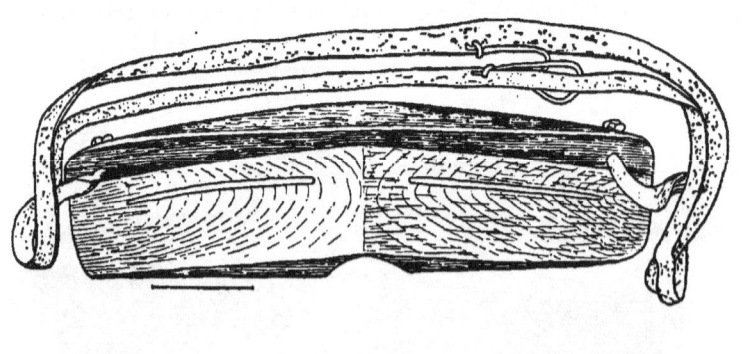

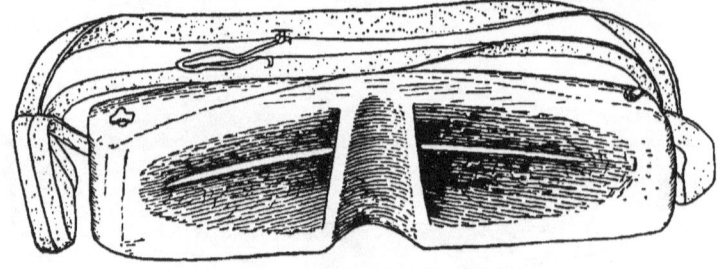

Fig. 19.
SNOW GOGGLES USED BY THE ESKIMO OF CUMBERLAND GULF.
Cat. No. 29978, U. S. N. M.   Collected by W. A. Mintzer.

tion above the eyes are Cat. Nos. 90184, 90185, U. S. N. M., from the same area. The length of this example is 5¼ inches.[1]

Nos. 29976–29978 in the U. S. National Museum are from Cumberland Gulf, and conform to the eastern type illustrated in the foregoing figures. The only characteristics in this example to which attention should be drawn is the heavy form of the goggles, the chamfered or sloped undersurface of the visor, and the additional little string between the two back portions of the head strap to prevent their spreading too wide apart. Length, 5¼ inches; height, 1¾ inches. Collected from Niautilik Eskimo, by W. A. Mintzer, U. S. N. (fig. 19).

[1] Cf. Eleventh Ann. Rep. Bureau of Ethnology, p. 222, figs. 46, 47.

In regarding the relation between these eastern examples and the environment it is well to put them into comparison with another apparatus in the same region, say the Ulu, or woman's knife. Turner's Ungava ulus look like harness makers' knives made and riveted in England or the United States. The other Hudson Bay, Cumberland Gulf, and Fury and Hecla pieces, out of foreign woods remind one of the patched up compound bows, the poorly hafted ulus, manufactured under the overshadowing influence of the whaler.

Between Fury and Hecla Strait and Cape Bathurst, just east of the mouth of the Mackenzie is a region unknown to the U. S. National Museum. Through the great generosity of Messrs. Robert MacFarlane,

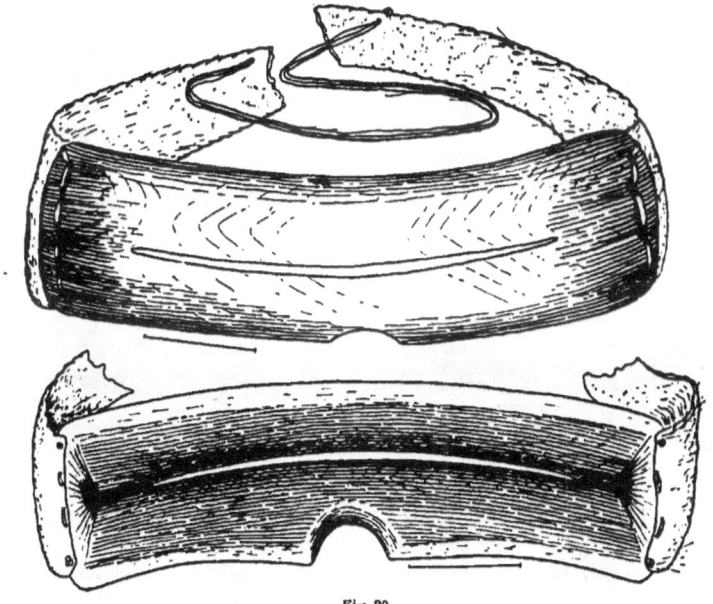

Fig. 20.

SNOW GOGGLES USED BY THE ESKIMO OF ANDERSON RIVER, CANADA.

Cat. No. 1650, U. S. N. M.   Collected by R. MacFarlane.

B. R. Ross, C. P. Gaudet, Robert Kennicott, and others, especially the agents of the Hudson Bay Company, the Museum possesses rich treasures from the Mackenzie River district.

There are two well-marked types of goggles collected in this region, that with a single continuous eye slit and no visor and that with two independent disks. Both of them are seen elsewhere, but neither of them occurs in the east, so far as the U. S. National Museum collection goes. The former is just as rude and primitive as it can be; the latter is seen in regions easily accessible to traders.

No. 1650 in the U. S. National Museum is from Anderson River, east of Mackenzie River (fig. 20). It consists of a long tray-shaped block of wood, red on the outside and blackened on the inside. It is roughly blocked out to fit in front of the eyes and to rest on the bridge of the nose. The headband is a broad strip of dressed skin sewed to the ends of the goggles. Especially should the student notice the continuous slit, for it is rare in Alaska on eye shades north of the Bristol Bay region. This specimen is 5¼ inches long, was made by the Kopagmut, and stands for the tray-shaped type of goggles to be noticed again.

Example No. 2167, from Anderson River, is carved in the shape of a trough, neatly polished, shaved out on the lower margin to fit the nose, but furnished with two long and quite neatly cut eye slits. The headband is a strip of dressed hide. Length, 5¾ inches. Gift of R. Mac-Farlane.

The second type, first appearing in the Mackenzie region and neighborhood going westward, is shown in fig. 21. The apparatus consists of two little wooden trays, with slits across their bottoms, attached to each other by being sewed upon a broad strip of dressed hide.

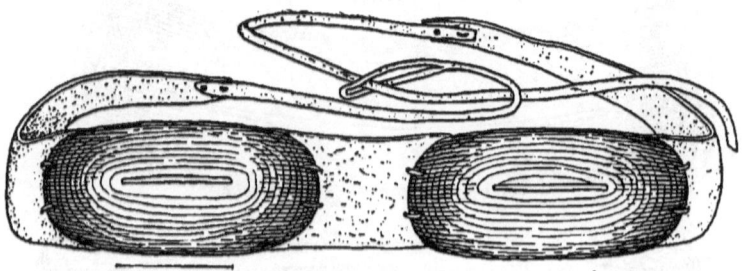

Fig. 21.

DOUBLE SNOW GOGGLES USED BY THE ESKIMO OF ANDERSON RIVER, CANADA.

Cat. No. 2147, U. S. N. M.   Collected by R. MacFarlane.

To the ends of this strip are attached rawhide strings to complete the headband. This very simple device will reappear farther west in more elaborate form, and attention will be later directed to the incorporation of the dish-like eyepieces into goggles made of one piece. Mr. MacFarlane sent also from Anderson River No. 1651, a visor cut out of a single piece of wood. In the Museum collections there is no visor coming from Canada east of the Anderson River. But the East Greenland specimens shown in Holm's plates 34–36 must not be overlooked. This peculiar type abounds about Sledge Island (Aziak) and the Bering Strait. Length, 7 inches. It may be said here as well as elsewhere that other collections may contain different types from the regions named, and forms like the one just described may have been brought from Aziak to Anderson River in trade. The author can give his patient care only to reporting things as they are represented.

Captain Herendeen, an experienced whaler, says that the goggles with separate disks are to be seen at Point Barrow. This is not strange, since the natives know their relatives at the Mackenzie mouth and trade as far west as St. Lawrence Island. The Ray party brought to the U. S. National Museum specimens of goggles from Point Barrow. These are of two kinds, the elongated dish-shaped variety, and a form soon to be described made of a single piece but suggestive of the style consisting of two disks.

No. 89701 is from Point Barrow and is mentioned by John Murdoch. Some specimens seen by him are of wood, and he describes one taken from a gravel bed 27 feet under ground in the process of sinking a shaft to obtain earth temperatures. But the example here figured (fig. 22) is of antler following the natural curve, divided longitudinally, with the softer tissue hollowed out. Mr. Murdoch never saw an example of this kind in actual use. It was obtained from a native, and there was no account of it given.

The second variety from Point Barrow, described by Mr. Murdoch,

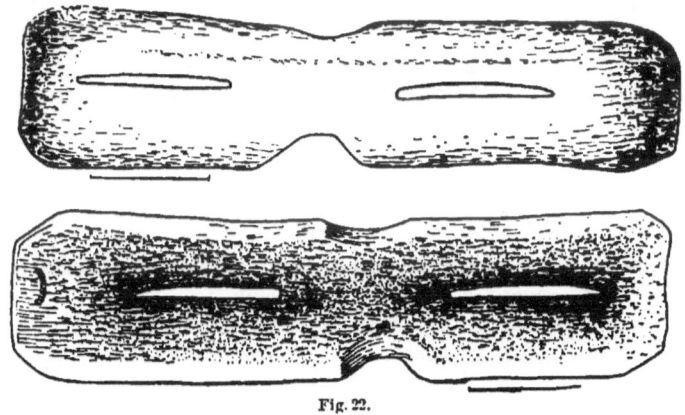

Fig. 22.

OLD SNOW GOGGLES OF ANTLER USED BY THE ESKIMO OF POINT BARROW, ALASKA.

Cat. No. 89701, U. S. N. M.   Collected by Capt. P. H. Ray, U. S. A.

have along the top a horizontal brim about one-half inch high. Above this are two oblique holes opening into the cavity inside, which are for the purpose of ventilation to prevent the moisture of the skin from being deposited as frost on the inside of the goggles or eyelashes. Mr. Murdoch did not see these worn. He also calls attention to the appearance of air holes in specimens from Norton Sound and Ungava, and compares the visor with that on the eastern specimens[1] (fig. 23).

Following up the single-slit specimen from Anderson River, Dall sent to the U. S. National Museum from Cape Lisburne (68° 50', 166° NW.) wooden goggles (No. 46041) with a continuous aperture for vision. It is a compromise between the trough-shaped northern specimens and the hollow-visored type in the south. Indeed, it is a good example of the northern double visor, with wide continuous slit, over which the upper

[1] Ninth Ann. Rep. Bureau of Ethnology, p. 262, figs. 259–261.

side of the visor projects a little. Sinew cord is used to hold the apparatus on the head. Collected by William H. Dall and S. Bailey. It

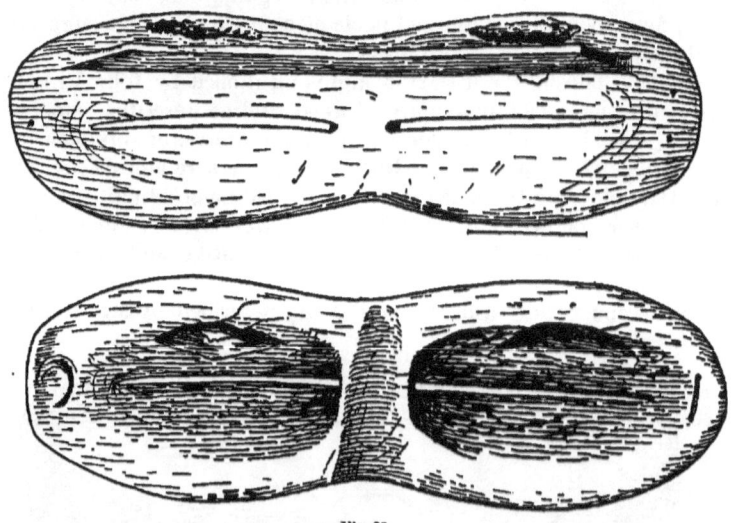

Fig. 23.

SNOW GOGGLES WITH VENTILATORS USED BY THE ESKIMO OF POINT BARROW, ALASKA

Cat. No. 89703, U. S. N. M.   Collected by Capt. P. H. Ray, U. S. A.

is of wood, and measures 5¾ inches in length and 2¾ in height. The Eskimo at this point are called Nunatogmut.

Through the kindness of Lieut. G. M. Stoney, U. S. N., the U. S. National Museum has goggles from Kotzebue Sound, north of Bering

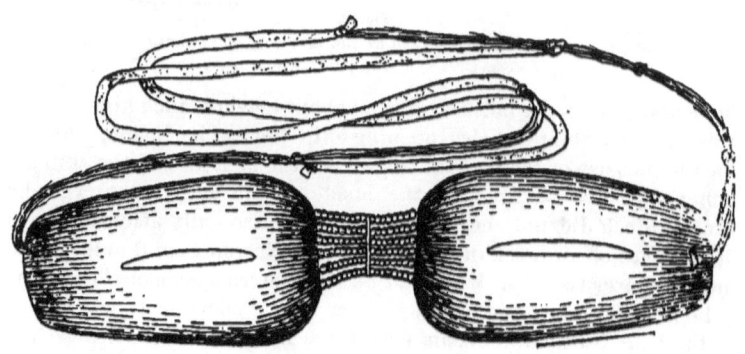

Fig. 24.

DOUBLE SNOW GOGGLES USED BY THE ESKIMO OF KOTZEBUE SOUND, ALASKA.

Cat. No. 127907, U. S. N. M.   Collected by Lieut. G. M. Stoney, U. S. N.

Strait, No. 127907. They consist of two little wooden disks or trays, oval in outline, with rather broad eye slits (fig. 24). These trays are joined together neatly by means of six strings of beads sewed into the margin of the disks and held in place in the middle by the threads passing through a "spreader" of rawhide. This device is common on beadwork farther south. The headband consists of sinew yarn and two little thongs of rawhide for the back of the head.

Example No. 63825 is from Point Hope. It has a single wide slit between a visor-like part above and a receding portion below, on the rear of which the notch for the nose is cut. The specimen is in essential particulars like the Cape Lisburne example, No. 46041.

Passing south from Kotzebue Sound to Bering Strait, Diomede Island, and Cape Prince of Wales, the U. S. National Museum does not possess an aboriginal specimen of goggles from this area. Instead, Nelson brought home a modern adaptation (fig. 25). It consists of a rectangular block of wood, with a shallow nose slit in the middle. The back of the block is gouged out roughly, and further cutting away provides two elliptical eye cavities. In front of the block is a rectangular bit of canvas,

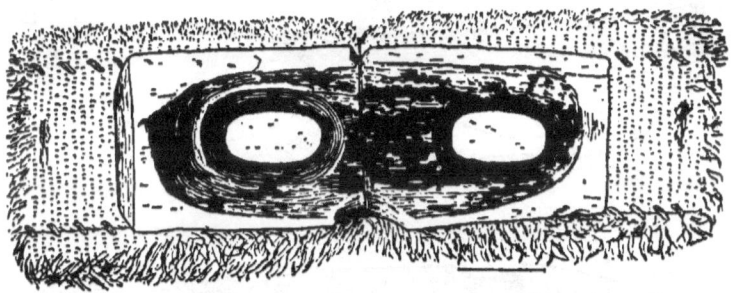

Fig. 25.

MODERN SNOW GOGGLES FROM DIOMEDE ISLAND, BERING STRAIT.

Cat. No. 63696, U. S. N. M. Collected by E. W. Nelson.

doubled and fitted with colored glass in front of the eyeholes in the wood. It is raveled around the edges and effectively excludes the light and air.

This is an interesting specimen, since it shows how thoroughly the most exposed places to foreign contact exhibit the greatest departure from the fundamental or primitive forms. The specimen figured is No. 63626, U. S. National Museum, and measures four and a quarter inches in length.

Just south of Bering Strait is Port Clarence, always an important location in Eskimo life and now the point at which the United States Government is making the experiment of introducing Siberian reindeer into Alaska. From this locality, through the kindness of Dr. Tarleton H. Bean, the U. S. National Museum possesses a very elaborate specimen of wood carving in the shape of snow goggles, No. 46137. The framework is in three pieces. This is easily accounted for since Port Clarence is in the land of driftwood. The upper and lower halves of the body of the apparatus are joined by means of neat lashings of rawhide thong and strips of baleen. The visor is also a separate piece closely fitted and joined in the same manner. The especial characteristic of this specimen and its congeners not far away is the amount of carving in the round in front. In the rear the deep eye and nose cavities and in front the visor suggest Eastern examples. But the last named are angular and do not reveal the countenance. In the Port Clarence type

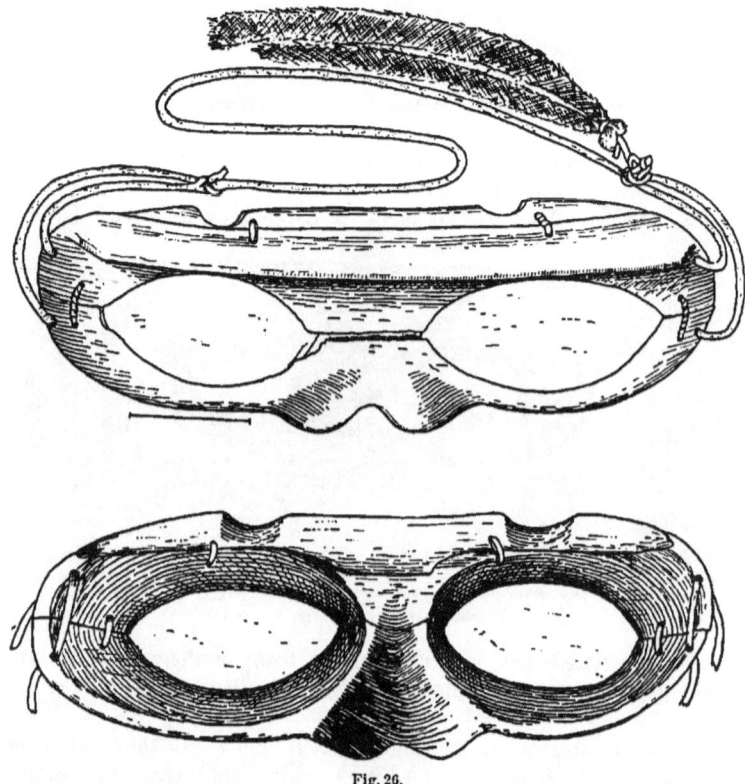

Fig. 26.

CARVED SNOW GOGGLES WITH VENTILATORS USED BY THE ESKIMO OF PORT CLARENCE, ALASKA.

Cat. No. 46137, U. S. N. M. Collected by Dr. Tarleton H. Bean.

every unnecessary scrap of wood is cut away outside about the nose and eyes. The effect of this is to reduce the weight and to give the appearance of a mask. The connection of the whole class with mask wearing would not be difficult to trace. The headband consists of a single string back of the head to which double strings are attached at each end in order to connect with the wooden frame. This specimen was worn by Dr. Bean in his Alaskan explorations for the U. S. Fish Commission (fig. 26). It is similar in typical characteristics to a number of specimens in the U. S. National Museum collection from that point, excepting that the eye slits in the aboriginal specimens take the place of the glass. It should be also noted that in such examples this slit though continuous in front, as may be seen in the Bean specimen, is not continuous in the rear, being interrupted by the wood that forms the nose cavity. Mr. Tylor would say that this groove on the outside across the bridge of the nose is a survival of the old primitive continuous slit apparatus. Certainly it performs no function and does not add to the beauty of the specimen. Similar to this specimen are Nos. 45075, 45076, 45077, and 44769, from Sledge Island (Aziak), a little southwest of Port Clarence, sent to the U. S. National Museum by E. W. Nelson, and No. 44257 from Cape Darby on the northern shore of Norton Sound. From Port Clarence southwestward to Cape Darby is a continuous area. The specimen here figured is 5½ inches in length.

Example No. 45080 is from Sledge Island. It is a very light and neatly made specimen. Its characteristics are the continuous slit in front, interrupted by the nose portion behind, the visor having a gracefully curved surface above, the outer portion carved in form of the face. Length, 6 inches. Collected by E. W. Nelson.

Example No. 45079, also from Sledge Island, is related to the northern hooded or visored type, only the wide eye slit is continuous and the notch for the nose is cut from the lower margin. The two Sledge Island specimens, Nos. 45079 and 45080, are excellent for comparison. The former is the double-visored type, trough-like and deeply hollowed on the back. The former is like the eastern examples, with separate eye and nose cavities in the rear and the eye slits only seem to be continuous in front. Length of the former, 6 inches. Collected by E. W. Nelson.

Sledge Island, or Aziak, is a small island between Port Clarence and Cape Nome (64°, 30′, 168° NW.). Through the energy of the indefatigable collector, E. W. Nelson, the U. S. National Museum is rich in specimens from this region. It will not be surprising to find here a complex art, since this little projection from the sea is a middle ground for the Norton Sound, also from Sledge Island and Bering Strait region.

The specimen (fig. 27) here figured (Cat. No. 44768, U. S. N. M.) is very beautifully finished off, sandpapered and polished, colored red on the outside and black within, as most examples are. The specimen suggests the types already mentioned at the north, consisting of two disks like spoon bowls fastened together, this time not by beadwork but by a narrow bridge of wood. The eye slits are wider open on the inner ends, a characteristic quite common. Above the eye slits is a narrow visor delicately carved. Length of specimen, 4½ inches.

Example No. 44349 is a visor from Norton Bay made of a single block of spruce wood in shape of the front of a seaman's cap. Similar in form is No. 46309 from Port Clarence, collected by Dr. Bean; also, Nos. 45071, 45072, 45073, and 45074, from Sledge Island; No. 44144 from Cape

Darby; and No. 49068 from Rasboiniksky collected by E. W. Nelson
This type of eye protectors is better fitted for use on the water.
Similar forms occur on Norton Sound and about the Alaskan Penin-
sula. The Aleuts wear specimens of unusually large size, and there
are decorated forms used also in their ceremonial performances.
Length, 6 inches.

From St. Lawrence Island, the middle ground or Cyprus between the
American and the Asiatic Eskimo area, the U. S. National Museum possesses a specimen of the dish-shaped goggles, No. 63269, in which the
continuous slit does not appear, but has been replaced by two irregu-

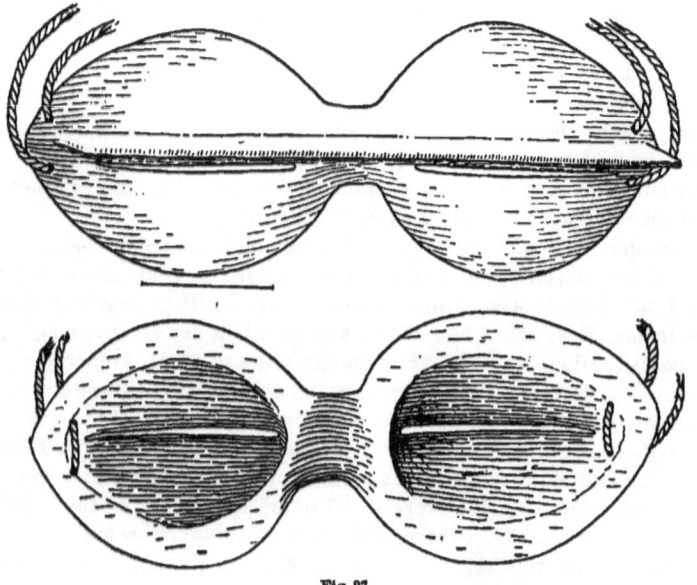

Fig. 27.

SNOW GOGGLES FROM SLEDGE ISLAND, ALASKA.

Cat. No. 44768, U. S. N. M.   Collected by E. W. Nelson.

larly cut holes for the insertion of smoked or colored glass. Collected
from the Kikhtogamut Eskimo by E. W. Nelson; length, 5½ inches. It
is not to be supposed that this aberrant specimen exhausts the native
ingenuity on St. Lawrence Island. The smooth finish of the object, its
normal shape, the holes for the headband, and the thong are entirely
Eskimo. Even the little knot shown on the left of the bottom figure
(fig. 28) is thoroughly savage, being made by cutting a slit in a thong
half an inch from the end and then thrusting the end through the slit.
It may be seen in many Eskimo implements where a button or toggle is
needed to fit into a countersink in wood or ivory. But the eyeholes are
bungling afterthoughts, many of which appear on Eskimo articles traded
to the whites.

Cape Nome, just southeast of Sledge Island, should be represented in the U. S. National Museum collections, but unfortunately it is not. A creditable number of specimens, however, come from Cape Darby at the entrance of Golovina Sound and Bay (64°, 20′, 163° NW.).

Example No. 44256 is from Cape Darby. Carved front and rear and resembling a masquerader's disguise, fitting the face neatly behind and cut away to a parallel surface in front. Over the eye slits is a visor three-fourths of an inch wide, which is not flat on top in this or any related specimens, as we have in the eastern type, but sloped up by a

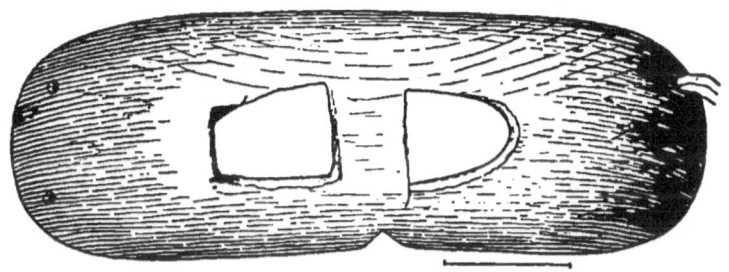

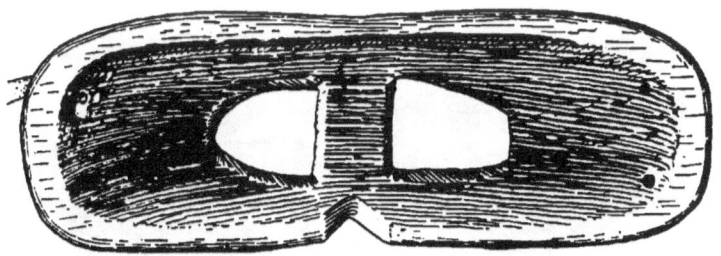

Fig. 28.

ESKIMO SNOW GOGGLES FOR COLORED GLASS, ST. LAWRENCE ISLAND, ALASKA.

Cat. No. 63269, U. S. N. M.   Collected by E. W. Nelson.

curved surface to follow the lines of the eyebrows. Length, 6¼ inches. Collected by E. W. Nelson.

Norton Bay is in the northeast corner of Norton Sound. From this area comes, through E. W. Nelson, another set of goggles, No. 43929, of two separate disks. Two oval plates or trays of wood fit over the eyes with narrow aperture for vision. These are connected by means of three short sinew strings or cords. Length, 6¼ inches. Made and used by the Kaviagmut. In another specimen, No. 44329, the disks for the eyes are connected by a bridge of wood. The object is neatly carved and so symmetrical that it may be used either side up. It should be compared with No. 1650, from Anderson River and figures 24 and 27.

From the same area Nelson procured the specimen No. 44349 (fig. 29a), one of a series of plain visors like that on the front of a cap. From this point to Kadiak, south of Aliaska or the Alaskan peninsula, the visor becomes larger and larger until it entirely covers the head like a hat and extends in front 6 or more inches. In fact this sort of visor is in that area an equipment of the mariner, and will be more properly con-

Fig. 29.

(a) HUNTING VISOR USED BY THE ESKIMO OF NORTON BAY, ALASKA. Collected by E. W. Nelson.
(b) GOGGLE AND EYE SHADE MADE OF THE SKIN OF A RINGED SEAL'S HEAD (PHOCA FŒTIDA). Gift of R. MacFarlane.
(c) EYE SHADE OF CARVED WOOD USED BY THE ESKIMO OF ANDERSON RIVER, MACKENZIE RIVER DISTRICT, CANADA. Gift of R. MacFarlane.

Cat. Nos. 44349, 7733, and 1651, U. S. N. M

sidered in the chapter on aboriginal water travel. The specimen is engraved with geometric lines.

With this visor must be compared a specimen from Anderson River, No. 7733, made of the skin from the face of a seal with the hair on, the eyeholes fitting over the man's eyes. This again leads up to the decoration upon No. 1651, U. S. National Museum, which is a visor of pine wood, upon the front of which the wearer has painted in blue lines the countenance of the seal. The specimens here shown (fig. 29b and c) are the gift of R. MacFarlane.

As one might imagine, the greatest variety of goggles are received from St. Michaels and Norton Sound. No lessons in geographic distribution are to be drawn from these offhand. For the past one hundred years and more this region has been the entrepôt of Russian and Federal occupation. Hereabout the cunning natives early became acquainted with steel knives, hammers, saws, files, and boring tools, and here their creative and adaptive minds were first excited and modified by seeing new objects and forms to copy. Turner, Nelson, and others have sent to the U. S. National Museum pretty specimens

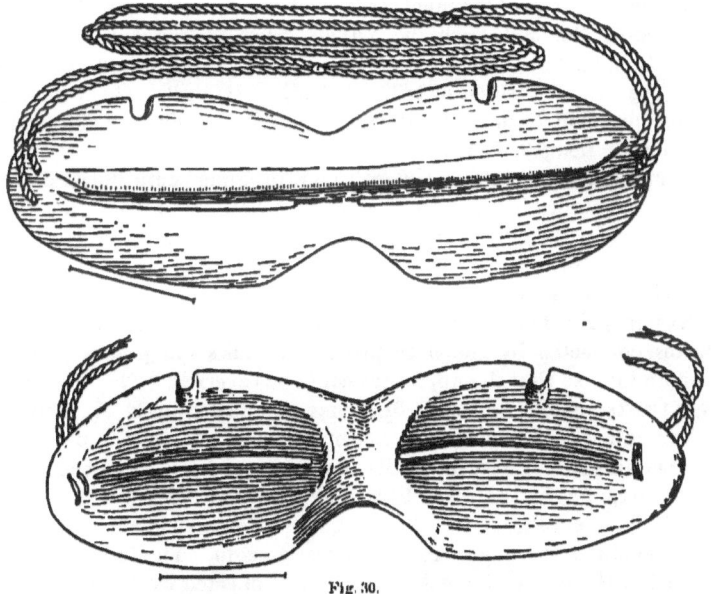

Fig. 30.

ESKIMO SNOW GOGGLES WITH VENTILATORS, NORTON SOUND, ALASKA

Cat, No. 32942, U. S, N. M. Collected by E. W. Nelson.

of goggles, consisting of two disks united by means of beadwork, No. 24339. Leather thongs also replace the beadwork as in No. 24686, made by the Unaligmut on St. Michaels. Length, 6 inches. By the first-named collector was secured a specimen on the same order, in which a narrow bridge of wood replaces the beadwork. In this specimen there is also a projecting ledge across the front above the eye slits. Length, 5¼ inches, Unaligmut. Nelson also contributes a double specimen from the Unaligmut, No. 32944. The specimen from Norton Sound, No. 32942 (fig. 30), is worthy of special study in relation to this area as the southern limit of certain types. There are in it suggestions of the elongated dish or tray shaped body of the extreme north, of the two trays fastened together by means of beadwork, of the separate eye cavities and notch for the nose, of the narrow ridge or visor, and especially to be noted is the occurrence of neatly cut notches above the eyes, apparently for'ventilation. It is a very daintily made specimen. No. 24340, from Unalakleet, resembles in front this example, the cavities are deeper in the rear, and there are no notches for ventilation. No. 32948 has also separate eye and nose excavations, but in front the visor is flat and the eye slits are similar to those farther north. Length, 5 inches.

Example No. 24341 is from Norton Sound, and is a mixture of the Sledge Island example, with the quasi continuous eye slit, and the northern example, with disk-like eyepieces. This specimen has a hood or visor over the eye slits, and is also remarkable for the projection or sharp curve outward, as much as 2½ inches. Length, 5¼ inches.

Example No. 5581, from the Yukon River, is trough-shaped, much curved outward, having no projections or decorations, and one continuous eye slit. Collected in 1868 by William H. Dall. This example is as primitive in form as those made from antler above mentioned by Murdoch. Length, 7 inches.

Example No. 5579, from Yukon River, in fundamental form, like No. 5581, but notches for the nose above and below and a slight hood over the two eye slits give variety to the form. A slight furrow connects the eye slits in front, as in No. 45080. Length, 5½ inches. Collected by William H. Dall.

Example No. 44328 is cut from a single piece in form of two disks or dishes, connected by the nose piece. The slits are precisely along a median line, so that the apparatus could be reversed. The head string is of twisted sinew. Length, 5½ inches. Collected by E. W. Nelson.

Example No. 72906, from the Lower Yukon, is cut out of a single piece of wood in general form of the Kuskokwim specimen. The comparison ends there, for in the piece here described the block is hollowed out interiorly, a notch cut for the nose, and a long, wide slit with square ends separates the upper from the lower margin. The former does not project in the least. Length, 7½ inches. Collected by E. W. Nelson.

Example No. 44330 is also a pair of goggles of two separate dish-like eye covers, united by means of sinew thread, decked with red and white beads. This is a very pretty specimen and has seen much use.

Example No. 43929, from Yukon River, is made of two oval dish-like pieces, with narrow eye slits in the bottoms, and fastened together by means of sinew twine; the headband of hide thong doubled. These and others of the same type are neatly made, and cut away very thin just behind the eye slit. Length, 6½ inches. Collected by E. W. Nelson.

Example No. 36351 (fig. 31) is lorgnette-shaped and was brought from Kushunuk, Bristol bay. The place where it was worn is unknown. A piece of wood is deeply hollowed in the rear so as to form two prolonged tubes. In front the wood is cut away in shape of the interior, and large openings are left for vision or for smoked glass. Collected by E. W. Nelson.

On the Lower Yukon River, in the delta that forms the southern boundary of Norton Sound, reappears a type of goggle described from Sledge Island, No. 48724, U. S. National Museum. That is, the eye slit is uninterrupted in front, but across the nose it is cut in only one-eighth of an inch and there is interrupted in the rear by the piece that forms the bridge of the nose. With this should be compared No. 38251, both collected by E. W. Nelson. Length, 6 and 6½ inches. From the Ekogmut Eskimo.

In addition to this marked type Nelson sends from the Yukon other patterns varying away from it into single slit forms; those in which the mask feature is suggested and rude pieces of degenerate style. In the Museum of Natural History, New York, Mr. Saville reports the three varieties from Norton Sound and Lower Yukon area, namely, two separate disks (No. 287, Emmons); solid block with slits or glass (Emmons 49297, 49430, and Terry, 22247 and 22248); and visor or hood

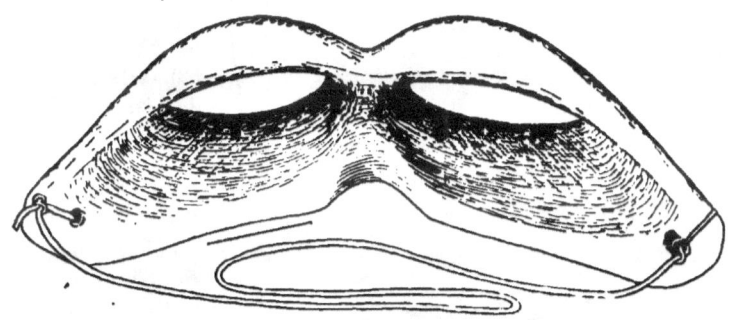

Fig 31.

VISOR SNOW GOGGLES USED BY THE ESKIMO OF KUSHUNUK, ALASKA
Cat. No. 36351. U. S. N. M. Collected by E. W. Nelson

(Emmons, 39, 47, 52, 53, 148, 455). Some new special features are presented by the New York pieces.

So far as the true goggles with narrow eye slit are concerned, the apparatus is not represented in the U. S. National Museum south of the Yukon mouth. Dall brought no specimens from the Nunivak and Nelson Island region. The next specimen southward in the U. S. National Museum collection is from the Kuskokwim region, carved out of a single piece of wood and strongly suggestive of the projecting shades made of wire gauze worn in civilized communities by persons suffering with weak eyes, as in example 36351. The specimen is quite maskoid, with huge eyebrows, and deep cut cavities. The whole is trimmed away in front to make the apparatus lighter to the wearer. Length, 6 inches. Collected from the Eskimo of Kushunuk, at the mouth of the Kuskokwim River, by E. W. Nelson. There is no evidence of glass having been used on this specimen. The long tubes in front of the eyes are blackened.

Lately, Mr. I. C. Russell, of the International Boundary Survey between Alaska and Canada, brought to the U. S. National Museum two pairs of goggles, No. 153427, from the Athapascan tribes on the upper Yukon. They are evidently birch-bark makeshifts on the suggestion of the double goggles of the northern area. Each specimen is made of two "pill boxes," of birch bark with diamond-shaped holes cut in the bottoms. These are joined together by a strip of birch bark sewed on.

Following up the idea that the Kuskokwim specimen was not designed for glass, the student comes to the typical Bristol Bay eye-shade (Ihug-ach-shu-duk). On top this apparatus is no more nor less than a common visor, seen all about Bering Sea and over the northern arctic zone, where wood abounds. If a visor an inch thick were hollowed out, cut away a little for the nose in one place, pared away on its under edge in front, blackened on the inside, that would be the double visored eye

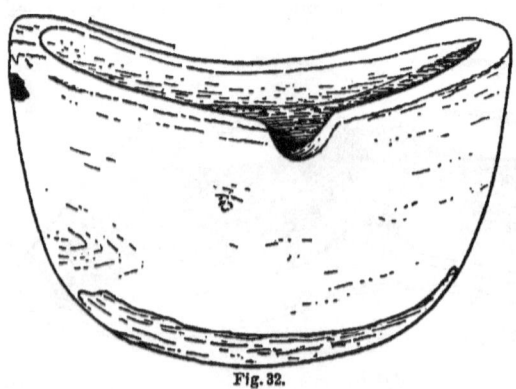

shade or goggles of Bristol Bay. The figure here given is of No. 127781 (fig. 32), collected by W. J. Fisher. The U. S. National Museum contains a great variety of this type. With this example should be compared No. 55930 collected by C. L. McKay, Nos. 127477 and 127478 from Togiak River, collected by Apple-

Fig. 32.

VISOR SNOW GOGGLES FROM KUSKINAK, ALASKA.
Cat. No. 127781, U. S. N. M. Collected by Wm. J. Fisher.

gate, and No. 72515 collected by W. J. Fisher. The last named is an oddity, and is probably of very modern manufacture. Length of figure, 5½ inches.

Example No. 55930 from Bristol Bay is in effect a typical double visor or a thick visor mortised through and painted black inside, the lower margin cut to fit the nose. In front the apparatus looks like the slightly opened mouth of a big fish. Most of the visor-like goggles are fastened with rawhide thongs. Length, 6 inches. Collected by C. L. McKay.

. The accompanying illustrations (figs. 33 and 34) exhibit the structure of the double visor or elongated goggles. It is here recalled that at the extreme north this form does not occur, owing to absence of wood, and that at the extreme south the goggles with slits for the eyes are not to be found.

Indeed, while the goggles, the visor, and the double visor are all to be worn on the eyes, the first-named is to prevent ophthalmia in the hunter walking over the snow.

The second is the Arctic form of the universal sunshade, hat brim, eye shade, having a different technical treatment for every people and culture region.

The third is this likewise, and by its lower shelf is also a device for looking a long way down into the water. Many of Holm's East Greenland specimens having a visor top, and a deep curtain of wood around the margin enables a hunter lying on his stomach on the ice to see far down into the water and to guide the long-handled harpoon held by his companion. The wearers of the western examples are kaiak people who hunt their game with bladder harpoons, and it is essential that they should be able to follow them with the eye. Our modern deep-sea fishermen use a common bucket with a pane of glass in the bottom for looking down into the ocean.

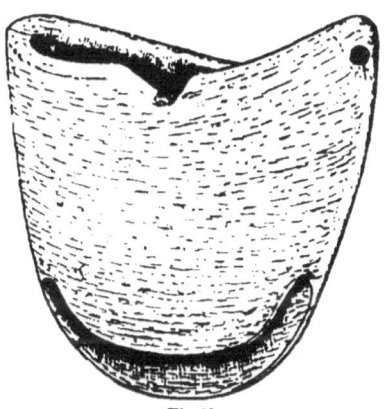

Fig. 33.

VISOR SNOW GOGGLES USED BY THE ESKIMO OF BRISTOL BAY, ALASKA.

Cat. No. 127784, U. S. N. M. Collected by Wm. J. Fisher.

The Aleut dress according to Strong was similar to that of the Koniagas, with the addition of a high peaked hat made of wood or leather. This hat had a long brim in front to protect the eyes of the wearer from the glare of the sun upon the water and snow, and was ornamented at the back by hanging upon it the beards of sea lions. The front was usually carved to represent some animal and the surface was overlaid with ivory carvings.[1]

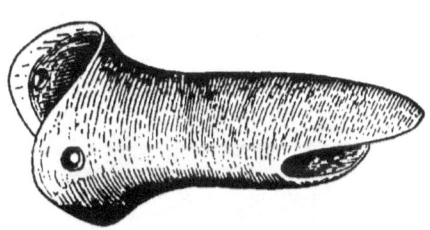

Fig. 34.

VISOR SNOW GOGGLES USED BY THE ESKIMO OF BRISTOL BAY. (SIDE VIEW).

Cat. No. 127784, U. S. N. M. Collected by Wm. J. Fisher.

Nansen recommends the common goggles with slits, but objects that the snowshoer should be able to look vertically as well as horizontally; but C. W. Remington figures a set of native snow goggles of the Barren Ground, in which a narrow T-shaped slit admits of both horizontal and vertical sight.[2]

From Fort Hall, Idaho, the U. S. National Museum possesses another

[1] Strong, "Wah-kee-nah and Her People." New York, 1893, Putnam, p. 101.

[2] Harper's Magazine, 1895, XCII, p. 26, and F. Nansen's "First Crossing of Greenland," London, 1890, I, p. 50.

aberrant specimen of snow goggle or eye shade, No. 153545, collected by Mr. Danilson (fig. 35). This specimen is said to have been used by the Shoshones and Bannocks, who belong to the great Uto-Aztecan family; but the apparatus is made from harness leather, punched with a steel punch, cut out with a keen steel knife, and held on with worsted braid. The adjustable shutter is also a device somewhat above any-

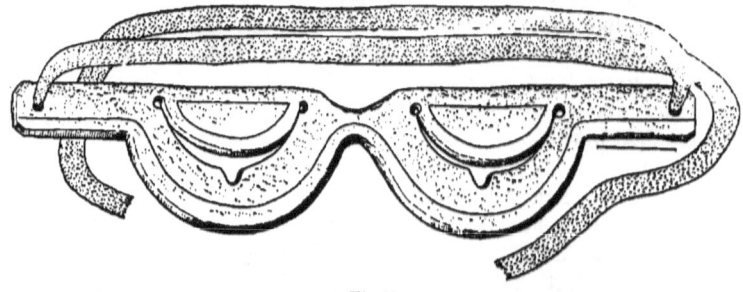

Fig. 35.

SNOW GOGGLES USED BY THE BANNOCK AND SHOSHONE INDIANS OF IDAHO.

Cat. No. 153545, U. S. N. M.   Collected by W. H. Danilson.

thing in the way of eye screens exhibited by savagery. It serves the purpose of emphasizing what has been many times repeated by the present writer, that civilization modifies the working principles of savagery. This specimen furnishes a fitting close to the study of an implement that the whalers and fur hunters modified and carried from place to place. Local forms are not nearly so fixed as those of the throwing stick.

EYE SHADES AND SNOW GOGGLES IN THE U. S. NATIONAL MUSEUM.

Museum number.	Specimen.	Locality.	By whom contributed.
168938	Large wooden eye shade, plain	East Greenland	Captain G. Holm.
168939	Hooded eye shade, ornamented	...do	Do.
168940	Tray-shaped, triangular eyeholes, large.	...do	Do.
90176–90188	Angular type, more or less visor	Ungava	L. M. Turner.
10292	Angular type, flat visor	Frobisher Bay	Capt. C. F. Hall.
29976–29978	Angular type, visor flat	Cumberland Gulf	W. A. Mintzer.
68141	No visor, machine made	Hudson Bay	J. T. Brown.
10200	Angular type, flat visor	Fury Strait	Capt. C. F. Hall.
2167	Plain tray shape, two slits	Anderson River	R. MacFarlane.
1650	Plain tray shape, single slit	...do	Do.
1651	Visor, with face painted on	...do	Do.
2147	Two small separate disks	...do	Do.
7733	Visor and goggle, skin of seal's head.	...do	Do.
7478–7479		Mackenzie River	Do.
89701–89702	Tray shape, two slits, antler	Point Barrow	P. H. Ray, U. S. A.
89703	Two slits, visor, ventilators	...do	Do
89694	Goggles from gravel bed	...do	Do.
46041	Double visor, ventilators	Cape Lisburne	W. H. Dall.
63825	Tray shape, single slit, visor	Point Hope	E. W. Nelson.

Eye Shades and Snow Goggles in the U. S. National Museum—Continued.

Museum number.	Specimen.	Locality.	By whom contributed.
127907	Two ovate disks separate	Kotzebue Sound........	G. M. Stoney, U. S. N.
63626	Wood, canvas cover. glass eyes	Diomede Island	E. W. Nelson.
63269	Dish-shaped, eyeholes for glass	St. Lawrence Island....	Do.
46309	Large visor	Port Clarence..........	T. H. Bean.
46101	Maskoid type, glass eyes............	....do	Do.
46137	....do	....do	Do.
45071–45074	Large, plain visors................	Sledge Island....	E. W. Nelson.
45075–45077	Maskoid with visor.................	....do	Do.
45078	Maskoid, visor, ventilators	....do	Do.
45079	Double visor like, single slit	....do	Do.
45080	Tray shape, visor..................	....do	Do.
44768	Two disks and visor in one piece....	....do	Do.
44769	Sledge Island type................	....do	Do.
44144	Plain visor........................	Cape Darby..........	Do.
44256	Maskoid, visor, Sledge type	....do	Do.
44257	....do.............................	....do	Do.
44329	Tray shape, one slit, reversible	....do	Do.
44328	Double disk, slits in visor..........	Norton Bay..........	Do.
44330	Two separate disks	....do	Do.
44349	Plain visor........................	....do	Do.
24339	Separate disks	Unalakleet	L. M. Turner.
24340	United disks	....do	Do.
43029	Separate disks	Norton Sound	E. W. Nelson.
24341	Double disk and visor..............	....do	Do.
24686	Two separate disks................	....do	L. M. Turner.
33136	Visor and frog mask...............	....do	E. W. Nelson.
33137	Visor and headband	....do	Do.
32942, 32944	Double disk, single slit, air holes....	....do	Do.
32943	Tray shaped, slight visor...........	....do	Do.
37351–37353	Visors, lorgnette style	....do	Do.
37619	Plain visor........................	....do	Do.
49102	Visor and headband................	Pastolik	Do.
48684	Conical hat, with ornament	St. Michaels	Do.
153784	....do.............................	....do	J. H. Turner.
5581	Plain tray, single slit	Yukon River	J. Y. Dyer.
5579	Maskoid, Sledge Island type........	Mablemut	W. H. Dall.
11441	Visor	Lower Yukon	Do.
38251	Slightly maskoid, two slits.........	....do	E. W. Nelson.
38329	Visor	....do	Do.
38704	Tray shape, one slit visor..........	....do	Do.
38710–38712	Visor and headband...............	....do	Do.
38837	Visor	....do	Do.
38658	Tray shape, maskoid	....do	Do.
48724	Tray shape, one wide slit..........	....do	Do.
48996	Maskoid, no visor	Sabotnisky	Do.
49068	Visor and headband	Rasboinisksky.........	Do.
72906	Double visor, coarse...............	Lower Yukon	Do.
16221	Visor and headband	Nunivak.............	W. H. Dall.
38659	Visor	Kuskokwim..........	E. W. Nelson.
55930, 55931	Double visors, coarse..............	Bristol Bay.........	C. L. McKay.
36351, 36352	Lorgnette shape	Kushunak...........	E. W. Nelson.
37351	Lorgnette leather visor............	....do	Do.
36404	Conical visor hat, ornament........	....do	Do.

Museum number.	Specimen.	Locality.	By whom contributed.
38713–38718	Visor hats, plain	.....do	E. W. Nelson.
127477, 127478	Double visors......................	Kassian	I. Applegate.
90444	Conical visor hat, ornament.........	Kadiak	W. J. Fisher.
72515	Quadrangular visor	.....do	Do.
74720	Conical visor hat...................	.....do	Do.
127780, 127781	Double visor	Kuskinak...............	Do.
72515	Visor hat	Ugashik	Do.
1131	Visor hat, conical	Aleut..................	Capt. Bulkley, U. S. A.
5772	Painted visor hat	.....do	Capt. W. A. Howard.
11377	.....do.............................	.....do	Vincent Collyer.
154073	.....do.............................	.....do	Mrs. M. M. Hazen.
153427	Birch-bark spectacles, 2 pairs.......	Upper Yukon	I. C. Russell.
22286	Goggles from harness leather	Fort Hall, Idaho........	W H Danilson
131053	Eye screen or network	Northeast Tibet........	W. W. Rockhill.
167159	Eye shades and case	Lhasa	Do

FOOT WEAR USED IN TRAVEL AND TRANSPORTATION.

Among the five typical classes of industries (page 237) the barefooted man and woman are common in the first two and the last two. The shoe is especially an accessory of travel; it belongs to the road. Even nowadays men wear their shoes to the field and work in the field barefooted. The same is true of women in all their drudgeries. Barefooted men and women are glorified in art, and in old religions both priest and worshiper remove the shoes. Ratzel has also noticed that sandals are rather peculiar to the road, and thinks they are more commonly made of hide than of wood or bast. He also calls attention to their wide extent.[1]

Locations will be found where the traveling class are barefooted, but a close inspection of them will show that the people are maritime or that the climate is opposed to clothing the feet. Furthermore, it is difficult and seems useless to make the foot a decorative part of the body. Unclothed the foot is usually plain.

Bush speaks of Giliaks whom he met as far north as the Amur mouth with naked feet and legs in September.[2] They wandered over the jagged stones on the beach as though their feet were soled with iron, while the cold seemed to have no effect upon them whatever. Upon a stump of driftwood 6 feet long, six of them sat with their feet drawn up under their bodies. But when these same people go away from home, they and all other hyperboreans exhaust their ingenuity on foot wear and foot gear. It is said that in southern China the children's feet are seared to harden them.[3]

---

[1] "Völkerkunde," Leipzig, 1887, I, p. 67.
[2] "Reindeer, Dogs, and Snowshoes," pp. 81 and 104.
[3] Chinese Repository, Canton, 1833, I, p. 29.

As previously mentioned.the anatomy of the foot has excited some attention, but it is a wonder that no one has dwelt upon the foot as an instrument of human industry. There are multitudes of able dissertations upon the foot as a characteristic in comparative anatomy, but here the organ is regarded in the light of an instrument of locomotion, whose place saddles, wagons, cars, and the like were invented to fill, and whose burdens dogs, reindeer, llamas, camels, elephants, asses, horses, and oxen were domesticated to share. In this light its power, versatility, adaptability, recuperative attributes, elasticity, and endurance are beyond our praise. But in this chapter the foot itself is the starting point of a wonderful series of inventions.

In all countries where mere protection of the foot was the motive, those substances were chosen that were abundant and from which in a few moments new shoes could be constructed with a little knack and no special tools. Mackenzie says that the women who attended his Indians were constantly employed in making fresh moccasins of elk skin. Travelers in the tropics also note that when the foot demands protection, the material is always at hand, and that the natives have no trouble in providing themselves during their resting spells with an entirely new outfit.

Under the general name of foot gear must be included all that is attached to the foot and lower leg in walking, running, or carrying, for industrial purposes. Sandals, slippers, shoes, sabots, boots, stockings, greaves, snowshoes, ice creepers, and others to be mentioned, may be comprehended in a genus and treated as objects in natural history of which we may study:

(1) The structure, materials, methods of production and of application to the foot, varying from region to region.

(2) The elaboration, or evolution, or phylogeny, taking the more complex varieties and tracing them to their pristine forms, as a patent attorney would proceed in showing the serial development of a modern machine.

(3) Environmental influences. Since foot gear is devised for the double purpose of defending the foot from wear and tear, and of protecting it from the cold or heat, on mountain, plain, and bog; on open sward, volcanic slag, thorny undergrowth, and burning sand; from poisonous plants and noxious creatures, each and all of these have claimed a hearing from the inventor and stimulated ingenuity, giving endless variety to what would else appear barefooted monotony.[1]

(4) Ethnic peculiarities. These are they that put the last finishing touches on all human productions. Anatomical form of the foot, the survival of old fundamental structures useful in their day and in some other region, the tribal art conceptions, stitches, knots, patterns, forms; the traditional and mythic emblems; names that are repeated in things— all these come out in an intensive study regarding any class of inventions.

---

[1] Cf. The author's " Origins of Invention," London, 1894, Walter Scott, Chap. x.

The anatomy of the sandal includes the following parts or characteristics. Some of the parts may be absent, but that fact should be
noted:

(1) The materials and technique.

(2) The sole, its form, material, and structure.

(3) The toe piece, a thong or peg between the great toe and the next
one or between other toes; a cap or cover or string over the toes—that
is, the vamp or the primeval device that answered its purpose.

(4) The instep pieces or straps, rising from the sole in front of the
heel and uniting over the instep. In many oriental varieties there are
short loops attached to the sole, and the lacing performs this function.

(5) The heel, wanting from sandal and slipper or is turned down,
especially in lands where one has to remove the foot-wear quickly,
for social, political, or religious motives. This is true in Japan, and
notably in countries under Mohammedan influences.

So there is an endless variety of thought expressed in the heels
of sandals, as the material is vegetable or animal, according to the
environment of the people and their work. Starting from the points
on the margin of the sole just below the ankles, two short straps may
run up to an ankle band, or a loop over the heel may join the sole
at these points, or the lacing may run over the heel through loops at
these points.

(6) The thong or lacing. It seems to one giving heed to the matter,
that the shoemakers of old were more troubled and racked their brains
more over the lacing of the sandal than on the structure of the sole.
The desiderata are, to have a sole securely and flexibly attached to the
foot, not to lacerate the foot unnecessarily, and to get the object off
with as little trouble as possible. The Turkish slipper, worn slipshod
or down at the heel, and the Japanese sandal, with toe string and instep
bands simply, fulfill the conditions of easy removal—the former for
ceremony, the latter for cleanliness.

There are two theories of lacing a sole to the foot—with toe strings
and without them. In the last-named process a sole of leather has a
number of slits cut about the margin and a sole of fiber has a number
of loops woven in the same places. Through these slits or loops the
lacing passes as on a skate or high shoe. By the first-named the toe
string is the starting point of fastening, and the question whether
there shall be any lacing at all is a matter of nationality.

Example No. 22192, from Yokohama, Japan, stands for a very numer
ous type of foot wear (fig. 36).

These very coarse examples (sandals) are made from the bark of
walnut, or some very dark-colored bast. They are woven on a warp
of four strands of the same material. There are six loops for lacing
in front, two on the margin at the arch of the foot and four at the
heel. These loops are made in the course of weaving, and are, in
fact, a part of the selvage. At the proper place the material is car-

ried beyond the outside of the warp and doubled; the weaving then goes on as usual, but when the weft returns to form the next stitch on the selvage a half hitch is made around the loop to hold it fast in place, and then the weaving proceeds normally. The lacing is of coarse rope crossed over the toes, over the instep, and carried around the heel through the four heel loops as shown, and brought back over the instep and tied. Length of foot, 11½ inches. Collected by Hon. Benjamin S. Lyman.

A widely disseminated form of sandal consists of the following parts:

(1) Sole of rawhide, single or double, cut rights and lefts.

(2) A toe piece passing up through the sole between the great and the fore toe. This piece is fastened underneath by a toggle or frog, cut out of the leather or rawhide itself, and flattened parallel with the sole or by a single knot in the end.

(3) Side strap: in this class of examples formed by cutting two slits about an inch long at the margins of the sole under the arch of the

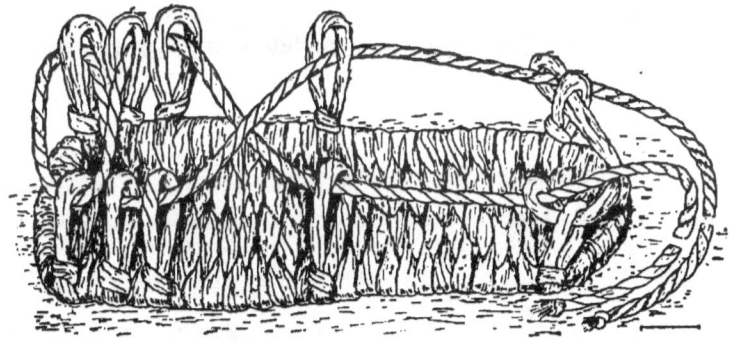

Fig. 36.
SANDAL OF BAST FROM YOKOHAMA, JAPAN.
Cat. No. 22192, U. S. N. M. Collected by Benjamin S. Lyman.

foot. A bit of rawhide passes down through one slit across the sole beneath and up through the other slit. The two ends extend 2 inches straight upward and are slit to receive the lacing.

(4) The lacing: a thong of leather slit at one end. Commencing at the little toe it passes backward through the slit in the side strap on that margin, making a half hitch. Thence it passes back of the heel and through the other side strap, and makes a half hitch. Thence it passes through the slit in the toe piece and through the slit at its own starting point, and is fastened off. Length, 9½ inches in the example (figs. 71, 72) from Bolivia. Collection of Mrs. Fanny B. Ward. Other examples from Bolivia are made of rawhide, and two thicknesses are pegged together, the rows of pegs mimicking the stitching on the better class of Turkish shoes. Under the term Baxeae in Smith's Dictionary of Greek and Roman Antiquities, two sandals of vegetable fiber are figured—one rounded in front, the other pointed, one woven

diagonally, the other in close wicker. These have three points of attachment—one for the toe strap and two at the margin under the ankles.

The shoe is a sandal that has grown up over the foot. The North American Indian moccasin is the simplest modern illustration of this. In a great collection of them it is hard to say where the sole leaves off and the upper begins. The evolution of this important element of clothing may be traced in two directions, forward or backward. Commencing with the first efforts to bring the sandal sole a little way over the foot or by dissecting a modern elaborate shoe and observing where, in what form, and from what motives each element made its appearance.

Tristram says that the word used for shoe (in the East) is different

Fig. 37.

LEGGING OF RUSHES IN TWINED WEAVING, KLAMATH INDIANS, NORTHERN CALIFORNIA.

From a figure in Mason's "Ray Collection from the Hupa Reservation," Report of the Smithsonian Institution, 1886.

from that for sandals. The latter are simply soles of undressed hide, with the hair on the upper surface, and fastened with thongs, always carried by the traveler, who walks barefoot on sandy or grassy ground, but who finds them absolutely necessary for the rocky and stony paths of the hill country. Shoes, or rather as we should call them, slippers, have upper leathers and heels, and are made of softer material. They are worn by horsemen, and for use in the house are frequently brightly colored.[1] It is more than probable that the rawhide sandals with single toe-string came to Latin-America from this region via Spain.

The legging must next be studied in this connection. It may have a separate existence, as in our modern examples. It may form an elongated portion of the shoe, as in Eskimo boots. It may be attached immediately to a sandal and become a boot, as in northern Japan. It may extend uninterruptedly from a rawhide sole to the hip, being shoe top, boot leg, and breeches, as in the Pueblo country. Finally, shoe, legging, and breeches may be continuous, as in the woman's boots of the Eskimo and the Mackenzie River costumes, or in the modern night drawers of children.

Example No. 24080 in the U. S. National Museum (fig. 37) is a legging worn by a Klamath Indian in California, made of coarse rush and woven together by twined weaving precisely as in the Alaskan grass sock and the Tate Yama boot (fig. 44). The Klamath country as well as the Aleutian Islands having been more or less exposed to Asiatic influences during the past half century it is quite within the possible that both

---

[1] Tristram, "Eastern Customs in Bible Lands," London, 1894, p. 50.

the socks and the leggings are late acculturations. Omitting this, the reader is left to decide the question of original suggestion in three separate areas.

Examples Nos. 150645 to 150649 are leggings (hose) worn by the Ainos and collected by Romyn Hitchcock. They are made of Japanese white or blue cotton cloth, each embroidered with cotton yarn of the other color. Two pairs are of the ohiyo or ehu bark (*Ulmus montana*). The ornamentation is produced partly in the weaving with differently colored yarns and partly in the use of the embroidered Cupid's bow or double line of beauty, so marked in all Aino ornaments.[1] It is only one step to the boot. By uniting the legging to the moccasin and sewing the sandal on to the bottom of that, the modern boot is in progress. There is not yet the complete outfit of sole and welt and insole; of vamp and quarters; of heel with a series of lifts; of top and extension top and straps; besides a dozen ornamental parts. But it will be seen that most of these parts, or something more elaborate and quite as effectual, have been thought out by downright savages.

As previously mentioned, the moccasin is of little or no use in a wet country, in bogs, or on the seashore. The high-heeled shoes of actors and of palaces had their origin in a necessity. The aborigines of America above the Arctic circle had recourse to sealskin cured without sweating and fish skin to keep the feet dry. The clumsy sole of the Asiatic Pacific Coast is the result of a struggle in the same direction. But the sabot, the clog, the chopine show how western Europe wrestled with the problem and thousands of persons still find employment in their manufacture. In England, the clog or patten is one step in advance of the sabot. A sole of maple or ash has an upper of leather riveted or nailed on. The survival of the clog is seen in great establishments like tanneries, where it is desirable to keep the feet above wet and muddy floors. Professor Morse draws my attention to the thousand and one styles of stilted sandals or quetta in use among the Japanese, and these point westward to the Caspian drainage for their congeners.

No one fails to remark the extreme roughness on the inside of most primitive foot gear. Now, since the sole of the foot, like the back and the neck of a horse, is the vital point to the footman and the carrier, it is reasonable to suppose that this was an object of constant care. In fact, the foot itself has wonderful adaptedness and the sole of the barefoot man becomes extremely callous. This is nature's contribution. In the U. S. National Museum are wooden sandals adorned on the sole with rows of brass-headed upholsterer's nails and the tough feet of the owners have actually worn furrows in the wood between the nails. But the inventive faculty has not been idle.

The Japanese weave a neat and smooth little insole of rushes or other soft fiber to fit above the regular sole in the common or diagonal

---

pattern seen in chair bottoms. In a large series of shoes the student gets a good notion of inventive progress through these insole devices and the method of their attachment.

The wearers of sabots are in the habit of eking out the foot by padding of some kind to prevent chafing. In every case the remedy is made effective with the best help of the environment. These devices are provisions simply against hurt or bruises. Temperature is not considered. In most regions under consideration the foot would be injured by bandaging or covering. A little further on it will be seen that packing the foot in soft grass is a provision for warmth and to prevent making that member too delicate. But there is a zone, an isothermal belt, between the complete double boot and the sandal, where the temperature for at least a part of the year is not cold enough for the hyperborean boot and packing, but where it is too cool for the unprotected foot. Here was elaborated the stocking or the double shoe top, or something to keep the foot and lower leg warm. It is interesting to note how exactly elevation above sea level tallies with latitude in determining this special article of dress.

The middle and western Asiatics, for religious and other considerations, holding on to the use of the sandal (easily removed), worked out the mitten sock with divided toes, the regular sock or stocking, and the inshoe or boot, over which the other shoe fitted. One may imagine such people moving northward or higher up and developing the double boot and the overshoe by simply thickening the material or adopting the thicker material supplied by nature.

In Korea, as well as in China, the stocking turns out to be a very complicated affair. A double bag of coarse cotton or other fabric is stuffed with a mass or waste half an inch thick. This is doubtless a luxury for those who do not travel, rendering the foot entirely too tender for work. (Cat. No. 167711, U. S. N. M., from Korea, collected by H. B. Hurlbert.)

The Samoyed men and women both wear the lieup thieu, or skin stocking, and the pimmies, or long deerskin boots. The only difference in the latter is that the crossbar is just above the instep in the woman's pimmies and just below the knee in the men's. In wet snow unsweated sealskin pimmies are worn. The Samoyed woman, it is said, is very careful of her husband's skin boots, turning them inside out, hanging them up to dry and putting grass into them in the morning.[1]

Eskimo men at Point Barrow, according to Murdoch, wear stockings of deerskin with the hair in. He figures the pattern of this sock, and says that they are made of very thick winter deerskin and substituted for the outer boots when the men are out deer hunting in winter in the dry snow, especially when snowshoes are used.[2] The same device is to

---

[1] Jackson, "The Great Frozen Land," London, 1895, pp. 27, 64.
[2] Ninth Ann. Rep. Bureau of Ethnology, p. 129, fig. 74, showing patterns; also F. Nansen, "First Crossing of Greenland," II, p. 275.

be seen in other fur wearing regions, and the selfsame custom projects itself into northwestern Canada, only the buckskin has been tawed. Nansen describes the double sealskin boot of the Greenland Eskimo.

The Eskimo also have a fashion of placing little bundles of dried fiber or fur in the boots, especially where the foot is chafed.

The East Greenland Eskimo use grass in their shoes, according to Nansen. He gives an amusing account of this in speaking of his Lapp companions, Balto and Ravna, who had the selfsame custom.[1]

The straw socks in the national collection (Nelson, No. 49082-'3) are said by him to be made along the lower Yukon and adjacent tundra to the south, perhaps to the Kuskokwim. Unaleet name, Athl uk shat.

Example No. 8784 is a pair of grass socks worn by the Premorska Indians of Alaska, collected by William H. Dall. They are regularly constructed by process of twined weaving; the warp is vertical, and the stocking is made to fit the foot by the insertion of extra-warped threads where they are needed. Beginning at the middle of the sole a series of twined weavings proceeds in a spiral around the bottom and the top of the foot for about an inch, when the lines begin to extend from the heel over the top of the instep. Separate lines of weaving are inserted across the back of the foot between the toes and the instep. This kind of weaving is very common all over the world, but its particular application to foot gear should be compared with No. 73091 from Tate Yama, Japan (fig. 44). Length of foot, 10½ inches. Precisely similar weaving is to be seen on the numerous grass wallets collected at St. Michaels.

STOCKINGS IN THE U. S. NATIONAL MUSEUM.

Museum number.	Specimen.	Locality.	By whom contributed.
49200	Socks (odd)	Alaska	E. W. Nelson.
48696	Socks, straw	Sabotnisky, Alaska	Do.
38813, 38814	Socks (or shoes), straw	Lower Kuskoquim	Do.
55972	Socks, woven grass	Bristol Bay, Alaska	Charles L. McKay.
1698	Socks, fox skin	Anderson River	R. Mac Farlane.
68143	Socks, child's	Hudson Bay, Eskimo	J. T. Brown.
5136	Socks, man's deerskin	Mackenzie River	R. Mac Farlane.
70999	Socks or shoe (Moki)	Arizona	Maj. J. W. Powell.
153045	Stockings, woolen	Persia	Pinkas Hanuka.
76386	do	do	Otis Bigelow.
164943	Socks, leather, worn with chaplies	Kashmir, India	Dr. W. L. Abbott.
167711	Socks, child's	Korea	H. B. Hurlbert.
151396	do	Wenchow, China	Dr. D. J. McGowan.
126875	Stockings	China	Miss Dollie Leech.
55826	Socks, felt, for women	Manchuria, China	Chinese Centennial Commission.
49082, 49053	Socks, straw	Lower Yukon, Alaska	E. W. Nelson.
49199	Socks, grass	Alaska	Do.
8784	do	Premorska Indians	W. H. Dall.

[1] F. Nansen, "First Crossing of Greenland," London, 1890, i, p. 362.

The interoceanic area, with its Australian, Negroid, Polynesian, and Malay peoples, is par excellence the barefooted region. On the shore the wet sands would render any foot clothing for which nature there furnishes material very uncomfortable. Life in the boat or canoe and in the shallow waters creates no demand for shoes. In recent pictures of the Malagasy army the soldiers are barefooted. These islands are volcanic and the coasts are lined with coral reefs. For walking over the one or for fishing along the other, some protection is necessary. The Polynesians, therefore, wore a tufted sandal of bast of the *Hibiscus*[1] in fishing on the coral reefs (fig. 38). Or, as in example No. 92884 in the National Museum, from the Sandwich Islands, leaves of pandanus are braided into a poor sandal for walking over the warm slag. The thick butt ends of the leaves are imbricated under the soles so as to leave quite a thick pad between the feet and the rough, hot ground.

Example No. 130639 is a sandal from New Zealand made of cordyline fiber, and consists of three pieces—the sole, the selvage or series of loops extending quite around the sole, and the lacing. The sole is of very coarse fiber, woven in diaper pattern diagonally. The selvage consists of a coarse vine fastened at the heel, and at intervals of 3 inches looped into the edge of the sole. Along the margin a small vine is carried and tied to the joints of this selvage by a clove hitch at each junction with the sole, and the lacing passes backward and forward across the foot, and around the heel through these selvage loops. The heel is made by a series of bands of very coarse fiber, passing backward and forward from one selvage loop to another, and tied with a single knot at each turn.

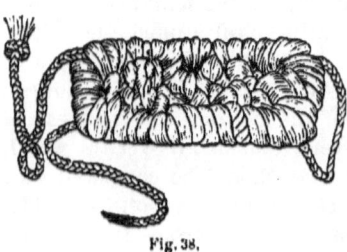

Fig. 38.

SANDAL OF BAST OF HIBISCUS FROM SAMOA.

From a figure in Ratzel's "Völkerkunde."

The noticeable points in this specimen are the diaper weaving, the complicated selvage, and the curiously built-up heel. This specimen must have belonged to a very large man (fig. 39). Length, 13 inches. Collected by the Royal Gardens of Kew, England.

This type of sandal exists elsewhere, and it must not be understood that it is a native New Zealand product. The absence of the string or strap between the first and the second toe will help to suggest certain culture centers from which it was not derived. In Korea and among the Ainos it is found, especially the border loops for the lacing. But an interesting similarity will be noted between this specimen and the figure of a cliff-dweller's sandal drawn by Nordenskiöld.[2]

---

[1] Figured by Ratzel in "Völkerkunde," II, p. 165.

[2] Cf. Hitchcock, Rep. Smithsonian Inst. (U. S. Nat. Mus.), 1890, pl. XCVII. Wiener does not figure anything of the kind in "Pérou et Bolivie."

Example No. 130640 is a pair of very primitive sandals of taromba spathe (*Arenga saccharifera*) from Borneo. The strings are made of the bast of the timbarua tree. This is the simplest form of shoe that can possibly be constructed. A bit of the spathe of the arenga is cut out in form of the foot, one hole is bored at the toe and two under the heel. A bit of twisted bast of the artocarpus is knotted and drawn through the front so as to pass between the toes, after the manner of the Caucasian or Mediterranean stocks or the Japanese; this is the lacing. Another bit of the same material doubled passes through the two holes under the heel to form loops. The lacing passes between the toes, across the back of the foot to the loop on the outside, around the heel through the loop on the inside, and across the instep to be fastened. Length, 11 inches. Collected by Royal Gardens of Kew, England.

In tropical America below the Piedmont regions, that is in the eastern portions and on the lowlands, the aborigines were barefooted. Indeed, though the question of origin is not here at all discussed, it will be further seen when the shod American is studied that it is very difficult nowadays to distinguish the New World from the Old World sandal in that area. Looking through such careful works as Von den Steinen's one sees no picture of foot gear and no allusion to it in the index.[1]

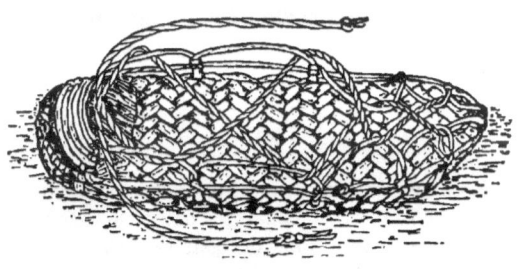

Fig. 39.

SANDAL OF CORDYLINE FIBER FROM NEW ZEALAND.

Cat. No. 130639, U. S. N. M. Collected by the Royal Botanic Gardens, Kew, England.

What has been said concerning the Indo-Pacific peoples and America may be repeated of negroid Africa, that is the part south of the Sahara. There is no climatic reason for shoes, the country is not volcanic, and the noxious animals are less able to injure the unclothed foot. There is an enormous amount of going about and of trading along beaten and cleared paths, hundreds of thousands of natives are all the time tramping to the trading center and to the coast, and yet we are told that they never cover the feet. In all books of travels and in photographs the natives are represented barefooted. This has given rise in Africa, and in Borneo as well, to a peculiar weapon, the foot-path splinter, small splints of cane sharpened, cut nearly in two, and stuck in the trail or public highway, a kind of aboriginal caltrop. The U. S. National Museum, though well supplied with African material and specially rich in foot wear, is extremely poor in examples from negroid Africa. An interest-

---

[1] "Unter den Naturvölkern Zentral-Brasiliens," Berlin, 1894.

ing chapter could be written on the deformations produced by cramping the foot of the African into white men's shoes.

The Hottentots, according to Ratzel, wear sandals of woven filaments and of rawhide. In the former the toes pass under a looped cord which extends up the middle of the instep, is knotted at the ankle, and fastened down at either side of the heel. In the rawhide specimens there is in addition a separate heel piece.[1]

Weiss's "Kostumkunde" figures a Hottentot sandal made of a piece of hide drawn up about the side of the foot and laced. He quotes Neibuhr on the Arab practice of cutting up the hide of a dead donkey on the road for sandals. Two Arab figures of Weiss's have loops or inclosures for one or more toes (fig. 101, *d* and *e*). This last has (1) quadrilateral sole; sewed with single thong; (2) heel strap separate, sloping up from sole; (3) instep band; (4) toe band, across all toes; (5) toe strings, inclosing three middle toes and running back to (3) to be tied. Feature 5 has some résemblance to Central American types.

When the Hottentots drive their herds to pasture, says Kolben, they put on a kind of leather stocking to secure their legs from being scratched by briars, etc. When they are to pass over rocks and sand, they put on a kind of sandal cut out of the rawhide of an ox or elephant, each consisting of only one piece, turning up about half an inch all around the foot, with the hairy side out, and fastened on with strings.[2] Nothing could be simpler to protect the sole of the foot. Aboriginal peoples, having access to animals with thick skins, naturally resort to this simple device of a bit of pelt cut larger than the foot, and while green or soaked turned up around the edge of the sole. This method of constructing a shoe or boot sole will appear again away up in the higher grades of the art. This specimen must be compared with a South American example further on.

Ratzel also figures a sandal from Unyoro, after Baker, somewhat dish-shaped, in which there is no distinction of sole and upper, and yet the material rises well up about the sole of the foot and above it for nearly an inch.[3] The sandals of this type are held onto the foot by the rudest kind of lacing, generally rove backward and forward through gashes cut in the upper margin. As the Sandwich Island sandal is among the rudest of vegetal foot gear, this type ranks lowest among those made of skin. Similar sandals are worn on the high plateaus of Peru made from the skin of the llama or of coarse vegetable fiber (fig. 40).[4]

Sir Samuel Baker figures a Unyoro sandal of rawhide. It is a shallow tray or dish, into which the foot is fitted. A strap loop in front fits the great toe; at the sides, on the margins, under the ankle bones

---

[1] Ratzel, "Völkerkunde," Leipzig, 1887, 1, p. 91, four figures.
[2] Kolben, "Voyage to Cape Good Hope," IV, p. 14.
[3] Ratzel, "Völkerkunde," Leipzig, 1887, 1, p. 65.
[4] Wiener, "Pérou et Bolivie," p. 679.

there are projections upward, slashed for the reception of a thong or lacing that passes over the instep and backward over the heel.

In central Soudan, Kanembu and Manga warriors wear sandals made of a sole of hide fastened on by a thong passing between the toes straight back to the ankle, where it meets a thong passing around the ankle and down to the sole at the arch, as in a spur. Indeed, the whole fastening is one continuous thong. This variety adds the toe strap, so common in all lands immediately or remotely touched by Caucasian influence. This feature will be noted further on.

Ratzel figures examples made from leather among the Herero. The type has toe strap extended and looped behind the ankle and attached to two side straps.[1] The specimens figured are quite ornate, and belong rather to social life than to the road. The characteristics also are from a region farther north.

Example No. 72716 is a low shoe from Morocco. The sole is of rawhide, curved up, and formed while wet so as to fit around the margin of the foot and over the toes, where the two edges are united to form a point decorated with an insertion of red morocco. The narrow upper margin, of black leather, is sewed on all around and doubled under at the edge. The string or strap passes through slashing in

Fig. 40.

PERUVIAN SANDALS OF LLAMA HIDE AND TEXTILES, FROM ANCON AND PARAMONGA.

From a figure in Wiener's "Pérou et Bolivie."

the heel and at the sides of the ankle. The noticeable features are the sole made of one piece and the simple manner in which the pointed toe is formed. Length, 10 inches.

Example No. 72716 is a shoe from Morocco, the gift of the Museum für Völkerkunde, Leipzig. It is made of light-brown leather, which has been stretched over a last when wet and permitted to dry into shape. The toes are pointed, and into them are inserted strips of red leather bound with black. They are secured to the foot by a leather thong, which ties across the instep. Length, 9¾ inches. The pointed toe is ornamental and leads away from the road. Its distribution in time and place is not difficult to trace.

The Mohammedan influence in west Soudan, added to the North African propensity for fine leather, is expressed in embossed and bedecked slippers. Symmetry overcomes the desire to follow the shape of the foot. The toe strap is attached to cross straps rising from the arch of the foot. There are no heel straps, and the sandal has only a slipshod attachment to the foot.[2] The stilt sandal, with toe peg, exists among

[1] Ratzel. "Völkerkunde," Leipzig, 1887, i, p. 328.
[2] Museum für Völkerkunde, Berlin. Figured by Ratzel, Ibid., iii, pp. 187, 277.

the Mandingos, but is useless for traveling purposes and came with the Mohammedans.

Example No. 43073 is a pair of sandals from Monrovia, Liberia, constructed on the plan of shoes generally worn in Mohammedan countries. Several thicknesses of leather are sewed together with a single thong in the form of stitch called "running." A small string passes up through the front and is connected with the lacing, which passes between the toes. The shoe is held in place by broad bands attached to the sole under the heel, and crossing each other on the back of the foot. A large button or rosette is placed on top of the foot below the instep. The surface of this rosette consists of diagonal weaving of red and black leather and palm leaf in very pretty geometric patterns. Length, 9¾ inches. Collected by J. H. Smyth, United States minister.

Mr. L. M. McCormick purchased at a bazaar in Aden a pair of sandals which show little or no signs of wear (example No. 175228 in the National Museum). The soles are quadrilateral, of two thicknesses of old leather, the lower much tougher. Under the heel of each is an additional piece, wedge-shaped, and between the soles an old sole for packing. These soles are sewed together by thongs of leather, making short stitches on top and long stitches underneath, about the margin and halfway down the middle. So much for the soles.

There are four parts connected with the lacing, which may be called (1) the toe string, (2) the buckle, (3) the heel strap, and (4) the lacing. The toe strap, or string, passes through two slits in the upper sole, so as to go between toes 1 and 2 and 3 and 4, and the two ends are then drawn up through separate slits in the leather buckle, tied in a single knot, and laid down flat. The buckle, so called, is a quadrilateral piece of leather, having two narrow slits for the ends of the toe string and two wider ones for the lacing. This buckle lies on the top of the foot below the instep.

The heel strap is of the very common sort, a strip of leather nearly an inch wide, passing through two slits on the margins of the upper sole. Its ends stand up an inch or more, and have double slits or slashes for the lacing.

The lacing is interesting (1) for its function in the "buckle," to hold the toe string in place and for the deft way in which the ends of the toe strings are tucked under, and (2) for the knots in the lugs or ends of the heel strap made on one side by a double loop in the lacing rove through the slits, and for the other side by the tucking in of the ends, which can be shown only by a drawing.

Example No. 175227 is a pair of sandals without location, consisting of compound soles, toe strings, toe loop, instep band, and side straps at the arch of the foot, besides a variety of ornamentations. As the sandal furnishes a type, it may be more minutely described:

(1) The sole in its top layer is complete, the next layer reaches from the heel nearly to the tip, the next two are complete, and they finish

the upper series. The heel is cut like that of a modern shoe. Under the ankles two broad side straps extend outward for purposes of lashing. The front portion widens out very broad, and the specimens are rights and lefts.

(2) Beneath this series is another, of the same dimensions at the heel, receding half an inch under the front of the foot. The heel has two or three extra layers, but there has been some patching.

(3) The ankle pieces extending from the sole are double on either side, and a double ankle band, the upper layer cut and stamped into lace work, is sewed by its ends between the ankle pieces.

(4) The toe fastenings are noteworthy, consisting of a loop for the great toe, and triple or double toe strings between 1 and 2 and 4 and 5.

These toe strings are gathered between the instep band by means of strings having false buttons of leather decorated with brass. The sewing is done in the universal southern Asiatic fashion by punching holes and reeving a leather thong through them, making neat stitches above and long ones beneath. In the English Illustrated Magazine for October, 1895, page 83, may be seen a Somali man wearing the peculiar, heavy, thick soled, curved sandals, with the curious sideboards visible on the feet of some Assyrian sculptures. On page 85 a queer looking lot of boys are similarly set out. In riding, the men use a rawhide loop for stirrups.

"In Egypt," says Erman, " men and women, young and old, almost always went barefoot, even when wearing the richest costumes. Under the old and the middle empire women seem never to have worn sandals, while great men probably only used them when they were needed out of doors, and even then they generally gave them to be carried by the sandal bearer who followed them. Sandals were more frequently used under the new empire; still they were not quite naturalized, and custom forbade that they be worn in presence of a superior. Consequently sandals were all essentially of the same form. Those here represented have soles of leather, of papyrus, reed, or palm bast; the two straps are of the same material, one strap passes over the instep, the other between the toes. Sometimes a third strap is put behind round the heel in order to hold the sandals on better; sometimes the front of the sandal is turned over as a protection to the toes. The sandal with sides belongs to a later period."[1]

The Egyptian sandals in the Metropolitan Museum, New York, are of the following kinds:

1. No. 351, center of sole of leather bordered with rows of coiled weaving in vegetal fiber; toe string of vegetal fiber.

2. No. 298 is woven, warp transverse, the texture resembling the coiled basketry of the Interior Basin of the United States, wherein the filaments split through one another; the border consists of two rows of coil; toe string of fiber, knotted underneath.

---

[1] Erman, " Life in Ancient Egypt," London, 1894, pp. 226–228, with ten figures in the text.

In the Douglas Egyptian collection of the same museum, one example is woven diagonally of papyrus, but has a sewed border; there is a hole for the toe string. One pair has wooden soles, one-eighth inch thick, holes for toe strings, and little posts or standards of wood beneath the ankle; the lacing passes from the toe string across the top of the foot to these posts. In drawings little curtains of ornamental stuff depend from the lacings. These sandals are not for the road. No. 45 in the Douglas collection has a strongly turned-up toe, pointed, the continued point meeting the toe string; a side, or vamp and quarter in one, extends from the toe quite around, inclosing the foot; the inside is lined with diagonally woven matting. These shoes resemble many Chinese examples.[1]

The sandal on the statue of Rameses II, in Turin, has a flat sole, toe string between 1 and 2, going straight up the top of the foot to a much-raised instep band reaching up from the sole under the heel. Other examples much turned up after the manner of the Somali type in front have the same elements with decorated instep band. Weiss[2] figures the greatest variety in this instep piece. There are practically five types of Egyptian shoe according to this author:

(1) Sole, toe string, instep strap.

(2) Sole of vegetal fiber, toe string bifurcated, instep strap.

(3) Toe strap, ankle band, vertical side straps.

(4) Wooden soles, ankle posts, ankle band sloping downward to the top of the post, and toe string passing to ankle band in two parts, from which hang curtains.

(5) Double sole, curled toe, toe strap, instep strap. From the instep strap to the toe, as in a Canadian toboggan, a curtain hangs down the sides.[3]

The ancient Hebrew wore a sandal with sole of leather, felt, cloth, or wood, occasionally shod with iron. From a passage in the Mishna it would seem that a heel strap was used in addition to the lacing [latchet] (Jebam., XII, 1). In accordance with the general statement that the shoe is an implement of travel, the Hebrews wore the sandal chiefly on the road. It was the Gibeonites who used the condition of their footwear as an indicator of distance traveled, "Our shoes have become old by reason of the very long journey" (Joshua IX, 13).

The modern Semito-Hamite pays great attention to the sandal and the shoe. The Hittite statue at Jerabis has on its feet boots, the sole

---

[1] The modern Egyptians wear red and yellow Turkish shoes; red outer shoes, murkoo'b; inner yellow shoes, mezz. The former are worn slipshod, and taken off upon stepping on a carpet or rug. (Lane, "Modern Egyptians," London, 1846, I, p. 44.)

[2] "Kostümkunde," Stuttgart, 1860, 2 vols. For the many ways in which ankle band may become heel and instep band by having its ankle parts elongated and drawn down to the sole, cf. Erman, "Ægypt," Tübingen, 1885, pp. 138, 159, and elsewhere.

[3] Weiss, "Kostümkunde," I, p. 37.

stopping under the ball of the foot. There is a distinct quarter over the heel and a top reaching up and constructed much as in the Athapascan moccasin.[1]

In the U. S. National Museum there is an interesting pair of sandals (example No. 5499), which have been in its possession a great many years. The locality given is Arabia, but many of the older numbers of the collection are not absolutely reliable. The notable features are the sole, the lacing, and the ornamentation. The sole consists of four thicknesses of leather, the middle one being the thickest. These are sewed together by means of a leather thong passing backward and forward, so as to make the alternation of stitches and vacant spaces quite regular around the upper border. No care is bestowed upon the bottom in this particular. This form of sewing or running bits of leather together is a type to be observed. The lacing is thus applied: the toe strap consists of three thicknesses which pass down through the sole and are fastened off below. Two of these thicknesses serve this function and no other. The third strap passes up between the toes, turns to the outer side of the foot, is attached to a loop or lug on the side by a single half hitch, passes across the instep down to a lug on the opposite side where it is again fastened, and then up over the side of the foot above the great toe, where it passes through the three thicknesses of leather and is fastened off by a sort of Turk's-head knot. The ornamentation consists of diagonal patterns and lines in white and green leather formed by sewing or back-stitching with a very narrow thin filament or thong of leather. The top of the sole, a broad band going across the foot, and a little narrow tongue of white, green, and brown leather on the instep over the lacing are all decorated after this fashion. Length, 10 inches.

Bare feet are very common in Chaldean and Assyrian sculptures, but foot gear is not uncommon. Boottees, high shoes, a little difficult to make out, and sandals with borders turned up, are worn in processions and about the royal palace.[2]

Assyrian sandals shown in sculptures have (1) sole of leather, single or double, flat generally; (2) heel inclosed by "quarter" piece, sloping down frontward; (3) cross straps and lacings from the quarter piece over the back of the foot and to the margins frontward; (4) loop over great toe, alone or attached to lacing.

Three kinds of foot gear are shown at Khorsabad. Two of them are sandals and one is a laced boot. In one form of sandal the heel and plantar arch are closed in, the instep and toes are bare, and three straps or three turns of a lacing connect the heel piece or low quarter across the instep. In the second sandal this heel is prolonged forward. The toes are strapped down and lacings pass across the metatarsals and over the instep. The laced boot has a sole curved up all round like

[1] William Wright, "Empire of the Hittites," New York, 1884, pls. I, II.
[2] Perrot et Chipiez, "Chaldea," London, 1884, II.

that of a Canadian lumberman and the top is sewed to this and laced all the way up the front. The Eskimo boots and the lauparsko of the Lapps are on the same model.

The Assyrian of high rank wore a sandal with sole of wood or thick leather. The upper consisted of a heel piece, sloping forward and reaching to the ball of the foot, where it runs out and leaves the toes and back of the foot uncovered. Lugs, or eyelets, on the margin of this piece served for lacing, passing two or more times over the instep. The lacing also crossed on the instep, and was passed round the great toe and between it and the adjoining toe.

For the common people the sandal was a sole, with a sloping heel band extending to the ball of the foot, laced over the instep with a thong passing through eyelets. Between the lacing and the instep a pad was held in place by the lacing running through slashes in the pad. This kind of sandal, reaching only to the toes and held on by a heel band, occurs in hundreds of figures in the Mexican codices. It is a little difficult to understand how a bare foot would be benefited by such gear. In the finest American snowshoes the open space in the netting for the accommodation of the toes also suggests itself. Layard also tells us that the enemies of the Assyrians differ from them in foot gear. On some feet the sole is attached by bands passing over the instep and around the heel. In other examples there seems to be a sole turned up and the upper rim united by crossbands, the upper part being left exposed.

The warriors' boots in the Khorsabad sculptures are not so difficult to comprehend. The sole was turned up all around the margin, the vamp and legging were, perhaps, in one piece, and sewed to the sole. The legging was doubtless open in front, as may be seen in a great many northern examples in our day.[1] See figure boot of the Tate Yama hunter. Mr. Rockhill brought from Tibet a long scroll, covered with painting of the various western barbarous nations coming to pay their tribute to the Emperor of China. The footwear in most of them agrees with the specimens brought home by him. The primitive efforts at boot making with the toe well curved up and the typical Turkish slipper predominate.

The Assyrian sandal shown in the bas-reliefs has a leather sole of several thicknesses sewed together. The toe string passes between 1 and 2, is bifurcated and reaches the margin of the sole under the arch of the foot, as in the Japanese sandal. There is also a band across all toes well in front, in a side view seeming to be looped only over the first toe. Frequently the heel cover is a solid leather quarter sloping forward and giving out at the margin under the ball of the foot.

In the Cesnola collection, Metropolitan Museum, New York City, several pieces of pottery from Cyprus show the boot or shoe form, or

---

[1] Cf. Layard, "Nineveh and its Remains," New York, 1849, II. See figure opposite p. 236.

the ornamented moccasin. In one or two examples the toe string between 1 and 2, and the additional band across all toes appear.

Some idea of the foot gear of the Caucasian in his ancient culture may be gained from carvings and sculptures or monuments and from ornaments on vases. The lesson is the same. The soldier is shod, for he is the man of the road, and whether he is portrayed in combat or idealized in sculpture or apotheosized in temple adornment, he knows no holy ground where he must take the shoes from off his feet. A modern officer of high rank when borne to his grave, accompanied by his horse, has the boots still attached to the stirrups.

The Greek κρηπίς, Latin *crepida*, occupied a middle position between a closed boot and a plain sandal. Its simplest form was a high and strong sole often studded with nails. Other forms had a low upper creeping up over the foot and becoming a shoe. In .the dramatic costumes the κρηπίς assumed the form of a soft shoe worn by women.[1] The *crepida* belonged to working people and soldiers, chiefs among roadsters. About the heel there was a series of loops into which the thong was laced across the top of the foot and through the toe strap. One form of Assyrian sandal has the same suggestion of an upper.

The Roman *sandalium*—Βλαῦται or σανδάλιον in Greek—were originally wooden soles secured to the feet with thongs. During the Homeric age they were worn only by women; later in Italy and in Greece they were used by both sexes. *Solea* was the military sandal. A sandal with a leather toe piece, ὑπόδημα, was the ancestor of the now universal sandal of the world. By a regular transition the lower form became the shoe, *calceus*. Indeed, the last term covers ὑπόδημα, the laced sandal, shoes, and boots.

The *barea* of the Romans were sandals made of vegetable leaves, stems, twigs, or fibers. The figures in Smith show both plain and wicker weaving.[2] In both examples there is the toe strap between the first and the second toe, a selvage border more closely plaited, and the two varieties of sharp toe and round toe that have divided shoes and snowshoes into two opposite camps always and everywhere. No heel strap appears on these simple devices, and they evidently take their places in the class with the heelless slipper.

In a work published in Amsterdam in 1667, entitled "Balduinus de Calceo Antiquo et Negronius de Caliga Veterum," the following styles of sandals are figured:

(1) A scoop-shaped piece of leather, extending under the foot to the ball and up the sides and about the heel an inch or so, is abruptly cut off, leaving the toes free as on a moccasin snowshoe. Loops pass from side to side across the top of the foot.

(2) A stiff sole fitting the foot has four lugs or loops on the margin, two opposite the toe joints, the others under the instep; a single lace is used.

---

[1] Smith, Dictionary of Antiquities, s. v. "*Crepida*," with figure.
[2] Ibid., s. v. "*Barea*."

(3) A flat sole, with one or two bands across the foot at right angles to its axis. Under soles of this pattern blocks of wood and stilted appliances are put.

(4) A sole, with toe string between the first and second toe. On reaching the top of the foot this toe string is variously treated (*a*), splitting and proceeding over the foot to the margin of the sole under the instep, Japanese fashion; (*b*) going straight to the ankle band; (*c*) becoming part of straight across lacing. In a Roman sandal on the Arch of Constantine the toe string does both, splits and passes to the margin, and by another branch passes straight to the ankle band, locking with all crossbands on its way. On Trajan's Column both kinds are shown, with toe string and without it.[1]

Examples of medieval shoes are in the Baker collection, Metropolitan Museum, New York. The slipshod and the plain low shoe are affairs of fashion, however, and the ancient forms held the road till much later.

Example No. 130835 (fig. 41) is an Afghan sandal, consisting of the sole and the upper lacing. The sole is built up of three thicknesses of leather, that is, a heavy, coarse strip lined above and below with thin leather. At the heel two additional thicknesses of the thin leather are added below. These are all sewed

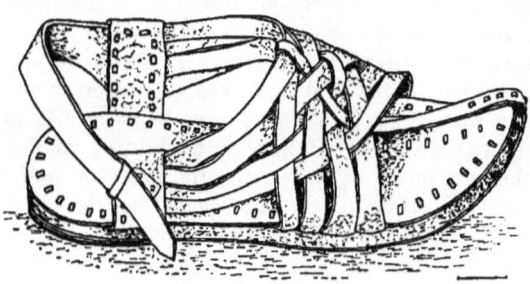

Fig. 41.

LACED SANDAL OF LEATHER FROM AFGHANISTAN.

Cat. No. 130835, U. S. N. M.   Gift of Barnet Phillips.

together by three lines of stitching, in which the sewing is done, not with thread, but with a string of leather one-eighth of an inch wide, passing through the three soles backward and forward in what is called a running stitch.

The upper part or lacing is thus effected; a strip of leather 2 inches wide is sewed in with the parts of the sole on both sides of the ball of the foot, these are then slit into four divisions or ribbons, braided together by a four-ply braid to go across the back of the foot. The ends are then gathered up and sewed into the upright ankle straps, which were also attached to the soles when they were sewed together. Between the two upright ankle straps a horizontal strap is carried back of the heel and buckled into the one on the other side. The toe is pointed, and from this point a narrow loop of leather is carried backward over the back of the foot and woven in strips before mentioned.

[1] Greig, "Old-fashioned Shoes," Edinburgh, 1889, pls. XVI, XVII.

This peculiar attachment of strings running from the point of the toe should be compared with the similar feature of some Oriental sandals. Length, 10½ inches. Gift of Barnet Phillips.

In many western Asiatic pictures on stone and pottery and paper the men are wearing buskins or a kind of moccasin of greater or less height and thickness.

Example No. 153347 is a pair of sandals called cinpal, from Singapore. This is an ornamental shoe, the parts fastened together with rivets. The upper part, however, preserves the band between the toes made of a cord bound with red morocco and sewed.

An interesting feature of this example is the fact that in the construction of the modern complex sole the shoemaker, instead of carrying his knot of the toe strap down through the sole and fastening it off under the bottom has brought it partly through the sole and out again on top to form an ornament. It might be well to remember this characteristic in accounting for the long-toed shoes worn extensively in medieval times. Length, 9½ inches. Collected by Hon. Rounsevelle Wildman. The common sandal of India consists of (1) a leather sole of more than one layer, sewed with a single thong; (2) the single toe string; (3) instep band, meeting the toe string on the back of the foot, the joint covered with large rosette. The elevated wooden sandal, with toe peg or knob, carved and inlaid, is here also perhaps under Mohammedan or Aryan influence.

In the U. S. National Museum there are a pair of chaplies or sandals worn in Kashmir, India, No. 164944. They are said by Dr. W. L. Abbott to be exceedingly comfortable. They consist of the sole, the toe strap, the upper and the heel strap, similar to No. 130835. A stocking or sock of soft leather is worn with these sandals; it is made of soft dressed sheepskin, and has two nearly equal divisions in front for the toes. The sole is a separate piece of leather. The vamp and the quarters are sewed on to the sole as in a European shoe. The divided toe is to be compared with the Japanese type. Dr. Abbott says that the socks are generally used without the split toes, and the brass eyelets or grommets are inserted for the lacing. This last should be regarded as a European production. It is an Aryan type of shoe, and it reminds one of the form in vogue in Europe. Length, 12½ inches. Gift of Dr. W. L. Abbott. In Dr. Abbott's collection the moccasin-like sole with puckered margin is common on boots. The Museum is further indebted to Dr. Abbott for a pair of woman's low boots from Leh Ladak, No. 175104, woolen throughout, in many colors and patches, toes turned up and pointed; a pair of children's pabboos, same materials and style, No. 175105; boots or chirroks from Yarkand and worn by both sexes, No. 175118. These last have white leather soles turned up two inches, the long, brown legs are inserted and blind stitched to the sole. There is a loop on the back of the sole for a lacing. The leg and sole unite without intervention of an upper. From Baltistan Dr. Abbott sends boots of like type but wretchedly made with leather soles patched and coarsely puckered, the tops being of the coarsest kind of woolen fabric, No. 164978.

The chapli, or shoe of Bombay, is a mitten for the foot, having a separate stall for the first toe. This shoe exists as a stocking in the Himalayas and the Kashmir and also in Japan, where the sandal with toe string demands such inside wear.

Example No. 16695 is a leather shoe worn by the Telugus, in southern India, consisting of three layers of very coarse leather sewed together with a white leather thong in the same stitch as most of the examples from this region. The great toe is inclosed in a separate loop. Two small straps pass from the front backward between toes 1-2 and 4-5, and a broad band is attached to the sole on either side of the arch of the foot and passes over the instep; the two narrow straps from the front are inserted through this band. This is a very coarse piece of work.

Fig. 42.

KOKO NOR BOOT.

Cat. No. 131072. U. S. N. M.   Collected by W.
W. Rockhill.

Length, 8½ inches. In this connection it should be noted that in the sandals from East Africa there are two toe straps, one between the first and second toe and one between the fourth and fifth.

The collections of Hon. W. W. Rockhill in the U. S. National Museum admirably show some of the transitions of the Tibetan foot wear. In the rudest form there is a clumsy combination of the turned-up and puckered sole with the vamp, just as in the Eskimo sealskin boot. Above the vamp is the boot leg with fore and hind seam and any number of transverse seams. This part is coarsely lined with woolen cloth.

The Koko Nor boot, on the contrary, proceeds upon another plan. Coarsely it is a boot in all essential points, in fact a Chinese shoe with thicker soles and leather top and an additional sole of leather beneath (fig. 42). This type may be seen in various parts of the Chinese Empire and represents the climax of the art there.

Other specimens in this same collection are worthy of study. Example No. 167179, No. 5 in Rockhill's plate in his "Mongolia and Tibet," page 14, is a llama boot with top of red russian leather stamped with small checkerwork. Only one seam, and that in the back; but on one side of the front half a vamp is inserted, making a seam on top of the foot and down diagonally on one side. The toe is the regular Chinese form, with projection. To unite this top with the sole the lower edge of the top is bound with a strip of green leather, like a welt, only the margin turns out instead of in. The sole consists of two parts, a thick upper layer of felted yak hair quilted together an inch thick and bound also

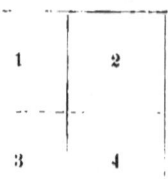

BOOTS OF TIBET AND NEIGHBORING REGIONS.

In examples brought to the United States National Museum by Mr. W. W. Rockhill and Dr. W. L. Abbott are to be studied the endeavors of the bootmaker to secure warmth, protection, and durability in relation to environment. The Chinese compound and padded sole, the hyperborean turned up and puckered sole, the uppers of cloth, felt, and leather, the legs with several tops, and the garters are in great variety. Some elements are original, some Siberian, and others are derived from China, Mongolia, and from Turkestan.

Fig. 1. TIBETAN BOOT AND GARTER. Sole of stiff, white yak leather, turned up all around as in Siberian and Eskimo boots and puckered very little. Upper of several thicknesses of white cotton cloth, closely quilted together and attached to the sole by running stitches, short on the outer side and long on the inside. There are three parts to the leg; one of very coarse, garnet, woolen cloth called "truk;" one, of gaudy striped flannel; and the other, of blue cotton cloth. Continuous with a gore in front of the upper, there is an opening along these three tops, and into this is inserted an ornamental stripe of different-colored woolen stuffs. Lining, of very coarse woolen cloth, woven diagonally. Length 10 inches. Collected by W. W. Rockhill.

(Cat. No. 131045, U. S. N. M.)

Fig. 2. TIBETAN BOOT AND GARTER. Similar in design to the specimen shown in fig. 1, with sole of white yak hide whipped on to the upper, which is of black leather run on to the woolen top. In this specimen also is a series of tops in different colors, with insertion or embroidery worked into the slit in front of the leg and upper. Length 10 inches. Collected by W. W. Rockhill.

(Cat. No. 131045 (a), U. S. N. M.)

Fig. 3. TIBETAN BOOT. Made of cowhide, after the Chinese pattern. Sole, of several thicknesses, attached by an ingenious sort of welt which is sewed to the upper and joined to the under layers by another row of sewing deeper in. The parts are generally fastened together at the heel and front by enormous nails which are clinched on the inside. The upper is attached to the leg by a double piping of leather between them. In the seam that extends from the front of the toe, far up on the leg, occurs also a double piping, and the edges of the leather are turned outward in the seam. Worn on the borders of Koko Nor. Length 11 inches. Collected by W. W. Rockhill.

(Cat. No. 131072, U. S. N. M.)

Fig. 4. TIBETAN BOOT.—SIBERIAN TYPE. The sole is of yak rawhide with the hair on. It is turned up and slightly puckered, pointed and bossed in front. The upper is of dressed leather and fitted inside the margin of the sole and attached by blind stitching. The leg consists of three tops; the first is of yellow leather fitted inside the upper and backstitched; the second is of light-brown leather, inserted inside the first, and sewed over and over; the third is of coarse leather with the flesh side out. The upper and all of the tops are split for the insertion of several narrow bands or pipings of colored leather. In this regard the specimen should be compared with many beautiful examples from Alaska, secured by E. W. Nelson. One of these is mentioned on page 340 (Cat. No. 43345). The lining is of coarse woolen cloth. Collected by W. W. Rockhill.

(Cat. No. 167303, U. S. N. M.)

BOOTS OF TIBET AND NEIGHBORING REGIONS.

Rockhill, "Notes on the Ethnology of Tibet," Pl. 2, Report of the Smithsonian Institution (U. S. National Museum), 1893.

about the margin with green leather. The under sole is a thick piece of hard leather, attached to the upper sole and the top by a stitching of stout twine that passes down through all and back, holding the parts together. The ornamentation is worked on the surface in various colors of narrow silk braid. There does not seem to be any originality in the Tibetan foot clothing. Here Mongol elements obtrude; there Chinese and frequently Russian influence obscures all the others. One may see in Lapland and Finland characteristics of boots suggestive of Tibet, and again among the Eskimo other marks call them to mind. As this desert land can not have been the prolific source of cultures, it must be the desolate suburb into which they have been driven.

Example No. 131045 is a pair of Tibetan boots (pl. 2, fig. 1). The sole is white yak rawhide, puckered as in the Eskimo boot. The upper consists of two pieces of white cotton cloth doubled several times, united at the toe and at the heel, about 2½ inches high. On the top of this upper a rectangular space has been cut out from the instep down. The top of the boot is of red woolen cloth called truk and is sewed on the margin of this upper, and also fills the rectangular space adorned with insertions of white and green and red. The red truk top is continued in a strip up to the margin of the boot leg. Above the red top is a broad band of green woolen material, and above this a band of blue cotton stuff. Inside of this complicated top is sewed a lining of very coarse woolen blanketing in diagonal weaving. The boot leg is split open at the back down as far as the upper margin of the red top. Length, 11 inches; height of upper, 2 inches; height of red flannel top, 4 inches; height of green top, 5 inches; height of blue top, 4 inches.[1]

Example No. 131202 is a pair of shoes from Mongolia, made of leather and puckered in front, drawn and sewed together in a T-shaped seam at the back of the heel, a flap being turned up and fastened down. The vamp is a piece of leather fitting under the margin of the crimped portion and bound to it by the puckering string. This rude example must be compared with the example (No. 20797) from Sitka, being similar to it in the puckering of the front and the peculiar formation of the heel and the vamp. There is no heelpiece sewed on above, as in the Sitka specimen. Length, 11 inches. Collected by W. W. Rockhill.

Example No. 131044 is a pair of sandals from Sechuan, made of bast upon four warp cords, with filaments of straw. The sole is woven in wicker-work. In passing across, the outer threads are finely twisted, but across the middle of the sole above and below they are left plain, and on the bottom are cut off at each turn just below and parallel with the margin all around, leaving a sort of fringe work or tuft. At the heel and toe the cords forming the outer margin of the warp are turned up for an inch or two and wrapped with twine or with braid. Upright strands to the number of three or more extend for an inch or two along the outside of the great toe, the little toe, and at the sides of the heel.

---

[1] Figured in Rockhill's "Journey through Mongolia and Tibet."

Through these are rove the long lacing which is tied above the instep. As regards the upper lacing, this shoe should be compared with No. 131198 from Kansu, China, collected by W. W. Rockhill. Length, 11 inches.

In most respects these two examples are like No. 116211 (p. 331), from Yokohama, Japan, collected by S. Kneeland.

Mr. Rockhill brought from Kansu, in northwestern China, a pair of shoes (No. 131198, U. S. N. M.) that represent a type. The sole is made of sennit or braid of hemp strands, half an inch or more wide. Beginning in the central line of the sole the sennit is coiled backward and forward six or more times. The whole fabric is held together by sewing through from side to side with stout twine. Sailors make the same kind of soles from manila yarn braided into sennit and the very same sole exists in Spain and Peru. The upper part of the shoe is a very complicated affair, but the style is common. At the toe and the heel stout cords are inserted between the last two turns of the sennit and extend in front up over the middle toes, dividing on the back of the foot below the instep. In the rear these cords, to the number of five or more, extend well up on the heel. Both sets, front and rear, are sewed together with a common weaving finer cord. The lacing of the shoe is rove through loops at the ends of the upright cords. At the sides of the toes and of the heel a series of small cords pass from the sole up to the lacing, which is doubled and are neatly woven into it. In many Chinese and Korean shoes this system of upright cords like a delicate balustrade is common. In the U. S. National Museum there is an Athapascan Indian moccasin upon the bottoms of which a sole of coiled sennit has been securely sewed. Mr. Rockhill says that you rarely see Chinese go barefooted. The poorest of them wear straw sandals. This is for northern China, but Dr. Graves says that many of the coolies go barefoot. Many wear sandals, which on the road do not last very long, but they are cheap and may be found at stalls and shops by the roadside. Others wear leather sandals that are more lasting.

Example No. 55864 is a pair of shoes from China, each consisting of two parts, the sole with its lacings and the upper. This is a very important specimen in connection with No. 116211 and No. 131044 (fig. 43) because it explains the use of the pointed portions at the heel and at the toe. The sole part is built up of rice straw upon four twines laid down in the same way as No. 116211 and the warp is of coarsely woven rice straw. The projection at the toe, the loops at the sides of the toes and at the sides of the heel are precisely as in the examples mentioned, but the upper part of the shoe is a slipper made of plantain leaf folded together ingeniously to fit the foot. This slipper also fits into the straw sole and is lashed on by means of lacing passing over the toe, through the loops, and above the heel. In looking at the ordinary sandal of this kind it is difficult to see how it could be made comfortable on the

KOREAN SHOES AND SANDALS.

The intermediate position of Korea with reference to Mongolia, China, and Japan, as well as the geological and social conditions about the people, produce a great many kinds of footwear. In the U. S. National Museum are the following varieties:

1. The Chinese low shoe with thick sole made fine or coarse, and often foxed with leather or cloth of different colors.

2. The stilted shoe with endless variety of form in Japan, but having an upper more like a sabot, modeled after the Chinese low shoe.

3. The straw openwork low shoe (*chip-seki*). This is shown in three examples on the plate. The woven sole is similar to that of the Japanese and Chinese. The upper never has strings between the toes nor loops about the margin of the sole, but is built up of any number of vertical twine filaments united at the top by means of a horizontal twine. As will be seen in the plate, rags cooperate with the straw twine to form a padding. The rope on the back of the foot is attached to upright ankle loops and a rope heel-band wrapped with bast or cloth. There are several examples in the U. S. National Museum, collected by Ensign J. B. Bernadou, U. S. N.

PLATE 3.

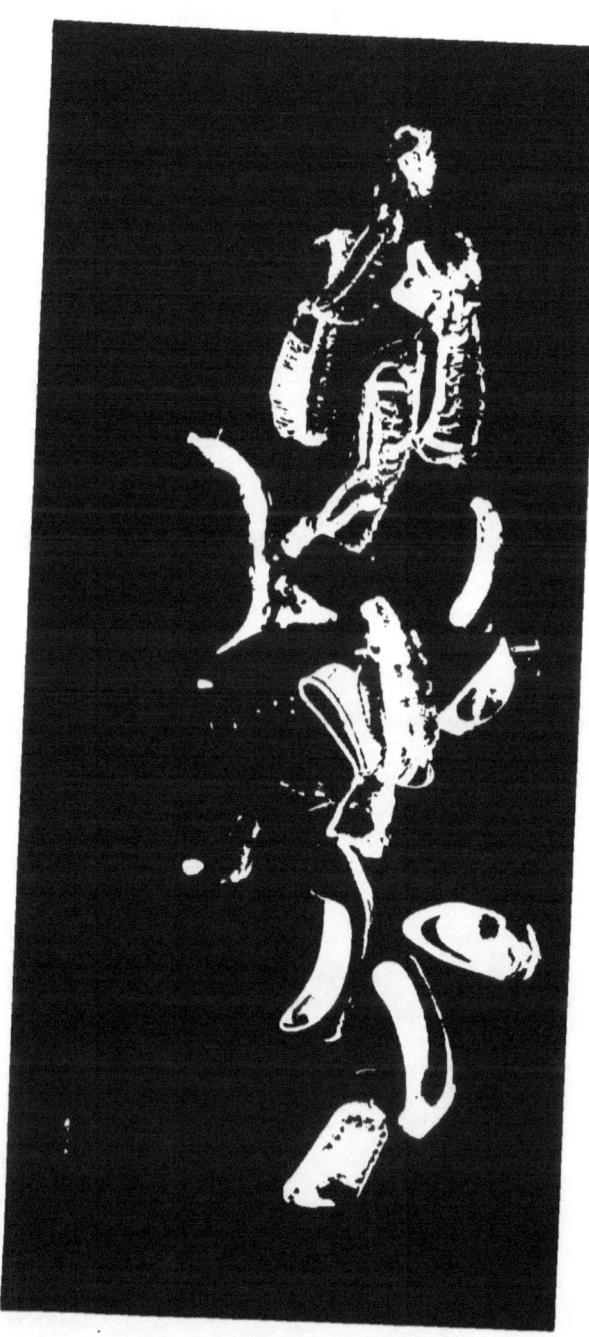

KOREAN SHOES AND SANDALS

PLATE 3. The Following Articles and their Kind in the collection of the U.S. National Museum, the National Museum

foot, but this example explains all the parts of the sole. It is also to be noted as a very coarse, first step, in the invention of the stocking. Length, 13½ inches.

One of the Korean sandals shown in pl. 3 has the sole made of a warp of six coarse cords upon which is woven in wicker style a weft of twisted rushes. Two of the twines extend up and back of the heel. From the top of this extends quite across the upper margin of the foot a cord, like a rail about a boat. From this descend to the sole stout lashing on each side of the arch of the foot, and a close arrangement of parallel cords all around the front half of the foot. There are no lacings. A child's sandal of this type (No. 151146, U. S. N. M., 6 inches long; Seoul) is identical with Chinese specimens before described.

Dr. Hough describes and figures the following types of Korean shoes:

(1) Rain clogs' or sabots, with stilts beneath. This feature may be traced in western Asia; the stilted shoe, beautifully inlaid and adorned, abounding in Persia and India.

(2) Felt shoes, lined with leather, Chinese types.

(3) Travelers' sandals, with straw soles, upper border like a balustrade connected with the sole by many parallel twines. This class exists in many styles,[1] and is perfected in China.

The Japanese sandal with single toe string and padded bands over the back of the foot will be referred to as of Tartar origin.

The Japanese laced sandal, based on Chinese motives, involves two types of manufacture, one for the sole and one for the upper. The weaving on the sole is based on four warp filaments, ropes, or bundles of straw. The weaving on the sole is done with long, coarse filaments in wicker style. The warp being rigid, the weft presents a coarse appearance as in corded goods. Practically, the shoemaker takes two bundles of filaments or two small ropes more than twice the length of the foot, doubles them at the middle, and unites the bends at the toe; or he takes one long rope or twine, and at its middle forms a couple of loops 3 or more inches long. The two halves of the cord are carried forward to the toe and beyond it. Here they are doubled back and the four strands securely and neatly wrapped together. This forms the projecting portion at the toe, to be later mentioned again. The two ends are carried back to the heel and crossed at the starting point. The weft of the sole is then woven in; the extended ends of the warp ropes, a foot or more long, will serve for lacing.

In the simplest sandal the sole constitutes the chief part of the object. But in the development of the most beautiful examples there has been improvement in two directions simultaneously, to wit, in the workmanship and material of the sole and in the creation and perfecting of the upper. In the coarsest sandals the soles are of bark or

---

[1]Hough, "The Bernadou, Allen, and Jouy Korean Collections in the U. S. National Museum," Rep. Smithsonian Inst. (U. S. Nat. Mus.), 1891, pl. XX.

bast, evidently made in a few minutes. They are as ugly as a garment could well be. In the finest examples, the bundles of warp filaments are nicely laid cylinders and the weft is a neat and uniform cord of rushes or straw.

The provision of what in the modern shoe corresponds to the welt, or middle piece between sole and upper, has evidently been the occasion of much thought among shoemakers in all ages and regions. The material at once drives welt makers apart—the workers in hide, felt, and the like taking one road, the workers in fiber quite another. The Japanese maker of fiber shoes has two expedients ready at hand; he can utilize the loops and ends of his warp filaments in securing the top of the shoe or he may, as he goes on weaving, gather into the selvage along its upper margin loops of bast or rush with the free ends projecting upward any distance desired. Indeed this is done. So that at the finishing of the sole there would be projecting from its margin upward a fence or hedge of fiber ready to become twine of an open upper or warp of a closed texture.

Let us suppose that a closed upper is in mind. Of these there are many varieties, but they may be divided into two, namely, those with heels, becoming slippers or low shoes, and those without heels. In the example with heels as many rows as are desired of twined weaving in rush or straw or bast are worked around on the warp filaments rising from the soles. In a great many examples this weaving is boustrophedon, and in the best specimens in colored and uncolored fine filaments the effect is that of chain stitch in embroidery; but even in the coarse sandals for road work the effect of the weaving is always pleasing. There are examples of this variety in which the rows of twined weaving forming the heel equal in number those across the front. In such examples the effects of the twining are in bands and lines of colored and uncolored material, varied with geometric and diaper patterns, to which this style of technique cleverly lends itself. But in most examples in the U. S. National Museum the heels are low. In such, four or five rows of twined weaving pass entirely around the sandal, then the vamp is woven boustrophedon, and finally a finishing row passes entirely around. There remain now the whole set of warps of the upper, sticking up an inch or more. These are braided to form an ornamental border and then turned down flat inside the shoe. The braiding is done in three ply; at each braid one filament is laid down and one taken up until the entire border is completed.

The heelless sandal or slipper without lacing is for house wear chiefly, and resembles the other except in the treatment of the heel, and may be dismissed with a brief mention. In a pretty example in the U. S. National Museum (No. 92861) the first row of twined weaving in rather coarse twine is carried entirely around the margin of the sole, but at the heel it passes down and under the sole a little way, and four short rows of this weaving border the heel, the last scarcely rising to the level of its upper surface. The upward projecting elements at the heel are then inclosed in a pretty flat fabric of twined weaving boustrophedon. In many fine examples the tip is a circular insertion like a projecting transom, the weaving is the same, however, only this hooded or projecting tip is always plain colored. As hinted above, the motive in this type of shoe is from the Chinese and Korean area.

Example No. 116211 is from Yokohama, Japan (fig. 43). These sandals are built on a warp or foundation of coarse straw cord. A single cord 10 feet long is doubled in the middle around the front of the foot, the two ends are carried back the length of the foot and 4 inches to form the heel loops. Here they are both doubled and carried back between the outer border cords over the first loop, and extend outward 30 inches to form the lacing. With the four warp strands thus provided for, the

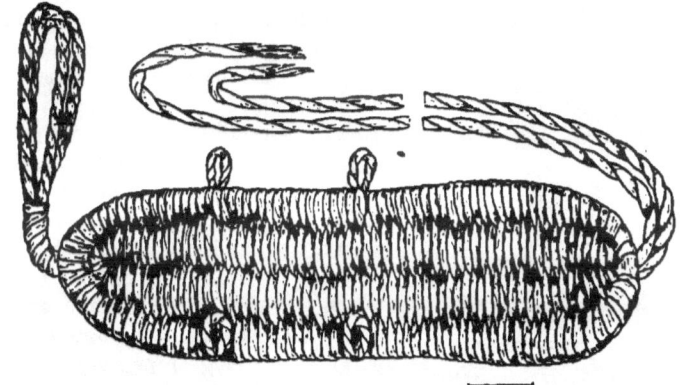

Fig. 43.

WICKER SANDAL OF STRAW FROM YOKOHAMA, JAPAN.

Cat. No. 116211, U. S. N. M.   Collected by S. Kneeland.

weft consists of a close wicker weaving of very slightly twisted bunches of straw fiber packed closely together at the margins of the heel and just in front of the arch of the foot. On each side loops are formed in the course of the weaving by extending the weft filaments a little way. These loops extend about an inch beyond the border of the sandal. The lacing proceeds from the tip of the sandal across the foot, through the loops on the side, passed back through the heel loops, and back again through the side loops and over the instep, where it is tied. These cheap sandals carefully studied form the type or foundation characteristics of the more refined foot gear of the Japanese. Length of sandal, 9 inches; of foundation twine, 5 feet. Collected by S. Kneeland.

Example No. 73084 is a pair of sandals brought to the U. S. National Museum from Nikko, Japan, by P. L. Jouy. They are each made of two thin and one thick piece of ox hide, closely sewed together by a flat thong of the same material near the edge. The hair has been left upon the upper layer as a protection to the foot. Under the heel is a thin semicircular plate of iron, which receives the wear as the sandal is dragged along the ground in making the forward stride. The sandal is secured to the foot by a round, soft strap, which passes from the sides near the heel up over the back of the foot to an upright piece of hide secured to the sole and passing between the first and second toe. This style of attaching the sandal by means of two round, padded bands passing from the thong between the toes over the back of the foot to the margin of the sole under the ankle joints has a restricted area in space, and it also has social characteristics. Those of this type in the U. S. National Museum collection are mostly for house wear, although the specimens here described are for hard service, and this style of

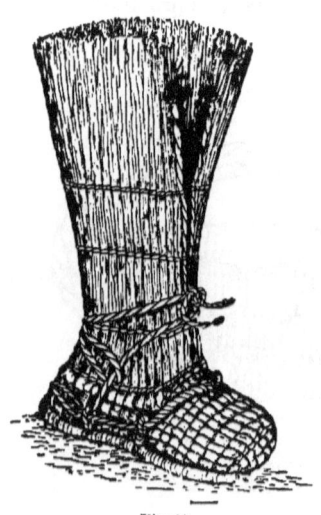

Fig. 44.

SANDAL AND BOOT TOP OF STRAW UNITED,
FROM TATE YAMA, JAPAN.

Cat. No. 73091, U. S. N. M. Collected by P. L. Jouy

sandal is universal on the road. The trailing heel may also be remarked as an incident in shoe wearing which finds its more exaggerated occurrence in the action of the snowshoe and skee. The language of Japan is believed to be Tartar. Certainly, the divided stocking, the sandal with toe string, and the high-posted shoe are not of eastern Asia. If the collection in Washington speaks truly and comprehensively, none of these are used there outside of Japanese influence. The chapli, the high wooden shoes, and the sandal with a single toe string or peg are not seen again after leaving Japan until the explorer reaches the Caspian and Aral drainage. This statement is subject to modification, being based merely on the specimens in hand.

Example No. 73091 (fig. 44) is from Tate Yama, Japan. This interesting specimen of footwear worn by hunters is made of rice straw, and shows precisely how the sandal and the legging unite in a very primitive fashion to form a boot. The sole of this boot is, in fact, a sandal, with five loops for the lacing or attachment, one at the back of the heel, two at the side of the heel, and two opposite the instep. It is built upon four longitudinal warped cords with small ropes, and wisps or bunches of rice straw are woven backward and forward over this warp and form a sole a half inch thick. These four warped cords, continued outward from the heel, form the two long heel loops. The top of the boot is also woven of bunches of rice straw, forming a checkered pattern over the foot and around the heel, in which the meshes are about half an inch square (see figs. 45–47), just on a level with the instep. These straws are left free for the boot top, excepting in four places they are gathered together, and held in place by single rows of twined weaving, absolutely identical with the stitch common all over America and in certain parts of Africa.

The lacing on this foot gear is worthy of study. The loop at the heel is formed of two long bends braided together and fastened off in the sole. There is a lacing of two-ply coarse twine, made of straw, on each side; the long, loose end passes first through the loop on the side of the heel, then through the long loop at the back of the heel, then back again through number one, then through the loop below the instep, then twined with the extended end of the lacing belonging to the other side of the boot. The two lacings form a four-ply cord or rope across the foot knotted into the fabric just below the instep on the back of the foot, and extending down to the loops below the instep on the sides where it is fastened off into the sole. This knot on the back of the foot is the extremity of a toe string passing down through vamp and sole, and in the simple Japanese sandal is to be found under the tip of the toe. The loose ends, after being drawn tight through the loops, are brought together and tied at the instep. Length of sole, 11 inches; height of boot, 14 inches. Collected by P. L. Jouy.

Example No. 150644 in the U. S. National Museum is a pair of sandals (shitukeri), made of walnut bark, from the Ainos of Piratori, Yezo, collected by Romyn Hitchcock. They are woven on the plan of the Japanese sandal, with loops on the side and no toe strap. In most of the specimens of Aino sandals in the U. S. National Museum, and shown in their photographs, there is a flat sole of textile or hide and a toe strap connected with two padded bands passing over the top of the foot and attached to the sole just under the arch of the foot after the manner of the Japanese.[1]

Example No. 150637 in the U. S. National Museum is a pair of Aino boots from Yezo, collected by Romyn Hitchcock. They are made of fishskin. The foot is not unlike that of a moccasin. The leg is of several upright strips sewed together in all but one seam to admit the foot. Around the top is a band of material doubled. It is interesting to note that they are fastened about the ankles by a cord attached to a loop on the back of the boot precisely where the loop occurs on the sandal in figure 43.[2]

The U. S. National Museum possesses a large collection of Finnish ethnographic material collected by Consul-General Crawford. Among the specimens are a number of shoes in braided or woven birch-bark strips or splints. Dr. Gustave Retzius contributed to the Revue d'Ethnographie a memoir on the uses of birch bark among the Finns. In this memoir are figured[3] three forms or fashions of foot gear that

[1] Hitchcock, "The Ainos of Yezo, Japan," Rep. Smithsonian Inst. (U. S. Nat. Mus.). 1890, pls. LXXXIX, XCII, XCV.

[2] Ibid., pl. XCVII.

[3] Rev. d'Ethnog., Paris, 1882, I, pp. 81-93.

are here reproduced (figs. 45, 46, 47). The first and simplest is an attempt in birch-bark checker weaving to produce a sandal that will

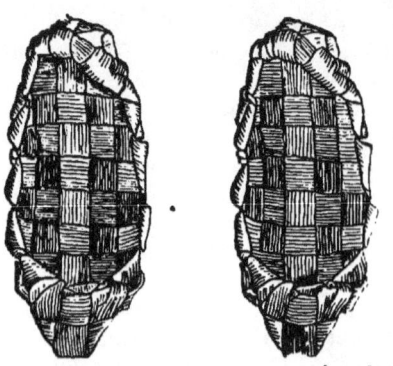

hang on to the foot or will roll up at the sides and incase the toes and the heel and furnish loops for lacing if desired. This is one way of reaching the result achieved by the Africans and Peruvians in the use of rawhide and the Ainos and Japanese in the use of bast and other vegetable fiber. A bit of art is thrown in by alternating the outer and the inner side of the bark.

The next step in the evolution is a low shoe or moccasin in bark. The Pueblo Indians likewise weave shoes or moccasins in the split leaf of the yucca.

The third step is the production of a boot reaching as high up the leg as the rigidity of the material would admit. There is no preparation for a lacing on these specimens. These examples should be compared with the boots from Tate Yama, Japan (fig. 44), collected by P. L. Jouy. The question of early Finnish influence in northern Japan might be raised.

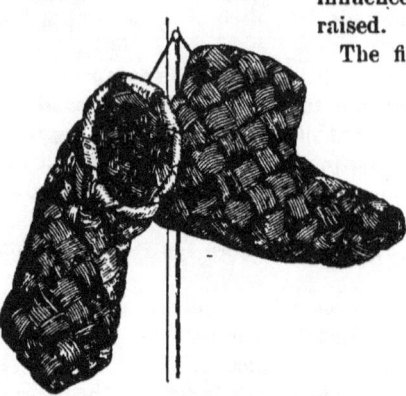

Figs. 45, 46, 47.

SLIPPERS, LOW SHOES, AND BOOTS MADE OF PLAITED BIRCH BARK, FINLAND.

From Retzius, in the Revue d'Ethnographie.

The fishskin boot may be traced entirely around the salmon-fishing area. Speaking of the Amur people and their use of fishskin as waterproof material, Ravenstein says that though dangerous as a constant article of food, the fish of these rivers (Usuri and Amur) are invaluable on account of the imperishable garments made of their skins. In boots made of such fishskins you may wade through rivulets and walk in the snow as on the dry ground, equally protected against the cold and moisture.[1]

[1] Ravenstein, "Russians on the Amur," London, 1861, p. 96.

Bush found among the Yakuts, who are Tartar, that their torbossas or boots of heavy tanned deerskin were made "to fit the foot snugly and at the toe to arch over the foot like the bow of a skate." Welts are sewed in the seams, and "at the ankle two very long and broad strips of buckskin are fastened, to be wound snugly about the leg half way up to the knee."[1] These characteristics agree with the Kashmir and Tibetan specimens of Rockhill and Abbott.

According to Lansdell, Tartar men and women wear top boots and generally leather goloshes over them, so that on entering a house or mosque they have only to slip off the goloshes to secure clean shoes.[2] There are specimens of these in Dr. W. L. Abbott's collection in the U. S. National Museum.

The torbossas of the Kamchatkans are fur boots reaching to the knees, made of the skin on the deer's legs, as being tougher and having shorter hair, soled with bearskin or sealskin, tied about the knee and ankle with thongs. Chazees, or fur socks, are made of dog, reindeer, or wolf skin, worn with the fur next the foot, and are not intended to fit snugly.[3]

The foot covering of the Chukchi consists of reindeer or sealskin, which above the foot are fastened to the trousers in the way common among the Lapps. The soles are of walrus skin or bearskin, and have the hair side inward. On the other part of the pantaloons the hair is outward. Within the shoes are sealskin stockings and hay.[4] The summer coverings of the lower extremities are often as long in the leg as our sea boots.

From whatever cause, the fact remains that there is no break between the foot covering of the Chukchi and that of their eastern neighbors in Asia and northwestern America. The Eskimo examples will be studied geographically, commencing with the west. Mr. John Murdoch has with great care worked out the pattern, the making, and the varieties of the Point Barrow boots, and his types may be used in studying the rest.[5] The boots and shoes of the Point Barrow Eskimo have uppers of two kinds—those with the hair on and those made of black dressed sealskin fitted to heelless, crimped moccasin soles of different material. The crimped soles are of three sorts of material:

(1) White, urine tanned, snow-bleached seal skin for winter wear when the snow is dry; not suited for rough and damp salt-water ice.

(2) Sealskin dressed with the hair on and worn flesh side out; best for summer boot soles on wet ground and melting snow.

[1] Bush, "Reindeer, Dogs, and Snowshoes," New York, 1871, p. 161.
[2] Lansdell, "Through Siberia," Boston, 1882, pp. 58–59.
[3] Bush, "Reindeer, Dogs, and Snowshoes," New York, 1871, p. 61.
[4] Nordenskiöld, "Voyage of the Vega," 1881, 11, pp. 98–99.
[5] Murdoch, "Ethnological Results of the Point Barrow Expedition," Ninth Ann. Rep. Bureau of Ethnology, figs. 72–82.

(3) Waterproof soles of oil-dressed walrus, bearded seal, polar bear, or best of all white whale.[1]

The cutting out and making of the boot, as well as the process of turning up and crimping the sole, are minutely worked out by Murdoch.

Example No. 74042 (fig. 48) is a pair of woman's pantaloons (kûmûñ) from Point Barrow, Alaska, collected by Captain Ray and carefully illustrated by Murdoch. They may be thus described: Soles of white tanned

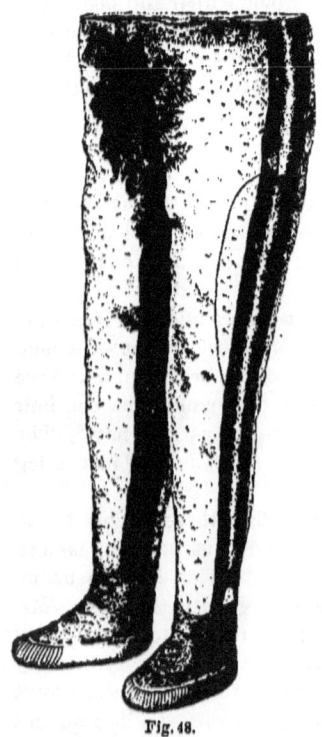

seal skin turned up and puckered or crimped about the margin. Uppers of deerskin in two pieces (vamp and quarter), trousers of deerskin, made from the short-haired skin from the deer's legs. The pantaloon in America is found only among western Eskimo and Athapascans. Murdoch says that these pantaloons are always worn with the hair out, and usually over a pair of underpantaloons of the same shape but of softer skin with longer hair, worn next the skin with stocking feet. In summer the inner ones are worn, the feet being protected by sealskin waterproof boots, shown in pl. 4.[2]

Example No. 56750, from Point Barrow, is a man's boot (fig. 49) with deerskin leg and seal-skin sole. The leg and upper are in four pieces—back, two sides, and front. There are strings attached to the sole on the margin below the ankle joint. These are brought up above the heel around in front and laced about the lower part of the leg. Collected by the Ray expedition. Murdoch, in describing the structure of this specimen, says that this is a type of the everyday pattern. The bottom is cut off accurately to fit the sole; there is no insertion of orna-

Fig. 48.

WOMAN'S PANTALOONS, USED BY THE ESKIMO
OF POINT BARROW, ALASKA.

From a figure in Murdoch's "Ethnological Results of the
Point Barrow Expedition," Ninth Annual Report of the
Bureau of Ethnology.

Cat. No. 74042, U. S. N. M.

mental bands or piping, but they are often made of a pattern like that of the lower part of the women's pantaloons, that is, with the uppers separate from the leg pieces, shown in fig. 48 and in pl. 4, fig. 6.

---

[1] Cf. Murdoch, "Ethnological Results of the Point Barrow Expedition," Ninth Ann. Rep. Bureau of Ethnology, p. 130, referring to Crantz, I, p. 167, and Simpson, pp. 242-266.

[2] Ibid., p. 127, with references to Petitot, Bessels, Egede, Crantz, Parry, and Franklin.

ESKIMO SHOES AND BOOTS FROM NORTON SOUND REGION AND MACKENZIE RIVER DISTRICT.

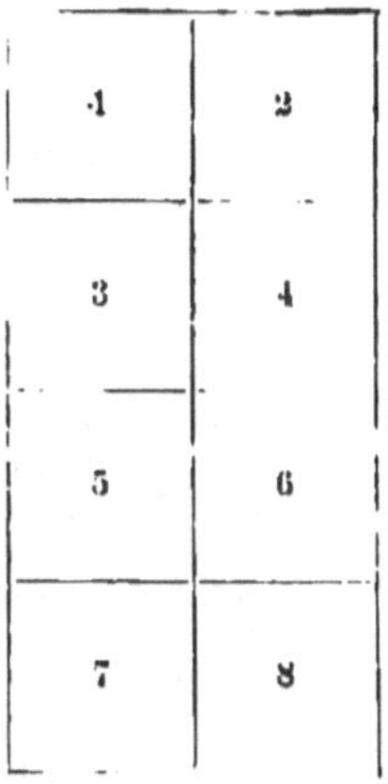

ESKIMO SHOES AND BOOTS FROM NORTON SOUND REGION AND MACKENZIE RIVER DISTRICT.

Fig. 1. SUMMER BOOTEES. Puckered sole of white sealskin; upper and leg of seal pelt, hair side in; gore in front of seal skin painted red. The lacings, of seal pelt, embroidered in quill work, are attached to the margin of the gore on the top of the foot, pass through loops under the ankles, cross on the back of the shoe, and are tied in front. · Collected at Norton Bay by W. H. Dall.

(Cat. No. 7591, U. S. N. M.)

Fig. 2. LOW SHOES OF BLEACHED SEALSKIN. Puckered well up over the foot. These shoes have a gore and tongue piece on the top of the foot and drawstrings about the upper margin, suggestive of Athapascan moccasins. Collected from Anderson River, Mackenzie District, Canada, by R. MacFarlane.

(Cat. No. 2009, U. S. N. M.)

Fig. 3. WINTER BOOTS. The sole and footing are of sweated seal hide, bleached on the snow, hair side out and neatly puckered. Above this a band of dark hide, with the hair side out, is sewed in a water-tight joint. This is attached to the deerskin top by means of a puckered seam. The top is ornamented with tabs and strips of hide neatly inserted vertically. Collected from the Anderson River Eskimo by R. MacFarlane.

(Cat. No. 3663, U. S. N. M.)

Fig. 4. WINTER BOOTS. These are similar to those shown in fig. 3, but are more ornamental, bands of skin with hair on being inserted vertically. Gift of R. MacFarlane.

(Cat. No. 3670, U. S. N. M.)

Fig. 5. MAN'S SEALSKIN WATERPROOF BOOTS. The puckered soles of sealskin are cured with the hair on and are unhaired by friction. The uppers are of unhaired oiled hide. The seam across the instep is the joint of the two edges of the top, made almost of one piece. There is a drawstring in a hem around the upper margin. Gift of C. P. Gaudet. From Anderson River, Canada.

(Cat. No. 1322, U. S. N. M.)

Fig. 6. MAN'S WATERPROOF BOOTS. Sole, of black seal hide puckered and run on to a narrow strip of soft white hide all around; top, of deer pelt in two pieces; leg, of vertical strips of deer pelt; border, of several strips of variously colored pelt; all from parts of the Caribou skin, selected for ornamental effect. Between this border and the boot top is a fringe of wolverine fur. The connection between upper and top should be compared with fig. 48. The lacings proceed from the margin of the sole below the ankle bones, and are wrapped about the heel and the ankle. Eskimo of Anderson River, Canada. Gift of R. MacFarlane.

(Cat. No. 3980, U. S. N. M.)

Fig. 7. ESKIMO WOMAN'S WINTER BOOTS. These boots have (1) a sole and footing of white sweated sealskin, bleached in the snow, and puckered nearly all around; (2) a narrow upper of seal hide, flesh side out; (3) tops of deerskin, having the seam ornamented with a strip of embroidered hide. There is a drawstring in a hem on the upper margin. Anderson River Eskimo. Gift of R. MacFarlane.

(Cat. No. 3983, U. S. N. M.)

Fig. 8. WATERPROOF SEALSKIN BOOTS. These boots are from Yukon River and consist of six parts—the sole, upper, leg, extension top, ornamental band, and lacings. The sole is of black dried sealskin from which the hair has been carefully removed by shaving. It is turned up and molded into shape so that the crimping has almost disappeared. The upper is of brown oiled leather, its lower border is turned up all around inside of the margin of the sole, and the two upturned edges are run together, the stitches being caught over a cord on the inside, as in birchbark sewing. The two vertical edges of this upper are joined together by a diagonal seam, as shown in fig. 5 of this plate. This diagonal joint is sometimes sewed only on one side, as in fig. 53. In specimens from Greenland, collected by Dr. C. Hart Merriam, the seam extends on both sides of the instep. Above the upper, the leg consists of a broad band of white sealskin cured by sweating and bleaching in the snow. On top of this band, or between it and the extension top, is a pretty insertion of brown and white sealskin with piping. The extension top is of white sealskin. Collected by J. T. Dyar.

(Cat. No. 10486, U. S. N. M.)

Example No. 56759 is a pair of man's dress boots of deerskin. These differ from the common boot in the insertions of different colored hide alternating along the horizontal and vertical seams. The soles are of white sealskin, neatly crimped, with the edges coming to a point at the toe. Between the upper and the sole are five bands of seal hide, the hair black and white alternately. The leg is hemmed at the top for a drawstring, and there are lacings at the ankles (fig. 50).

Example No. 89834 (fig. 51) is a pair of man's dress boots from Point Barrow, Alaska. The tops are made from the skin of the mountain sheep (*Ovis montana*). The soles are much turned up all round, and, like the last described pair, recall the crimped moccasin of the Athapascans. There are three ornamental bands of sealskin—black, white, and black—between the sole and the upper. Strips of mountain sheepskin and dark-brown deerskin, tagged with red worsted, fringe the side seam of the leg. Little tags are also cut in the edge of the side piece on its hinder margin. Mr. Murdoch says that this pair of boots was brought from the east of Point Barrow by one of the Nuwuk trading parties in 1882, and this may account for the material and the shape of the sole. His conjecture is confirmed by comparing the specimen here described with figures 3, 4, and 7 in plate 4.

Fig. 49.

MAN'S BOOT AND TROUSERS UNITED, USED BY THE ESKIMO OF POINT BARROW, ALASKA.

From a figure in Murdoch's "Ethnological Results of the Point Barrow Expedition," Ninth Annual Report of the Bureau of Ethnology.

Cat. No. 56750, U. S. N. M.

Example No. 56749 is a pair of man's dress boots from Point Barrow, with soles crimped high up. The ornamental bands are inserted in the same manner between sole and upper, and similarly pointed above the phalanges. There is a difference in the side seam, and the insertion of a larger piece to increase the size of the leg above, let in by an oblique seam across the calf.[1] These, according to Murdoch, fairly represent the style of full-dress boots worn with loose-bottomed breeches, as in his figure 69, page 125. They all have drawstrings just below the knee, and often have no lacings about the ankles. He calls attention to the drawstring as an eastern fashion, but prefers the Point Barrow style of tying the breeches down over the tops of the boots. The Smith Sound

---

[1] Murdoch, "Ethnological Results of the Point Barrow Expedition," Ninth Ann. Rep. Bureau of Ethnology, p. 133.

natives are said to tie the boots over the breeches. The boots are all joined with reindeer sinew by fitting the edges together and sewing them "over and over" on the "wrong" side (fig. 52).

Example No. 153892 is a very pretty specimen of the Eskimo boot from Point Barrow, with the sole puckered in front and at the heel after the manner of the Athapascan shoe. The vamp and heel are separate, as in a modern boot; the upper margin of the vamp, the heel, and the outer leg of the boot are sewn together. The leg consists of alternate strips of white and brown reindeer hide. The upper part of the boot is made of eight rows of deerskin having different colored hair, bordered below with a strip of skin of the arctic fox (*Vulpes lagopus*). Length, 10 inches. Collected by John Murdoch.

Example No. 76182 (fig. 53) is a pair of woman's waterproof boots. The tops are of black dressed sealskin reaching to the knee. Murdoch says that they are made full at the instep and ankles to reduce the number of seams and the chances of leaking. This single seam on one side of the instep appears in Greenland. No. 151668, collected by C. H. Merriam. Soles of white whale skin; leg and upper all of one piece, having one double, water-tight seam in front of the leg and across the instep to the sole at the ankle joint. The upper is joined to the sole in such manner that the insides of both come together; the two are then run together with fine stitches. A band of white sealskin run on ornaments the top, and a drawstring is inserted in a binding of black sealskin. Lugs or loops of white whale skin for lacing are attached to the margin of the sole on either side at the ball of the foot and beneath the ankle joint. Murdoch says that the ends of the string are passed through the front loop so that the bight comes across the ball of the foot, then through the hinder loops, and are crossed above the heel, carried once or twice around the ankle and tied in front. The waterproof boots from Alaska have the seam on both sides of the instep.

Murdoch describes the manner of sewing a waterproof seam among the Eskimo: "The two pieces are put together, flesh side to flesh side, so that the edge of one projects beyond the other, which is then blind stitched down by sewing it over and over on the edge, taking pains to run the stitches only part way through the other piece. The seam is then turned and the edge of the outer piece is turned in and run down to the grain side of the under with fine stitches that do not pass through to the flesh side of it. Thus in neither seam are there holes through both pieces at once." [1]

This same notion of blind stitching may be seen on Atha-pascan shoes, even among the Hupas in California.

Lieutenant Schwatka says that a certain kind of boot for use in the water is found among the Alaskans, made of seal or fish skin, which is almost if not fully as impervious as those made of rubber by more civilized people. [2] His travels were about the Yukon River.

Example No. 43345 is a pair of shoes or boottees from Golo-vina Bay, consisting of three parts—the sole, the vamp, and the heel piece. The soles are of black seal skin, turned up

Fig. 52.

MAN'S DRESS BOOTS OF DEERSKIN, USED BY THE ESKIMO OF POINT BARROW, ALASKA.

From a figure in Murdoch's "Ethnological Results of the Point Barrow Expedition," Ninth Annual Report of the Bureau of Ethnology.

Cat. No. 56749, U. S. N. M.

all around and puckered in front and in the rear, looking like an old man's chin. The vamp is of white sealskin and is quite ornamental. Its lower edge, where it is attached to the upper margin of the sole, con-sists of seven bands of sealskin of different colors and varying widths, making an extremely elaborate device. From this the vamp extends upward quite well on the foot. The heel is a piece of plain white seal-skin, which is sewed to the margin of the sole and extends to the top of

[1] Murdoch, "Ethnological Results of the Point Barrow Expedition," Ninth Ann. Rep. Bureau of Ethnology, p. 134.

[2] Schwatka, "Military Reconnoissance in Alaska," p. 105.

the boot. The border at the top is of the same color and has below it a little band of sealskin with the hair on. All the parts are united by means of cording or piping of different-colored leather. The lacing is attached to the front loops on the sole by sewing. They are crossed above the back of the foot, passed through two lugs of white leather at the side of the heel, then across the instep, where they are tied. Length, 9½ inches. Collected by E. W. Nelson.

Example No. 129822 is a pair of boots from St. Michaels, Alaska. The sole is made from sealskin, turned up and puckered; the margin on the toe

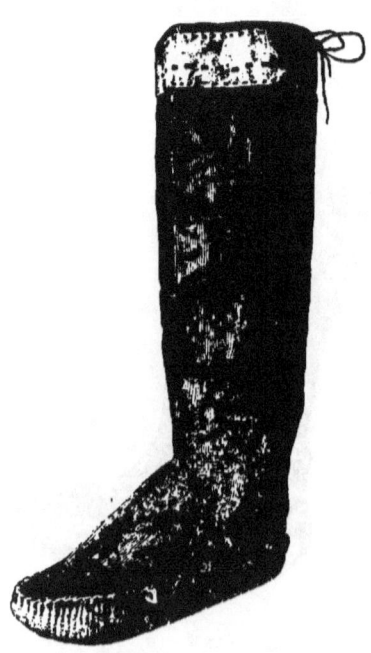

Fig. 53.

WOMAN'S WATERPROOF SEALSKIN BOOT, USED BY
THE ESKIMO OF POINT BARROW, ALASKA.

From a figure in Murdoch's "Ethnological Results of the Point Barrow Expedition," Ninth Annual Report of the Bureau of Ethnology.

Cat. No. 76182, U. S. N. M.

and heel turned out so as to form the profile of a human chin. The lugs consist of straps, as on a boot, and the front pair are sewed on to the lacing. The top is of brown dressed sealskin and is run on to the margin of the sole more than half way round in front by a piping or welt. This top consists of a front, or vamp, and the heel, which extends from the border of the sole to the upper margin of the boot. Between the vamp and the leg is a gore or insertion of white skin, and a band of white skin is let in between the sides of the vamp and the leg; on that two narrow borders of dark leather have been run. From this vamp to the upper margin the front of the leg is decorated in the following manner: A piece of hide is inserted between the two margins of the top, and between these margins a piece of white leather doubled up for a piping, then the other parts are sewed together with a thong or leather string. The upper border is decorated with a piece of white hide; this is adorned with a narrow strip of dark hide run on, and at the juncture of this band with the top the second row of stitches has, alternating with the white, little bits of dark leather one-half inch wide sewed on. Length, 10½ inches. Collected by General Hazen, U. S. A.

There is in the National Museum a shoe similar to No. 43345, but the strips of different colored skin inserted between the vamp and the sole are wider, more numerous, and are decorated with geometric figures effected by running narrow strips of leather into the texture of the body of the shoe, a very common style of ornamentation in Greenland. This specimen is from Norton Sound, and is one of the most beautiful examples of the shoemaker's art. Length, 8½ inches. Collected by E. W. Nelson.

Example No. 10467, from the Yukon River district, has the following marks: First, the sole is a stout piece of seal hide, dressed without the hair; puckered around the toes and heel in exactly the same fashion as the sole of the Navajo shoe, No. 9549. To this margin is sewed a strip of red sealskin, flesh side out, about an inch wide all around, and to this is whipped the top of the boot made up of twenty-five pieces or bits of deerskin sewed together. Just above the ankle there is a dividing line between the shoe proper and the leg. This latter part is very ornamental, consisting of skin from different parts of the deer's leg, with patches of wolverene skin front and back; the upper part consists of several bands of skin from the leg of the deer, the hair being white and trimmed close above the seams. Drawstrings are inserted between the sole and the red strip, just below the ankles, and these are brought up over the heel and instep and around the ankle to bind the shoe to the foot. Length, 9¾ inches. Collected by J. T. Dyar.

Example No. 38771 is a pair of boots from Unalakleet, Yukon district, Alaska, consisting of a heavy black sole turned up all around and puckered at the ends. The upper part consists of the vamp, the heel in a single piece, and the upper border. The vamp, before being back-stitched to the upper margin of the sole is ornamented more than half way round with a pretty band of brownish leather, into which two rows of narrow stitching of rawhide thread are run making a web-like ornament; it extends well up above the instep and the heel. A little higher still, and the two join together by a very neat seam, in which piping is introduced in leather of a different color. The border of the boot is a separate strip of leather run on to the top, and a very narrow band of brown leather is inserted at this point. Around the top is a little strip of deerskin with the hair on. The lacing consists of two straps sewed on to the upper margin of the sole opposite the ball of the foot. These are crossed over the instep and passed down to the sides of the heel through two loops of leather; they are then brought around the back of the heel and tied in front over the instep. Length, 10 inches. Collected by E. W. Nelson.

Example No. 7612 is a pair of shoes from Nunivak Island. Soles made of sealskin turned up and crimped. The upper part consists of a broad strip passing entirely around the foot, with the leg attached above that. The tongue is inserted between the leg and the vamp and the lacing. The lacing and the tongue are ornamented with embroidery in quill work, which shows a little contact between the Indian and the Eskimo. Length, 10 inches. Collected by W. H. Dall.

In the early spring the Eskimo women, of Ungava, north of Labrador, are busily engaged in making boots for summer wear. The skins of the seals have been prepared the fall before and stored away till wanted. The method of skin dressing is the same as practiced by Eskimo elsewhere. If it is designed to make boots for a man, the measure of the height of the leg is taken. The length and width of the sole is measured by hand, stretching so far and then bending down the middle finger until the length is measured.[1]

The foot wear of the Hudson Bay Eskimo, collected by Lucien M. Turner, has the following characteristics:

The boots and shoes differ in material and pattern for different seasons of the year. In all the styles the stout soles turn up an inch or two all round the foot, a tongue piece covers the top of the foot and above the sole and the tongue the top varies in height, either being long enough to reach the knee or else rising a little above the ankle. The low-top half boots are worn over fur stockings in warm weather. These stockings are made of short-haired deerskin with the hair worn inside. These low-top boots are worn outside the long boots in severe weather. The Hudson Bay Eskimo also wear Indian moccasins, sometimes over a pair of inside shoes and sometimes as inside shoes. The Indians in proximity with the Eskimo here are the Nascopi and Montagnais Algonquian, and features of Algonquian moccasins are to be seen in the more northern boots. The wearing of overshoes, of stockings and overshoes must not be overlooked in primitive life, and may be kept in mind in the interpretation of ancient pictures and sculptures. The Hudson Bay Eskimo use for waterproof soles the skin of the beaver or of the harp seal, and prefer the former. For indoor shoes or for those to be worn in cold, dry weather, the skin of the white whale was chosen. The skins of the smaller seals are made into soles, either with the flesh or the hair side out. They are comparatively waterproof if the black epidermis be allowed to remain. The creamy white leather made by allowing the skins to ferment until hair and epidermis may be scraped off and then stretching and drying them in the cold air does not exclude the water and can be used for soles only in perfectly dry weather. Buckskin or deerskin soles are worn with snow shoes, as the feet are not so liable to slip, and the porous skin allows the moisture of the feet to escape more readily.

The tongue and the heel band of the Hudson Bay shoe are generally made of dressed sealskin; the legs or uppers are of sealskin with the hair on.

Example No. 90359 (fig. 54), collected by Lucien M. Turner, is a pair of boots with buckskin feet and tongue and sealskin tops. The combination of Eskimo and Indian is noteworthy. Throughout Mr. Turner's Ungava collection there are many specimens of this character. As in

---

[1] Cf. Turner, " Ethnology of the Ungava District, Hudson Bay Territory," Eleventh Ann. Rep. Bureau of Ethnology, p. 206.

Alaska the arts of the Yukon pass insensibly from Indian to Eskimo, so here.

Example No. 90356 (fig. 55) is a pair of low shoes from Hudson Bay Eskimo, with white sealskin soles, black sealskin tongue and heel band, and deerskin tops. The tawed and smoked reindeer skin for the tops was purchased from the Nascopi Indians. The noticeable features of these specimens are the similarity of the white skin sole with those of the western Eskimo, the pointed tongue or upper, and the narrow inserted heel band between sole and top. In some of the more elegant western forms of boots half a dozen band welts and pipings of particolored skin and fur are inserted.

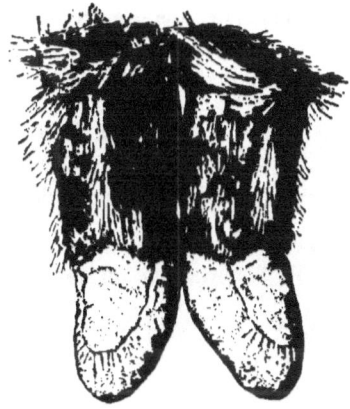

Fig. 54

SHORT BOOTS OF UNGAVA BAY ESKIMO.

From figure in Turner's "Ethnology of the Ungava District, Hudson Bay Territory," Eleventh Annual Report of the Bureau of Ethnology.

Cat. No. 90359, U. S. N. M.

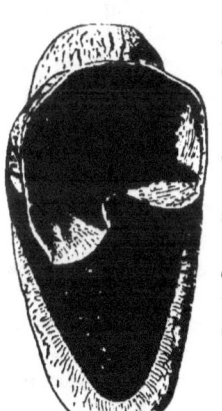

One kind of foot gear of these Eskimo consists of a bird skin short sock with a padding of grass nicely distributed over the sole. Outside of this comes a bearskin leg sewed with great skill to the natural sole of the plantigrade and abundantly wadded about the foot with dry, nonconducting straw.[1]

Fig. 55.

LOW SHOE OF UNGAVA BAY ESKIMO.

From a figure in Turner's "Ethnology of the Ungava District, Hudson Bay Territory," Eleventh Annual Report of the Bureau of Ethnology.

Cat. No. 90356, U. S. N. M.

Stearns thus minutely describes the process of boot making by Indians of Old Fort Bay, Labrador: "From a lot of sealskins one is selected, either from a harbor seal with the hair on or a large harp seal from which the hair has all been scraped off. In either case the skin, to be the most serviceable, must be well scraped of fat on the inside and dried for two or three months on some frame on which it has been stretched to its fullest extent in the sun, exposed on the wood pile or roof of the house (after the hair has been taken off, if a harp seal, and with

[1] Dr. E. K. Kane, "Arctic Explorations," Philadelphia, 1856, pp. 22–24.

the hair on, if a harbor seal). These dry skins will not shrink, and for every purpose of wear are infinitely better than the shoes sold in large numbers, made of quickly dried skins, sewed upon wooden forms, which shrink and tear, while they soon wear useless. Out of them the boot leg is cut from a pattern of any kind the wearer may choose. All or nearly all bottoms are cut from like patterns to fit a foot of any shape, but invariably from the dried skin of the harp seal, the drier and older the better, since they stand more wear the older they are. The pattern of the sole is an oblong oval, while the tongue or top piece is more or less lance shaped. After soaking over night in water to soften it, the sole is taken and the whole edge for about an inch and a half is bent inward; then the toe is puckered in creases, as is also the heel, while the tongue fits the space left after the boot leg is temporarily fastened on, all the pieces overlapping enough to allow for sewing. These puckerings are made by simple creases of the needle at the time of sewing. All seams are made—if the sewing is done in a skillful manner, and not simply to sell the boot—by the simple overlapping of the two pieces and sewing each edge tightly to the part beneath, while the ridge thus made by the seam, if rubbed with a piece of wood, shoemaker fashion, will be hard and shiny as well as very tight. In all sewing the skin is so thick that the needle can be run through it and out the same side without perforating the skin; thus a seam admits no water through the sewing if the thread and overlapping pieces are drawn tight. The upper border of the boot leg has a doubled piece of cloth sewn around its edge, though sometimes sealskin replaces it, through which a piece of tape or braid of any color to suit the wearer, about a yard and a half long, is threaded, and the skin being quite flexible when on the foot is drawn tightly about the leg, the braid wound about twice and tied with the string end hanging outward. This secures the boot firmly and yet not painfully to the foot by the leg, and, though the string often gets loose and the boot leg often slips down, it seldom gives much trouble to the wearer. A noteworthy operation that might escape one's attention, as well as a curious fact in connection with this operation, is that the puckerings of the heel are held together by running two, three, or four small threads at about equal distance from each other, the stitches being taken through the bend in the creases on the inside of the boot from side to side around the heel, where they are drawn tight and fastened to the seam above; another fact is that the creases of the toe are not thus fastened." [1]

The types of the Eskimo foot wear are:

1. The straw shoe or stocking, between Bering Strait and Kadiak..
2. The moccasin-shaped low shoe.
3. The moccasin sole with boottee top.

---

[1] W. A. Stearns, "Labrador," Boston, 1884, pp. 162, 163. The boots of the east Greenlanders are of similar make, and are described by Holm and by Nansen, "First Crossing of Greenland," II, p. 272 et seq.

4. Boottee with sole; vamp and legging separated from the sole by one or more bands or welts of different color and width.

5. Crimped soles united immediately to the seal or other skin tops. These are winter boots.

6. Waterproof boots with crimped soles united immediately to the vamp and quarter. These two parts are joined, sometimes with a seam on one side and sometimes with a seam on both sides, and above the vamp and heel piece are tops, and sometimes extension tops, either of waterproof or of white sealskin.

7. Double boot (outer boot with crimped sole united to a long leg of sealskin or deerskin with the hair side out and inner boot or stocking with the hair side in toward the foot).

Where the Eskimo have been in contact with the Russians, the whalers, and with the Scandinavians, various foreign elements have been introduced, as the welt in the seams, additional strips and decorative piping between the different parts, and the addition of bead work and fine embroidery on the surface. While certain elements and materials characterize various culture regions, the going about of the Eskimo themselves and the acculturations above mentioned have greatly mingled the characteristics of the foot wear.

On leaving the Eskimo region in America and traveling southward one passes from the land of sealskin foot gear into that made from the dressed hides of land mammals. This class of foot wear goes by the generic name of moccasin, from an Algonquian word having a similar sound. Some features of the moccasin may be seen in Eskimo land, and Eskimo features will appear in Athapascan and Algonquian shoes especially; so also on the south border of the moccasin areas there is no sharp line dividing it from the sandal and the bare foot.

Moccasins have their dispersion in those areas of North America where the great mammals were in abundance, and where the ground was adapted to their usage. The people were ever on the move. In the Canadian region where the caribou was the prevailing mammal and no good thick hide could be found for soles, the shoe was cut from a single piece. The eastern Canadian Indians cut the skin from the heel of a caribou or moose with extensions above and below, for the leg and the foot of a rude moccasin, called botte sauvage.

The land of the buffalo and of the elk, because of the quality of the hide and the exigencies of region, occupation, and climate, had another set of types.

On arriving in the cactus country the Indian had to guard his feet and his legs as well, and found in the ample folds of an entire deerskin for each foot, and a thick sole well turned up in front, the protection he needed. The patch of leather on the Mexican sandal lacing is for the same end. In point of fact there were and are three principal classes or species of the moccasin:

1. The Athapascan type, a soft gaiter coming well up on the ankle,

made of a single piece with decorated tongue in front, lapels of flannel and buckskin over the lacing behind, and the gaiter top. Found in Canada and on the west coast.

2. The low, much decorated slipper moccasin of the plains and of the United States east of the Rockies, with endless tribal varieties.

3. The boot, with long top to wrap about the limbs.

There were, in addition to the environmental suggestions, fashions of moccasins that were purely tribal. For instance, among the Siouan tribes the Ponka moccasin sole was nearly symmetrical, broad across the ball of the foot, and bluntly pointed in front. The Omahas made a moccasin the sole of which was almost straight along the inside of the foot and pointed like our latest fashion, while the Páni style was curved very irregularly along both edges and sharply pointed. But styles were mixed from tribe to tribe.

Moccasins were generally made in summer, since the hides of buffalo slain during that season were without thick hair. In the making the women pulled out the hair, as they did in the manufacture of leggings. They were cut out by a pattern, made over a rude last, and sewed with thread made of sinew from the leg or the fiber from the muscular fasciae of the back and the shoulder. Before the introduction of beads dyed porcupine and bird quills were employed in ornament, and it is worthy of notice that now the old patterns are repeated faithfully in beadwork. The making of the moccasin is a matter of ethnical and geographical study, as will be observed in the drawings and descriptions. They are white, yellow, brown, black, or green; they are very low, with margin turned down, or fitted closely to the foot; they are plain or covered with symbols of totemism and mythology; they have trailers differing in pattern, number, and length. In a region so vast as all Canada south of Eskimo and all the United States excepting the southwestern corner, the resources and exactions of nature would in the same tribe effect many varieties and styles.

Commencing at the far north, example No. 7613 is a pair of moccasins of the Kutchakutchin Indians on the Yukon, consisting of three parts, the covering of the foot, the tongue, and the heel (fig. 56.) The first-named piece is cut out in rectangular form, mitered in front and the two edges sewed together or joining a tongue piece. In the heel the two edges are brought together and sewed downward about 3 inches, then for the rest of the way the leather is doubled so as to form a T-shaped seam, and this provides for the flattening out of the sole. The tongue, like that of a modern shoe, is sewed in with a piping, but the heel curtain is here omitted from the margin of the shoe. The edge of the bottom of the heel is cut off square and leaves no trailers whatever. No 1336, collected by C. P. Gaudet (fig. 57), is similar to this, excepting on the top of the shoe a piece of white leather or false tongue is added for ornament, and the seam gathered with beautiful quill work of red and blue. Also on the back of this example the inserted leather hangs an inch below the seam like a curtain and is cut out neatly into a castellated ornament. Length of foot. 10½ inches; height of boot, 9 inches. Collected by W. H. Dall.

Example No. 166964 is a shoe of the Athapascan form worn in the interior of Alaska on the Yukon, described also under No. 1336, but to the bottom of this Indian moccasin is sewed a thick sole, made of sennit constructed out of old manila rope, frayed and braided after the manner of the Tibetan shoe No. 131198. The union of the Indian moccasin with the Chinese and Tibetan sole in the same specimen is an excellent example of the way in which one people borrow the inventions of another. This shoe is evidently an adaptation made by an American sailor or by a Chinaman recently living in Alaska. Length, 10½ inches. Collected by J. H. Turner.

Fig. 56.

MOCCASIN OF KUTCHAKUTCHIN INDIANS, ALASKA.

Cat. No. 7613, U. S. N. M. Collected by William H. Dall.

In winter, according to Mackenzie, the dress of the Chippewyan is composed of the skins of deer and their fawns, dressed as fine as any chamois leather in the hair. In summer the same, except without the hair. Their shoes and leggings are sewed together, the latter reaching upward to the middle and being supported by a belt, under which a small piece of leather is drawn, the ends of which fall down both before and behind. In the shoes they put the hair of the moose or reindeer with additional pieces of leather as socks. The shirt or coat when girted around the waist reaches to the middle of the thigh, and the mittens are sewed to the sleeves or are suspended by strings from the shoulders. A ruff or tippet surrounds the neck, and the skin of the head of the deer forms a curious cap.

Fig. 57.

MOCCASIN OF ATHAPASCAN INDIANS, ANDERSON RIVER, NORTHERN CANADA.

Cat. No. 1336, U. S. N. M. Collected by C. P. Gaudet.

A robe made of several deer or fawn skins sewed together covered the whole. This dress is worn single or double, but always in winter the hair within and without. The dress of the women differs little from that of the men.[1] The U. S. National Museum, through the kindness

---

[1] "Mackenzie's Voyages," pp. cxv and 120–122.

of R. MacFarlane, B. R. Ross, Robert Kennicott, C. P. Gaudet, and others, possesses a number of rare specimens of this shoe, stocking and long legging all in one piece, made of excellent tawed caribou skin and richly decorated with beadwork.

The Carriers (Athapascans) of Stuart Lake, British Columbia, originally wore a moccasin of elk skin (*Cervus canadensis*). But the poorer classes made shoes of untanned marmot skin, or even of the skin of the salmon. They are now of dressed caribou or of moose skin among the Carrier and the Tse'kéhne and of deerskin among the Tsilkoh'tin.

These tribes went barefooted in rainy weather, the women and children still adhering to the custom. No Carrier would now undertake a journey without the traditional moccasins.[1]

The Nascopi Indians of Labrador, contiguous to the Eskimos, have

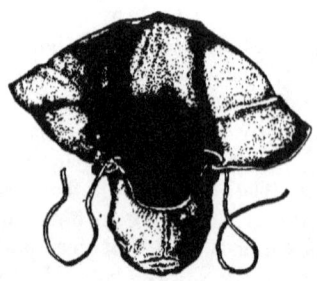

Fig. 58.

MOCCASINS OF NASCOPI (ALGONQUIAN) INDIANS, LABRADOR.

From a figure in Turner's "Ethnology of the Ungava District, Hudson Bay Territory," Eleventh Annual Report of the Bureau of Ethnology.

Cat. No. 90062, U. S. N. M.

been studied by Lucien M. Turner, who sent to the U. S. National Museum examples No. 90062 and 90063. According to Mr. Turner the deerskin moccasin is thus constructed: "The footing is cut out first in the shape of a parallelogram; the edges are then turned up and creases made around the part that covers the front of the foot. The puckers are held in position by a stout sinew thread run through each one and around from side to side to prevent their 'bagging' over the toes. The sides of the footing and the heel are not creased, as the heel seam takes up the slack." The heel seam is T-shaped, the horizontal portion resting on the ground. In the example figured by Turner there is no "trailer." At the tip of the toe there is, contrary to Athapascan fashion, a T-shaped seam also (fig. 58). This mark has a curious distribution and may be of little account. The tongue or upper is sewed to the edges of the creases on the sole or bottom portion, but between the upper and the sole oftentimes a narrow welt or piping of skin or

[1] A. G. Morice, "Notes on the Western Dénés," Trans. Canadian Inst., IV, p. 163.

cloth is inserted. The superfluous edges of the sole are then trimmed off and the gaiter top is sewed on. This is a long, narrow strip of inferior skin of sufficient size to overlap in front and come well above the ankles.

Just below or at the margin of the top a long thong of reindeer hide is inserted through several holes, which allows it to pass around the heel and below the ankles, bringing the ends in front over the tongue. One end of the top is carefully laid over the other and wrapped round by the ends of the thong.

Certain portions of the hide make better foot wear than others. The neck is too thick and stiff to crease, but is useful for tongues; the flanks are too thin. The sides of the hide are useful for bottoms; the flanks and back, scarred by grubs, serve for tops and strings.

For wear about the tent the gaiter top is omitted and a slipper moccasin worn, which is held on the foot by means of a drawstring. This low form is adopted largely among the Canadian white population.

A single deerskin will make five to seven pairs of moccasins for an adult, and as they last but two or three weeks as many as fifteen to twenty-five pairs are necessary for each.

The Nascopi are of the Algonquian family, and the chief characteristics of their moccasins may be expected in all the tribes of the United States east of the Mississippi and north of the thirty-fifth parallel.

The moccasin of the Iroquois, ah ta qua o weh, was made of deerskin. In the modern moccasin the front part is worked with porcupine quills, after the ancient fashion, while the lapel which falls down upon the sides is embroidered with beadwork, according to the present taste.

The legging, giseha, which was fastened above the knee and descended upon the moccasin, was also made originally of deerskin and ornamented with quill work upon the bottom and side, the embroidered edge being worn in front. In later times red broadcloth, embroidered with beadwork, has been substituted for deerskin in most cases. Much ingenuity and taste were displayed in the designs and in the execution of the work upon this article of apparel. The warrior might well be proud of this part of his costume.[1]

Of the tribes west of the Mississippi, Carver says that the shoes of the Naudowessies are made of the skin of the deer, elk, or buffalo; these, after being sometimes dressed according to the European manner, at others with the hair remaining on them, are cut into shoes and fashioned so as to be easy to the feet and convenient for walking. The edges round the ankle are decorated with pieces of brass or tin fixed around leather strings about an inch long, which being placed very thick, make a cheerful tinkling noise either when they walk or dance.[2] In point of fact during the good old days of the buffalo the Sioux moccasin of the trail and the hunt was chiefly of buffalo hide. The

---

[1] Lewis H. Morgan, "League of the Iroquois," 1851, pp. 263–265.

[2] Carver, "Three Years' Travels," Philadelphia, 1796, p. 146.

large proportion of Indian foot gear exposed for sale in the last few years have been made by the women of this stock. A full set from any one tribe includes very many designs. There seems to have been no collector who gave attention to completing such sets. The U. S. National Museum is rich in Sioux material, but has nothing near a perfect series from any Sioux tribe.

Example No. 8535 is a modern Sioux moccasin, consisting of a sole of rawhide and upper of dressed buffalo hide all in one piece, the only seam being at the back. The sole is a piece of an old pemmican case, showing the paintings in green and red, attached to the upper by whipping along its margin so as to leave the lower half of the margin projecting downward and raise the upper above the ground. The tongue is a separate piece. The ornamentation consists of a tribal symbol in blue, green, yellow, red, and white beads sewed on separately. A lacing of buckskin thong passes through slashes around the heel and ties in front of the instep. The trailer is two strings close together, about an inch and a quarter long. Length, 10 inches. Collected by S. M. Horton, U. S. A.

Example No. 152855 is a pair of moccasins belonging to the Kiowa Indians and collected by James Mooney, of the Bureau of Ethnology. The uppers are of soft leather, dyed blue, and ornamented with beadwork and cut fringe. The fringe is a marked character on the Kiowa moccasin. The sole is of hard rawhide sewed on with sinew. Mr. Mooney says that the tongue in the moccasin, and the long, fringed trailer are worn by both Kiowa and Comanche (Shoshonean stock).

Example No. 165811 is an Arapahoe moccasin, consisting of a separate sole of rawhide, cut from an old parfleche case, and an upper made of a single piece of buckskin. The manner of attaching the upper to the sole should be observed: The margin of the thick sole is split for a little way all around, and the margin of the buckskin upper is attached to that portion of the border of the sole that is above by whipping; in this way the stitching does not come in contact with the ground, but the sole stands off as in a regular shoe; in fact, by splitting the margin of the sole the Arapahoe Indian woman has provided herself with a quasi welt. This same process of splitting and sewing is shown in an interesting manner in a California shoe figured in the report of the Ray collection. The only seam that appears in the upper part of the shoe is at the heel, from the bottom of which extend two long trailing strings close together. The lacing is of rawhide thong passing through slashes between heel and ankle. The tongue of the moccasin is sewed on separately, and for ornament there are three rays of blue, red, yellow, and white beads. Length, 10 inches. Collected by James Mooney. Compare the Sioux example, No. 8535, above described.

Lieutenant Abert, U. S. A., describes the Cheyenne moccasin as made of buffalo hide dressed without the hair, the fronts ornamented with beadwork. This moccasin has only one seam; that is on the outer side of the foot, the material being doubled over and made to fit. But it will be seen that this style of seaming is in use with the Nez Percé and the Shoshone. The inside line is perfectly straight, as among the Omahas and some Poncas. Another style is of antelope skin and has trailers attached to the heel. Abert says that these are worn by horsemen and that the Cheyennes believe the trailer to be a protection from the rattlesnakes.

Examples 6987 and 6988 are buckskin moccasins made in one piece, cut out so that the seams extend down the back of the heel and over the top of the foot, with puckering. This form of moccasin is peculiar to the Caddo of Texas. Collected by Edward Palmer.

Frequent reference is made in this paper to the "trailer," or hiⁿ-be-ga-ceg-che, of the Sioux. It consists of one or more little rawhide strings about an inch long trailing behind the heel of a certain type of Indian moccasin. When the woman cuts out the skin for the shoe she leaves hanging on the edge of that part which forms the horizontal seam at the bottom of the heel the little tags, strings, or tassels that will form the trailer. Each tribe had a different number and order of this part, so that a good scout is said to have been able to tell the tribe to which an Indian belonged by the mark of his trailer in the snow. Mr. Dorsey once told the writer that the Omahas had a habit of omitting or disguising the trailer as a part of their strategy in war. For many examples of the low, beaded moccasin of the East, Catlin's and other works should be consulted.

Turning away from the Atlantic to the Pacific drainage, it will be necessary to commence at Mount St. Elias. The Kwakiutl and other tribes of the British Columbia coast go barefooted the year round, according to Boas. This might be declared of all primitive maritime peoples in regions where the want of warmth did not stimulate the invention of waterproof foot gear. In maritime Europe the sabot lifts the foot above the wet sand and mud. This maritime or barefooted region stretches from Mount St. Elias to the Columbia River. It is the home of the Koluschan, Skittagetan, Chimmesyan, Wakashan, and coast Salishan families; the route of the Pacific gulf stream; the region of abundant sea food and great forests; the culture region of the great dugout canoes.

Example No. 20797 (fig. 59) is a moccasin from Sitka, consisting of three pieces—the footing, the vamp, and the leg piece. The sole is probably of soft elkskin cut into long rectangular form and rounded in front. In the rear two wedge-shaped gores are cut out at the corners, leaving a right trapezoid extending as in a dovetail. When the two edges of the rear are brought together they are doubled so as to form a T-shaped seam and the trapezoidal piece extends outward to form the trailer of the shoe. The horizontal seam of the T provides for the flat sole, and the vertical part provides for the extension of the material well up around the heel and the front of the foot as in an ordinary slipper. The front of this shoe is gathered and puckered so as to cover the ends of the toes and the margin of the foot. The vamp or back piece is sewed to the margin of the footing and extends well upward on the leg; the seam connecting this with the sole, and also the two edges of the sole in the rear, have inserted between them a narrow piece of buckskin acting as a piping. The heel portion of the leg is whipped on to the upper margin of the sole in such a way that a small portion of it extends below the seam like a lapel. The vamp and the heel piece extending well up on the leg are wrapped around it and held in place by cord or some kind of a garter. Length, 10½ inches. Collected by J. G. Swan.

Example No. 23854 is a pair of moccasins said to have been worn by a Nez Percé Indian, consisting of two parts; that which covers the foot and a short legging around the ankle. The body of the shoe is

Fig. 59.

ATHAPASCAN TYPE OF MOCCASIN, FROM SITKA, ALASKA.

Cat. No. 20797, U. S. N. M.   Collected by J. G. Swan.

made of a single piece of hide cut out like the finger of a glove, sewed around the toe and along the outer margin of the foot to the heel where the two edges of the rear end of the pattern are sewed together to form the upright portion of the heel and also a horizontal seam with trailers at least 1¼ inches apart. The upper border or legging is sewed on to the upper margin of the shoe, and a portion of the leather of the shoe extends backward to form a tongue. The top of the foot is ornamented with beadwork in white, black, and blue beads. Around the ankle is a strip of red flannel ornamented with blue and white beads. The strings are formed of buckskin thong. The formation of this shoe should be especially observed, as it differs from those in the regions about in the manner in which the seam is carried around from heel to great toe. Length, 10 inches. Collected by J. B. Monteith.

Example No. 673 is a pair of shoes from the Chinook Indians at the mouth of the Columbia River. This shoe consists of three parts—the sole, the upper, and the legging. The sole is of thick rawhide and sewed on to the upper by a series of blind stitches, just as in a modern, cheap slipper or eastern moccasin. The upper is of buckskin and has only one seam at the back. At the lower end of this seam is a trailer, in which a single rawhide string, one-eighth of an inch wide, is supplied nearly all the way. The upper is extended into a long tongue, passing to the top of the legging. The legging is a band of buckskin about 4 inches wide, sewed to the top of the upper. The shoe string passes through slashes in the upper on either side of the heel, and at the instep as in the Athapascan and after passing once or twice around the ankle, is tied in front. They are ornamented by beadwork in red, white, green, blue, and pink beads. The designs are entirely European. They are rights and lefts. Length, 9½ inches; height, 7 inches. Collected by George Gibbs.

The moccasin of the Shoshone is of the deer, elk, or buffalo skin, dressed without the hair, though in winter they use the buffalo skin with the hair side inward, as do most of the Indians who inhabit the buffalo country. Like the Nez Percé moccasin, it is made with a single seam on the outer margin and sewed up behind, an opening being left at the instep to admit the foot. It is variously ornamented with figures wrought with porcupine quills, and sometimes the young men most fond of dress cover it with the skin of a polecat and trail at their heels the tail of the animal.[1]

Fig. 60.

PATTERN AND BLIND STITCHING OF HUPA MOCCASIN.

Example No. 165147 is a Shoshone moccasin, from Wyoming, made of smoked deerskin. As described by Lewis and Clarke, this specimen, collected by James Mooney, is all in one piece, with the seam at the side, instead of having a separate sole like the moccasins of the prairie tribes. Example 165148 from the same tribe has the T-shaped seam on the toe. Example 22018 is a buckskin moccasin made in one piece cut out so that the seam extends down the back of the heel and around the outer margin of the foot quite around the toes. The edges are sewed together with a piping in the seam. Short tongue sewed on as in a modern slipper, lacing through slashes about the heel. Long trailers from seam, and short ones from horizontal seam of the heel. Length, 9½ inches. Wind River Utes, collected by Major J. W. Powell.

The shoes of the Hupa (Western Athapascan) and of the other Indians of northern California are made high like gaiters and are cut from a single piece of buckskin sewed up at the back rather carelessly by a buckskin cord, as in basting. Down the instep a curious seam is formed as follows (fig. 60): The two edges of the leather are slightly

[1] "History of the Lewis and Clarke Expedition," 1893, II, New York, pp. 564-568.

split. They are then brought together as in joining the edges of
a carpet. A loose cord of sinew is laid along the two edges and a
whipped stitching of sinew made to join the .two inner margins of
the edges of the buckskin, inclosing at the same time the loose cord of
sinew.

When the shoe is rounded out, the two outer margins of the leather
come together on the outside of the shoe and conceal the sewing altogether. A coarse sandal of the thick portion of the elk hide or of twined
matting is worn by some tribes (fig. 61), and also a nicely woven legging of soft basketry. The latter, however, belong to full or ceremonial dress.[1]

Example No. 24079 (fig. 62) is a sandal of rushes worn by the Klamath
Indians of northern California (Lutuamian family), collected by L. S.
Dyar. It is only half finished, and shows the method of construction.

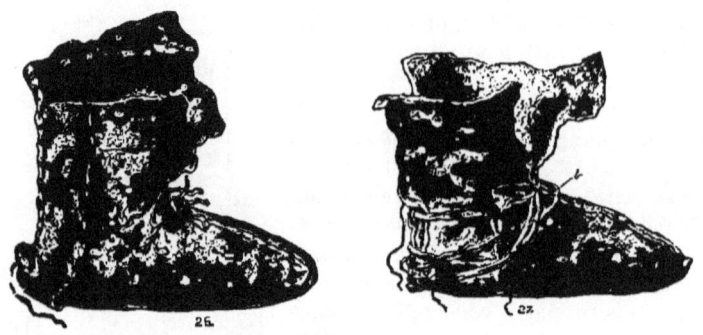

2 5.

Fig. 61.

MOCCASINS OF CAHROC AND HUPA INDIANS, NORTHERN CALIFORNIA.

Cat. Nos. 21437 and 79197, U. S. N. M.   Collected by Stephen Powers and Capt. P. H. Ray, U. S. A.

The foundation is laid on eleven twine warp strands, as in the Japanese
sandal of thread, spreading apart toward the toes. The weft, however,
is in twined weaving, and the work is carried up to cover the toes as
in a light slipper, as will be seen on Korean and Chinese examples.
Along the margin of the sole loops have been left, as in the Asiatic specimens figured and described.[2] Especial notice must be taken of this
specimen occurring in northern California because-it is the first intimation at the north of the sandal, which will a little later on usurp the
place of the moccasin.

Example No. 9549 (fig. 63) is a pair of Navajo moccasins from New
Mexico (Southern Athapascan), consisting of three parts—sole, vamp,
and heel. The sole is of rawhide turned up in front of the great toe
and about the foot for a half inch or more around the entire margin.

[1] Mason, "The Ray Collection from Hupa Reservation," Rep. Smithsonian Inst.,
1886, p. 210.

[2] Ibid, pl. VI.

The vamp is of brown deerskin, or smoke-cured deerskin, very neatly sewed to the margin of the rawhide sole all the way around, and the stitches are all finely puckered. This work is suggestive of the Eskimo shoemaker. The heel (or what is commonly called the quarters and legging) consists of a broad strip of buckskin attached to the sole back of the arch of the foot, having a long, wide flap which passes from the inner side of the foot across the instep, and is buttoned at the ankle on the outside. No. 9550 (fig. 64) is of the same character, excepting the quarter piece is fastened with a thong rather than with buttons. Length, 10 inches. Collected by E. Palmer.

It is worth noticing, in passing, that the gaiter tops of the Navajo, who are Athapas-can, is here modified to a modern style, and that the soles are of such primitive fashion that they may be said to stand for the first of all rawhide foot wear. The Apache boot, as a protection against the thorny plants of their desert country, resembles the classical *endromis*, figured in the third edition of Smith's Dictionary. But it is after all the Athapascan legging and moccasin, combined with the addition of a rawhide sole having a broad point turned up in front. Now, the Apache is also an Athapascan. The long seam down the inside of the leg is made by turning one margin down for half an inch, laying the other margin against the crease and whipping the doubled and the single edge together with sinew thread. For attaching the upper to the sole the raw edge of the former is doubled, the upper margin of the latter is beveled, the two are whipped together, and then the sole projects outward to conceal and protect the seam.

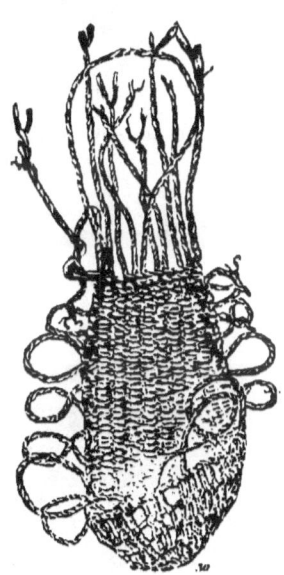

Fig. 62.

WOVEN GRASS SANDAL OF KLAMATH (LUTUAMIAN) INDIANS, NORTHERN CALIFORNIA

Cat. No. 21079, U. S. N. M. Collected by Capt. P. H. Ray, U. S. A.

The following types of moccasins may be noted:

1. Athapascan type, with gaiter or extension top. Footing of one piece, with seam at the heel and straight up the back or top of the foot to an ornamental tongue piece. The extension top is sewed to the footing so as to extend downward in a curtain to conceal the lacing.

2. Tlingit type, like the Athapascan, but without seam in front, the tongue piece covering almost entirely the back of the foot. Top not extending downward to cover the lacing. Trailers are present.

3. Algonquian type, very similar to the Athapascan, but having a cross seam in front of the toes, meeting the seam from the front of the tongue piece. These three forms merge into the Eskimo at the north and the low moccasins at the south.

4. Iroquoian pattern. Footing slipper like, with lapels at the side; embroidered. The tongue piece is set into the puckered border of the footing. In modern examples linings are introduced.

5. Siouan pattern. In recent times with rawhide sole, beaded top, and lapels. The Shoshonean variety of this type has a seam from the heel around the outer margin of the foot, quite to the inside of the great toe, and this was doubtless the earlier Siouan form. Frequently heavy buckskin fringes adorn the heel seam and the top of the foot.

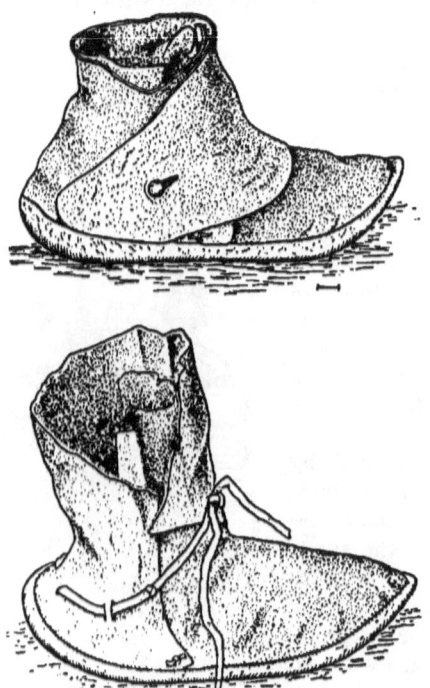

6. Desert type. Found in the Great Interior Basin from Utah to Mexico; characterized by a heavy rawhide sole turned up in a peculiar manner to protect the end of the great toe from thorns.

7. The Caddoan type. Gaiter form, with straight seam all the way up the heel and entirely across the top or back of the foot, with seams often elegantly puckered on the toes.

At this point it is necessary to make an abrupt stop on the borderland of the Spanish territory. Passing the moccasin, the student arrives at the land of the sandal, just on the southern boundary of Colorado and Utah. Here he encounters two radically different types of sandal, the one now in common use throughout Latin America, having, as in Japan, a single toe string

Figs. 63 and 64.
MOCCASINS OF NAVAJO (ATHAPASCAN) INDIANS, NEW MEXICO.
Cat. Nos. 9549 and 9550, U. S. N. M.   Collected by Edward Palmer.

between the first and the second toe, and the older, aboriginal, and now quite disused type having a toe loop or two toe strings, one between 1 and 2, the other between 3 and 4. Through the courtesy of Prof. F. W. Putnam, Mr. Marshall Saville, and Mr. Stewart Culin, I am able to extend the rather meager collection of the U. S. National Museum.

Example No. 13013, Museum of the University of Pennsylvania, is a sandal from the cliff dwellings of Arizona. It consists of sole, lining, and lacing. The sole is in yucca leaves, diagonally woven or plaited six ply. On top of the sole is an insole or lining of corn husk.

The lacing consists of a series of loops around the margin of the sole, through which a tie of yucca string passes, as in the Indian cradles and sleds. The heel loops pass from two of those before mentioned around the heel and down to the sole under the ankle. (Pl. 5, fig. 1.) Sandals from the Kentucky caves should be studied in this connection.

Example No. 12155b, in the Peabody Museum, is a coarse sandal of yucca fiber, collected by Edward Palmer in an abandoned camp in Utah. It is in the form of an openwork slipper, made up of a fore-and-aft warp held in place by nine rows of cross-twined weaving at varying distances apart. The lacing is gathered into the outer margin of the sole. The Utes are adepts at the twined basketry, and in this example possibly have attempted to imitate a low shoe or moccasin after their own fashion. (Pl. 5, fig. 2.)

Example No. 22192, in the U. S. National Museum, is a sandal from Yezo, worn by the Ainos, and here introduced for comparison with American examples, devoid of toe strings and fastened on entirely by lacing through loops on the side and heel loops. (Pl. 5, fig. 3.)

Example No. 12155c, in the Peabody Museum, is a sandal of yucca fiber found in an old Ute camp. It is much dilapidated, but shows elements of twined weaving, side loops, and cross lacing. Inside is stuffed an old rag, part of a knit stocking. (Pl. 5, fig. 4.)

In an old abandoned camp in southern Utah, in the cedar forests near Mount Trumbull, Edward Palmer found a number of Pah-Ute sandals which, by the kindness of Professor Putnam, I am privileged to describe. All of them are of yucca fiber, and are as coarsely made as sandals can be. Two of them, examples Nos. 12155a and 9439, are of Asiatic pattern, and two of them are in coarse-twined weaving. These will be better described.

Example No. 20929, U. S. National Museum, is an old sandal from Utah, made of coarse yarn of yucca fiber, woven on a warp of two strands of the same material in figure of 8 pattern, the loose ends always left underneath. The toe strings that projected from the end of the sole are gone, and there is left of the lacing only the loop that encircled the heel. (Pl. 6, fig. 1.)

Example No. 12155a, in the Peabody Museum, is an extraordinary specimen. The double warp is the same as in fig. 4 of this plate, and so is the heel covering and overtoe lacing arrangement, but there is in addition a series of loops on the side between the toe and the ankle as in other sandals. We have here a combination sandal, all the elements of which are to be seen in the Japanese types. (Pl. 6, fig. 2.)

Example No. 128173, U. S. National Museum, precisely similar to example No. 116211, figured and described on page 331 of this paper, is here introduced for comparison of the overtoe string, lugs on the sides, heel loops, and especially the wicker weaving. All loose ends are in this shaved off on the bottom. This specimen was presented by the Japanese department of education. (Pl. 6, fig. 3.)

Example No. 9439, in the Peabody Museum, is a sandal from southern Utah, built after one of the Japanese patterns. A coarse bundle of yucca fiber 3 feet long is doubled in the middle, and on this as a warp the sole of the sandal is woven from other bundles in a figure of 8 wickerwork, the coarse ends always appearing underneath. At the heel the fiber is wrapped around the bend of the warp. The sole is 9 inches long. At the tip the two ends of the warp are tied in a single knot, the remainder serving as lacing. For heel and instep strap a bundle of twisted fiber 2 feet long is doubled in the middle back of the heel, the two ends drawn down and passed inside the warp strands beneath the ankle and are then brought up over the instep and tied. The lacing is attached to this, but passes over the toes instead of between them, just as in some Eastern examples. (Pl. 6, fig. 4.)

Example No. 22717, Peabody Museum, is a child's sandal from Aca-tita Cave, Coahuila, Mexico, made from unshredded yucca leaf. The warp is a leaf bent in the middle, the two ends projecting at the heel and shredded. The weft is a very coarse wicker of yucca leaf. The whole is bound together by a leaf brought up through the sole near the heel (a), down again near the toes (b), forward and up around the front, spliced through itself at b, under the sole and spliced through itself at a. The two toe strings have their front ends tied together in a square knot underneath, are spliced through the binding piece to go between toes 1 and 2, and 3 and 4, are attached to the margin under the ankle, and then pass up and around the heel in the usual manner. (Pl. 7, fig. 1.)

Example No. 45610a is a sandal from Mexico. It is built upon two yucca leaves bent double in front, the one overlying the other. In each, the under half is warp; the upper half is doubled down on top and used to strengthen the whole. The toe strings inclose 1 and 2, and 3 and 4, and do not cross on the back of the foot. Heel strap missing. (Pl. 7, fig. 2.)

Example No. 45610, U. S. National Museum, is a child's sandal from a cave near Silver City, N. Mex. It is in figure of 8, or wicker weaving on two-warp filaments. All lashing is absent. (Pl. 7, fig. 3.)

Example No. 22833, in the Peabody Museum, is an old sandal from Coyote Cave, Coahuila, Mexico. In this specimen the yucca warp is carelessly laid along and held together by means of cross sewing with the same material. On top of all a spliced wide leaf occurs, as in figs. 1 and 2. A neat two-ply cord forms the toe string, doubled in the middle, rove through the fabric near the front, so as to go between toes 1 and 2, and 3 and 4, back to the sides of the sole under the ankle, where the ends pass through the heel string and are fastened off with a single knot. The heel string is a very pretty piece of square plaiting, as in whip lashes. Its ends are attached to the ends of a separate twine

EXPLANATION OF PLATE 5.

1	2
3	4

SANDALS WITH MARGINAL LOOPS FOR LACING. CLIFF-DWELLERS OF ARIZONA.

Fig. 1. SANDAL OF YUCCA FIBER. Insole of corn husk and lacing of yucca strips. Lent by Mr. Stewart Culin.

(Cat. No. 13013, Museum of the University of Pennsylvania.)

Fig. 2. SANDAL FROM AN OLD CAMP IN SOUTHERN UTAH. The warp is of shredded yucca fiber and the weft in twined weaving of the same material.

(Cat. No. 12155 (b), Peabody Museum, Cambridge, Mass.)

Fig. 3. SANDAL OF BAST FIBER WOVEN IN WICKER PATTERN. Lacing of straw, twined. (To be compared with fig. 1.) Worn by the Ainos of Yezo.

(Cat. No. 22192, U. S. N. M.)

Fig. 4. SANDAL FROM SOUTHERN UTAH. This is similar to the specimen shown in fig. 2. Inside is a portion of a knit stocking in cotton yarn. The lacing is the same as that shown in the other figures of the plate. The specimen was found in an abandoned camp.

(Cat. No. 12155 (c), Peabody Museum, Cambridge, Mass.)

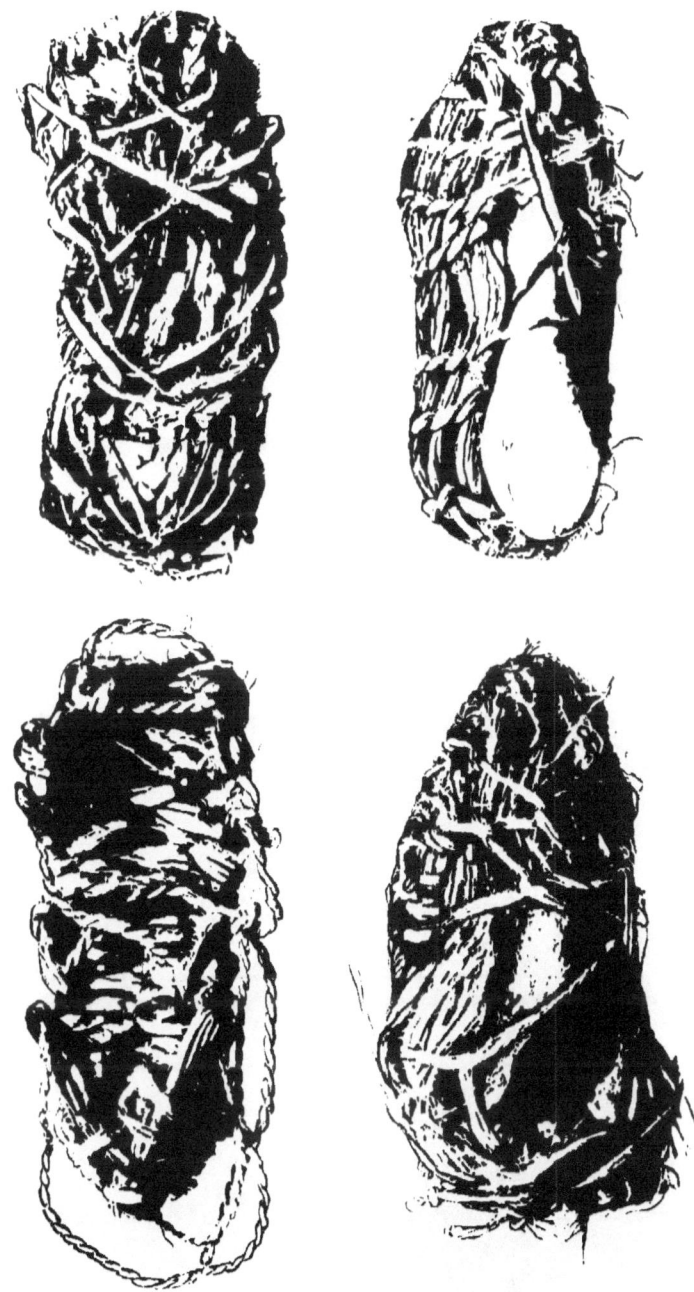

SANDALS WITH MARGINAL LOOPS FOR LACING.
Cliff-dwellers of Arizona.

1'   2

|-

3   4

SANDALS WITH OVERTOE LACING.

Fig. 1. SANDAL OF SHREDDED YUCCA FIBER. Made on a warp of two strands. Southern Utah.

(Cat. No. 2069, U. S. N. M.)

Fig. 2. SANDAL OF SHREDDED YUCCA FIBER. Based on a string of the same material doubled, the ends of which, drawn over the toes, serve as lacings through the loops along the margin. The loop over the heel is of the same material.

(Cat. No. 12155 (a), Peabody Museum, Cambridge, Mass.)

Fig. 3. JAPANESE SANDAL MADE OF STRAW. The foundation is a long twine of the same material, twice doubled, to form at its middle two loops extended at the heel and at its ends to constitute the lacing, which passes over the two toes, through the loops or lugs at the sides, through the heel loops and over the instep, where they are fastened. From the Japanese Department of Education.

(Cat. No. 128173, U. S. N. M.)

Fig. 4. SANDAL OF SHREDDED YUCCA FIBER. This sandal is built up, like those shown in figures 1 and 2, by wicker weaving on a warp of coarse twine of the same material, the ends of which form the overtoe strings. After being laced around the heel they are tied over the instep.

(Cat. No. 9680, Peabody Museum, Cambridge, Mass.)

PLATE 6.

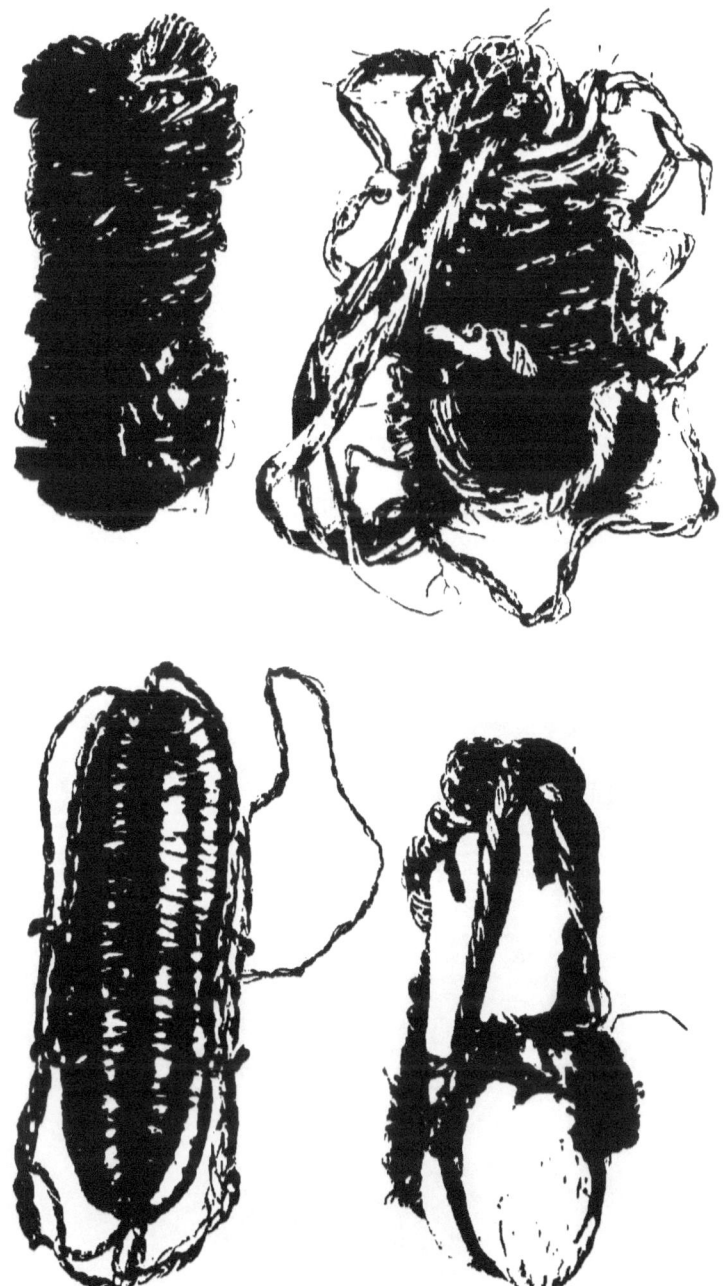

SANDALS WITH OVERTOE LACING.

SANDALS WITH DOUBLE TOE-STRINGS.

Fig. 1. CHILD'S SANDAL OF YUCCA LEAF. This sandal is based on a single leaf, doubled. The wicker weaving is held together by another leaf doubled and spliced over all longitudinally. A lacing of strips of yucca leaves passes between toes 1 and 2, and 3 and 4. The heel band is missing. From Acatita Cave, Coahuila, Mexico.

(Cat. No. 22717, U. S. N. M.)

Fig. 2. CHILD'S SANDAL. This specimen is of similar construction to that shown in fig. 1, but is much worn. No lacing is shown. Mexico.

(Cat. No. 45610 (a), U. S. N. M.)

Fig. 3. CHILD'S SANDAL. This specimen is from a cave near Silver City, New Mexico, and is of the same material and construction as the specimen shown in the preceding figure.

(Cat. No. 45610, U. S. N. M.)

Fig. 4. SANDAL OF SHREDDED YUCCA FIBER. The specimen is similar in original design to fig. 1 in warp, weft, and spliced binding, but it has been much worn and repaired. The lacing is of fine twine and braiding. It consists of the toe strings between 1 and 2, and 3 and 4. The heel strings are of braid, and the ankle strings of the same material. All of these are attached to one another just below the ankles. From Coyote Cave, Coahuila, Mexico.

(Cat. No. 22831, Peabody Museum, Cambridge, Mass.)

Fig. 5. SANDAL FROM A MUMMY. Constructed precisely like the specimen shown in fig. 4, and found in the same cave.

(Cat. No. 22850, Peabody Museum, Cambridge, Mass.)

SANDALS WITH DOUBLE TOE-STRINGS.

rove through the fabric of the sole, the latter being tied with the clove hitch. (Pl. 7, fig. 4.)

Example No. 22850, Peabody Museum, is a sandal from a mummy in Coyote Cave, Coahuila, Mexico. This example shows very clearly the carelessly laid warp and the cross weaving and sewing, which are doubtless repairs of a much worn sandal. The toe string in this case is continuous, passing between 1 and 2, and 3 and 4, back through the sole; the ends make half hitches and are continued to form the heel string. (Pl. 7, fig. 5.)

The sole of the cliff dweller's, the Utah man's, the New Mexican mound and cave man's sandal, as may be seen by the plate, is of vegetal fiber, Indian hemp (*Apocynum*), yucca of many species, and hene quen, sisal, or agave (*Ixtli*).

For the most part, they are rights and lefts, but not a few of them that are built on a warp are quadrilateral.

In texture, they are either in corded weaving, with warp and weft variously treated; or if the material be coarser, they are in wicker-work, or they are plaited or woven diagonally, but one and all have a toe loop or string that pierces the sole in two places and passes up between toes 1 and 2, and 3 and 4. This forms the basis of a lacing, and is variously treated, but a description of the figures will make the matter perfectly plain.

Example No. 13014 is from a cliff dwelling in Arizona. The warp and weft are of a fiber strongly resembling that of *Apocynum cannabinum*. The weft is finely spun, laid close, colored in narrow stripes, and on the under side the meshes are caught into a continuous loop or coil of coarser thread, making that part more durable. At the front the projecting ends of the warp are concealed in a continuous braiding of a single thong of buckskin. Two perforations show where the toe loop came through. Unfortunately, this part is wanting, but the rest of the lacing down to the ankle loops and up over the heel, returning to the knot on the instep, make the whole treatment plain. (Pl. 8, fig. 1.)

In the collection of Mrs. T. T. Childs, of Washington, is a sandal woven in wicker pattern from a two-ply twine of *Apocynum*. The heel strap and lacing are administered precisely as in fig. 1, but the loop in front of agave fiber, twined, seems to have included the first and second toes. This is an uncommon form of toe loop. The under side of this sandal also is worthy of study, for the weaver has tied single knots in her cord all around the under margin, and also at proper places under the heel and under the ball of the foot where the strain would come. This ingenious device stands for the hobnails in peasants' shoes of more advanced peoples. The selvage of the Childs specimen is formed by an ingenious turning in of the twines in the course of the weaving or plaiting. A woven heel also is somewhat turned up.

Example No. 13015 is from a cliff dwelling in Arizona and is perfect in all its parts, which are four—the sole, the toe loop, the heel loop, and the lacing. The sole is of yucca leaf (*Yucca angustifolia*) woven or plaited diagonally, and needs no explanation. The toe loop is a separate part, gathered at its ends into the texture of the sole, and is double. The heel loop is precisely like it, caught into the margin under the ankles and hooked over the heel. The lacing starts from the instep, and from this point makes three loops, to wit, about the toe string and about each side of the heel string, returning to the starting point, where it is knotted. (Pl. 8, fig. 2.)

Example No. 45609 is of yucca fiber coarsely plaited, from a cave near Silver City, N. Mex. All the lacing above is in one continuous string, starting on the back of the toes, passing down through the sole, and up, where a single knot is tied. The long end then makes an excursion to the ankle loops and around the heel, coming back to the single knot over the toes, where an additional square knot is tied. The treatment at the heel can not be made out, owing to the torn condition of the specimen. (Pl. 8, fig. 3.)

Example No. 13016, from a cliff dwelling in Arizona, is of shredded yucca fiber. The under side shows the structure better. There is a warp of four ropes, and the weft is woven into this like wicker, all the loose ends being purposely left long on top to afford a soft bed for the foot. The great majority of Japanese straw sandals happen to be woven in precisely the same manner, only in Japan the loose ends are cut off underneath. All the lacing is gone from this splendid specimen save the well-defined toe loop. (Pl. 8, fig. 4.)

Example No. 22716 in the Peabody Museum is a sandal from Acatita Cave, Coahuila, Mexico, an old and exceedingly interesting form. The thick sole is closely woven in twisted yucca fiber in checker pattern and the bottom is soaked in pitch or gum. There are two toe strings, knotted on top and passing between 1 and 2 and 3 and 4, crossed, perhaps, over the top of the foot, hitched into the sole at the margin below the ankle and passing behind the heel. This should be compared with example No. 10119. (Pl. 9, fig. 1.)

Example No. 22718 in the Peabody Museum is a substantial sandal from Acatita Cave, Coahuila, Mexico, made of yucca fiber, and loaned by Professor Putnam. The underside is shown in the photograph. The structure is a little obscure, but there seems to be a mass of fiber felted, and sewed together with coarse yucca yarn, long stitches beneath and short stitches above, precisely as on the compound soles of the Orient. The border is strengthened by stitching all round. The specimen is not ancient and may have been constructed under European motives. (Pl. 9, fig. 2.)

Example No. 22183 in the Peabody Museum is a sandal from Coyote Cave, Coahuila, Mexico, loaned by Professor Putnam. The outline is that of a modern round-toed shoe. The fabric is of yucca fiber, the warp laid along loosely in wisps, little twisted, but the loose ends are all underneath. This warp is held in position by a continuous boustrophedon twined weaving of two-ply string in crooked rows from half an

SANDALS WITH STRINGS INCLOSING SECOND AND THIRD TOES.

Fig. 1. SANDAL MADE OF INDIAN HEMP. The specimen is closely woven after the pattern of California basketry. The toe string is missing. The heel string and lacings on top of the foot show the method of administration. From a cliff-dwelling of Arizona. Lent by Mr. Stewart Culin.

(Cat. No. 13014, Museum of the University of Pennsylvania.)

Fig. 2. SANDALS OF YUCCA LEAF IN DIAGONAL WEAVING. Toe string, heel string and lacing of the same material and in the same pattern as fig. 1. From a cliff-dwelling of Arizona. Lent by Mr. Stewart Culin.

(Cat. No. 13015, Museum of the University of Pennsylvania.)

Fig. 3. SANDAL OF COARSE YUCCA FIBER IN DIAGONAL WEAVING. Toe string, heel string, and lacing of the same material.

(Cat. No. 45609, U. S. N. M.)

Fig. 4. SANDAL OF SHREDDED YUCCA FIBER. Wicker weaving based on a warp of four ropes, the shredded ends on top; toe string, of double twine; heel string and lacing missing. From a cliff-dwelling of Arizona. Lent by Mr. Stewart Culin.

(Cat. No. 13016, Museum of the University of Pennsylvania.)

SANDALS WITH STRINGS INCLOSING SECOND AND THIRD TOES.

ANCIENT AND MODERN SANDALS FROM MEXICO.

Fig. 1. SANDAL OF YUCCA FIBER. Checker weaving, double toe string. From Acatita Cave, Coahuila, Mexico. Collected by Edward Palmer.

(Cat. No. 22716, Peabody Museum, Cambridge, Mass.)

Fig. 2. SANDAL OF SHREDDED YUCCA FIBER. Woven so as to leave a portion of the long pile on top. Perforations for double toe string. From Acatita Cave, Coahuila, Mexico. Collected by Edward Palmer.

(Cat. No. 22718, Peabody Museum, Cambridge, Mass.)

Fig. 3. SANDAL OF SHREDDED YUCCA FIBER IN TWINED WEAVING. This sandal is made in the shape of the foot and has a double toe string. From Coyote Cave, Coahuila, Mexico. Collected by Edward Palmer.

(Cat. No. 22813, Peabody Museum, Cambridge, Mass.)

Fig. 4. MODERN SANDAL OF BAST FIBER. Plain weaving, with double toe string crossing over the back of the foot, fastened to the ankle string on either side beneath the ankles and looped over the heel. Worn by the Mohave (Yuman) Indians, Arizona. Collected by Edward Palmer.

(Cat. No. 10119, Peabody Museum, Cambridge, Mass.)

Fig. 5. TYPICAL LEATHER SANDAL. European pattern, with single toe string. Worn by Indians of Coahuila, Mexico. Collected by Edward Palmer.

(Cat. No. 22863, Peabody Museum, Cambridge, Mass.)

PLATE 9.

ANCIENT AND MODERN SANDALS FROM MEXICO.

inch to an inch apart. The border is further strengthened by sewing all round with a yarn of yucca fiber. The sandal is nearly worn out, and the toe strings have been set back as though for a smaller foot. Enough of the lacing remains to show that two toe strings passed between 1 and 2 and 3 and 4. (Pl. 9, fig. 3.)

Example No. 10119 of the Peabody Museum is a quadrilateral sandal of the Mohave Indians, Yuman stock, in southwestern Arizona, loaned by Professor Putnam. The sole is a coarse example of checker weaving in strips of cottonwood bark. The warp consists of a series of strips doubled at the toe, so that all ends project at the heel. In finishing off these are turned up and folded on top where they are held in place by whipping. The whole lacing is of one strip of bast, doubled in the middle, which is beneath the sole at the toes. The ends are brought up through two holes in front to inclose toes 1 and 2, and 3 and 4, crossed over the top of the foot, rove through the margin of the sole under the ankle and then twisted onto the other to make a heel band. In older forms farther south the toe-strings do not cross on the top of the foot. (Pl. 9, fig. 4.)

Example No. 22863 in the Peabody Museum is a rawhide sandal from Coahuila, Mexico, consisting of two parts: (1) A simple flat sole with a hole in front for the toe string and two gashes under the ankle for the lacing; (2) the lacing, a strap half an inch wide, knotted underneath the sole, passing up for a toe string over the foot and down to the gash under the outside of the ankle, making a half hitch there, passing around the heel to the gash on the inner side and making a half hitch, and thence up to the instep, where it is tied. Collected by Edward Palmer in 1880. (Pl. 9, fig. 5.)

If the reader will consult the illustrated works of Charnay, Maudslay, Schmidt, and the earlier travelers to Mexico and Central America, he will find that in every case where the artist has not erred, there are two toe-strings or a loop between toes 1 and 2, and 3 and 4. Imagine the knot in the third figure of my plate to be drawn further up toward the instep on the back of the foot, and the thing is done. Mr. Alfred P. Maudslay writes that in all cases the strings pass between toes 1 and 2, and 3 and 4. In the codices, the sandal on the feet of the men is not easily made out. The sole seems to recede and to leave the toes free, but in no case is the single-toe-string visible.

Example No. 41828 (fig. 65) is a shoe worn by the Wolpi Indians of northeast Arizona (Hopi or Moki pueblos). The sole is dish shaped, well turned up around the foot. The upper is sewed to this, and is wrapped around the ankle precisely as in the modern "uppers" or false gaiter tops. This gaiter top is made fast by knots at three separate points, and, in addition, a thong passes about the heel through lugs or loops on the sole just in front of the arch of the foot, and is tied over the instep. At once the similarity will be noted between this example and those from the Navajo encamped in the same region.

Example No. 68657 is a shoe from the Zuñi pueblo, New Mexico, collected by J. W. Powell, Director of the Bureau of Ethnology. It is made from the fronds of the Spanish bayonet (*Yucca elata*) split and woven diagonally. As this form of moccasin is not common in the region and is unique in the national collection, it stands for an innovation by the Zuñi in imitation of modern shoes. Length, 8½ inches; height, 6 inches. A very similar form is example No. 70999, from the Moki or Hopi pueblo in northeastern Arizona. Indeed, these seven towns have preserved to us all the types of basket weaving in the United States.

In seeking to trace the southern limit of the moccasin or shoe, as against a plain sandal, it is well to remember Vaca's saying that the

Fig. 65.

MOCCASIN OF WOLPI PUEBLO INDIANS, ARIZONA.

From a figure in the Second Annual Report of the Bureau of Ethnology. Cat. No. 41828, U. S. N. M.

Pueblo Indians also wore shoes. He had not mentioned the shoe before and was surprised at their appearance, so it is evident that from Florida to western Texas people went barefooted. The cactus desert may account for the change.[1]

The Papago and other Yuman tribes in southwestern Arizona and in northwestern Sonora are sandal wearers now, and their foot-gear is akin to that of the South and of Spain. Example No. 174450 (fig. 66) is one of half a dozen pairs collected by W J McGee, of the Bureau of Ethnology, and may be thus described:

(1) Soles of cow rawhide, hair beneath, pointing indifferently; rights and lefts, cut around the foot.

(2) Pierced for toe string and slit in two places below the ankles for the ankle strap, as in a skate.

(3) Toe string buttoned under the sole by a ratchet produced by leaving a portion of hide to be turned down. The other end of the toe string is slit and provided with loose toggle.

(4) Ankle strap, a strip of hide with ends passing up through the slits. These are perforated for the fastening of the lashing, which passes over the foot, through this ankle strap, behind the heel, through the other ankle strap and back to the toe string, where it is fastened off. The peculiar button or ratchet beneath the sole, to keep the ankle strap in position, is worthy of a cultured brain.

Examples 19763 and 73001 are sandals of Diegeños and La Costa Indians, California. They are made of *Agave deserti* fiber woven in coarse filaments over a warp consisting of two strands of coarse twine

[1] Davis, "Spanish Conquest of New Mexico," p. 101.

of the same material. There are two loops at the heel and one loop at the ball of the foot passing from side to side over the top of the foot. The warp strands are tied together at the toe, drawn up over the foot under the loop back of the heel, then come in front and tie around the ankle. Length, 12 inches. Collected by Edward Palmer.

One type of Mexican sandal sole has five points of attachment for the lacing—one between the toes, one on either side opposite the metatarsals, and one on either side under the heel. The lacing passes around

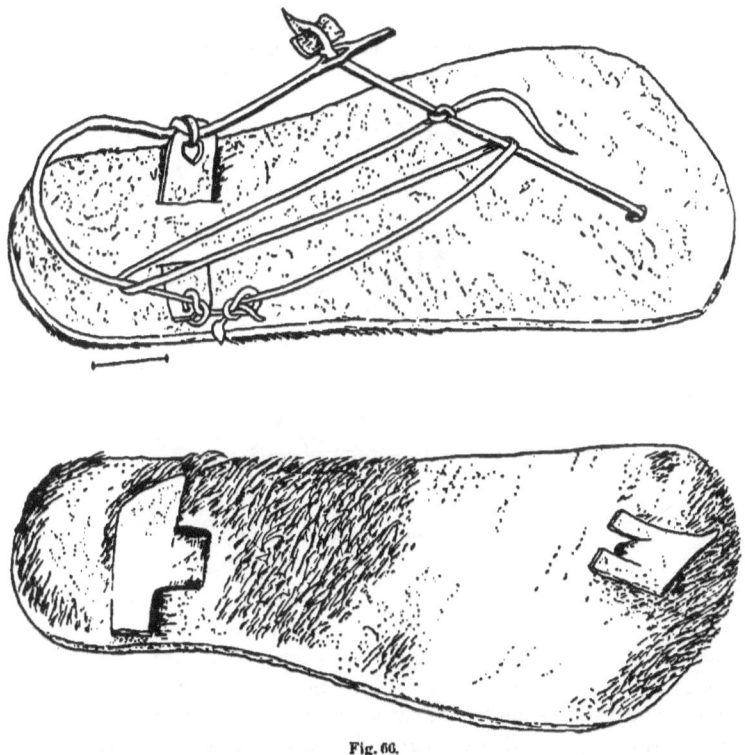

Fig. 66.

RAWHIDE SANDAL OF PAPAGO (PIMAN) INDIANS, SOUTHWESTERN ARIZONA.

Cat. No. 174450, U. S. N. M. Collected by W J McGee.

the heel and below the instep across the front part of the foot, connecting with the five attachments above mentioned. This is very important in the study of the Mexican shoe. In the cliff dwellers and in the Klamath examples the side lacings also appear.

Example No. 17698, in the Peabody Museum, is a pair of sandals from San Luis Potosi, Mexico, consisting of sole and lacing. The former is a strip of harness leather worn smooth side up. They, like most other Mexican specimens, are cut rights and lefts. There are three slashes along either margin, between the ball of the foot and the point beneath the ankle. The lacing is a strap half an inch wide, looped into the front gash on the inside and passing diagonally to 2 on the outside, to 2 on the inside, to 1 on the outside, to 3 on the inside, and around the heel.

A sandal from Puebla, Mexico, has a sole of rawhide cut to fit the foot roughly, the margins of which are turned up. Along each side six good-sized holes are cut. Beginning at the front left-hand hole a strap one-fourth of an inch wide is woven backward and forward from margin to margin, passing under and over. The last three pairs of holes on each side are devoted to forming a heel by a system of half hitches. Pieces of soft leather slashed and woven onto the lacing protects the back of the foot and the heel. Length, 10½ inches. Collection of Mrs. Fannie B. Ward.

Example No. 152732 is a pair of sandals from Colima, Mexico (fig. 67). These consist of a sole and upper lacing. The sole is a piece of tanned leather, cut somewhat in the shape of the foot. Five holes are pierced

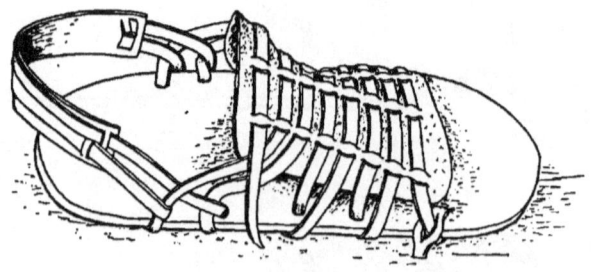

Fig. 67.

MODERN LACED SANDAL OF LEATHER, FROM COLIMA, MEXICO.

Cat. No. 152732. U. S. N. M. Collected by Edward Palmer.

through each side margin of the sole for the lacing. The lacing consists of a continuous leather string one-eighth of an inch wide, which is attached to one side of the sole, and is woven backward and forward through three pairs of holes in the margin of the sole, on the fourth round a half hitch is made and the string carried backward to form the heel, forward by a half hitch through the sole, and then over the foot to the other side, where another half hitch is made, and another string, passed around the sole through a hole in the margin and back again, is fastened off in a pad on the top of the foot. The lacing at each excursion passes through three slits cut in a soft piece of leather, which lies between the foot and the lacing. This shoe should be compared with patterns in South America collected by Mrs. Fannie B. Ward. Length, 9 inches. Collected by Edward Palmer.

Example No. 30382, in the Peabody Museum, Cambridge, is a pair of sandals worn by the Maya of Yucatan, which are rights and lefts; sole double, with extra heel lift beneath; sewed together with single thong; lugs, or loops on the margin under the ankle. The tapering rope lacing

passes up between toes 1 and 2, and then through the loop over the instep
and heel as usual.   Length, 9½ inches.   These are modern and Latin
American, doubtless.   But Maudslay figures elegantly in Biologia Central Americana—Archæology—statues of gods wearing sandals.   In the
photographs, so far as they can be made out, and in the lithographs,
where the artist has followed the original, the double toe strap passes
down between toes 1 and 2, 3 and 4, or 1 and 2, 2 and 3.[1]

In the American Museum of Natural History are two portions of jars
showing the strap between toes 1 and 2, 4 and 5.   One from Orizaba
(No. 300) has the inclosed heel, shown on the Codices, with separate
strings running between the toes to the ankle band.   The other
example (No. 207), from Guerero, is more complete.   The leg is incased
like a Zuñi woman's; strings pass from this leg band down between
the toes.   An examination of any collec-
tion of pottery from Middle America re-
veals the fact at once, if the human foot
is portrayed, that the single toe string
was not anciently known.[2]

In one of the sculptured monoliths of
Copan, figured by Dr. Julius Schmidt,
the feet of the god are incased in sandals
very much like those of the Codices, consisting of a sole and the quarters of a
shoe without the vamp (fig. 68).   In the
monolith, however, the thong passes between the first and the second toe.[3]   In
the succeeding monolith[4] the left toes
are broken off, but the right limb presents a square front view.   The thong
passes between the first and the second
and the third and the fourth toe, and is
apparently looped or concealed in a ring
or horseshoe-shaped object, though this
may be only an artist's flourish, the two
ends approaching each other, turning

Fig. 68.

FOOT OF STATUE AT QUIRIGUA, GUATEMALA,
SHOWING DOUBLE TOE STRING.

From a figure in Meye and Schmidt's "Stone Sculptures
of Copan and Quirigua."

outward and terminating in braids in which a loop is caught which
descends from a highly ornate rosette in front of the ankle.   According to Meye's drawing, the sandal is unfastened by detaching the last-
named loops from the braids on the ankle ring.   The Eskimo fashion of
attaching a similar device is to bring the upper loop under a ring
and over a nail head or stud.   Mr. Saville confirms these statements
from original drawings.

[1] Cf. Part II, pls. 34, 37, 45, and 46, and Part IV, pls. 77, 79, and 82.

[2] Cf. Charnay, "Ancients Villes," p. 49, and elsewhere.

[3] Meye and Schmidt, "Stone Sculptures of Copan and Quirigua," New York, 1883,
Dodd, Mead & Co., pl. III.

[4] Ibid, pl. III.

In pl. IV of Meye and Schmidt's work the feet of the image are turned sidewise, and the sandals exhibit only the heels attached to the soles. The feet of the figure in pl. V are said in the description to be clothed in thick-soled shoes fastened with bows, but the appearance is of a moccasined foot resting on a sandal. The squatting figures in the succeeding plates are barefooted and wear bandages of some kind about the ankle. Pl. XIII (fig. 19 b) shows a masked figure, wearing bands wrapped four times about the lower leg, suggesting the leggings of the pueblo women. In pl. XV, depicting a monolith in Quirigua, the feet are gorgeously covered, either with a shoe consisting of sole, vamp, and decorated quarters, or, in what would be more American, they are clothed in moccasins that rest on a heeled sandal. The thickness of the sole in these figures leaves one puzzled whether this feature is only a sculptor's decoration, but the heel band is still worn in Moki dances.[1]

Mr. im Thurn says of the Guiana Indians that they make sandals from the leaf stalk of the æta palm (*Mauritia flexuosa*), to be worn in traveling over stony ground. The string passes between the great toe and

the next, and when the sandal is much worn the skin is made callous by the string. In a few hours the sandals are worn out and new ones cut from the nearest æta palm.[2] Mr. im Thurn also speaks of the neatness with which they fit the foot. This form is of Spanish introduction. Fray Simon, speaking of the Indians encountered on the Orinoco by Aguirre's party, says that they were naked, but had on the soles of their feet pieces of deerskin, fastened like the sandals worn in Peru or like those seen by him in the provinces of the Government of Venezuela.[3]

In Whymper's "Great Andes of the Equator," page 143, is a figure of a sandal, with sole of sennit sewed together, and the upper made of woven stuff (fig. 69). There probably would be no doubt in the mind of any student that this foot wear was actually made in Spain. The National Museum possesses a great number of examples of this peculiar type, and the following description of the Spanish example may be compared with the Whymper specimen.[4]

---

[1] Very great caution should be used in the practical interpretation of sculptors' and painters' costume and implements. In Catlin's drawings and paintings of moccasins the very decorative features of the sandals on the statues here referred to are produced, though they have no existence in fact.

[2] "Indians of British Guiana," London, 1883, p. 195, quoted by Mason, in his work on the "Origins of Invention," Chapter x.

[3] Bollaert, Publications of the Hakluyt Society, 28, 1861, p. 105.

[4] For the sennit sole, cf. Wiener, "Pérou et Bolivie," p. 680; also Reiss and Stübel, "The Necropolis of Ancon," pl. 88, fig. 4.

The braided-sole sandal of Spain has in it some noteworthy characteristics. The sole nowadays is made of esparto grass, braided, coiled ingeniously to fit the bottom of the foot and sewed through with a stout twine of different material, the stitches being about half an inch apart. The heel and toe are the noteworthy parts. At a cursory glance these, when made of coarse material, resemble in their manipulation the twined weaving of savage and barbarous peoples, but the effect is produced by "darning." For instance, the heel cover is made up by forming a band of warp twines—that is, passing a series of twines backward and forward, catching them under the braided sole as the thrifty housewife proceeds in laying the foundation for darning a stocking. This is done with a long twine, which is afterwards made a quasi weft by sewing it across the band of warp twines, running between the strands of each one, but not in any regular manner. At one excursion this cord extends entirely the length of the foot, pierces the band of cords across the toe, returns through them and then takes up its excursions through the heel band. In an example in the U. S. National Museum the heel is built up of a series of three-ply loosely twisted hemp cord. The embroidery of the weft pierces the warp twines so as always to leave one strand outside the heel and two strands inside, rendering the inside much softer.

There is a low side strip running between heel and toe on the outer upper margin of the sole made up of two or three rows of "button hole stitches" or "half hitches," each row looped into the one beneath it. It may be a Spanish device, or at least a Latin American device, being found in the netted bags of Latin America everywhere. It also occurs in the fish baskets of Tierra del Fuego. Essentially it is coiled work, only the moving part, instead of running on by a coil, passes under or behind the standing part each time. In no other corner of aboriginal America outside the Latin area has the author seen any such work. The Fuegians, in addition to the endless chainwork of half hitches, use a continuous rod running through the links to give body to the basket. As mentioned elsewhere, a lacework effect is produced by passing the moving part two or more times about the standing part. This is also common from the Southern California Papago through Latin America to Peru.

Reiss and Stübel's gorgeous work on "The Necropolis of Ancon" is poor in figures of foot wear. In Volume I, "Pérou et Bolivie" pl. 25, fig. 26 is the picture of a very interesting sandal of leather. On the margin of the sole on either side a flap is turned up and pierced for the lacing. This specimen should be compared with Assyrian and Somali forms and with the sandal of La Paz, Volume II, pl. 16, fig. 9.

Whymper draws attention to a curious economic distinction in Ecuador, where the carriers "were paid in advance and had to be provided with shoes. Although natives of all sorts were continually met with trudging barefoot along the roads, whenever one was hired, he found himself unable to walk without shoes."[1]

Wiener relates that the Indians who dwell on the high plateaus of South America, obliged to walk at times over the snow, are in the habit, when they skin a llama, to cut out a piece of the green hide, to fit it upon the foot and to keep it bandaged there during twenty-four hours or more to dry into shape and take the form of a low slipper. The wool is left on the outside. Mummies have been found wearing similar foot gear, the foot also enveloped in a sock-like cover. The Indians of the Ceno de Pasco preserve this custom.[2]

Example No. 127572, from Pachacamac, Peru, is a pair of sandals (fig. 70) from a mummy. These are of a very simple pattern; each one consists of a single piece of rawhide of the llama. When the hide was in a wet or green condition it was stretched over the toe and up about the margin of the foot, slightly rising to a height of 2 inches. Back of

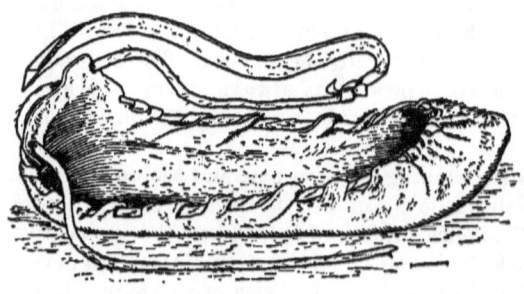

the heel a series of slits were then cut all around the upper margin and a drawing string of rawhide passed through all of these slits, beginning at the left side of the heel, passing across to the right side, then around the margin through the holes, back across the heel and through

Fig. 70.

RAWHIDE SANDAL WITH PUCKERED MARGIN, FROM PACHACAMAC, PERU.

Cat. No. 127572, U. S. N. M.   Collected by William E. Curtis.

the left side. The loose ends of this rawhide form the string which passes around the instep, where it is tied or looped. Length, 9½ inches. Collected by W. E. Curtis.

Wiener figures the following foot gear from Peru, partly industrial and partly ornamental (pl. 10):

(1) Cord, metal ring, broidered stuff, about the ankles, said to prevent cramps and accidents.

(2) Sole, with toe strap, joined with two straps passing in front of instep down to the border of the sole in front of the heel.

(3) Toe strap, or cord, meeting cord passing around the instep, which is looped onto a heel cord.

(4) From the border below the instep two loops extend, one about the heel, one over the lower instep.

(5) Sandal of braided, in Maguey fiber, coiled like a chenille mat.

(6) Regular sandals and slippers, European models.

---

[1] Whymper, "Great Andes of the Equator," New York, 1892, p. 39.
[2] Wiener, "Pérou et Bolivie," Paris, 1880, p. 679.

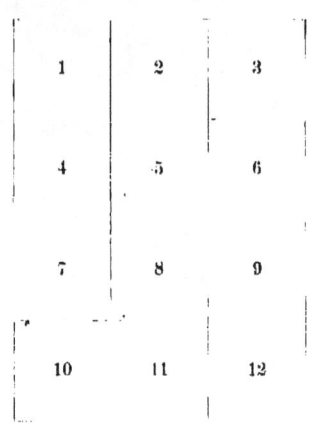

FOOTWEAR FROM PERU.

Fig. 1. FRINGED ANKLE BAND, Embroidered material. Ancon.

Fig. 2. LEATHER SANDAL FROM ARICA, PERU. Single toe strap, bifurcated on the back of the foot and attached to the margin of the sole half way back, as in Japanese specimens.

Fig. 3. SANDAL OF LEATHER. Found at the foot of the Cerro de la Horca, Paramonga. Single toe string passing through a broad loop in each end of the heel band and fixed at the margin of the sole beneath the ankles.

Fig. 4. LEATHER SANDAL FROM CHIMBOTE. Single toe strap bifurcated on the back of the foot. Attachments not shown. Rosette at the joining of the straps.

Fig. 5. LEATHER SANDAL FROM SANTA. Sole held on by two loops fastened under the instep, one passing over the back of the foot, the other behind the heel.

Fig. 6. SANDAL FOUND IN THE ARENAL OF PARAMONGA. Single toe cord bifurcating an inch or two from the toes and passing to the middle of the heel loop on either side. The extreme variation of this form is in the Mediterranean sandal, in which a band clasps the lower leg, the ankle strings are perpendicular, and the toe string is carried singly across the back of the foot to the leg band.

Fig. 7. SANDAL FOUND IN THE NECROPOLIS AT GRAN-CHIMU. The especial features are the absence of the toe-string, and the wrapping about the ankles of a series of straps attached to the margin of the sole at various points.

Fig. 8. ORNAMENTAL SANDAL FOUND AT CHANCAY. This sandal is of little use in travel, but is of the same general style as that shown in fig. 7.

Fig. 9-12. SANDALS FROM CAJAMARCA, CAJABAMBA, AND VIRACOCHAPAMPA. These specimens all have slashed tops.

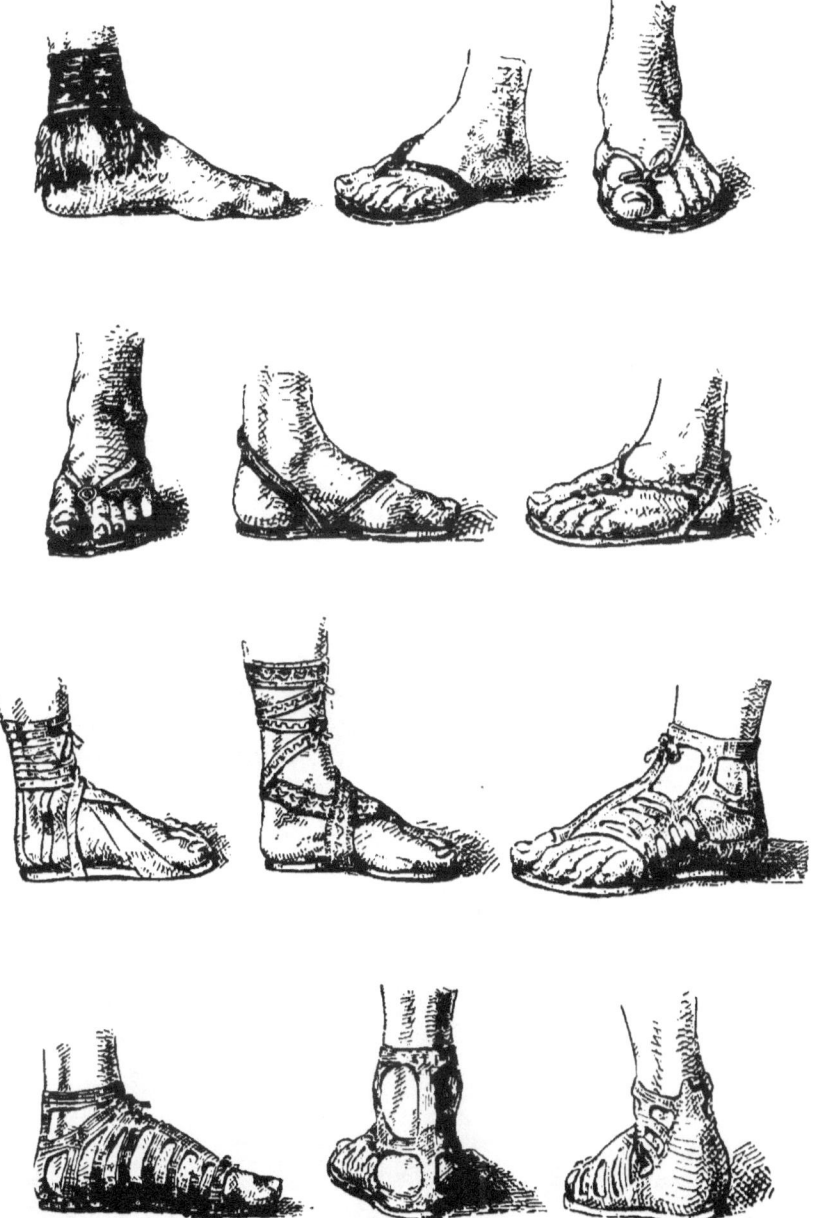

FOOTWEAR FROM PERU.

From Wiener, " Perou et Bolivie."

In Mrs. Ward's collection from Bolivia is a sandal (figs. 71 and 72) worthy of close study. The leather sole is double, and sewed or "run" together by means of leather thongs after the most approved Moham. medan style everywhere seen south and east of the Mediterranean. The toe strap is separate, passing up through the sole, keyed or tog. gled under the bottom and slit at the upper end for the passage of the thong. A "quar. ter" or arch strap just beneath the ankles, gashed at each end, passes down through the sole at one margin and rises through the other side. The lac-

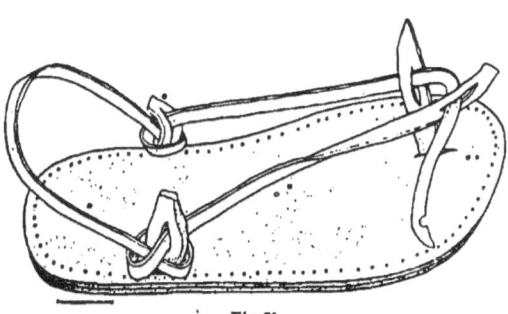

Fig. 71.

MODERN LEATHER SANDAL FROM BOLIVIA.

Collection of Mrs. Fannie B. Ward.

ing of hide slit at one end at the toes passes back to the quarter strap, where it takes a half hitch about and through the slit. The lacing thence passes about the heel to the quarter strap on the other side, where it is fastened by another half hitch and thence is continued through the slit in the toe strap and is fastened off in the slit at the beginning.

Bandelier sent to the American Museum, New York, four sandals from Arica, Peru, having rawhide soles slashed similarly and provided with looped short straps, gashed at the four ends for receiv- ing the lacing.

In Mrs. Ward's collection there may be seen another type of sandal from Bolivia (fig. 73) in which there is no strap between the first and the second

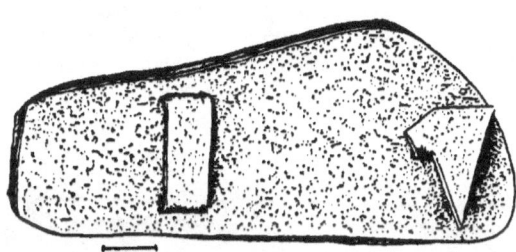

Fig. 72.

BOTTOM OF BOLIVIAN SANDAL, SHOWING ATTACHMENTS.

Collection of Mrs. Fannie B. Ward.

toe. On the other hand, the quarter or heel strap is repeated under. neath the ball of the foot, and its gashed ends come up over the toes as does a skate strap. The lashing is practically the same as in the last example.

The Patagonians (Tehuelche stock) wear potro boots made of the skin stripped from the knee and hock of a horse or large puma not unlike the bottes sauvages of Canada mentioned on page 345; over these they sometimes wear overshoes made of the skin from the hock of the guanaco. The footmarks made by them when thus shod would be abnormally large, which gave rise to the name Patagon, or big foot.

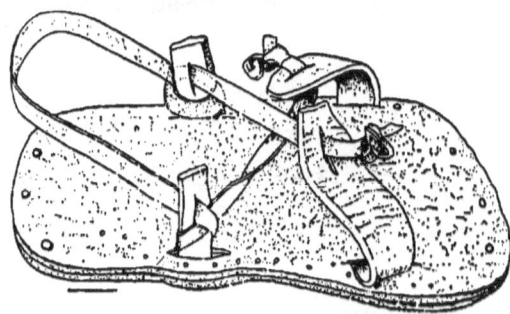

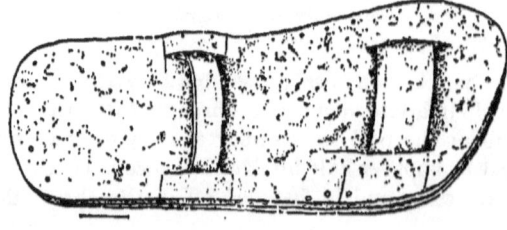

Example No. 55860 is a pair of man's shoes from Portugal. Uppers and soles are in one piece finished at the top with a softer leather; the upper border in front is puckered. The top is sewed together at the heel in a T-shaped seam, but the extra piece of leather is turned up inside. This shoe must be compared with the Eskimo shoes for the puckering, and with those of the interior Indians for the manner of joining the edges at the heel. The same style of foot wear made of very

Fig. 73.

BOLIVIAN LEATHER SANDAL, WITHOUT TOE-STRAP.

Collection of Mrs. Fannie B. Ward.

similar material, namely, thick uncolored hide, is in general use among the Canadian and New England lumbermen. The history of Portuguese foot clothing is not well enough known to enable the student to decide whether this style was adopted from the American moccasin. The road would be a round about one, since the Portuguese in America were very far away from the northern moccasin made all in one piece.

Example No. 128069 (fig. 74) is a wooden

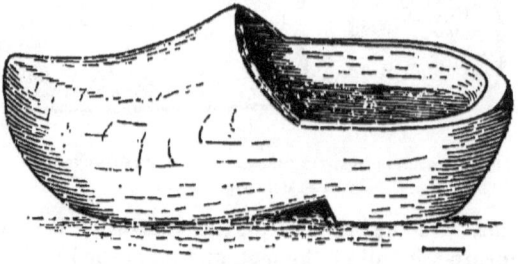

Fig. 74.

SABOT OR WOODEN SHOE, FROM MINNESOTA.

Cat. No. 128069, U. S. N. M. Collected by Reuben Wright.

shoe from Minnesota (called sabot). It is made from poplar wood and is a typical example of the wooden shoe of northern and western Europe, especially in the Netherlands and Scandinavian countries. This example was made and worn in Minnesota by a Dane. Excellent wood for these shoes is found throughout the Mississippi Valley from the Gulf northward, and factories have been established for their manufacture, whence they are shipped to supply the European market. Length, 13 inches. Collected by Reuben Wright. The sabot in modern Europe has two or three motives of geographic expansion. In the Netherlands it lifts the foot above the wet ground. It is found in the countries where extremely light wood abounds. It is durable, and above all, in modern economics it is cheap, a man being able to shoe his whole family a year for what it costs for a single pair of leather foot wear in one of our cosmopolitan cities. The antiquity of the sabot is difficult to trace.

SANDALS, SHOES, AND BOOTS IN THE U. S. NATIONAL MUSEUM.

Museum number.	Specimen.	Locality.	By whom contributed.
75051	Sandals, clogs with toe bands.	England	New Orleans Exposition.
75052, 75053	Shoes, wooden	....do	Do.
126956	Clogs, shoes for laborers	....do	Do.
126957	Shoes	....do	Do.
126958	Hobnail shoes	....do	Do.
150876	Wooden clogs	....do	Edward Lovett.
175473	Rude hide sandals	Shetland Islands	Do.
76381	Shoes, lauparsko	Norway	Otis Bigelow.
13144	Wooden shoes, Danish	Greenland	Frank Y. Commagère.
76635	Shoes, wooden, Swedish (fig. 74)	Michigan	R. E. Earll.
128069	Wooden shoes, Swedish	Minnesota	Reuben Wright.
75055	....do	Belgium	
75056–75059	Shoes	....do	
76491	Shoes, carved, wooden	....do	Max Potschak.
76492, 76493	....do	....do	Do.
129417	Shoes, wooden	Holland	Mrs. E. S. Brinton.
151282	Wooden clogs	Switzerland	W. W. Rockhill.
55830, 55860	Leather moccasins (p. 371)	Portugal	Centennial Commission.
55857	Leather leggings	....do	Do.
73124	Sandals, Alpargatas	Spain	Do.
167007	Child's sandals	Madrid, Spain	Walter Hough.
167008	Man's sandals	....do	Do.
129414	Child's rag shoes	Northern Italy	Mrs. E. S. Brinton.
129418	Slippers	Germany and Italy	Do.
129416	Red shoes, Turkish pattern	Athens, Greece	Do.
129415	Wooden sandals	Island of Rhodes	Do.
168009–168011	Shoes, thick soled	Bulgaria	Sophia Museum.
126937	Slippers, felt and fur lined	Russia	State Department.
126940	Lady's felt boots	....do	Do.
126941	Men's felt boots	....do	Do.
126942	Lady's kid shoes, buttoned	....do	Do.
126944	Child's cloth shoes	....do	Do.
126945	Lady's half slippers	....do	Do.
43073	Sandals, Afghan type (p. 318)	Monrovia, Africa	Hon. J. H. Smyth.
168052	Stilted clogs, toe string	Mandingo, Africa	J. F. Cook.
168876	Sandals, Mandingo	Angola, Africa	Colonization Society.
174689	Boots, red legs	Kongo, Africa	Dorsey Mohun.
174767	Wooden sandals with toe pegs	....do	Do.
151741	Slippers, Portuguese	Angola, Africa	Heli Chatelain.

SANDALS, SHOES, AND BOOTS IN THE U. S. NATIONAL MUSEUM—Continued.

Museum number.	Specimen.	Locality.	By whom contributed.
175213, 175214	Sandals, types with toe strings....	Somali, Africa	Glenn Island Museum.
76383	Shoes, yellow morocco ....?.....	Northern Africa	Otis Bigelow.
72716	Shoes, colored leather (p. 317)	Morocco	Museum für Völkerkunde, Leipzig.
5500	Yellow embroidered morocco slippers.	....do	J. Varden.
129412	Shoes, colored leather	Tunis...............	Mrs. E. S. Brinton.
129413	Slippers, slipshod	....do	Do.
76409	Wooden clogs with toeband.......	Tripoli................	State Department.
5499	Sandals, type (p. 521)	Arabia	J. Varden.
76385	Lady's outer shoes	Cairo, Egypt	Otis Bigelow.
74636	Slippers or in-shoes	Palestine	Dr. G. W. Samson.
76973, 76974	Red leather shoes, embroidered ...	....do	State Department.
76382	Shoes, red morocco	Syria	Otis Bigelow.
76470	Boots............................	....do	State Department.
76471	Half boots, children	....do	Do.
76472	Half boots, yellow leather........	....do	Do.
76473	Shoes, worn over 76472	....do	Do.
129411	Slippers. Damascus...............	....do	Mrs. E. S. Brinton.
926	Outer shoes, types...............	Turkey	Charles Laszlo.
927	Shoes, types	....do	Do.
5498	Slippers, types	....do	J. Varden.
5502	....do	....do	Do.
76384	Slippers, yellow morocco..........	....do	Otis Bigelow.
4830–4832	Man's Turkish slippers ..:......	Constantinople.........	Isaac Y. Westervelt.
130614	Mud sandals, Chirrok	Kerkook, Kurdistan	Rev. A. H. Audrus.
130605	Shoes with nails, Koords	Eastern Turkey	Do.
130635	Sandals, over toe string (fig. 41) ...	Afghanistan	Daniel Phillips.
164944	Chaplies (p. 325)...................	Kashmir, India........	W. L. Abbott.
164978	Shoes (p. 326)....................	Baltistan	Do.
175117	Woman's boots	Eastern Turkestan.....	Do.
175118	Boots, Chirrocks (p. 325)	....'.do	Do.
175119	Child's boots....................	....do	Do.
175104	Woman's boots, Pabboos (p. 325) ..	Leh, Ladakh..........	Do.
175105-	Child's boots, Pabboos (p. 325)	.....do	Do.
153044	Shoes............................	Persia	Pinkes Hanuka.
150877, 150878	....do	....do	Ed. Lovett.
126834	Slippers, types..................	India	W. H. Dall.
93150	Wooden sandals with toe peg.....	Calcutta.............	Do.
16693	Wooden sandals..................	Burma..............	Burma Mission.
16696	Leather sandals (p. 326)	....do	Do.
76465–76467	Wooden sandals..................	Singapore............	State Department.
153347	Sandals (p. 325).................	....do	R. Wildman.
168760	Wooden sandals.................	Ceylon...............	Commission of Ceylon.
154158	Grass shoes.....................	Malay	R. Wildman.
168223	Wooden clogs	Java................	World's Columbian Exposition.
130640	Sandals (p. 315)	Borneo..............	Royal Gardens. Kew, England.
130639	Sandals, of cordyline (p. 314)	New Zealand	Do.
3919	Woman's shoes	China...............	Lieut. Wilkes, U. S. N.
4800	Shoes	....do	Lieut. Geo. T. Emmons, U. S. N.
4826	....do	....do	Dr. G. J. McGowan.

SANDALS, SHOES, AND BOOTS IN THE U. S. NATIONAL MUSEUM—Continued.

Museum number.	Specimen.	Locality.	By whom contributed.
5497	Shoes	China.	J. Varden.
15674	....do	....do	Chinese Centennial Commission.
34764	Shoes, small	....do	Hon. Horace Dane.
55827	Shoes, woman's	Amoy, China	Chinese Centennial Commission.
4827	Shoes, grass	Canton	G. W. Robinson.
55847, 55848	Fancy cloth shoes, men's	Amoy, China	Chinese Centennial Commission.
55849	Straw shoes, men's	....do	Do.
55828	Shoes, velveteen	Cheefoo, China	G. W. Robinson.
55829	Cotton cloth shoes, men's	....do	Do.
55830, 55831	Felt shoes, men's	....do	Do.
55833	Deerskin shoes	....do	Do.
55835	Cotton cloth boots	....do	Do.
55836	Deerskin boots, men's	....do	Do.
55837	Cloth and velvet shoes	Shantung Province	Do.
55838	Straw shoes, men's	Kiang Su, China	Do.
55839	Straw shoes, woman's	....do	Do.
55841	Wooden clogs, women's	Shanghai, China	Do.
55842	Sandals, men's	....do	Do.
55843	Wooden shoes, men's	Shantung, China	Do.
55844	Wooden shoes, boy's	....do	Do.
55845	Leather shoes, men's	China	Do.
55846	Straw shoes, men's	....do	Do.
55850	Hobnailed boots, men's	Shanghai, China	Do.
55851	Hobnailed shoes, boy's	....do	Do.
55852	Yellow leather hobnailed half boots, man's.	....do	Do.
55854	Leather boots	....do	Do.
55855	Leather boots, half	....do	Do.
55856	Straw shoes	....do	Do.
55863	Straw overshoes, woman's	China	Do.
55864	Plantain leaf and straw shoes(p.328)	....do	Do.
55865, 55866	Straw sandals	....do	Do.
76476	Lady's shoes	....do	State Department.
131044	Sandals, wicker (p. 327)	Kansu, China	W. W. Rockhill.
131198	Sandals, sennit (p. 328)	....do	Do.
151281	Shoes	China	Do.
151383	....do	....do	Mrs. E. J. Stone.
131045	Boots (pl. 2)	Tibet	W. W. Rockhill.
131065	Boots, felt	....do	Do.
167179	Lama boot (p. 326)	....do	Do.
167181	Sandals	....do	Do.
167303	Leather boots	....do	Do.
55832	Velvet shoes, men's	Manchuria, China	Do.
55840	Felt shoes, man's	....do	Do.
131072	Boots and garters (fig. 42)	Mongolia	Do.
77011	Shoes, grass	Seoul, Korea	Ensign J. B. Bernadou.
77012, 77013	Shoes, rice straw	....do	Do.
77014	Shoes	....do	Do.
77015	Wooden shoes, men's	....do	Do.
77016	Blue felt shoes	....do	Do.
77081	Child's shoes	....do	Do.

SANDALS, SHOES, AND BOOTS IN THE U. S. NATIONAL MUSEUM—Continued.

Museum number.	Specimen.	Locality.	By whom contributed.
151146	Child's sandals (p. 329)	Korea	W. W. Rockhill.
167706	Shoes, man's	do	H. B. Hurlbert.
167707	Shoes, woman's	do	Do.
167708	Shoes, child's	do	Do.
167709	Sandals, child's	do	Do.
167710	Clogs, child's	do	Do.
73107	Antelope-skin shoes	Japan	P. L. Jouy.
73986	Shoes	do	Col. Alex. Johnston.
116211	Straw sandals (fig. 43)	do	Bureau of Ethnology.
128161-128173	Last and straw sandals	Tokio and Yokohama	Japanese Government.
150487	Straw sandals	Japan	Romyn Hitchcock.
150637	Fishskin shoes, with snowshoes (p. 333).	do	Do.
150644	Sandals (p. 333)	Yezo, Japan	Do.
5797	Gaiters	Japan	Perry expedition.
22192	Sandals (fig. 30)	Ainos, Japan	Benjamin S. Lyman.
73082	Snowshoes, hunter's	Tate Yama, Japan	P. L. Jouy.
73084. 73085	Sandals	Nikko, Japan	Do.
73091	Boots straw (fig. 44)	Tate Yama, Japan	Do.
73092	Straw boots, hunter's	do	Do.
167961	Moccasins, woman's, birch bark (figs. 45, 47).	Finland	Hon. J. M. Crawford.
167968, 167969	Shoes	do	Do.
167970	Shoes, child's	do	Do.
167976	Slippers, woman's	do	Do.
73026	Long boots, tarbossas	Kamchatka	Leonhard Stejneger.
153524	Boots	Siberia	Lieut. G. B. Harber, U. S. N.
2438	Boots, Alaskan type	Chukchi	Commodore Rodgers.
2440, 2441	Water-proof boots	do	Do.
73025	Dressed-skin boots, soles of sea-lion flippers.	Bering Island	Leonhard Stejneger.
44686	Summer boots, many insertions	Cape Nome, Alaska	E. W. Nelson.
49167	Waterproof boots, winter	Diomede Island, Alaska.	Do.
44347	Toy sealskin boots	Norton Bay, Alaska	Do.
43344	Boottees, waterproof	Golovina Bay, Alaska	Do.
43345	Boots, sealskin (p. 340)	do	Do.
7581	Boots, deerskin, winter	Unalakleet, Alaska	W. H. Dall.
17591	Boottees, sealskin (pl. 4)	Norton Bay	Do.
36194	Boots, dressed sealskin	do	E. W. Nelson.
38771	Boots, waterproof (p. 341)	do	Do.
49063	Man's fancy boots	do	Do.
76338	Fishskin boots	Norton Sound, Alaska	Do.
7583	Riding boots, dogskin	St. Michaels, Alaska	W. H. Dall.
38703	Grass shoes	do	E. W. Nelson.
129344	Shoes, high, elegant	do	L. M. Turner.
129821	Woman's boots	do	General Hazen.
129822	Boots, skin	do	Do.
38097-38699	Boots, toy	Fort Yukon, Alaska	E. W. Nelson.
38700	Shoes, toy	do	Do.
38370	Boots, fishskin	Lower Yukon, Alaska	Do.
153737	Half boots, woman's	Yukon, Alaska	J. H. Turner.
8784	Straw shoes, Eskimo	Premoraka	W. H. Dall.
38794	Boots, fishskin	Anvik, Alaska	E. W. Nelson
43903-43906	Boots, salmon skin	do	Do.

SANDALS, SHOES, AND BOOTS IN THE U. S. NATIONAL MUSEUM—Continued.

Museum number.	Specimen.	Locality.	By whom contributed.
48130, 48131	Boots, fishskin	Anvik, Alaska	E. W. Nelson.
5594, 5595	Boots, child's	Yukon River, Alaska	W. H. Dall.
5591	Boots, salmon skin	do	Do.
10486	Boots, sealskin (pl. 4)	do	J. T. Dyar.
10487	....do	do	Do.
11440	Boots, skin	do	W. H. Dall.
36206	Shoes, child's, fine	Alaska	E. W. Nelson.
153735	Boots, waterproof	Yukon, Alaska	J. H. Turner.
153736	Boots, half	do	Do.
16389	Boots, sealskin	Nunivak, Alaska	W. H. Dall.
38779	Boots, deerskin, soles flat	Kuskokwim, Alaska	E. W. Nelson.
7954	Boots, reindeer skin	Nushagag, Alaska	Dr. T. T. Miner.
38871	Boots, winter, deerskin	do	E. W. Nelson.
43280, 43281	Boots, tarbossan	do	Do.
20921	Boots, winter, decorated	Aleutian Islands	J. G. Swan.
48102	Boots, waterproof	Unalaska, Alaska	E. W. Nelson.
168295	Shoes, grass (fig. 44)	Attu, Alaska	Lieut. G. T. Emmons.
127332	....do	Togiaknmut, Alaska	J. Applegate.
90460	Moccasins, fishskin	Igiagik River	William J. Fisher.
55071	Boots, waterproof, fishskin	Bristol Bay, Alaska	Charles L. McKay.
56061	Boots, men's	do	Do.
72503, 72504	Moccasins, women's	Kenai Indians	William J. Fisher.
49164	Boots, deerskin	Kotzebue Sound	E. W. Nelson.
129661, 129002	Boots, sealskin bottoms	do	Lieut. G. M. Stoney.
127950	Boots	Putnam River, Alaska	Do.
56749, 56750	Boots, men's (figs. 49, 52)	Point Barrow, Alaska	Lieut. P. H. Ray.
74042	Woman's pantaloons (fig. 48)	do	Do
76182	Boots, woman's waterproof (fig. 53).	do	Do
89834	Boots, skin of mountain sheep (fig. 51).	do	Do.
128409	Boots, man's winter	do	E. P. Herendeen.
153892	Boots, reindeer (p. 338)	do	John Murdoch.
912, 915	....do	Anderson River	Robert MacFarlane.
916	Boots, muskrat skin	do	Do.
1332	Boots, sealskin, waterproof (pl. 4)	do	C. P. Gaudet.
1333	Boots, deerskin	do	Do.
1669	Boots, fox skin	do	Robert MacFarlane.
1683	Boots, deerskin	do	Do.
1692	....do	do	Do.
1718	Boots, sealskin	do	Do.
2056	Shoes, child's	do	Do.
2050	Boots, Eskimo, man's	do	Do.
2060	Shoes, man's (pl. 4)	do	Do.
2061	Shoes, child's	do	Do.
2219	Boots, Eskimo	do	Do.
2220	Boots, without tops	do	Do.
2222, 2223	Shoes, child's	do	Do.
2226	Shoes, woman's	do	Do.
2227	Overshoes, fur	do	Do.
3979	Boots, woman's winter (pl. 4)	do	Do.
3980	Boots, man's winter (pl. 4, fig. 6)	do	Do.
3981	Overshoes, Eskimo (pl. 4)	do	Do.
3982	Boots, man's	do	Do.
3983	Boots, man's summer (pl. 4)	do	Do.

SANDALS, SHOES, AND BOOTS IN THE U. S. NATIONAL MUSEUM—Continued.

Museum number.	Specimen.	Locality.	By whom contributed.
3985	Soles, man's sealskin boots........	Anderson River........	Robert MacFarlane.
7721–7725	Boots, deerskin	....do	Do.
7648	Boots, part of deerskin..............	....do	Do.
2053	.....do...:	....do	Do.
3977	Shoes, child's	....do	R. Kennicott.
864	Boots, Eskimo...................:..	Mackenzie River	Do.
865	Boots, Eskimo	....do	Do.
1717	Boots, men's deerskin	....do	Robert MacFarlane.
1720	Shoes, child's	....do	Do.
1721–1723	Boots, men's deerskin, sealskin, and fox skin.	....do	Do.
127951	Boots, man's	....do	Do.
10189	Models of Eskimo shoes	Repulse Bay..........	Capt. C. F. Hall.
10379	Boots, sealskin, waterproof........	Hecla Strait	Do.
68115	Boots, sealskin, fur	Hudson Bay............	J. Temple Brown.
68116	.....do	....do	Do.
68117	Overshoes, sealskin	....do	Do.
68121	Boots, woman's, deerskin, fur inside	....do	Do.
68122–68124	Boots, waterproof.................	....do	Do.
68142	Shoes, child's, waterproof........	....do	Do.
553, 554	Boots	Upernavik, Greenland..	Dr. I. I. Hayes.
558, 559	Boots, long, double	....do	Do.
567	Boots, man's	....do	Do.
13133–13138, 13152	Boots, sealskin..................	Greenland	F. Y. Commagére.
36966	Boots, fur lined	....do	Governor Fenckner.
36967	Shoes	....do	Do.
127137	Boots, long, ornamented..........	South Greenland........	Mrs. Octave Pavy.
127138	Slippers, sealskin	....do	Do.
151668	Boots (four pairs)................	Greenland	Dr. C. H. Merriam.
151665	Boots, sealskin, double............	....do	Dr. F. M. Hoadley.
168921, 168922	Boots, man's	East Greenland........	Royal Museum of Northern Antiquities, Copenhagen, Denmark.
168933, 168934	Boots, woman's	....do	Do.
74487	Gaiter shoes	Ungava, Labrador	L. M. Turner.
90062, 90063	Moccasins, Tinné type.............	....do	Do.
90066–90070	Shoes, child's, T-shaped toes (p. 348)	....do	Do.
90076–90081	.....do	....do	Do.
90189–90193	Shoes, corrugated soles............	....do	Do.
90356, 90357	Shoes, child's, winter (p. 343)......	....do	Do.
90358–90365	Boots, type set, models (p. 342).....	....do	Do.
90366	Boots, toy, hair inside.............	....do	Do.
150890	Shoes, child's, waterproof........	....do	Miss Anna L. Ward.
151667	Boots, outside.................	....do	Dr. C. H. Merriam.
153507	Moccasins	....do	Henry G. Bryant.
153516	Boots	....do	Do.
74435	Moccasins, Tlingit Indian	Southeastern Alaska....	J. J. McLean.
129354	.....do	Interior Alaska	L. M. Turner.
153865	Moccasins, child's.................	....do	J. H. Turner.
839	Moccasins, man's.................	Fort Good Hope	R. Kennicott.
840, 841	Shoes, man's	....do	Do.
5051	Moccasins	....do	Do.
577	Shoes, porcupine quill work	Fort Simpson, Canada..	B. R. Ross.

SANDALS, SHOES, AND BOOTS IN THE U. S. NATIONAL MUSEUM—Continued.

Museum number.	Specimen.	Locality.	By whom contributed.
578	Shoes, ornamental...............	Fort Simpson, Canada..	B. R. Ross.
1336	Moccasins (p. 346)...............	Anderson River........	C. P. Gaudet.
2221	Moccasins, child's	....do	R. MacFarlane.
7612	Moccasins	Yukon River..........	W. H. Dall.
7613–7615	Moccasins (p. 346)..............	....do	Do.
160062–160065	Moccasins (p. 347).............	....do	J. H. Turner.
11390	Moccasins, child's..............	Southeast Alaska.......	Vincent Colyer.
20920	Boots, Indian	....do	Jas. G. Swan.
21580	Moccasins	....do	Dr. J. B. White.
2018, 2043	Moccasins, Chippewayan	Fort Simpson, Canada..	B. R. Ross.
8694	Moccasins	Fort Good Hope........	R. Kennicott.
131095	Moccasins, bear's feet...........	Fort St. James, Canada.	R. MacFarlane.
674	Moccasins, Blackfoot	Saskatchewan	Geo. Gibbs.
30842	Moccasins, low, with lapels.......	Cognowaga, Canada.....	Dr. G. Brown Goode.
76562–76565	Boots and shoes...............	Canada	State Department.
151388	Moccasins, Oneidas............	New York	Mrs. E. J. Stone.
74201	Moccasins, Iroquois............	North Carolina	F. H. Cushing.
130478	Moccasins, Cherokee...........	....do	Bureau of Ethnology.
153506	Moccasins, Montagnais	Labrador	Henry G. Bryant.
30837	Moccasins, Micmac	Shubenacadie, Nova Scotia.	Dr. G. Brown Goode.
30838	....do	....do	Do.
30839	Moccasins, heavy bead work.....	....do	Do.
30840, 30841	Moccasins, bead and porcupine work	....do	Do.
8544	Moccasins, Arapahoe	Nebraska	Medical Museum, U.S.A.
151934	....do	....do	Capt. J. G. Bourke, U.S.A.
153052	....do	Oklahoma	Emile Granier.
165140	....do	Wyoming..............	Bureau of Ethnology.
165786	....do	Indian Territory	H. R. Voth collection.
165804–165811	Moccasins, Arapahoe (p. 350)		Do.
6986	Moccasins, Cheyenne		E. Palmer.
8350	....do		Medical Museum, U.S.A.
130797	....do		Mrs. J. G. Bruff.
165914	Moccasins, girl's................	Indian Territory	H. R. Voth collection.
165981, 165982	Moccasins, woman's	....do	Do.
165983, 165984	Moccasins, man's	....do	Do.
165985	Moccasins, woman's	....do	Do.
165986–165989	Moccasins, man's.............	....do	Do.
165990–165992	Moccasins, woman's..........	....do	Do.
165993–165998	Moccasins, child's...........	....do	Do.
166008	Moccasins, toy	....do	Do.
166009	Moccasins and leggings, woman's.	....do	Do.
10110	Moccasins, Ponca Indians.........	Fort Randall..........	Asst. Surg. A. J. Comfort, U. S. A.
151991	....do	....do	Capt. J. G. Bourke, U.S.A.
7090	Moccasins, Ogallala Sioux	....do	Lieutenant Belden, U. S. A.
165022–165026	....do	....do	Bureau of Ethnology.
154319	Moccasins, child's..............	Leech Lake, Minn	Dr. W. J. Hoffman.
8869	Moccasins	Kansas ....:...	Medical Museum, U.S.A.
154354	Moccasins, Crow	Montana..............	Dr. W. J. Hoffman.
154355	Moccasins, man's, beaded	....do	Do.
30260	Moccasins, beaded. Sioux........	Missouri..............	Dr. R. Mueller.
1897	Moccasins, Sioux................	....do	Lieut. G. K. Warren.

378   REPORT OF NATIONAL MUSEUM, 1894.

SANDALS, SHOES, AND BOOTS IN THE U. S. NATIONAL MUSEUM—Continued.

Museum number.	Specimen.	Locality.	By whom contributed.
1898-1901	Moccasins, Sioux	Missouri	Lieut. J. K. Warren.
1902	Moccasins, child's, Sioux	do	Do.
8364	Moccasins, Sioux	Red River	Robert E. Williams.
164820	....do	Pine Ridge Agency	Mrs. E. C. Sickels.
21670	....do		Dr. J. F. Boughton, U.S.A.
166688	....do	Arizona	James Mooney.
166689	Moccasins, child's, Sioux	do	Do.
152855	Moccasins, Kiowa (p. 350)	Indian Territory	Do.
152926	Moccasins, toy, Kiowa	do	Do.
152967	Moccasins, Kiowa	do	Do.
152968	Moccasins, boys, Kiowa	do	Do.
153567	Moccasins, child's, Kiowa	do	Capt. R. H. Pratt, U.S.A.
153568	Moccasins, man's, Kiowa	do	Do.
165238	Moccasins, man's, Kiowa, type	do	James Mooney.
23740	Moccasins, Sioux	Devils Lake, Dakota	Paul Beckwith.
31037	Moccasins, beaded, Dakota		War Department.
31038	Moccasins, child's, Sioux		Do.
130799	Moccasins, Sioux		Mrs. J. G. Bruff.
131353	....do		Mrs. A. C. Jackson.
151387	Moccasins, child's, Dakota		Mrs. E. J. Stone.
153569	Moccasins, men's, Sioux		Capt. R. H. Pratt, U.S.A.
153991	....do		Mrs. M. M. Hazen.
153992	Shoes, Sioux		Do.
154356	Moccasins, beaded, boy's	Montana	Dr. W. J. Hoffman.
154363	Moccasins and leggings, child's	Crow Agency	Do.
2107	Moccasins, Omaha Indians	Omaha	Rev. Wm. Hamilton.
127619	....do	Nebraska	Mrs. J. O. Dorsey.
165024	Moccasins, Assiniboine Indians		Lieut. Cook, U. S. A.
8348	Moccasins, Sioux		Medical Museum, U.S.A.
8362	Moccasins, Dakota		Do.
8505	Moccasins, Sioux	Dakota	Do.
13143	Moccasins		Dr. E. Coues.
153993	Moccasins, child's, Sioux		Mrs. M. M. Hazen.
153994	Moccasins, unfinished, Sioux		Do.
164819	Moccasins, Sioux		Miss E. C. Sickles.
165145	....do	South Dakota	James Mooney.
165146	....do	do	Do.
160042	Moccasins, boy's	do	Dr. Z. T. Daniels.
8535	Moccasins, Sioux (p. 350)	Nebraska	Medical Museum, U.S.A.
165023	Moccasins, Brulé	Dakota	Lieut. Cook, U. S. A.
165025	....do	do	Do.
165239	Moccasins, Kiowa	Indian Territory	James Mooney.
1466	Moccasins	Texas and Mexico	Lieut. Couch, U. S. N.
1471	Moccasins, Comanche	do	Do.
6983	Moccasins and leggings, Comanche	do	E. Palmer.
6984, 6985	Moccasins, Comanche	do	Do.
130798	....do	New Mexico	Mrs. J. G. Bruff.
152816	....do	Indian Territory	James Mooney.
131201	Moccasins	Texas	Minor Kellogg.
131202	Moccasins, child's	do	Do
9005	Moccasins, Pawnee	Nebraska	L. W. Platt.
6986, 6987	Moccasins, Caddo (p. 351)		E. Palmer.
6989	Moccasins, Wichita		Do.
76785, 76786	Moccasins, Chetemacha, type	Louisiana	C. E. Whitney.

SANDALS, SHOES, AND BOOTS IN THE U. S. NATIONAL MUSEUM—Continued.

Museum number.	Specimen.	Locality.	By whom contributed.
56748	Woman's pantaloons, buckskin	Kenai Indians	Wm. J. Fisher.
7955	Boots, reindeer skin	Chilcat, Alaska	Dr. T. T. Minor.
11386	Moccasins	Wrangell, Alaska	Vincent Colyer.
20815–20817	Moccasins, Stikine Indians	do	J. G. Swan.
20795, 20796	Moccasins	Sitka, Alaska	Do.
20797	Moccasins (p. 351)	do	Do.
2129	Boots, child's	Northwestern coast of America.	Commodore W. Lilkes, U.S.N.
2131	Shoes, grass	do	Do.
9059	Moccasins	Fort Colville, Wash	Dr. James T. Ghiselin.
673	Moccasins, Chinook (p. 352)	Columbia River	George Gibbs.
34073–24078	Moccasins, Klamath	Oregon	L. S. Dyar.
24079, 24080	Shoes for winter, Klamath	do	Do.
23855	Moccasins, Nez Percé (p. 352)	Idaho	J. B. Monteith.
167726, 167727	Moccasins, child's, Bannock	do	Ed. Palmer.
131243	.....do	do	Dr. George M. Kober.
151715	.....do	do	Prof. C. H. Hitchcock.
165147	Moccasins, Shoshone	Wyoming	James Mooney.
22011	Moccasins	Northern Wyoming	Maj. J. W. Powell.
22018	.....do	.....do	Do.
22020	.....do	.....do	Do.
1197, 1198	Moccasins, plain	.....do	Do.
12066, 12067	Moccasins, Pai-Utes	Southern Utah	Do.
12068, 12069	Moccasins, womens' Pai-Utes	.....do	Do.
14384–14391	Moccasins, Pai-Utes	..... do	Do.
17217. 17218	Moccasins	Utah	Do.
19831	.....do	.....do	Do.
19836	.....do	.....do	Do.
19841	.....do	.....do	Do.
165148	Moccasins, Shoshone	Wyoming	James Mooney.
19628	Moccasins, child's	Walker Lake, Colo.	S. Powers.
21347	Moccasins, Hupa Indians	California	Do.
21721	Moccasins, McCloud River Indians	.....do	Livingston Stone.
21722, 21723	.....do	.....do	Do.
10778	Moccasins, Ute Indians	Colorado	Maj. J. W. Powell.
10779	Moccasins, beaded, Ute Indians	.....do	Do.
10780	Moccasins, with long leggings	.....do	Do.
10788, 10789	Moccasins, Ute Indians	.....do	Do.
11105, 11106	Moccasins, Moki	Arizona	Do.
11193, 11194	Boots, hide soles	.....do	Do.
45607	Sandals, straw	Silver City, N. Mex	Henry H. Rusby.
45609	Sandals, large (a fragment) (pl. 71)	.....do	Do.
45610	Sandals, child's (pl. 7)	.....do	Do.
20929	Sandals, yucca fiber (p. 357)	St. George, Utah	E. Palmer.
5555	Boots, Apache	Arizona	Do.
5556	Boots, Tonto Apache	.....do	Do.
7314	Moccasins and leggings, Apache	.....do	Maj. W. H. Mills.
11321	Boots, long, Apache		W. F. M. Army.
21533–21535	Moccasins, with legs, Apache	Arizona	Dr. J. B. White, U. S. A.
77824	Moccasins, girls', Shoshone	Utah	Maj. J. W. Powell.
115380–115388	Moccasins, Gosh Utes	.....do	Do.
115383–115385	Moccasins, child's	.....do	Do.
151443	Moccasins, used in Mormon church	.....do	George Woltz.
152569	Moccasins, Utes		Lewis Engel.

SANDALS, SHOES, AND BOOTS IN THE U. S. NATIONAL MUSEUM—Continued.

Museum number.	Specimen.	Locality.	By whom contributed.
73001	Shoes, mescal fiber, La Costa Indians.	Lower California	H. C. and Chas. R. Orcutt.
19848	Moccasins	Utah	Maj. J. W. Powell.
19856	.....do	.....do	Do.
19859	.....do	.....do	Do.
19863	.....'do	.....do	Do.
19866	.....do	.....do	Do.
19871	.....do	.....do	Do.
22001	Moccasins and leggings, woman's.	Northern Utah	Do.
27820	Moccasins, boy's, Shoshone	Utah	Do.
68657	Overshoes, basket, Zuñi (p. 361)	New Mexico	Do.
127702	Moccasins, Zuñi	.....do	Bureau of Ethnology.
166619	Moccasins, Hopi Indians	Arizona	James Mooney.
166638	.....do	.....do	Do.
166789	Moccasins and leggings, Hopi Indians.	.....do	Do.
166791	.....do	.....do	Do.
166793	Moccasin straps, Hopi Indians	.....do	Do.
166805	Moccasins, red tops, Hopi Indians.	.....do	Do.
22818	Moccasins	Tusayan, Ariz	Maj. J. W. Powell.
22830, 22831	Moccasins, boy's, Moki	.....do	Do.
22903	Moccasins, winter, Moki	.....do	Do.
23156	Moccasins, Moki	.....do	Do.
41723	Moccasins, woman's, Moki	.....do	Col. J. S. Stevenson.
41828	Moccasins, man's, Moki (fig. 65)	.....do	Do.
41829–41832	Moccasins, child's, Moki	.....do	Do.
68969	.....do	.....do	Do.
68970–68974	.....do	.....do	Do.
68976–68978	.....do	.....do	Do.
84283	Shoes, child's, Moki	.....do	V. Mindeleff.
166682	Moccasins, child's, Moki	.....do	James Mooney.
166685	.....do	.....do	Do.
166687	Moccasins, child's, Moki	.....do	Do.
11790, 11791	Moccasins, Oraibi		Maj. J. W. Powell.
128957	Shoes, woman's, Oraibi		Mrs. M. E. Stevenson.
1057	Sandals, Indian	Casa Grande, Gila River.	Col. Paston.
9364	Last for moccasins	Arizona	E. Palmer.
174450	Sandals, rawhide (fig. 66)	Sonora, Mex	W J McGee.
166596	Moccasins and leggings, Navajo	Arizona	James Mooney.
166597	Moccasins, driller's, Navajo	.....do	Do.
166621	Moccasins, black, silver button, Navajo.	.....do	Do.
17349	Moccasins	New Mexico	G. M. Wheeler.
76896	Sandals, plaited	Huaguechila	Mexican Commission.
130711	Moccasins, child's	Pueblo	Rev. Father Walter.
17346	Moccasins, Zuñi	New Mexico	G. M. Wheeler.
21540	Sandals, hide, Zuñi	Arizona	Dr. J. B. White, U. S. A.
21541, 21542	.....do	.....do	Do.
24215	Sandals, willow bark, Mohave	Colorado River	E. Palmer.
24222	.....do	.....do	Do.
8357	Moccasins	New Mexico	Medical Museum, U. S. A.
9979	Shoes and leggings, woman's	.....do	E. Palmer.
17350	Moccasins, child's	.....do	G. M. Wheeler.
47177	Shoe	Santa Domingo, N. Mex.	Maj. J. W. Powell.

SANDALS, SHOES, AND BOOTS IN THE U. S. NATIONAL MUSEUM—Continued.

Museum number.	Specimen.	Locality.	By whom contributed.
153160	Soles of sandals	Rio Grande, Mexico	Capt. J. G. Bourke, U.S.A.
152732	Sandals (fig. 67)	Colima, Mexico	E. Palmer.
174484	Sandals, rawhide	Sonora, Mexico	W J McGee.
31039	Moccasins, Apache	Yuma, Ariz.	Maj. W. H. Brown, U.S.A.
152519	.....do		Capt. J. G. Bourke, U.S.A.
153566	Moccasins, woman's, Apache		Capt. R. H. Pratt, U.S.A.
8356	Moccasins, Navajo Indians	New Mexico	Asst. Surg. John Brooke.
9549, 9550	Moccasins, Navajo Indians (figs. 63 and 64).	.....do	E. Palmer.
16503	.....do		Gov. W. F. M. Arny.
17347, 17348	.....do	New Mexico	Lieut. G. M. Wheeler.
128114	Shoes, Navajo Indian	Arizona	A. M. Stephen.
166593	Moccasins and leggings, Navajo Indians.	.....do	James Mooney.
73908, 73909	Sandals, Merida	Yucatan, Mexico	Louis H. Ayme.
175185	Shoes, child's	Venezuela	R. M. Bartleman.
32091	Rubber shoes	Central America	Hon. E. K. Hart.
32092	.....do	.....do	Do.
128397	Sandals	.....do	V. O. King.
127572	Sandals from mummy, fur skin	Peru (fig. 70)	W. E. Curtis.
4828	Slippers, wooden sole	Brazil	W. W. Carter.
4829	Slippers, woman's	Lima	Do.

SNOWSHOES AND DEVICES FOR TRAVELING OVER THE SNOW AFOOT.

The snowshoe is a device for sustaining the body of one traveling on the top of the snow. It will be seen at a glance to be absolutely necessary to the welfare of hyperborean peoples in walking, hunting, pulling a sled, or in driving a team attached to the sled. Every Arctic culture area has its own use for this article. According to the timber supply and the life to be led, the snowshoe varies from place to place. In association with its kindred implement, the sled, the snowshoe was the apparatus for most rapid land transit known to man before the age of steam.

Snowshoes are of two kinds: (1) Those of wood, the skee or its equivalent; (2) the netted snowshoe. The wooden snowshoe varies from people to people, but there are, in a general sense, but two kinds, the skee proper, or wooden skate (fig. 75), useful in rapid transit, and the compound skee, lined beneath with pelt, useful in draft and also for uphill work (fig. 77).

The smooth skee is to be seen in two forms, one having grooves beneath acting as a keel or keel board, the other being perfectly flat and smooth beneath.

The netted snowshoe grows out of two needs, that of timber sufficiently large and strong from which to make them, and the demand for a footgear that will help the wearer in an emergency to draw a heavy load. There is a great variety of netted snowshoes, the differences among them depending partly upon the form and quality of the frame, and partly upon the material the kind and fineness of netting.

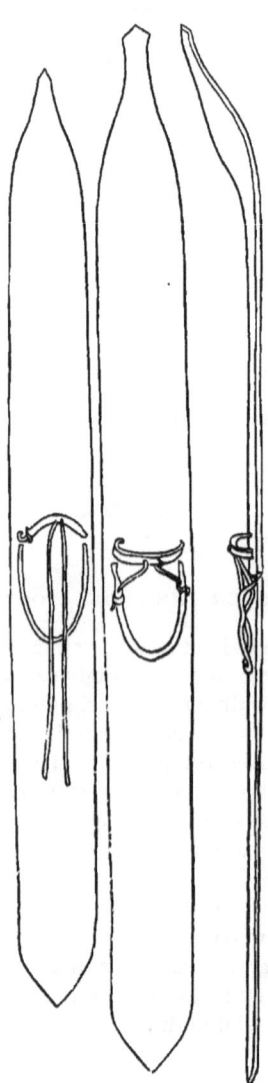

Fig. 75.
WOODEN SNOWSHOES USED BY THE GILIAKS ON THE AMUR.
From a figure in Schrenck's " Reisen und For-schungen im Amur-Lande "

(1) The simplest form of frame is a hoop of wood, made from a scion or sapling, trimmed very little, and bent into a form more or less round, without crossbars. Examples of this type are shown in pls. 17 and 21.

In the Caucasus and in the Aino country a nearly round frame is made by telescoping one half hoop into another and binding the ends together. In the Adirondacks the wealthy hunters wear a very pretty and costly kind with circular frames.

(2) An advance upon the first form is a hoop or ellipse, with two opposite points drawn toward each other, more in shape of the foot or like an hour glass; also without crossbars. This form has a restricted area and is shown in fig. 76.

(3) A third type does not differ essentially from No. 2, except that the outline is oval and the rear part occasionally constricted, as in a hand glass. The oval form is illustrated by an example in the U. S. National Museum from the northwest coast of America, collected long ago by Captain Wilkes. No. 2728, fig. 92, is the type specimen.

A type slightly differing from No. 3 is from Ungava, eastern Canada. The ellipse is the fundamental form; the rear is constricted into three local varieties, described by Turner, to wit, the beaver tail, the swallow tail, and the round end forms. The Ungava specimens are neatly made, as if by machinery, and they have crossbars and fine webbing of thong and provision for the toes inclosed in a soft shoe.

(4) This type has a frame in one piece, but the front end is bent sharper and the rear ends lashed together, forming a trailer. All of this looped variety in the National Museum have crossbars set in after the manner to be described. The variations in this class of frames are in the turning up or not of the front, the length of the trailer, and, in the latest voyageur and Canadian examples, the curve of the front.

(5) The Chukchi and the natives of St. Lawrence Island make a frame of two pieces of wood bowed and lashed together at the ends in lenticular form. Anciently, all Eskimos wore this sort of snowshoe. These specimens are necessarily provided with crossbars. There is one example in the National Museum in which a two-part frame is rounded in front and trailed behind. In the Iroquois and Sioux country, and also among the voyageurs, the two-part frame reaches its perfection, being neatly made and gracefully turned up in front.

In order to give room for all questions that may arise in separating snowshoes into their species, and varieties on ethnical, technical, and geographical grounds, the following characteristics must be examined:

1. *Material.*—Driftwood, lumber, sapling, bone, antler, etc.

2. *Outer frame.*—Number of parts, relation to symmetry and the manner in which they are bound together.

3. *Cross section of the frame.*—Round, squared, pointed oval, etc.

4. *Outline and shear.*—Circular, elliptical, oval, pointed oval, lenticular; also flat, warped, turned up, etc.

5. *Crossbars.*—Number, material, form, and attachment.

6. *Netting.*—Rude or woven; wrapped, rove, or worked on a border line; of thong, babiche, twine of sinew, twine of babiche, vegetable twine; toe netting, heel netting, foot netting.

7. *Measurements.*

The netted snowshoe may be traced into the United States quite well to the southward in the States east of the Plains; but it practically disappears from the horse tribes or regions. Old frontiersmen say that the horse Indians were not fond of snowshoes, and did not care to use them.

The snowshoe line southward is on the isotherm of northern New York in winter. There was an abundance of raw material for making them, and the question was one of demand. If the snow was too soft to sustain the wearer, it mattered not how deep it lay, that only made matters worse. There was also a northern limit of good snowshoes. It lay within the Arctic Circle, where the snow became hard enough in the long winter nights to sustain the hunter without them. There, it will be seen, they became poorer as we get farther north.

Snowshoes are not known to have been used south of the Klamath River in California. They are not spoken of as occurring in South America. Here and there further south netted and fur overmoccasins occur.

Nansen[1] mentions in his matchless chapter on the Skee the use of mud boards on the feet for crossing a marsh, and contrasts the lifting of them in stepping with the gliding of the Skee and the peculiar motion of the skater.

The Guaraon, of the Orinoco, run with extreme address on muddy lands, where the European, the Negro, or other Indians except them-

---

[1] "First Crossing of Greenland," London, 1890, i, p. 76.

selves would not dare to walk; and it is, therefore, commonly believed that they are of lighter weight than the rest of the natives. The ease with which they walk in places newly dried without sinking in, when even they have no planks tied to their feet, seemed to me the effects of long habit.[1]

The Norwegian snowshoe, skee (called *she*, pl. skier, skilöber, snowshoer; skilöbning, snowshoeing), is a strip of hard wood from 5 to 8 feet long, 4 or more inches wide, and not more than an inch thick, on the average. Many of them are ornamented, but essentially they are pointed and turned up at both ends, having a strap back of the middle for the foot. On the underside may be a groove, acting like a keel or centerboard. The skee was formerly accompanied with the staff, useful especially in steering or guiding the traveler. This type is found in Norway, Sweden, Finland, Russia, and on the Amur. In Kamchatka the sled rests on skees. The Norwegian truger is the counterpart of the netted snowshoe, worn by men and horses and also by Alpine peasants. It is made of an oblong osier hoop, 12 to 16 inches in length, bound to the foot with the simplest lashings.[2]

Nansen devotes a chapter to the spread of the skee argued on philological grounds. The origin is found thereby in the Altai from Baikal Lake southwestward. He names four types:

1. Sok, tok, hokh, from Japan Sea to Lapland.
2. Sana, tana, hana, among Buriats and northwest Samoyeds.
3. Solta, tolde, among Golde, Tungus, Ostyak-Samoyeds.
4. Lysha, gola, kalku, etc., of Aryan parentage.

In northeastern Siberia outstanding names are given.

The interesting fact is also stated that the transition from the fur-lined to the smooth skee is not abrupt. In Österdalen, Norway, the one on the left foot is long and smooth; the other short and lined beneath with skin. With this may be compared the skater on one foot.[3]

The great dexterity shown by professionals on this apparatus and its introduction into civilized sport must not be noticed here except to call attention again to the universal tendency of old drudgeries to become by and by pastimes and fine arts. Nor does the skee escape the common lot of apotheoses, since in the Norse mythologies heroes are made to travel on this wise; and it is the boast of a northern chieftain that he could traverse the snow upon skates of wood.[4]

In 1865 Henry Elliott and the Intercontinental Telegraph party traveled 25 miles in two hours across Stuart's Lake, Canada, on skates made from cedar boughs, using blankets for sails.

---

[1] Humboldt's Travels, London, 1852, Bohn., I, p. 332.

[2] F. Nansen, "First Crossing of Greenland," London, 1890, Longmans, I, pp. 3, 10, 39, with figure; also Illustrated London News, 1895, 106, p. 172.

[3] "First Crossing Greenland," London, 1890, I, Chap. III, pp. 73–114, with figures and map.

[4] Olai. Worm. Lit. Run., p. 129, cited by Strutt, "Sports and Pastimes of the People of England," p. 153.

Bone skates from Iceland are figured in "The Reliquary,"[1] made from the radius, metatarsal, metacarpal bones of the ox or horse, shaved off to fit the foot on one side and trimmed at the ends on the lower side. Holes are pierced through the ends and a cord is looped through the front hole by its middle. The two ends cross on the instep, pass down to the hole through the heel, where they cross and are brought up to the ankle and fastened around the limb. The bone skate is only a kind of skee. The forward motion is obtained by means of a rod shod with iron or by sailing before the wind.

A Scandinavian, far from home, at Meadow Lake, Nevada County, Cal., has reproduced the skee with a longitudinal groove underneath from end to end, and has sent an example to the Museum of Natural History, in New York.

Rasmus B. Anderson speaks of the Laplander making snowshoes, and also as being expert in the use of the skee, or long wooden snowshoe.[2]

The kinship of the skee to the sledge, shown in the traveling apparatus of Kamchatka and the Canadian toboggan, is also illustrated by Conan Doyle in a pleasure trip over the Alps: "The guides undid their skier, lashed their straps together, and turned them into a rather clumsy toboggan. Sitting on these, with our heels dug into the snow and our sticks pressed down hard behind us, we began to move down the precipitous face of the pass."[3]

Hendrick Hamel says that the cold was so intense in Korea in 1662, and there fell such a quantity of snow, that the people made ways under it to pass from house to house; and to go on it they wore small boards like battledores under the feet.[4]

Batchelder must be thinking of still another style used by these northern aborigines of Japan. He says the snowshoes of the Aino are of wood; each consists of a single piece neatly covered with sealskin. They are 5 feet 7 inches long, 7½ inches in breadth, and fastened to the feet by means of a rawhide thong.[5] They are almost identical with those of the Amur.

Whales abound in the Channel of Manchuria, but are only got by the natives of Saghalin when washed ashore. They sell the oil to the Japanese, and make use of the whalebone for their sledges, bows, and snow-

---

[1] J. Romilly Allen, The Reliquary, London, 1886, II, pp. 33–38, quoting Leland's Itinerary, London, 1772, VIII, p. 45; Strutt, "Sports and Pastimes of the People of England," and C. Roach Smith, Archæologia, XXIX, p. 397. See also R. Munro, Proc. Soc. Antiquaries of Scotland, XXVII, p. 185.

[2] Senate Ex. Doc. 73, 53d Cong., 2d sess., p. 148. See illustration in Frank Leslie's Monthly, Feb. 2, 1894.

[3] McClure's Magazine, New York, 1895, IV, p. 352.

[4] Quoted by W. E. Griffis in "Korea, Without and Within," Philadelphia, 1885, p. 114.

[5] Batchelder, "Ainu of Japan," Chicago, 1893, p. 187, with figure. Cf. Schrenck.

shoes.[1] All the Japanese snowshoes in the U. S. National Museum
are of the hooped variety.

Examples Nos. 22195 and 22196 are snowshoes sent from Yokohama,
Japan, by the Hon. Benjamin Lyman. The frames are hoops of wood
drawn together in the shape of a long oval constricted in the middle.
The lashing under the foot is made of rawhide thongs. Length, 18½
inches; greatest width, 10 inches. Worn by the Aino, of northern
Japan. One of these specimens is shown in fig. 76. In the collection
of Romyn Hitchcock, No. 150643, U. S. National Museum, is a pair
of Aino snowshoes made of wood and lashed with thong of bearskin. The general shape is an oblong oval. The frame consists of two

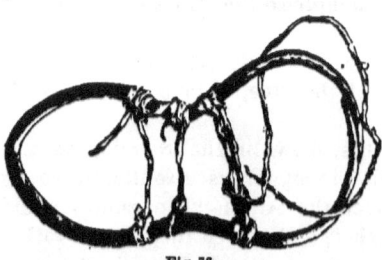

Fig. 76.

RUDE SNOWSHOE FROM YOKOHAMA, JAPAN.

Cat No. 22196, U. S. N. M.   Collected by Hon. Benjamin S. Lyman.

bent sticks, rounded at the bends
and squared along the limbs.
The one forming the heel portion
"telescopes" into the other, and
the two are lashed together by
the webbing of bearskin. This
is all of one piece, and passes
around the two side sticks by a
double loop, as in many American specimens. The knot is the
same. Commencing at one margin near the toe the loop is made.
The thong passes diagonally across and makes another loop, then across
again and back, so that when completed it makes a monogram of M
and W. The toe strap or loop is simply the fastening of the remaining
thong. These are worn with fishskin boots.[2]

In Brockhaus's Atlas of Ethnography, there is figured a snowshoe
of the telescoped form used by the Swanen, in the Caucasus, and Hitchcock brought from Tate Yama a telescoped frame with wooden wedges
beneath, without foot netting (fig. 93, p. 411).

The Samoyed skees are wider and shorter than the Norwegian, being
about 6 feet long and 6 inches wide. They are made of light wood, and
have deerskin stretched over the sole. They can make 35 miles a day
on their "olen lœgia" or "kaminus lœgia."[3]

The Giliaks have two kinds of snowshoes—small, lahk; and large, cuj.
The small snowshoe is made from a thin board without covering, 4½
feet long and 5 to 6 inches wide, bent up and more or less pointed in
front. In different regions it assumes modifications of form in the end.
These are of universal use as sleds, as shovels, and even as dishes, on
a pinch. The large snowshoe is longer, wider, and covered on the
bottom with hide of the seal, the hair pointing backward[4] (fig. 77).

[1] Ravenstein, "Russians on the Amur," London, 1861, pp. 323–324.

[2] Rep. Smithsonian Institution (U. S. Nat. Mus.), 1890, pl. XVII.

[3] Jackson, "The Great Frozen Land," London, 1895, p. 69.

[4] Schrenck, "Reisen und Forschungen im Amur-Lande," St. Petersburg, 1891, K.
Akad. d. Wissensch., III, 475, pl. XXXV, 9 flgs.

On the Usuri the Yupitatze or Fish Skins hunt only during winter. The snowshoes are planks cut from the pine trees, one-fourth inch thick, 5 inches broad, 6 feet long, sloping upward at both ends, lined beneath with deerskin, and bound tightly to the feet by means of two straps. On these the Yupitatze will skim lightly over the snow, follow the track of the game, and go 20 to 25 leagues in a short winter day. He climbs the mountains with ease. The deerskin is set on with the hair pointing backward, and this serves as a ratchet.[1]

The Tungusian snowshoe is a skee, about 5 feet long and 10 inches wide, hewn very thin and bent up at the toes. They are soled with skin from the seal or the legs of the deer or horse, with the hair on and pointing backward.[2]

At Oudskoi men and boys slide down hill on them, descending steep declivities at almost lightning speed. The snowshoer always carries a staff as a rudder, a brake, and a balance or fulcrum.[3]

The snowshoes of the Koraks, about Ghijigha, are different from those farther south. They consist of wooden bows, rounded and raised in front, and pointed at the rear, over which a network of seal thongs is interwoven, but very clumsy, and not as buoyant as those used by the Yakuts and Tungus.[4]

This change of snowshoe is the result of natural causes.

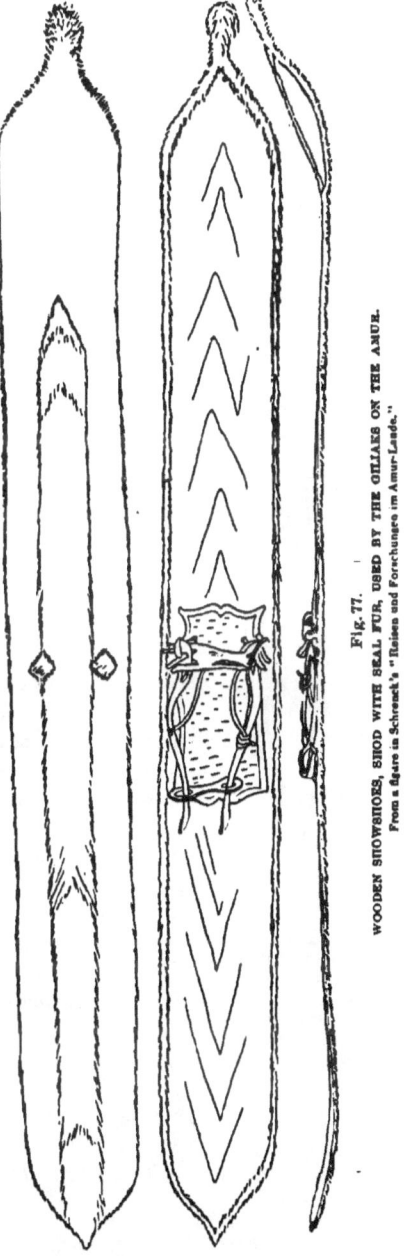

Fig. 77.

WOODEN SNOWSHOES, SHOD WITH SEAL FUR, USED BY THE GILIAKS ON THE AMUR.

From a figure in Schrenck's "Reisen und Forschungen im Amur-Lande."

---

[1] Ravenstein, "Russians on the Amur," London, 1861, p. 94.
[2] Bush, "Reindeer, Dogs and Snowshoes," New York, 1871, p. 166.
[3] Cf. John Bell, "Lives of Celebrated Travelers." Harper's Magazine, 1835, II, p. 145.
[4] Cf. Bush, "Reindeer, Dogs and Snowshoes," New York, 1871, p. 356.

There is not enough good, tough wood in all northeast Siberia to make one skee.

The Kamchatkans hunt sable on snowshoes with trained dogs, drive them into holes which they surround with nets, and then, forcing them out with fire and ax, kill them with clubs.[1]

The Kamchadale snowshoes are really a necessary accessory to the sled driver to enable him to quit the vehicle for hunting or working about it, and for the protection of the road. They are made of thin board, 4½ feet long, 7 inches broad, sloped to a point at both ends, curved up in front, and arched up a little in the middle. On the underside sealskin is fitted with the hair pointed backward, to serve as a ratchet. The straps are nearer the front. Langsdorff speaks of them as extremely useful in going up and down hill.[2]

Fig. 78.
COARSE SNOWSHOE WITH
POINTED TOE AND HEEL,
WORN BY THE CHUKCHI OF
NORTHEASTERN SIBERIA.
Cat. No. 2442, U. S. N. M. Collected
by Commodore John Rodgers,
U. S. N.

"The Chukchi snowshoes are 2 feet long, broad and flat, front 8 inches wide, tapering to a point behind, where to prevent sinking in the snow a piece of baleen 4 inches wide and 18 inches long is attached. This widening out of the trailer by inserting a wedge-shaped piece is to be seen on New England examples. The nettings are of seal or walrus hide."[3]

Examples Nos. 2442 and 2443 are two pairs of Chukchi snowshoes from northeast Siberia, collected by Commodore John Rodgers, U. S. N. The frames are of oak roughly squared, the ends are pointed, the fronts turn up, and there are braces or crosspieces of wood and bone. The netting over the central space is of coarse caribon skin, rove through the sides and wrapped about the crosspieces. There is no toe or heel netting. Length, 35½ inches; breadth, 6¾ inches. One of these specimens is shown in fig. 78.

The wide Amur type of snowshoe reaches the northern border of the Chukchi country. Of this, Nordenskiöld says that a Chukchi man drove past his vessel in February, and offered him a pair of immensely wide skates of their wood, covered with sealskin and raised at both sides.[4]

Of the Chukchi with whom he came in contact, Nordenskiöld says that both men and women use snowshoes in winter. Without

[1] Kennan, "Tent Life," p. 159.
[2] Langsdorff, "Voyages," London, 1814, II, p. 291.
[3] Hooper, "Tents of the Tuski," London, 1853, p. 184.
[4] "Voyage of the Vega," New York, 1882, Macmillan & Co., p. 475, with figure.

them they will not undertake willingly any long walk in the snow. The frame of the snowshoe is of wood, and the netting of stout thongs. In the figure given by the author the frame is in two parts, with two crossbars, pointed at both ends and much turned up in front.[1]

Examples Nos. 63602 to 63604 (the latter being shown in fig. 79) are snowshoes from Icy Cape. The frames are roughly whittled and pointed at the heel. Netting fine, babiche woven open and strong, and rove through the frame. The foot is supported on strong rawhide thong laid rectangular. Length, 30 inches; width, 10¼ inches. Collected by E. W. Nelson.

The Eskimo about Bering Strait make their snowshoe frames from willow and alder, the only growing trees about that vicinity. They are like those just described from the Chukchi area. Indeed, the typical Eskimo snowshoe has always coarse netting. There are two pairs of these double pointed, rude snowshoes from about Bering Strait in the Museum of Natural History, New York. They are in excellent condition, and one of them has a line nicely served extending from the toe point to the front bar. The netting is of coarse thong, and forms regular parallelograms under the feet. These have been examined through the courtesy of Professor Putnam and Mr. Marshall Saville.

Example No. 15605 is a set of three snowshoe frames from Ponook, a little island east of St. Lawrence Island, Bering Sea, collected by Henry W. Elliott. They are short, made of two pieces, thin and straight, in cross section. The braces are broad and flat, ends pointed and sharply curved up in front. The lashing is with thongs of seal or walrus hide. Length, 21 inches; breadth, 9 inches. Other examples, collected by E. W. Nelson (Nos. 63236, 63242),

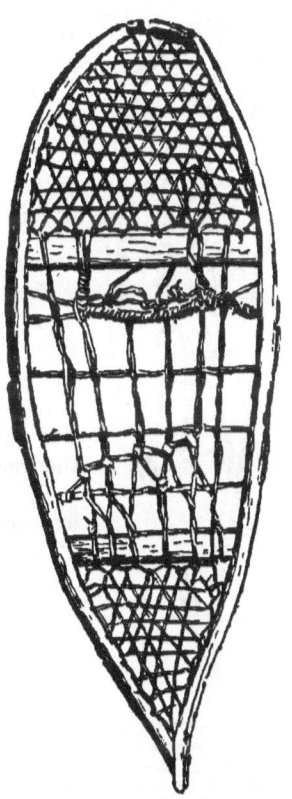

Fig. 79.

NETTED SNOWSHOE FROM ICY CAPE, ALASKA.

Cat. No. 63604, U. S. N. M. Collected by E. W. Nelson.

are nearly flat, the frame coarsely made in two pieces, the netting of walrus-hide thong. An average length is 4½ feet.[2]

The Innuit snowshoe is small and nearly flat, seldom over 30 inches long. They are always rights and lefts. Ingalik, larger; Kutchin, same

[1] "Voyage of the Vega," New York, 1882, Macmillan & Co., p. 475.

[2] See also Whymper, "Travels and Adventures in the Territory of Alaska," p. 183.

style; Hudson Bay, 30 inches in length.[1] They are from 2 to 3 feet long, 1 foot broad, and slightly turned up in front.[2]

Example No. 48092 (fig. 80) is a pair of snowshoes from Cape Darby, Alaska, north of Norton Sound, collected by E. W. Nelson. Frame in two pieces, rounded in cross section, and cut small in front. The toe is rounded and sharply curved up; heel pointed. The foot netting, strong seal-thong rove through the frame. Both shoes are alike. Length, 36 inches; width, 10½ inches. This coarse shoe is a connecting link between the ruder Asiatic and the finer Athapascan forms. In this one the round toe has taken the place of the pointed toe, and there is a trace of toe netting.

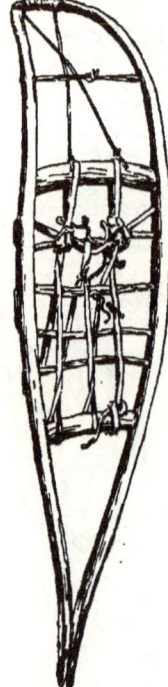

Example No. 48103 is a pair of snowshoe models from Norton Bay, Alaska, collected from the Mahlemut Eskimo by E. W. Nelson. The frame is rounded, in section, wide in front, and strongly curved up. The netting is of deerskin thong twisted into twine. Length, 19½ inches; width, 4⅝ inches.

Example No. 45400 (pl. 11) is a pair of snowshoes from Norton Sound, Alaska, collected from the Ingalik Indians (Kai yuh kha tana) by E. W. Nelson. The frame is made of two pieces spliced in front and rounded in section. The netting is made of deer sinew twisted and attached to loops rove through the frame; strongly curved up in front and pointed at the heel. They are rights and lefts, a slight difference being made in the frames. The method of attaching by the toe and heel loop is described by Murdoch, page 391. Length, 46 inches; width, 10½ inches. In the transition from the rectangular and shapeless meshes to hexagonal meshes in the three spaces, this specimen fills a gap. The toe netting is tolerably good hexagonal weaving. The foot netting is still as poor as any of its square-woven type, and the heel space is filled with a warp of thong converging at the trailer, held in position by a line of "bird-cage" weaving athwart its middle.

Fig. 80.
NETTED SNOWSHOE FROM CAPE DARBY, ALASKA.
Cat. No. 48092, U. S. N. M. Collected by E. W. Nelson.

The Kai yuh kho tana of Dall and Ingalik of the Russians (a corruption of the native or Eskimo word meaning Indians) occupy the low tundra on and about the Yukon and the Kuskokwim. They are Athapascan. Dall says that their habits vary with their environment, some being fishermen, others hunting the moose and the deer. On the Yukon the southernmost settlements trade dry fish and wooden ware, in making

---

[1] Dall, "Alaska and its Resources," pp. 190–191.
[2] Seeman, in "The Zoology of the Voyage of H. M. S. *Herald* during the years 1845-51," London, 1853, II, p. 60.

NETTED SNOWSHOES.

These specimens are somewhat short and wide. The frames are of two pieces of wood, spliced in front, round in cross section and turned up at the toe, having pointed heel and crossbars let into the frame. The perforations of the frame for the cord to which the netting is attached, are in pairs, separated on the inside and coming together on the outside just below the surface, so that the foundation thong may be tied in a series of single knots, concealed on the outside and forming a line of loops on the inside of the frame.

The netting or filling in front is in hexagonal weaving through the foundation thong above mentioned. The netting in the rear space consists of ten filaments passing through the vertical holes in the rear of the hindmost crossbar, and converging toward the heel where they are fastened off in the thong that binds the frame together. Midway of these longitudinal filaments a cross thong is wrapped in bird-cage style to hold them in place. The netting in the foot space is of stout thong, rove through the frame at the sides and running parallel. It is wrapped twice about the front crossbar and four times about the rear crossbar or cross lashing, making meshes which are a compromise between rectangular and hexagonal weaving. Norton Bay, Alaska. Collected by E. W. Nelson.

(Cat. No. 45400, U. S. N. M.)

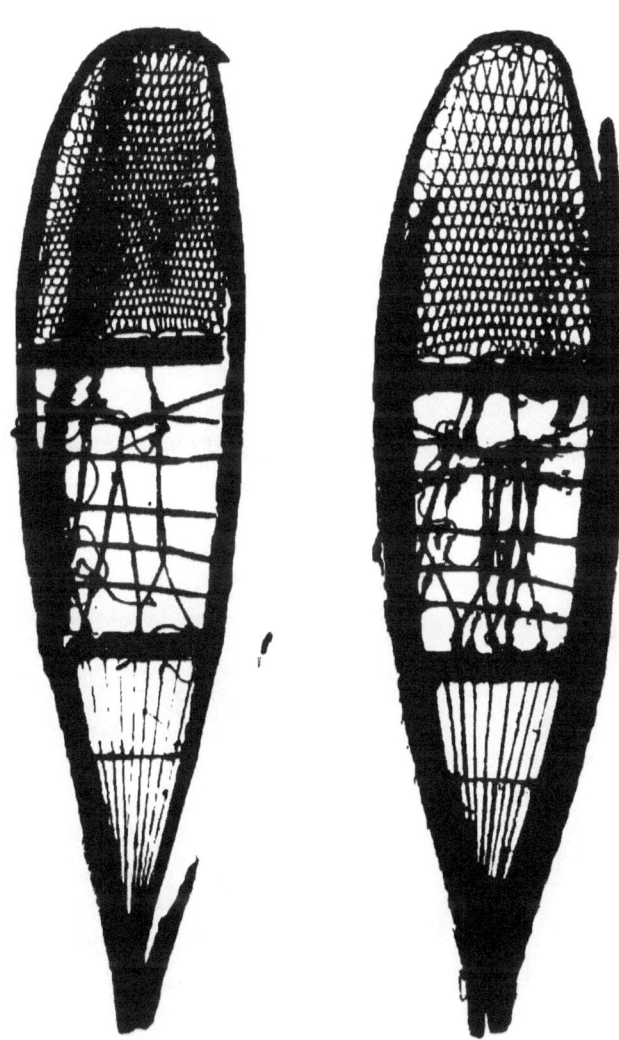

NETTED SNOWSHOES.
Norton Bay, Alaska.

NETTED SNOWSHOES.

These shoes are broad in front. The frames are made of two pieces of rounded wood, spliced and turned up at the toe, pointed at the heel, and having three crossbars let into the frame. There are perforations in the frame around the front space and hinder spaces passing vertically through a keeled projection, as in lacrosse sticks. The frame alongside the middle of the foot space has six holes bored quite through for the cross lashing. The main crossbars have vertical perforations on the margins away from the foot space. The short crossbar is not perforated and the frame sticks do not bulge out at this point.

The netting, front and rear, is of babiche in hexagonal weaving, done into a set of loops around the inner margin of the frame and tied by single knots into V-shaped perforations.

The foot netting is of stout rawhide in parallel or rectangular weaving, the fore-and-aft lines being doubled and twisted about the transverse set. This specimen is a transition form between the irregular and the hexagonal style of footing.

Ingalik of Nulato, Alaska. Collected by E. W. Nelson.

(Cat. No. 49009, U. S. N. M.)

PLATE 12.

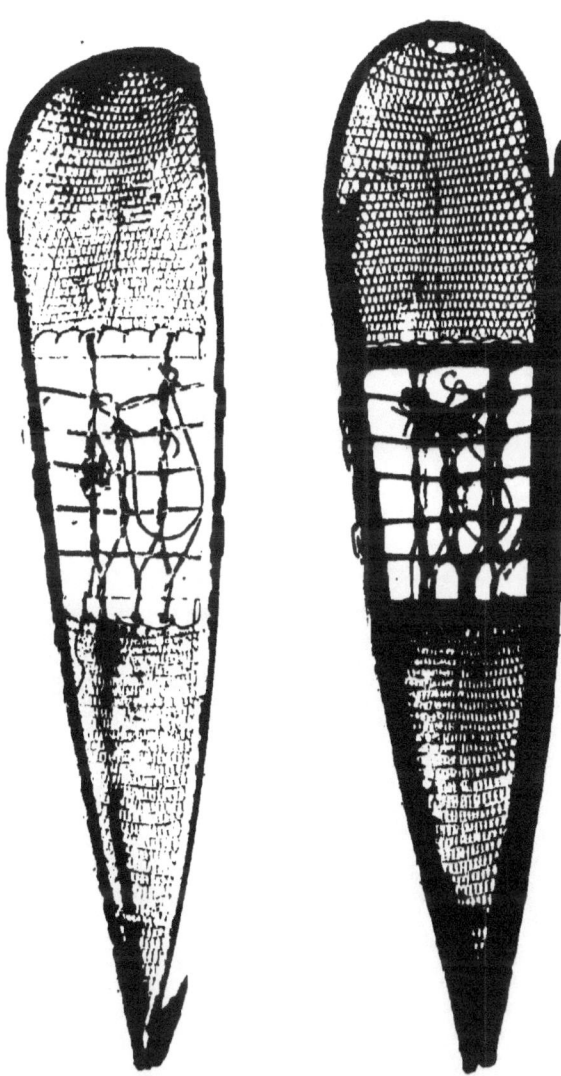

NETTED SNOWSHOES.
Ingalik of Nulato, Alaska.

which they are very expert, and strong birch bark canoes with the upper Yukon and Shagelnk people.

Example No. 38873 is a pair of snowshoes from the mouth of the Yukon River, Alaska, collected from the Eskimo by E. W. Nelson. They are nearly flat, the frame rounded in section and roughly made. Toe rounded, heel pointed. Toe and heel netting destroyed, but formerly made of sinew twine; the foot netting of hide thong. Both shoes alike. Length, 36½ inches; width, 9½ inches. The noteworthy feature in these specimens is the manipulation of the foot thong, which is rove through the front crossbar and the sides of the frame, and is carried around the hind crossbar. The first meshes in the rear are suggestive of hexagonal weaving, but this design is arrested by the second cross line, and the six fore and aft strands are made parallel in pairs. These by simply rising and falling as in a common warp hold the cross lines from sagging. The rest under the ball of the foot is simple and effective, and affords an explanation of the more elaborate construction of this part elsewhere.

Example No. 49099 (pl. 12) is a pair of snowshoes from Nulato (64°, 40', 158°, NW.), Alaska, collected from the Ingalik Indians (Athapascan) by E. W. Nelson. Round toe, strongly curved up; long, pointed heel. Toe and heel netting of twisted deer sinew; foot netting and foot loop of thong. Rights and lefts. Example No. 8812, collected by Dall, is similar to the foregoing. The short crossbar near the trailer should be noticed as leading up to a similar device further on with a new function.

Example No. 127941 is a pair of snowshoes from Putnam River, Alaska, collected by Lieutenant Stoney, U. S. N. The frame is in cross section, rounded at the toe and curved up; the heel is long and pointed; toe and heel netting of twined deer sinew; the foot netting and loops of strong walrus-hide thong. Length, 54 inches; width, 8½.

Simpson, in his journal, says that snowshoes are so seldom used in the North where the drifted snow presents a hard surface to walk upon that not half a dozen pairs were in existence at Point Barrow at the time of his sojourn (1853–55),[1] and those were of an inferior sort. Murdoch thinks the Point Barrow Eskimo learned to make the finer sort from the people of Kuwuk River, who have trading relations with the Indians, and in Simpson's time the Kuwuk people used the Indian shoe. Murdoch thus describes the present Point Barrow shoe:

Snowshoes (tûgln) of a very efficient pattern and very well made are now universally employed at Point Barrow. Although the snow never lies very deep on the ground, and is apt to pile up in hard drifts, it is sufficiently deep and soft in many places, especially on the grassy parts of the tundra, to make walking without snowshoes very inconvenient and fatiguing. I have even seen them used on the sea ice for crossing level spaces when a few inches of snow had fallen. Each shoe consists of a rim of light wood bent into the shape of a pointed oval, about five times as long as the greatest breadth, and much bent up at the rounded end, which is the toe. The sides are braced apart by two stout crossbars

---

[1] Simpson, "Narrative of Discoveries of the North Coast of America," p. 243.

(toe and heel bar), a little farther apart than the length of the wearer's foot. The space between these two bars is netted in large meshes (foot netting), with stout thong for the foot to rest upon, and the spaces at the ends are closely netted with fine deerskin "babiche," or sinew thread (toe and heel netting). The straps for the foot are fastened to the foot netting in such a way that while the strap is firmly fastened round the ankle the snowshoe is slung to the toe. The wearer walks with long, swinging strides, lifting the toe of the shoe at each step, while the tail or heel drags in the snow. The straps are so contrived that the foot can be slipped in and out of them without touching them with the fingers, a great advantage in cold weather.

Example No. 88912 is a pair of snowshoes from Point Barrow collected by Captain Ray and described by Murdoch. (Fig. 81.) The rim is of willow, 51 inches long and 10½ inches wide at the broadest part, and is made of two strips about 1 inch thick and three-fourths of an inch wide, joined at the toe by a long lap-splice, held together by four short horizontal or slightly oblique stitches of thong. Each strip is elliptical in section, with the long axis vertical, and keeled on the inner face, except between the bars. Each is tapered off considerably from the toe bar to the toe, and slightly tapered toward the heel. The two points are fastened together by a short horizontal stitch of baleen. The tip is produced into a slight trailer, and the inner side of each shoe is slightly straighter than the outer—that is to say, they are "rights and lefts."

The bars are elliptical in section, flattened, and have their ends mortised into the rim. They are about a foot apart, and of oak, the toe bar 9.2 inches long and the heel bar 8.5. Both are of the same breadth and thickness, 1 inch by one-half inch. There is also an extra bar for strengthening the back part of the shoe 10 inches from the point. It is of oak, 4.8 inches long, one-half inch wide, and three-tenths of an inch thick (fig. 82). The toe and heel nettings are put on first. Small equidistant vertical holes through the frame run round the inside of each space. Those in the rim are drilled through the keel already mentioned, and joined by a shallow groove above and below. Those in the bars are about one-half inch from the edge and joined by a groove on the

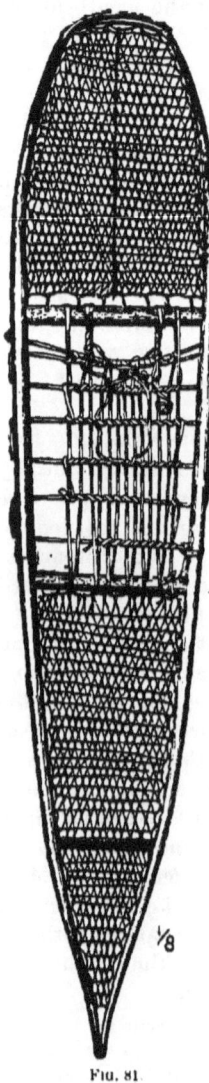

⅛

FIG. 81.

FINELY NETTED SNOWSHOE FROM POINT BARROW, ALASKA.

From a figure in the Ninth Annual Report of the Bureau of Ethnology.

Cat. No. 89912, U. S. N. M

under side of the toe bar only. Into these holes is laced a piece of babiche, which is knotted once into each hole, making a series of beckets about three-fourths of an inch wide round the inside of the space. There are no lacing holes in the parts spliced at the toe, but the lacing passes through a bight of each stitch. At the toe bar the lacing is carried across from rim to rim about three times, the last part being wound round the others.

On the left shoe the end is brought back on the left-hand side, passed through the first hole in the bar from above, carried along in the groove on the underside to the next hole, up through this and round the lacing, and back through the same hole, the two parts being twisted together between the bar and lacing. This is continued, "stopping" the lacing in festoons to the bar, to the last hole on the right, where it is finished off by knotting the end round the last "stop."[1]

Example No. 89913 is a pair of snowshoes from Point Barrow, shorter and broader than those just described. The hinder bar is of walrus ivory. They are 48½ inches long and 11 broad. The two shoes are not perceptibly different in shape. The lacing, which is of sinew braid, is put on in the same way as on the preceding pair, except that it is fastened directly into the holes on the toe bars. The whole of the heel netting is in one piece, and made precisely in the same way as the point nettings of the first pair, the end being carried up the middle to the point of the heel, and brought down again to the bar, as on the toe nettings, but fastened with

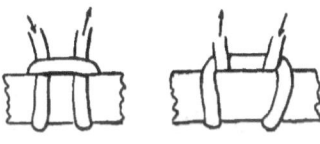

Fig. 82.

KNOT ON REAR CROSS BAR OF ESKIMO SNOW-
SHOE.

From a figure in the Ninth Annual Report of the Bureau of Ethnology.

marling hitches. The number of strands is the same in each shoe—twenty-three in each set. The toe nettings follow quite regularly the pattern of the preceding pair.

The shoes are not quite the same size, as the right has 35, 35, and 28 strands, and the left 33, 33, and 25, in each set, respectively. There is no regular rule about the number of strands in any part of the netting, the object being simply to make the meshes always about the same size. The foot netting is made of stout and very white thong from the bearded seal. These shoes have no strings.

No. 89914 [1738] is a pair of rather small shoes from Utkiavwïñ, one of which is shown in fig. 83. They are rights and lefts, and are 42 inches long by 10 broad. The frame is wholly of oak, and differs from the type only in having no extra hind bar, and having the heel and toe bars about equal in length. The points are fastened together with a treenail, as well as with a whalebone stitch. The heel nettings are put on with perfect regularity, as on the pair last described, but the toe

[1] Cf. Murdoch, Ninth Ann. Rep. Bureau of Ethnology, pp. 344–352, figs. 350–354, for minute details of making and weaving.

nettings, though they start in the usual way, do not follow any regular rule of succession, the rounds being put on sometimes inside and sometimes outside of the preceding, till the whole space is filled. The foot nettings are somewhat clumsily made, especially on the right shoe, which appears to have been broken in several places, and "cobbled" by an unskillful workman. There are only five transverse strands which are double on the left shoe, and the longitudinal strands are not whipped to these, but interwoven, and each pair twisted together between the transverse strands. There is no wattling back of the toe hole, and one pair of longitudinal strands at the side of the latter is not doubled on the left shoe. The strings are put on as on the type, except that the ends are knotted instead of being spliced. This pair of shoes was used by Mr. Murdoch during the winters 1881–82 and 1882–83, while serving on the International Polar Expedition as naturalist and observer.

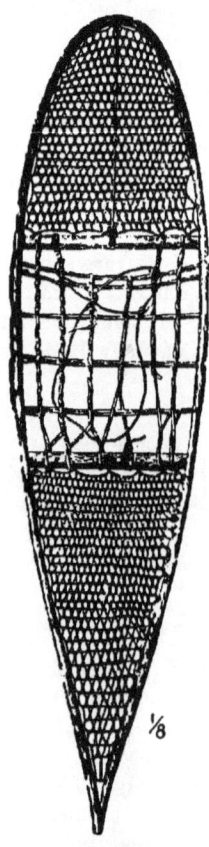

Fig. 83.
SMALL NETTED SNOWSHOE FROM POINT BARROW, ALASKA.
From a figure in the Ninth Annual Report of the Bureau of Ethnology.
Cat. No. 89914, U. S. N. M.

Example No. 38874 is a pair of snowshoes from Lake Iliamna (59°, 154°, NW.), Alaska, between Bristol Bay and Cooks Inlet, and at the eastern extremity of Alaskan Peninsula, collected from the Kenai Indians by E. W. Nelson. Frame rounded in section, netting of deer-sinew twine rove through the frame. Toe round and strongly curved up; heel pointed. Rights and lefts. Length, 51½ inches; width, 12¼.

Examples Nos. 72240 and 72241 (pl. 13) are snowshoes from Bristol Bay, Alaska, collected from the Indians (Tinné). The frame is square in section, toe rounded and strongly curved up, heel long and pointed. Toe and heel netting of twined deer sinew, foot netting of strong rawhide thong, all rove through the frame. They are rights and lefts, and have the typical toe and heel straps. Length, 44 inches; width, 9¾.

Example No. 63558 (pl. 14) is a pair of snowshoes collected at Sitka, Alaska, by J. J. McLean. It must be remembered that Sitka is the marine entrepôt for all the surrounding region. Trade goes to the interior of the continent up Lynn Canal and Chilkat River, and over the passes to the headwaters of the Yukon River. The snowshoes here described, and others, therefore, are Tinné, or Athapascan. The long, slender frame, rounded section, round toe bent up, and long, tapering heel are typical. Toe and heel netting of babiche close and fine. Foot

NETTED SNOWSHOES.

These specimens are not mates. They are spatulate in form, each space having its peculiar shape. The frame is in two pieces neatly spliced in front, round in section, much turned up at the toe, long pointed at the heel, and has three crossbars let into it. In this example each crossbar modifies the outline. There are V-shaped perforations about the front and rear spaces, in the middle of the long crossbars, as well as in their outer margins, and quite through the frames alongside the foot space. The short crossbar is not perforated.

The netting is hexagonal in front, built up on a thong knotted into V-shaped perforations of the frame and into the vertical perforations of the crossbar. In the rear space, owing to its elongated triangular form, the weft, as it might be called, is twined once from warp to warp, which is neatly let into V-shaped borings through the frame. In this Bristol Bay type the foot rest is in rectangular weaving with double and twisted longitudinal filaments. The rest for the ball of the foot and opening for the toes is formed by neatly wrapping the rawhide thong at this point.

Bristol Bay, Alaska. Collected by Charles L. McKay.

(Cat. No. 72421, U. S. N. M.)

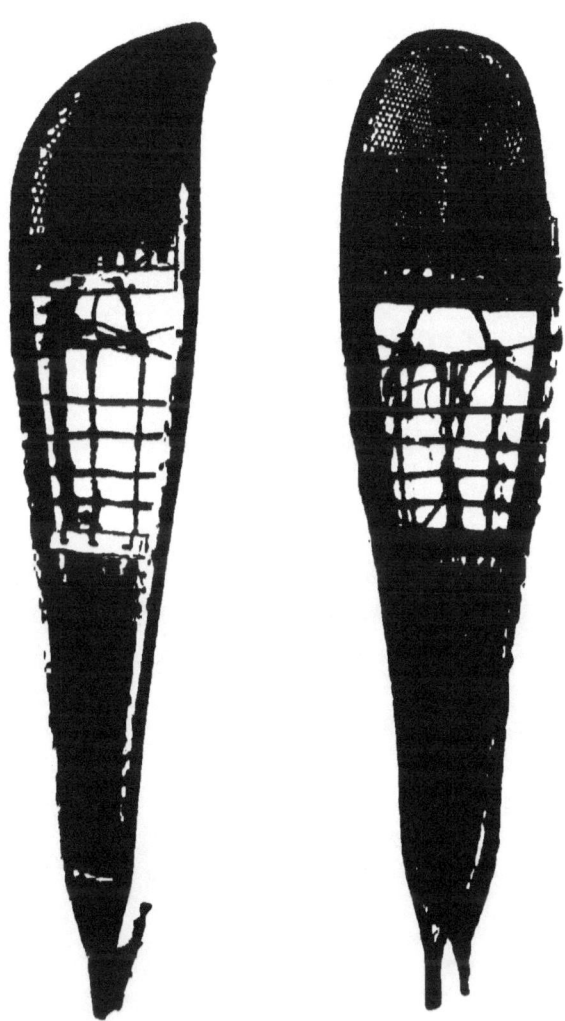

NETTED SNOWSHOES.
Bristol Bay, Alaska.

NETTED SNOWSHOES.

These specimens are leaf-shaped, suddenly tapering at the heel, and are not mates. The frames are in two pieces, spliced and neatly wrapped in front, pointed oval in section, and well turned up at the toe. This is much more the case in one specimen than in the other. They are bluntly pointed at the heel and have three crossbars. The perforations of the frame run vertically through a keel on the inner side of the front and hind space quite through at the sides of the foot space, while there are none whatever in the crosspieces, except a long slit for obvious reasons in front of the toe openings.

Netting, hexagonal, front and rear, and quadrangular in the foot space.

The leaf-shape and the abrupt heel curve should be noted.

Sitka, Alaska. Collected by J. J. McLean.

(Cat. No. 63558, U. S. N. M.)

PLATE 14.

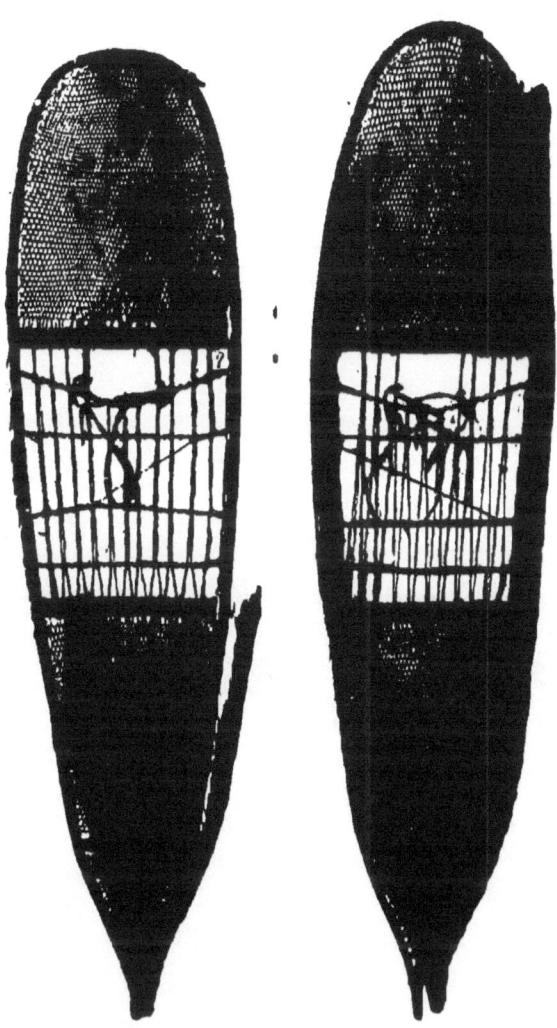

NETTED SNOWSHOES.
Sitka, Alaska.

NETTED SNOWSHOES.

These specimens are long and irregular. The frames are in two pieces, spliced and lashed together in front, pointed oval in section, and much turned up at the toe, having three crossbars and being wedge-shaped behind the third. The perforations of the frame around the front and rear spaces are vertical. There are no perforations for the foot lashing in the frames or crossbars. A slit is cut in the front crossbar before the toe space.

Netting, in hexagonal weaving, done on a thong knotted into the vertical perforations and about the long crossbars. Foot netting, in coarse hexagonal weaving wrapped about the crossbars and frame. Extra thong and wrapping form the rest for the ball of the foot and toe space.

Sitka, Alaska. Collected by J. G. Swan.

(Cat. No. 20783, U. S. N. M.)

NOTE.—Snowshoes are not worn in Sitka. Specimens brought there are from the Chilkat country and the head waters of the Yukon.

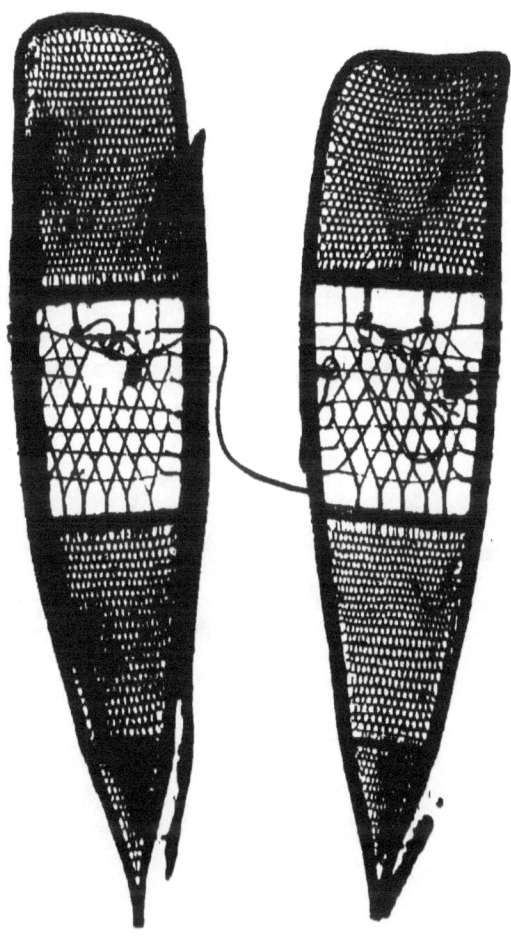

NETTED SNOWSHOES.
Sitka, Alaska.

NETTED SNOWSHOES.

The frames are of two pieces of wood squared and tapered, spliced and lashed together in front, nearly sharp and much turned up at the toe, pointed at the heel with short trailers. There are four crossbars, three of which are in front. The perforations of the frame are V-shaped in front and rear. and wanting about the foot space, excepting three in the crossbar in front of the foot lacing.

The netting in all the spaces is hexagonal, and of different fineness. In the front and rear spaces, by omitting cross threads and twining the diagonals, a beautiful lace-work effect is produced. The lacing of the foot rest is about the framework, excepting the two front cross lines under the ball of the foot. Those are rove through the frame, doubled and twisted. The decorations are tufts of red yarn gathered into the knots of the thong into which the network is done. The device to prevent the toe of the moccasin from wearing the loops of the front netting is noteworthy.

Fort Simpson, Mackenzie River District. Collected by B. R. Ross.

(Cat. No. 5047, U. S. N. M.)

PLATE 16.

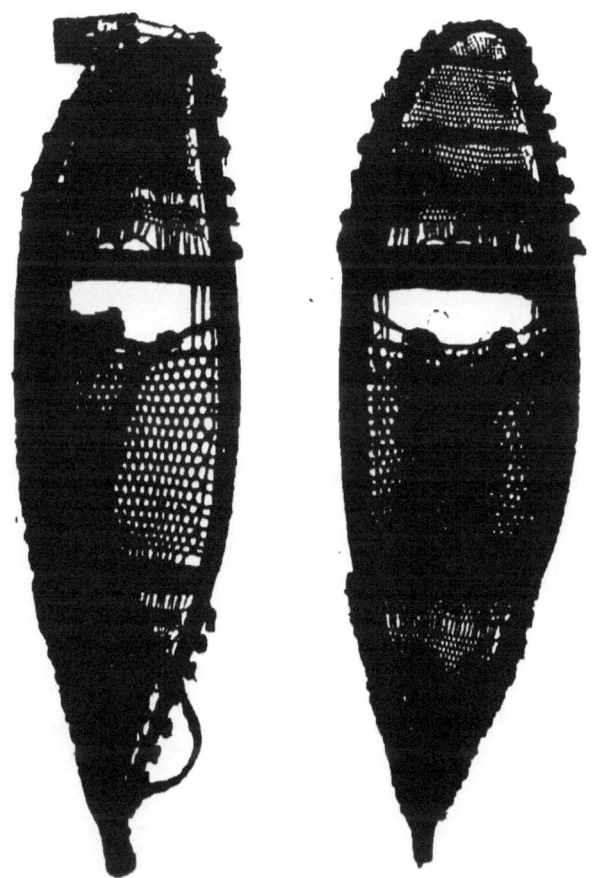

NETTED SNOWSHOES.
Hudson Bay Company's pattern. Fort Simpson, Mackenzie River District, Canada.

netting of raw hide rove through the frame. Painted and ornamented with beads. Rights and lefts. Length, 49 inches; width, 11¾.

A second pair, collected by McLean from the Chilkat, has the netting of sinew twine instead of babiche (No. 72462).

Example No. 20783 (pl. 15) is also Chilkat, collected in Sitka by James G. Swan, the lacing being of sinew twine. Paymaster Webster collected here a specimen, No. 127614, of the three-brace type, the netting of babiche. The Emmons collection in the Museum of Natural History, New York, contains an excellent example of the Chilkat transitional type of snowshoes. The frame is in two pieces, Athapascan in type, much curved up at the toe, and even incurved or emarginate at the extreme front. The toe and the heel netting are of babiche, and not of sinew thread. The foot netting is of coarse rawhide thong, but is woven with hexagonal mesh. Underneath the inner margin of each shoe the black tip of a goat horn is lashed so as to incline backward and catch in the snow. It is in this respect unique.

Example No. 20783 is a pair of snowshoes procured in Sitka by J. G. Swan. They are of great interest in this connection. The frame and crossbars conform to the customary plan of the Kutchin snowshoe. At the heel the crossbar marks, as in other examples, a sudden change in the curve. The toe is properly turned up. But in one particular the shoe is typical. The network is not of coarse rawhide laid in quadrangular meshes, but is coarsely woven in the hexagonal mesh. The specimen is in fact a transition between the Eskimo foot netting and the refined hexagonal netting of the interior, which grows more and more delicate and symmetrical as the Siouan, Chippewa, and Iroquoian areas across the boundary between Canada and the United States are reached where steel knives are in vogue.

Example No. 1974 is a pair of snowshoes from the Chippewayan Indians, Mackenzie River, collected by B. R. Ross, used as far as the Arctic Coast. The frames are squared in section, in two pieces, pointed at both ends, sharply curved up in front. Netting of babiche, close and fine, the foot netting being wrapped about the frame and coarser than the rest. The frames are painted and ornamented with tufts of worsted on the outside. Length, 33½ inches; width, 7½ inches. Mr. Ross also collected examples Nos. 2046 and 5647 (pl. 16), model of Chippewayan shoe used as far north as the Arctic Coast by the Hudson Bay Company's voyageurs.

Robert Kennicott collected among the Yellow Knife Indians at Fort Resolution, Canada, a pair of the pointed models just described, example No. 2045, and examples Nos. 860, 861, and 5646 at Fort Good Hope. Of these he says that those of smaller size are for walking behind dog sledges. He also says that the voyageurs sometimes use the round-toed shoe, but that they prefer the pointed kind.

In the Catlin collection, example No. 73310 National Museum, is another example of this type. The foot lacing wrapped about the frame is protected by an additional seizing of cloth. The shoes are fastened to the feet by a soft strip of deerskin instead of the hard thong.

Mackenzie says of the Chippewayan that their snowshoes are of superior workmanship. The inner part of the frame is straight, the outer one is curved, pointed at both ends, and turned up in front. They are also laced with great neatness with thongs made of deerskin.[1] Especially noteworthy in this connection is the squared frame, lenticular outline pointed at both ends, the number of crossbars in front, the close netting in the foot space, and the soft band of the foot straps.

An old, worm-eaten specimen in the National Museum from the Catlin collection exhibits the ingenious manner in which the frames are bored for the cord or line to sustain the toe and heel netting. It will be remembered that in the Athapascan type the holes are usually vertical through a keel or molding on the inside of the frame. But in the Voyageur specimens, which are an Algonquian intrusion into an Athapascan area, two small holes are made in the frame, at the middle of the inner face, near together, and so inclined as to meet about the middle of the wood on the outer face. One of the holes continues on through to enable the workman to push the thread through and back, coming out at a hole other than the one in which it entered. The thread is then pulled tight and tied in a single knot. This laborious process is repeated at intervals of an inch on the frames for the foot and heel netting. The holes in the crossbars are bored down straight through.

The sort of weaving practiced on all the Athapascan and Algonquian snowshoes is paralleled in the cedar bark weaving of the north Pacific Coast and in Japan. The filaments pass in three directions, crossing each other at an angle of 60 degrees and leaving hexagonal interstices. But in the old example now considered, features of textile work are introduced that are seen in the net work of the Yuma tribes of southern California, and thence southward, also in grass work from the Aleuts, and occasionally in bark work from the Pacific Coast. The regular three direction or hexagonal weaving is interrupted here and there by the omission of a cross filament. In such case the two diagonal filaments make a half turn, a whole turn, a turn and a half, and so on about each other, leaving elongated hexagons flanked by twine. By an alteration in the spacing along the crossbar, rows of wider spacing are carried diagonally across the netting.[2]

The Cree snowshoe is flat, squared off in front, sharp behind, has two broad crossbars, and is finely netted in the three spaces.

The Chippewayan snowshoes are of superior workmanship, and are rights and lefts, pointed at both ends, turned up in front, and laced with thongs of deerskin.

Example No. 1975 is a pair of snowshoe models. Frames rounded

---

[1] Mackenzie, "Voyages from Montreal through the Continent of North America," Philadelphia, 1802, p. cxx.

[2] Compare figures of carrying baskets from Japan and figure 92.

in cross section, toe rounded and slightly curved up; long, broadened heel, terminating in short, sharp point. Toe and heel netting of babiche, or fine line cut from deer hide. Foot netting of rawhide thong, painted red by rubbing with earth and ornamented with beads. Length, 21 inches; width, 4⅜; collected on the Yukon River from the Koyukon Indians (Athapascan) by B. R. Ross and W. L. Hardisty. Example No. 5569 from the Koyukon, collected by W. H. Dall, differs little from the above.

Examples Nos. 7470 and 7471 are snowshoe models from the Kutchin Indians, Fort Anderson, northern Canada, collected by R. MacFarlane. Frame rounded in cross section; toe round pointed, sharply curved up; broad heel, terminating in sharp, short point. Netting of babiche, close and fine, rove through frame. Foot net of babiche, but coarser and more open. The frames are painted and the netting is ornamented with beadwork in blue, red, and black. Length, 33 inches; width, 9. Especial attention is asked to the fact that east of the Yukon drainage the foot netting changes and becomes like that of the toe and the heel space, while those already described have the foot netting like the Eskimo and Aino types.

Example No. 1330 is a pair of snowshoe models from the Kutchin Indians, on the Yukon River, collected by Robert Kennicott. The frame is rounded in cross section. Toe rounded and slightly curved up; heel abruptly tapered from a short crossbar. Toe and heel netting of babiche, close and fine. Painted and ornamented with line of blue and red beads in middle of toe and heel netting. Length, 29½ inches; width, 5½. Another example, No. 896, from Peels River, collected by R. Kennicott and C. P. Gaudet, possesses the same characters.

Example No. 877 is a pair of snowshoes from La Pierre House, Rocky Mountains. Frames rounded in section; toes round and strongly turned up; heel terminating abruptly from short crossbar. Toe and heel netting of babiche, closely woven; foot netting of rawhide rove through frame and about the crossbars; they are rights and lefts; collected by Robert Kennicott. They are worn by the Louchenx Indians, of Canada. None of these people use the voyageur pointed shoe. According to Kennicott the small amount of underbrush in the woods renders the pointed shoe unnecessary. The type of snowshoes is essentially Athapascan. They are found in Alaska, inland all around the coast, but they are essentially Indian, though found with Chilkats or with Eskimo on the Yukon or at Point Barrow. The framework is not of driftwood, but of alder, birch, or willow, cut green and seasoned into shape. Each frame is in two parts, rounded and spliced at the toe, pointed at the heel and held into form by flat oval crossbars let into the sides. The number of bars varies, and it is quite common to notice a short bar near the heel let into a gash or "saw cut," at which point the frames are abruptly bent toward each other. The amount of upcurve at the toe varies greatly. In some localities the shoe is nearly flat, in others the toe stands up more than 6 inches. The cross section is well noted by Murdoch, being an elongated ellipse standing vertically, with the middle of the inner side angular or keeled to admit of the vertical perforations through which is rove and knotted the line or thread on which the netting is built up. Of the netting of these shoes the toe and heel fabric is similar in all. The foot webbing is partly Eskimo or Asiatic, and partly of Southern type. The reason is plain. The thinner the shoe sole, the finer the webbing must be. The moccasin is the occasion of the finer and finer web of the South under the foot. The material in some examples is of sinew thread or twine, in others of babiche or finely cut deerskin dressed. In those areas where the deerskin is not depilated the sinew thread is used.

Snowshoes in the Barren Ground country of Canada are made of birch wood and babiche. The former is cut wherever and whenever opportunity offers, the trapper never losing a good specimen. The wood is worked into shape at leisure. The babiche is cut by the women, who spend their leisure thereat, very much as our women do at knitting.

C. W. Whitney, in Harper's Magazine, figures a pair of snowshoes from the Saskatchewan,[1] which are a compromise at the toe between the Athapascan round toe and the Hudson Bay sharp toe.

The carriers on Stuart Lake, British Columbia, are Athapascans, and are said by Father Morice to have four styles of snowshoes (aih) under different names.

(1) Khé la pas (moccasin end rounded). Frame in one piece, pointed oval, long with trailer, similar to the Algonquian and Iroquoian shoes about Quebec and Montreal; the frame of Douglas pine (*P. murrayana*), mountain maple (*Acer glabrum*), or mountain ash (*Pyrus americana*). Cross sticks of willow or birch, fine lacing of caribou babiche, foot lacing of moose-hide thong.

(2) Let'lu (stitched together). This is the voyageur and the typical Sioux snowshoe. Frame in two pieces, turned up in front, pointed at both ends, additional crosspieces used, and a line from the toe to the long crossbar. The frame is bent by wrapping strips of willow bark around it and heating, by cooking it in boiling water, or by pouring boiling water on it.

(3) Aih za (snowshoe only). Frame of two pieces, spliced, rounded and turned up in front; crossbars, two. In fact, it is the typical Athapascan shoe of the North, more commonly used than the others.

(4) Seskhe (black bear foot). Frame of a single hoop spliced at the heel, elliptical, crossbar inserted into a hole through either side. In this shoe the elements of weaving are reproduced with coarse thong in a clumsy manner.[2]

Father Morice asserts that the double-pointed snowshoe was little known among the Tacullies, or Carriers, until thirty or forty years ago.

[1] New York, 1895, xcii, pp. 10, 364.
[2] Morice, Trans. Canadian Inst., 1894, iv, pp. 152-155, figs. 141-145.

but they were worn by the Tsĕ′kĕh ne from time immemorial. He also says that before Mackenzie (1793) snowshoes were unknown in the western Déné country, except among the Sekanais and Nah′anes.[1]

From Point Barrow around to Bristol Bay, as has been seen, the Eskimo wears Indian snowshoes. The same is true of the Eastern Eskimo, as will be seen in the Turner collection.

Of the Cumberland Gulf Eskimo, Kumlien says that in traveling over the frozen wastes in winter they use snowshoes. These are half-moon shaped, by which is meant that they are asymmetrical, or rights and lefts, and made of whalebone; that is, the bones of the whale, not baleen, with seal-thongs drawn tightly across. They are 16 inches long.

Another pattern is merely a frame of wood, about the same length and 8 or 10 inches wide, with sealskin thongs for the feet to rest on.[2] This form associates itself with the rude types about Bering Strait.

Turner describes five varieties of snowshoes about Ungava, but reduces the forms to four: (1) Swallow tail, with tail or trailer; (2) beaver tail, kite shaped, with nipple-like projection behind; (3) round end kite shaped, without trailer; (4) single bar, frame oval, crossbar in front. The single bar specimens have also round end. Of these there are two varieties, that in which the crossbar comes in the middle of the foot and that in which it is in front of the toes (fig. 84).

In addition to these there comes from Little Whale River a snow-

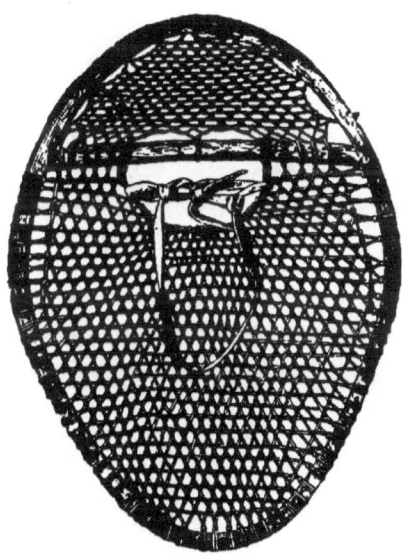

Fig. 84.

NETTED SNOWSHOE, SINGLE BAR, WORN BY THE NENENOT INDIANS, LABRADOR.

From a figure in the Eleventh Annual Report of the Bureau of Ethnology.
Cat. No. 90023, U. S. N. M.

shoe of spruce wood, No. 90145, U. S. National Museum (fig. 85). It is shaped like the single bar or round end pattern and looks as though it might have been cut out of a toboggan or flat sledge, common in all Canada. Two pieces of thin board are fitted together along their margins and sewed together with thong. Across them near the front and the rear a batten is sewed by a continuation of buttonhole stitches or half hitches. Just behind the front batten is the hole for giving free action and grip to the toes. In use the shoe is turned smooth side down and battens up. Turner says that this variety is used on soft

[1] Proc. Canadian Inst. (Series 3), VII, p. 131.
[2] Bull. U. S. Nat. Mus., No. 15, 1879, p. 42.

snow. In the spring the netted shoe becomes clogged. These may be
made in a few hours, while the netted shoe requires several days of
arduous labor.[1]

The reader must look in the hyperborean region of the Old World
for the skee or snowshoe made of boards.

Example No. 90151 is a pair of snowshoes from Ungava, Canada,
collected by Lucien M. Turner (fig. 86). In the specimen here studied,
two staves of pine, whittled into rectangular cross section, were spliced
in front and bent into a kite shape, with somewhat square body and
three rounded corners. At the fourth or hinder corner or heel the ends,

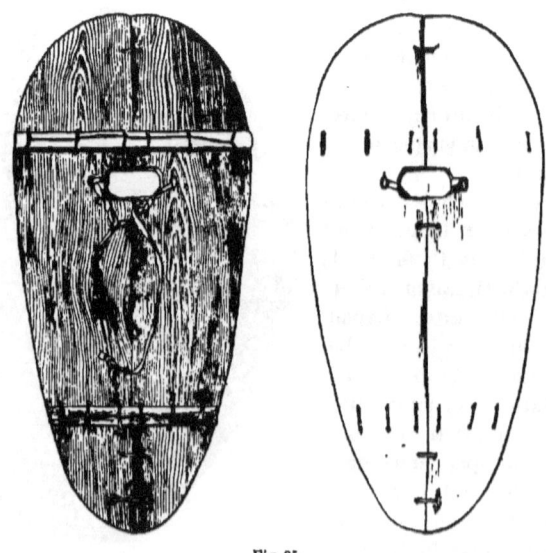

Fig. 85.

WOODEN SNOWSHOE WORN BY THE INDIANS OF LITTLE WHALE RIVER, LABRADOR.

From a figure in the Eleventh Annual Report of the Bureau of Ethnology.

Collected by L. M. Turner.

instead of being spliced, are pushed outward to form a tail, or trailer,
and sewed together through countersunk holes. This framework is
not of uniform thickness, but is thickest at the sides, somewhat smaller
at the toe, and much thinner at the trailer. There are two crossbars
mortised or let into the frame, flat oval in section and curved outward
from the foot slightly. This specimen, like all others in Mr. Turner's
collection, lies flat on the ground.[2]

---

[1] Eleventh Ann. Rep. Bureau of Ethnology, p. 312.

[2] For the detail, cf. Murdoch, Ninth Ann. Rep. Bureau of Ethnology.

The babiche netting of toe and heel is attached by regular hexagonal weaving to a border cord which is rove through the frame and obscured in countersunk cavities on the outside. Along the crossbars the toe and foot netting are laced into a border cord laid under the loops of the foot netting, excepting in front of the foot space where the border cord is rove through the crossbar. The netting of the foot space is woven hexagonally out of coarser babiche. Especially noteworthy is the tough band of hide forming the front border of this network, passing straight from either side of the frame to the foot space, where it is curved backward and held in form by stout bracings of hide. Under the toes it is sewed with babiche. On the right and left margins the network does not pass entirely outward to a border cord rove through the frame, but the bends make double loops about the frame at each excursion and are gathered into a straight selvage. This central web is also looped to the crossbars. The shoe is attached to the foot by a soft band of buckskin forming toe and heel loop.[1]

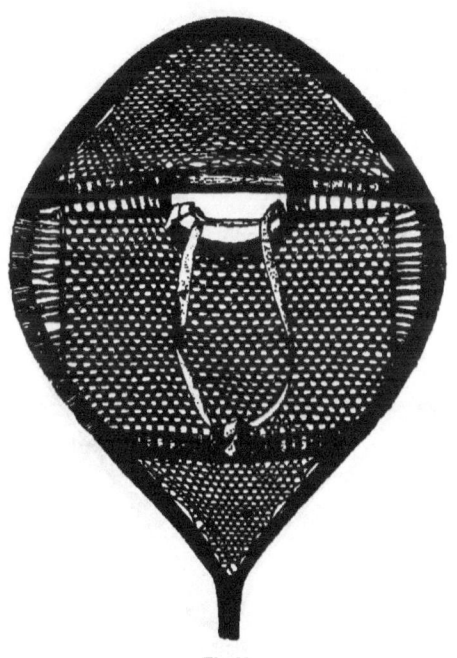

Fig. 86.

NETTED SNOWSHOE, SWALLOW TAIL PATTERN, WORN BY THE NENENOT INDIANS, LABRADOR.

From a figure in the Eleventh Annual Report of the Bureau of Ethnology.
Cat. No. 90151, U. S. N. M. Collected by L. M. Turner.

Example No. 90149 (fig. 87) is a pair of snowshoes collected in Ungava, north of Labrador, by Lucien Turner. In most particulars this specimen resembles that last described, excepting that the width is still more disproportionate to the length and near the heel the frame on either side bends outward and then sharply inward, forming a tongue-shaped end, and quite aptly called a beaver tail. Many of the long, slender Athapascan shoes reverse the process and near the heel begin suddenly to narrow. In this example the shoe is made of two pieces of wood in form of a loop or oxbow spliced together on the sides of the foot space, the hinder bow laid inside the forward bow precisely as in the Aino specimen. The spliced portions are held in position by the loops of the

[1] Turner, Eleventh Ann. Rep. Bureau of Ethnology, pl. xi.

foot netting passing around them. Examples Nos. 90145 to 90153, collected by Turner, are also of the same general form and finish. One of these is shown in fig. 88. They are from Ungava, and were used, as were the others just described, by the Nenenot. In these examples the frames are made in one piece, spliced at the side of the foot space and held fast by the loops of the netting which encircle it.

In all of the specimens gathered by Lucien M. Turner the mechanical work is excellent. The babiche is very white and clean and uniform in each space. The attractiveness is in the uniformity. No. 90022 (fig. 89) is called by its collector a single-bar snowshoe. The frame is of

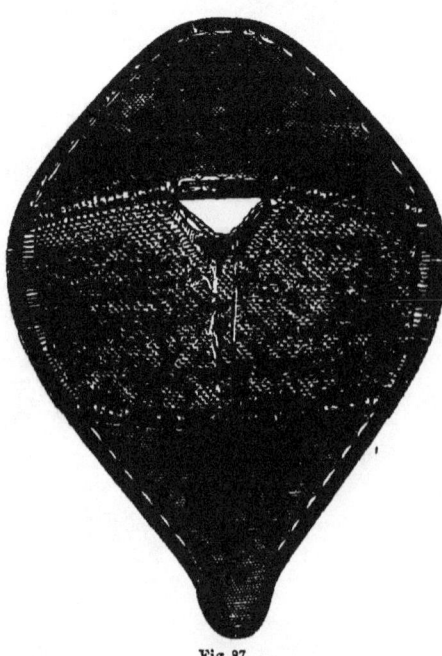

Fig. 87.

NETTED SNOWSHOE, BEAVER TAIL PATTERN, WORN BY THE NENE-
NOT INDIANS, LABRADOR.

From a figure in the Eleventh Annual Report of the Bureau of Ethnology.
Cat. No. 90149, U. S. N. M.

a single piece of wood. For these birch is preferred, but spruce and larch are generally used. The framework is rectangular in cross section, with rounded corners. The crossbar is a wide piece of wood mortised at its ends into the framework and rounded up along its middle. Four eyelets are worked in the texture for the lacing. The arch of the foot of the walker rests on the bar. This is a novel idea in American snowshoes.

Example No. 90023, as in fig. 84, is another type of Nenenot single-bar snowshoe collected by Mr. Turner. The framework is of two pieces spliced at the front and rear. The crossbar is mortised into the frame near enough toward the front to allow the foot to rest on the network in the middle of the shoe. It will be noticed by the drawing that the lacing of deerhide thong is rove through the frame in front and looped around the frame in the rear portion, which is both foot space and heel space. The Eskimo name for the round shoe is ablakatautik.

The Montagnais of Labrador wear clothing of tawed deerskin. As nearly all the skins of the reindeer are used for garments, the northern stations about Fort Chimo furnish great numbers of these skins in the

1

2

NETTED SNOWSHOES.

Fig. 1. MODERN ELLIPTICAL FORM USED BY HUNTERS IN THE ADIRONDACKS.
Broad, short type. The frame is of one piece of squared and tapered
wood, bent. It is spliced and lashed with rawhide at the heel, perfectly
flat, slightly oval, and has two broad crossbars let into the frame. There
are no perforations in the frame, but eight holes are bored through the
front crossbar for the twisted thongs that support the footing. The foot
space occupies nearly all the interior, the front and the rear space being
insignificant.

The netting is of tough rawhide in hexagonal weaving, the thong
being fastened at each round by a loose knot or double half hitch
around the frame, crossbar, or footing. The thong is rove through
the front crosspiece, and twined between it and the footing. The shoe
is fastened on with buckled bands and straps. Collection of Maj.
Charles Bendire, U. S. A.

(Cat. No. 126830, U. S. N. M.)

Fig. 2. NETTED SNOWSHOE OF ALGONQUIAN INDIANS OF NORTHERN LABRADOR
AND UNGAVA: Broad, oval type. The frame is of one piece of squared
and tapered wood, bent, spliced, and lashed together at the side, perfectly flat, oval or kite shaped, having two stout, curved crossbars let
into the frame. The curves are set to take the strain of the foot netting.
There are V-shaped perforations in the frame around the front and rear
spaces, and three holes are bored through the front crosspiece over
against the footing.

The lacing is of very fine babiche or deerskin thong, woven in hexagonal pattern over a selvage thong, knotted into the V-shaped holes
continuously about the frame, and caught under the foot-space loops
along the crosspieces. The netting of the central space is caught around
the frame and crossbars by double half hitches, as in the foregoing specimen, but also neatly looped about the footing thong. This example is
fastened to the foot by a soft buckskin thong. Collected by Lucien
M. Turner.

(Cat. No. 90147, U. S. N. M.)

PLATE 17.

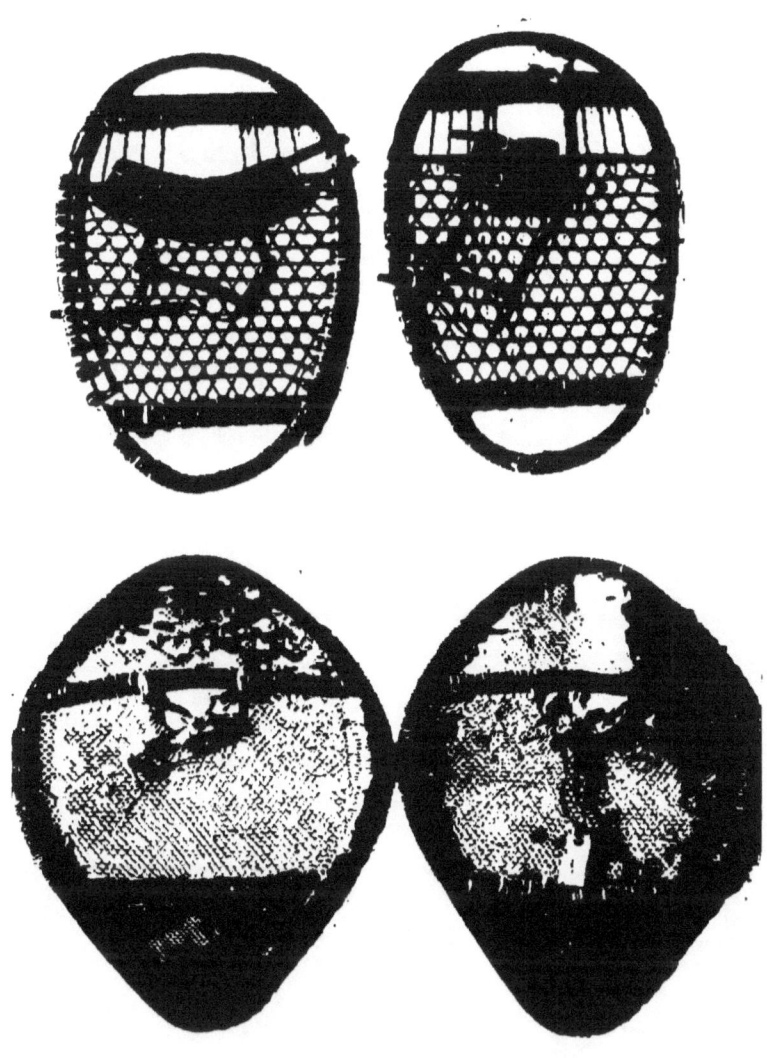

NETTED SNOWSHOES.

parchment condition to be purchased by the mountaineers, who cut them into fine lines for snowshoe netting and other purposes.[1]

Mr. Henry G. Bryant, of the University of Pennsylvania, brought from the interior of Labrador a pair of Montagnais snowshoes almost circular, conforming to the pattern of those figured by Turner. There are two strong braces and a short trailer.

In this same connection should be introduced a modern snowshoe, example No. 126839 (pl. 17, figs. 1 and 2), collected in the Adirondacks by Major C. E. Bendire, U. S. A. The frame is of hard wood, probably oak, bent into oval form, a little wider in front, and spliced at the heel by a series of half hitches.

It lies flat on the ground, as in the Nenenot examples from Ungava. The crossbars are very near the toe and the heel, and there is no attempt at netting. The netting of the foot space is of the best rawhide laid on by hexagonal weaving, as in all the other specimens from Canada. The netting is not worked about the space for the toes, but the stout thong of the foot-rest passes straight across and is sustained by continuing the diagonal filaments of the network and reeving them through the crossbar. At the heel they form double loops about the crossbar, and at the side the fastening is by half hitches. The foot is held in place by a leather band with buckles, an adjustable strap passing around the heel.

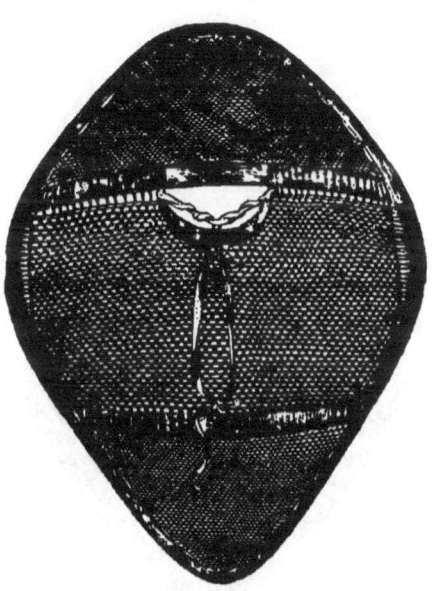

Fig. 88.

NETTED SNOWSHOE, ROUND END, WORN BY THE NENENOT INDIANS, LABRADOR.

From a figure in the Eleventh Annual Report of the Bureau of Ethnology. Cat. No. 90147, U. S. N. M.

The principle of attachment is the same everywhere.

According to Lewis H. Morgan, the Iroquois wore a wide snowshoe, as will appear in the following description:

The snowshoe, ga-weh-ga, is nearly 3 feet in length by about 16 inches in width. A rim of hickory, bent round with an arching front, and brought to a point at the heel, constituted the frame, with the addition of crosspieces to determine its spread. Within the area, with the exception of an opening for the toe, was woven a network of deerskin strings, with interstices about an inch square. The ball of the

[1] Turner, Eleventh Ann. Rep. Bureau of Ethnology, p. 181.

foot was lashed at the edge of this opening with thongs which passed
also around the heel for the support of the foot. The heel was left free to
work up and down, and the opening was designed to allow the toes of the
foot to descend below the surface of the shoe, as the heel is raised in
the act of walking. It is a very simple invention, but exactly adapted
for its uses. A person familiar with the snowshoe can walk as rapidly
with it on the snow as without it upon the ground. The Senecas affirm
that they can walk 50 miles per day upon snowshoes, and with much
greater rapidity than without them, in consequence of the length and
uniformity of the step. In the bear hunt, especially, it is of the greatest
service, as the hunter can
speedily overtake the bear,
who, breaking through the
crust, is enabled to move but
slowly.[1]

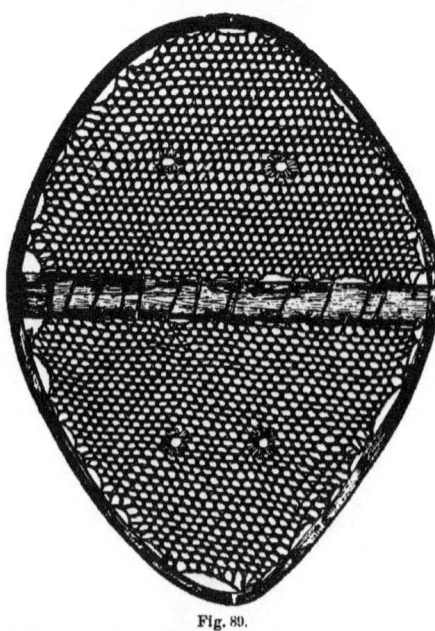

Fig. 80.

NETTED SNOWSHOE WITH CENTRAL BAR, WORN BY THE NENE-
NOT INDIANS, LABRADOR.

From a figure in the Eleventh Annual Report of the Bureau of Ethnology
Cat. No. 90022, U. S. N. M.

Examples Nos. 24788 (pl.
18) and 24789 are modern
snowshoes used by hunters
and trappers of St. Law-
rence Valley and manufac-
tured by Renfrew & Co., of
Quebec. The frame is made
of a single stave of hickory,
rectangular in cross section.
The two braces are of beech
or oak. In form the shoe is
elongated, kite-shaped, with
a trailer 9 inches long. It
is broad across the middle,
bluntly rounded at the toe,
and slightly curved up. The
netting is said to be of the
stripped and untwisted
sinew of the Caribou (*Ran-
gifer tarandus*). The foot
netting is looped about the
frame at the sides and passes about the braces by single turns. At
the distance of an inch or more from the framework there is a selvage
where the weaving commences, and outside of this the filaments are
twined and act as a series of slings. The same is true of the toe and
heel netting. There is first a border cord rove through a series of
double holes in the frame, countersunk on the outside, but not so well
concealed as in the old voyageur specimen. This border cord passes
along the outer margin of the crossbars, between the wood and the
loops of the foot netting. Indeed, both sets of network hang on this

---

[1] Lewis H. Morgan, "League of the Iroquois," 1851, pp. 376–377.

MODERN CLUB SNOWSHOES FROM MONTREAL.

The frame is of one piece of squared and tapered wood, bent at the toe, and united at the heel by a thong rove through two perforations, quite flat, abruptly rounded at the toe, with two crossbars let into the frame. The perforations in the frame are V-shaped, but in the front crossbar three holes are bored for the netting thong or selvage.

The netting is of fine rawhide thong, woven hexagonally about the knotted thong or about the framework. The netting does not in any one of the spaces reach the woodwork, but at the end of each excursion the filament is twisted a definite number of times. The edge of the woven space is afterwards whipped around with a separate thong. This makes a neat and pretty ornament. Gift of Renfrew and Company, manufacturers.

(Cat. No. 21788, U. S. N. M.)

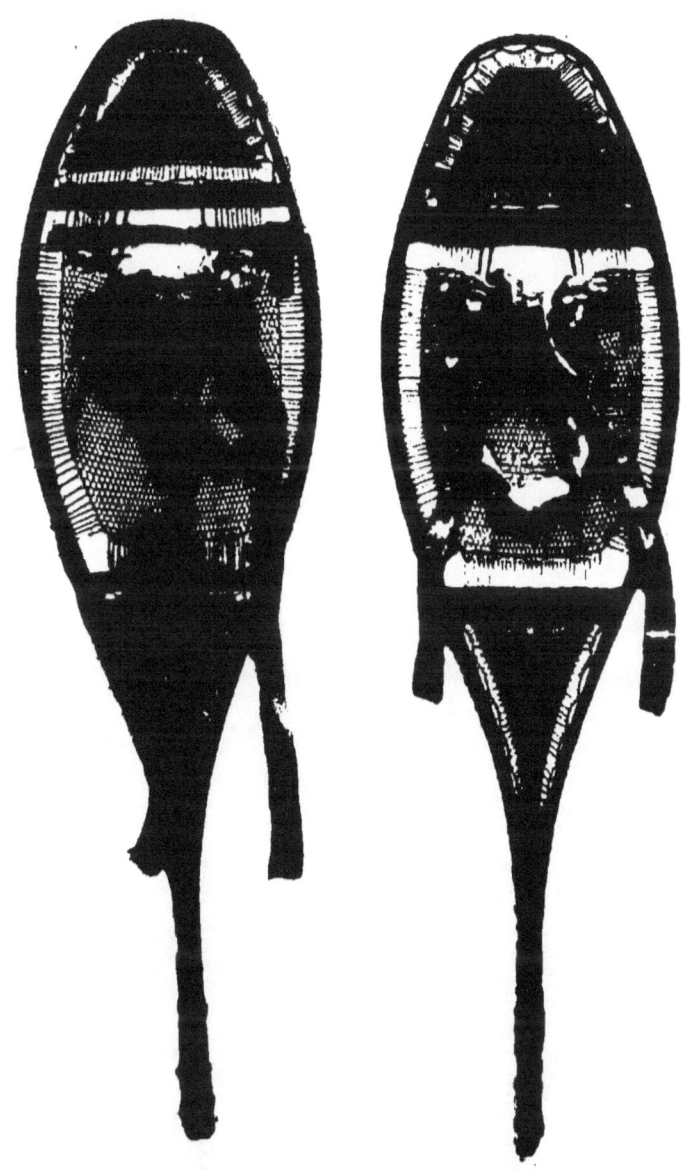

MODERN CLUB SNOWSHOES.
Montreal, Canada.

NETTED SNOWSHOES.

This is an old pair found in the Varden collection, United States Patent Office. The frame is of one piece of squared and tapered wood, bent, and joined at the heel, forming a short trailer. It is quite flat, and is provided with two crosspieces let into the frame. The perforations in the frame for the selvage thong of the netting, are V-shaped, and, as in all the other examples, they meet a little way within the outer side of the frame, so that the bend in the thong is countersunk or concealed. There are no holes at all about the central space, hence this was a very strong shoe.

The netting is all of buckskin thong, thicker in the foot space. The weaving is done immediately through the selvage thong about the frames, but it is twisted and looped around an additional thong athwart the crosspieces. On the hinder bar this added thong is caught under the double ends of the central space weaving, and furthermore is held in place by an extra winding of thong.

The netting of the central space is looped about the frame and crossbars by a curious knot, consisting of a half hitch, and a plain wrap instead of the conventional loop knot. (See plate 18, fig. 1, rear crossbar.) The cross thongs that form the footing are swung to the front crossbar by six stout thongs, doubled twice, and neatly wrapped with the same. Instead of perforations in the front crossbar, a stout thong is wrapped about the middle, to hold the front netting and prevent abrasion by the moccasin.

Canada. Collected by J. Varden.

(Cat. Nos. 1755, 1756, U. S. N. M.)

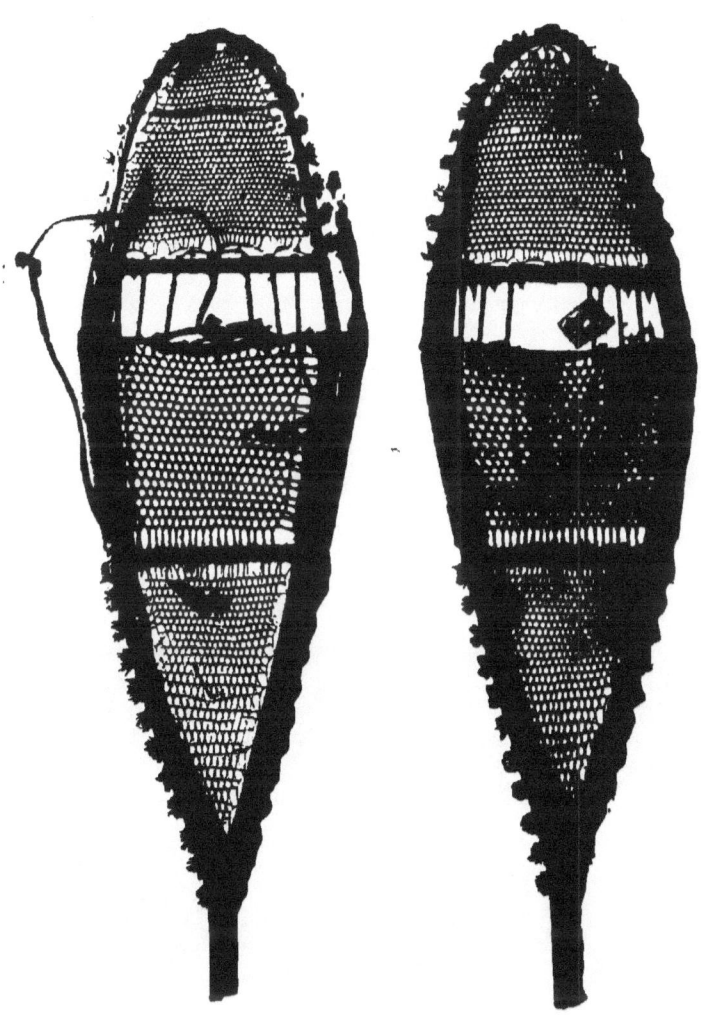

NETTED SNOWSHOES.
Canada.

cord. At the ends of the crossbars and in the middle of the front bar the cord is rove through and knotted with a single tie.

The footband is a broad strap of soft buckskin, under which the toe of the moccasin passes. The ends of this band pass through eyelets worked in the netting and then are laced about the heel and ankle. These eyelets appear on one of Turner's single-bar snowshoes from Ungava. Length, 42 inches; width, 12½ inches. Other examples of this type in the National Museum are Nos. 1755 and 1756 in the collection of the National Institute, and No. 18826 from the St. Regis Iroquois Reservation, New York (pl. 19).

The Cree Indians around Winnipeg, on the authority of Dr. E. R. Young, have two or three pairs of snowshoes each. They are of the turned-up and pointed variety, formed of two pieces. One pair is made just the height of the man. These are for long journeys after deer, etc. The hunter will carry in his hand a long pole, to the end of which is lashed his hunting knife, and when he runs down the game he soon dispatches it with his extemporized lance. Another pair of snowshoes is used for home hunting, and the third pair around his home. The women do not wear a different shoe from the men. The shoes are rights and lefts.

Example No. 73308 in the National Museum, in the Catlin collection, is of the same type.

Two of the oldest and most interesting specimens of snowshoes in the National Museum from the Algonquian are Nos. 1755 and 1756, above-mentioned. The frame is rectangular in the cross sections, and consists of a single piece, smallest at the toe, widening and thickening toward the foot rest, and tapering again toward the trail. There are three crossbars, one small one in front and two rounded sticks bordering the foot space. The netting of the toe and heel space is in hexagonal weaving attached all round by a series of loops rove through the frame on the sides and caught under the lashing of the foot space along the crossbars. This weaving is made of very finely cut deerskin (or babiche) woven with great care. The netting of the foot space is of coarser babiche, and passes around the crosspieces and the frame on the outside. The hexagonal weaving and the strong rawhide piece on which the ball of the foot rests are all swung from the frame by a twine an inch long on the sides, and in front 3 inches long, the front lines being also wrapped or marled with rawhide. The knots by which the foot netting is attached to the frame on the sides are called the clove hitch, and along the front foot bar the knots are fastened off with half hitches. The small line to which the front netting is attached, and also the cross line which forms the sling of the foot netting, in passing from one knot to another is fastened down with what sailors call the marline hitch. Around the border of the foot netting—in order to strengthen it—there is an additional twining or wrapping of babiche to keep the meshes in place.

Examples Nos. 19116 to 19119 are modern snowshoes made in Marquette, Mich., and given to the National Museum by T. Meads. A pair

of these is shown in pl. 20. They represent the western Canadian idea of perfection as the Renfrew examples do the eastern. The frame is rectangular, flat, squared in front and cut a little thicker in the middle of the front. They are wide in the middle, taper more abruptly than the eastern specimens and have not such long trailers. Furthermore, the babiche is finer and the netting goes snug up to the frame everywhere excepting the front and hinder margin of the foot net. The square-toed snowshoe is geographically located south of the double-pointed voyageur type and west of the flat, round front type. It is the snowshoe of the Western lakes. Examples in the Museum are Nos. 73307–73310, Catlin collection, possibly Chippewa No. 2651 from the War Department, no tribe given; and Nos. 154369–154371 collected among the Menimonee by Dr. W. J. Hoffman.

In Glen Island Museum of Natural History, New York, are exhibited Nick Stoner's snowshoes, of the double-pointed type. They are square in cross section, turned up in front, the two pieces riveted together with iron. There are two crossbars, no toe and heel netting, and the rawhide lacing is wrapped around frame and crosspieces.

Again and again it was said, when studying the Mackenzie River snowshoe, that the voyageurs and white agents of the Hudson Bay, while they walked on the round-ended shoe, preferred these sharp at the ends for tripping. In Catlin's pictures (Smithsonian Report 1883, II, pl. 99), this pointed shoe occurs with Siouan label. Indeed, this variety may be called temporarily the Siouan type (fig. 90). It is an exalted form of the Chukchi type, consisting in this case of the outer frame

Fig. 90.

NETTED SNOWSHOE, POINTED AT BOTH
ENDS, PROBABLY SIOUX.

Cat. No. 2730, U. S. N. M.　Collected by the War
Department.

of two pieces square in cross section, irregularly lenticular in outline and turned up at both ends and resembles that of the Tsekehne.

The frame is of one piece of squared and tapered wood, cut in ogee curve on the inside of the toe. It is bent almost square in front, and joined together at the heel with a short trailer; flat, somewhat short and broad, and having two crossbars set well front and back. The front and rear netting is very light, and is attached to the knotted selvage thong in the usual way. The ingenuity of the maker has exhausted itself on the long central space. The noteworthy features are:

(1) The hexagonal weaving in stout thong.

(2) The double loop knots about the frame.

(3) The single loops about the crosspieces, inclosing at the same time the selvage thong of the front and rear netting, and the long twisted ends that form these loops.

(4) The quadruple cross thong for the footing.

(5) The neat slings holding the footing to the front crossbar.

(6) The absence of holes in the wood anywhere about the middle space.

The ornamentation on the outside is formed by tufts of different-colored yarns, caught under the knots in the selvage thong where it is tied through the frame.

Grand Rapids, Mich. Gift of Mead and Company, manufacturers.

(Cat. Nos. 19116-19119, U. S. N. M.)

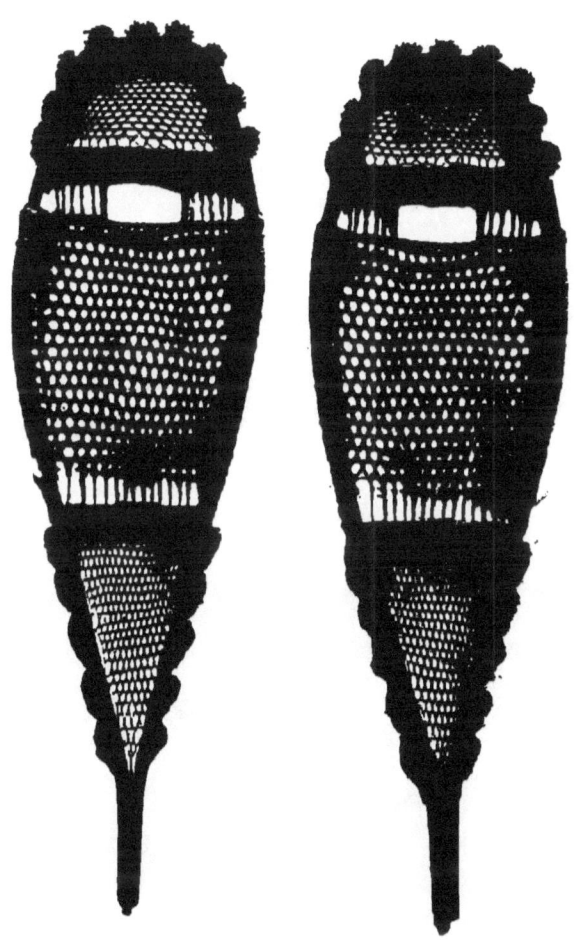

MODERN NETTED SNOWSHOES.
Grand Rapids, Michigan.

RUDE SNOWSHOES.

These are old specimens from the western territories. The frames, the breadth of which is greater than the length, are made of rough poles, skinned, spliced, and clumsily wrapped at the front. There are no crosspieces nor perforations. The entire interior is like the central space of the Alaskan ruder forms, and must be so studied. The foot rest is at the front, made by doubling and twisting the thong. It is quite possible that long handling may have disturbed the radiating thong. The twist, which is so beautifully handled in better specimens, is here in embryo. The curious loop of single turn and half hitch may be noted. Mr. Eells describes in the "American Antiquarian" (vol. x) precisely this form of snowshoe among the Salishan tribes from Puget Sound eastward. Snowshoes are also reported from the cliff-dwellings of the Mesa Verde. Collected by the War Department.

(Cat. No. 2729, U. S. N. M.)

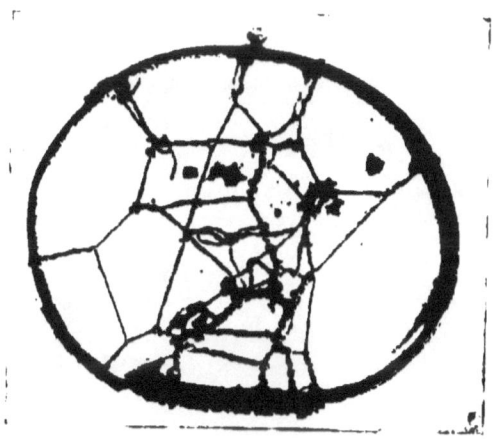

RUDE SNOWSHOES.

No example of snowshoe is in the National Museum from the Indians of Alaska, Canada, or the eastern United States that was not made with metal tools. No remains of an ancient and purely Indian type have been recovered. Therefore, with the utmost caution, the skill of the tribes long associated with French and English as trappers, should be set over against that of others whose snowshoes were ruder. The very fine babiche is the production of the curved steel knife, and the refinement of the snowshoe seems to date from its introduction.

In the western slopes of the Rocky Mountain region, and thence over the Sierras to the Pacific Ocean, will be found the most primitive types of American Indian snowshoes, and yet the Renfrew, the Turner, and the Meads examples are illuminated by these rude specimens. Example No. 2729 (pl. 21) in the National Museum is a pair of snowshoes collected among the Utes, of Utah, in 1841, by Capt. H. Stansbury, during the

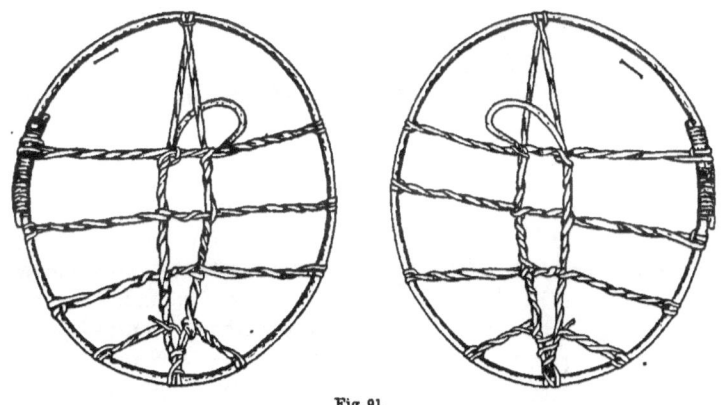

Fig. 91.

PRIMITIVE SNOWSHOE, WORN BY THE KLAMATH (LUTUAMIAN) INDIANS OF CALIFORNIA.

Cat. No. 24109, U. S. N. M.   Collected by L. S. Dyar.

Rocky Mountain exploring expedition. The frame is a bent pole, the hoop being wider than long, the ends roughly spliced and lashed with rawhide in front. There are no crossbars, but an intimation of structure in the position of the foot rest. The two elements of the perfected snowshoe, here exhibited in their nakedness, are the double loop about the frame, as in figure 82, and the twined thong acting as a set of slings for footing. The network is a series of half hitches made by the thong wherever it crosses itself. The two shoes are not even alike. Length, 16½ inches; width, 20.

Example No. 24109 (fig. 91) is a pair of snowshoes collected on the Klamath River Agency, Oreg., by L. S. Dyar, Indian agent. The framework is a hoop made of a pole and is lashed together at the side with buckskin, with very little splicing. The network is all of one piece of rawhide passed backward and forward, commencing at the lower right-hand corner and fastened to the hoop, not by a double loop, but by a half hitch and single turn and then twined about the standing part. Diameter, 14 inches.

To complete the western series is example No. 2728 (fig. 92), a very old specimen marked "West coast of America" and collected by the Wilkes Exploring Expedition. The frame is an elongated oval and irregular hoop of pole, spliced and wrapped at the heel. The two shoes are not quite alike in shape. There are no cross-bars, but three turns of the raw-hide netting are served together and answer precisely to the rest under the ball of the foot in the eastern specimens. In this speci-men may be seen a rude and primitive form of the Renfrew foot netting set in a series of slings made of twined babiche and caught around the frame with a half hitch and single-turn knot. In the irregular and ar-tistic spacing of the slings will be seen the foreshadowing of the open-work ornamental lacing on the elaborate voyageur speci-men (pl. 16), which is made in the same manner, namely, by omit-ting the filaments that pass straight across in a triangle that is longer than it is wide.

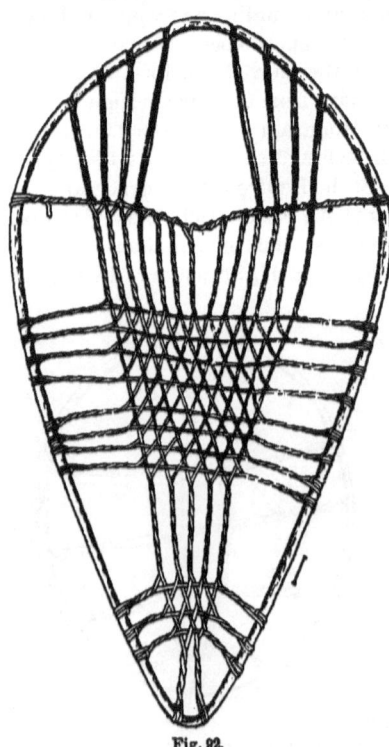

Fig. 92.

PRIMITIVE TYPE OF SNOWSHOE FROM COLUMBIA RIVER, WASHINGTON.

Cat. No, 2728, U. S, N. M.   Collected by Wilkes Exploring Expedition.

Mr. F. W. Hodge says that the Zuñi and other pueblo tribes make an overshoe of goatskin, worn over the moccasin in the snow, with the hair side out. Snowshoes are also reported in the cliff-dwellings.

SNOWSHOES IN THE U. S. NATIONAL MUSEUM.

Museum number.	Specimen.	Locality.	By whom contributed.
167801, 167892	Skees	Finland	Hon. J. M. Crawford.
169274	.....do	Minnesota	Theo. Roosevelt.
22195	Snowshoes, Ainos(p. 386)	Japan	Hon. B, S. Lyman.
22196	Snowshoes (fig. 76)	Yokohama, Japan	Do.
150043	Snowshoes (p. 386)	Yezo, Japan	Romyn Hitchcock.
63602, 63603	Snowshoes (p. 389)	Siberia	E. W. Nelson.
63004	Snowshoes (fig. 79)	Icy Cape	Do.

SNOWSHOES IN THE U. S. NATIONAL MUSEUM—Continued.

Museum number.	Specimen.	Locality.	By whom contributed.
2442	Snowshoes (fig. 78)...................	Chukchi.................	Commodore Rodgers.
2443	....do................................	....do	Do.
15605	Snowshoes (p. 389)...................	St. Lawrence Island, Alaska.	H. W. Elliott.
45732, 45733	....do................................	....do	Capt. C. L. Hooper.
63236	Snowshoes (p. 389)...................	....do	E. W. Nelson.
44265	Snowshoes, toy......................	Cape Darby, Alaska	Do.
48092	Snowshoes (fig. 80)..................	....do	Do.
45400	Snowshoes (pl. 11)..................	Norton Bay, Alaska	Do.
48103	Snowshoes (p. 390)	....do	Do.
896	Snowshoes, Kutchin Indians(p. 397)	Alaska	C. P. Gaudet.
5509	Snowshoes (pl. 12)	Yukon River, Alaska...	W. H. Dall.
49099	Snowshoes (p. 391)..................	....do	E. W. Nelson.
8812	Snowshoes, Ingalluk Eskimo(p. 391)	....do	W. H. Dall.
38873	Snowshoes (p. 391)..................	....do	Do.
90455	Snowshoes, Kenai Indians........	Cooks Inlet............	W. J. Fisher.
90456	....do................................	....do .:..............	Do.
38874	Snowshoes (p. 394)..................	Alaska.................	E. W. Nelson.
72420, 72421	Snowshoes (pl. 13).................	Bristol Bay, Alaska...	C. L. McKay.
89012–89914	Snowshoes (fig. 81).................	Point Barrow, Alaska...	Lieut. P. H. Ray.
877	Snowshoes (p. 397).................	Anderson River........	R. Kennicott.
571	Snowshoes, Kootcha, Kutchin	Northwest Canada	W. L. Hardisty.
862	Snowshoes...........................	Yukon River, Alaska...	R. Kennicott.
127941	Snowshoes (p. 391).................	Putnam River, Alaska..	Lieut. G. M. Stoney, U. S. N.
127614	Snowshoes, Tinnei Indians(p. 395).	Alaska.................	Lieut. E. B. Webster, U. S. N.
153488	....do................................	Upper Yukon, Alaska..	J. C. Russell.
153489	....do................................	....do	Do.
153651, 153652	Snowshoes...........................	Yukon River, Alaska ...	J. H. Turner.
7470	Snowshoes (p. 397).................	Fort Anderson, Canada..	R. MacFarlane.
7471	Snowshoes (p. 397).................	....do	Do.
530	Snowshoes, Chippewayan	Mackenzie River, Canada	B. R. Ross.
1974	Snowshoes (p. 395).................	....do	Do.
1975	Snowshoes (p. 396).................	....do	Do.
2046	Snowshoes (p. 395).................	....do	Do.
528	Babiche or snowshoe line..........	....do	Do.
568	Snowshoes, Slave Indians	....do	Do.
569	Snowshoes, Chippewayan Indians.	....do	Do.
2044	Babiche for snowshoes	Fort Simpson, Canada ..	Do.
5647	Snowshoes (pl. 16).................	....do	Do.
860	Snowshoes of voyagers, for walking behind dog sledge (p. 395).	Mackenzie River, Canada	R. Kennicott.
861	Snowshoes, Slave Indians (p. 395)..	....do	Do.
5646	Snowshoes, Slave Indians (p. 395)..	....do	Do.
536	Snowshoes, Yellow Knife Indians.	....do	Do.
2045	Snowshoes, Yellow Knife Indians (p. 395).	....do	Do.
1330	Snowshoes (p. 397).................	....do	C. P. Gaudet.
72462	....do................................	Chilkat, Alaska	John J. McLean.
20783	Snowshoes (pl. 15).................	Sitka, Alaska..........	J. G. Swan.
63558	Snowshoes (pl. 14).................	....do	John J. McLean.
158509	Snowshoes, Montagnais	Labrador	Henry G. Bryant.
90019, 90020	Snowshoes, small	Ungava Bay, Labrador..	L. M. Turner.

SNOWSHOES IN THE U. S. NATIONAL MUSEUM—Continued.

Museum number.	Specimen.	Locality.	By whom contributed.
90023	Snowshoes (fig. 84)	Ungava Bay, Labrador..	L. M. Turner.
90145	Snowshoes (p. 402)	....do	Do.
90146–90153	Snowshoes (figs. 86–88, pl. 17)	....do	Do.
2651	Snowshoes, Chippewa (p. 406)	Wisconsin	War Department.
154370	Snowshoes, Ojibwa	Minnesota	W. J. Hoffman.
154371	Snowshoes, girl's	....do	Do.
19116–19118	Snowshoes (pl. 20)	Marquette, Mich	T. Meads.
19119	Snowshoes, small model (p. 406)	....do	Do.
154369	Snowshoes (p. 406.)	Menominee, Wis	W. J. Hoffman.
126839	Snowshoes, hunter's (p. 403)	Adirondacks	Maj. C. E. Bendire, U. S. A.
24788, 24789	Snowshoes (pl. 18)	British North America..	G. R. Renfrew & Co.
1755	Snowshoes (pl. 19)	Eastern part of British North America.	J. Varden.
1756	Snowshoes (p. 405)	....do	Do.
2730	Snowshoes, Sioux Indians (fig. 90).		War Department.
73307–73310	Snowshoes, Catlin collection (p. 406)		
2728	Snowshoes, Indians of the North-west Coast of America (fig. 92).		Captain Wilkes, U. S. N.
24109	Snowshoes, circular (fig. 91)	Klamath	L. S. Dyar.
2729	Snowshoes, Coast Indians (pl. 20)..	Columbia River	Lieut. Wilkes, U. S. N.
165588	Snowshoes	Klamath, Cal	A. S. Gatschet.

ICE CREEPERS.

The ice creeper is a device of some kind worn under the boot in winter to enable the traveler to walk over smooth ice or snow crust without slipping. The snowshoe prevents the traveler from sinking in the snow and at the same time in many places, especially in America and northeastern Asia, affords a ratchet to prevent the foot from slipping backward. The creeper, however, does not prevent the foot from sinking in the snow, but simply acts as a ratchet or stop to prevent its slipping in any direction. This result is achieved in different ways by different peoples. The Russians, the Chinese, and the Mongols attach sharp-headed nails, sometimes of immense size, to the bottoms of their boots. The eastern Eskimo quilt the bottom of the shoe, leaving loops of rawhide projecting underneath which serve the purpose, but the ice creeper (par excellence) is a device fastened under the shoe and not a part of it, provided with sharp points beneath, which keep the foot from slipping.

There is a small area of distribution for this type of objects, as exhibited by the collection in the U. S. National Museum, partly in northeastern Asia and partly in northwestern America. It is a question, not yet settled, whether both sets of peoples owe the existence of this invention to the presence of the Russians in that quarter.

In America ice creepers precisely like those of the Eskimo, Chukchi, and Kamchadales, made, however, of leather and iron, are worn extensively in winter throughout the Northern States.

The U. S. National Museum does not possess any specimens from Russia, but doubtless such things are used there abundantly.

The Roman soldier at times wore under the bottom of his caliga or sandal sharp spikes, like harrow teeth, so that if literally men were not mangled under harrows, it was just as painful to be tramped to death thus. Greig reproduces one of these sandals from Balduinus de Calceo Antiquo, etc.[1]

Example No. 55850 is a mandarin's boot from north China to be worn in icy weather. The legs and uppers are of soft, black leather lined with blue cotton. The front seam extends from the sole in front to the top of the leg. The back seam, as in our boots, reaches from the sole to the top, and in both seams is a neat piping of thin leather. The noticeable feature here is the existence of a thick extra sole and heel, the former having sixteen rifle-bullet shaped iron points, the latter twelve projecting downward half an inch, as though two Kamchatkan ice-creeper frames had been nailed beneath each boot.

The Aino rode on broad Amur-skees drawn by the reindeer. Nordenskiöld figures, from an old Japanese book, an Aino man, bareheaded, dressed in fur, wearing skin boots, standing on a pair of skees and holding the staff or balancing pole in his hand. In front of the man trots a reindeer having a rawhide line about its neck, the other end of which is tied around the man's waist.[2]

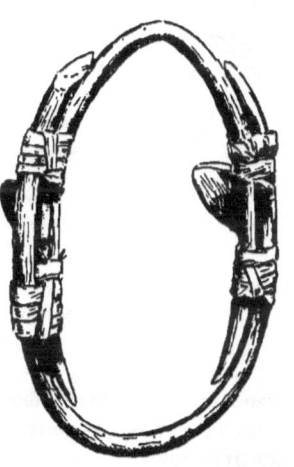

Fig. 93.

COMBINED SNOWSHOE AND ICE CREEPER WORN BY THE AINOS OF JAPAN.

Cat. No. 73092, U. S. N. M. Collected by Romyn Hitchcock.

Example No. 73092 (fig. 93) is a snowshoe frame and ice creeper combined. The framework consists of two bent sticks in shape of an oxbow, one telescoped into the other and bound with spruce root tucked in at the ends. Secured between the two bows, at the side, are wedge-shaped pieces sharp at the bottom so as to be driven into the snow crust, or surface, or rough ice. The structure of this specimen is the same as that of the snowshoe before mentioned from the Caucasus.

The Kamchatkans use in hunting the ice shoe, consisting of two small parallel "splines" 3 feet long and 7 to 8 inches apart, united at each end, and having crossbars; they have the same curve at each end, and are arched in the middle the same as snowshoes, and like them fastened on with straps. The splines are set underneath with pointed bones to stick into the ice. This example may be compared with the Finland

[1] T. W. Greig, "Old-Fashioned Shoes," pl. XVI.
[2] "Voyage of the Vega," New York, 1882, p. 475.

skee, which has a midrib or keel the whole length underneath. The Kamchadal who live in the neighborhood of ice hills or glaciers make use of sharp-pointed irons, called posluki,[1] which they fasten to the foot.

"For smooth ice or snow the Tuski use 'creepers' of carved ivory, having serrated edges, fastened under the moccasin, which prove of great service."[2]

Example No. 2433 (fig. 94) is an ice creeper from northeastern Asia collected by Admiral John Rodgers. It consists of a piece of walrus ivory cut in rectangular shape and having a rectangular piece removed from the middle. Around the underside of the remaining piece are ten projections or blunt points. This

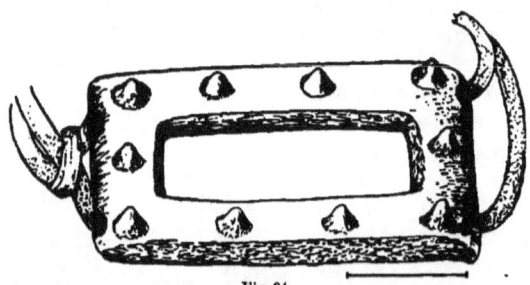

Fig. 94.

ICE CREEPER OF IVORY FROM NORTHEASTERN SIBERIA.

Cat. No. 2433, U. S. N. M. Collected by the Rodgers Expedition.

piece of ivory is tied under the instep of the boot by means of a thong passing though holes bored at either end. The student in looking at this piece will hardly fail to recognize that it is copied from something else, and in reading the description of the wooden frame with spikes beneath, worn under foot by Kamchadal, will see at once whence the motive came.

Example No. 46261 (fig. 95) is an ice creeper from Plover Bay, in northeastern Asia, collected by W. M. Noyes. It is well known that the people of Plover Bay are Eskimo who have gone over there in times not remote to take up their abode, and this specimen, therefore, was worn by an Eskimo. It consists of an oblong, rectangular piece of ivory cut out in the middle and having four-

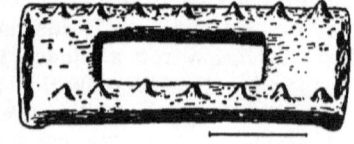

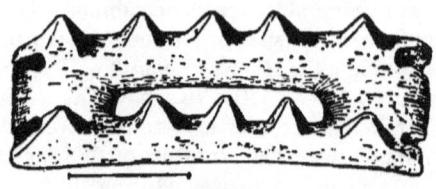

Figs. 95 and 96.

ICE CREEPERS OF IVORY FROM PLOVER BAY, SIBERIA.

Cat. Nos. 46261 and 46260, U. S. N. M.   Collected by E. W. Nelson.

teen little obtuse points or projections beneath, and is fastened to the foot in exactly the same manner as the foregoing. Short rude snowshoes are used for ice creepers by Chukchi and Eskimo about Bering Strait.

---

[1] Langsdorff, "Voyages," London, 1814, ii, p. 292.

[2] Hooper, "Tents of the Tuski," London, 1853, p. 185.

Example No. 46260 (fig. 96) is another specimen from the same locality, which is interesting because of the variation in detail. The shape is rectangular in outline on top, but is chamfered beneath around all of its margins, and also the margin of the cavity in the middle has been chamfered, so that beneath were left two long edges, like sled

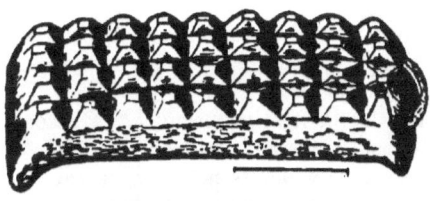

runners; by cutting away notches in these pyramidal points were formed. The lashing is similar to those before named.

Example No. 63881 (fig.97) is from St. Lawrence Island, and exhibits another stage in the process of elaboration. The general shape is quadrangular. The upper part is cut so as to fit around the foot a little better. There is no excavation from the middle, but by a series of furrows filed on the underside, three longitudinally and eight laterally, a series of thirty-six pyramidal projec-

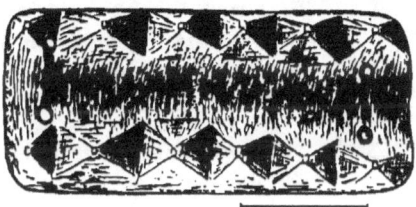

Figs. 97 and 98.
ICE CREEPERS OF IVORY, FROM ALASKA.
Cat. Nos. 63881 and 44761, U. S. N. M.   Collected by E. W. Nelson.

tions are effected. The lashing or attachment to the foot is exactly as in the preceding one.

The last step in this evolution, or practically fading out of a type of invention, is a specimen from Sledge Island, No. 44761 (fig. 98), collected by E. W. Nelson. This is also a rectangular specimen. The edges are chamfered all around. Underneath a broad furrow is gouged longitudinally through the middle and ridges remaining are filed across, leaving two rows of projecting pyramids. So far as the collections in the U. S. National Museum are concerned, this peculiar device does not seem to have gone any farther southward on the American side.

Murdoch says that in early spring, before it thaws enough to render waterproof boots necessary, the surface of the snow becomes very smooth and slippery. To enable themselves to walk on this, the natives make a

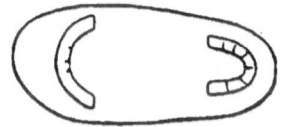

Fig. 99.
ICE CREEPER ATTACHED TO BOOT SOLE.
Point Barrow, Alaska.
From a figure in the Ninth Annual Report of the Bureau of Ethnology.

kind of creeper of strips of sealskin, doubled lengthwise and generally bent into a half moon or horseshoe shape, with the folded edges on the outside of the curve sewed on the toe and heel of the sealskin sole.[1]   (Fig. 99.)

----

[1] Cf. Ninth Ann. Rep. Bureau of Ethnology, p. 135, fig. 82.

In example No. 56750, a pair of boots from Point Barrow, Murdoch draws attention to a large round patch of seal skin with the hair on, and pointing toward the toe, to prevent the wearer from slipping. These patches are carefully "blind stitched" on so that the sewing does not show on the outside. On the Amur snowshoe the hair is pointing backward to prevent slipping.[1]

At Point Barrow, says Herendeen, the Eskimo make an ice creeper by rolling up rawhide and sewing the strips across the boot, which should be compared with the Ungava plan.

The boots of the Northern Labrador Eskimo are peculiar. The soles are often made with strips of sealskin thongs sewed on a false sole, which is attached to the undersurface of the sole proper. The strips of thong are tacked on by a stout stitch, then a short loop is taken up and another stitch sews a portion of the remainder of the strip. This is continued until the entire undersurface consists of a series of short loops, which, when in contact with the smooth ice, prevent the foot from slipping; not made in any other portion of the district.[2] (Fig. 100.)

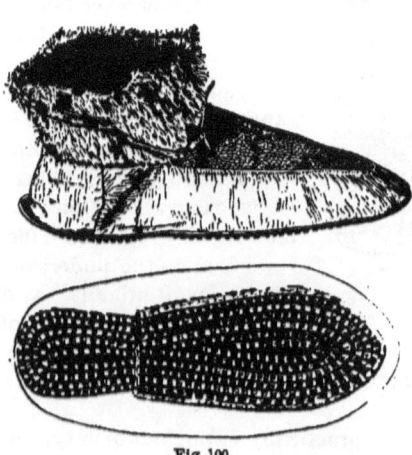

Fig. 100.

ICE CREEPER ON BOOT SOLE.   HUDSON BAY ESKIMO.

Collected by L. M Turner.

From a figure in the Eleventh Annual Report of the Bureau of Ethnology

An interesting example of the fading out of a device is seen in the wipka or skeleton shoes of the Klamath Indians, example No. 165588 in the U. S. National Museum. Their god kuukamtihiksh wore them. It is not a snowshoe at all in the sense of sustaining a person on the snow, but a net in the form of a moccasin drawn over the latter as an overshoe. It is made of coarse twine, in twined weaving, with a mesh about an inch wide. A similar makeshift, example No. 165558 in the U. S. National Museum, is from the Moki pueblo.

ICE CREEPERS IN THE U. S. NATIONAL MUSEUM.

Museum number.	Specimen.	Locality.	By whom contributed.
73002	Snowshoe and ice creeper (fig. 93) ...	Aino, Japan	R. Hitchcock.
2433	Ice creepers, ivory (fig. 94)	Chukchi................	Commodore Rodgers
46260–46262	Ice creepers, ivory (figs. 95, 96)	Plover Bay, Siberia	W. M. Noyes.
63300	Ice creepers, ivory	St. Lawrence Island, Alaska.	E. W. Nelson.
126982	.....do.................	.....do	Do.

[1] Cf. Ninth Ann. Rep. Bureau of Ethnology, p. 132.
[2] Ibid., p. 179.

Ice Creepers in the U. S. National Museum—Continued.

Museum number.	Specimen.	Locality.	By whom contributed.
63881	Ice creepers, ivory (fig. 97)	St. Lawrence Island, Alaska.	E. W. Nelson.
44361	Ice creepers, ivory	Cape Nome, Alaska.....	Do.
44559	.....do............................	Sledge Island, Alaska ..	Do.
44761, 44762	Ice creepers, ivory (fig. 98)	.....do	Do.
49176	Ice creepers, bone..................	Alaska	Do.
153439	Ice creepers, Eskimo.................	.....do	J. C. Russell.
90189–90193	Shoes with crimped soles	Ungava, Canada........	L. M. Turner.
105588	Twined-over-moccasins ....·......	Klamath Indians, California.	Bureau of Ethnology.

PRIMITIVE MAN AS A CARRIER.

Among the numerous epithets applied to man it must not be forgotten that he is a carrying animal, an emigrating animal. Other species carry objects, but they make no carrying devices; fishes and birds especially are migratory, but they go in annual circuits, many of which they have

Fig. 101.

VIRGINIA NEGRO ON THE ROAD.

From a figure in the Report of the Smithsonian Institution (U. S. National Museum), 1887.

been repeating since the glacial epoch. Many animals are provided by nature with pouches and carrying organs. So men also have excellent hands and arms, relieved of the toilsome work of walking so that they may be more free to grip and hold.

In this chapter it is designed to trace the progress of early and more primitive forms of invention as applied to the carrying industry. Nowadays one may see men in the double rôle of carrier and of rider; they carry and are being carried, which gives rise to the two generic terms, freight and passengers. The freight of the world as well as its passengers are either carried or hauled, and these separate functions divide men into pack animals and traction animals.

For carrying on the head or toting, according to the shape of the load and the skill of the bearer, there may be (1) nothing to hold the load on; (2) one or both hands may grasp the burdens; (3) the forearm may rest between load and head; (4) a pad, having many patterns from land to land, may sustain the load on the head and support it when placed on the ground; (5) the receptacle may be made convex at the bottom by an added rim or by punching up.[1] Finally, the load may be hung from the head by means of a headband and slings or straps. In such cases there is a double resting place for the back and shoulders and hips, all assist in sustaining the burden. Furthermore, the student will notice that the head strap rests against the forehead in some instances and against the bregma in others, as in the Apache water carrier. This same head or forehead band will occur in certain tribes as an instrument of traction. Toting as against carrying with the headband will also be found to have relation to natural resources, and hence to tribal and ethnic custom.

It should be noticed in this connection by craniologists that among savages that carry loads on the head or use the burden strap or other devices about the forehead, children are taught and compelled just as soon as they can walk to carry loads. Small jars, baskets, frames, or packs are loaded upon them at first, and these are increased with age. Again, in many tribes carrying methods are a matter of sex, so that if any modification of the skull takes place by the act it would show itself in one sex and not in the other.

CARRYING PADS FOR THE HEAD IN THE U. S. NATIONAL MUSEUM.

Museum number.	Specimen.	Locality.	By whom contributed.
77189	Head pad for packing	Hupa Valley, California.	Lieut. P. H. Ray, U. S. A.
126907	Head pad, leather and grass twine ..	California	Do.
84107, 84108	Belt for carrying burdens, Moki.....	Arizona	V. Mindeleff.
84109, 84110	Head pad, Moki Indians	...do	Do.
22828	Rope for carrying wood, Moki.......	...do	Maj. J. W. Powell.
70962–70974	Head pads (thirteen), Moki Indians .	...do	Col. Jas. S. Stevenson.
40473	Head pads (fig. 161) Zuñi	New Mexico...........	Do.
41760	Carrying strap, Moki and Zuñi......	...do	Do.
41761	Carrying strap, hood rope, Moki	...do	Do.
42156	Carrying band, plaited, Moki........	...do	Do.
76980	Headband..........................	Mexico	New Orleans Exposition.
152720	Carrying gourd and yoke	Colima, Mexico	Edward Palmer.

[1] Ratzel figures a Schilluk woman, barefooted, with a jar on the head, supported by the wrist of the right hand and grasped at the rim with the left.

CARRYING-YOKES AND HEADBANDS IN THE U. S. NATIONAL MUSEUM.

Museum number.	Specimen.	Locality.	By whom contributed.
167783	Yokes	Finland	Hon. Jno. M. Crawford.
73386	Carrying strap	New Guinea	D. S. Spaulding.
151120	Carrying pole	Sandwich Islands	Mrs. Sibyl Carter.
153361	Carrying bands	India	W. H. Dall.
153557	Carrying rope, goat's hair	Kashmir, India	Dr. W. L. Abbott.
150679, 150680	Carrying band	Yezo, Japan	Romyn Hitchcock.
150683	.....do	.....do	Do.
150757	Carrying band and stick	.....do	Do.
77112	Headband	Seoul, Korea	J. B. Bernadou.

The shoulders and back are favorite places for men's burdens; women a little more commonly prefer " toting." The roustabouts and wharf men set all sorts of sacks upon the shoulder for short distances. The sack holds its own as a carrying utensil on their account. The shoulder not only lends itself to actual burden bearing, but has been the occasion of inventions in the following directions:

(1) In the utensil that fits and holds the load—the receptacle or package (fig. 134).

(2) In the carrying device itself, the vehicle.

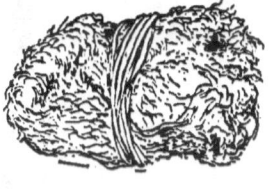

(3) In the attachment of the burden to the man, the harness (fig. 102).

These are not always separate, and not even ever present, but the operation must always embrace the use of something answering to these and out of which they were elaborated.

Carrying is done on one shoulder, on both shoulders, and on the shoulders and neck.

All the eastern Asiatics and the Polynesians carry a load first on one shoulder, then on the other, by means of a shoulder pole.

The race of peddlers and of men with little impedimenta in Europe and America go about with their belongings in a pack borne on the end of a stick, resting near its middle on the shoulder and grasped by the hand at the other end (fig. 101).

Fig. 102.

CARRIER'S SHOULDER-PADS FROM MU-HAMBA, AFRICA.

Cat. No. 151132, U. S. N. M. Collected by the U. S. Eclipse Expedition.

African porters, as will be seen, have their load on one shoulder, either with or without carrying-frame, and relieve that shoulder by putting the middle of the staff on the other shoulder and catching the lower end of the staff beneath the load behind (fig. 103).

Finally, the Caucasian literally wears a yoke, so carved out that it rests on both shoulders and the atlas at once (figs. 108, 109).   The "porter's knot" is an invention which combines head, atlas, and shoulders into one resting place for enormous burdens (fig. 110).

But, somehow the back has come proverbially to be the seat of the human load, so as to leave the arms free.   Knapsacks, carrying frames, porters' packs, and the thousand and one devices for long marches are designed for the back, especially in Europe and aboriginal America.

The head-strap load, the breast-strap load, the shoulder-strap load,

Fig. 103.

ANGOLA NEGRO CARRYING ON THE SHOULDER.

From a photograph in U. S. National Museum.

the sack held over the shoulder by its mouth, all rest against the leaning back, and are sustained upon the center of gravity of the body. Allied to this back load is the burden on the hip and on the thighs.

Besides these wholesale methods there is the infinitely varied retail method of bearing small packages on the hands, arms, breast, stomach, and knees, which together afford room for regional, racial, and cultural variations of apparatus.   One will see in pictures of Brazil, for instance, a servant carrying a bottle of wine or fruit on the head as a feat of agility in toting.   In another place, men are trained to the knack of carrying after other fashions, until they seem to take on certain gaits and styles of walking. But it is along the docks and retail streets that one will witness the survival of all modes of burden bearing in vogue since human history began.

The devices for carrying loads will first receive attention; after that the carrying of children and adult persons. Following the method of the former chapter, it seems more convenient, from a museum point of view, to continue the geographic order, regarding—

(1) Africa in its negroid portions.

(2) Caucasian Africa, Europe, and Asia.

(3) Semitic and southern Asia.

(4) Northern Asia and its appendages.

(5) America.

This order is generally followed so as to bring geographic areas into contact where there has been also industrial contact.

A common sight in the landscape of negroid Africa is that of a woman with an immense jar on her head, steadied not by her hair or by a carrying ring, but by her naked forearm resting between the head and the jar or gourd. Her other hand may or may not hold to the rim. These toting negroes are now all over the warm portions of the world. No sight is more common in the streets of Washington than that of an old negress with an immense bundle on her head. In their native countries the negroid tribes have invented apparatuses for carrying.

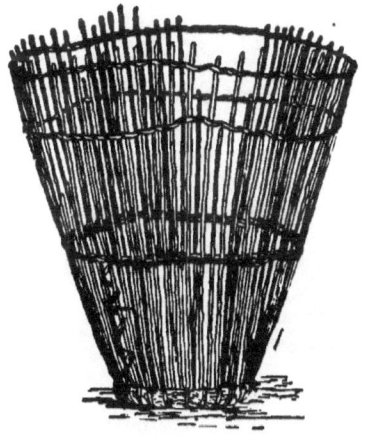

Fig. 104.

CARRYING-CRATE FROM ANGOLA, AFRICA.

Cat. No. 151129, U. S. N. M. Collected by Héli Chatelain.

Example No. 151129 (fig. 104) is a rude carrying or packing basket from Angola. The bottom is made in form of a mat or head pad. The warp is a series of rods, and the weft is in twined weaving, common in Africa, in eastern Asia, and in the Pacific States of North America north of the Pueblo country. The lower row of this twining should be noticed as a bare suggestion of which the bird-cage baskets of California and Oregon are the fine art. It is designed to introduce a little more rigidity into the texture. In this specimen the complete carrying baskets of many lands appear almost as a skeleton, and there are many variations of this type in West Africa.

A carrying basket from the Herero African tribe in the Berlin Museum für Völkerkunde is a little on the plan of the typical bean basket of the Mohave, but much shallower. Its motif is hoops and sections of hoops in three series held in place by windings of bast. At

the top is a wooden hoop. To this hoop are lashed three segments of
hoops outside, their ends close together on opposite sides, like meridio-
nal lines. Inside these are laid segments of hoops of smaller size,
at right angles to the three and parallel to one another, like the wires
in a rat trap.[1]

Example No. 152612 (fig. 105) is from the French Kongo, the gift of the
Cincinnati Museum Association. In this specimen the common wicker-
work is used; that is, a rigid warp and flexible filling. It is seen in
America in three culture regions, that of the birch, ash, and oak splint,
that of the split cane, and in one Pueblo in northeastern Arizona made
from little twigs of *Hilaria Jamesii.* The plaited headband of the
specimen here figured would also be familiar in America.

Baker furnishes excellent examples of varied carrying among the
Madi negroes: Four men bearing a house-frame on their heads and
spears or bows in their hands; woman with hamper on the head and

child astride the hips; woman with
hamper on the head and gourd in net
borne in left hand; bottle in net and
child clasped in the arms against
the stomach; man with great bundle
of long poles on back, shoulders, and
head, held in place with both hands,
the small ends dragging on the
ground; the whole party are driving
a herd of cattle.

Knapsack straps and headband
combined are given by Du Chaillu
in the picture of an Aschira negro
carrier. The man is naked, save a
loin cloth; holds a staff in his hand
and bears on his back a crate, shown

Fig. 105.

WOMAN'S CARRYING-BASKET WITH HEADBAND.
Cat. No. 152612, U. S. N. M. Collected by C. Steckelman.

with board bottom and latticed sides. The crate is supported by a
band across the forehead and a strap over each shoulder, attached to
the borders of the crate. This should be compared with a picture in
v. d. Steinen's "Unter den Naturvölkern Zentral-Brasiliens," pl. VI, and
page 237.[2]

Ratzel reproduces from Cameron a Mrua man barefooted, wearing only
a cloth about the loin, carrying a plain or self bow in the right hand, a
spear in the left hand, and three arrows under his left arm. On his back,
knapsack fashion, is a bale of goods, and suspended on his left side
from his left shoulder hangs a fish basket and scrip or small haversack.[3]

Example No. 169128 (fig. 106) from Kongo Free State, Africa, is a carrying frame or basket, collected by J. H. Camp. The essential parts, as of
many others in the U. S. National Museum from the area of African

[1] Figured by Ratzel, "Völkerkunde," Leipzig, 1887, I, p. 333.
[2] Cf. Ratzel, "Völkerkunde," Leipzig, 1887, I, p. 596.
[3] Ratzel, "Völkerkunde," Leipzig, 1887, I, p. 92.

porters, are the two substantial bamboo rods along the bottom; around this a network of bamboo fillets in twined weaving is constructed, and the flat border finished off in diaper weaving. The staff always accompanies this device, not only to support the carrier, but to place on the vacant shoulder as a fulcrum in order to help support the frame.

Example No. 151132 is a Muhamba carrying frame from Portuguese West Africa, collected by Héli Chatelain. The fundamental parts are the rods and the sides. The rods are two poles about 6 feet long, laid parallel, like the frame of a bier upon which the apparatus is built up. In the economy of the carrier 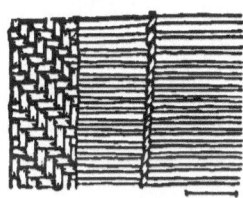 these poles serve as foundation for the frame, as holds for the hands, and the projections of the rods enable the carrier to set his load upon the ground and to resume it without much stooping. The sides of the apparatus are two-netted hoops. Each hoop is a stick bent into an elongated ellipse, and lashed to

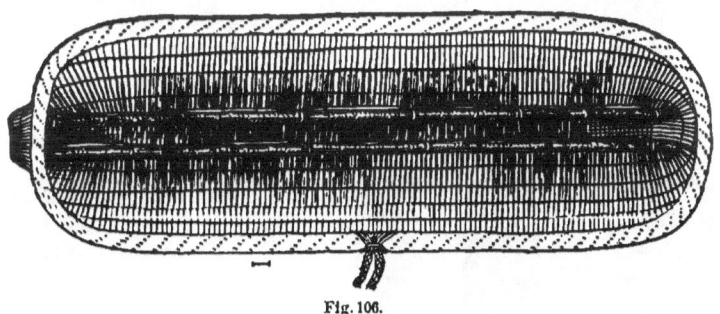

Fig. 106.
CARRYING-CRATE OF CANE FROM KONGO, AFRICA.
Cat. No. 169128, U. S. N. M.   Collected by J. H. Camp.

the poles. The network consists of quadrilateral meshes made of cane splints served neatly all over with finely split cane. Between the chief meshes and subdividing them is a series of meshes in wrapped style of weaving. The poles are held in place by cross-pieces, and the space padded beneath to protect the shoulders. These frames are convenient in packing, and the load is required to be put up in such manner as to fit them.[1]

Serpa Pinto figures a Biheño carrier with his regulation pack fastened between the parts of a forked stick and borne on the shoulder. His belt is a regular arsenal and commissary.[2] This may be compared with the West African and Kongo pack.

Example No. 72708, received from the Museum für Völkerkunde, Leipzig, is the most interesting specimen of this type of frame for the reason that it is constructed from two palm leaves and may be made

[1] Cf. Steinen, "Unter den Naturvölkern Zentral-Brasiliens," pl. VI, p. 72.
[2] Ratzel, "Völkerkunde," Leipzig, 1887, I, p. 194.

without the use of metal tools by laying the stems parallel and a few inches apart. The leaflets on the sides of the stem that are toward each other are interwoven, which forms a prolonged webbing on which the load may rest. The leaflets on the outside of each stem are twisted for a few inches and their ends are braided down together to form a continuous upper border of the apparatus. This construction will be best seen by examining fig. 107. Nothing could be simpler than this device, and yet it is an attractive object, containing all of the elements of the most finished carrying frame from the African region.

There are over one hundred thousand carriers on the Kongo. They are almost naked African savages, and yet the produce they bring is on its way to the great streams of world commerce. Each one of them carries a load of 75 pounds 12 or more miles a day, making in round numbers a unit of 1,000 pounds 1 mile.

Among the Kasai and other wooly-haired tribes, as well as in the Papuan area, the women carry water jars on the shoulder. The reason seems to lie in the great care that is taken of the hair. Enough material does not exist in the U. S. National Museum to test the question whether Friedrich Müller's division according to hair is tallied by the two customs of head carrying and shoulder carrying respectively. The jars are always round bottomed and the roads tolerably level.

Fig. 107.

PRIMITIVE CARRYING-FRAME OF BRAIDED PALM LEAF.

Cat. No. 72708, U. S. N. M.

These same round jars or gourds, in order to be carried in other ways, must be protected. The most common and natural style of sling or lashing for a rotund jar or gourd consists of two small circles of some flexible material near the top and the bottom united like the snare of a drum so that they can not move either way. A cord attached to either of them or around the bottom and united with them will be efficient. The jar and the gourd being frail, the sling has often padding added or protection at exposed points and extra bottoms are attached to the lower ring.

In the rattan region this inclosure of the gourd is most efficient and elaborate. In many examples the network is tastefully knotted and ornamented and provided with a bottom and a bale. The vessel may be carried then after any fashion; may be set down and will support itself; is guarded against destruction by a blow. The U. S. National Museum possesses a great variety of such vessels, which are usually devoted to the transportation of water, oil, milk, etc.

A very elaborate mounting for carrying a gourd bottle, in the U. S. National Museum, is No. 5587, from the Kongo. A conoid carrying basket is formed of a warp of bent rods crossing at the bottom, fitted to the gourd and held in place by weaving in leather thong and cotton thread. Palm oil, animal fat, milk, and other food liquids, as well as pombé and native fermented drinks, are kept for immediate use in such inclosures. They are well known to collectors by their indestructible rancid odor.

Example No. 76281 is a long carrying gourd from the Kongo, collected by Hon. W. P. Tisdel. It is mounted by boring a hole in the side near the small end, cutting off the end and running a noose up from the former hole through the latter. The knot at one end of the noose forms

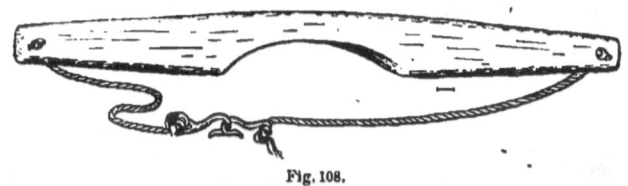

Fig. 108.

ENGLISH CARRYING-YOKE.

Cat. No. 131093, U. S. N. M.   Collected by Edward Lovett.

the toggle and the bend the means of attachment. The gourd is about 30 inches long and 3 inches thick.

It will be convenient to insert here some of the survivals of primitive carrying apparatus and methods in vogue in Europe. Indeed, every form of transportation may be witnessed on the farm and garden, about the docks, and along the commercial streets, and especially in the markets. Every part of the body fit to carry any object is harnessed. Every kind of harness for attaching the load to the person is in use. Every sort and shape of receptacle for holding loads and holding them on survives. Finally, in the great commercial centers, all things that have been carried elsewhere must be borne again.

The carrying yoke (example No. 131093, fig. 108), from England, is a type of harness widely dispersed in northern Europe and among the colonists from that area. Dr. W. J. Hoffman found the Indians of Wisconsin and Minnesota carrying water and maple sap in buckets made of birch bark on their backs by means of this yoke. The parts of the utensil are the horizontal piece, or the yoke itself, and the slings. The yoke itself is wider than it is thick, is rounded on all corners, for ease to the carrier, and tapers toward the ends to reduce weight.[1] It

[1] Rep. Smithsonian Inst. (U. S. Nat. Mus.), 1887, p. 285, fig. 40.

also serves another purpose in common with all other carrying poles,
it holds the loads away from the body. Whoever has tried to carry
two pails of water with his hands alone knows this. It is a common
thing in the country to see the boys and women using a hogshead hoop
as a spreader. In the cities two ice men carry an enormous block by
both holding to the hooks and one pushing against the shoulder of the
other for a brace. This triangulation of lift and push is excellently
illustrated in the style of carrying in vogue among the peasantry of
Europe. The yoke is practically reversed. A strap or rope about 6
feet long, with a hook at each end, is worn over the neck and the hooks
attached to the bales of the buckets to be carried (fig. 109). This enables
the bearer to use both arms and neck, for the hands may grasp either

the handles of the hooks or the
bales of the buckets. In order
to hold the loads away from the
person four sticks are framed
together, and the two crossbars
are laid against the bales of the
bucket on the side next to the
carrier.[1]

Example No. 131091 in the U.S.
National Museum (fig. 110) is a
"porter's knot," procured in London by Mr. Edward Lovett. This
specimen is a hard pillow, after
the general plan of a horse collar.
A band passes around the forehead and the knot or pad rests
on the shoulders and the back.
Its uses are twofold, first to protect the head and body from injury, and to perfect this function a
cap of stout leather is worn. The
chief use, however, is to enable

Fig. 109.

SUBSTITUTE FOR NECKYOKE USED BY WOMEN IN
NORMANDY.

From a figure by Dupré.

the carrier to take any kind of load at will—boxes, bags, furniture, in
short, every sort of freight that is hauled in London or Liverpool and
carry it to and from the wagon or car. The rather crude drawing of a
knot collected on Thames street, London, will help the reader to see
that the porter may use and rest in turn the head, the back, or either
shoulder. The modern packing box or barrel, with ugly corners, nails,
hoops, and hoop iron, are also kept from lacerating the flesh. The combined activity of these thousands of carriers by whose agency great
piles of freight appear and disappear incessantly reminds one of the
silent power of those great rivers at whose bidding islands of débris
are formed and carried away.

The bearing of burdens on the scapulæ (fig. 111), as among the Eng-

---

[1] "Art of the World," D. Appleton & Co., New York, p. 76.

MARKET WOMAN IN DRESDEN SELLING VEGETABLES.

The noteworthy features in this connection are:

(1) The wicker carrying basket, strong and flexible, for the back.

(2) The knapsack straps, made fast to the upper edge of the basket and buttoned at the lower end under the projecting ends of the frame posts, making it perfectly easy for the woman to harness or unharness herself.

(3) The hamper basket, with two handles, for field work and not for the road, carried in front of the body or upon the shoulder or nape of the neck.

(4) The pack or bundle, easy to carry on the arm, in the hand, or on the shoulder.

In this picture is an example of the most active folk industries in one of the most enlightened cities of the world.

From a photograph in the U. S. National Museum.

MARKET WOMAN IN DRESDEN SELLING VEGETABLES.
From a photograph in the U. S. National Museum.

lish porters, must be very old, for it was long ago æstheticized in the Atlantides and Telamones, the first term relating, doubtless, to Atlas, who bore up the vault of heaven on his shoulders, and the second to the Telamonian Ajax.[1]

While the southern Europeans and the races allied to them affect the toting habit, the northern Europeans, especially the German race, carry burdens on the back. The soldier and his knapsack, the peasant, and the drudgery woman with her basket furnish the ever present picture.

The German carrying basket (pl. 22) is a model of convenience. It exists in many materials, sizes, degrees of finish, and it varies somewhat in form according to special functions. But all of them are practically knapsacks. The side of the basket next to the carrier's back should be somewhat flat. The straps for the shoulders are attached near the top of the apparatus, and they both have a loop or eyelet at the bottom to fit over the ends of the frame sticks which project downward below the basket to receive them. These loops and projections are of the greatest possible convenience, for the carrier does not have to rise painfully with her load. She sets it upon any accessible rock or table, turns her back to it, brings the straps over her shoulders, and buttons the eyelets over the projections at the bottom of the basket. She has nothing more to do than to bend her back, adjust herself to the load, and walk off. Other modes of carrying are in vogue, practically, every other, and the mode here described exists elsewhere, but the

Fig. 110.
PORTER'S KNOT, AS SEEN ON THAMES STREET, LONDON.
Cat. No. 131091, U. S. N. M. Collected by Edward Lovett.

peaceable knapsack is, after all, the favorite style of burden bearing with the Germanic people.[2] In periodicals one will now and then see a picture of a German woman carrying dirt in a knapsack basket up a hill, and children drawing her along by means of a rope working round a pulley.[3] The occasion of this is as follows: The constant working down hill of the light loam by farming and by the rain impoverishes the hilltops. In order to enrich them again the men carry the fertile dirt uphill in baskets on their backs and the women resort to the device above

---

[1]Smith, Dictionary of Greek and Roman Antiquities, s. v., *Atlantides.*

[2]Cf. U. S. Consular Report No. 103, March, 1889, p. 431; Mason, "Woman's Share in Primitive Culture," New York, 1894, p. 124, and "The Human Beast of Burden," Rep. Smithsonian Inst. (U. S. Nat. Mus.), 1887, p. 285.

[3]Zeitschrift des Vereins für Volkskunde, Berlin, 1894, v, pl. I.

spoken of. In the figure given by Miss Rehsener, there is a tripod shown on the top of the hill and a pulley attached to the crossbar. One woman at the foot of the hill is filling a basket with rich dirt by means of a shovel. A long rope is attached by one end to the basket on the back of the woman. The middle of the rope is around the pulley, and three children are drawing at the other end. The cooperation in this simple process is perfect. One basket is being filled, one is on the carrier's back, and a third is being brought to the starting point by the children.

Example No. 28155 (fig. 112) is a Lapland wallet made of spruce root. This is a species of network made as follows: A two-ply twine for about 9 inches forms the foundation along the middle of the bottom. From that point, as the twine proceeds in a coil, at every turn one of the strands is extended or expanded into a loop, which passes backward around the preceding twine by a double twist, and then the original twining proceeds for another loop and double turn, when strand number two is expanded to form the next loop or mesh, and the whole process consists in twining and alternately making both the strands a loop around the cord of the preceding coil. The whole operation is a process of alternate twist and loop, making meshes about three-fourths of an inch square. The handle consists of a three-ply rope made of the same spruce root. One single cord makes both handles knotted on one side to form the double loop. Depth of the basket, 9 inches.

Fig. 111.

MADEIRA WINE CARRIER USING FOREHEAD, SHOULDERS, AND BACK.

From the Report of the Smithsonian Institution (U. S. National Museum), 1887.

This species of twining and looping is essentially hand work, and is rather netting than weaving. That is, there is no warp and weft, but the two are one, built up mesh by mesh with the fingers. The wallet is useful for all carrying purposes, being tough and light.

As remarked, the melanochroic peoples of Europe, in their devices for carrying, resemble the North Africans and the Semito-Hamites generally. The women carry loads on the head; the men over the backs like peddlers, or on a shoulder pole, as did the ancient Egyptians, the Irish peasantry, especially the women. The writer has seen a young woman toting a pail of milk on her head and carrying one in each hand, thirty quarts in all, seemingly with great pleasure.

The Greek and Roman *asilla* was a pole of wood held on one or both shoulders for carrying burdens, which were attached to the two ends. Smith figures a dwarf, a grasshopper, and a faun, each bearing loads therewith, showing how this drudgery thing had become a motif in art and mythology.[1] In Greece the term ἀναφορεός is applied to every carrying device, strap, pole, yoke, etc. This southern European carrying pole, however, is not the English yoke. It may be seen in hundreds of pictures of Egyptian laborers, and has its greatest development in eastern Asia, south of the great divide.

The carrying yoke laid on both shoulders or biceps is shown in Roman art.[2] The Egyptian clay and brick bearers seem to be wearing the yoke after the Chinese fashion.

The Greek κάλαθος was the basket in which women placed their work,

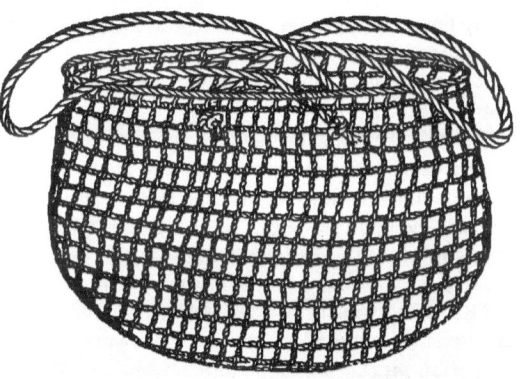

and is figured like the waste basket at the office desk, a truncated cone or cylinder of wicker. It was also a religious emblem and is found associated with Minerva, who taught women the art of weaving; with Demeter or Ceres, the goddess of harvest; with Tellus and other divinities, as an emblem of abundance. It was frequently placed on the heads of divinities in ancient statues, and is thus called modius by archæologists. Carried on the heads of young women in processions it gave rise to the Caryatides.[3]

The Roman *ferculum* was a platform on which the images of the gods were carried in procession. Spoils of war and prisoners were borne in triumph on the same device. On the

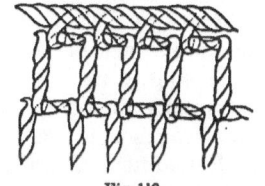

Fig. 112.

LAPLAND CARRYING-WALLET, MADE OF SPRUCE ROOT.

Cat. No. 24155, U. S. N. M.

arch of Titus at Rome soldiers are figured as carrying the golden candlestick of the Jews on a *ferculum*.[4]

---

[1] Dictionary of Greek and Roman Antiquities, s. v., *Asilla*, with 3 figs.

[2] Smith, Dictionary of Greek and Roman Antiquities, s. v., *Corbis*, illus. from Herculaneum.

[3] Smith, Dictionary of Greek and Roman Antiquities, s. v., *Calathus*, with figure of Calathus on chariot and on the head of Serapis. Reference is made to Saglio's Dictionary, for description of priestesses wearing the Calathus.

[4] Figured in Smith's Dictionary of Greek and Roman Antiquities, s. v. *Ferculum*.

The enormous loads borne incessantly on the heads of women in Italy are shown in a painting by Gioli, exhibited at the Art Exposition at Venice in 1887. The women are all barefooted and poorly clad. They have immense bundles of brush upon their heads, and for the double purpose of staff and prop for the load each holds in the right hand a stout stick.[1]

Upon the monuments and paintings of Egypt, as well as in the scenes of modern life, carrying may be seen in the following varieties:

(1) On the head, with or without head pad: with or without support from hand or arm.

(2) Picking up and carrying bricks with both hands, in the kiln and at the building. The carriers are in every attitude, and the study of them exhibits excellently the versatility of the human body in this industry.

(3) On the shoulder, in box or tub; in sack, and by means of the carrying pole, like the Chinese coolie.

(4) In the hand; with satchel, or in the infinite variety seen about the bazaars.

The salver or charger held in the right hand, extended in the presence of gods and great men, is one of the commonest appearances on ancient monuments. This practice has a ceremonial motive as well as that of convenience and respect. It is not right for a menial to touch the food of a superior, and the ceremonially unclean must not touch the food of those that have been purified regardless of rank.

The form of carrying food and drink on a waiter or charger resting on the two extended palms held forward, occurs again and again on Egyptian mural paintings and sculptures and survives in the waiters at most hotels.

Montfaucon has a picture of men in rows holding up and carrying the throne of a Persian King upon their uplifted hands.[2]

Herodotus mentions, as an example of the contrary ways of the Egyptians, that the women carry burdens on the shoulders while the men bear them on the head. But on the monuments even the testimony of Herodotus is reversed. And the women of the lower orders in our day carry water in large vessels on their heads. Now, as anciently, the women do the bulk of the carrying.[3]

The methods of carrying in ancient and modern Egypt are those also of Syria and Palestine. The multitudes of asses and camels in use lift the burdens from the heads of women and from the backs and shoulders of men, the former for short haul, the latter for long haul. Tristram speaks of the shepherds in Palestine carrying lambs not only under the arm, but in the hood of the ábeih, or cloak.

---

[1] Mason, "Woman's Share in Primitive Culture," New York, 1894, fig. 36.
[2] "L'Antiquité expliquée," Paris, 1722, p. 183, pl. II.
[3] Lane, "Modern Egyptians," 1846, I, p. 267; Erman, "Life in Ancient Egypt," London, 1894, pp. 99 and 276.

For professional carrying and the daily round of burden bearing, as connected with the transportation of water, two inventions are in vogue, the pottery vessel and the skin bottle. In Egypt, where the donkey is also aquarius, the sharp-bottomed jar made to fit in a saddle pack may also be carried in a sling on the back. But, in the Holy Land, the use of the head in carrying water necessitates an entire change in the form of the utensil.

The water skin is simply the hide of the goat or some other animal, drawn off with great care; the openings all but one are closed tight, and straps added for the convenience of the bearer, according to whether he may live in a headband country or one addicted to shoulder or breast straps.

It is a common sight in Constantinople to see eight stout fellows carrying a tierce of wine by means of two parallel poles (fig. 113). The tierce rests in two rope slings. Each end of each rope is attached to the middle of a piece of wood, the ends of which are swung under both the

Fig. 113.
WINE BEARERS OF CONSTANTINOPLE.
An illustration of cooperative carrying.
From a photograph in the U. S. National Museum.

poles. This divides the load into eight equal parts. The poles extend beyond the tierce at either end, so that the men have no difficulty in walking. Elsewhere this cooperative carrying is still further amplified, and its survival may be seen at barn raisings, about shipyards, foundries, navy-yards, and in handling ordnance in the open.

Of the Arab women about Mosul, Layard says that they looked after their children, made bread, fetched water, cut and carried wood home on their heads. They did all the weaving, struck and raised the tents, loaded and unloaded the beasts of burden when they changed camp, drove cattle to pasture and milked them at night. When moving, they carried the children on the back as well as when about the daily toil. The weight of the large sheep or goat skin filled with water is considerable. It is hung on the back by cords strapped over the shoulders, and upon it was frequently a child unable to follow the mother afoot. The bundles of firewood brought from afar were enormous, concealing head and shoulders of the bearer. The author speaks of one athletic girl, Hadla, who, having finished the task imposed by her mother, would assist her neighbors for pastime.[1] A good picture of such an athlete would in art stand for the genius of work. Emil Schmidt figures the Tamil women of southern India carrying loads upon their heads, at the same time bearing their children upon the arm and the hip.[2]

The following kinds of carriers appear on the black obelisk of Shalmaneser: (1) With hands held out in front; (2) with hamper held in both hands in front; (3) with wallet in right hand and sack held on left shoulder with left hand, most common; (4) with load held aloft over head in two hands; (5) with bundle of rods hugged in both arms; (6) with load held on shoulder in sack, like the wharf porter; (7) two men with pole between them on the shoulder, load swinging; (8) with lead and driven camels; (9) with box or pack on the shoulder. No one is using headband, breast strap, knapsack straps, or any other device for fastening the load.

Fig. 114.

CARRIER WITH WATER SKIN, FILTER, AND BOTTLE.

From a photograph in the U. S. National Museum.

On the Chaldean and Assyrian monuments the diversity of carrying is well shown. For example: (1) The bearing of fans, fly brushes, umbrellas, food, and drink before gods and princes; (2) the sack over either shoulder; (3) the satchel in the right or the left hand; (4) the shield on either arm; (5) bow in left, arrows in right hand, great shield supported on the back; (6) all sorts of loads borne on the head, two men with carrying pole, the load above, between, or below the supports.

In the figures of Kouyunjik gallery the men are building a mound, carrying earth in baskets on their backs. The lower tier of men are running down hill with empty baskets. In the photographs in the U. S. National Museum none of the groups show the endless-chain method of passing light objects along a line of men and women. The Polynesians practiced such economy. In the Hawaiian legend of the Royal Hunchback it is related that on the arrival of Pili in the islands, Paao, the high priest, removed with him to Kohala. At Puuepa he erected a large *heiau*, the stones of which were passed from hand to hand a dis-

---

[1] Layard, "Nineveh and its Remains," New York, 1849, p. 29L.

[2] Schmidt, "Reise nach Südindien," Leipzig, 1894, p. 10.

tance of 9 miles.[1] MacRitchie mentions a similar custom among the Picts. It was in vogue not many years ago at fires in villages, and in the Southern States watermelons and other fruits and fruit packages are handed along for considerable distances.

The use of the hides of animals in raising, carrying, and holding of liquids is confined chiefly to the Caucasian race, and is especially seen in their Mediterranean, Asiatic, and African areas (fig. 114). The goat's skin is particularly chosen because of its size and its texture. The hide is drawn off with as few openings as possible; these are tied up and calked and a harness of leather is attached for carrying, suspending,

and emptying. In the illustration here given the skin is brought into proximity with the jar that in its form succeeds the goatskin in some lands. By comparing the harness with that of the Mexican aguador and others it will be seen that the strap for dumping, which is absolutely necessary in the skin, survives as of doubtful utility on the jar.[2]

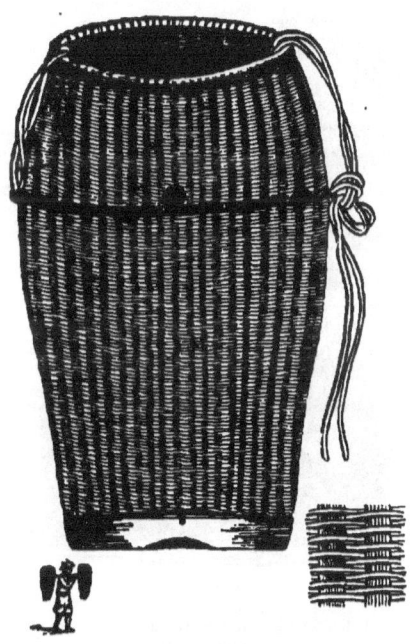

In the Rig Veda leather water bottles, like those in use at this day, are mentioned.

India, southern Asia, and the Malayo-Polynesian islands may be considered seriatim on the notion of contiguity, regardless of race and environment. The carrying pole or Hindu *banghy* is omnipresent. Here a load on the hinder end is sustained by the hand in front. There the man in the middle sustains the pole with a load on either end, and in a third view, the load is

Fig. 115.

SIAMESE WICKER CARRYING-BASKETS, BORNE IN PAIRS WITH SHOULDER POLE.

Cat. No. 27613, U. S. N. M. Presented by the King of Siam, through Gen. John A. Halderman.

in the middle and there is a man at each end. Other changes are rung on each of these. The methods of attaching the load to the poles are quite as numerous.

Example No. 27613 (fig. 115) is an elaborate carrying apparatus presented by the King of Siam. It consists of a pole and two baskets. Each end of the pole pierces a basket from side to side, holes having been provided for this purpose. The material of the structure is split rattan done in wickerwork. Cords are provided for packing the load

[1] Kalakaua, "Legends and Myths of Hawaii," New York, 1888, Webster.
[2] See also Rep. Smithsonian Inst. (U. S. Nat. Mus.), 1887, p. 284, fig. 38.

and blocks of wood are attached to the bottom of each hamper to protect the weaving.

With this may be compared a precisely similar fashion from the Sandwich Islands. A photograph in the U. S. National Museum represents a Kanaka carrying two bundles after the manner of the Siamese,
having thrust through each one of them an end of his carrying pole
(fig. 116).

The U. S. National Museum possesses a number of immense gourds
holding each several gallons, the gift of Mrs. Sybil Carter. In the
absence of all pottery from the entire Polynesian area these gourds
are the universal receptacle of
things to be carried, clean or

Fig. 116.
CARRYING POLE.
Sandwich Islander carrying two bales by means of a
shoulder pole.
From a photograph in the U. S. National Museum.

Fig. 117.
PRIMITIVE SHOULDER POLE.
Burmese boy carrying Jack fruit (*Artocarpus
integrifolia*).
From a photograph by Rev. R. M. Luther.

unclean, liquid or solid. On the testimony of travelers and missionaries these gourds are slung in network and suspended from each end of
the carrying pole. Wilkes says that the people are so wedded to this
method of burden bearing as to use stones to balance the weights in
the two packages. The stick is made of the *Hibiscus tiliaceus*, used
also by the Kanaka in creating fire by the plowing method. Covers
of gourd are sometimes fitted over the bottom ones to prevent the rain
from wetting the contents. The gait of the carrier is a quick trot, with
short steps.

The U. S. National Museum is indebted to Rev. R. M. Luther for
the description and photograph of the most primitive form of the
carrying pole and double load from Burma. A Karen boy is return-

ing home with two jack fruits attached to a stem of the same tree. (Fig. 117.) The drawing fails to show that the fruits are adhering to the original stem, but in fact they are, and this is the last analysis of the shoulder pole in which the stick, the perpendicular strings, and the weights are in one piece made by nature.

Weights are never carried on the head by the Nicobarese, but are invariably slung on a stick or pole and borne over the shoulder. A woman may occasionally be seen carrying on her head for a few yards, from her hut to the jungle, a basket containing a light load of pandanus drupes, but this is the only instance in which anything is borne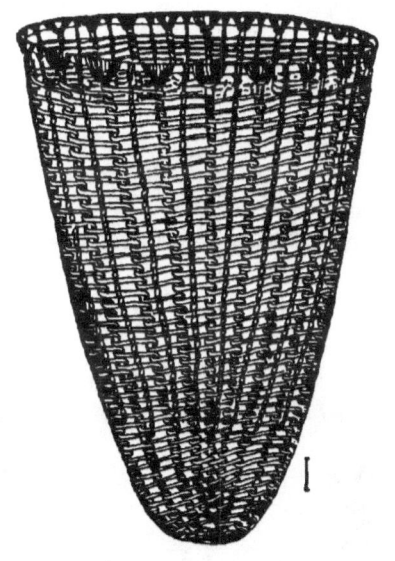
on the head. As they are not in
the habit of distressing themselves by taxing their powers of
endurance, the distance that a
man or woman will carry a maximum load without a rest rarely,
if ever, exceeds a few hundred
yards; in fact, it would appear
that, though the physical powers
of the average Nicobarese exceed
those of the average Burman or
Malay, there are many tasks performed by the latter from which
the former would shrink as irk-
some and fatiguing.[1]

Example No. 164745 (fig. 118)
is a carrying basket from Jarawa,
Andaman Islands, the gift of En-
rico Giglioli. The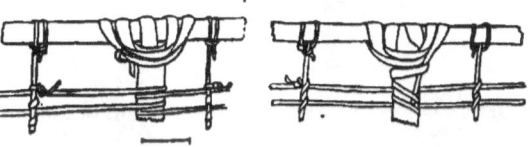
texture of this
specimen is a re-
markable study.
It should be com-
pared with the
Mohave carrying
basket from south-
western Arizona.[2]

Fig. 118.

WOMAN'S CARRYING-BASKET, FROM THE ANDAMAN ISLANDS.

Cat. No. 164745, U. S. N. M.   Collected by E. H. Man.   Gift of Prof. Enrico Giglioli.

The upper rim is a rigid hoop. From this depend bamboo rods, doubled in the middle and attached to the hoops by their ends. These doubled rods cross at the bottom as the meridians do at the pole, in such manner as to lay the foundation for an inverted cone. Between these rods depend subsidiary and smaller ones, reaching down not quite to the bottom and

---

[1] E. H. Man, Journ. Anthrop. Inst., London, 1889, xviii, p. 376.
[2] Rep. Smithsonian Inst. (U. S. Nat. Mus.), 1887, p. 264, and Third Ann. Rep. Bureau of Ethnology, p. 403.

forming the warp of a weave soon to be described. The weft of the basket is a continuous splint of bamboo passing round and round outside the warp and wrapped once around the warp rods as each one is passed, crossing the subsidiary rods without winding around them. This wrapped style of weaving is seen also in some impressions left on mound pottery, and in specimens from the Lake Dwellings. It reaches its modern expression in wire gauze, where both elements are equally flexible, and a two-ply twine at the joint is the result.

Further detail of the weaving is necessary. The subsidiary vertical rods are crossed by the weft splints and are held to them by a third and still smaller splint coiled or seized so as to make one turn about each crossing of warp and weft. This style exists in its highest perfection in Vancouver Island and Washington State, and is most skillfully combined with twined weaving by the Yokaia Indians of central California.

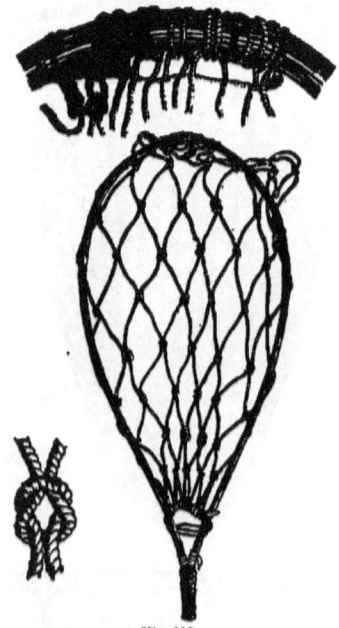

Fig. 119.

CARRYING-NET AND FRAME FROM NEW GUINEA

Cat. No. 73386, U. S. N. M.   Collected by A. P. Goodwin.

The fastening off of the warp rods at the bordering hoop is worthy of study. The little subsidiary rods are fastened by a double loop, as may be seen on snowshoes and in hundreds of other objects.

The main warp rods are chamfered or whittled away thin so that the hoop may rest solidly on their tops, and the remaining splint is wrapped around the hoop and then makes a half hitch about it, first on the right then on the left of the rod two or three times, producing a firm and ornamental joint.

Example No. 73386 (fig. 119) is a carrying net from New Guinea, consisting of a network of stout cord attached to a pole bent in the form of a pointed oval or broad snowshoe. This is to be filled with portable objects and borne on the shoulder or back and not on the head or carrying pole. The method is more nearly allied to the African methods of the Kongo. There are also tribes in the interior basin of the United States that carry in nets.

Powell says of the negroid women of New Britain that they carry on their backs two or three cocoanut bags full of merchandise.

The water carriers of Port Moresby, New Guinea, are women (fig. 120). They wear skirts of fringed leaf, dyed a reddish brown. They make a globe-shaped vessel, which they carry very gracefully on the shoulder well around on their necks, using the right hand to grasp it by the mouth and hold it steady. A small gourd is used in filling the vessel. In some areas on the Kongo, where the hair of the people is bushy and woolly and the coiffure is a matter of pride, this method of setting the round-bottomed water jar on the shoulder is to be seen.

The Philippine Islanders are a composite people of Negrito, Malay, and Sinitic elements, existing in all varieties of mixture. These Indonesians make pottery, and carry water therein. The round-bottomed vase is made to harmonize with the delicate and slightly pilose head by means of the headband, consisting of a scarf or sash deftly rolled up. In a collection of photographs made by Consul A. R. Webb the women are shown in various attitudes of holding, placing, poising, and removing the jar (figs. 121 and 122).

In this connection it is not difficult to understand how art is the glorification not of nature alone, but of industry. These caryatides have for their motive not some natural object, but a common human experience.

Example No. 74506 (fig. 123) is a carrying stick of bamboo, with baskets of bamboo. The pole is a piece of split bamboo, wider in the middle and notched at the ends to prevent the slipping of the load. The baskets of this

Fig. 120.

PAPUAN WOMEN CARRYING JARS ON THE SHOULDER.

From a photograph in the U. S. National Museum.

particular specimen are rather elaborately made of whole and split stalks, and paneled with the same materials. The inside is provided with cleats, on which shelves or drawers may slide, for holding and serving a number of dishes. The special treatment of the bamboo in making fast joints without nails or lashing will be better shown in the carrying chair from China, illustrated in this paper (fig. 229).

Example No. 54174 (fig. 124) is part of a carrying apparatus made of two bent bamboo splints, with a latticed floor on which to set the load. This and the specimen just before described were the gift of the Chinese Centennial Commission. It would be impossible to describe and figure the practically endless variety of inventions in China for the utilization of the shoulder pole. The bamboo also is a great blessing, since it lends itself to the inventor's mind with a plasticity almost equal to that of clay and with a toughness, according to weight, that can not be excelled by any other material.

Dr. R. N. Graves, long time missionary in China, contributes the following notes on the Chinese carrying trade in general:

The carrying poles of the Chinese coolies are of stout bamboo, about 6 feet long, or they use a pole of smooth, strong, flexible wood, about 2 inches broad by 1 thick, a long ellipse in section. A peg at each end, and the stick being somewhat widened, prevents the ropes or rattan slings from falling off. They shift the burden from one shoulder to another by means of the staff, and never use a yoke resting on both shoulders, as is seen in Europe. The skin on the shoulders becomes thickened and hardened, but not infrequently becomes sore and galled. They are truly beasts of burden.

Fig. 121.

PHILIPPINE WOMAN "TOTING" WATER.

From a photograph by Consul Alexander R. Webb.

Fig. 122.

PHILIPPINE WOMAN LIFTING JAR FROM THE HEAD.

From a photograph by Consul Alexander R. Webb.

As to the rate of travel and annual amount of goods carried, no definite information can be given. Most of the carrying is between the villages and towns 15 or 20 miles away and shorter distances. Formerly, before the opening of the Yang Tze to foreign trade, a great deal of tea was brought across the mountains from the central provinces, several days' journey, to the head waters of the Canton River, but this is discontinued. Most of the merchandise in South China is carried for long distances by the waterways. In the more thinly settled hills and mountainous districts it is carried on men's shoulders.

The Chinese wheelbarrow (fig. 125) is, in fact, a camel or donkey pack-saddle with its balanced, two-sided load. The wheel and the coolie's legs are the locomotory part of the device. If the wheel be removed, the two sides of the burden would fit over the back of any pack beast and the track need not be widened. The Chinese do not at present extensively use this mode of transportation except in the cities, but the Tibetans employ both the yak and the horse. The camel is not far distant on the northwest, and in the Chinese tribute-pictures horses, asses, camels, elephants, and pack reindeer are seen. Hereabouts there are two other examples of the beginning of the wheel. The Baschkir cradle in Orenburg, Russia, with two little wooden block wheels, is figured by Pokrowski. The Korean carrying chair has often beneath it a single wheel, a very laborious device for taking a load from the back of an animal instead of putting it on.[1] In the exaltation of the royal person, ceremony decides the form of the vehicle. In the freight and passenger barrow of the Chinese there is no social distinction created between passenger and barrow man.

The women of western Tibet are healthy and hardy, and carry weights of 60 pounds over the passes. They wear shoes of felt and of straw.[2]

The Tibetans are very quick over their work. Each time they raise a heavy load they force out the air from their lungs by a vigorous hiss. They handle great weights with considerable ease, for

Fig. 123.

CHINESE CARRYING-BASKETS AND SHOULDER-POLE OF BAMBOO.

Cat. No. 74506, U. S. N. M. Gift of the Chinese Centennial Commission, Philadelphia, 1876.

their arms, though not muscular, are tough and set in solid shoulders, which are supported by deep necks, the length of their forearm being remarkable. Lamas, stick in hand, give their orders and reprimand them; but these savages do their work cheerfully and are obedient and respectful to the lamas, to whom they listen in the most humble posture, with back bent and hanging tongue.[3]

The Aino usually carry burdens by means of a braided band of the bark of ohiyo (*Ulmus montana*).

[1] Pokrowski, Revue d'Ethnographie, 1889, p. 34.
[2] Bishop, "Among the Tibetans," Chicago, 1891, p. 44.
[3] Bonvalot, "Across Tibet," New York, 1892, Cassell, p. 270.

Example No. 22254 (fig. 126) shows the manner in which this elaborate contrivance is constructed. Hough figures one of them in use (pl. 23), and says that these bands, called tara or pickai-tara, are also employed to sustain the babe upon the back. Sometimes the two ends of the headband are tied to the ends of a stick resting on the lumbar region, and upon this the burden rests. The Korean extends the ends of the stick, and then has a kind of yoke resting on the lower part of his back. The Aino women make constant use of the tara. They carry heavy loads with them, and even bring large tubs of water to their homes.[1]

Example No. 22254 is a carrying band collected in Yokohama by the Hon. B. S. Lyman. A similar specimen, collected by Wilkes on the northwest coast of America, is unfortunately labeled Africa.[2]

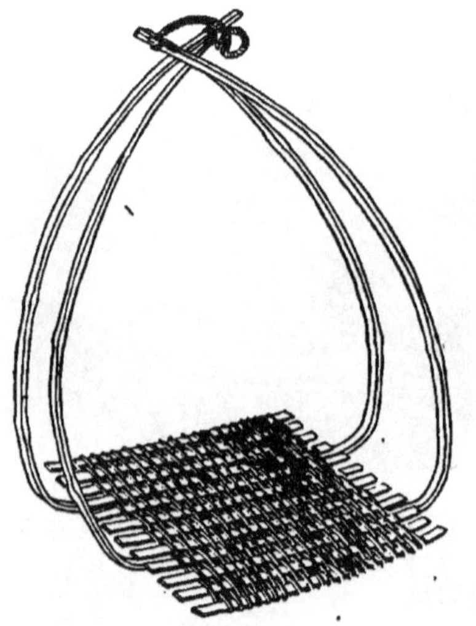

Fig. 124.

CHINESE CARRYING-CRATE.

Cat. No. 54174, U. S. N. M.   Gift of the Chinese Centennial Commission, Philadelphia, 1876.

Prof. E. S. Morse speaks in the greatest praise of Japanese backs, both as to their strength and flexibility. This people also are expert in the hexagonal weaving of carrying devices in bamboo splints. This enables them to produce a receptacle (fig. 127) which combines perfectly the strength and lightness that are needed. The same hexagonal plan of weaving exists in the U. S. National Museum upon specimens of snowshoes in Canada and cedar-bark wallets of southeastern Alaska and British Columbia, but nowhere on basketry in America south of the Canadian line and east of the coast range.

The Japanese also have borrowed from China the shoulder pole or stick of bamboo for all sorts of short-distance carrying (fig. 128). The exigencies of Japanese commerce do not demand the extensive coolie system. The epoch of the human back, however, was at its climax when the islands were first visited. The people were singularly devoid of beasts of burden. In the figures from life here reproduced the clever tricks for using the pole are made manifest, for in such matters the Japanese are extremely ingenious. Owing to a climate not at all rigorous, the professional carriers are not overclad.

Example No. 73093 (fig. 129) is a carrying frame from the province of Tate Yama, Japan, collected by P. L. Jouy. It is a ladder or frame-

[1] Cf. Rep. Smithsonian Inst. (U. S. Nat. Mus.), 1890, p. 464, pl. cv.
[2] Cf. Rep. Smithsonian Inst. (U. S. Nat. Mus.), 1887, p. 287, fig. 42.

KOREAN PEDDLERS.

The one on the left hand with the rectangular box is a seller of confectionery and small articles, his load resting against his body in front and supported by a strap or band hung from the nape of the neck. This method of carrying is universal among hawkers of small ware, and is said to be omnipresent in Korea.

The carrier to the right wears the knapsack frame supported on the back by shoulder straps or braces.

KOREAN PEDDLERS.

Hough, "The Bernadou, Allen, and Jouy Korean Collections in the U. S. National Museum,"
Pl. VI, Report of the Smithsonian Institution (U. S. National Museum), 1891.

work of wood, not unlike that of some American Indian cradles. To render the framework soft to the back and to hold it in place, it is

Fig. 125.

CHINESE BARROW OR DOUBLE SHOULDER-PACK, MOUNTED ON A WHEEL.

From a photograph in the U. S. National Museum.

entirely wrapped and concealed in a continuous sennit or braid of straw. The arm bands are of the same material and are braided like

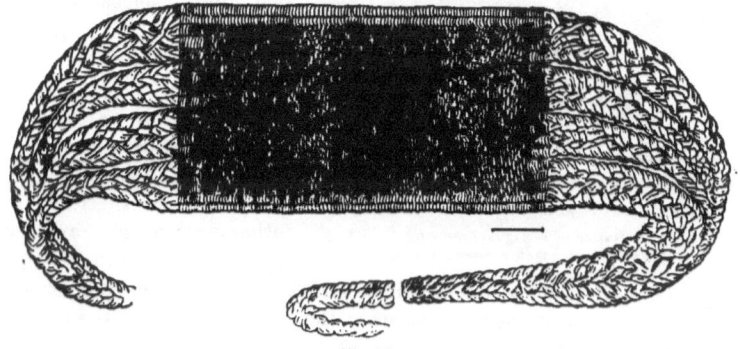

· Fig. 126.

JAPANESE HEADBAND AND CARRYING-ROPE, BRAIDED AND WOVEN.

Cat. No. 22254, U. S. N. M. Collected by Hon. B. S. Lyman.

a whip-lash, thickest where the pad is needed. These bands are to be worn knapsack fashion, and are tied by their extremities to the wooden framework. The lashing for the load is also of sennit.

The Tate Yama carrying rack or ladder appears in Korea without the wrapping of sennit, but with pieces framed in near the bottom pointing outward at right angles to form a shelf like that on the glass peddler's frame. A staff or rest may be attached to enable the carrier to relieve his back without setting the burden on the ground. (Fig. 130.) Hitchcock brought from the Aino country photographs of a precisely similar device. It is worn knapsack fashion, which refers the reader to Japan.[1]

The carrying pole in Korea (fig. 131) is not always used on the shoulder, but after a fashion that recalls two or three inventions in different areas. The pole rests on the lower back and is suspended from a band attached to its middle and passing up under one arm, over the shoulder, back of the neck, down in front of the other shoulder, and back to the starting point. Children in England and America harness one another thus in playing horse; but this is the only example known to the author where the scheme is in serious use. Hooks are suspended from the ends of the pole, and from these hang jars slung neatly in splints. The detachable feature of the sling on the jar is also quite original, as will be noted in Carles's figure.[2]

From Carles it is also seen that the order of transportation is sometimes reversed in Korea, in that the woman may carry merchandise on the head and the man become packer for merchandise and passenger-bearer at the same time, using the double bandolier (fig. 132).

Example No. 150768 is a carrying band and seat from Shikotan, in the island of Yezo, collected by Romyn Hitchcock. It is used by women for carrying children on their backs. The apparatus consists of two parts—a woven band which passes over the chest of the bearer,

Fig. 127.
JAPANESE CARRYING-BASKET WITH SHOULDER-STRAPS.
Illustration of hexagonal weaving.
From a photograph in the U. S. National Museum.

[1] Cf. Carles, "Life in Korea," New York, 1894, Macmillan & Co., p. 67.
[2] Ibid., p. 30.

to each end of which a line is attached, and a slightly curved wooden seat, to the ends of which the line is made fast. The child sits on the seat as in a swing, and its feet straddle the hips of the mother.[1] (See fig. 133.)

Among the causes that have produced pluck and physical strength in men, perhaps the carrying trade is preeminent. The pick, the hammer, the plane, develop muscle. Art, commercial pursuits, and the enjoyments of life usually render men delicate. The toughening of the legs and back and arms, the development of lung and heart power, and the ability to endure winter's cold as well as summer's heat come from the carrying and traveling industry.

So far we have been in the land of the professional carrier, where men have been compelled to transport burdens and to haul loads professionally.

Fig. 128.

JAPANESE CARRIER, WITH SHOULDER-POLE AND LOADS.

From a photograph in the U. S. National Museum.

Coming to the American continent, the reader will still be witness to a great deal of heavy drudgery in this department, but the human back is greatly relieved by the fact that few of the industries of this continent were in the world's great streams of progress before Columbus, and therefore the amount of burden bearing was restricted to limited culture areas. It is fitting at this point, and speaking of this enormous amount of professional carrying, to take into consideration the effect of this successive work upon the bodies of men.

Dr. Robert Fletcher calls my attention to the fact that studies in this line have been instituted by the French Government upon what is called "l'homme moteur" by Dr. Bezy, of Toulouse. Dr. Fletcher refers

---

[1] Rep. Smithsonian Inst. (U. S. Nat. Mus.), 1890, p. 426, fig. 67.

to the enormous amount of work done by man power, especially in times of war. It seems that the railroad hands at Toulouse had made complaint of being compelled to carry on the back bags of flour weighing from 100 to 122 kilos (say, 240 pounds) from the car to the quay, a distance of 21 meters, on uneven ground, continuously. One man made twelve trips, but at the last one broke down and was unable afterwards to work.

Dr. Bezy found that the railroad companies had not used the dynamometer in examining men for the work, and, furthermore, the following interesting results were obtained. A man weighing 85 kilos can walk on a horizontal road at the rate of 1.50 meters per second for a space of ten hours. A traveler with his baggage on his back can carry 40 kilos at the rate of 0.75 meters per second for seven hours. A porter, carrying a load on his back and returning empty handed for a fresh load, can carry 55 kilos at the rate of 0.50 meters per second for six hours.

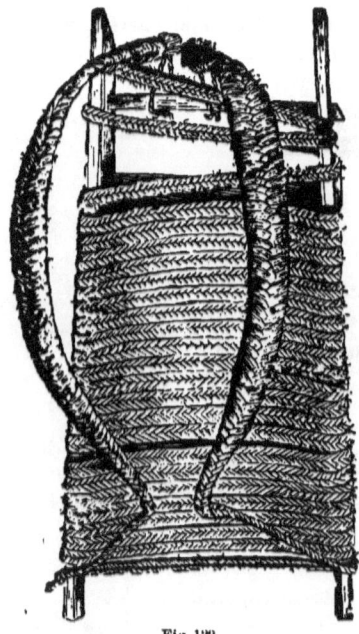

Fig. 120.

NORTHERN JAPANESE CARRYING-FRAME, WITH SHOULDER-BANDS.

Illustration of plaited work.

Cat. No. 73093, U. S. N. M. Collected by P. L. Jouy.

Dr. Fletcher also calls the author's attention to Quetelet's table of the standard of lifting strength to the rule that a man should not carry a load greater than his own weight.

Excessive carrying is made more injurious by increasing the time, or age, or speed, or roughness of the path, or by decreasing nutrition.

On passing northward into eastern Siberia the student comes upon the pack reindeer, the sledge reindeer, and the dog. Women have their own fashions of carrying children, as will be seen later; but men are too much burdened with clothing, and relief is too near at hand for them to continue the old-time slavery of the back.

The Eskimo in carrying loads use the band across the forehead as well as across the breast. Having their little hand sledges, they are given more to traction than to carrying. The women have strong backs, and upon them falls the duty of burden-bearing. In the "Cruise of the Corwin" is an account of a woman who, by rolling and the use of her boat, succeeded in transporting an anchor stone weighing, it was supposed, 300 pounds.[1]

---

[1] Haley, "Cruise of the Corwin," Washington, 1885, p. 49.

Turner says that he has seen the Ungava Eskimo place a barrel of flour on their shoulders and carry it up a hillside so steep as to require one not burdened to pick his steps with care. [1]

Crantz says that the women of Greenland are the butchers and cooks, and also the curriers to dress the pelts and make clothes, boots, and shoes out of them, and for all this business they use nothing but a knife in form of a half-moon, such as cooks mince meat with, which they use also at the table, and have neither shears nor knife besides; a bone or ivory slice, a thimble, a couple of coarse and fine needles, and their own teeth, with which they pull the skins and supple them both at dressing and sewing. They build and repair the houses and tents quite alone, as far as relates to the masonry. The men very coolly look on while the women bring heavy stones that are ready to break their backs. [2]

The enormous amount of energy and endurance in the Eskimo arrested the attention of Nansen. He has collected in his second volume a number of narratives in which are described West Greenlanders who have gotten into straits and who have performed prodigies of energy. [3]

The Babines, a subtribe of carriers in British Columbia, have a frame for the back called tchen-est'lú (sticks interwoven). It is like a rough arm chair without legs, made of stout split sticks of willow (*Salix longifolia*) joined by thongs. The Déné women pack this frame from the forehead with

Fig. 130.

KOREAN BRUSHWOOD CUTTER USING RISING-FRAME WITH SHOULDER-STRAPS.

From a figure in Carles' "Life in Korea."

a skin line broadening in the middle, and if the load is heavy the ends of the line are passed across the chest. Father Morice has seen among the Hwotsn' tinne, a fraction of the Babines, a woman thus packing her invalid husband, a man of more than average size and weight. [4]

[1] Turner, "Indians and Eskimo of Ungava," p. 104.
[2] Crantz, "History of Greenland," London, 1767, p. 164.
[3] Nansen, "First Crossing of Greenland," London, 1890, II, p. 285.
[4] Trans. Canadian Inst., 1894, VII, p. 118.

Example No. 150406 is the model of a similar packing frame (ka-ni-ko n-hua) from the Onondaga Iroquois, procured by Mr. Hewitt. It is made of hickory rods bent like a wooden flail, and resembles two backs of bent-wood chairs, one vertical, the other horizontal, the parts united by means of tough hickory bark. The rack for trunks on the back of a country stage coach seems to be a survival of this angular packing frame. Father Morice points out its occurrence in the ancient Mexican codices. It may be seen on the backs of porters at Panama and in Peru. The Patagonian mother has a similar device for her baby, and

Fig. 131.

KOREAN MAN CARRYING WATER BY MEANS OF A POLE RESTING ON THE LUMBAR REGION AND SUPPORTED
BY A BAND PASSING OVER THE SHOULDER AND AROUND THE NECK.
From a sketch in the U. S. National Museum.

Hitchcock, as has been said, photographed the type on the backs of his Aino carriers for the U. S. National Museum.

Father Morice reports that the carriers of Stuart Lake (Athapascans) are inferior workmen, and that they fabricate carrying pails from the bark of the birch (*Betula papyracea*) and of spruce (*Abies nigra*). The method of construction is given, with working patterns.[1]

Among the carriers the wallet or packing bag of the men, t'lul-en'-kez', is made from the caribou skin cut in fine strips or the skin of beavers when found so decomposed that the fur has lost its value.[2]

___

[1] Trans. Canadian Inst., 1894, IV, Chap. VII. The whole paper can not be too highly commended.

[2] Ibid., 1891, IV, p. 160.

The regular packing wallet (lu'-kéz) of the carriers is made of undressed moose hide and tanned caribou skin. The packing band is of moose skin, broad in the middle for the forehead and quite long. On each end of the wallet is a lug or ear of tanned hide pierced with two holes. The ends of the carrying band pass through the upper holes and are drawn forward and tied across the breast, so that the position of the burden may be changed at will.[1] Salmon skin often replaces the hide. Women are the principal carriers.

Of the Athapascan woman Father Morice says that her capacity for

Fig. 132.

KOREAN METHODS OF CARRYING.

From a figure in Carles' "Life in Korea."

carrying heavy burdens lies in her ability to preserve an accurate balancing of the load rather than in any great muscular strength. The pack rests on the back, between the shoulders, supported by a leather line which passes in a broad band across the forehead and is secured by the ends of the line being tied across the chest.[2]

The professional carriers about Lake Nipigon, Canada, are described by Ralph, who says that each man uses a tumpline, or long stout strap, which he tied in such a way around what he meant to carry, that a broad part of the strap fitted over the crown of his head (fig. 134).

[1] Trans. Canadian Inst., 1891, IV, p. 147, fig. 135.
[2] Proc. Canadian Inst., 1889, XXV, Nos. 124 and 152.

Thus they "packed" the goods over the portage, their heads sustaining the loads, and their backs merely steadying them. When one had thrown his burden into place, he trotted off up the trail with springing feet, though the freight was packed so that 100 pounds should form a load. For bravado one carried 200 pounds, and then all the others tried to pack as much, and most of them succeeded. All agreed that one, the smallest and least muscular-looking one among them could carry 400 pounds.[1]

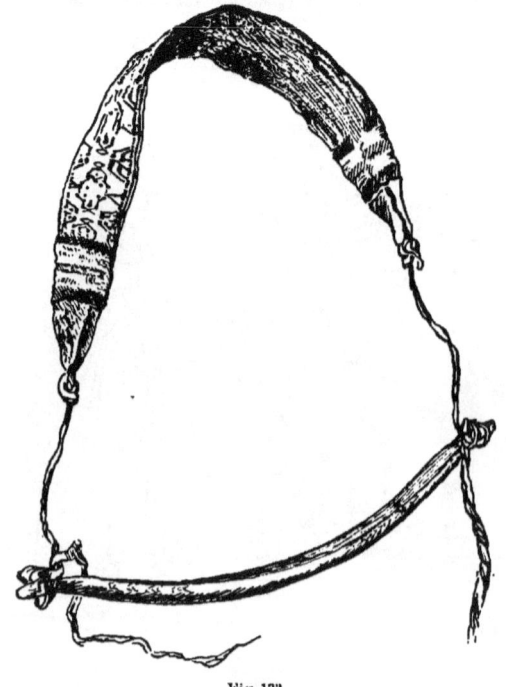

Fig. 133.

AINO HEAD-STRAP AND SEAT, FROM SHIKOTAN, YEZO.

From a figure in the Report of the Smithsonian Institution (U. S. National Museum), 1890.

Cat. No. 150768, U. S. N. M

Mackenzie tells of men who carried seven packages of 90 pounds each across a portage half a league long without stopping.[2]

The Kutchin woman cuts and hauls the firewood for her husband; she hauls his lodge, kettles, and property when the camp is moved; she hauls the meat to the camp in winter and carries it in summer. During the warm weather she dries the meat, carries him water, makes his clothes, laces his snowshoes, and indeed does all the drudgery of the camps. The men always cook. If a wife will not obey her husband

[1] Julian Ralph, "On Canada's Frontier," New York, 1892, p. 188.
[2] "Voyages from Montreal through the Continent of North America," p. LVIII.

she gets a good beating. Children are generally well treated by their parents.[1]

The watersheds and river systems of Canada and the northern United States, together with the fact that nature supplied excellent material for very light and capacious water craft, rendered this whole territory accessible from any point of it and made it possible for single stocks of Indians to occupy large territory. Portages were of several kinds:

(1) The voyageurs unloaded their canoes, carried the goods on their backs by means of headbands or on their shoulders, from open water to open water, making as many trips backward and forward as necessary. The canoe was towed up and past the obstruction by means of strong lines.

(2) If the water would not permit the towing of the boat, it had to be carried around the obstruction, a distance of a few feet or of miles. In fact, in former time this sort of carrying was called portage, the carrying of goods alone was called décharge.

(3) In descending, the boat with its cargo, or partly lightened, was "shot" through moderate rapids by skillful steersmen, or let down by means of lines and guided past dangerous points.

Portages varied also in their length, in the nature of the surrounding hills, in the depths of the water according to season. Mackenzie speaks of portage à la vase, which is the same as the English mud portage, or the poling, dragging, forcing of the vessel through

Fig. 134.
CANADIAN PACKER WITH TUMPLINE.
From a figure in "Canada's Frontier," by Julian Ralph.

mud flats. Now and then a natural canal was helpful, and then for a quarter of a mile or more the navigation was a comprehensive example of all the species of human effort.[2]

Of his carriers Mackenzie says that when leaving Montreal they arrived at the Grand Portage, which is 9 miles over; each of them had to carry 8 packages (90 pounds). "So inured are they to this kind of labor, that I have known them to set off with two packages and return with two others of the same weight in six hours, a distance of 18 miles over hills and mountains."

The canoes of the Hudson Bay Company were navigated by four to six men, and carried on an average 3,500 pounds. Each had a foreman

[1] Jones, Rep. Smithsonian Inst., 1866, p. 326.
[2] Mackenzie, "Voyages from Montreal through the Continent of North America," Philadelphia 1802, p. xxxiii.

and a steersman, and enough additional men to form a crew capable of carrying the boat.

The justification among the Chippewas for loading the backs of their women with grievous burdens is found in their mythology. They derive their origin from dogs. At one time, as the story goes, they were seized with such reverence for their canine ancestors that they entirely ceased to employ dogs in drawing their sledges, greatly to the hardship of their women, to whom the task fell.[1]

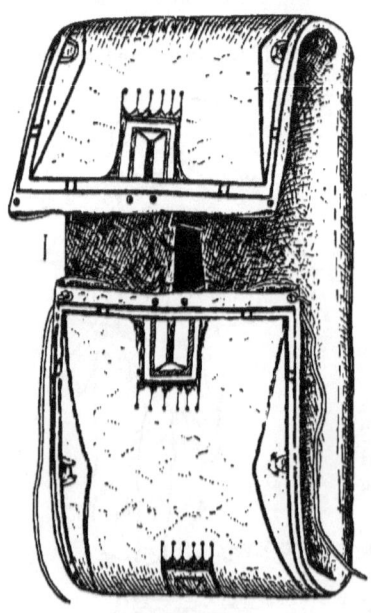

Fig. 135.
RAWHIDE PACKING OR PARFLECHE CASE.
Cat. No. 165918, U. S. N. M.   Collected by H. R. Voth.

Maximilian saw Cree Indian women returning in all directions from the forests, panting under the weight of large bundles of wood, which were fastened on their backs.[2]

Example No. 165918 in the U. S. National Museum is the universal packing or parfleche case of the Cheyenne Indians of the Algonquian stock. It is made from a single piece of buffalo hide, cured as rawhide and not tawed. A hide was first sweated so that the hair would come out and then cleaned and stretched until nearly dry. It was then cut into shape, doubled up into wallet form, useless folds were cut away, and was then fitted with strings and painted in green, black, yellow, and blue to the gentile pattern. The U. S. National Museum possesses a large variety of these packing cases from every one of the stocks on the plains—Siouan, Algonquian, Caddoan, Kiowan, and Shoshonean.

The function of the parfleche was to preserve articles and food in the tent and to become a packing case for man, for dog's back, dog travois, horse travois, and horse's back in the daily or the annual move (figs. 135 and 136).

"In winter time," says Wood, "the New England Indian women were their husbands' caterers, trudging to the clam banks for their timber, and their porters to lug home their venison which their laziness exposes to the wolves till they impose it upon their wives' shoulders."[3]

Loskiel says that the Delaware women carried everything on their

[1] Bancroft, "Native Races of the Pacific States," New York, 1874–1876, I, p. 118.
[2] Maximilian, "Travels in the Interior of North America," London, 1843, p. 203.
[3] Wood, "New England's Prospect," Prince Soc. Publications, Boston, I, p. 108.

heads, fastened by a thong round their foreheads. By means of this they frequently supported above a hundredweight, the load being placed so as to rest also upon their backs.[1]

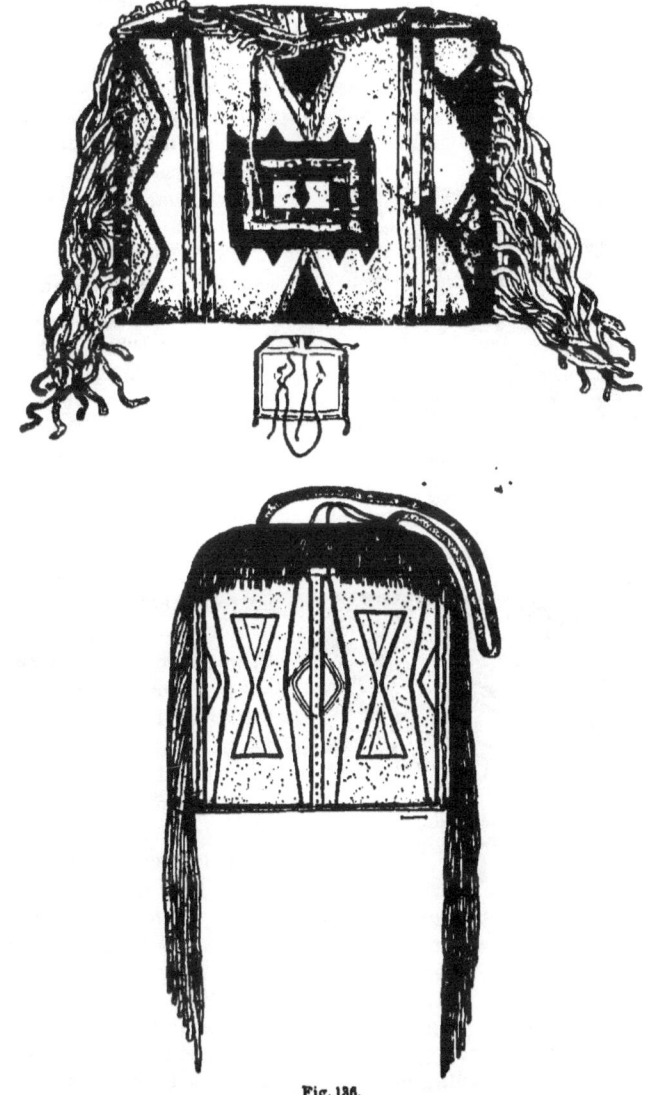

Fig. 136.

RAWHIDE PACKING OR PARFLECHE CASES.

Cat. No. 165129, U. S. N. M.   Collected by James Mooney.

The U. S. National Museum possesses an old carrying basket, example

[1]Loskiel, "History of the Mission of the United Brethren," 1794, pp. 107–108.

No. 8430 (fig. 137), from the Arikaree Indians, of Dakota, who are of the Pânian or Caddoan stock. The basket is quadrilateral, widest at the top and longer than wide. Four bent poles constitute the frame, each one forming the basis of a side or end. The end ones, much like ox-yoke bows, project below the others to form a rest for the basket. At the top the ends of the poles are held in place by means of a hoop. In a former paper the weaving was said to resemble that of the British Columbia tribes in cedar bark and other flat material, and so it does. But it is

Fig. 137.

CARRYING-BASKET OF ARIKAREE (CADDOAN) INDIANS.

Cat. No. 8430, U. S. N. M.   Collected by Dr. Washington Matthews, U. S. A.

more significant here that it also resembles that of the Muskhogean and other southern stocks of the United States. It is diagonal weaving in narrow strips of birch and other tough bark, varying in color. The distribution of this type of weaving belongs to the study of the industries of the American aborigines.

The cacique of Patofa gave to Soto guides, 700 Indians to bear burdens, and maize for four days' journey. Soto traveled six days by a path, which narrowed more and more until it was lost altogether. All through Georgia the Indians obeyed their ladie to furnish bearers. From that it is inferred that the professional carrier had been developed.[1]

Example No. 91508 (fig. 138) is a form of carrying basket quite common among the Choctaw Indians of Louisiana. It is a hamper holding a bushel or more, wider at top than at bottom. It is made of the common cane, split and woven by diagonal weaving, the universal method among the southern tribes of the United States upon all baskets whatever. The headband of leather is attached to the sides of the basket.

On the west coast of America, south of the peninsula of Alaska, the sled, the kayak, and the portable canoe disappear, and the porter at once assumes his carrying devices, and does not lay them aside again until the Straits of Magellan are reached. Both head and breast band are brought into play. With the former the reader is familiar.

The breastband is a flat piece of textile or hide extending from a

---

[1] "Discovery and Conquest of Terra Florida," Publications of the Hakluyt Society 1851, p. 52.

load on a man's back across his arms and breast. Sometimes it is seen quite up to the collar bone, again it crosses almost down to the elbows. A good picture of this device is given by Krause. He figures a Chilkat man, barefoot, wearing trousers and blouse, and carrying a pack supported by a headband and breastband. Between the former and the forehead lies a soft pad.[1] (Fig. 139.)

Schwatka was astonished at the endurance of the Alaskan carriers, and says that the Indian packers over these mountain passes usually carry 100 pounds, although one he had witnessed walked along readily with 127, and a miner informed him that his party employed one that carried 160. The cost of carriage of a pack (100 pounds) over the Chilkoot trail for miners has been from $9 to $12, and the Indians were not inclined to see him over at any reduced rates, despite the large amount of material re quired to be transported, some 2 tons. By giving them two loads, or doubling the time over the portage, a slight reduction could be had, not worth the time lost in such an arrangement, and he made contracts with enough of them to carry his effects over at once. "Mr. Spuhn was also very energetic in his efforts to secure for me better terms, but without avail, and after I crossed the

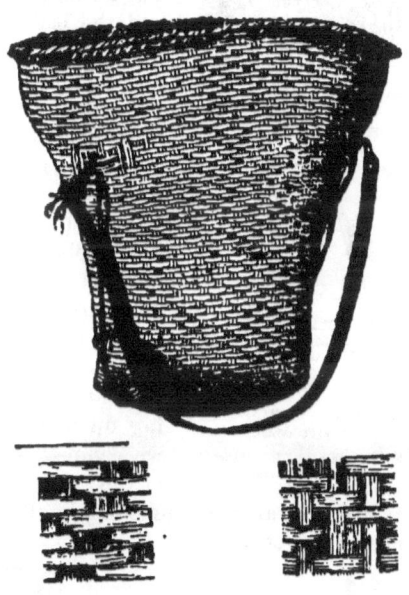

Fig. 138.

CHOCTAW CARRYING-BASKET, COMMON AMONG MUSKHO-GEAN TRIBES.

Cat. No. 91508, U. S. N. M. Collected by Edward Palmer.

trail I in no way blamed the Indians for their stubbornness in maintaining what seemed at first sight to be exorbitant, and only wondered that they would do this extremely fatiguing labor so reasonably."

Schwatka gives a view on Payer portage, representing a Chilkat Indian with two ammunition boxes going over the pass. The amount some of these packers will carry seems marvelous, and makes estimates for pack mules or trails therefor seem superfluous. Their only packing gear is a couple of bands, one passing over the forehead where it is flattened out into a broad strip, and the other over the arms and across the breast. The two meet behind on a level with the shoulder, and are there attached to lashings more or less intricate,

---

[1] Aurel Krause, "Die Tllnket-Indianer," Jena, 1885, p. 101.

according to the nature of the material to be transported. If a box or stiff bag, the breast band is so arranged in regard to length that when

the elbow is placed against it (the box), the strip fits tightly over the extended forearm across the palm of the hand bent backward. The head-band is then the width of the hand beyond this. Schwatka saw a few Indians arranging their packs and their harness according to this mode. The harness proper will not weigh over a pound, and the lashing according to its length. The strip across the head and breast is of untanned deerskin, about 2 inches wide, with holes or slits in the ends protected from tearing out by spindles of bone or ivory.[1]

"It seemed marvelous beyond measure how these small Indians, not averaging, I believe, over 140 pounds each, could carry 100 pounds up such a precipitous mountain, alternately on steeply inclined glacial snow and treacherous rounded bowlders where a misstep in many places could have hurled them hundreds of feet down the slope or precipices.

Fig. 139.

CHILKAT (KOLUSCHAN) PACKER WITH LOAD.

From a figure in "Die Tlinket Indianer," by Krause.

"The Indian would chase a goat, almost keeping up with him, down into the valley where we camped, and up the steep mountain slopes of the eastern side equally as high as those mentioned, and all this immediately after he had carried over 100 pounds across the trail."[2]

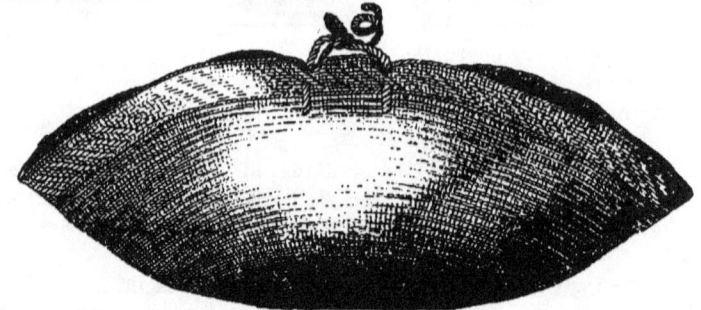

Fig. 140.

CARRYING-WALLET OF SPRUCE ROOT, MIXED PLAIN AND TWINED WEAVING.

Southeastern Alaska.

Cat. No. 168163, U. S. N. M. Collected by Herbert Ogden.

Example No. 168163 (fig. 140) is a wallet of spruce root from south-eastern Alaska, near Fort Wrangell. It is a shallow bowl or tray,

---

[1] Schwatka, "Military Reconnoissance in Alaska," 1883, p. 23, fig. 8.
[2] Ibid., pp. 17–18.

circular in outline, and flexible. The noteworthy characteristic is the mixture of art in its production. In the weft every alternate row is twined and the next plainly woven. Now Dixons Entrance is the point of contact of the Koluschan or Tlingit, the Skittagetan or Haida, the Chimmesyan and the Wakashan or Haeltzukan families, and Salishan tribes are not far distant. On the north of Dixons Entrance twined weaving in split spruce root attains its perfection. On the south of it, in the cedar-bark country, plain weaving and diagonal or diaper weaving have their develop-

Fig. 141.

PLAITED CARRYING-BAND AND LINE, USED BY THE MAKAH (WAKASHAN) INDIANS, NEAH BAY, WASHINGTON.

Cat. No. 1292, U. S. N. M.   Collected by James G. Swan.

ment. In this specimen a Tlingit woman might have woven one row and a Wakashan woman the alternate row. On a great many trade baskets and fanciful articles, such as covered bottles, this alternation reappears. The handle is a loop of spruce-root rope on one margin and a loose end on the other margin to fit therein.

Speaking of the necessity of carriers from the coast, Seton-Karr says that when the Chilkats are all gone, those interior regions which are only attainable on foot with pack-carriers or packers will become more difficult of access, because now these Indians, broken as they are by disease, can yet carry heavier packs than a white man. They can travel farther on foot and endure greater hardships. They do not

Fig. 142.

PLAITED AND WOVEN HEAD-BAND, USED BY THE CLALLAM (SALISHAN) INDIANS.

Cat. No. 23472, U. S. N. M.   Collected by James G. Swan.

require so much in the shape of clothes and bedding. Their dried salmon, which they carry as food, weighs little, and they are satisfied with that. They are able, moreover, to supplement this with many kinds of roots, herbs, and fruits which are eatable.[1]

Mrs. Allison says of the Similkameen:

Before there was any regular means of transport over the mountains lying between Hope, on the Frazer, and the Similkameen, the Indians used to be employed to pack provisions over on their backs. Their packs were suspended by means of a band or strap passed over their foreheads [see figs. 141 and 142], and I have known some of them to pack three sacks of flour (150 pounds) on their back while traveling on snowshoes for a distance of 65 miles over a rough, mountainous road, with a depth of 25 feet of snow on the summit of the Hope Mountain, over which the trail ran. Some-

[1] Seton-Karr, Proc. Roy. Geog. Soc., London, 1891, XIII, p. 73.

times a whole family would start out on one of these packing expeditions, the children as well as their parents, each taking a load and accomplishing the journey in six or eight days, according to the state of the road. If an unusually violent snowstorm overtook an Indian while traveling in the mountains he would dig a hole in the snow, cover himself with his blanket, and allow himself to be snowed up; here he would calmly sleep until the snow had passed, then he would proceed on his journey.[1]

Mayne's testimony is to the same effect:

The things were then divided into bundles or packs, of as even weight as possible, giving some 50 or 60 pounds to each man. Arranging these packs is a matter of no little difficulty, for the Indian has a great objection to altering his load after he has started, so that you have to give the men carrying the provisions, which grow lighter daily, a heavier load at starting than those who have the canteen or the tent to carry.

They generally stop for some five minutes' rest every half hour. This they do with surprising regularity. They generally squat near a ledge of rock on which they can rest their burden without removing it. They carry everything the same way, viz, with a band over the forehead, the pack resting on their shoulder blades or a little below.[2]

Of the Columbia Indians Lewis and Clark speak:

The morning was cool; the wind high, from the northeast. The Indians who arrived last night took their empty canoes on their shoulders and carried them below the great shoot, where they put them in the water and brought them down the rapid, till at the distance of 3¼ miles they stopped to take in their loading, which they had been afraid to trust in the last rapid, and had therefore carried by land from the head of the shoot.[3]

Fig. 143.
INDIAN WOMAN CARRYING WOOD WITH BREAST-BAND AND PARBUCKLE.
Montana.

From a photograph in U. S. National Museum.

The men and women about Stillwater, Mont., carry loads in a similar way. (Fig. 143.) The packer takes a reata or rope about the size of one's finger, made out of Buffalo skin or braided elk skin (three plait), lays it on the ground in shape of a loop, and places the load across it. They generally get a little rise in the ground or a cut bank; but if on the level of a prairie they are helped by one of their number to raise it or else work over on their side until they can get upon their knees, when they are all right. After placing their load of 100 pounds each of flour or a quarter of a buffalo or steer or a bundle of dry wood they, with their back against it, take the curve or bend of the rope over their head,

[1] Allison, Journ. Anthrop. Inst., London, 1892, xxi, pp. 305–306.
[2] Mayne, "British Columbia and Vancouver Island," pp. 100–101.
[3] "History of the Expedition under the command of Lewis and Clark," New York, 1893, ii, p. 684.

down across the breast and across the shoulders, and then, taking one of the ends in each hand, bring them up behind their back, catch the rope on top of the load by running each end under; then, pulling the ends over each shoulder, tighten the load, if loose, and then raise on one side, then the other, to make it more secure, and with a heave forward the carrier comes to the knees before getting on the feet. The load or burden rests on the back and shoulders. When moving, the body is bent forward, and the heavier the load the more the body is inclined. I have seen them carry wood over 4 miles in this way, resting whenever they find a suitable place, like a cut bank or washed gully, so the load will be even with the place and can be taken again in a minute or so.

It will be observed that the regulation carrying strap is for the professional packer. When good textiles abound along the shores and inland, from Sitka southward, the carrying wallet and conical basket come into vogue. In the land of the giant cedar and of the soft grasses the former prevails. Under the domination of more rigid material the cone comes into play. The freight also is different. Most of the dwellings of the fishing people are by the water side, the freight can not be packed and the haul is short.

Example No. 127843 (fig. 144) is a carrying wallet from the Quinaielt Indians, a Salishan tribe in Chehalis County,

Fig. 144.

CARRYING-WALLET AND HEAD-BAND.

An example of twined weaving, with horizontal warp.

Cat. No. 127843, U. S. N. M. Quinaielt (Salishan) Indians, Washington. Collected by Charles Willoughby.

Wash., collected by Charles Willoughby. By reference to the illustration it will be seen that the apparatus is a combination of the head band and line, a kind of inverted sling, with a bag. The band is braided in the same manner as in the foregoing figure.

The construction of the wallet is of interest. The general texture is precisely that of the typical Chilkat blanket and the Sitka wallets, only the material is twine, the weaving is loose and flexible, and the warp is horizontal. At the top are one or two interesting features introduced to strengthen the border. Two rows of close-twined weaving are laid on outside as in the style called "bird-cage" stitch. The ends of the weft are braided down into one another, drawn tight and cut off.

Example No. 19026 (fig. 145) is a conical carrying basket used by the Clallam Indians. It was collected by James G. Swan. It is introduced to show how the savage inventor would convert a soft wallet of the north into a hard cone of the south. The web of the basket is from rushes united by twine weaving, by braiding, and by the plaiting of a single filament. This soft, open network is converted into a light but strong cone by the insertion of a hoop into the top and the fixing of six vertical rods to the hoop at equal distances, uniting their ends at the bottom of the cone, and sewing them to the texture of the wallet inside.

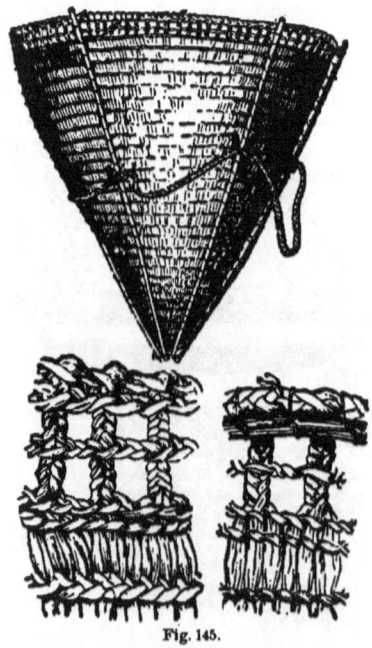

Fig. 145.

CONICAL CARRYING-BASKET WITH RODS AND PLAITED HEAD-BAND FROM PYRAMID LAKE, NEVADA.

Cat. No. 19026, U. S. N. M.   Collected by Stephen Powers.

Example No. 19289 (fig. 146) is a burden basket used by McCloud River Indians, California, collected by Livingstone Stone. In the Clallam basket just noted, the headband encircles the cone about the middle, raising the load high on the back, after the manner of the Oriental water carriers. Indeed, the conical basket and the conical jar should be studied together as for the back instead of the head. Farther south it will be seen that the Pueblo women make their jars for the head, while the Papago make theirs for the back, hence the variety in form. (Fig. 146.)

The California woman has abundance of rhus, hazel, willow, pine root, and other rigid material and may decorate the surface with different fern stems, straw, and dyed splint. So she makes her baskets in twined weaving, having rigid switches or small stems for her warp. But in this central California region there is a device of strengthening the texture not sufficiently explained in the drawing. It is, in fact, the union of what has been called the twined stitch with the bird-cage stitch.

There are three elements: (1) The fundamental or vertical warp of twigs; (2) across this at right angles a horizontal subsidiary warp of twig carried around in the process of weaving, and (3) a web or weft of twined weaving uniting the two. Dr. Hudson, of Yokaia, Cal., the best authority on such matters, draws attention to the fact that all the northern stitches culminate in the Sacramento Valley and parts adjacent, and that the Yo-kaian stock are very adept at this composite style of texture. The top of this basket is strengthened by a hoop, to which the carrying band is attached. The bottom is strengthened by close weaving.

The Pomo Indians use a conical basket for carrying, held on the back in a sling, the headband of which passes over the carrier's brow. Dr. Hudson once saw an old woman carry 3 bushels of potatoes in this manner through mud and rain to her home 2 miles distant. Greater loads are not unusual to the men, and as a consequent result of such customary labor the Digger Indian is abnormally developed in the dorsal and the anterior cervical muscles,

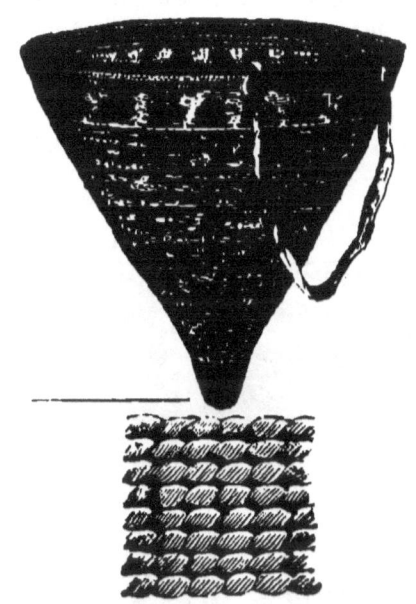

Fig. 146.

CONICAL BURDEN-BASKET USED BY THE MCCLOUD RIVER INDIANS OF SHASTA COUNTY, CALIFORNIA.

Cat. No. 19299, U. S. N. M. Collected by Livingston Stone.

besides having a chest magnificent in proportions.[1]

Example No. 126907 (fig. 147) is an elaborately constructed headband worn by the Natano band of Hupa Indians, Athapascan stock, living on the reservation of the same name in northern California. It consists of a loosely woven, visor-like pad to fit on the forehead, and is held in place by a rope made of the warp of the pad, served with twine made from the native hemp. This apparatus is first placed on the head, and then the headband of the load or of the tracking line is worn over it. It must be remembered that the Hupa are the kinfolks of the Carrier Indians of Canada and Alaska. Collected by Capt. P. H. Ray, U. S. A.

Fig. 147.

FOREHEAD PAD WORN BY THE HUPA (ATHAPAS-CAN) INDIANS OF CALIFORNIA.

Cat. No. 126907, U. S. N. M. Collected by Capt. P. H. Ray, U. S. A.

Farther southward and in the mountains north of San Francisco Bay

---

[1] J. W. Hudson, Overland Monthly, 1893, XXI, p. 573.

dwell the most exquisite of American basket makers. They use the conical carrying basket, and from each of the stocks the U. S. National Museum has a large collection. They also make globular baskets in large quantity and of many sizes, but these are quiet holders of things, not carriers. If they were they would sit on the head after the manner of a Zuñi vase.

In the companion pictures here given (figs. 148 and 149) the two styles of weaving are shown, the open and the close, though both have

Fig. 148.

POMO WOMAN CARRYING CONICAL BASKET.
California.

From a photograph in the U. S. National Museum by H. W.
Henshaw.

Fig. 149.

YOKAIA MAN CARRYING WOOD IN CONICAL BASKET.
California.

From a photograph in the U. S. National Museum by H. W.
Henshaw.

the same stitch. In the administration and mingling of the twine and the coil the natives of central California developed as many as seven distinct varieties of weaving, which will be minutely described in a paper on the industrial arts of the aboriginal Americans. The man is a Yokaia, reduced to poverty by the new régime, and is seen carry-ing wood. The staff is of great help to the bearer with the headband. The other picture represents a Pomo woman bearing a lighter load in a conical basket. The headband encircles the middle of the utensil, and passes across the woman's forehead well up. The basket is woven by the twined process, and ornamented in bands and triangles with split stems of maidenhair fern.

Example No. 42155 (fig. 150) is one of a large number collected among the Utes of Utah by Maj. J. W. Powell. The Utes belong to the Shoshonean stock, stretching from the northern border of Mexico to Costa Rica. In each culture area they will be found adapting themselves to circumstances and yet preserving their originality:

(1) In the north they carry luggage in folders or cases of rawhide, as do the Sioux and other dependents on the buffalo.

(2) In the Great Interior Basin, of which they were practically the owners in aboriginal days, the Ute-Shoshoneans were gleaners of all sorts of grass seeds: the women went out with conical baskets, stood them on the point behind a bunch of goose foot or other plant, with a fan knocked the seeds into the cone until it was full, hung the load on their backs by means of the headband, and carried it home. The contents were winnowed, ground, and cooked by the same industrious women.

(3) In the pueblo country the Utes are represented by the mixed Moki pueblo, where, as will be seen, four or five quite distinct types of carrying baskets are made.

(4) In Mexico and southward the Aztecan becomes the greatest of burden bearers.

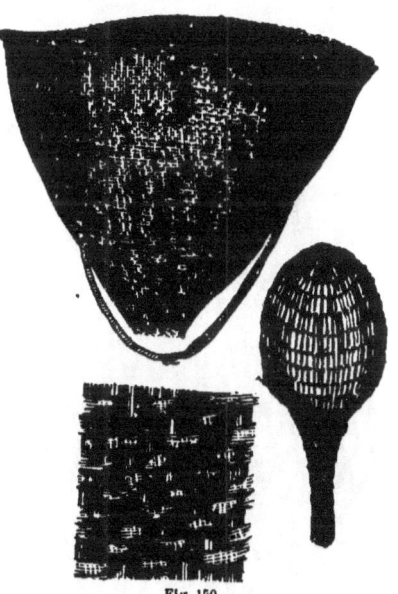

Fig. 150.

UTE SEED-BASKET AND GATHERING-FAN.

Cat. No. 42155, U. S. N. M. Collected by Maj. J. W. Powell.

The cones here described are made of split osiers, rhus stems, and the scions of other plants not identified, worked into twined weaving, leaving a very rough surface on account of the harshness of the material. Once in a while a narrow band of black varies the monotony. But nothing is more striking in the immense Powell collection of Ute material than the lack of variety in the color of the buckskin clothing and the uniform hue and texture of the carrying baskets and bottles.

Examples Nos. 131139 and 18897 (figs. 151 and 152) are carrying nets from the Missions in California. The latter is marked Temecula, who are Shoshonean; the former is simply accredited to the Missions. In the Powell collection from Utah is another carrying net, No. 11244. Each of these is a strip of open netting with fixed meshes, gathered up at the ends into an eyelet or loop like a hammock and provided with a carrying rope of the same kind. The nets are of bast fiber, probably *Apocynum*. The knots of two of them are the standard-mesh knot, bowline on a bight, in nautical phrase; the other is square. The geographic distribution of knots will be considered later, but the reader practically bids adieu to the rigid mesh knot with the Pueblo region and takes up the plain coil, half-hitch, wrapped filament of all America south. This is seen in carrying nets and hammocks.[1]

Before leaving the Shoshonean sphere of influence, it is necessary to

Fig. 151.

CARRYING-NET USED BY THE MISSION INDIANS OF
CALIFORNIA.

Cat. No. 131130, U. S. N. M.   Collected by Stephen James.

Fig. 152.

CARRYING-NET MADE OF AGAVE FIBER, USED BY
THE TEMECULA INDIANS OF CALIFORNIA.

Cat. No. 18897, U. S. N. M.   Collected by Edward Palmer.

mention another carrying device whose texture and material are the same as that of the Ute conical burden basket. Example No. 42129 is one of a large number of tight carrying bottles or jars, used in the transportation of water. After being closely woven the vessel is dipped in hot pitch, and this closes every chink. These vessels are much stronger than pottery; indeed, it seems impossible to break one in the ordinary wear and tear. In the course of the weaving lugs or loops are left on the side for the carrying band. These water bottles in their

---

[1] Cf. Rep. Smithsonian Inst. (U. S. Nat. Mus.), 1887, p. 369, fig. 75.

use are not confined to the Utes, being seen in the hands of Apaches and Pueblo peoples. The Apaches are Athapascans, and are most expert in coiled basket bowl weaving. It is fair to infer that they possess this type of water jar by trade or that they were early taught the art of making them in their new homes.[1] (Fig. 153.)

Davis speaks of Indian women carrying water along on the march for the Spaniards to drink.[2]

Vaca says of the Arbadaos, a tribe of Indians in western Texas, that they go naked, and tear their flesh in passing through the woods and

Fig. 153.

APACHE WOMAN CARRYING WATER IN BASKET BOTTLE.

From a photograph in the U. S. National Museum.

bushes. They were obliged to carry heavy loads of wood upon their backs, and the cords which bound it on cut into their flesh. This refers to Vaca's party[3] in this instance, but shows the common method of carrying in this region.

Vaca also speaks of a separate class of emasculated men among some

[1] Cf. Rep. Smithsonian Inst. (U. S. Nat. Mus.), 1887, p. 268, fig. 14. Apache woman carrying water bottle.

[2] "Spanish Conquest of New Mexico," Doylestown, 1869, p. 89.

[3] Ibid., p. 77.

Texan tribes who, among other functions, carried heavy burdens. They were more muscular and taller than other men and bore burdens of great weight.[1]

The Apaches also use a modified conical basket, example No. 21489 (fig. 154). The material and the stitch are precisely those of the Utes, but there are three noticeable features. The basket is oblong, like a northern pack; the surface is decorated by plain colored and checkered bands, and hanging from the top and the bottom are fringes of buckskin, at the ends of which are the false hoofs of deer and bits of tin rolled up.

The reader is now in the midst of the arid region including the cliff

dwellings and the pueblos. Into it have come tribes from the four quarters and introduced every form of carrying apparatus known thereabout. They also preserve to us forms obsolete elsewhere. In addition to this, for three hundred and fifty years, Spanish influence has been at work producing modifications and making additions. The women who go to the mesa for clay now bring it home in old blankets in good European style, slung over one shoulder like a peddler's pack. Mr. Cosmos Mindeleff calls the attention of the writer to a curious shifting of the industrial center in those pueblos where the men collect wood in the adjoining plains, carry it by toilsome journeys up the mesas just to burn it for the ashes. The creating of fires in the plain would disturb all the social economy of the mixed populations.

Fig. 154.
ORNAMENTED CARRYING-BASKET USED BY THE APACHE INDIANS OF ARIZONA.
Cat. No. 21489, U. S. N. M. Collected by J. B. White.

The Moki or Hopi pueblos, seven in number, in northeastern Arizona, have been carefully studied by many ethnologists, latterly by the Bureau of Ethnology and by Dr. J. Walter Fewkes. These tribes, of mixed linguistic affinity, have several marked varieties of basketry, especially for carrying: (1) wickerwork, warp rigid, weft flexed; (2) diagonal weaving, of split yucca leaf; (3) coiled work, in meal plaques, etc.; (4) twined work, in water jars.

Example No. 70937 (fig. 155) is one of a large number of carrying baskets from Moki in wickerwork, the same manipulation being practiced on pretty plaques and flat, quadrilateral mats. The material is the unbarked twigs of little shrubs yet undetermined. The

[1] Davis, "Spanish Conquest of New Mexico," Doylestown, 1869, p. 83.

quadrilateral form and framework of these baskets recall the Arikaree specimen before described. The headband is attached to the ends one-third of the distance from the top.

Example No. 42153 is figured by Stevenson, in connection with a plaque having woven center and wicker border.[1]

Example No. 42199 (fig. 156) is a carrying basket of split yucca fiber leaf in diagonal weaving, collected by James Stevenson. There are a great many specimens of this ware in the U. S. National Museum vary-ing in form from a flat tray to a deep fruit-picking basket. All of them are coarse, light, strong, and often made to be quite ornamental by the variation of the stitch and alternating of the two sides of the leaf, one green and the other whitish. The headband is attached to the rim. The various styles are figured by Colonel Stevenson.[2]

Example No. 42129 (fig. 157) is a water-tight jar for carrying water, collected at Wolpi, one of the Moki pueblos in northeastern Arizona, by James Stevenson. It is of split

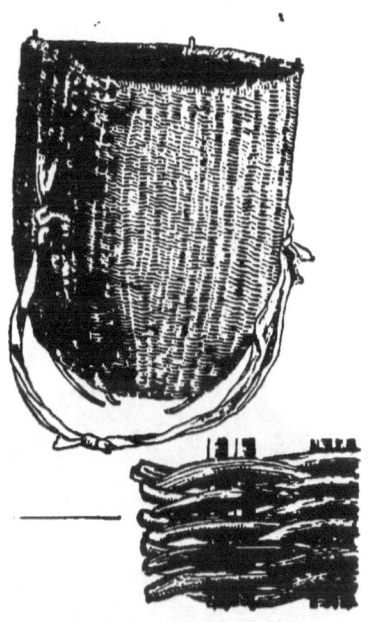

Fig. 155.

FRUIT-PICKER'S BASKET FROM TUSAYAN, ARIZONA.
Cat. No. 70957, U. S. N. M. Collected by James Stevenson.

Fig. 156.

BASKET FOR GATHERING YUCCA FRUIT, FROM TUSA YAN, ARIZONA.

Cat. No. 42199, U. S. N. M. Collected by James Stevenson. From a figure in the Second Annual Report of the Bureau of Ethnology.

osiers made in coiled work, after the fashion of the Apache trays, and dipped in hot pitch. Lugs of horse-hair are attached to the sides for the headband. This should be com-pared with Ute and Apache speci-mens, the more especially since these make no pottery, while the Moki are excellent potters.

The basketry of the Zuñi In-dians, in New Mexico, as it exists in the U. S. National Museum is of very rude and ordinary form, doubtless owing to poverty of ma-terial and motive to its construc-tion. The twined, coiled wicker, and diagonal or plaited styles exist, but no original fashions are developed.

[1] Second Ann. Rep. Bureau of Ethnology, figs. 539, 540.
[2] Ibid., figs. 543-545.

Example No. 22971 (fig. 158), collected by James Stevenson, is built up on corner bows and warp of three sticks together: the filling is in wicker and the ends are fastened off very neatly by tucking them in.[1]

Example No. 40093 (fig. 159) is a modern specimen of Moki pottery collected by James Stevenson, and is one of a large number illustrating the control of the carrying function over form. It may be called an aboriginal canteen and could have been influenced in shape by those of civilized peoples. At any rate, the mouth has relation to filling and emptying, the flat side to the convenience of the carrier; the lugs are for the headband, for the Moki wears the canteen on the back and not on the hip with the strap over the shoulder. Finally, the whole motive of ornamentation is controlled by the industrial form. The axis of ornament has revolved outward 90 degrees from the mouth to the apex of the outer side. In the great variety of canteens figured by Stevenson this is true.[2]

Fig. 157.

WATER-BOTTLE FROM TUSAYAN, ARIZONA, MADE OF COILED BASKETRY AND COVERED WITH PITCH.

From a figure in the Second Annual Report of the Bureau of Ethnology.

Cat. No. 42129, U. S. N. M.   Collected by James Stevenson.

Water jars, globose in form, with wide open mouths and receding bottoms to fit the carrier's head (fig. 160), exist by thousands in Zuñi and other pueblos.[3]

Carrying on the head is not an American Indian native custom. There are thousands of Pueblo water pots and jars with concave bottoms to facilitate carrying them on the head. But these are all post-Columbian. Not all the Pueblos even in our day practice toting, keeping up the good old custom, once in vogue from Smith Sound to Patagonia, of bearing loads on the back held in place by a band across the forehead or the breast. No ancient American water jars seem to have concave bottoms, but the circular padded ring is found in Arizona and New Mexico, and occurs in some collections from ancient sites. Dr. J. Walter Fewkes has found only one fragment of a small jar punched up at the bottom. It is therefore possible that the ancient inhabitants of Tusayan may have carried water on the

[1] Figured also in Rep. Smithsonian Inst. (U. S. Nat. Mus.), 1884, fig. 80; and in Second Ann. Rep. Bureau of Ethnology, figs. 484–488.

[2] Second Ann. Rep. Bureau of Ethnology, 1883, figs. 385–397.

[3] Op. cit., figs. 359–384. The papers of Holmes on the development of form and ornament should be examined.

head in jars convex or rounded on the bottom by means of the padded ring. The presence of the rings does not prove this altogether, since their function may have been to uphold the jar but not to carry it.

The head and the breast band, the shoulder and atlas yoke, and toting seem to have divided the earth among them in early times as carrying methods, and their areas are quite contiguous.

Example No. 40473 is called a carrying pad, hä kin ne, of the Zuñi Indians. It is made of the dried leaves of the *Yucca baccata*, split and plaited as in making a whip. These rings are made to fit the head comfortably, and serve the double purpose of sustaining a jar of water on the head and holding it upright on the ground. They also preserve the soft pottery from wearing away.

Fig. 158.

COARSE GATHERING-CRATE USED BY THE ZUÑI INDIANS OF NEW MEXICO.

Cat. No. 22971, U. S. N. M. Collected by James Stevenson.

Example No. 40466, collected in the pueblos of Arizona and New Mexico, illustrates a variety of head pads used in carrying jars. The Irish milkmaid catches up a kerchief or cloth and by a quirk or two converts it into a ring or crown which she places on her head before setting thereon the brimming pail. The Zuñi water carrier provides herself with a thick ring of bark, or especially of closely braided yucca, and on this she sets her round-bottomed jar. The

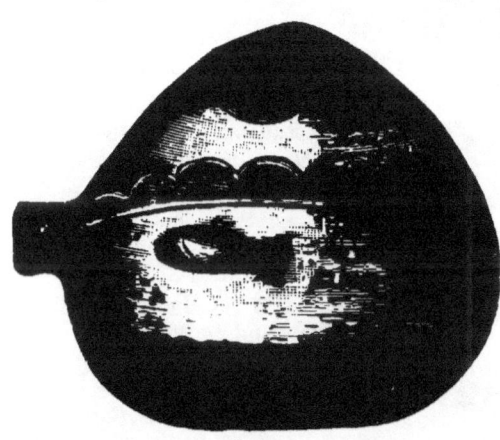

Fig. 159.

CANTEEN OF POTTERY, USED BY THE MOKI INDIANS OF ARIZONA.

Cat. No. 40466, U. S. N. M. Collected by James Stevenson.

same ring serves also in keeping the jar upright on the floor of her room.

H. Mis. 90, pt. 2——30

The making of jars with receding bottoms modifies the size and function of the ring[1] (fig. 161).

Fig. 160.

VASE USED FOR CARRYING AND STORING WATER BY THE ZUÑI INDIANS OF NEW MEXICO.
Cat. No. 41150, U. S. N. M. Collected by James Stevenson.

Coronado (1540) wrote to his superior in Mexico: " I send your lordship two rolles which the women in these parts are woont to weare on their heads when they fetch water from their wells, as we used to do in Spain; and one of these Indian women with one of these rolles on her head will carrie a pitcher of water, without touching the same, up a lather."[2]

Fig. 161.

HEAD-PADS USED BY THE PUEBLO WATER-CARRIERS OF NEW MEXICO.
Cat. No. 40465, U. S. N. M. Collected by James Stevenson.

Leaving the pueblo country the student may transfer his investigations among the unclassed Mission Indians, the Yuman, and the Piman families, all about the Colorado mouth. The U. S. National Museum is indebted to the Pasadena Association and to Miss Picher for some observations among the Mission carrying people. It is a singular fact that Indian women cut grass with such old knives as they may get, dry it,

[1] Cf Second Ann. Rep. Bureau of Ethnology, 1883, fig. 486; Rep. Smithsonian Inst. (U. S. Nat. Mus.), 1887, fig. 19, Zuñi woman carrying water vase.
[2] Publications of the Hakluyt Society, London, 1890, III, p. 454.

and sell it as hay to the Government. The huge bundles are rolled up and tied, and are carried on the top of the back, being held up in a variety of ways. In one case the good woman thrusts the end of a stick under the binding rope and holds onto that. In another, the woman attaches the ends of her carrying strap to the wrapping cord of the bundle, using the stick for a cane, and in a third case she uses both headband and staff, holding onto the latter with both hands above the shoulders (fig. 162).

Rockhill figures a woman of Imamu Chuang carrying a bundle of fagots on her back by means of a shoulder band.[1]

Fig. 162.

MISSION INDIAN WOMAN OF SOUTHERN CALIFORNIA CARRYING HAY.

From a photograph in the U. S. National Museum by Miss Annie B. Picher.

Example No. 19742 (fig. 163) is a basket for carrying cactus fruit, collected among the Diegeños Indians, of the Yuman family, on the Mission Reservation, in Lower California. As will be seen, it is in twined weaving of the rudest sort, a globose wallet, strikingly similar in shape to the great pottery ollas made and used by the neighboring tribes. The noteworthy character about the specimen is the occurrence of twined weaving so far south. On the testimony of the national collections there does not exist a tribe south of this line that practices it.

Example No. 24145 (fig. 164) is one of the most interesting specimens in the world. It is the carrying frame and net of the Mohave Indians,

[1] "Diary of a Journey through Mongolia and Tibet," 1894, Smithsonian Inst., p. 81.

of the Yuman stock, dwelling about the mouth of the Colorado River, in Arizona. They live largely upon the mesquite bean, which they gather, pod and all, and grind for bread. Two poles 8 feet long bent in the form of an oxbow and crossing each other at right angles form the ground work. These are held in place by lashing at the bottom and by a hoop at the top. Four or five strong twines of agave fiber pass from the hoop above to the bottom of the framework between each pair of uprights. These and the uprights constitute the warp. The weft is a new type of Indian textile on the Pacific Coast called "wrapped" weaving. A single twine is coiled round and round the frame, making meshes with the warp half an inch wide. Every time this weft passes the warp strings or poles, it is simply wrapped once around. The roughness of the agave fiber holds the wrap from slipping and preserves a tolerably uniform mesh. Foster describes the finding of cloth in a mound in Butler County, Ohio, and figures a specimen in which the twines are wrapped in the same manner.[1] The headband is a rag tied to two of the upright sticks. This should be compared with the Jarawa basket, p. 433.

Fig. 163.

BASKET FOR GATHERING CACTUS, USED BY THE DIEGEÑOS (YUMAN) INDIANS OF CALIFORNIA.
Cat. No. 19742, U. S. N. M. Collected by Edward Palmer.

The Pima women make of native twine a kind of carrying basket or hod called kiho. Bandelier finds mention of it in the tradition of the Casa Grande.[2]

The principle is the same as that of the Mohave carrier just described, and the functions and environments are the same, but the structure is different. The Pimas dwell in the northwestern corner of Mexico, contiguous to the Yuma. They are by some considered a separate family, by others to be allied to the Nahuatl or Uto-Aztecan. At any rate, their weaving on the kiho or carrying basket is of the south.

Example No. 126680 (fig. 165) is a kiho of the Pimas collected by Edward Palmer. It consists of four straight sticks 4 feet long, tied

[1] Foster, "Prehistoric Races," Chicago, 1873, p. 225, fig. 29.

[2] Bandelier, Archæological Inst. Am. (Am. Series), III, 1890, p. 255.

together at one end for the bottom of the utensil, and fastened to a hoop at the other end for the top.

The network is done with a needle, and not with the fingers. It is netting or lace work, and not weaving at all. There is nothing to serve as a warp. The whole surface of the frame is covered by a continuous coil of agave fiber twine from bottom to top. Each coil is looped into the one beneath it by a "buttonhole stitch" or "half hitch," as shown in the drawing. In the Mexican hammocks each coil is simply caught under the preceding at regular intervals, while in more pretentious work the moving part is wrapped once, twice, or three times about the standing part as in Canadian snowshoes.

Accompanying this specimen and every other one of the kind in actual life is the staff, which serves a multitude of purposes to be explained later.

The Pimas and their neighbors make use of gourds as well as of pottery in carrying water and more compact freight.

Example No. 76047 (fig. 166) is a carrying gourd from the Pima country, collected by Edward Palmer. It is interesting in this connection on account of the net in which it is inclosed. About the bottom the twine is laid in the style of the Pima kiho. It is coiled in "half hitches." About the top it is served around the gourd itself in a series of half hitches. The headband is a rag caught into the network.

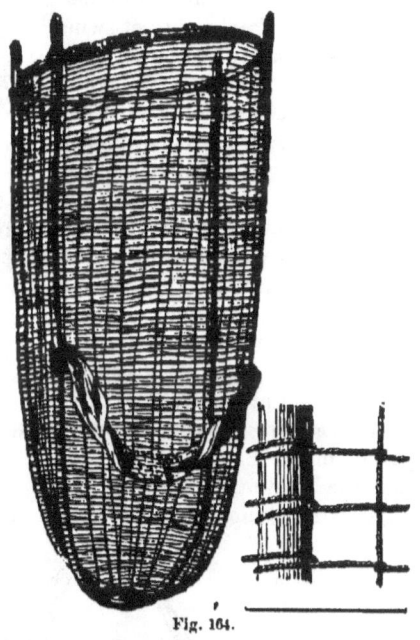

Fig. 164.

CARRYING-BASKET, WRAPPED WEAVING, USED BY THE MOHAVE INDIANS OF ARIZONA.

Cat. No. 24145, U. S. N. M. Collected by Edward Palmer.

Example No. 19478 is a globular gourd from San Diego, Cal., Mission Indians. It is mounted in two zones of leather above and below, with lashing of rawhide rove through holes cut along their inner border like the snare of a drum, holding about a gallon.

The Papago Indians of northwestern Mexico make a very elaborate carrying device also called "kiho." Example No. 76033 (fig. 167) is a small-sized kiho collected by Edward Palmer. Four sticks and a hoop, as in the specimen last described, form the ground work, but they are disposed quite differently. Two of them, forming the back of the utensil, are 6 feet long, and extend below the kiho for legs and above it for binding the top load. The front pair of sticks start from the back pair a foot, more or less, from the ground and are lashed to the hoop which forms the upper border. This hoop is so adjusted to these four sticks that when the woman is leaning forward with the load on her back the hoop shall be horizontal.

Covering the space between the hoop and the junction of the four sticks is a pyramidal bag of network starting from a ring of twine at the bottom and wrapped about the hoop at the top. This network is like that on the Pima basket, but is rendered ornamental by varying, according to a predetermined plan, the number of times the moving part shall be wrapped about the standing part. The Papago Indians of the Piman stock have been lately studied carefully by Professor McGee, of the Bureau of Ethnology, and excellent descriptions and pictures of the carriers secured. It is a puzzle in technographic studies that the lacework on their carrying frame, or kiho, commonly called

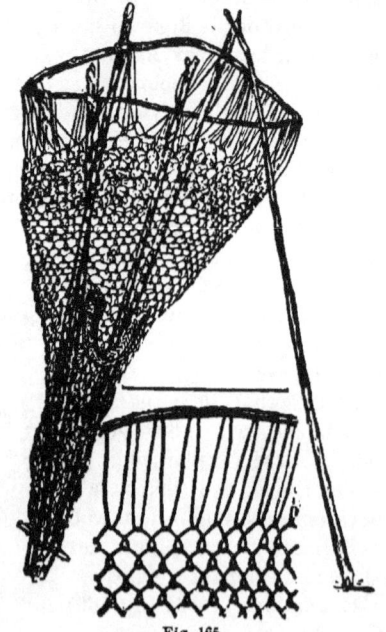

Fig. 165.

CARRYING-BASKET OF COILED NETTING, USED BY THE PIMA INDIANS OF ARIZONA.

Cat. No. 126680, U. S. N. M.   Collected by Edward Palmer.

the buttonhole or half-hitch stitch, finds its most northern extension among the Piman stock. Nowhere in the Pueblo tribes is it found, according to the collections of the U. S. National Museum. But south of the Piman it occurs in Central America, in Latin South America as far south as Tierra del Fuego, where it will be found to be the only attempt at textiles. The open-work pattern is produced by enlargement and multiplication. The half hitches may be longer laterally

Fig. 166.

CARRYING-GOURD IN NETWORK, USED BY PIMA INDIANS OF ARIZONA.

Cat. No. 76047, U. S. N. M.   Collected by Edward Palmer.

or centrifugally; that is, each one or a series of them may be made on a larger gauge. The multiplication takes place in the number of winds of the moving about the standing part in each stitch. The pattern is in fact a matter of counting and a fair indication of progress in arithmetic and geometry made by the Papagos.

This network is woven from a ring or loop of cord about 6 inches in diameter, and spreads out tent like to fit a hoop 2 or 3 feet in diameter. This hoop is attached to 3 or more poles of varying length, which act as spreaders, stays, foot rests, handles, stancheons, etc. To complete the outfit a mat of diagonal weaving in yucca fiber extends along one side of the apparatus, to act as a pad to protect the back, and a headband is fastened by its ends to two of the upright sticks.

Accompanying the kiho always is a staff about 4 feet long, with a short crotch on the top. Mr. William Dinwiddie, who accompanied Professor McGee, secured excellent photographs of a woman rising with the kiho, loaded with pottery and other objects (figs. 168–170). The kiho is stood upon its two short legs while the woman sits down with her back against it and draws the headband across her forehead. Virtually, she harnesses herself to the load. Taking her staff firmly in the right hand and grasping the hoop with the left hand, she leans forward and throws the load upon her back. Rising thereafter is

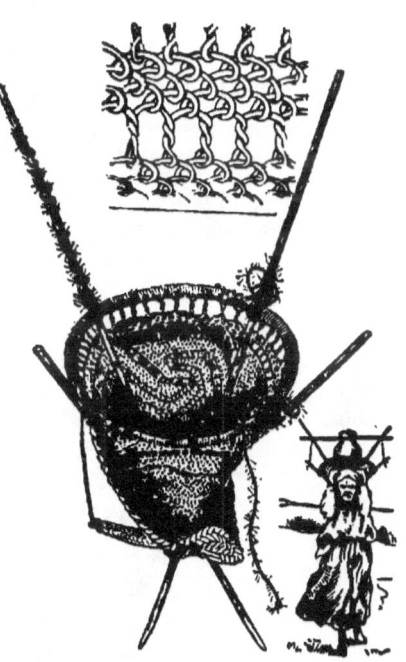

Fig. 167.

KIHO, OR PAPAGO CARRYING-FRAME, IN LACE WORK.

Cat. No. 76033, U. S. N. M. Collected by Edward Palmer.

a matter of several movements, in which the good right hand and the staff play a prominent part. She is now ready to walk away with her load.

The professional carriers of Mexico, men and women, use two kinds of headband and the breastband, either singly or combined, and the kinds of receptacles that are attached to the body thereby, as well as the varieties of merchandise therein, are innumerable. The loads shown on their backs in the U. S. National Museum collection of photos are bales of hemequin fiber, bales of goods formed up to suit the carrier, coops of poultry, all sorts of marketing and retail merchandise, furniture, pottery, basketry, water and pulque, frequently many times more bulky than the porter himself.   The water carrier is

Fig. 168.
PAPAGO WOMAN ADJUSTING KIHO.
From a photograph in the Bureau of Ethnology.

a man whose neck muscles are marvels of toughness, for he supports a globular canteen on his back by means of a headband across his fore-

Fig. 169.
PAPAGO WOMAN RISING WITH KIHO.
From a photograph in the Bureau of Ethnology

head at the same time that he supports a pitcher in front of him by means of a strap over the bregma.   This process is better shown in a

MEXICAN WATER PEDDLER.

The man wears the sun and rain hat, and the old-time sandals without the single toe string. The long vessel derives its form not from the imitation of a natural object, but from several exigencies. It is to be slung below the center of gravity, to fit the back somewhat, to be carried by means of a band across the forehead, to enable the bearer to empty the liquid by bending his back. The straps about the neck of the vessel, held by its other end in his left hand, are for the purpose of drawing down and guiding the mouth of the can.

The plate is from a photograph in the U. S. National Museum by Rev. F. F. X. Cleveland, of Dundee, Ill., who says that this is the method of distributing water in Guanajuato, and that the metric system of measures is employed in selling, as may be seen by the cup at the top of the can. The town is in a valley between precipitous hills. A delightful spring on the side of the mountain is conducted to reservoirs, whence the carriers obtain their stock.

MEXICAN WATER PEDDLER.

From a photograph in the U. S. National Museum presented by Rev. F. F. X. Cleveland.

sketch of a butcher made for the author by W. H. Holmes (fig. 171). The economy of supporting force is equaled by the economy of points of attachment. This man is at once Pueblo Indian, packer, and the inventor of a new method of self-imposition in the form of a load hanging in front.

Illustrating the carriers of liquids there is in the U. S. National Museum a photograph of a water peddler of Guanajuato worthy of closest study, for he looks as though he had dropped in from Cairo (pl. 24).

Fig. 170.

PAPAGO WOMAN WITH KIHO PROPERLY MOUNTED.

From a photograph in the Bureau of Ethnology.

He has on his back a jar 4 feet in length slung in leather straps and hung to himself by a headband attached to the bottom of the jar. To the top of the jar is fastened a strap the other end of which he holds in his left hand. In order to deliver his water he uses his spine as a pivot by which the jar can be brought to a horizontal position and guided by the straps.

"The cargadores are trained from boyhood to carry heavy burdens over great distances. Don Pepe expected them to travel 8 leagues a day. But when carrying lighter loads they will sometimes travel for several consecutive days at the rate of nearly 40 English miles a day. When the cargo bearers were moving in single file with their burdens, they looked like the Tamemes bearing tribute to Montezuma, as represented in the ancient pictures. It is probable that these men were enduring labors similar to those that had been performed by their ancestors for centuries before the arrival of the Spaniards."[1]

The Mexican carrier enters into serious competition with all modern schemes to improve his country. Over the devious and painful trails of the mountains he knows the shortest cuts. Once in a while his

Fig. 171.
MEXICAN BUTCHER USING TWO HEAD-BANDS.
From a sketch by W. H. Holmes.

trail lies across the railroad, which he pauses for an instant to contemplate, and then he proceeds on his way, a bit of the olden time crossing the path of the nineteenth century (fig. 172). As in the drawing, his load on his back may be supported by breastband, or the more ancient headband may be in vogue. Some of his dress is modern, but his hat, or migratory house to defend his head from heat and rain and his eyes from the beating sun, is old; it is a survival. His sandals, especially dedicated to the travel and transportation industry, are old in form, but the coming of the Spaniard brought him horses and cattle and rawhide,

[1] Lindesay Brine, "The American Indians; Their Earthworks and Temples," London, 1894, pp. 283–284.

which he did not have previously, and so there is about his feet just a
suggestion of Mediterranean influence. On the very top of his load is
his water flask of gourd, that the ingenious horticulturist has compelled
to grow with a constriction about its middle for the sole occupation of
its carrying strap. Beneath that is his poncho or shawl, at once cloak,

Fig. 172.
PROFESSIONAL CARRIER.
Mexico.
From a drawing by W. H. Chandler.

bed cover, and umbrella. On his back between it and the load is a soft
padding, prelude to all saddle blankets.

The U. S. National Museum is indebted to E. F. X. Cleveland for
a photo of the Mexican carrier in the last act of his drama (fig. 173).
In this he has quit his mountain path and rivalry of the locomotive and
freight car in one, and is in the act of carrying coal to feed the iron horse.
His old-time hat gives place to the porter's cap. The visor is only the

shadow of the luxurious brim of his native sombrero. He can not discard the headband. His limbs are as bare as he is allowed to wear them, and his sandals have antique elements.

The carrying pole has a place in the Mexican transportation industry. Example No. 126592 (fig. 174) is a carrying device of great interest from Guadalajara, Mexico. The yoke is a flat piece of wood, slightly bent and pierced at the ends for slings or nooses. There is no cutting away to fit the shoulder, but the utensil may be worn as a Holland yoke or as a Chinese pole ad libitum. The sling at each extremity is of leather, attached by passing the bend through the hole and over the end. The noose or slipknot at the other end of the sling is for attach-

Fig. 173.

MEXICAN COAL CARRIER.

From a photograph in the U. S. National Museum by E. F. X. Cleveland.

ment to the top of a jar. In this specimen form is determined by function. But the apparatus has another interest, for it lies exactly on the boundary line between the man carrier and the donkey carrier. The jars should have been drawn with round bottoms. They fit into a wooden rack, one-half of which is shown in miniature in the drawing. By fastening two of these together and throwing them over the back of a donkey four jars full of liquid may be carried, or, as one may see every day in San Luis Potosi, the four jars rest in a rack, beneath which is a wooden wheel suggestive of the Chinese type. In point of fact, the student is witness to the two transfers of loads, to wit, that onto the wheel and that onto the beast.

"The Indians of central Yucatan are accustomed to carrying, which their fathers pursued before them from time immemorial, and they not only carry merchandise and the baggage of travelers, but travelers themselves."[1]

The mozos or porters of Guatemala are obliged, when ordered by the comandancia, to carry burdens not to exceed four arrobas (100 pounds). Their pay is 3 reales, and they must not be sent beyond their district. They support the burden with the mecapal, a rawhide strap, against the forehead. The frame is called carcaste by the Quiché.[2]

"The women have a certain kind of dignity in their manner, caused, in a great measure, by their usage of carrying water jars and pans of crockery poised upon their heads. They therefore walk slowly and hold themselves upright. This custom, which begins from early childhood and forms part of their daily life, has the result of giving them good figures and a particularly graceful movement.

"The men, on the contrary, have a crouching appearance, caused by the method in which they have been accustomed from boyhood to carry their burdens. They relieve the pressure of the weight on their backs by means of a broad band passed over the forehead, and thus, by bending forward, the load is made less oppressive. The men and boys consequently contract a stooping posture, and this presents an

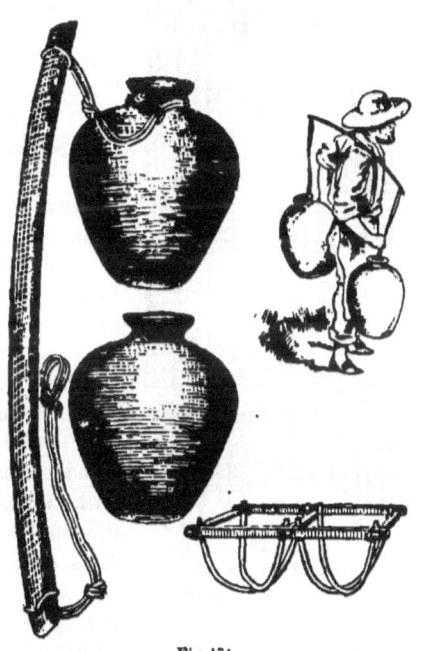

Fig. 174.

CARRYING-JARS, WITH POLE AND CRATE FOR SAME.
Guadalajara, Mexico.

Cat. No. 128597, U. S. N. M.   Collected by Edward Palmer.

unfavorable contrast to the women, whose bearing is precisely the reverse. There is another circumstance which has its influence in shaping the figures of the women. They carry all small things on the open palm of the left hand, which is thrown back and held well raised up. In fact, the same causes which affect the appearance of the Indians in North America are present here, but with the difference that there it is the squaw who contracts the stooping and bent figure, through carrying

[1] Morelet, "Travels in Central America," New York, 1871, p. 279.
[2] Brigham, "Guatemala," New York, 1887, p. 78; figure, p. 98.

her children and other burdens, and it is the man who maintains the upright figure and dignified manner."[1]

Example No. 129654 (fig. 175) from Honduras, is a simple net made of twine in one continuous piece, wrapped backward and forward to form the warp and then woven through plainly for the weft. Leaving a few inches for attachment the selvage at each end is formed by twined weaving almost out of place in this area. The square netting is also rare, most of the bags and hammocks being in the netted style.

Fig. 175.

CARRYING-NET FROM HONDURAS.

Cat. No. 129654, U. S. N. M.   Collected by C. F. Townsend.

Example No. 126805 (fig. 176) is a carrying frame from Honduras, collected by Consul A. E. Morlan. To the student of comparative technography it is worthy of close attention. It is framed on two poles, on which rests a structure suggestive of the California baby cradles, and of the porters' frames of West Africa. The sides and border are of wood, panneled with a textile in diagonal weaving. It is quite within the area of probability that in this device there are borrowed African features.

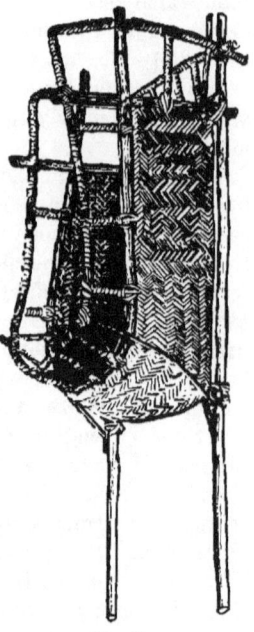

Fig. 176.

CARRYING-FRAME FROM HONDURAS.

Cat. No. 126805, U. S. N. M.   Collected by Consul A. E. Morlan.

That the negro race, introduced at the beginning of the sixteenth century into middle America, modified and in places crowded out the aboriginal arts is easily proven. In the museum of the Peabody Academy in Salem is a carrying frame labeled Panama, which I here produce through the kindness of Prof. E. S. Morse (fig. 177). It consists simply of two palm fronds in which the stalks are the basis sticks, and the network is made up of the leaflets twined together. A headband of cotton cloth completes the outfit. This specimen is almost identical with fig. 107, from West Africa.

---

[1] Lindesay Brine, "The American Indians; Their Earthworks and Temples," London, 1894, pp. 188–189.

"About St. Pierre, in Martinique," says Lafcadio Hearn, "the erect carriage and steady, swift walk of the women who bear burdens is likely to impress the artistic observer * * * and the larger part of the female population of mixed blood are practiced carriers. Nearly all the transportation of light merchandise as well as of meats, fruits, vegetables, and food stuffs to and from the interior is effected upon human heads. * * * Packets are loaded and unloaded by women and girls—able to carry any trunk or box to its destination. At Fort de France the great steamers are entirely coaled by women, who carry coal on their heads, singing as they come and go in processions of hundreds. The highest type of professional female carrier is to the charbonniere, or coaling girl, what the thoroughbred racer is to the draft horse—

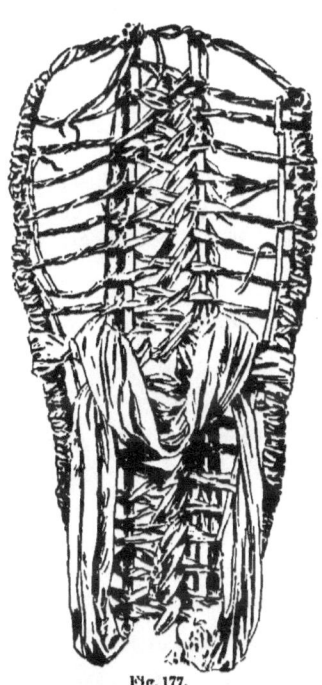

Fig. 177.

CARRYING-FRAME OF PALM FROND, FROM PANAMA.

From a specimen in the Peabody Academy, Salem, Mass.

the type of porteuse selected for swiftness and endurance to distribute goods in the interior parishes, or to sell on commission at long distances.

Fig. 178.

PORTEUSE, OR CARRIER IN LESSER ANTILLES.

From a figure in Hearn's "Midsummer in the Tropics."

"At a very early age she learns to carry small articles upon her head, a decanter of water, or an orange in a plate. At 9 or 10 she is able to tote a tolerably heavy basket or a tray weighing from 20 to 30 pounds and to walk barefoot 12 or 15 miles a day. At 16 or 17 she carries a tray and burden of 120 to 150 pounds' weight or walks 50 miles a day as an itinerant seller. * * * The weight is so great that no well freighted porteuse can unassisted either load or unload herself. She can not even sit down under her burden. * * *

"She wears no shoes. She must climb thousands and descend thousands of feet every day; march up and down slopes so steep that the horses of the country all break down after a few years."[1]

In St. Pierre itself women carry burdens on the head, "peddling

[1] Hearn, "Two Years in the French West Indies," New York, 1890, p. 103.

vegetables, cakes, fruit, ready-cooked food, from door to door (fig. 178).
* * * These women can walk all day long up and down hill in the
hot sun, without shoes, carrying loads of from 100 to 150 pounds on their
heads, and if their little stock sometimes fails to come up to the accus
tomed weight, stones are added to make it heavy enough. * * *
I have seen a grand piano carried on the heads of four men. With the
women the load is seldom steadied with the hand."[1]

The coaling at Kingston, Jamaica, is done by women. They lift the
baskets upon their heads and walk on board the ship, and as they go
round the plank and come out there is a little brass piece given each
one. These women are very skillful in Curaçao. They have been

known to take numerous clothes baskets on their heads and march along.
You hear them paddling all day long;
it is a continuous clatter. One of the
curious things about them is the fact
that the poorest of them will have
their pure white clothes, and a friend
writes that in the Spanish islands
you can buy from them just as much
with a 3-cent piece as with a 10-cent
piece. They bore a hole through it
because they fear that travelers will
spend it again. Coal is transported
to these islands; the steamer comes
right up alongside the wharf, and
women carry the freight.

In the South American Cordilleras
the carrying art has little new information to offer. This much is true,
that the configuration of the country
and the political and commercial conditions resulting therefrom multiplied

Fig. 179.
NAPO INDIAN CARRIER.
Ecuador.
From a figure in Stanford's Compendium.

the number of backs that had burdens to bear, made of them a class
or caste, organized them into more complex social units, and greatly
increased the length of the journey. Long roads were laid out, paved
in some places, bridges were thrown over deep chasms, and a system
of relays was established.

Humboldt, speaking of the carriers in his day, says:

In those times of oppression and cruelty (sixteenth century) which have been
described as the era of Spanish glory the commendatorios (encomienderos) let out
the Indians to travelers like beasts of burden. They were assembled by hundreds,
either to carry merchandise across the Cordilleras or to follow the armies in their
expeditions of discovery and pillage. The Indians endured this service more
patiently because, owing to the almost total want of domestic animals, they had

---

[1] Hearn, "Midsummer in the Tropics," New York, 1890, p. 40.

long been constrained to perform it; though in a less inhuman manner under the government of their own chiefs.[1]

The explorers of the Isthmus of Panama found the Indians engaged in commerce, and upon their backs laid the timbers of the first boats ever sailed on the Pacific by Europeans. In Stanford is the picture of a Napo Indian carrier (fig. 179). The scant costume, the basket of cane, the headband, the two staves, are of old. The shabby dress replaces the old-time clothing of bark cloth universally donned by the natives of tropical America formerly.

Hassaurek says that the Indians of Ecuador carry everthing on their backs, the load being tied to their forehead. Their strength lies in the muscles of the neck and not in their arms. They carry stone, brick, sand, lime, furniture, vegetables, meat. etc., and pass along laughing or talking, or in sullen silence, but you never hear them sing.[2]

Near Quito the traveler is surprised by the sight of many an Indian woman, who not only carries a load on her back, with a babe tied to the top of the carga, but also spins cotton as she trots along.[3] Mrs. Fannie B. Ward says that she has seen Peruvian women and men walking along by the side of a llama spinning the wool that the animal was shedding, using the creature for a natural distaff.

Whymper figures a man carrying a huge jar of water (fig. 180). He is barefooted and clad in European dress. Upon his lower back rests a pad of cloth and on the top of this the vessel, round bottomed and inclosed in a sling or network in which the two rope rings rest against the sides of the jar instead of around the neck and the bottom. These are

Fig. 180.

DEVICE FOR CARRYING WATER JAR ON THE BACK.
From a figure in Whymper's "Great Andes of the Equator."

united by cross lines so as to retain the vessel from all directions. A strap passes from the network around the man's breast. There is no headband.[4]

The aboriginal water carrier of Cajamarca figured by Wiener is clad partly in native and partly in European rags; but his water jar is of the universal type, globose, with lugs on the side, through which a braided rope passes and thence over the right shoulder and under the left arm.[5]

---

[1] Humboldt's Travels, Bohn, II, p. 31.
[2] Hassaurek, "Four Years Among Spanish Americans," New York, 1867, pp. 89-90.
[3] Hassaurek, op. cit., p. 89.
[4] "Great Andes of the Equator," New York, 1892, Scribner, p. 169.
[5] "Péron et Bolivie," p. 128.

Raimondy says the Jivaro of northern Peru carry loads of a hundredweight with case over the worst of mountain tracts. The women use a covering for the lower portion of the body, called the pampanilla, protecting sometimes the upper portion with a mantle, in which they generally carry their children before them. The Llameo, Cocama, and Omagua of Nanta are land carriers and boatmen.[1]

Fig. 181.

CARRYING BASKET, COILED IN HALF HITCH OR BUTTONHOLE STITCH.

Straits of Magellan.

Cat. No. 131722, U. S. N. M.

On the Brazilian coast Hawkins (1593) says that "the women fetch the water and do all drudgerie whatsoever. Their childe they carry in a wallet about their necke, ordinarily under one arme."

If one kills any game in hunting he does not bring it home, but strews leaves to mark his path and sends his wife back after it. On a journey or going to war the women carry all.

Example No. 131222 (fig. 181) in the U. S. National Museum collections, from Sandy Point, Straits of Magellan, is the model of a carrying basket made of rushes, a specimen of which is to be found in every Fuegian bark canoe. The notable feature about the specimen is that while it is a coiled basket it also has the peculiar characteristic of the Central American netted bagging. As in all spiral basketry, the foundation is a rod or a bunch of fiber coiled continuously from bottom to top. These coils are held together, not by a continuous whipping or sewing, but by a series of half hitches or buttonhole stitches. The Japanese lunch baskets carried by school children have a similar stitch, but the weft is wider and more closely woven. The handle of the basket is plaited.

Fig. 182.

COFFEE CARRIER OF RIO

From a figure in Wilkes' "Narrative of the United States Exploring Expedition during the years 1838-1842."

The Patagonians are said to build up their hair with a "hair lace of ostrige feathers, and make it a stoar house for all things * * * a quiver for their arrows, a sheath for their knives, a box for fiersticks, etc."[2]

---

[1]Raimondy, "Indian Tribes of the Great District of Loreto, Northern Peru," Anthrop. Rev., London, 1863, I, No. 1, pp. 31-36.

[2]Drake, "The World Encompassed," Publications of the Hakluyt Society, London, 1854, pp. 50, 52.

Mr. im Thurn says that in Guiana the hard work falls to the women. They clean the house, fetch water and firewood, cook the food, make the bread, nurse the children, plant the fields, dig the produce, and when the men travel the women carry whatever baggage is necessary. The women bring water for the house in clay bottles or gourds (goobies), or they take surianas, large baskets fitting on the back and supported by a band across the forehead, and fetch heavy loads of firewood.[1]

Carrying on the head is most common in Brazil. M. Biard gives a great variety of methods of submitting the head to a load, among them a single negro toting five empty wine casks, and a company of six bearing a grand piano on the head, keeping time to the sound of a rattle.[2]

According to Wilkes the slaves are almost the only carriers of burdens in Rio Janeiro. They go almost naked, and are exceedingly numerous. They appear to work with cheerfulness, and go together in gangs, with a leader who carries a rattle filled with stones (fig. 182). With this he keeps time, causing them all to move on a dogtrot. Each one joins in the monotonous chorus, the notes seldom varying above a third from the key. The words they use are frequently relative to their own country; sometimes to what they heard from their master as they started with their load, but the sound is the same. The coffee carriers go in gangs of twenty or thirty. In singing, one-half take the air, with one or two keeping up a kind of hum on the common chord, and the remainder finish the bar. These slaves are required by their masters to obtain a certain sum according to their ability, say, from 25 to 50 cents a day, and to pay it every evening. The surplus belongs to themselves. In default of not gaining the requisite sum, castigation is always inflicted. The usual load is about 200 pounds.[3] The methods employed are from the Old World and especially negroid.

Fig. 183.
CARRYING-FRAME, FROM UPPER SHINGU, BRAZIL.
From a figure in von den Steinen's "Unter den Naturvölkern Zentral-Brasilens."

Fig. 184.
CARRYING-BASKET OF COILED NETTING, FROM BRAZIL.
Cat. No. 152507, U. S. N. M. Collected by F. G. Fry.

---

[1] im Thurn, "Indians of British Guiana," I, p. 216; Wallace, "Travels on the Amazon," p. 254,; H. H. Smith, "Brazil," New York, 1879, p. 371.

[2] "Le tour du Monde," Paris, IV, p. 15.

[3] Wilkes, "Narrative of the U. S. Exploring Expedition during the years 1838–1842," I, p. 52.

One of the most striking resemblances possible in culture objects in two hemispheres is the carrying frame from the Shingu (fig. 183) and from the west coast of Africa, almost opposite on the South Atlantic and not very far away, and both under Portuguese influence. The apparatus consists of a circular hoop for bottom, with coarse lacing of fiber and three elongated ellipses of the same style for the sides and bottom.[1] The African specimen is carried on the back and shoulders, sustained by the

Fig. 185.

COOPERATIVE CARRYING.

Men on the Shingu launching canoe.

From a figure in von den Steinen's "Unter den Naturvölkern Zentral-Brasiliens."

staff, while the Brazilian specimen has had to submit itself to the local attachment of the headband.

Example No. 152507 (fig. 184) is a carrying bag, said to come from Brazil. By examination of the texture it will be seen that the construction is precisely that of the Mohave carrying crate, of many examples from the Central American States and of the Fuegian carrying

---

[1] von den Steinen, "Unter den Naturvölkern Zentral-Brasiliens," p. 237.

basket minus the warp or foundation rod. Now, all such ware is made on a spacer or gauge of different sizes. One has only to imagine the gauge left in the mesh to see how the Fuegian and the other varieties could be transformed one into another.

A lively scene in the portage or transportation of a woodskin, or bark canoe is figured by von den Steinen.[1] A dozen stout men, naked excepting a girdle, are merrily bringing the canoe on their shoulders and in their hands. The picture is a remarkable one for the variety of ways in which the men are at work. (Fig. 185.)

CARRYING APPLIANCES IN THE U. S. NATIONAL MUSEUM.

AFRICAN TRIBES.

Museum number.	Specimen.	Locality.	By whom contributed.
4809	Haversack....	Africa	John Cassin.
4947	Bag, grass	....do	National Institute.
4948	....do	....do	Do.
4949	Haversack, leather	....do	Do.
4965	....do	....do	Do.
5155	....do	West Africa	R. R. Gurley.
151129	Packing basket (fig. 104)	Angola	U. S. Eclipse Expedition.
151130–151131	Carrying basket, long	Gold coast, Africa	Stewart Culin.
76536–76537	Wallet for fruit	Africa	New Orleans Exposition
151132	Carrying barrow and outfit	....do	Stewart Culin.
151133	Wallet	West Africa	Do.
151203	....do	East Africa	W. L. Abbott.
151248	Haversack, Masai	....do	Do.
141825	Wallet	....do	Do.
152612	Carrying basket Balumbo (fig. 105)	....do	Carl Steckleman.
164874	Carrying basket	Gaboon, Africa	Rev. A. C. Good.
166135	Shoulder cloths	West Africa	Heli Chatelain.
166143	Carrying basket	....do	Do.
166146	Carrying basket, Angola	....do	Do.
168867	Wallet, leather, Mandingo	Africa	Colonization Society of Washington, D. C.
168907	Straps, carrying	East Africa	W. A. Chanler.
168911	Bag, traveling	....do	Do.
167500	....do	....do	W. H. Brown.
166222	Basket, carrying	West Africa	Heli Chatelain.
166128	Carrying frame (fig. 106)	Kongo	T. H. Camp.

EUROPEAN PEASANTRY.

131091	Porter's knot and cap (fig. 110)....	London, England	Edward Lovett.
131092	Yoke for carrying	....do	Do.
131093	Yoke and carrying ropes (fig. 108)	....do	Do.
126800	....do	Russia	New Orleans Exposition.
167006	Net bag for carrying eggs	Madrid, Spain	Walter Hough.
167007	Porter's strap	....do	Do.
164803	Yokes for carrying water	Venice	H. H. Giglioli.
150833	Carrying baskets	Morocco	Royal Ethnological Museum, Berlin.

[1] "Unter den Naturvölkern Zentral-Brasiliens," Berlin, 1894, pl. x, opp. p. 120.

CARRYING APPLIANCES IN THE U. S. NATIONAL MUSEUM—Continued.

EUROPEAN PEASANTRY—continued.

Museum number.	Specimen.	Locality.	By whom contributed.
167787–167788	Carrying tray	Turkey	R. J. Levy.
28155	Open wallet (fig. 112)	Lapland	Russian Government.
167820	Carrying basket	Finland	Hon. John M. Crawford.
167821	Knapsack	...do	Do.

ASIATIC AND INDO-PACIFIC PEOPLES.

164745	Carrying basket (fig. 118)	Andaman Islands	Enrico Giglioli.
27189	Basket, fruit	Siam	King of Siam.
27613	Carrying baskets (fig. 115)	...do	Do.
165410	Vessel, wooden, for milk	Manila	Alex. R. Webb.
4451	Basket, provision	Fiji Islands	Captain Magruder, U. S. N.
3239–3251	Basket haversack	...do	Lieutenant Wilkes, U. S. N.
4419	Basket haversack	...do	Do.
4538	Basket haversack	...do	Do.
23978–23980	...do	...do	Isaac M. Brower.
73386	Carrying net (fig. 119)	New Guinea	A. P. Goodwin.
3397	Haversack	Samoan Islands	Lieutenant Wilkes, U. S. N.
130770	...do	...do	Lieut. W. E. Safford, U. S. N.
3842	...do	Penrhyn Islands	Lieutenant Wilkes, U. S. N.
76500	Wallet, Maori seed	New Zealand	New Orleans Exposition.
3501–3504	Baskets, grass	Sandwich Islands	Lieutenant Wilkes, U. S. N.
151113	Haversack, banana and maidenhair roots.	...do	Mrs. Sibyl Carter.
3538–3540	Large gourds, with network	...do	Lieutenant Wilkes, U. S. N.
3776	Bag, traveling	New Zealand	Do.
129760	Haversack	Easter Island	W. J. Thomson.
1535	Satchel	Australia	C. R. Raymond.
54171–54174	Basket, market (fig. 124)	China	Centennial Commission
74506	Carrying pole (fig. 123)	...do	Do.
73093, 73094	Basket, hunter's and fisherman's	Tate Yama, Japan	P. L. Jouy.
150684	Bag, carrying	Yezo, Japan	Romyn Hitchcock.
150768	Headband and seat (fig. 133)	...do	Do.
22254	Headband (fig. 126)	...do	Do.
28189	Basket, fish	Japan	Japanese Commission.
169034	Chair, lady's carrying	Korea	Korean Commission.
153613	Carrying-cloth, with cover	...do	Ensign J. B. Bernadou, U. S. N.

ESKIMO AND ALASKAN INDIANS.

44685	Traveling bag, Man's, Nerpa skin	Cape Nome, Alaska	E. W. Nelson.
43334	...do	Golovina Bay, Alaska	Do.
36025	Strap for back load	...do	Do.
38074–38075	Haversack, grass	...do	Do.

CARRYING APPLIANCES IN THE U. S. NATIONAL MUSEUM—Continued.

ESKIMO AND ALASKAN INDIANS—continued.

Museum number.	Specimen.	Locality.	By whom contributed.
38467	Haversack, grass, small	Golovina Bay, Alaska	E. W. Nelson.
37630	Haversack, grass	St. Michaels, Alaska	Do.
43480	Bag, hunting	do	Do.
30184	Satchel, fishskin	Kushunnk, Alaska	Do.
37640	Haversack, sealskin	Chalituut, Alaska	Do.
24084	Haversack, grass	Norton Sound, Alaska	L. M. Turner.
32901–32905	Satchel, straw	do	E. W. Nelson.
32971–32974	Bag, traveling, straw	do	Do.
894	Bag, hunting	Yukon, Alaska	R. Kennicott.
8782	Haversack, fishskin	Yukon River, Alaska	W. H. Dall.
48832	do	Lower Yukon, Alaska	E. W. Nelson.
38304	Wallet, bladder	do	Do.
38305	Haversack, grass	do	Do.
38309	Wallet, fishskin	do	Do.
38316	Bag, leather, and fishskin	do	Do.
38465	Wallet, rush, long	do	Do.
38003	Wallet, bladder	do	Do.
38308	Sack, fishskin	Alaska	Do.
38790	Sack, sealskin	Anvik, Alaska	Do.
37871	Bag, fishskin	Askeennk, Alaska	Do.
37872	Sack, grass	do	Do.
36185	Satchel, fishskin	do	Do.
7580	Bag, sealskin	Cape Romanzoff, Alaska	W. H. Dall.
7778	do	do	Do.
36183	Satchel, fishskin	Kuskokwim, Alaska	E. W. Nelson.
67996	Haversack, beaded	Alaska	J. J. McLean.
16320	Straps, packing	Nunivak Island, Alaska	W. H. Dall.
38466	Basket, grass, large	Kuskokwim, Alaska	E. W. Nelson.
37401–37404	Sack, fishskin	Nusbagag, Alaska	Do.
127325–127326	Breast yokes	Togiakmut, Alaska	S. Applegate.
55946	Breast collars	Bristol Bay, Alaska	Charles L. McKay.
38843	Sack, straw, large	Nushagak, Alaska	E. W. Nelson.
73055	Wallet, of fur	Alaska	Charles L. McKay.
72496–72497	Pouch, hunting	do	William J. Fisher.
72500–72502	do	do	Do.
38306	Wallet, rush	Big Lake, Alaska	E. W. Nelson.
14976–14980	Wallet, sea grass, ornamented	Aleutian, Attu Island, Alaska.	W. H. Dall.
30990–30992	Basket, mat	do	L. M. Turner.
76346	Wallet	do	T. H. Bean.
168296	Wallet, grass	do	Lieut. G. T. Emmons.

INDIANS OF EASTERN NORTH AMERICA.

Museum number.	Specimen.	Locality.	By whom contributed.
1979	Wallet	Arctic coast	B. R. Ross.
2041	Bag	Mackenzie River	Do.
2549–2550	Haversack, ornamented	Fort Simpson	W. L. Hardesty.
2608	Basket, grass	do	Do.
2020	Bag, hunting	do	B. R. Ross.
2047	do	do	Do.
2609	Satchel, birch bark	do	W. L. Hardesty.
5112	Pouch, hunting	do	Do.

CARRYING APPLIANCES IN THE U. S. NATIONAL MUSEUM—Continued.

INDIANS OF EASTERN NORTH AMERICA—continued.

Museum number.	Specimen.	Locality.	By whom contributed.
542	Haversack (Yellow Knife Indians)	Fort Resolution	R. Kennicott.
2048	Bag, hunting (Yellow Knife Indians).	.....do	B. R. Ross.
2551	Bag, hunting	Fort Rae	Strachon Jones.
548	Bag, skin	Mackenzie River	B. R. Ross.
527	Bag, hunting	Fort Simpson	Do.
127140	Bag, sealskin (square)	South Greenland	Mrs. Lilla Pavy.
127141	Bag, sealskin (hand)	.....do	Do.
128079	Bag, leather (hand)	Greenland	Do.
153505	Pouch for gun caps	Labrador	Henry G. Bryant.
153506	Wallet (Montagnais Indians)	.....do	Do.
54404–54441	Wallet, porcupine quill	Canada	J. Varden.
1937–1939	Wallet, large leather, ornamented (Sioux).	Upper Missouri River	Lieut. G. K. Warren. U. S. A.
154320	Wallet of grass and bark	Leach Lake, Minn	Dr. W. J. Hoffman.
152963	Parfleche case (Kiowa Indians)	Indian Territory	Jas. Mooney.
164821	Bag, hunting	Pine Ridge Agency	Miss E. C. Sickels.
164823	Bag, traveling	.....do	Do.
168408	Satchel	Kansas	F. W. Clarke.
8553	Haversack, buffalo skin	Nebraska	S. M. Horton.
154035	Haversack (Sioux Indians)	Montana	Mrs. M. M. Hazen.
165840	Parfleche case, small (Cheyenne Indians).	Wyoming	H. R. Voth.
165918	Parfleche case, clothing (Cheyenne Indians) (figs. 135, 136).	.....do	Do.
6910	Sack, provisions (Comanche)		Edward Palmer.
91508	Basket, carrying (Choctaw) (fig. 138).	Alabama	Do.
91509	Basket, berries (Choctaw Indians)	.....do	Do.
8430	Carrying basket (fig. 137)	Arikaree Indian	Dr. W. Matthews, U.S.A.

WEST COAST INDIANS.

168293	Wallet, beaded	Alaska	Lieut. G. T. Emmons. U. S. N.
21560	Basket, large, Kolnschau Indians.	.....do	Dr. J. B. White.
60227–60228	Packing straps, hide	Southeastern Alaska	J. J. McLean.
11410	.....do	British Columbia	V. Colyer.
168163	Wallet, spruce-root (fig. 140)	.....do	Herbert Odgen.
60330	Pouch, hunting, fur	Southeastern Alaska	J. J. McLean.
20808	Pouch, hunting, beaded	Prince Wales Island, Alaska.	J. G. Swan.
20811	Pouch, hunting, small	.....do	Do.
4123	.....do	Northwest Coast, America.	Do.
648	Basket, carrying	.....do	George Gibbs.
685	.....do	.....do	Do.
2552–2553	Pouch, hunting	.....do	Lieutenant Wilkes, U. S. N.
23477–23478	Baskets, Towanahoo Indians	Hooda Canal	J. G. Swan.
168288	Wallet	Alaska	Lieut. G. T. Emmons.
168294	Wallet, gut	.....do	Do.

CARRYING APPLIANCES IN THE U. S. NATIONAL MUSEUM—Continued.

WEST COAST INDIANS—continued.

Museum number.	Specimen.	Locality.	By whom contributed.
2127	Wallet, waterproof.................	Northwest Coast, America.	Lieutenant Wilkes, U. S. N.
153550	Wallet.....................	Baffin Land............	Dr. Franz Boas.
1289	Wallet, sea grass.................	Washington............	J. G. Swan.
23360	Wallet, bark-woven..............	Neah Bay, Washington.	Do.
76634	Wallet, cedar-bark	Washington............	Do.
151452	.....do......................	.....do	Dr. Franz Boas.
127843	Carrying wallet (fig. 144)...........	Quinlault, Wash........	Charles Willoughby.
165137	Valise of rawhide	Wyoming.............	Jas. Mooney.
166541	Case (parfleche)...................	Washington	Dr. E. L. Morgan.
1292	Straps, for carrying load..........	.....do	J. G. Swan.
130970	.....do......................	.....do	E. C. Chirouse.
23479–23480	Basket, carrying (Clallam Indians)	.....do	J. G. Swan.
19020	Carrying basket (fig. 145)	.... do	Do.
1778	Satchel, strips of bark	Columbia River........	Dr. Suckeley, U. S. A.
24104	Basket for carrying roots (Klamath Indians).	Oregon	L. S. Dyar.
24116	Satchel, made of tuli (Klamath Indians).	.....do	Do.
24122	Sack, carrying grain...............	.....do	Do.
18897	Net, agave fiber (fig. 151)..........	California............	Edward Palmer.
19700	Net, carrying	.....do	Stephen Powers.
19472	Basket, cactus fruit...............	.....do	Edward Palmer.
19743–19744	Basket, fruit (fig. 163)	.....do	Do.
19745	Basket, acorns	.....do	Do.
19769	Bag, fruit, etc...............	.....do	Do.
19770	Bag, cones of pine	.....do	Do.
24166	Basket, carrying	.....do	Do.
131139	Carrying net (fig. 152), Missions...	.....do	Do.
131148	Basket and strap, carrying (Hupa Indians).	.....do	Jeremiah Curtin.
131161	Basket for acorns	.....do	Do.
126907	Headband (fig. 147), Hupa Indians.	.....do	Lieut. P. H. Ray, U. S. A.
167410	Basket, carrying, conical...........	.....do	H. W. Henshaw.
165687	Basket, carrying (Pima Indians)...	.....do	F. W. Hodge.
126680	Basket, carrying (figs. 165), Pima Indians.	.....do	Edward Palmer.
174523	Basket, carrying (Papagos).......	Arizona	W J McGee.
10351	Basket, for seed...................	Fort Mohave, Colorado..	Edward Palmer.
168412	Satchel, beaded	Colorado...............	F. W. Clarke.
152528	Pouch, hunting.................	....	Lewis Engel.
70929–70937	Basket, carrying (fig. 155), Moki ..	Arizona	Col. Jas. Stevenson.
128013	.....do......................	.....do	Mrs. T. E. Stevenson.
160707	Basket, carrying (Zuñi Indians)..	New Mexico............	Jas. Mooney.
68465–68475	.....do......................	.....do	Col. Jas. Stevenson.
68544–68550	.....do......................	.....do	Do.
68701–68714	Gourd, for carrying water (Moki Indians).	.....do	Do.
71020	Basket, water-tight (Moki Indians)	.....do	Do.
84263	Strap, carrying, with hair ropes...	.....do	V. Mindeleff.
9540	Rope, woolen, for carrying wood (Zuñi Indians).	.....do	Edward Palmer.
68698	Carrying bands (Zuñi Indians)...	.....do	Col. Jas. Stevenson.

CARRYING APPLIANCES IN THE U. S. NATIONAL MUSEUM—Continued.

WEST COAST INDIANS—continued.

Museum number.	Specimen.	Locality.	By whom contributed.
68655–68656	Shoulder pad (Zuñi Indians)	New Mexico............	Maj. J. W. Powell.
27827	Net basket, prop stick, headband..	Arizona	Mrs. Geo. Stout.
1804	Cushions, for carrying (Mohave Indians).	.....do	Lieutenant Whipple, U.S.A.
1514	.....do	Mexico	Dr. Berlandier. .
73934	Head strap (Yucatan)...............	...do	L. H. Aymé.
73974	Packing rope........................	....do	Do.
24145	Basket, carrying (fig. 164), Mohave.	California	Edward Palmer.
9981	Net, to carry burdens	Colorado River	Do.
12004	Haversack (Pai Utes)	Southern Utah..........	Maj. J. W. Powell.
14382	.....do.............................	....do	Do.
14397	Haversack, beaded, with strap	....do	Do.
14493	Bladder, for carrying water.........	....do	Do.
14664–14675	Baskets, for fruit and seeds.......	....do	Do.
17196	Haversack, rawhide (Ute Indians).	.....do	Do.
42155	Carrying basket (fig. 150), Utes....	Utah	Do.
19026	Basket, large, conical, for seeds, etc	Pyramid Lake, Nevada .	Stephen Powers.
134422–134429	Baskets, gathering fruit	New Mexico............	Col. Jas. Stevenson.
84139–84143	Gourds, for carrying dry articles (Moki Indians).	.....do	V. Mindeleff.
5564	Basket, gathering (Apache Indians).	Arizona	Edward Palmer.
152711	Haversack (hide)	Colima, Mexico	Do.
126680	Basket and rest stick; also head band.	.....do	Do.
126591, 126592	Carrying yoke and jars (fig. 174)...	...do	Do.
77006	Basket, slung over the back........	Cozumel Island.........	J. E. Benedict.
78955	Bag, packing, large	Mexico	Louis H. Aymé.
73956	Bag, packing, small	...do	Do.
129652	Carrying net.......................	Central America........	Chas. H. Townsend.
129654	Carrying net (fig. 175)..............	....do	Do.
152507	Carrying net (fig. 184).............	Amazon River..........	Mrs. F. G. Fry.
126805	Carrying frame (fig. 176)	Honduras..............	A. E. Morlan.
1864	Wallet (Comanche Indians).......	New Mexico............	Lieutenant Couch, U.S.A
7926	Wallet, mat	Mexico	Dr. Sartorius.
7927	Wallet, mat (double)	....do	Do.
76918–76919	Wallet, basket (palm).............	...do	New Orleans Exposition.
43121	Wallet, grass (double)	United States Colombia.	Thomas Moran.
131222	Carrying basket (fig. 181).........	Straits of Magellan	Leslie Lee.

THE CARRYING OF CHILDREN.

Next to getting about and carrying things comes the activity of carrying persons, or passenger traffic, and this commences with the transportation of helpless children.

Invention has had in this art an opportunity of elaboration along the lines of geographic conditions in obedience to the commands of ethnic peculiarities, but the most primitive method resorts to no machinery whatever. (Fig. 186.)

The traffic of the world in the present day is always numbered in millions, whether of persons, of miles, of tons of freight carried or coal consumed, or of dollars invested. It began with naked mothers carrying naked children, without the expenditure of one dollar. To study this art from its simple to its complex forms one must commence with tropical peoples who have never been elsewhere. Here the infant is transported upon the person of the mother, both of them clinging one to the other by a semiautomatic habit or instinct. In this paper little attention will be paid to the bed and wrappings of infants. That subject has already been discussed.[1]

African mothers, on the testimony of the U. S. National Museum, have never invented a single device for their tiny passengers, who are usually gathered into the folds of the sash or shawl or mantle. Doubtless this garment is worn frequently to give the child a resting place, and netting tied about the neck furnishes support to the nestling; but it is practically true that the spirit of invention in Africa has not been awakened by the necessity of carrying infants.

Schurtz figures a Masakara negro woman in the interior of Africa, grinding grain on the metate, with a muller, at the same time bearing an infant in the folds of the shawl upon her back.[2] And the union of the manufacturer with the carrier is one of the commonest occurrences there.

Ratzel gives an interesting picture, after Falkenstein, of a Loango mother, barefooted, wearing a head handkerchief, hoeing in the field, and carrying a sleeping infant on her back, securely held in place by a cloth or shawl, tied around her body under the arms and above the breasts, and reaching to her ankles.[3]

Fig. 186.
WOMAN OF BRITTANY CARRYING CHILD.
From sketch by W. K. Chandler.

Holub, in his illustrated catalogue of the South African Exposition in Prague, pictures a Bechuana woman engaged in the same double exercise, and illustrated books and journals describing the west coast of Africa show the usual position of the African babe riding astride

[1] E. Pokrowski, Trans. Soc. Friends of Nat. Sci., Moscow; Mason, "Cradles of the American Aborigines," Rep. Smithsonian Inst. (U. S. Nat. Mus.), 1887, pp. 164–212; J. H. Porter, "Notes on the Artificial Deformation of Children among Savage and Civilized Peoples," ibid., pp. 213–235; H. Ploss, "Das Kind in Brauch und Sitte der Völker," Leipzig, 1884, 2 vols.

[2] "Katechismus der Völkerkunde," Leipzig, 1893, p. 180.

[3] "Völkerkunde," Leipzig, 1887, I, p. 155.

the mother's hips and enfolded in the loose garment. (Fig. 187.) In many places the attachment to her body is reduced to a mere string.

The Zulu mother carries her babe in a shawl, or wide sash, which passes around her body above her breasts, close under her arms, and reaching quite down to her hips.[1] The child sits in the shawl as in a swing, which passes about the loins above the center of gravity.

The Hottentot women generally wear the krass—a square piece of the skin of a wild beast, generally a wildcat, tied on with the hairy side outward—around their shoulders, which, like those of the men, cover their backs and sometimes reach down to their hams. Between two krasses they fasten a suckling child, if they have one, with the head just peeping over their shoulders. The under krass prevents their bodies being hurt by the children at their back.[2]

Fig. 187.

AFRICAN METHOD OF CARRYING CHILD.
From a photograph in the U. S. National Museum.

Ratzel figures Abyssinian women in the double function of carrying children and carrying freight. In the former, the tiny passenger rests in the folds of the dress on the back. In the latter, the load is borne on the back and sustained by ropes, knapsackwise.[3]

In European countries for the most part, the child has been consigned to a wheel carriage of some kind. The simplest form of this is the Baschkir Kuné, which is merely one form of California cradle (fig. 188), with wheels on the hindmost cross bar, and a hood of birch bark instead of reed mat.[4]

A forked stick is the frame of the cradle and hounds of the axle. On this rests an oblong cylinder of birch bark, ovoid in horizontal outline, and having a lattice bottom. The hood is of birch bark, and not unlike that of a common wagon.

A differentiation has also taken place among cradle frames, one form dropping the suspension strings, by means of which it became now a bed to be swung, now a vehicle to be carried, assumes the rockers or wheels and is no longer lifted from the ground; the other remains in the condition wherein it may be now a swinging bed, now a carrying frame.

The carrying of children on the person has been affected in European

---

[1] Ratzel, "Völkerkunde," Leipzig, 1887, 1, p. 150.

[2] Kolben, "Voyage to the Cape of Good Hope," IV, p. 14.

[3] "Völkerkunde," III, p. 229.

[4] Cf. Pokrowski, Rev. d'Ethnog., 1889, fig. 27, p. 34, with Rep. Smithsonian Inst. (U. S. Nat. Mus.), 1887, p. 180, fig. 12.

countries by this differentiation. Wherever the old-time carrying frame and swing becomes a rocking cradle or a wagon, the process of carrying the child reverts to the most primitive type, chiefly on one arm, after the manner of the African mother.

The commonest sight and often a painful sight in the poorer settlements of any modern city is that of a girl, often quite young, lugging an infant on the left arm, distorting her body hopelessly.

Likewise may be seen among the folk in sport or in serious humor and in the pastimes of children survivals of past practices in the car-

riage of infants. In art, as has been previously stated, the drudgeries of life are glorified. If the caryatid and atlas are the æstheticising and apotheosis of burden bearing on head and back, the many renditions of the Madonna exalt in art and religion the transportation of the human infant on the left arm.[1]

Hercules was cradled in his father's shield: Dionysius in a winnowing fan, which has the same shape. The Greeks do not seem to have carried children in cradles, but the Romans had gotten so far, although the figures resemble the Sioux shoe-shaped device without the wooden support.[2]

The Semite mother who carries her child about her neck puts it astride one shoulder, shifting it to the other as occasion demands (fig. 189). No device or invention is used, but a semi-automatic habit, a kind of instinct for clinging to each other, keeps the young passenger in position. This should be compared with the position of the child among other peoples.

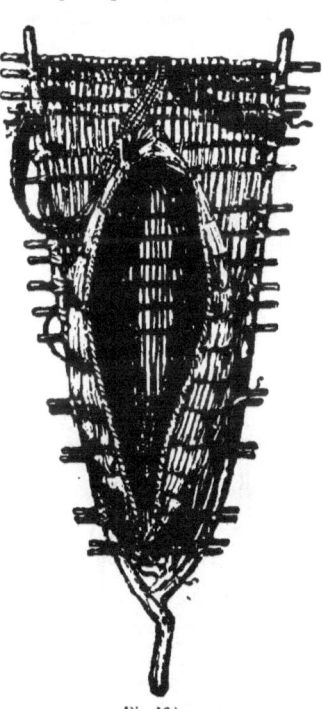

Fig. 188.

CRADLE OF RUSHES, WITH HANDLE, USED BY KLAMATH INDIANS OF CALIFORNIA.

In Egypt the young children of both sexes are usually carried by their mothers and nurses, not in the arms, but on the shoulder, seated astride as in fig. 190 (see Isaiah, XLIX, 22), and sometimes, for a short distance, on the hip.[3] The Nestorian woman bears her child in a bundle on her back.

In the Indo-Pacific area there is little change, only local modifications

[1] Cf. "Woman's Share in Primitive Culture," New York, 1894, p. 186, fig. 50. Woman of India carrying burden and child.
[2] Smith, Dictionary of Greek and Roman Antiquities, s. v., *Cunae.*
[3] Lane, "Modern Egyptians," London, 1846, I, p. 79.

in the primitive method of having as little machinery as possible involved in the transportation of the infant. Of course none of these peoples have ever so much as thought of differentiating the carriage device from the sleeping device.

The siwela, or cradle of Timor, is a flattish basket made of woven rattan ropes, suspended so as to rock over a fire placed beneath, with only the spathe of a palm under the child's back, its head generally lying on rough rattan, and with a small piece of rag thrown over its stomach. The fire below the cradle, which not unfrequently sets fire to it, is partly to keep off the mosquitoes and partly to keep the child warm during the night. The smoke is often so great as almost to suffocate the infant.[1]

Turner says that the Samoan mothers carry their children not on the arm but astride the hip. He pronounces it much safer than on the back and less tiresome to the nurse, and it gives the child a lest constrained posture.

The New Guinea baby may be said for some time to practically live in a net; it is carried in one suspended to the mother's neck, dangling low down in front of the woman; it sleeps in a net bag, and when it awakes and cries and can not change its position in the bag, which is probably suspended from the roof of the veranda, it presents a most comical appearance.[2]

The Australians of Carpentaria Gulf carry the young children under the arm, in a trough of ti bark, with a string under the center and over the shoulder, the arm pressing it on the outer side to keep it close. When a little grown, the child is carried across the hip, supported with one arm, and afterwards across the neck, holding itself on by the mother's hair.

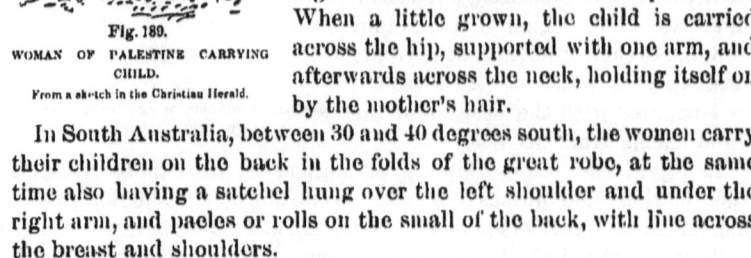

Fig. 189.
WOMAN OF PALESTINE CARRYING CHILD.
From a sketch in the Christian Herald.

In South Australia, between 30 and 40 degrees south, the women carry their children on the back in the folds of the great robe, at the same time also having a satchel hung over the left shoulder and under the right arm, and packs or rolls on the small of the back, with line across the breast and shoulders.

When a Darling River mother is about to carry her child she leans her body forward, and taking hold of the child by its arms swings it over her left shoulder and places it between her shoulder blades with its

---

[1] H. O. Forbes, "Ethnology of Timor-laut," Journ. Anthrop. Inst., London, 1884, XIII, p. 12.

[2] Journ. Anthrop. Inst., London, 1892, XXI, p. 203.

hands around her neck. She then throws a fur rug around herself and the child, and afterwards a netted bag (nunyuncka) is drawn tight under the seat of the child with one end brought over each shoulder of the mother and tied together under her chin to keep the child and rug in their position; so a pouch is formed to hold the infant while it is being carried about. The men generally carry children on their shoulders, as do the Eskimo men.[1]

In a photograph taken by Romyn Hitchcock at Osaka, Japan, a woman is represented as carrying a 3-year-old child pickaback (fig. 191).

The very same method of carrying is practiced by both men and women among the Eskimo of Port Clarence, Alaska.

The child's bed and carriage in one piece exists in Russia, in all the countries under her sway, and in the lands along the southern border of these. It had a wide development in America. This combination carriage and bed exists in two forms—that in which the whole body of the child is bandaged, legs and all, and that in which the body is swaddled and the legs are partly free. These two have relation to climate and pedagogic notions and superstitions; but they have profound relations also to the nomadic and hunting life of the people.

Pokrowski traces the rigid cradle wherein the child is laid upon its back and strapped therein so as often to produce deformation among the Georgians, Nogaïs, Sartes, Kirghiz, Kalmuck, Yakut, Buriat, Ostiak, and Samoyed.[2] He says that it is the most ancient and widely spread. In central Russia it is formed of four planks about a finger

Fig. 190.

EGYPTIAN WOMAN CARRYING CHILD.

From a photograph in the U. S. National Museum.

and a half high, in shape of a box, 1 meter long and 80 centimeters wide, on which is fixed a cloth bottom, and from the corners are ropes which unite in a ring above for suspension. In fact, it is a wooden hammock that has lost its carrying function. But Pokrowski affirms that these cradles often preserve the ancient form that they may be carried about as well as hung up in the house. They are both carriage and swinging cradle in one. The cords from the two borders of the cradle cross over the woman's breast as in the bandolier[3] (fig. 192).

[1] F. Bonney, "Customs of the Aborigines of the River Darling, New South Wales," Journ. Anthrop. Inst., London, 1884, XIII, p. 126.

[2] Mém. Soc. d. Amis d. Sc. Nat., 1886. See also Rev. d'Anthrop., 1885, p. 364; 1887, p. 238.

[3] Rev. d'Ethnog., Paris, 1889, p. 10.

The cradle of the Lapps is a very ingenious structure, admirably suited for its purpose under the ordinary circumstances of Lapp existence. "These cradles," Friis tells us, "are hollowed out of a log, and have a hood which protects the child's head. From this hood down to the end a light network of thongs or cord is stretched over the child, and over this net a handkerchief or other covering can be spread in such a manner that the child can be in complete shelter without hindrance. A strong strap is fastened from one end of the cradle to the other, by means of which it can be slung on the back or set to swing from the branch of a tree (fig. 193). It may be thrown on the ground and rolled about without injury to the child, and it will, moreover, keep out cold of 20° below zero." [1]

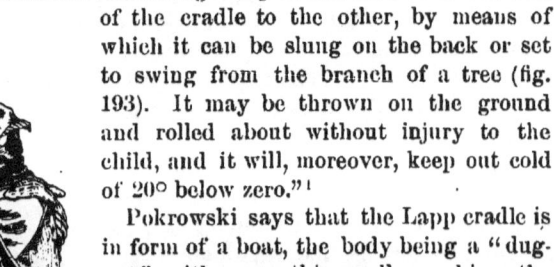

Fig. 191.
JAPANESE WOMAN CARRYING CHILD.
From a photograph by Romyn Hitchcock.

Pokrowski says that the Lapp cradle is in form of a boat, the body being a "dugout" with very thin walls, making the apparatus very light and easy to carry. Outside is stretched a covering of reindeer leather, very thin. Moss is used for the bed, and over it is spread the fur of the young reindeer. Rawhide lines, stretched from the hood to the foot, sustain the curtain of leather hung over all. A strap attached to the foot and the front serves for suspension, and enables the mother to support the child in front or on her back, or on one hip, the strap resting on the opposite shoulder.

The Ostiak have two kinds of cradles, those for the new born and another kind for more advanced children. The former are trays of birch bark, oblong, shallow, high at the head, rolled over about the margin and decorated with great taste. The cradle is provided with cords, by means of which it may hang in front of the mother (fig. 194).

The cradle for the more advanced infant is deeper, and provides for seating it more erect. This is carried on the back of the mother (fig. 195).

The children of the Giliak, as among the Goldi, are strapped down on a kind of board serving as a cradle, and hung up in that position to

[1] Journ. Anthrop. Inst., London, 1885, xv, p. 228.

a rafter of the hut.[1]   Schrenck should also be consulted about the Giliak cradle and method of carrying the infant.[2]

Bush says of the Giliak cradle that near one end of the shed was a babe tightly bandaged in a wooden box or cradle, somewhat like those used by our American Indians, but with its little legs from the knees downward unfettered.   This cradle was suspended from the ridge pole in an upright position, by four leather thongs that were just long enough

Fig. 192.
WOMAN OF LITTLE RUSSIA CARRYING CHILD.
From a figure in the Revue d'Ethnographie.

to enable the little one to reach the ground with its feet, by which it swung itself back and forth without assistance.[3]

Of the Samoyed cradle Jackson says:

It was amusing to see the baby, which had been sitting up and had eaten a fairly good supper of raw meat, put to bed by its mother.   She first wrapped it in furs, then placed it in a box shaped like a coffin, and laced it with narrow strips of hide, so

[1] Ravenstein, "Russians on the Amur," London, 1861, p. 391.
[2] "Reisen und Forschungen im Amur-Lande," pl. XII.
[3] Bush, "Reindeer, Dogs, and Snowshoes," p. 123.

that it was not only impossible for it to fall out, but also very difficult for it to move.[1]

Infants are kept among the Mangun and Orochou in an oblong box; while the Goldi strap them down in a basin-shaped cradle, ornamented with small coins, and suspended by means of an iron hoop to a rafter in the house.[2]

The Yakut cradle, according to Lansdell, resembles a coal scuttle.

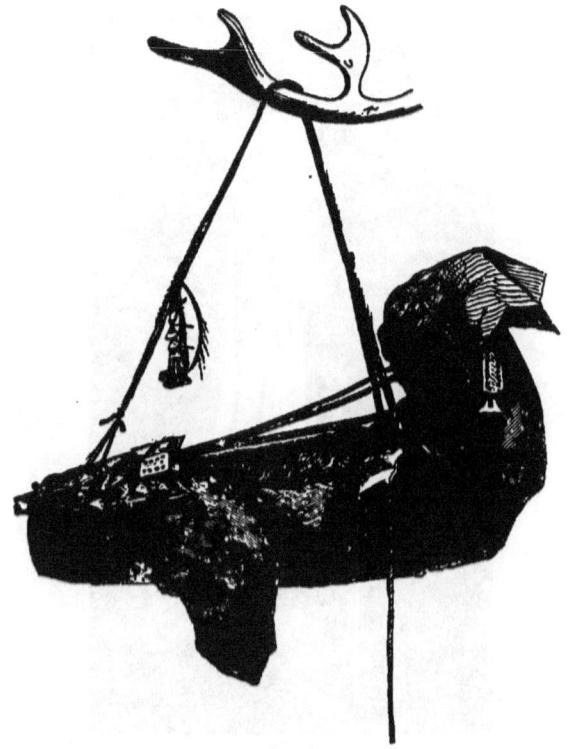

Fig. 193.
LAPP CRADLE.
From a figure in the Revue d'Ethnographie.

When traveling they suspend it at the side of the reindeer as the Sioux women hang their cradles from the pommel of the pony saddle.[3]

On the northwestern border of the Okhotsk Sea dwell the Tungus and the Lamut. They, owing to the rugged condition of their country, saddle the reindeer and use it both for riding and packing instead of

[1] F. G. Jackson, "The Great Frozen Land," London, 1895, p. 108.
[2] Ravenstein, "Russians on the Amur," London, 1861, p. 386.
[3] Lansdell, "Through Siberia," Boston, 1882, p. 303.

draft to the sledge. The infant is neatly stowed in a cradle lined with reindeer fur (fig. 196). This cradle shuts up, and ventilation is provided through a valve of leather which the mother controls. This device may also be suspended from the human body The Tungus, says Bush, have a novel way of carrying children on reindeer back. Two of them are lashed together and thrown over the pack saddle like two packages. Each is sewed up in a single garment, jacket, pants, boots, mittens, and cap all in one piece, made of heavy reindeer fur, with no part of them visible but the small, shining black eyes and little red noses

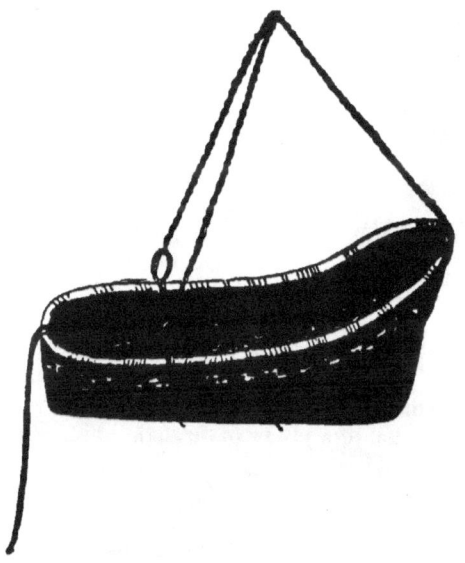

Fig. 194.

OSTIAK CRADLE.

From a figure in the Revue d'Ethnographie.

peering over the fur. Perchance a baby may be balanced by a kettle, etc. The youngsters do not seem to mind the cold.[1]

Says N. Width:

I remember from my boyhood that the women carried their infants in a box on the back, the box well provided with reindeer skin. These boxes were fastened on poles, and when the women entered a store in the town for shopping the poles were stuck in the snow and the babies left there for hours.[2] * * *

In Sheldon Jackson's report on the introduction of tame reindeer into Alaska there is a native drawing of a cradle or bed for an infant, swung from the ceiling by four cords. This should be compared with

[1] Bush, "Reindeer, Dogs, and Snowshoes." New York, 1871, p. 240.

[2] Senate Ex. Doc. No. 73, Fifty-third Congress. second session, p. 150.

the Cape Breton and the Seminole cradle, and a photograph by Boas of the Kwakiutl.[1] The same author gives a plate showing a crowd of

Chukchi; in several of the figures the children are borne pickaback, as among the western Eskimo.

The author has not been able to find the cradle board or frame among the Eskimo. So far as he is informed this device does not exist in Mexico or anywhere in the tropics. If the collection of the U. S. National Museum be complete (and he is sure it is not) the cradle does not exist in either of these areas. A few general statements may be predicated upon the scanty material in the U. S. National Museum collection.

The American aboriginal cradle is influenced by climate. It can not exist in extremes of heat or cold. In one case the child would be smothered, in the other it would be frozen.

Fig. 195.

OSTIAK WOMAN CARRYING CHILD.

From a figure in the Revue d'Ethnographie.

Again, whatever may be the material, whether birch bark, rawhide, a flat board, a dugout, a frame of rods, the infant's head is never placed in contact with it. There is always between the head and this hard frame or board a pillow of fur, hair, shredded bark, down, or

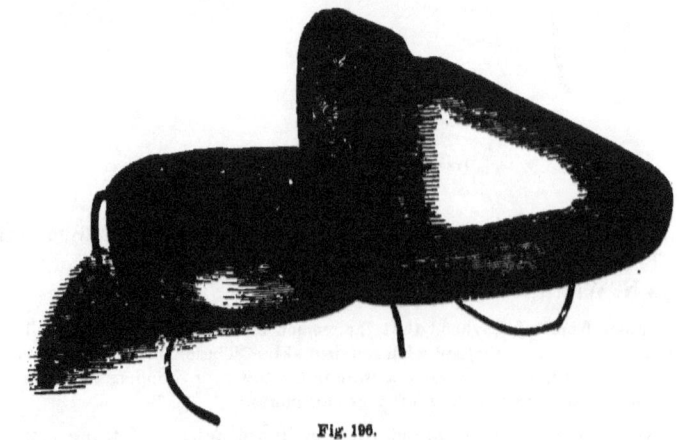

Fig. 196.

TUNGUS AND LAMUT FOLDING CRADLE.

From a figure in the Revue d'Ethnographie.

some other substance. It is idle, therefore, to collect cradles in order to study intentional and undesigned head flattening unless we secure

[1] Senate Ex. Doc. No. 70, Fifty-third Congress, second session, p. 101.

also the pillow. One cradle, from the Yumas, has two little pads about 4 inches apart to catch the head of the infant; another has a regular pillow, and so on.

Finally, all the U. S. National Museum cradles are made to stand up or to hang up. A great many persons who are familiar with the subject have been questioned, and it seems to be true that Indian cradles are very seldom laid flat on the ground. In that case the head is perfectly free, and after the child is a few weeks old, excepting during sleep, the head does not touch the pillow at all.

As explained elsewhere, the exigencies of climate prevent the Eskimo from carrying their children in open frames. But the Lamut and Tungus devices just named exist in a climate as cold as any endured by the Eskimo. It is necessary to seek the explanation of the absence of any device among the Eskimo in the difference of the culture grade. The Asiatics are herdsmen and hang the children to the saddlebow. The Eskimo have generally no good wood for frames and no good reason to separate the infant from the mother. When the child is young it rides in the mother's hood, between her fur coat and her skin (fig. 197). To prevent the young passenger from getting lost Boas intimates that a strap is worn about the mother's waist. The costume of this unique people over many hundreds of miles of coast east and west is uniform in this regard.[1]

Fig. 197.
ESKIMO WOMAN OF POINT BARROW CARRYING CHILD.
From a photograph by Captain Healy, U. S. R. M.

When children are about a month old they are put into a jacket made from the skin of a deer fawn having a cap of the same material, their legs remaining bare, as they are always carried in their mother's hood. In some places, where large boots are in use, they are said to be carried in these.[2]

The hood of the jacket is much the larger in that of the women, for the purpose of holding a child. The back of the jacket also bulges out in the middle to give the child a footing, and a strap or girdle below this, secured round the waist by two large wooden buttons in front, prevents the infant from sliding down.[3]

The mode of treating infants is one of the national customs of a people that changes most slowly says Richardson.[4]

---

[1] Sixth Ann. Rep. Bureau of Ethnology, p. 556.
[2] Ibid, p. 556.
[3] Ibid, p. 557.
[4] Richardson, "Arctic Searching Expedition," New York, 1852, p. 218.

Peary says that the woman of North Greenland, like the man, wore the ahtee and netcheh, made respectively of bird skin and sealskin. They differed in pattern from those of the man only in the back, where an extra width is sewed in, which forms a pouch extending the entire length of the back of the wearer and fitting tight around the hips. In this pouch or hood the baby is carried; its little body, covered only by a shirt reaching to the waist, made of the skin of a young blue fox, is placed against the bare back of the mother, and the head, covered by a tight-fitting skull-cap made of seal skin, is allowed to rest against the mother's shoulder. In this way the Eskimo child is car-

Fig. 198.

ESKIMO WOMAN CARRYING CHILD.

From a photograph in the Bureau of Ethnology.

ried constantly, whether awake or asleep, and without clothing except the shirt and cap, until it can walk, which is usually at the age of 2 years; then it is clothed in skin and allowed to toddle about. If it is the youngest member of the family, after it has learned to walk, it still takes its place in the mother's hood whenever it is sleepy or tired, just as American mothers pick up their little toddlers and rock them.[1]

When the Eskimo babe is large enough to escape from the hood and walk it has still to be carried a great deal. Of this sort, both father and mother take the youngster by one arm and one leg, give it a toss, and in a twinkling the youthful rider is sitting pickaback astride the parent's neck (fig. 198). The author has seen both men and women carrying young children after this fashion.

Women carry their young astride their backs. The child is held in place by a strap passing under its thighs and around over the mother's breasts.[2]

When a child is born in Ungava, on the authority of Lucien Turner, the mother wraps it in the softest skin she is able to procure and during its infancy it is carried in the ample hood attached to her coat.

The carrying devices for infants among the American Indians, as

[1] J. Peary, "My Arctic Journal," New York and Philadelphia, 1893, p. 43.
[2] John W. Kelly, "Ethnographical Memoranda Concerning the Arctic Eskimos of Alaska and Siberia," Bureau of Education, Circular of Information No. 2, 1890, p. 18.

distinguished from the Eskimos, may now be examined in the following families and tribes: (1) The Athapascan family, of Alaska and
Canada; (2) the Algonquian family, of Canada and the United States;
(3) the Iroquoian family, north to south; (4) the Southern Indians
of the United States; (5) the tribes of the plains of the Great West,
especially the Siouan family; (6) the Pacific Slope tribes of southeast
Alaska and British Columbia; (7) the tribes of the Pacific Slope from
Vancouver Island southward; (8) the Great Interior Basin and the
Pueblos; (9) Mexico and Central America; (10) the Cordilleras of
South America; (11) the Amazonian area and southward; (12) the
Caribbean area.

The Athapascans of the north are the inland neighbors of the
Eskimo and by the Rev. A. G. Morice are thus classified:

Northern Dénés.—Loucheux: Lower Mackenzie River and Alaska;
Hares: Mackenzie, Anderson, and MacFarlane rivers; Bad-People:
Old Fort Halkett; Slaves: west of Great Slave Lake and Macken-
zie River; Dog-Ribs: between Great Slave Lake and Great Bear
Lake: Yellow-Knives: northeast of Great Slave Lake; Cariboo Eat-
ers: east of Lake Athabaska; Chippewayans: Lake Athabaska, etc.;
Tsé'kéhne: both sides of Rocky Mountains; Beavers: south side of
Peace River; Sarcees: east of Rocky Mountains, latitude 51° north;
Nah'ane: Stickeen River and east; Carriers: Stuarts Lake, north and
south; Tsilkoh'tin: Chilcotin River.

Southern Dénés.—Umkwas, Totunies, and Kwalhiokwas: Oregon;
Hupas: Hupa Valley, California; Wailakis: northern California;
Navajo: Arizona; Apache: Oklahoma, Colorado, New Mexico, and
Arizona: Lipans: New Mexico.

Mackenzie somewhere intimates that the Chippewayan mothers make
their upper garments full in the shoulders. When traveling they carry
their infants upon their backs next the skin and convenient to giving
them nourishment. This is a transition habit between Eskimo and
Indian and not prevalent among the Athapascans.

"The Kutchin women," says Richardson, "do not carry their infants in
their hoods or boots after the Eskimo fashion, nor do they stuff them
into a bag with moss, as the Chippewayan and Crees do, but they place
them in a seat of birch bark, with back and sides like those of an
armchair, and a pommel in front resembling the peak of a Spanish
saddle. This hangs at the woman's back, suspended by a strap which
passes over her shoulders, and the infant is seated in it, with back to
hers, and its legs, well cased in warm boots, hanging down on each side
of the pommel. The child's feet are bandaged to prevent their growing,
small feet being thought handsome; and the consequence is that short,
unshapely feet are characteristic of the people."[1]

The Lower Yukon trough-shaped cradle of birch bark (example No.
32986, in the U. S. National Museum, fig. 199) is made of three pieces, the

---

[1] Richardson, "Arctic Searching Expedition," New York, 1852, p. 227.

bottom, the top or hood, and the awning piece. The two parts constituting the body of the cradle overlap an inch and a half and are sewed
together with a single basting of pine root, with stitches half an inch
apart. Around the body just under the margin, and continuously around
the border of the hood and awning, lies a rod of osier. A strip of birch
bark laid on the upper side of the awning serves as a stiffener and is
sewed down by an ingenious basting with stitches an inch or more
long which pass down through two thicknesses of birch bark, around
the osier twig just below the margin, and up again through the two

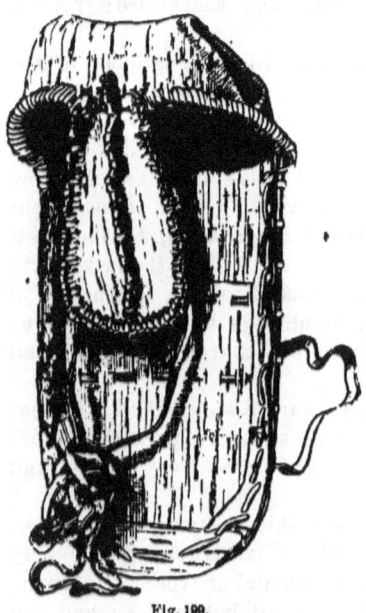

thicknesses of birch bark by another opening to form the next
stitch. The hood is formed by
puckering the birch bark after the
manner of a grocer's bag. The bordering osier is neatly seized to the
edge of the hood and awning by a
coil of split spruce root. Rows of
beads of many colors adorn the awning piece. In a country intolerable
by reason of the mosquitoes it is
not strange that provisions for sustaining some sort of netting should
be devised.

Immediately after birth, without
being washed, the Northeastern
Tinneh infant is laid naked on a
layer of moss in a bag made of
leather and lined with hare skins.
If it be in summer, the latter is dis-
pensed with. This bag is then securely laced, restraining the limbs
in natural positions, and leaving
the child freedom to move the head
only. In this phase of its existence

Fig. 199.
ATHAPASCAN CRADLE OF BIRCH BARK.
Yukon River, Alaska.
Cat. No. 32986. U. S. N. M.   Collected by E. W. Nelson

it resembles strongly an Egyptian mummy. Cradles are never used, but
this machine, called a "moss bag," is an excellent adjunct to the rearing
of children up to a certain age, and has become almost, if not universally,
adopted in the families of the Hudson Bay Company's employees.[1]

The Carrier women of Stuart Lake transported their babes in cradles
of birch bark, curved up at the narrow end or foot and prolonged at the
broad or open end as a support for the child's head. A hoop of willow
encircled the wide end, and the necessary lacings passed through a band
of buckskin bordering the apparatus on the outside. In recent times
modifications have been made in covers and in lacings. The Tsilkoh'tin
tribe make a cradle of willow twigs in form of a slipper, covered with

[1] Bernard R. Ross, Rep. Smithsonian Inst., 1866, p. 305.

deerskin and provide a hoop over the infant's face.[1] In this connection especial attention is called to the Yokaia and the Hupa cradles of California.   The shoe-shaped cradle of the Tsilkoh'tin resembles in form and motif the latter, the Carrier truncated cradle, in which the child's feet are free, recalling the former, even as to the material.[2]   The reader will not forget that the Hupa came long ago to California from the Athapascan country.

The Southern Canadian cradle is a board with two flaps of cloth which lace together up the center.   The child is laid on its back on the board, packed with soft moss, and laced firmly down with its arms to its side and only its head at liberty.   The cradle is strung on the back of the mother when traveling, or reared against a tree when resting in camp, the child being only occasionally released from bondage for a few moments.   The little prisoners are remarkably good.   No squalling disturbs an Indian camp.[3]

Catlin figures a Cree woman carrying a child on her right arm, and holding the buffalo robe around the child with the left hand.[4]   The Kickapoos, of the same stock, carry the small child on the back in the shawl (fig. 200).

Mr. Lucien Turner reports that the Nascopi of Labrador and Ungava, who are much affected by their proximity to Eskimo, use no cradle board for children.

The principal factor in the Chippewa infant's house, according to Kohl, is a flat board.   For this purpose poplar wood is selected; in the first place because it is light, and secondly, because it does not crack

Fig. 200.

KICKAPOO (ALGONQUIAN) WOMAN CARRYING CHILD.

After Hoppe.

or splinter.   On this board a small frame of thin, peeled sapling is fastened, much after the shape of the child's body, and stands up from the board like the sides of a violin from the sounding board.   It is fastened on with bast, because the Indians never use nails, screws, or glue.   The cavity is filled with very soft substances for the reception of the child.

[1] Cf. A. G. Morice, Trans. Canadian Inst., 1894, IV, p. 133, with two figures.
[2] See figures 210-212.
[3] Fitzwilliams, "The Northwest Passage by Land," p. 85.
[4] Catlin, "North American Indians," I, p. 33.

They prepare for this purpose a mixture composed of very fine, dry moss, rotted cedar wood, and a species of tender wool found in the seed vessels of a species of reed. This wool was recommended as a most useful ingredient in the stuffing, for it sucks up all moisture as greedily as a sponge, and hence there is no need to inspect the baby' continually. In this bed the little beings nestle up to the armpits—so far they are wrapped up tightly with bandages and coverings, but the head and arms are free. At a convenient distance above the head is a stiff circle of wood, also fastened to the cradle with bast. It serves as a protection to the head, and if the cradle happens to fall over it rests on this arch. In fact, you may roll an Indian tikinagan over as much as you please, but the child can not be injured. The squaws at times display extraordinary luxury in the gaily embroidered coverlid which they throw over the whole cradle.[1]

The Iroquois cradle, example No. 18806, has the backboard carved in imitation of peacocks and is painted in bright colors. It is square at the top and the awning frame is mortised at the ends, which allows them to slide over the awning bar held down and guyed by stays on the opposite sides; has a movable foot rest at the bottom and thongs along the sides for lashing the baby in. Length, 29¼ inches; width, top, 10½ inches, bottom, 8¼ inches; foot rest, height, 3½ inches; width, 6 inches. The St. Regis Iroquois, in the north of New York and near Canada, have for many years bought their cradle boards from the whites or made them of material bought from a white man.

Example No. 8894 is like the last, with gaudily painted and carved backboard, and awning frame carved. Length, 31 inches; width, top 11 inches, bottom 7¾ inches; height of awning frame, 12¼ inches; width of top 9¼, bottom 12 inches.

Morgan says that the Iroquois baby frame, "ga-ose-ha," is an Indian invention. It appears to have been designed rather as a convenience to the Indian mother for the transportation of her infant than, as has generally been supposed, to secure an erect figure. The frame is about 2 feet in length by about 14 inches in width, with a carved footboard at the small end and a hoop or bow at the head, arching over at right angles. After being inclosed in a blanket, the infant is lashed upon the frame with belts of beadwork, which firmly secure and cover its person, with the exception of the face. A separate article for covering the face is then drawn over the bow, and the child is wholly protected. When in use, the burden strap attached to the frame is placed around the forehead of the mother, and the "ga-ose-ha" upon her back. This frame is often elaborately carved, and its ornaments are of the choicest description. When cultivating the maize, or engaged in any outdoor occupation, the mother hangs the "ga-ose-ha" upon a limb of the nearest tree and left to swing in the breeze. The patience and quiet of the

---

[1] J. G. Kohl, "Wanderings round Lake Superior," 1860, pp. 6–7.

Indian child in this close confinement are quite remarkable. It will hang thus suspended for hours without uttering a complaint.[1]

East of the Mississippi River, north of the Tennessee and the North Carolina line, and south of Hudson Bay Algonquian and Iroquoian tribes all used a flat cradle board not far from 2½ feet long, 10 inches wide, and one-half an inch thick, tapering wider at the head. Example No. 18806 has the back carved in flowers and birds and painted blue, red, green, and yellow. The cleat at the upper end of the back is a modern chair round. The footboard is a small shelf or bracket on which the child's feet rest.

"In the towne of Dafemonquepenc distant from Roanoac 4 or 5 milles, the woemen are attired, and pownced, in fuch forte as the woemen of Roanoac are, yet they weare noe worathes vppon their heads, nether haue they their thighes painted with fmall pricks. They haue a ftrange manner of bearing their children, and quite contrarie to ours. For our woemen carrie their children in their armes before their brefts, but they taking their fonne by the right hand, bear him on their backs, holdinge the left thighe in their lefte arme after a ftrange and comnefmall fafhion."[2]

Hodgson's description is not clear. He says that as few of the Creeks are able to purchase many negroes, almost all the drudgery is performed by the women, and it is melancholy to meet them, as we continually did, with an infant hanging on their necks, bending under a heavy burden and leading their husband's horse while he walked before them, erect and graceful, apparently without a care. This servitude has an unfavorable effect upon the appearance of the women, those above a certain age being generally bent and clumsy, with a scowl on their wrinkled forehead and a countenance dejected.[3]

The Chetemacha of St. Marys Parish, southern Louisiana, had a peculiar method of fastening their infants in the cradle boards. They rocked them in such a way that the forehead was flattened, while the back of the head assumed a round shape by the rocking motion. This implies that the flattening pad, or short piece of wood, was fastened to the head only and not at the same time to the cradle board.[4] It also points to a fashion of cradling or carrying of that type which exists from the Columbia River mouth northward. The Choctaw custom should be studied in the same connection.

The frame of the Comanche cradle (Shoshonean) belongs to the latticed type, as in figure 202, and is thus made: Two strips of narrow

---

[1] Lewis H. Morgan, "League of the Iroquois," 1851, pp. 390–391, with illustration.
[2] Hariot, "Virginia," Holbein Soc., Manchester, 1888, pl. x.
[3] Hodgson, "Letters from North America," I, pp. 135–136. Compare the hammock cradle of the Seminoles (Fifth Ann. Rep. Bureau of Ethnology, p. 497) with Cape Breton cradle (Rep. U. S. Nat. Mus., 1887, p. 169) and drawing in Bruce's report. (Senate Ex. Doc. No. 73, Fifty-third Congress, second session.)
[4] Gatschet, Trans. Anthrop. Soc., Washington, 1884, II, p. 153.

board, often native hewn, wider and farther apart at the upper end, are held in place by crosspieces lashed on so as to accommodate the leather cradle sheath. The lashing is very ingeniously done. Four holes an inch apart are bored through the frame board and the cross-

pieces at the corners of a square. A string of buckskin is passed backward and forward from hole to hole and the two ends tied, or one end is passed through a slit cut in the other. The lashing does not cross the square on either side diagonally. Above the upper crosspiece the frame pieces project a foot and are sharpened on top like fence pickets. Disks of German silver and brass-headed nails are used in profusion to form various geometric ornaments. Upon the front of the frame, between the crosspieces, a strip of buffalo hide (with the hair side is sewn with raw-hide strings toward the cradle bed). The inclos-

ing case is a shoe-shaped bag made of a single piece of soft deerskin lashed to gether halfway on top in the usual manner, and kept open around the face by a stiffening of buffalo leather. This case is attached to the frame by thong lacings. Little sleigh bells, bits of leather, feathers, etc., complete the ornamentation.

Fig. 201.
COMANCHE CRADLE OF BEAR-
SKIN.
Cat. No. 6970 U. S. N. M Collected by
Edward Palmer.

Another Comanche example, No. 6970 (fig. 201), is the most primitive cradle in the U. S. National Museum. It is a strip of black bearskin, 30 inches long and 20 wide, doubled together in form of a cradle case. Along the side edges loops of buckskin are made to receive the lacing. The loops are formed as follows: A buckskin string is passed through a hole in the bearskin, and the longer end passed through a slit or cut in the shorter end. The long end is then passed through the next hole and drawn until a loop of sufficient size is left; a slit is made in the string near the last hole passed through, and then the whole lashing is drawn through this slit. This serves the

Fig. 202
TRELLIS CRADLE USED BY THE
BLACKFEET INDIANS OF
MONTANA.
Cat. No. 6918, U. S. N. M Collected
by Edward Palmer.

purpose of a knot at each hole, as in many other cradles. A foot piece of bearskin is sewed in with coarse leather string.

The Blackfeet Indian women of Montana carried their more advanced children in their arms or in a robe behind their backs. When traveling the children were placed in sacks of skin on the tent poles. No cradle of any form was seen.[1] Maximilian also tells of a Minitaree woman who carried a little child wrapped in a piece of leather fastened with straps.[2] This occurrence of a frameless cradle in three spots east of the Rocky Mountains lends color to the statement that the introduction of the horse greatly modified the method of carrying infants.

Among the relics of the Catlin collection are two old cradles. Of one the following description will suffice: Backboard square at the top; carved and painted; awning frame bent and painted; covering cloth decorated with beads and tacked around the edge of the side board, brought up and laced in the middle like a shoe; length, 28¾ inches; width, 13 inches.

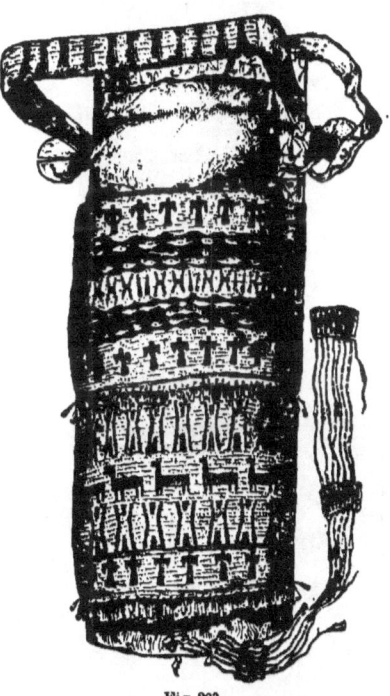

The description of the second example (fig. 203) is as follows: Backboard carved on front above; back brace with large, rounded ends extending outward; footrest low, curved around at the bottom; cradle covered over with quill work in red, white, and black patterns—lozenges, women, horses, etc.; decorated with iron bells; opening across the cradle covered in the middle with embroidered quilt; length, 31½ inches; width, 10¾ inches; head frame, 9½ inches; height, 13¾ inches.[3]

A plate from Catlin in the Report of the National Museum for 1885, is most significant. Here the Sioux woman carries a helpless infant in a cradle, laced

Fig. 203.
ALGONQUIAN CRADLE, DECORATED WITH QUILL WORK.
Collected by George Catlin.

down, feet and all. A second has an older child on her back infolded in her blanket. Further on the scene is changed. It is the epoch of the horse, and both women seem to be lifted from the ground bodily without changing the positions of their burdens. (Fig. 204.)

Example No. 75472 is an Ogallala Sioux cradle. The frame is made of two diverging slats painted yellow, held in place at the head and

[1] Stevens, Ann. Rep. Ind. Affairs, 1854, p. 204.
[2] "Travels in the Interior of North America," London, 1843, p. 180.
[3] Rep. Smithsonian Inst. (U. S. Nat. Mus.) 1887, p. 202.

foot by cross slats lashed as in the Blackfeet cradle, with this difference, namely, that the string crosses between the holes diagonally.

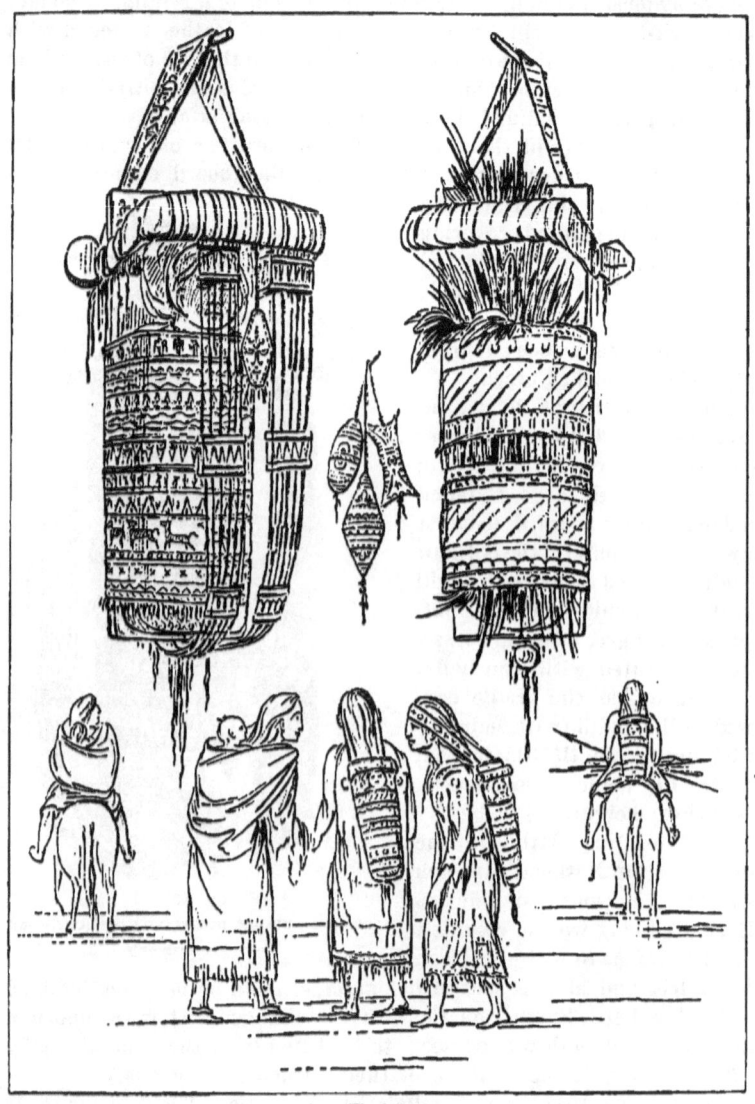

Fig. 204.

ALGONQUIAN CRADLES IN USE.

From a figure in the Report of the Smithsonian Institution (U. S. National Museum), 1885.

This may have no significance. The tops of the side piece project
above the cradle sack at least 18 inches, and are studded with brass-

headed nails in straight lines. As in the Blackfeet cradle, there is a bottom or mattress, but a quilt of calico, lined, supplants the buffalo hide. The baby case proper is shoe shaped, the part around the head and shoulders stiffened with a lining of buffalo leather. All over the outside beadwork is laid on in geometric patterns of blue, red, yellow, green, and blue black on a white ground. The beads are strung on a fine sinew thread in proper number and color to extend quite across the case. This string is then tacked down at inter-vals of three-fourths of an inch so regularly as to form continuous, creased lines extending from the foot longitudinally around the baby case to the foot on the other side to imitate porcupine-quill work. Streamers of colored tape and rib-bon take the place of old-fashioned fur and feathers. The edges of the lower half of the case are joined by four strings tied separately, instead of the universal lashing. There are about this cradle several marks of modifica-tion by contact with whites, which show at the same time the tenacity with which old forms remain and readiness with which they yield to pressure at the points of least resist-ance, indicating also where the points of least resistance are.

Fig. 205.

TRELLIS CRADLE OF THE OGAL-LALA SIOUX INDIANS.

Cat. No. 75472, U. S. N. M

The Dakotas had ornamented frames for cradles, to which they fastened the child with leather straps, one passing over the head, the other over the middle of the body. The workmanship of these leather straps was remarkably neat and curious, they being entirely covered with a ground of milk-white porcupine quills, on which figures of men, of a vermilion color, and black figures of dogs and other similar patterns, were most tastefully embroidered, and all of the most lively and well-chosen colors.[1] (Fig. 205.)

In another Sioux tent Maximilian found a child hung up in a leather pouch of very beautiful workmanship. These nests, which serve instead of cradles, were so large that only the child's head was visible. This pouch had on the upper side two broad stripes of dyed porcupine quills and several pretty rosettes with long strings of different colors, and was lined with fur.[2]

The Naudowessi women, according to Carver, placed their children soon after they were born on boards stuffed with soft moss, such as

[1] Maximilian, "Travels in the Interior of North America," p. 157.
[2] Ibid., p. 201.

is found in morasses or meadows. The child was laid on its back in one of this kind of cradles, and, being wrapped in skins or cloth to keep it warm, was secured in it by small bent pieces of timber. To these machines they fastened strings, by which they hung them to branches of trees; or, if they found no trees at hand, fastened them to a stump or stone while they transacted any needful business. In this position the children were kept for months, when they were taken out.[1]

As soon as the Sioux Indian baby is born, says Dodge, it is placed in a coffin-shaped receptacle, where it passes nearly the whole of the first year of its existence, being taken out only once or twice a day for washing or change of clothing. This clothing is of the most primitive character, the baby being simply swaddled in a dressed deerskin or piece of thick cotton cloth which envelops the whole body below the neck. The outside of the cradle varies with the wealth or taste of the mother, scarcely two being exactly alike. Some are elaborately ornamented with furs, feathers, and beadwork; others are perfectly plain. Whatever the outside, the cases themselves are nearly the same.

A piece of dried buffalo hide is cut into proper shape, then turned on itself, and the front fastened with strings. The face of the babe is always exposed. The whole is then tightly fastened to a board or, in the most approved cradles, to two narrow pieces of board joined together in the form of a ladder. It forms a real "nest of comfort," and as the Indian is not a stickler on the score of cleanliness, it is the very best cradle that they could adopt. To the board or slats is attached a strap which, passed over the head, rests on the mother's chest and shoulders, leaving the arms free. When about the lodge the mother stands the cradle in some out-of-the way corner, or in fine weather against a tree; or if the wind is blowing fresh it is hung to a branch, where it fulfills all the promise of a nursery rhyme.

When the baby is 10 months to a year old it is released from its confinement and for a year or two more of its life takes its short journeys on its mother's back in a simple way. It is placed well up between the shoulders; the blanket is then thrown over both, and being drawn tightly at the front of her neck by the mother, leaves a fold behind, in which the little one rides securely and apparently without the slightest inconvenience to either rider or ridden. A Nez Percé woman may be seen playing a vigorous game of ball with a baby on her back.[2]

Examining a collection of cradles from the United States east of the Rocky Mountains, the student is at a loss to harmonize the object with the old descriptions. Often the traveler speaks of a board being used, and this is true for cradles east of the Plains, or where timber abounds, but on the Plains the cradle is backed by lattice work, with sharp ends

---

[1] Carver, "Three Years' Travels," Philadelphia, 1796, p. 151.

[2] Dodge, "Our Wild Indians," Hartford, 1883, Worthington, pp. 185-186.

attention is called to the double method of suspending the cradle, though there may be only one way of carrying it. Dr. Boas has sent to the U. S. National Museum three photographs of the cradles of the Kwakiutl or Fort Rupert Indians of this stock, and in each of them the mother has suspended the object horizontally from a bough and is rocking it by means of a string with the hand or the toe.

As soon as a Similkameen child in British Columbia can sit alone it is placed on horseback, indeed before that it becomes familiarized with horses, for while a child is still bound on a "papoose stick," it is hung by a strap to the pommel of its mother's saddle, and away it goes flying with her over the bunch-grass hills, and they thus make good riders, with firm, easy, graceful seating.[1]

The Twana in Washington State have no cradles, but for young infants they have a small board about the length of the child, on which they place cedar bark, which is beaten up very fine, and on this they tie the child a large portion of the time. When the child is a little older but not strong enough to hold on its mother's neck, she wraps a blanket or shawl around it and herself and thus carries it on her back.

The cradle often lies down, but sometimes is hung on a small stick, a few feet high, which is fastened in the ground or floor, in a slanting direction, and acts as a spring. A string is fastened to it, and the mother pulls the string, which keeps the stick constantly moving and the cradle and child constantly swinging. This is done with the bare foot when the hands are busy at work.[2]

Example No. 1043 in the U. S. National Museum is a cradle trough rudely hewn out of cedar wood. A low bridge is left across the trough to strengthen it. Slats are put across to the level of the height of the bridge. The bedding is mats of cedar bark. On the lower end of the cradle is a handle. Around the sides are fastened strings. The compress for the head is fastened by means of cords to the sides of the cradle. It is woven of root and straw and stuffed tightly with cedar bark. In the cradle is a wooden model of a baby undergoing the process of head flattening. The covering is a cedar mat.

Length, 26 inches; width in the middle, 8¾ inches; length of end, 5 inches; upper, 6½ inches; depth, 4¼ inches; length of head compress, 10 inches; width of the stem, 3 inches expanded; end, 3¾ inches. Collected by J. G. Swan.

Example No. 1044 is a similar trough (empty).

The cradle of the Makah Indians, the most southern extension of the Wakashan stock, at Cape Flattery, Washington, is the cedar trough or ark prevalent further north and a little southward. Swan collected cradles from this tribe and conveys the important information that they are suspended horizontally by strings reaching from four corners to a

[1] Mrs. Allison, Journ. Anthrop. Inst., London, 1892, xxi, p. 306.
[2] M. Eells, Bull. U. S. Geol. and Geog. Surv., 1877, pp. 3,68,102.

pliant pole, and that is swung or rocked by the mother with her hand, or, if she be engaged at work, she does the rocking with her great toe.[1]

As soon as a Makah child is born it is washed in warm urine and then smeared with whale oil and placed in a cradle made of bark, woven basket fashion, or of wood, either cedar or alder, hollowed out for the purpose. Into the cradle a quantity of finely separated cedar bark of the softest texture is first thrown. At the foot is a board raised at an angle of about 25° which serves to keep the child's feet elevated or, when the cradle is raised, to allow the child to nurse, to form a support for the body or a sort of a seat. This is also covered with bark, he-se-yu. A pillow is formed of the same material just high enough to keep the head in its natural position, with the spinal column neither elevated nor depressed. First the child is laid on its back, its legs properly extended, its arms put close to its sides, and a covering either of bark or cloth laid over it, and then, commencing at its feet, the whole body is firmly laced up, so that it has no chance to move in the least. When the body is well secured a padding of he-se-yu is placed over the child's forehead, over which is laid bark of a somewhat stiffer texture, and the head is firmly lashed down to the sides of the cradle. Thus the infant remains, seldom taken out more than once a day while it is very young, and then only to wash it and dry its bedding. The same style of cradle appears to be used whether it is intended to compress the skull or not, and that deformity is accomplished by simply drawing the strings of the head-pad tightly and keeping up the pressure for a long time. Children are usually kept in these cradles till they are a year old, but as their growth advances they are not tied up quite so long for the first few months. The mother in washing her child seldom takes the trouble to heat water; she simply fills her mouth with water and when she thinks it warm enough spirts it on the child and rubs it with her hand. If the infant be very dirty, a wash of stale urine is used, which effectually removes the oil and dirt.[2]

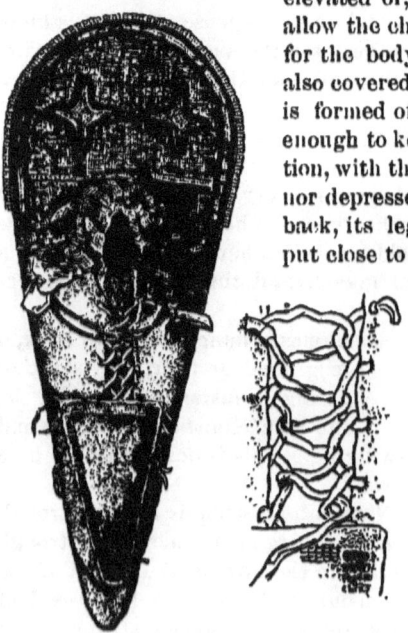

Fig. 207.

NEZ PERCÉ (SHAHAPTIAN) CRADLE.

Cat. No. 23845, U. S. N. M.   Collected by J. B. Monteith.

---

[1] J. G. Swan, "Indians of Cape Flattery," Washington, 1869, pp. 7-18.
[2] Ibid., pp. 18-19.

A cradle box and doll in the Emmons Tlingit collection illustrates what is meant by leaving the feet free. It is a coffin-shaped box, with sides curved out, headboard elevated, and a false bottom board that has one end under the child's thighs and the other cocked up on the top of a wooden image representing a man's head. The child is wrapped in fur, its face and feet bare.

In the same collection is a Kawitchin (Salishan) basket cradle. Seventeen strips of wood form the warp of the bottom. These are covered with coiled-weaving of split bark. The sides and ends of the cradle are similarly made and are eight strips high. The edge consists of a narrow beading. The upper side of the outside is overlaid with strips of straw and brown bark in geometric patterns. The child is laid at length in this apparatus. There is a short loop at one end for suspension vertically. For the purpose of carriage a string is tied to both margins in front, another is similarly tied across the foot of the frame. The carrying string or band is fastened to the middle of these two cross strings and the child is borne horizontally, precisely as in Russia and Siberia. This is a very beautiful object, and though collected among the Kawitchin, is in a style of weaving peculiarly Shahaptian.

The Walla Walla Indian women formerly sat astride a saddle made with high pommel and cantle. In traveling they carried their infants either dangling by the cradle strap to the pommel or slung in a blanket over their shoulders. Here, as elsewhere, a hoop was bent over the child's face to protect it from injury. In these cradles the feet of the children were bandaged and made straight for the coming swift and enduring runner.

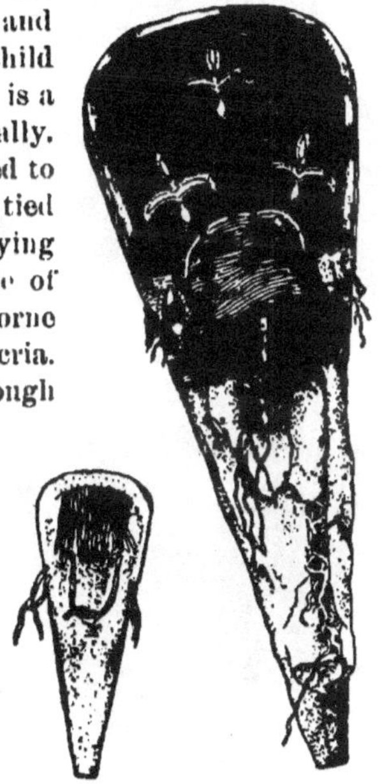

Fig. 208.
SPOKANE (SHAHAPTIAN) CRADLE.
State of Washington.
Cat No. 129675, U. S. N. M. Collected by Mrs A. C. McBean.

Example No. 23845 is a cradle of the Nez Percé, in Wyoming, and example No. 129675 a specimen from the Spokane Indians, both of the Shahaptian stock (figs. 207, 208). Although both tribes are in the Pacific drainage, they are away from the land of boats and in the area of great game. At present they are horse Indians, and they have been so during a long time. Their method of transporting children will, therefore, partake of two natures or spring from two motives.

The passenger is in fact encapsulated in a narrow leather inclosure, very much like the upper part of a passenger toboggan in the Hudson

Bay country. The basis of the cradle is a kite-shaped board 3 feet high. The exposed parts of the board, back and front, are covered with buckskin, and above the hood the front is adorned with beadwork. The opening for the child is left by the edges of the buckskin. A rigid lining to the hood forms the protection of the child's head. A strap on the back of the board serves for suspension on the mother's head, from the saddlebow, or upon a limb or hook.

In the making of a cradle by the Chinook Indians at the Columbia mouth, a block of cedar wood 30 inches long and 12 inches square was

Fig. 209.

CRADLE USED BY THE OREGON INDIANS.

Cat No. 2575, U. S. N. M.   Collected by the Wilkes Exploring Expedition.

roughly hewn in shape of a scow with bulging sides. At the foot, on the outside, was carved a handle. The bed was of shredded cedar bark, and the covering, a quilt of the same material roughly held together by twined weaving. A long pad was hinged to the headboard and so arranged as to be drawn down over the child's forehead and lashed to either side of the trough.

An interesting feature about this form of cradle is the appliance for lashing the child, as seen in example No. 2574, U. S. National Museum, fig. 206 (b):

1. A series of holes along the side just below the margin, parallel with the border most of the way, but sloping quite away from it at the head.

2. A cord of coarse root laid along next to these holes on the outside of the cradles.

3. On either side of the bedding a series of loops for the lacing string formed by passing a twine through the first hole, around the root cord on the outside, back through the same hole up to the middle of the cradle to form a loop, back through the next hole in the same manner.

4. The lacing string runs through these loops alternately from bottom to top.

The ornamentation of this type of cradle is chiefly by means of particolored basketry and furs. The Chinook were an advanced people in art, and many of their cradles were very prettily adorned. Mr. Catlin figures one in which the process of head flattening is going forward.[1]

Example No. 2575 (fig. 209) is a specimen collected by Wilkes. This cradle board is shaped like a trowel, with a short triangular handle. It

[1] Catlin "North American Indians," II, p. 110, pl. 210½, letter a.

is covered with buckskin in a single piece, secured around the bottom and up the axis of the cradle as far as the foot of the bed. The bed is a little mound in the middle of the board. Around its lower margin the buckskin covering of the cradle board is stretched by means of a rawhide string run quite through the board and outlining the bed on the back of the board. The flaps of buckskin are drawn up for the bed inclosure, and a series of the ordinary loops are tied along both edges to receive the lashing string. A triangular flap lashed at the three angles covers the legs and feet. A more ornamental flap forms the hood, notched and beaded, and is bound fast over the forehead. Along the top of the cradle are beautiful fringes of leather and beadwork.

The Modoc women make a very pretty baby basket of fine willow work, cylinder shaped, with one-half of it cut away, except a few inches at the ends. It is intended to be set up against the wall or carried on the back, hence the infant is lashed perpendicular in it, with its feet standing out free at one end and the other end covering its head like a small parasol. In one this canopy is supported by small standards spirally wrapped with strips of gay-colored calico, with looped and scalloped hangings between. The little fellow is wrapped all around like a mummy, with nothing visible but his head, and sometimes even that is bandaged

Fig. 210.

HUPA INDIAN CRADLE BASKET.

Cat. No. 126519, U. S. N. M. Collected by Capt. P. H. Ray, U. S. A.

back tight so that he may sleep standing. From the manner in which the tender skull is thus bandaged back it occasionally results that it grows backward and upward at an angle of about 45°.

The painstaking which the Modoc squaw expends on her baby basket is an index to her maternal love. On the other hand, a California squaw often carelessly sets her baby in a deep conical basket, the same in which she carries her household effects, leaving him loose and liable to fall out. If she makes a baby basket it is totally devoid of ornament, and one tribe, the Miwok, contemptuously call it the "dog's nest." It is among Indians like these that we hear of infanticides.

Example No. 126519 (fig. 210) is a cradle basket of the Hupas of northwestern California. A slipper-shaped, openwork basket of osier warp and twined weaving constitutes the body of the cradle. It is woven as follows: Commencing at the upper end, the small ends of the twigs are held in place one-eighth inch apart by three rows of twined weaving followed by a row in which an extra strengthening twig is whipped or served in place as in the Makah basketry. At intervals of 2½ to 3 inches are three rows of twined basketry, every alternate series having one of the strengthening twigs, increasing in thickness downward. The twigs constituting the true bottom of the so-called slipper continue to the end of the square toe and are fastened off, while those that form the sides are ingeniously bent to form the vamp of the slipper. This part of the frame is held together by rows of twined weaving boustrophedon.

Fig. 211.
YOKAIA CRADLE, FROM CALIFORNIA.
From a painting by Mrs. J. W. Hudson.

When two rows of this kind of twining lie quite close, it has the appearance of four-ply plaiting, and has been taken for such by the superficial observer. The binding around the opening of the cradle is formed of a bundle of twigs seized with a strip or tough root. The awning is made of open wicker and twined basketry bound with colored grass. This pretty flat cone resembles the salmon baskets figured and described in the Ray collection.

The child is not straightened out in this type, but sits with its feet partially exposed. The long toe of the frame holds the infant above the ground. At this point the horizontal and suspensory cradle leaves off and the standing cradle begins.

There is, in the U. S. National Museum, a cradle (example No. 19614) for a new-born babe from the McCloud River Indians, of California, belonging to the basket-tray type. It is shaped very much like a large grain scoop, or the lower half of a moccasin, and made of twigs in twined weaving. There are double rows of twining 2 inches, or such a matter, apart, and nearly all of them are boustrophedon, which gives the appearance of a four-ply braid.

The general shoe shape of the cradle is effected by commencing at the heel, which is here the bottom, and doubling the twigs by a continually sharper turn until, along the bottom, the rods simply lie parallel; that is, the rods that lie along the middle of the bottom terminate at the heel, while those from the sides and upper end are continuous. Around the border and forming a brace across the upper end is a border made of a bundle of rods seizing with tough bast or split root. The twigs themselves project upward, an inch or two from this brace, and are not fastened off.

Dr. J. W. Hudson says that the California coast Indians above San Francisco Bay do not suspend the cradle nor completely swaddle the infant, but they defend the base in order to stand the apparatus on its lower end. To this peculiar arrangement of the child in its bed, Dr. Hudson thinks, is due the bodily form of the people. The Sioux, Algonquian, and other interior tribes subject to long journeys, sudden changes of temperature, and rough handling more securely swaddle their children. The cradle board draws the cervical and spinal bones nearer the same line,

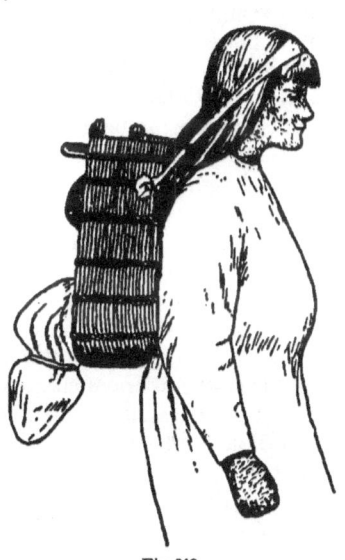

Fig. 212.

YOKAIA WOMAN CARRYING CHILD.
From a photograph in the U. S. National Museum.

flattens the dorsal surface (figs. 211, 212), rounds the thoracic muscles, and represses adiposity.

Example No. 21398 in the U. S. National Museum is a cradle from Potter Valley, California, of willow twigs laid closely together and held in place by an ingenious weaving to be explained further on.

The head of the cradle is a hoop of wood, 1 foot in diameter, quite open. It is fastened to the wickerwork by a continuous coil of twine passing around it and between the willow rods consecutively, being caught over the curious braid that holds the twigs together. In the example described the lashing is of cotton string, but in a more primitive form it would be of hemp or grass cord. The ends of the warp twigs are cut off flush with the hoop. The sides and bottom of the

cradle are scoop-shaped with high perpendicular sides, the twigs forming it all terminating at the head hoop.

The rods of the cradle frame are held together by a series of braids
about 2 inches apart. This braid is so constructed of a single string
as to resemble two rows of-coiled sewing on the inside and a close
double herringbone on the outside, and is made as follows: Commence
at one edge of the fabric and carry the twine along three osiers and
down through the warp, bring it back two and through to the front,
forward three, crossing number one; through and back two, and
through to the front, one rod ahead. Repeat this over and over, forward three, back two, forward three, back two, ready to start again.

Long leather loops are attached to the bottom of the cradle where it
joins the upright sides, to receive the lacing string which holds the
baby in place.

Example No. 21398 is a Pomo cradle, collected by Stephen Powers,
and there are similar specimens from the Concow and other tribes on
the Pacific drainage between Cape Mendocino and San Francisco. In
this peculiar type the climax of the free feet is reached. Dr. Hudson,
who has studied carefully the forms and types of basketry in the
region, presents a picture of the child fastened in the frame, and Mr.
J. N. Purcell furnishes the accompanying description:[1]

This is the baby-carrying basket used by most of the tribes of the
Pacific Coast from Cape Mendocino to San Francisco Bay. Being used
by them for carrying and nursing purposes, it is the child's almost constant home from the age of 2 weeks until it can stand alone; even then,
when the mother is traveling, the child is carried in this basket. After
having been dressed, the babe is set or laid in the basket, its face to
the opening, the buttock resting on the lower part. The feet hang over
the outer edge. The child is usually wrapped in a shawl, which comes
down over its feet.

It is fastened in by means of a cord or small rope run through the
buckskin loops attached to each side of the basket and wrapped snugly
around and around the body of the child. Commencing at the breast,
this lacing extends to about 6 inches below the feet. Thus the child can
not throw its feet about, nor can it fall out, for the six loops which are
run through with cord hold it securely in the basket. This apparatus
is carried on the mother's back, the buckskin strap securely fastened on
the bottom of the basket and passed around the mother's forehead or
breast. Thus the cradle rests securely upon the back and shoulders
of the mother. The child's face is, of course, out, and its head, neck,
and arms free, save the hoop around the top of the basket. This keeps
the head from injury. The small ear-like pieces extending above the
hoop on each side about 2 inches are for the purpose of fastening a veil
or covering over the face of the child. This is only done when the sun
is shining very hot. These baskets are usually made of ordinary creek

---

[1] See also Rep. Smithsonian Inst. (U. S. Nat. Mus.), 1887, p. 182, fig. 14.

willows, except the hoop and sometimes the two outside ribs, which are of redbud or oak. The pieces running semicircular around from one side of the basket to the other, with twine wrapped about them, are of willow. Instead of twine, sinew or wire-grass roots are most often used.

Example No. 19698 (fig. 188) is a cradle from the Tule tribe. The frame consists of three parts—the foundation, which is a forked stick; the cross-bars, lashed beneath; and the slat of twigs, upon which the bed is laid. Some parts of this frame demand description. The fork is a common branched limb, not necessarily symmetrical, with short handle, and prongs nearly 3 feet long, spreading about 16 inches at the distal end or top.

At the back of the fork are lashed 19 rods of wood projecting at their ends an inch or more beyond the fork. The lashing of the rods to the fork is by means of sinew skillfully crossed both in front and rear—that is, the seizing is partly parallel and partly cross-laced to give the strongest joint. These wooden rods seem to follow a rude plan of pairs, but the design is not clear.

The slat-work on the front consists of a separate transverse rod to which about 40 twigs are attached by bending the large end of each one around the rod and then holding the series in place by a row or two of twined weaving with split twig. To fasten this slat-work in place, the rod is put behind the two outer ends of the forked stick and the twigs

Fig. 213.

YOKAIA WOMAN CARRYING CHILD.

From photograph in U. S. National Museum by Mrs. J. W. Hudson.

laid in order on the front of the series of transverse rods so as to fill neatly the space between the forks. These twigs are held in place by lashing them here and there to the transverse rods and to the side prongs. This lashing crosses the twigs diagonally in front and the rods behind vertically.[1]

Upon this cradle rack or frame is fastened the true cradle, which in this instance is a strip of coarse mat made of soft flags, 1 foot wide, joined by crossrows of twined weaving 2 inches apart. This mat is bordered by a braid of flags, and the two ends are puckered or drawn

---

[1] By a misprint in a former paper the name Klamath is associated with this specimen. Rep. Smithsonian Inst. (U. S. Nat. Mus.), 1887, p. 180, fig. 12.

to a point. The cradle belongs to the open, unhooded type and is made by doubling the matting at the head and drawing it together to a point at the foot. The edge nearest to the cradle frame is joined and fastened to the frame, while the outer edge is allowed to flare open. In this little ark of flags or rushes the baby is placed.

Having escaped from the scoop-like half seat, half cradle, before described, the California child is still obliged to be a passenger. It does not ride pickaback, as the Eskimo, nor on the shoulder, as do the Caucasians, nor on the arm, as often seen in Africa; but it straddles the mother's hips and is held secure by her shawl or girdle (fig. 213), recalling rather the infants of Japan and thereabout.

Example No. 24146 in the U. S. National Museum is from the Mohave, in southern California and Arizona. The frame of this cradle is a prettily made ladder or trellis, built up as follows: A pole of hard wood about 7 feet long is bent in shape of an oxbow, the sides 7 inches apart at top and 5½ inches at bottom, so that the cradle is a little narrower at the foot. Eleven cross bars, like ladder rounds, connect and strengthen the frame, commencing at the bottom and ending near the bow. These rounds consist each of three elements—a rod or spreader between the two sides; a strap-like binding of two or three split twigs clasping the sides and laid along on the spreader; a seizing of tough twig holding fast the straps and spreader. The drawing of the reverse side clearly sets forth the manner of administering this light but strong cross bracing (fig. 214).

Fig. 214.

MOHAVE TRELLIS CRADLE AND BED.

Cat. No. 24146, U. S. N. M.   Collected by Edward Palmer.

Upon this ladder is laid the cradle bed of willow or mezquite bast, made as follows: Three bundles of stripped bast, each about an inch in diameter, are lashed at their middle with the same material. They are then doubled together concentrically and spread out to form a bed. On this is laid a little loose finely-shredded bast, like a nest, and the bed is ready for the baby.

A dainty quilt or counterpane of bast is made from strips 30 inches long, doubled and braided at the top like a cincture. This braiding is unique and so very neatly done as to demand explanation. Two strips of bast are seized about their middle by a single twist of the two elements of twined weaving. Of course, two halves will project above and two below the twist. Lay two more strips of bast in the second bight of the twist and draw down the first two upper ends, one to the right of and the other between the second pair of strips, seizing them in place by another half turn of the twines. Lay on a third pair of bast strips and bring down the second pair of ends projecting upward, as at first. The weaving consists of four movements, namely: Laying in a pair of bast strips, grasping them with a half turn of the two twining wefts, bending down the two upward strips just preceding, one between, the other outside of the last two strips, and grasping them with a half turn of twine.

The lashing belts of this cradle are 12 to 15 ply braids made up of red, green, white, and black woolen and cotton cords, plaited after the manner of the straws in hat making. Special attention is called to the peculiar type of ornamentation undesignedly originated by braiding with threads of different colors. On this belt of several colors the threads are so arranged as to produce a continuous series of similar triangles, filling the space between two parallel lines by having their bases above and below alternately. Not the worst of the ornamentation is the parallelism of the braiding threads, now to one side of the triangle and in the next figure running in a direction exactly at right angles. One of the commonest ornaments on pottery, rude stone, and carved wood is this distribution of lines in triangles.

Fig. 215.

CRADLE FRAME OF REEDS, USED BY THE YAQUI INDIANS OF SONORA.

Cat. No. 9396, U. S. N. M. Collected by Edward Palmer.

The floor of the Yaqui cradle (fig. 215) is of the slatted type, 30 inches long. A dozen or more reeds, such as arrow shafts, are fastened in the same plane by dowel pins. The reeds are not bored for the pins but simply notched in a primitive fashion. There is no cradle trough, but a bed of bast, shredded, is laid on longitudinally. The pillow consists of a bundle of little splints laid on transversely, at either end of which is a pad of rags. There is no awning, and the lashing material in this instance is a long cotton rag, taking the place of a leather strap, passing round and round baby and frame and fastened off in a martingale arrangement crossing the feet and tied to the lower corners of the cradle.

When a Pima child is able to stand alone, the mother allows it to mount upon the immense cinctures of bark worn on her back and to grasp her around the neck. On long journeys, says Edward Palmer, they use the cradle board.

Leaving the Pacific Slope and reverting to the Great Interior Basin, the Shoshonean tribes in the far north will be found adapting themselves to the surrounding Siouan, Salishan, and Shahaptian customs. They are on the drainage of the great Columbia and in the area of buckskin. For the most part, the basis of all Shoshonean cradles is of twig, a kind of open basketry with a warp of rods and a row of twined weaving here and there. Upon this grating the awning is built up for

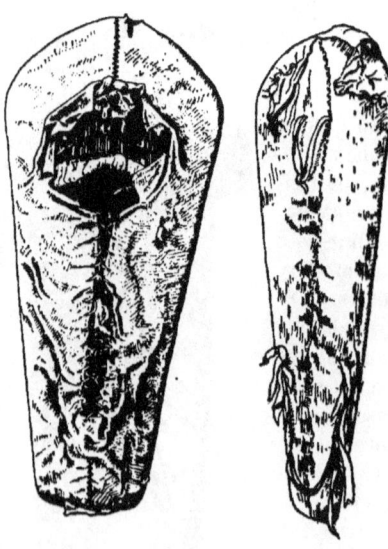

the face. Over it the covering of buckskin is stretched and to it the headband is attached as it is to the universal conical packing basket of the same culture area.

Example No. 128342 in the U. S. National Museum (fig. 216) is a cradle of the Uncompahgre Utes collected, with others, by Captain Beckwith, U. S. A. It is built upon a kite-shaped board. Special attention is called to the two suspension straps, one near the top for hanging in the cabin, the other lower down for the woman's forehead, to set the load well up on the back.

Maj. J. W. Powell collected a variety of Ute cradle frames in his early explorations. Example No. 14646, from the Colorado Utes, is shown in three views.

Fig. 216.

UTE CRADLE.

The frame is made of sticks covered with buckskin.
Cat. No. 128342, U. S. N. M. Collected by Captain Beckwith, U. S. A.

The frame is based on a dozen or more twigs, without bark, laid parallel. Underneath these is laid an ellipsoidal hoop, spread a little way beyond the rod at the sides. A stick is laid across under the rods and is fastened at its ends to the hoop and also to the rods by the wrapping of a filament. Two or three rows of twined weaving hold the rods in place at intervals. Over the frame a dainty awning is built and a covering of beautiful white buckskin incloses all. The carrying band is attached to the crossbar and goes over the forehead of the mother.

Example No. 14646 (fig. 217) is a cradle of the Utes of southern Utah. This cradle has the oxbow frame lathed along the back with twigs close together and held in place by a continuous seizing of sinew. It is a rude affair, but this is evidently due to the lack of material in a desert country rather than to want of taste in the maker. The awning for the face is a band of basketry, 4 inches wide, attached by its ends to the side frame of the cradle. This band is of twined weaving, the weft running boustrophedon. Notice especially that each half turn of the twine includes two warp twigs and that when the weaver turned backward she did not inclose the same pairs of warp twigs, but twined them in quincuncially, creating a mass of elongated rhomboidal openings, exactly as the Aleutian Islanders weave their marvelously fine grass wallets, while the Ute weaving is a model of coarseness in an identical technique with unaccommodating material. The headband of buckskin

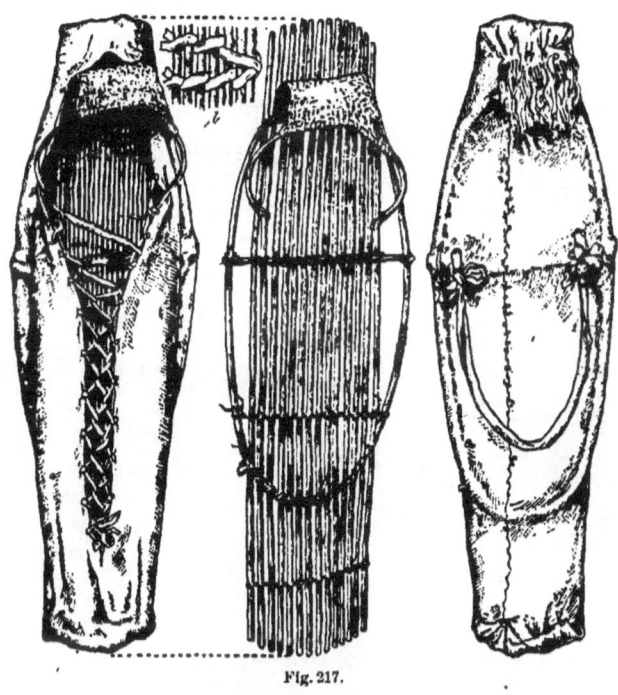

Fig. 217.

UTE CRADLE.

The frame is of rods covered with buckskin.

Cat. No. 14646, U. S. N. M. Collected by Maj. J. W. Powell.

is not tied immediately to the bowed frame, but is knotted to a loop made of a narrow string wound three times around the frame and knotted.

Pyramid Lake, Nevada, is on the border of California and adjoining to the Palaihnihan or Achomawi and Pujunan families of the last named States. Examples Nos. 19040 and 76734 (fig. 218) are from the Nevada Utes.

When the Ute babe leaves its swaddling frame, and before it comes to be entirely independent, it passes an intermediate stage, like the opossum, in an open sack. In this case the mother puts her shawl or robe about her, straps her bandolier around over one arm and under the other, and the young passenger has an apartment below which it can not go. Example No. 152252 (fig. 219) shows the Ute mother carrying a 2-year-old child.

The cradles of the cliff dwellers were made in the shape of an ellipse, constricted slightly at the sides. Small reeds or twigs were laid side by side lengthwise and on top of these crosswise, as in African shields

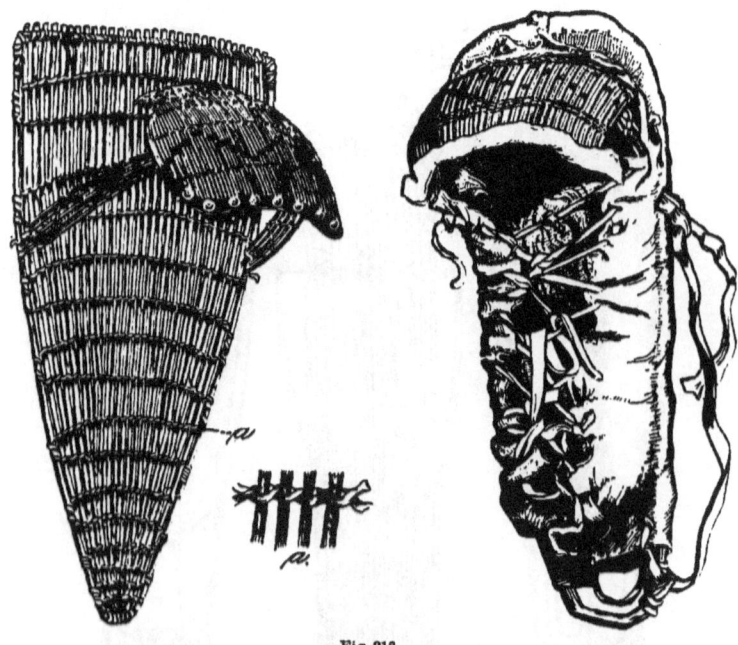

Fig. 218.

CRADLES OF NEVADA UTES, SHOWING CALIFORNIAN INFLUENCE.
Cat. Nos. 19040 and 76734, U. S. N. M.   Nevada exhibit, New Orleans Exposition.

On one side the sticks run up and down; on the other side they run crosswise. The two sets are held together by weaving in geometric patterns. On some of these cradles the hood is still preserved.

Example No. 21523 in the U. S. National Museum (fig. 220) is a very elaborate Apache cradle, the substantial part consisting of the frame and the hood. The frame is elliptical in outline, being formed by a pole of wood bent and the two ends spliced and lashed. Upon this ellipse are laid laths of pine, planed. Over the child's face is built the hood formed by bending two bows of supple wood to the required shape and overlaying them with transverse laths of pine laid close

together and tied down. The upper edges of these laths are beveled,
so as to give a pretty effect to the curved surface. The leather work
on the cradle consists of a crown of white buckskin to the hood, a
binding of brown buckskin to the bowed frame above the hood varie-
gated with narrow bands of white buckskin, and finally, the true sides
or capsule of the cradle, consisting of a strip of soft, brown buckskin,
say 10 inches wide, cut in a fringe along its lower border and edged
with fringe of white buckskin along its upper outer edge. This strip

Fig. 219.
UTE SQUAW CARRYING CHILD.
From a photograph in the U. S. National Museum.

is fastened to the cradle continuously, commencing at an upper margin
of the awning, carried along this awning, fastened to its lower margin
4 inches above the junction of awning and frame, passing on to the foot
and around to the other side as at first. Slits are made in the upper
edge of the brown buckskin just below where the white buckskin
fringe is sewed or run on, and back and forward through these slits a
broad, soft band of buckskin passes to form the cradle lashing. To
perfect the ornamentation of this beautiful object, tassels of buckskin

H. Mis. 90, pt. 2——34

in two colors and strings of red, white, and blue beads are disposed with great taste.

A simpler form of cradle, based, however, upon the elongated hoop, is shown in fig. 221, introduced here to illustrate all the details involved, to wit, the method of wearing the headband, the function of the awning as a cover and a place for toys, the border loops as on the margin of a sandal, the cross lacing, the free feet in accordance with the widespread west coast and northern habit, the modern style of wearing the blanket,

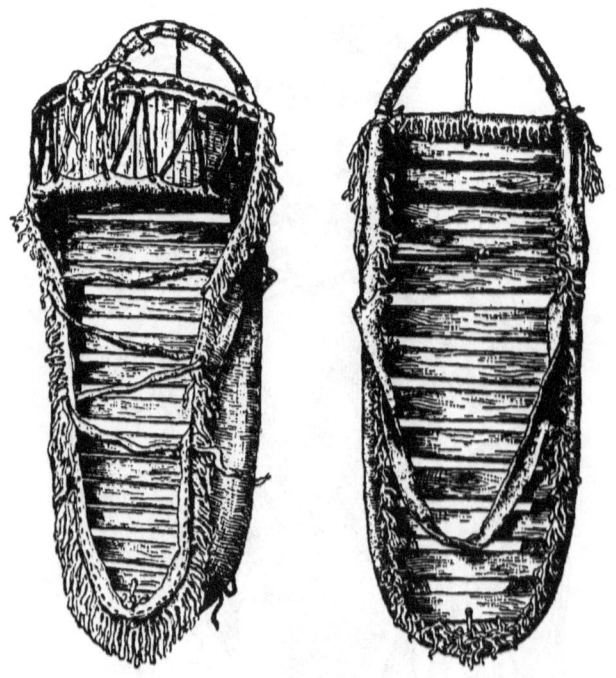

Fig. 220.

APACHE SLAT CRADLE, WITH HOOD.

Cat. No. 21823, U. S. N. M.   Collected by Dr. J. B. White, U. S. A.

the moccasins of the mother soled and having a protection against thorns in front, and, finally, her leggings, each one made of an entire deerskin.

The Navajo cradle, No. 127615, and the one with which it is compared (figs. 222 and 223), are built upon two strips of thin board, each pointed at the top, after the manner of the Indians on the plains. The awning of splint bows in figure 222 is suggestive of the buggy-top awning affected by the Zuñi Indians. This and many other introduced elements make it very difficult to discriminate what is truly aboriginal from what is not.

The packing, the lacing, the bedding, the pillow, and the headband are characteristic of the region. The cover or spread of buckskin and the foot rest are not so common. The former is of the north or of elevated and cool regions; the latter has a distribution not worked out. It will be seen on Iroquoian and other eastern forms, and on a Pitt River cradle from California, example No. 21411, figured upside down in the U. S. National Museum Report of 1887, page 180. This cradle of the Navajo Indians resembles the same article made by the Rocky Mountain tribes. It includes the flat board to support the vertebral column of the infant, with a layer of blankets and soft wadding to give ease to

the position, having the edges of the framework ornamented with leather fringe. Around and over the head of the child, who is strapped to this plane, is an ornamented hoop, to protect the face and cranium from accident. A leather strap is attached to the vertebral framework to enable the mother to sling it on her back.[1]

The Zuñi use a simple cradle board with parallel sides and the top either cut semicircular or notched in gradines in imitation of a kind of ornament much affected by these people in their decoration. Holes are bored along the sides for lashings and carrying strap. A block pillow, identical in form with the pillow blocks of many European peoples, performs the functions of a head rest and of a cleat There are many examples in the U. S. National Museum, of which Nos. 41184 and 69015 are types.

The elements of the Moki cradle frame, example No. 23154 in the U. S. National Museum (fig. 224), are the floor and the awning. The floor is of the oxbow type, having the bow at the foot and the loose ends projecting upward as in the Yokaia and other California frames. The Moki are the only savages west of the

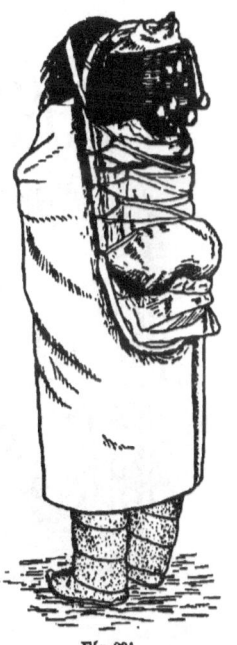

Fig. 221.

APACHE SQUAW CARRYING CHILD.
From a photograph in the U. S. National Museum, by A. Frank Randall.

Rocky Mountains known to the writer who make real wicker basketry. This cradle frame is covered with wicker of unbarked twigs, four rows on the floor and four on the awning. The warp of the floor is formed of series having two twigs each. There is a great variety in the delicacy, the number of warp strands, and the minor details in the Moki cradle floors. Indeed, while they are all alike in general marks, there are no two alike in respect to patterns. The awning is still more varied. Fundamentally it is a band of wicker basketry longer than the cradle is wide, its ends securely fastened to the frame sides by lashings of yucca

[1] Schoolcraft's Archives, IV, pp. 435–436; also Bancroft's Native Races, I, p. 501.

fiber or string.   Here and there stitches are omitted so as to effect an openwork ornamentation.   An additional strip frequently passes at right from the apex of the awning at the upper edge to the floor of the frame at its upper end.   (Fig. 225.)

The Quiché mother in Guatemala carries her babe on her back while she is at work and rocks it in a hammock while it is asleep.

The Muso and Colima, on the Magdalena, in Colombia, formerly laid their children in cradles made of reeds, just big enough to contain that

Fig. 222.

NAVAJO CRADLE BOARD.

From a figure in the Report of the Smithsonian Institution (U. S. National Museum), 1887.

Fig. 223.

COMPLETE NAVAJO CRADLE, WITH HOOD AND BUCKSKIN AWNING.

Cat. No. 127615, U. S. N. M.   Collected by Dr. R. W. Shu-feldt, U. S. A.

little body, binding their wrists and the brawny parts of the arms, as also their legs at the ankles and the calves, placing them with the head downward, and the feet up, the cradle resting against a wall stooping, that their heads might grow hard and round.[1]   Leaving out the last interpretation, it is certain that the Muso infant was laid in a little trough of reeds, which should be compared with those cradles made of a bit of skin rolled up and with the cylindroid cradles of wood in

---

[1] Antonio de Herrera, "History of America," VI, p. 183.

Siberia. The binding of the whole body, feet and all, in this region is interesting.

The Peruvians of old, it is said, used cradles of textile, not unlike those of California, but the Patagonians seem to be the only South Americans that actually strap their babies to a frame. On the pottery of Peru, children are seen lying in the lap, riding astride the neck, and sitting on the shoulder, but not fastened in cradles.

Wiener figures a barefooted woman at Andaymayo, Peru, with her child in a sash which passes around her waist and over the right shoulder. Both hands are active in carrying objects.[1]

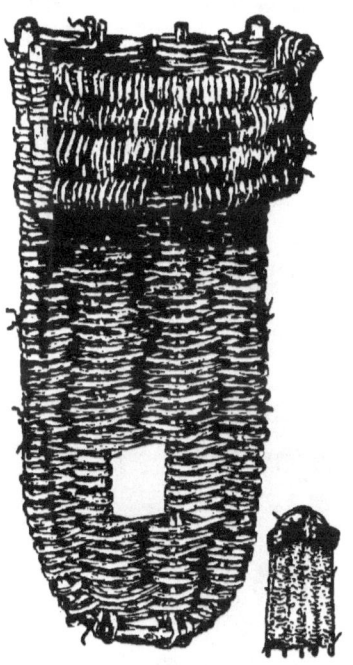

This fact should be considered in connection with the custom in the Tropics of wearing the infant about the naked body by the mother. On reaching elevated ground the cradle frame does not immediately appear, but the shawl or other garment becomes more and more the nesting place of the tiny passenger. Custom and climate play upon each other at every turn, and the typical plan is apparent at each.[2] But cradles did exist, made of reeds as shown, along the Cordilleras.

The Aymara Indian women of Tarapaca wear a long cotton garment, over which is a woolen dress, then a long mantle fastened by tupus or pins of silver, a long waistband, then the female poncho in which they carry their children behind them.[3]

The Araucanian infant is rolled up in bandages and put into a cradle frame which may be carried about by the mother or hung to a peg driven into the walls of the house or laid in baskets suspended from the roof so that they can be swung by a cord tied to the cradle.[4]

Fig. 224.

MOKI WICKER CRADLE WITH AWNING.

Tusayan, Arizona.

Cat. No. 23154, U. S. N. M. Collected by Maj. J. W. Powell.

In the smaller figure the awning is over the bowed end.

The Araucanian woman is often figured in the rôle of both passenger carrier and burden carrier (fig. 226). The child is laced on a rack and borne on the back by means of a headband. At the same time any amount of provisions may be stored in a netted bag suspended from the

[1] Pérou et Bolivie, p. 180.

[2] Excellent figure in Wiener's "Pérou et Bolivie," p. 395. The infant is snugly wrapped in a shawl tied across the mother's clavicles.

[3] W. Bollaert, "Ethnology of South America," p. 250.

[4] Wood, "Uncivilized Races," Hartford, II, p. 546.

shoulder by a bandolier. She carries her baby in a sitting posture; so do the Californian women, as opposed to the others whose children are prone in the frame. The Araucanian frame resembles in make-up that used by the Aino porter. It is worthy of inquiry whether the introduction of the horse into this region occasioned the rigid frame.

According to J. G. Wood, quoting Captain Bourne, the children of the Patagonians are laid in a square piece of guanaco skin, hung hammockwise by four ends to the rafters of the hut. During the daytime infants are packed in cradles made of pieces of board, between two pieces of guanaco skin. When the family is shifting quarters, the cradle is hung on the saddlebow of the mother's horse.

Bourne says that the papooses of the Indians of Patagonia, in traveling, are lashed to a kind of wooden sledge, rounded at the ends like sleigh runners, and crossed with narrow slats that bind the parts strongly together. The little ones are bound upon these machines, which are so shaped that their heads and feet are much below the general level of their bodies—a very uncomfortable position for the youngsters, if they have as much sensibility to pain as other children, of which there is much doubt, as they are inured from birth to almost every species of hardship. The sledge, with its living burden, is thrown across the horse's back, and made fast to the load.[1]

In Paraguay the cradle frame reappears after having passed out of sight throughout the entire tropical area. A hammock for little children is made of a hoop inclosing a net and supported by three short lines united as in a pair of scales and attached to a long line suspended from the roof.

The Indians of the Gran Chaco are expert swimmers. Of their movements across a stream, Wood says that they, with one hand, guide the horse, or hold to the spear with its light burden, and with the other paddle themselves across. The children and goods are conveyed in square boats or pelotas made of hide and towed by a rope tied to the tail of a horse or held in the mouth of a good swimmer.[2]

In comparison with the carrying frame of Guatemala should be

---

[1] Bourne, "Captive in Patagonia," Boston, 1853, p. 82; illustrated.

[2] Wood, "Uncivilized Races," Hartford, II, p. 572.

studied a frame from Guiana, called a cradle by J. G. Wood. It is in form of a scoop inverted, made of the split reed so common in the Carib art. The part nearest the carrier's back is widest, and the frame sticks project conveniently for the headband.[1]

Ratzel figures a boat-shaped cradle used by Brazilian Indians, with

Fig. 226.

ARAUCANIAN WOMAN CARRYING CHILD AND PROVISIONS.

From Simon de Schryver's "Royaume d'Araucanie-Patagonie."

apparatus for flattening the head, but there is not the slightest intimation of carrying it.[2]

In all pictures and descriptions of carrying children in Central Brazil no cradle is seen whatever. The naked child rides on the mother's hip or shoulder and may be clasped in the arms. Or again it will be seen astride her neck, precisely as appears in the pictures of the Eskimo.[3]

---

[1] Wood, "Uncivilized Races," Hartford, II, p. 609, with figure.

[2] "Völkerkunde," II, p. 622.

[3] von den Steinen, "Unter den Naturvölkern Zentral-Brasiliens," pl. IX, p. 112; also Fletcher and Kidder, "Brazil and the Brazilians," Philadelphia, 1857, p. 472.

CRADLES AND CRADLE-FRAMES IN THE U. S. NATIONAL MUSEUM.

Museum No.	Specimen.	Locality.	By whom contributed.
167899	Cradle with rockers	Finland	Hon. Jno. M. Crawford.
150768	Carrier, baby	Japan	Romyn Hitchcock.
32986	Cradle, toy	Norton Sound, Alaska	E. W. Nelson.
8894	.....do	St. Lawrence River	Dr. F. B. Hough.
18806	Frame, carved and painted	St. Regis, N. Y	Do.
18828	Frame, carved and painted	.....do	Do.
18829	Frame, carved and painted, beaded.	.....do	Do.
73311	Cradle, model, probably Sioux	Dakota	Catlin collection.
73312–73313	Cradle, probably Sioux	.....do	Do.
169009	Cradle, Kiowa Indians	Indian Territory	Jas. Mooney.
58607	Cradle, beadwork, South Cheyenne.	.....do	Col. R. J. Dodge, U. S. A.
152804	Cradle, Cheyenne Indians	.....do	Jas. Mooney.
165836	Cradle, beaded, Cheyenne Indians.	.....do	Voth collection.
153596	Cradle, Arapahoe Indians	Oklahoma	Capt. R. H. Pratt, U. S. A.
165774	Cradle, porcupine-quilled, Arapaho.	.....do	Voth collection.
152944	Cradle, Wichita Indians	Indian Territory	Jas. Mooney.
6918	Cradle, Comanche Indians	.....do	Edward Palmer.
6970	Skin bed, child's, Comanche	....do	Do.
73333	Frame for cradle, Haida Indians...	Queen Charlotte Island	Catlin collection.
9027	Cradle model, Nez Perce Indians..	Idaho	Dr. E. Storror, U. S. A.
129675	Cradle, Spokane Indians	Washington	Mrs. A. C. McBean.
1043–1044	Cradles, Makah Indians	.....do	J. G. Swan.
5366	Cradle, model	.....do	George Gibbs.
153548	Cradle, Chinook Indians	.....do	Dr. Franz Boas.
1757	Cradle board	Columbia River	Maj. Osborn Cross, U.S.A.
2574–2575	Cradle, models	Oregon	Lieut. Wilkes, U. S. N.
127616	Cradle, model, twined basketry ...	.....do	Mrs. J. O. Dorsey.
21337	Papoose basket, with shade, Hupa Indians.	Trinity River, California.	Stephen Powers.
21411	.....do	Pitt River, California	Do.
165679–165680	Papoose basket, Pomo Indians	California	Bureau of Ethnology.
167321	Cradle, model	.....do	L. L. Frost.
131109	.....do	.....do	N J. Purcell.
19617	Basket, papoose, model	Colorado	Stephen Powers.
150401	Cradle, Sac and Fox Indians	Ind. Territory	Frederick Starr.
168398	Cradle, baby dressed, Kiowa Indians.	Haworth collection	World's Columbian Exposition.
168416	Cradle, doll's, beaded	.....do	Do.
164811	Cradle, Sioux	Pine Ridge Agency	Miss E. C. Sickels.
154361	Cradle, beaded, Crow Indians	Montana	Dr. W. J. Hoffman.
152945–152946	Cradle, Kiowa Indians	Indian Territory	Jas. Mooney.
152947–152949	.....do	.....do	Do.
21398	Cradle, papoose	Potter Valley, California	Stephen Powers.
19697	Shade for cradle	Tule River, California	Do.
19698	Basket, papoose	.....do	Do.
22290	Board, papoose, Bannock and Shoshone Indians.	Fort Hall Agency, Idaho	Wm. H. Danilson.
151898	Cradle, doll's, Bannock	Idaho	Capt. Jno. G. Bourke, U. S. A.
19040	Cradle, papoose	Nevada	Stephen Powers.
10741	Bed, papoose, Ute Indians	Colorado	Maj. J. W. Powell.
10796	Cradle, Ute Indians	.....do	Do.
10797	Frame, papoose, Ute Indians	.....do	Do.

CRADLES AND CRADLE-FRAMES IN THE U. S. NATIONAL MUSEUM—Continued.

Museum No.	Specimen.	Locality.	By whom contributed.
19614	Basket, papoose, McCloud River Indians.	Colorado	Livingston Stone.
11222–11223	Cradle, papoose, Moki Indians	N. E. Arizona	Maj. J. W. Powell.
11909–11912	Cradle, Pai Utes	Southern Utah	Do.
14643–14646	.....do	.....do	Do.
14647	Cradle, toy, Pai Utes	.....do	Do.
76732–76734	Cradles (3), Pai Utes	Nevada	New Orleans Exposition, from Nevada State Exhibit.
128342	Cradle, Uncompahgre, Ute	.....do	Capt. Beckwith.
152564	Board, papoose, model	Utah	Lewis Engel.
11789	Crndle and doll, Moki Indians	Oraibi, Arizona	Maj. J. W. Powell.
166788	Cradle, Hupa Indians	Northern California	Do.
166813	Cradle, toy, Hupa Indians	.....do	Do.
166884	.....do	Arizona	Do.
40073	Cradle papoose, Zuñi	.....do	F. H. Cushing.
41184–41187	Cradle, toy and doll, Zuñi	.....do	Col. Jas. Stevenson.
152489	Cradle, Mohave Indians	.....do	Geo. A. Allen
27634	Cradle, with frame, Pima Indians	.....do	Mrs. G. Stout.
174438	Cradle, Papago Indians	.....do	W J McGee.
23134	Cradle, toy, Moki Indians	Northeastern Arizona	Maj. J. W. Powell.
23148	.....do	.....do	Do.
41725	Cradle, toy, Zuñi Iudians	.....do	Col. Jas. Stevenson.
41985–41986	Cradle, basket-work, with top, Moki Indians.	New Mexico	Do.
41987	Cradle, basket-work, without top.	.....do	Do.
41988	Cradle, Moki Indian	.....do	Do.
70957–70958	Cradle, toy, Moki Indians	Arizona	Do.
70959–70961	Head guard for cradle, Moki Indians.	.....do	Do.
84111	Cradle, toy, Moki Indians	New Mexico	V. Mindeleff.
160686	.....do	.....do	Jas. Mooney.
69391	Cradle, doll's, Zuñi Indians	.....do	Col. Jas. Stevenson.
18766	Cradle, portion of	Santa Cruz	P. Schumacher.
5566	Cradle, Apache Indians	Arizona	Edward Palmer.
21523–21524	Frames for papoose, Apache Indians.	.....do	Dr. J. B. White.
151909	Cradle, doll, Apache Indians	.....do	Capt. Jno. G. Bourke, U. S. A.
9545	Cradle, Navajo Indians	New Mexico	Edward Palmer.
10389	Basket, for papoose, Mohave Indians.	California	Do.
24146	Cradle, Mohave Indians	.....do	Do.
22545	Cradle, toy, Moki Indians	Northeastern Arizona	Maj. J. W. Powell.
9396	Cradle, Yaqui Indians	Sonora, Mexico	Edward Palmer.
127615	Cradle, Navajo Indians	Fort Wingate, N. Mex.	Dr. R. W. Shufeldt, U. S. A.
130650	Cradle, Yaqui Indians	Sonora, Mexico	Edward Palmer.

THE CARRYING OF ADULTS.

It was seen in the foregoing discussion that there are two periods in the carrying of children associated with two distinct types of activities:

1. The period of helpless infancy, calling for bed, swinging or rocking cradle, and carriage. The inventions associated with this period have passed through a wonderful evolution and elaboration, whose climax is all modern beds, cradles, baby jumpers, walking devices, carriages, and the great array of pediatric apparatus for the deformed.

2. The second period of infancy is devoted to learning the act of walking. About the home the child escapes from its cradle and soon finds itself going about. The mother, however, can not always wait for its slow locomotion and proceeds to carry it in an extremely primitive fashion, and allows it to mount her neck or back or hip without the aid of intervening devices.

In the earliest periods of culture or artificiality in living, there were no class conditions which demanded that one should be borne upon the backs of others by reason of rank.

The carrying of adults, or riding on human backs, was not in primitive times a world-wide enjoyment, and was never an industry until the climax of the hand epoch was reached. The dead were borne to

Fig. 227.

DIER USED BY THE SEMINOLES OF FLORIDA.

From a figure in the Fifth Annual Report of the Bureau of Ethnology.

their burial, helpless persons were assisted from the fight, and those who held some rank were carried on the backs or shoulders of men. But walking was the order of the day prior to the taming of the reindeer, camel, ass, horse, ox, and elephant. The Seminole Indians did not double up the corpse for burial, but laid it out straight. A long pole was placed above the body and securely tied thereto by bands at the neck, the middle, and the feet. Then two or more men lifted the pole and carried the dead to the last resting place (fig. 227). The single stick, with a passenger lying or sitting in a hammock beneath, is also the simplest form of carriage for the living. The next simplest device for bearing the living has for its manual part two poles instead of one. The Japanese use one pole, the Chinese and Koreans use two. In the Madeira Islands will be seen the single-pole hammock (fig. 228). But the double-pole riding chair was almost universal before good roads and wheel carriages and illuminated cities. It existed in several parts of semicivilized America. The U. S. National Museum possesses an example from Madagascar. The Caucasian subspecies in all its branches were familiar with it, and it was only a century ago, when streets were lighted at night sufficiently for carriages, that sedan chairs of most costly patterns went out of vogue.

The basterna was a kind of litter with two poles or shafts, in which women were carried in the time of the Roman emperors. It resembled

Fig. 228. -

HAMMOCK CARRIAGE, FROM MADEIRA, WITH TWO BEARERS.

From a photograph in the U. S. National Museum.

the lectica, or common litter, and the sedan chair, only the latter was carried by slaves while the basterna was supported by two mules,[1] the shafts running through stirrups on the saddle of each.

The ordinary bier is carried, not on the shoulders, but about a foot from the ground, by handles, but among the Maronites and other Syrian Christians, according to Tristram, the bier is borne aloft on the upstretched and reversed palms of a crowd of bearers, who rapidly relieve one another in quick succession.[2] The same method has been mentioned in the carrying of the throne chair of a Persian king aloft on the palms of bearers.[3]

The body of an Egyptian, when prepared for interment, says Lane,

---

[1] Smith, Dictionary of Greek and Roman Antiquities, s. v. *Basterna*, with woodcut.

[2] Tristram, "Eastern Customs in Bible Lands," London, 1894, p. 98.

[3] Montfaucon, L'Antiquité expliquée, Paris, 1722, ii, p. 183.

is placed in the bier, which is usually covered over with a red or other cashmere shawl. Three or four friends of the deceased usually carry it for a short distance; then three or four other friends bear it a little farther, and then these, are in like manner relieved.

The biers used for the conveyance of the corpses of females and boys are different from those of men. They are furnished with a cover of wood, over which a shawl is spread, as over the bier of a man, and at the head is an upright piece of wood, called a sháhid. The sháhid is covered with a shawl, and to the upper part of it, when the bier is used to convey the body of a female of the middle or higher class, several ornaments of female headdress are attached. On the top, which is flat and circular, is often placed a ckoor's (the round ornament of gold or silver set with diamonds, or of embossed gold, which is worn on the crown of the headdress); to the back is suspended the suf'a (or a number of braids of black silk with gold ornaments along each, which are worn by the ladies, in addition to their plaits of hair, hanging down the back). The bier of a boy is distinguished by a turban, generally formed of a red cashmere shawl wound round the top of the sháhid, which, in the case of a young boy, is also often decorated with the ckoor's and suf'a. The corpse of a very young child is carried to the tomb in the arms of a man, and merely covered with a shawl, or in a very small bier borne on a man's head.[1]

In ancient Egyptian burial and religious scenes nothing is more common than the same piece of furniture. But it is not certain that the function of bearing the dead thus is older than that of bearing the living, especially royal and sacred persons. Assyrian pictures are quite as full of living scenes in which men and women are thus borne.[2]

Example No. 160156 in the U. S. National Museum (fig. 229) is a Chinese carrying chair containing a great many separate inventions worthy of special notice. It is made of bamboo throughout, and almost without the use of pegs or lashings. For the legs and side bars of the seat two stout bamboos are chamfered out at the points where the tops of the legs should be, these gashes being as far apart as the width of the seat. The legs are bent down at right angles, inclosing in the chamfered part two other bamboos which form the front and the back bar of the seat. A few inches above the floor a bamboo is fitted snugly about the legs by the same chamfering and bending. The arm post and stirrups for the carrying bar on each side are chamfered and bent still more curiously. One piece serves as an additional side bar, as an arm post, and is then chamfered and bent down over the carrying bars. The seat above the lower encircling bamboo is boxed in with bamboo splints. The back is quite equal in motif to the Austrian bent-wood chair; the chamfering and bending, and lashing with split bamboo and inserting, when all other resources

---

[1] Lane, "Modern Egyptians," London, 1846, I, pp. 288, 297.
[2] Cf. Erman, "Life in Ancient Egypt," p. 65.

fail, together constitute a combination which is about as far as the inventor could go with his materials and his tools.

The awning frame is of smaller canes bowed at the top and so constructed that the vertical rods will fit snugly on the carrying bars.

The adjustable foot rest is a luxury built on in the same fashion as the other parts are made, getting the best strength and results with the least material. The carrying bars are movable, and when stood up in the corner they leave the passenger in his easy chair.

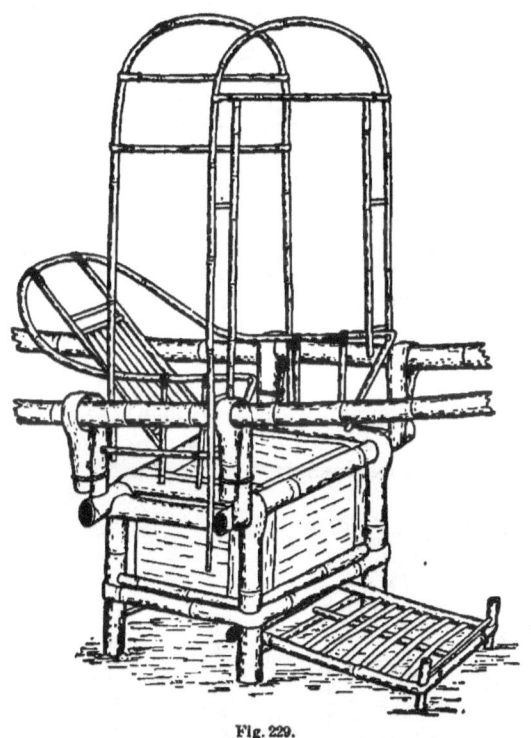

Fig. 229.

CHINESE CARRYING-CHAIR OF BAMBOO.

Cat. No. 160156, U. S. N. M. Gift of the Chinese Centennial Commission, 1876.

As in other arts, so in that represented by the litter, the Japanese have reached the acme of the hand epoch in carrying. It would take the student too far away from primitive methods to discuss all the varieties of apparatus in Japan by means of which individuals are borne about. In brief, there are two types, the hammock beneath a pole and the true litter inclosed. The two words "kago" and "norimono" are supposed to set forth these two, but Mr. Kota Nakahara, of the Japanese legation in Washington, says that "there is not very much difference between the words kago and norimono. We call norimono almost

every kind of kagos and jinriki and carriages which would transport us
from place to place, and call kago only the kind of kago proper, which
resembles the litter. It is thought both kago and norimono are what
we call kago. Of course, there is a special name for each different kago,
and those names are va-
ried according to the
localities. The word
norimono is the name for
the genus and kago is
for the species."

The Korean, according
to Carles, uses a rude
form of chair for trav-
elers not differing from
the Chinese and Japa-
nese types. The officials
are borne in a small open
chair, without legs, fas-
tened on the top of a pair
of carrying poles united
by cross bars, like a bier
without legs. Four men,

Fig. 230.
KOREAN CHAIR.
From a figure in Carles' "Life in Korea."

tandem, walk between these poles, two in front and two behind, and
hold up the great man by means of a short pole to each pair of bearers.
A fifth person walks at the side to steady the carriage (fig. 231).

The carrying of persons was known among the Muskhogean tribes in
the Southern States of
the Union. The gen-
tleman of Elvas de-
scribes the ladie of
Cutifachiqui as com-
ing out of the town
in a chair whereon cer-
tain of the principal
Indians brought her
to the river. The pre-
cise form of the chair
is not given, to enable
us to decide whether
it was a hammock or
swinging bed or a
litter borne by four.[1]

Fig. 231.
KOREAN OFFICIAL BORNE OF FOUR.
From a figure in Carles' "Life in Korea."

The pottery and tapestries of Peru show persons of distinction borne
by two, not in a chair slung between the poles, but in a chair or on a

[1] "The Discovery and Conquest of Terra Florida," Publications of the Hakluyt
Society, 1851, pp. 56, 67, 166.

platform quite above the poles.¹ Such a feat is impossible, and the omission of the other two indispensable carriers or a second pole must be due to ignorance of perspective. (Fig. 232.) In this connection Ratzel figures a curious little image from Colombia (fig. 233), in which the head-band is used in carrying a man.

"In this little town of the New World," (Santa Catharina, Brazil), says Langsdorff, "a sort of sedan chair is used, called cadeirinhas, in which the rich are drawn in state by their negro slaves. They are not like our sedan chairs, closed up with doors and glass windows, but rather resemble an easy chair with a high back. They have a canopy," etc.² (Fig. 234.)

Fig. 232.
CARRYING MOTIVE IN PERUVIAN TEXTILE.
One-third size.
From a figure in Wiener's "Pérou et Bolivie."

The bier, the sedan, and the litter become historically the travois for dog and horse, and after that the cart and the carriage. In one or two places in the world the carrying of men and women on human backs survives. This is especially true in mountains where there are no beasts to ride and two or more can not work together. In such places there is naught to do but for the tough and professional carrier to take his passenger upon his back, and this indeed he does.

In the Brockhaus Atlas of Ethnography (pl. 10) will be seen a Dyak carrying chair, very interesting in this connection. The Dyaks are in the habit of carrying

Fig. 233.
CHIRCHA CLAY FIGURE FROM COLOMBIA, SHOWING METHOD OF CARRYING BY MEANS OF A HEAD-BAND.
From a figure in Ratzel's "Völkerkunde."

¹ Wiener, "Pérou et Bolivie," pp. 609, 639; also Reiss and Stubel, "Necropolis of Ancon," pt. VII, and "Zeitschrift für Ethnologie," Berlin, 1895. XXVII, p. 307.
² Langsdorff, "Voyages and Travels," London, 1813, I, p. 47.

loads on the back in frames hung from the forehead by a strap, precisely after the American Indian fashion. Now the carrying chair is borne in the same way. It is a low seat, whose hind legs extend 3 feet, more or less, above the seat. The front legs are inclined backward and are

Fig. 234.

THE CARRYING-CHAIR IN BRAZIL.

From a figure in Langsdorff's "Voyages and Travels."

extended upward till their ends meet those of the hind legs, where they are securely fastened together. The *tamenes*, or porters, at Timbala, in Yucatan, carry a full-sized man on their backs in a chair or frame specially designed for that purpose.[1]

MAN IN TRACTION, AND THE DOMESTICATION OF RIDING AND HAULING BEASTS.

After inspecting the primitive man as the traveler in connection with his innumerable inventions, and also as a carrier, the study would not be complete without giving attention to man as a traction force.

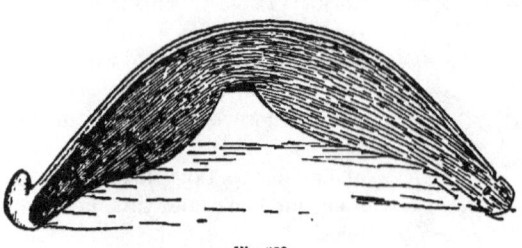

Fig. 235.

ESKIMO BREAST-YOKE USED IN HAULING.

Cat. No. 36025, U. S. N. M. Collected by E. W. Nelson.

It will be seen in a subsequent study on primitive domestication that the animal comes in merely to transfer the load from man's back to its own. The hauling of loads is in the same line. Before there were traction beasts there were traction men, and in our own day one can not go amiss for men and boys and women harnessed to objects dragged on the ground, on the snow, or along the water, or to sleds and wheeled vehicles. In order to perform this duty well there is need of harness for men (figs. 235 and

---

[1] Désiré Charnay, "Les Anciennes Villes," Paris, 1885, p. 433, with figure.

GROUP OF ASSYRIAN WORKMEN HAULING A WINGED BULL.

Only man power is involved, using the sled, the cart, cooperative traction, the roller, and the lever.

The following features must be noted:

(1) A low sled, or drag, with runners of heavy timbers, extra thick at the bottom, or shod.

(2) A rack or framework about eight feet high to steady the image. The uprights pierce the crossbars of the sled and are crossed by horizontal beams joining their tops or middles.

(3) Guy ropes and forked props attached to, and placed against, the top and middle rails, respectively, to steady the image on the sled. These are held at their lower ends by two men each, fourteen in all.

(4) Long drag ropes, four in number and double, fastened through eyelets in front and back of the runner, with men attached to them by means of bricoles. These men are evidently dragging the sled.

Those who saw the southern rivers before the civil war will remember that the slaves hauled ashore the heavy seines in precisely the same manner. It will be remembered also that in Holland the small boats are drawn up an incline from one canal to another by ropes attached to the stern and wound over a windlass. As soon as the center of gravity passes the summit of the causeway, the stern ropes are relaxed.

(5) Power is multiplied by the use of the lever and the roller in combination. Comparing this with another Kuyunjik inscription, it will be seen that a fulcrum is put beneath the lever near the sled, and that the men pry up that part by means of ropes over the long arm. This may be used as a walking lever to keep up continuous motion, or for the purpose of setting the roller under the sled and giving it a start. One may see nowadays two men moving a heavy locomotive along a track by steel crowbars worked between the track and the driving wheel.

It will be remembered that all the megalithic monuments of the world were erected in the hand epoch. No great teams of beasts are shown on the monuments, and no capstans with sweeps worked by animals. It was the weakness of the human body that necessitated cooperation.—strong ropes, lubricants, rollers, inclined planes, levers, wheels, etc., and these in turn provoked the highest expression of their capacity. (Layard, "Babylon and Nineveh," New York, 1853, Chapter V; also Rawlinson, "Herodotus," New York, 1872, frontispiece.)

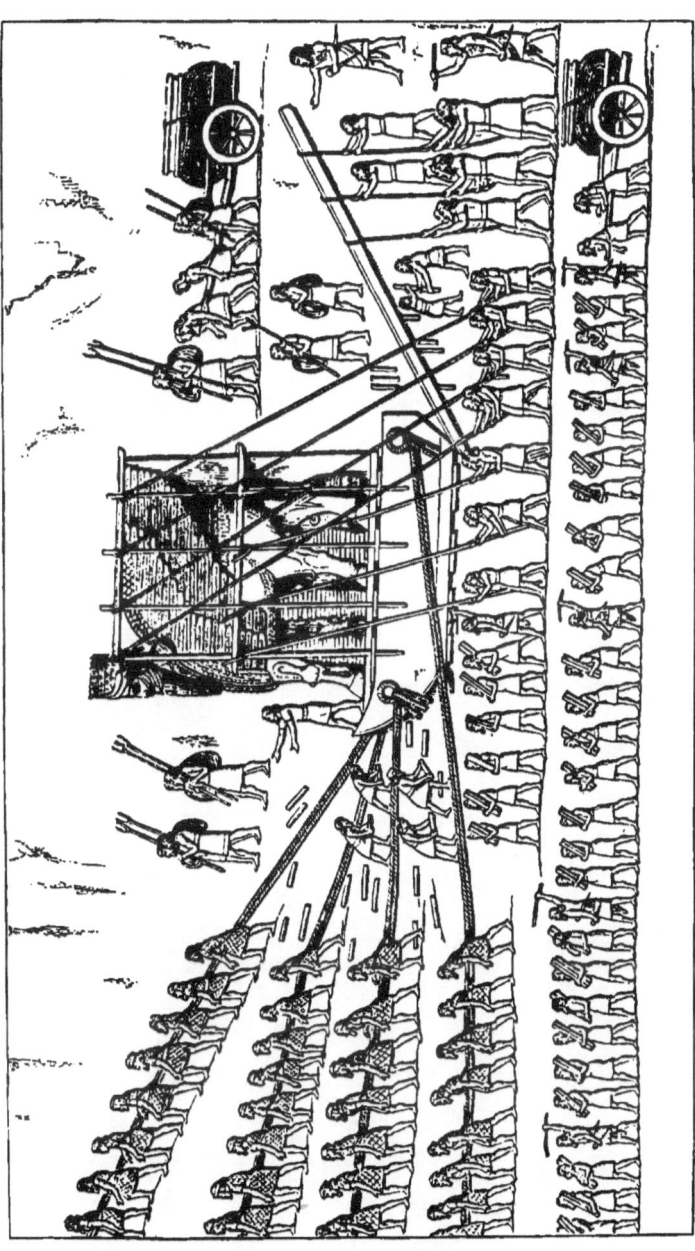

GROUP OF ASSYRIAN WORKMEN HAULING A WINGED BULL.

Layard, "Babylon and Nineveh"; Rawlinson, "Herodotus," frontispiece.

236), which, by and by, will become harness for dogs, reindeer, camels, yak and cattle, goats, elephants, horses, and mules, and the varied occupations thus engendered will have a splendid efflorescence in art and mythology.

The simplest harness for men is, in military phrase, the bricole, which is a loop to go over the head and a piece of loose rope or line extending therefrom constituting the single trace. The reindeer in Lapland now wear it, and so do men innumerable on the canals and at the fishing shores. In the old days of long seines the haulers could be seen wearing the bricole, now pressing with the breast, now with one shoulder, now with the other, now backing, with the loop athwart the neck or the shoulders so as to watch their work. There did not seem to be a contortion of the human body that could not usefully employ the bricole in traction. It was collar, breast strap, and breeching all in one. At the end of the loose rope or trace was a Turk's head knot, by means of which by a single overlap the seine hauler could hitch and unhitch himself from the cork line. The Eskimo have invented a variety of toggles, frogs, and buttons to facilitate attaching and detaching the hauler from his load, to be illustrated further on.

The number of locomotives in the world is 105,000, aggregating 3,000,000 horsepower, or 125,000,000 of menpower. The writer does not know the amount of horsepower in navigation, but it is very great. There are not over 200,000,000 able-bodied persons in the world, so the steam traction power and the power of human backs are about equal. But while steam

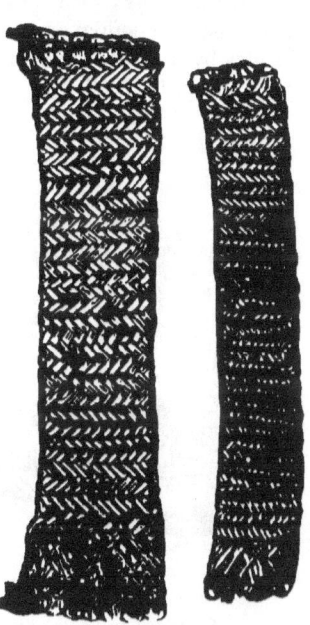

Fig. 236.

ZUÑI BREAST-BANDS USED IN HAULING.

Cat. No. 70968, U. S. N. M. Collected by James Stevenson

traction is the climax of the industry human traction is not superseded.

The first mechanical means of transport by land was doubtless the sled. It was employed by the Egyptians in the transfer of large masses of stone.[1] In one sculpture a statue drawn by 172 men is shown. There are oil men, bosses, and relays. In Assyria, also, the sled was used to haul heavy loads by means of a great multitude of men (pl. 25). There is no better example to be found of the two principles often mentioned in this paper—first, that it is the manual part of a device that is greatly modified by invention, and second, that the history of the past has been chiefly the evolution and glorification of the hand

---

[1]Lepsius, "Denkmäler," ii, p. 134; Erman, "Life in Ancient Egypt," p. 477.

or of the power of man. The industry of these two great nations was all anthropotechnic. Among the Eskimo there is no plainer looking sled than the ones shown by Wilkinson and Layard for moving the ancient gods; but there is an immense variety of activity going on to move the sled—concerted action, relaying, carrying, prying, and commanding. There is also a goodly and sufficient array of apparatus, ratcheted tracks, strong ropes, oil, levers, and shore poles to decrease friction and to increase power at the expense of time.

In the U. S. National Museum the sleds are associated with primitive life and with snow. But in many places in the United States and elsewhere sleds are employed to run over fallen grass and on the very steep hillsides by the backwoods farmers and lumbermen. As these harvesters of nature take all from the soil and restore nothing, their hauling is downhill and they have no difficulty in getting their forest product and their crops to the highway. Wagons would be out of the question unless the wheels were extremely low. The island of Madeira is quite famous in this regard, where sledding becomes a pastime (fig. 237).

Fig. 237.
PASSENGER SLED FROM MADEIRA.
From a photograph in the U. S. National Musem.

It must not be forgotten that in all countries where snow lies on the ground long enough to become packed, hauling and traveling over the snow are the easiest and swiftest. As far south in America as the New England and the Northwestern States hauling is preferably done in winter on sleds, largely with oxen. The frosts render the roads impassable in spring, and the common country road is disagreeable most of the year. It is also a season in which other work is dull. When one reads such works as Bush's Reindeer, Dog, and Snowshoes, it is pleasant to reflect on the little difference in this regard between many of the methods of cultivated New England and savage Siberia.

The characteristics of the best sled have to be studied out for each area. First and fundamentally, in sled-using lands sled-making material of the best quality is not always forthcoming. Men have to use what they can get—whale's jawbone in one place, driftwood in another, and poor standing wood in a third. Not discouraged in this, the fertile genius discovers and develops the qualities and versatility of rawhide, of braces, of splints, of form, of harness, of administration. No doubt a great many conferences and much cudgeling of the head have taken place. Captain John Spicer, who spent eleven winters among the Eskimo, tells of an inventional contest and debate between two sled builders in Cumberland Sound. The old-fashioned sleds have narrow runners, but one builder declared that broader runners would do better. To prove his assertion he made two sleds, loaded them exactly alike,

Fig. 238.

LAPLAND PULK, OR KEELED SLED.

Cat. No. 14800, U. S. N. M. Gift of the University of Christiania.

fastened each one to the end of a spar, hitched a line to the middle of the spar and pulled. The sled with broad tread moved first and easiest every time.

To make the sled runners broad and smooth, the wood and shoes are, by most peoples of Asia and America, treated to a coat of blood and water, and in one place of salt. This preparation is said to stick faster than merely frozen water; but almost universally the hyperborean

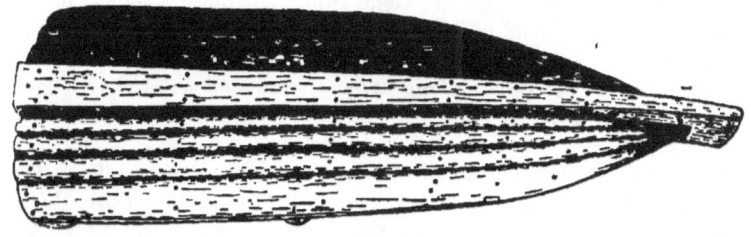

Fig. 239.

BOTTOM VIEW OF LAPLAND PULK.

teamsters go provided with the means of coating the bottom of the sled runners with a pellicle of ice, just as the drivers used to provide the tar bucket in days of wagoning.

The Norwegian sled is 10 feet long, 1 foot 6 inches wide, and 6 inches high. It is made of ash wood, and all the parts are firmly lashed together with rawhide. The runners are nothing else than a pair of skees, and are superior to the flat toboggan.[1]

Example No. 14800 in the U. S. National Museum (figs. 238, 239) is

---

[1] F. G. Jackson, "The Great Frozen Land," London, 1895, p. 132.

called a pulk or Lapland sled. As will be seen from the drawing, it is built up like a boat on a keel, above which rise on either side strakes of plank, wide at the rear and tapering to a point in front, where they disappear in the widened end of the keel. The whole is fastened together with treenails passing through stout wooden bows, the ends of which overlap at the widest part. The rear end is set in like the head of a barrel. The affair is decked over with movable sliding planks, so that it may instantly be adapted to freight or passengers.

The specimen here represented is the gift of the University of Christiania, and has with it a reindeer properly harnessed and the driver in costume sitting in the hold. At a glance he reminds one of an Eskimo sitting in a kaiak from which the stern has been sawed off.

As an element in the congeries of sled inventions, it is a compromise between the sled and the boat. The substitution of one runner for two, the rounding of the strakes on the outside to furnish a keel effect, however the vehicle might lean, especially the inclosed and comfortable passenger, all suggest settled life, short journeys, beaten roads, and social comforts.

The harness and the reindeer will be discussed in another paper. It is a very interesting fact that Nansen, in studying perfect economy in regard to his boat for landing in east Greenland, came upon the problem of the pulk or sled with a hull and runners in one.

The Samoyed sled is about 9 feet long and 30 inches wide, of pine, with large, thick runners curved up at the front 2 feet. On each side are four uprights, close together toward the rear and sloping inward. These are united by crossbars, which act as sills of the floor. Side frame pieces (called bereznias) extend from the top of the bend of the runners to the rear end of the sled. Baggage is heaped on the cross sills, and the driver sits thereon or upon a seat in front of it. The woman's sled is larger, and long strips of rawhide painted red hang from the bereznias.[1]

The Samoyed drives from two to five reindeer abreast. Each one is harnessed to the sled by running traces of seal hide attached by chulki, of which there is one at each side. The chulki is a tackle block or dumb sheave of ivory or wood through which the trace runs from the near to the off-side reindeer. Jackson figures four of them, and they may be compared with similar objects on Eskimo harness. But the Samoyed man, like the German woman with her dog team, does a good part of the work himself, and before the days of the tame reindeer he did it all.

Towing or tracking along the canals and on the rivers of China is done universally by men. Each coolie engaged wears over one shoulder and under the opposite arm a bricole or harness of bamboo, previously explained (page 545). From this becket or loop a piece of rope extends to the main line by which the load is hauled, after the same fashion as the negro seine haulers in Virginia fifty years ago.

---

[1] F. G. Jackson, "The Great Frozen Land," London, 1895, pp. 115, 118, figure.

Of the sleds about Berezovsk, in northeast Russia, it is said that those used for a long voyage have the form of a box, the interior being fitted with beds of feathers and furs. The little air openings are closed by broad curtains. The passenger lies down.[1] This form will be seen in every part of Siberia where the Russians have established themselves and their postal methods as far east as Kamchatka. The pavoshka is also suggestive of the inclosed toboggan of central and northern Canada.

Schrenck figures the Amur sled, and it will be seen that its form is quite the universal pattern. It may be seen in possession of children in civilized lands wherever there is snow. Its parts are, the runners, gently sloping upward; the posts, mortised into the runners; the cross-bars, set into the posts and held by lashing or pins; the top rail, into which are mortised the posts. The rail is securely fastened to the runner in front.

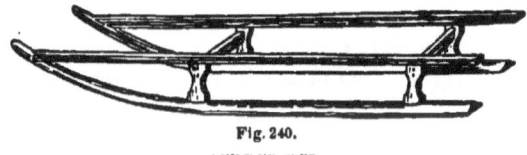

Fig. 240.

BUILT-UP SLED.

From a figure in Schrenck's "Reisen und Forschungen im Amur-Lande."

Omitting tenons and mortises, the framework is fundamental. (Fig. 240.)[2]

The narta, or sled, of the Tungus is from 8 to 10 feet long, 2 feet wide, and the floor is 1 foot above the snow. Above this a few inches is a light railing, on each side which keeps the load in place. The runners are of white birch, about 4 inches wide, flat-bottomed, and the parts are lashed together with rawhide thong. In front of each sled is a stout bow to which the long seal thong or trace is attached.

The Korak about Yamsk, on Okhotsk Sea, when the rough snow becomes destructive of sled runners, to protect them as well as to improve the running, every two or three hours turn the narta or sled over and with a piece of deerskin saturated with water, moisten the shoes and in a few minutes they are incased in ice. A bottle of water is carried by the driver beneath his furs next his body.[3]

Example No. 73018 in the U. S. National Museum (fig. 241) is a model of a Kamchatkan sled, consisting of the following parts: Runners, uprights, sills, bed or bottom rails, traction bow, and netting with its upper rail.

The runners are enlarged examples of the Lapland and Eastern skee turned up in front to the level of the bed or seat.

The posts perform the following functions: At the lower end they are inserted for a short distance into the upper margin of the runner by a shallow tenon and mortise. Each one is perforated above this point and a sinew cord is rove through these perforations, and holes

[1] Eve Felinska, "Le Tour du Monde," Paris, 1862, v, p. 236.
[2] "Reisen und Forschungen im Amur-Lande," IV, p. 492.
[3] Bush, "Reindeer, Dogs, and Snowshoes," p. 322.

bored through the runners diagonally in pairs so that the sinew cord on its lower loops is countersunk beneath the runners to prevent abrasion. Each upright is bored through its middle and the end of a sill fits exactly into the bore or auger hole. Above this point the upright extends far enough to receive the top rail.

The bed or seat of the sled is a long thin plank resting on the sills, and extending as far front as the flat portion of the runners.

The rail is a cylindrical rod or pole passing a short distance above and entirely around the sled, let into the tops of the upright pieces, and a network of sinew cord is laced through holes on the edge of the bed-piece and around the rails by a series of half hitches. The front of the bed is let into a stout piece of wood securely lashed to the traction piece, which is in the form of an oxbow, securely fastened in turn to the front of the runners, reaching back a short distance from the front to the bed and attached to the front pair of uprights by a cable extending from the end of the bow to a notch on the back of the upright.

Fig. 241.
BUILT-UP SLED WITH BODY OF NETWORK.
Kamchatka.
Cat. No. 73018, U. S. N. M.   Collected by Dr. Leonhard Stejneger.

Across the top of the bed from upright to upright there is a cable of sinew cords held together by a figure of eight seizing, common among the Eskimo in many of their harpoon lines.

Above the rail at the first pair of uprights is another bow like the traction piece in front, which the rider is said to hold firmly in going over precipitous or difficult places. Length, 21 inches. Collected by Dr. Leonhard Stejneger. Fridtjof Nansen speaks of a low hand sled, skikjaelke, on broad runners, resembling ordinary skees.[1]

Captain Cook says of the Kamchatkan passenger sled, that the length of the body is about 4½ feet and the breadth 1 foot. It is made in the form of a crescent, of light, tough wood, fastened together with wicker-work, and among the principal people is stained with red and blue, the seat being covered with furs or bearskins. It has four legs, about 2 feet in height, resting on two long, flat pieces of wood of the breadth of 5

---

[1] "First Crossing of Greenland," London, 1890, I, p. 33. Compare figure in "Zeitschrift für Volkskunde," Berlin, 1891, p. 430, and Senate Ex. Doc. No. 92, Fifty-third Congress, third session.

or 6 inches extending a foot beyond the body of the sled at each end. These turn up before somewhat like a skate, and are shod with the bone of some animal. The carriage is ornamented at the forepart with tassels of colored cloth and leather thongs. It has a crossbar, to which the harness is joined, and links of iron or small bells are hanging to it, which, by the jingling, are supposed to encourage the dogs.[1]

The riding sled of Kamchatka is a happy combination of a small hooded body on a pair of skees or Norwegian snowshoes for runners. There is one in the U. S. National Museum (Cat. No. 2811), all the parts fastened together with rawhide of different colors. The hood is a piece of brown leather, slashed and drawn through with particolored leather thongs so as to resemble weaving. The writer has seen the same imitation of weaving on Eskimo boxes and bags and on a box in Zuñi, New Mexico.

Langsdorff makes the important statement that the sleds of Kamchatka are of uniform width, so that when the track is once made all will run in the same lines. A good sled weighs about 20 pounds. There are two varieties, as shown above, the riding sled and the freight sled. The runners are a trifle farther apart in front. The driver always sits sideways, ready to spring out at any moment. The freight sleds, nardens, resemble a long bench, with a guard on each side set upon short feet. The runners are the same width apart as in the riding sled. Belonging to the sled is the oerstel, a strong stick, slightly angular, with a spud of iron at one end and thongs of leather at the other, into which iron rings are plaited for a rattle. If the driver wants to increase speed he rattles the oerstel, to stop the sled or to slow up he sticks the iron spike into the snow in front of one of the crosspieces. The oerstel also serves as a lever in upholding and righting the vehicle. In short, this implement is lever, brake, whip, and voice to the driver.[2]

The Chukchi sled runner is a long pole, cut away in the middle and bent until the two ends almost meet. In this stage of the manufacture either part would serve for top rail or runner.

Nordenskiold figures the essential parts of another style of Chukchi sled as follows:

1. Framework of curved "knees," four pairs.

2. Runners below and body rails above. framed to these knees.

3. A long, thin hoop passing on top of the body sill halfway and under the bottom of the runner all the way. The floor is of slats. These are for riding. The pack sleds are of stronger wood, with runners not bent back. Some of the light ones had a body of splints covered more or less with reindeer hide.[3]

The sled and its outfit occurs as a motive in the art of both Chukchi and the Eskimo. Over and over again on the drill handles and pipes

[1] Cook, "A Voyage to the Pacific Ocean, 1776–1780," III, p. 374.
[2] Langsdorff, "Voyages and Travels," London, 1814, III, p. 288.
[3] Nordenskiöld, "Voyage of the Vega," New York, 1882, p. 375, with figures.

teams of dogs are moving along with or without load. The Chukchi adds the reindeer team and shows the driver shaking the oerstel.[1]

Hooper, speaking of the Chukchi, says:

The Tuski traveling sled—for there are two other kinds—is constructed principally for speed, being exceedingly light and of elegant form. Six or nine arches of wood, let into flat runners, support a seat about 5 feet long and 14 inches broad, connected at the head with the runners by their springy curves. A sort of basket is formed at the back of the sled, and broad strips of whalebone are secured under the wooden runners. Braces and uprights further bind the parts together, and all are fastened with whalebone. * * * A single thong of seal hide from the under part of the seat serves to attach the dogs, which vary in number from two to ten; as far as eight they all run abreast, the single traces of the harness radiating from the main thong, to which they are secured by loops of ivory.

Hooper describes the dogs in full.[2]

Among the Eskimo in this last century, partly their own invention and partly introduced from the eastern continent, were to be found several classes of sleds. These, of course, are in addition to the makeshifts soon to be mentioned.

1. The bed on solid runners, the sled par excellence, repeated in the toy sled and in the common peasant examples. These are common further east and in hand work.

2. The bed on pairs of bent sticks or knees spliced together or arched, which serve for both posts and sills.

3. The bed resting on a square, mortised framework, and frequently made with great care.

4. The bed flat on the ground, the toboggan, or the common stone buck.

Nansen figures an ideal sled, with broad runners, curved at both ends, having a yoke for draft and bow behind, which should be compared with the Asiatic styles.[3]

To attach himself to his sled and to his load, the Eskimo uses his hand and a very simple harness or toggle now to be described.

Example No. 43717 in the U. S. National Museum (fig. 242 a, b) is a pretty toggle from Cape Prince of Wales, cut in imitation of a seal. The lines of feather ornament on the back and the prettily carved bands about the wrists are noticeable. The latter is in imitation of the embroidery around the tops of boots, with the fluffy band of Arctic fox fur. The holes are concealed on the underside, bored diagonally, so as to meet in the object and not appear above. The Eskimo are adepts at this "blind-stitching" method.

Example No. 43718 in the U. S. National Museum (fig. 242 c), of walrus ivory, is a button for many uses, carved to represent the head of a fish. On the end and on the underside holes have been bored at right angles, meeting to form a continuous cavity. The striations and the

[1] Figured by Nordenskiöld, "Voyage of the Vega," New York, 1882, p. 498.
[2] "Tents of the Tuski," London, 1853, p. 42.
[3] "First Crossing of Greenland," London, 1890, i, p. 31.

point work of the drill are neatly shown, as well as the use of the file or knife, to convert a conical hole into a cylindrical one.

Example No. 38551 in the U. S. National Museum (fig. 242 *d*) is an ivory hook with the eyelet in the plane of the hook. In this example the whip splice common among the Eskimo is shown. Where a knot in a greasy line that can not slip or jam is needed, this is, of course, the best. In some examples the splicing is continuous.

Example No. 37991 in the U. S. National Museum (fig. 242 *e*) is a good specimen of the Eskimo hook attachment carved from walrus ivory. The eye is bored transversely to the plane of the hook. One or more of these forms would be employed effectively by the Eskimo in lieu of tackle. The ivory is so smooth and the rawhide lines so saturated with grease that there is very little friction.

Example No. 44155 in the U. S. National Museum (fig. 242 *f*) is from Cape Darby, Alaska. The toggle represents a swimming seal. The holes are mortised across the line of the body. The ends are tied in a true lover's knot, and then the whole joint, as well as the parallel part of the line, are beautifully served with rawhide string.

Example No. 33673 in the U. S. National Museum is a drag or harness for a man, to attach him to any load he may have to draw. It is held in the hand, the line passing between the middle and the ring finger.

Fig. 242.

ESKIMO TOGGLES AND HARNESS OR CLOTHES HOOKS.

Alaska.

The toggle is a bit of walrus ivory, cut with pointed flutes. The two holes for the strap are joined outside by a double countersink. The two ends of the strap are united and the projecting extremities wrapped down with fine rawhide line. No. 38558 (fig. 242 *g*), from the Yukon district, is a plain example of the same construction, and there are many more in the collections.

Example No. 38552 in the U. S. National Museum (fig. 242 *h*) is the toggle of a drag from the Aleutian Islands, made of walrus ivory, in

imitation of a fox or wolf doubled up. The line hole is bored trans
versely. This object has seen much use, as the line has worn a deep
furrow in the ivory. No. 63819 is a precisely similar object from Point
Hope, in form of a seal.

Example No. 43848 in the U. S. National Museum (fig. 242 i) is a toggle
from Unalakleet, on the east shore of Norton Sound, representing a seal
floating on its back. This specimen was designed for hard work. Two
holes are mortised diagonally from the sides into the stomach. This
was done after the manner of the ancient carpenter, by boring holes at
the ends of the mortise and cutting away the intermediate material.

Example No. 45356 in the U. S. National Museum is a stop or toggle
on a loop or becket not here shown. The toggle or stop represents a
number of seals' heads. The object is perforated once longitudinally
and twice transversely. With lines through the latter it would become
a toggle. In its present form it is a stop for a running noose or ivory

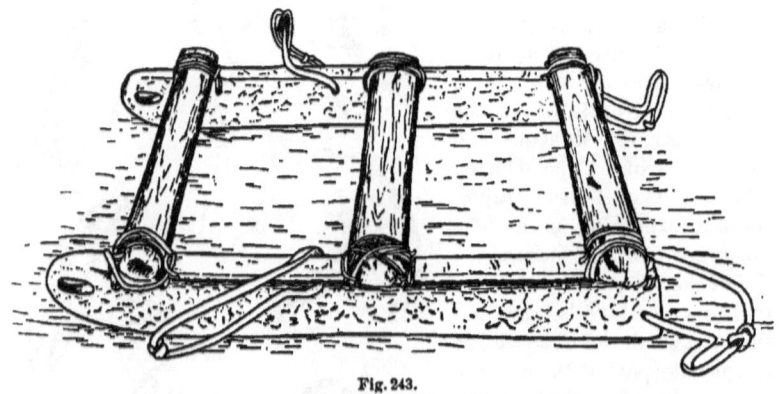

Fig. 243.
HAND SLED WITH RUNNERS MADE OF WALRUS TUSKS.
St. Lawrence Island, Alaska.
Cat. No. 63587, U. S. N. M.   Collected by E. W. Nelson.

eyelet of some kind. The rawhide line has its ends fastened together
in the usual way, but the longer bend is served with rawhide string by a
series of half hitches put on alternately by right and left turns, forming
a series of double loops. The effect is as pretty as the method is simple.

Concerning these traction hooks and toggles, it may be said that the
beautifully carved specimens of which those described are types, and
of which there are hundreds in the U. S. National Museum, are all
modern and effected with metal tools obtained from Europe and Asia.

Example No. 63587 in the U. S. National Museum (fig. 243), is a short
sled from St. Lawrence Island. The runners are two strips from enormous walrus tusks, thin below and winged or margined above. Each
one of these runners is pierced in nine places. At the front elliptical
holes are cut for the attachment of the harness. Three pairs of holes
are bored front, middle, and back for the lashing of the crosspieces, and

one hole is bored in the rear for rawhide loops or beckets. The ninth hole is bored just in front of the middle bar for additional beckets useful in lashing the load to the sled. These beckets are made of rawhide, one end slit, the other fastened through the slit by a weaver's knot. The three crossbars are made of driftwood, roughly cylindrical, somewhat flattened beneath to fit on the widened surface of the runner, and having two parallel notches cut almost around the upper part just above the runner. The crossbar is fastened to the runner by a lashing of rawhide which passes again and again through the runner over the end of the crossbar, back through the runner and over the other parallel notch of the crossbar, this process being repeated several times and fastened by simply tucking under. In the middle crossbars the end is

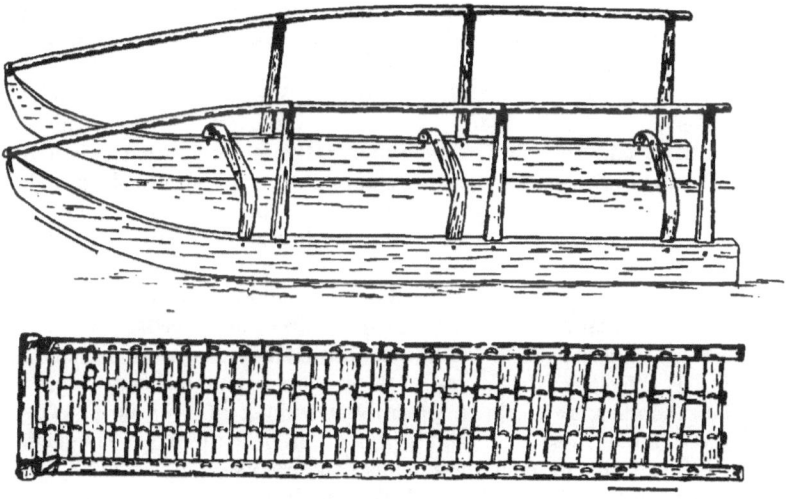

Fig. 244.
BUILT-UP SLED FROM NORTON BAY, ALASKA.
Cat. No. 45335, U. S. N. M.   Collected by E. W. Nelson.

fastened by a cross seizing, because the outside notch has been somewhat worn away. Such a vehicle takes the place of the wheelbarrow or common hand cart, and is used by man or dog traction in bringing in game short distances, and could never be utilized for long journeys. Example 15597, from Poonook, is double. Length of sled, 14 inches; length of crossbars, 15 inches. Collected by E. W. Nelson.

Example No. 45335 in the U. S. National Museum (fig. 244) is the model of a sled, consisting of runners, three pairs of knees, bed, uprights, and rails, from Norton Bay, Alaska. The runners are stout bits of wood turned up in front to the level of the bed. The knees are inserted or mortised into the upper margin of the runners in a crude way and fastened by pegs. The horizontal portions of the knees have been beveled so as to splice neatly and appear as a single piece extending from runner to runner. These are fastened together by lashings of rawhide.

The uprights are slender posts mortised into the runners and fastened by pegs just back of the point of insertion for the knees. The top rails fit into notches at the upper ends of these, and are held down by lashings. The bed or seat of the sled consists of four parallel slats or strips of wood extending from the rear to the front of the runners. Athwart these slats, above the two middle ones and beneath the two outside ones, are twenty-four cross slats fastened to the strips by a continuous sewing of sinew cord, which passes through perforations in the slats and cross-pieces all the way, excepting that underneath the outer slats the ends of the cross-pieces fit in a sling and are not perforated. These two pieces are attached to a stout block of wood, which, with the ends of the runners and the front of the floor or bed pieces, are joined by a firm lashing of rawhide. Length, 10⅝ inches. Locality, Norton Bay. Collected by E. W. Nelson.

Example No. 30771 in the U. S. National Museum is a sled model from Norton Sound, consisting of the following parts: Runners, knees, posts, floor, and top rails. The runners, like a series from this and neighboring regions, consist of two stout pieces of wood turned up with quite a sharp curve in front. The knees are three pieces of wood on each side, in the shape of a quadrate or ship's knee, mortised into the top of the runner and held in place by a treenail. These knees are chamfered and spliced neatly, so that the load of the sled rests upon three semicircular arches. There are also three posts mortised into the top of the runners back of the knees, and extending upward to hold a railing on the side. On the top of these posts a hand rail is fitted into shallow notches, and held in place by a lashing of rawhide passing over the rail and down through a perforation near the top of the post. This is a common form of joint among the Eskimo. The floor of the sled rests on two sills. Across these there are fourteen slats running at right angles to the sills, and over the ends of the slats and against the upright posts are two long strips of wood holding the slats in place. In front of the floor and against the runners is a stout piece of wood, to which the team is attached. The sills of the floor are fastened to this stout piece of wood by rawhide thongs running through holes bored in the crosspiece and in the sills; but the strips or cleats on top of the slats are mortised into this stout piece of wood. The posts and knees are held in place in the runners by pegs. The two knees of each pair are fastened together by pegs and by lashings of rawhide. The slats are sewed to the sills by a continuous rawhide line passing through a series of holes bored down through them and the sills, one stitch being taken in each. The slats are attached to the upper side strips in a somewhat similar manner, only the sewing passes through the strips of wood and around the ends of the slats, each one being grooved for that purpose. The posts are fastened also to these strips of wood by a lashing of sinew.

Finally, there is a network of rawhide which is laid on diagonally between the upper rail and the strip along the top of the floor. This line passes backward and forward around each piece by a single turn, without knots. The knots in this sledge are half-turn netting knots, or what is called a "single bowline". In many cases the ends are simply tucked under and drawn tight. Length of model, 9½ inches.

Example No. 48104, from Norton Bay, is of similar construction, except in minor details. In this model the parts are not sewed together with rawhide. Length, 23 inches. Collected by E. W. Nelson.

Example No. 169332 is the model of a sled in the U. S. National Museum, probably from St. Michaels, Alaska, consisting of runners, upright posts, sills or crosspieces, bed or seat rails, traction piece, and handle.

The runners are long, slender pieces of hard wood, broad below and narrow above, turned up in front twice as high as the level of the bed. There are five pairs of uprights mortised into the upper margin of the runners, raking backward at a slight angle and braced at the bottom with rawhide line seized through perforations in the upright and through the upper margins of the runners. This seizing is then neatly frapped and the ends tucked under. It is a very pretty piece of work.

The sills on which the floor or bed of the apparatus rests consist of pieces of hard wood, with their ends forming a cylindrical tenon fitting into an auger hole or round mortise.

The bed consists of two wide outer strips or framework, and between them six narrower pieces, parallel and equidistant. These middle pieces are not cut or bored at all, but the two wide outer pieces are mortised through for the insertion of the uprights. After the bed was in place a seizing of rawhide line was carried backward and forward, over and under the slats, and around the outside of the uprights, and a frapping passed around between the slats, so as to form a perfect brace in every direction, holding the slats firmly to the sills and forming a perfect separation for the parallel parts of the bed. The outer rails of the bed pass forward and are bent upward to correspond with the ends of the runners. This is a very neat piece of rawhide work.

The rail passes along the top of the uprights, which are mortised into them and held down by seizings of rawhide passing through the upright and over the rail, neatly frapped. The front ends of these rails bend downward from the foremost upright and are neatly seized to the outside rails of the bed. A network of rawhide joins the outside rails of the bed to the upper rail, formed by three parallel warp lines passing through the uprights, and a wedging made by a series of half hitches passing through the outer rail of the bed and the upper rail at equal distances, forming rectangular spaces.

The traction part consists of a bow seized to the foremost uprights, strengthened in front by a stout bit of wood just in front of the upper part of the runners.

The handle of the sled consists of a framework of wood very much like the handle of an old-fashioned horse rake. The ends pass down and are seized to the second pair of uprights. The side pieces of the handle are attached to a crosspiece at the rear end of the sled and reseized to the upper rail. Outside of the handle two rawhide lines double and cross each other, neatly served with the same material. This whole apparatus is of such extraordinary workmanship that it is easy to say that much was made with modern tools and that little is the work of the Eskimo. The form approaches that of the Kamchatkan sled, and the seizing and knots of the rawhide are thoroughly aboriginal.

Special attention is called to the very primitive fashion of network between the rail and the bed, in which the weaving is done by a series of half hitches. Length, 40 inches; width, 6 inches; height, 5½ inches.

Example No. 48147 is constructed somewhat on the plan of the last number, but is very rudely made. The floor consists of four slats running longitudinally between the sidepieces which constitute the frame-

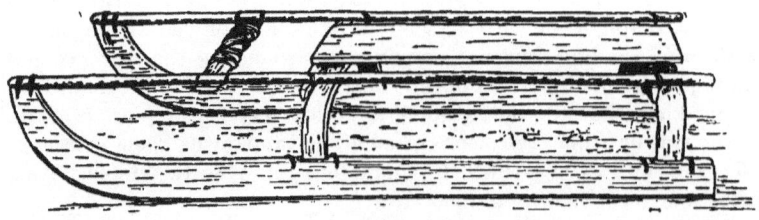

Fig. 245.

BUILT-UP SLED FROM TOGIAK RIVER, ALASKA.

Cat. No. 168567. U. S. N. M.   Collected by Dr. Tarleton H. Bean.

work. Length, 2 feet 3½ inches; locality, Anvik. Collected by E. W. Nelson.

Example No. 49111, from Tanana River, Alaska, is the model of a sled consisting of runners curved up at both ends and knees or supports for the floor or bed of the sled. There are three pairs of these supports, which are in the form of a ship's knee. They are slightly mortised into the upper part of the runner and secured there by a sewing of rawhide.

The two knees lie together parallel at the top and extend far enough to support the rails which form the bed. They are held together by a lashing of rawhide, which also holds down the rails in their places. At the ends the rails are mortised into the crossbars. The runners, the outside rails, and these crossbars, terminate together and are lashed with rawhide. This forms a very light but strong sledge. Length, 35 inches. Collected by E. W. Nelson.

On the Porcupine River, interior Alaska, Turner collected a sled (166974, U. S. N. M.) with the foundation like a toboggan and back and sides built up of dressed skins, and also a large lap robe of the same material. This should be compared with a precisely similar form in use in the Amur country.[1]

[1] "Le Tour du Monde," Paris, I, p. 106.

Example No. 168567, in the U. S. National Museum (fig. 245), from Togiak River, is a sled consisting of runners, two pairs of knees, and rails. The runners are stout pieces of wood, 1¼ inches thick above, 1 inch thick below, and 3 inches wide, shod with bits of antler and bone fastened on with pegs or treenails. They are turned up abruptly in front.

The knees are mortised into the upper margin of the runners and wedged in place. In order to bring the upper part of the knees closer

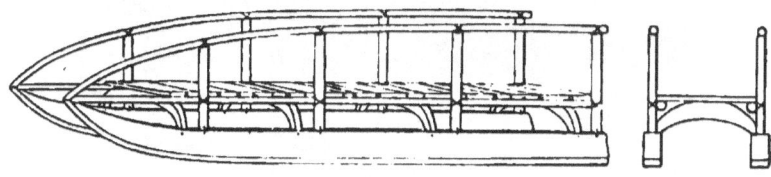

Fig. 246.

BUILT-UP SLED USED BY THE ESKIMO OF POINT BARROW, ALASKA.

From a figure in the Ninth Annual Report of the Bureau of Ethnology.

together, each one is chamfered and cut away so that the other can be partly let into it. These are then pegged together and sewed with raw-hide lashing.

The rail consists of a round pole extending from the top of the runner in front on a level backward and lashed to the extended upper ends of the knees. Along the upper margin of the runners holes are bored and loops of rawhide inserted for the attachment of the load and for bracing. For traction a line of braided sinew is provided.

Fig. 247.

ESKIMO FLAT SLED FROM POINT BARROW, ALASKA.

From a figure in the Ninth Annual Report of the Bureau of Ethnology.

This sled is said by the collector to be used in the transporting of kaiaks. Length, 6 feet. Collected by T. H. Bean.

The sled of the southeast Alaskan is said to be about 20 inches in breadth and 10 feet in length, a sort of rail work on each side, and shod with bone, put together with wooden pins or with thongs or lashings of whalebone.[1]

Murdoch describes two kinds of sleds at Point Barrow: (1) The kámoti, for carrying general freight (fig. 246): (2) the unia, low and flat, without rail or standards (fig. 247).

The kámoti consists of runners shod with strips of whale's jaw;

<hr>

[1] Cook, "A Voyage to the Pacific Ocean, 1776–1780," III, p. 23.

standards, four on a side; sills for the flooring of slats; crosspieces or knees connecting the runners and supporting middle floor; rail on top of standards, raised above the floor and meeting the front of the runner. All these parts are fastened together by seizings of seal hide.[1]

The second type of Point Barrow sled, the unia, is a small, low drag for conveying bulky objects and hauling umiaks across land ice.

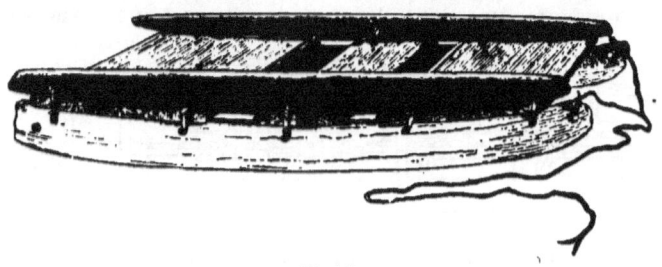

Fig. 248.
HAND SLED WITH RUNNERS OF WHALEBONE.
From a figure in the Ninth Annual Report of the Bureau of Ethnology.

Both kinds are made of driftwood and shod with strips of whale's jaw about three-fourths of an inch thick, fastened on with bone tree-nails. For carrying a heavy load over soft snow the runners are shod with ice. To each runner is fitted a shoe of clear ice, 1 foot high and 6 inches thick. From the ice on a pond they cut a piece the length of a runner, 8 inches thick and 10 inches wide. Into these they cut a groove

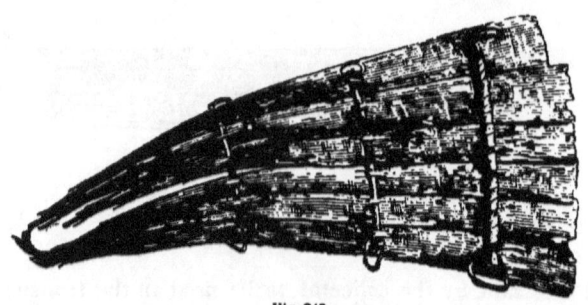

Fig. 249.
ESKIMO TOBOGGAN MADE OF BALEEN.
Point Barrow, Alaska.
From a figure in the Ninth Annual Report of the Bureau of Ethnology.

deep enough to receive the sled runner up to the crosspiece. The sled is fitted into the grooves and water poured in gradually. The sled is then turned bottom up and the ice shoes carefully rounded with a knife, then smoothed by wetting the naked hand and passing it over the surface until it becomes perfectly glazed.

[1] Ninth Ann. Rep. Bureau of Ethnology, p. 353.

Murdoch has carefully gathered the different methods of shoeing the sled. At Fury-and-Hecla Straits ice and snow are mixed. At Cumberland Gulf they pour warm blood on the under surface of the bone shoeing; water does not last so long and is more apt to chip off. About Repulse Bay they ice the runners by squirting over them water that has been warmed in the mouth. In eastern Labrador clay, tempered with hot water, is used first, and this is washed with water and polished with the hand. In the Mackenzie region also earth, water, and ice are used. At Pitlekaj, Nordenskiöld found the sled runners to be coated with a layer of two or three millimeters in thickness. Schwatka describes a custom in King-Williams Land similar to the Point Barrow fashion.[1]

Ray brought home from Point Barrow example No. 89889, U. S. National Museum (fig. 248), a small sled, with ivory runners 20 inches long and 13 broad. The bed or floor consists of three narrow boards laid crosswise, held down by a low wooden rail on each side. Each runner is a slice from a single large walrus tusk, with the butt at the back of the sled. The floor pieces, which are parts of a ship's paneling, are lashed

Fig. 250.

BUILT-UP SLED, USED BY THE KUTCHIN INDIANS.

From a figure in the Report of the Smithsonian Institution, 1866.

to the upper edge of the runners so as to project about one-half inch on each side. The rails flare slightly outward. The whole is fastened together by lashings of rather broad strips of baleen, passing through holes near the upper edge of the runner, around notches in the ends of the slats and holes in the slats inside of the rails. There are two lashings at each end of each broad slat or floor piece and one in the middle, at each end of the narrow one. The last and the ones at each end of the sled also secure the rail by passing through a hole near its edge, in which are cut square notches to make room for the other lashings. The trace is a strip of seal thong about 5 feet long and one-fourth inch wide, split at one end for about 1 foot into two parts. The other end is slit in two for about 3 inches. This is probably a broken loop, which served for fastening the trace to a dog's harness.[2]

Strachan Jones figures a Kutchin sled, turned up at either end. Upon this the women haul lodges, poles, and impedimenta.[3] (Fig. 250.)

Example No. 7472 in the U. S. National Museum (fig. 251) is a sled from Fort Anderson, Mackenzie River district, consisting of two parts—the solid runners and cross slats. The runners are in the form of broad planks hewed out thick above and thin below, with a longer

---

[1] Ninth Ann. Rep. Bureau of Ethnology, p. 353.

[2] Described and figured by Murdoch in Ninth Ann. Rep. Bureau of Ethnology, p. 355.

[3] Smithsonian Rep., 1866, p. 321.

H. Mis. 90, pt. 2——36

bevel in front than in the rear. The five crossbars are mortised through
the upper part of the runners in a very rude manner and fastened
down with pegs. The line for hauling is attached to the front ends of
the runners, just as in the case of the ordinary toy sled of boys in

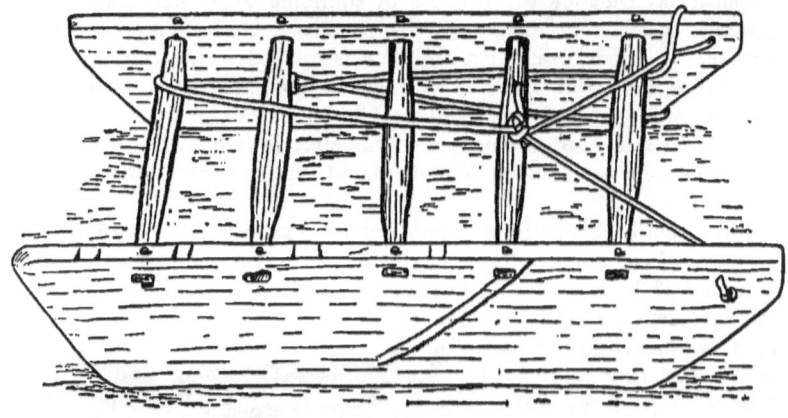

Fig. 251.

LOW SLED FROM FORT ANDERSON, MACKENZIE RIVER, CANADA

Cat. No. 7472, U. S. N. M. Collected by R. MacFarlane.

civilized countries. Although this was sent to the U. S. National
Museum with a large collection of most interesting objects, it does not
have the appearance of being an aboriginal form. Length, 7½ inches.
Collected by R. MacFarlane.

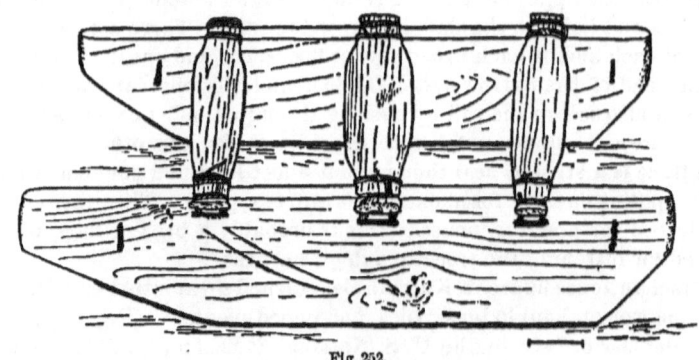

Fig. 252.

LOW SLED, FROM ANDERSON RIVER, CANADA.

Cat. No. 1638, U. S. N. M. Collected by R. MacFarlane.

Example No. 1638 in the U. S. National Museum (fig. 252) is the model
of a sled from Anderson River consisting of high solid runners and
crossbars. The runners have a long bevel in front and a short one in
the rear, and are sawed off at the ends. There are three crossbars,

broad in the middle and chamfered at the ends for the lashing. Near the upper border of the runners holes are gouged through the wood as long as the end of the crosspiece is wide. A double lashing passes over the end and through these holes so as to give a double bearing or brace. This is a very common method of attachment among the Eskimo. In the model the lashing is done with rawhide and sinew twine. This example reproduces with considerable faithfulness the construction of the aboriginal types. The shoeing on the bottom of the runners is fastened on with pegs of wood. Length, 12 inches. Collected by R. MacFarlane.

Example No. 7473 in the U. S. National Museum (fig. 253), is the model of a sled from Anderson River, northern Canada. The runners are wide, separate planks, curved up in front and beveled in the rear. Five crosspieces are attached to the top of the runners by means of sinew

Fig. 253.
BUILT-UP SLED FROM FORT ANDERSON.
Mackenzie River District, Canada.
Cat. No. 7473, U. S. N. M. Collected by R. MacFarlane.

cord passing over the ends of the slats and through very rudely executed mortises near the edge of the runners.

The winding of the thread passes over the slats outside and inside of the runner so as to form an excellent yielding brace. Mortising is very uncommon among aboriginal peoples, and therefore the needs of the fur traders are to be suspected.

The front crosspiece is fastened on through two sets of holes instead of mortises. Between the slats on top of each runner six posts are mortised and fastened down with treenails, and a similar post is mortised through the upper surface of the hind slat. Along the top of these posts, at the sides and at the rear, are tight rails which extend out and are fastened to the upturned ends of the runners. The rails are sewed to the posts by means of babiche. Length, 14 inches. Collected by R. MacFarlane.

Example No. 7474 is the model of a sled from Fort Anderson, Mackenzie River district, built up on knees, similar to example No. 49111. Length, 12 inches. Collected by Robert MacFarlane.

The U. S. National Museum possesses a large number of full-sized specimens of the Canadian toboggan. A model of one of them from Anderson River, northern Canada, example No. 1976 in the U. S. National Museum (fig. 254) is made of two separate thin planks of birch wood not more than three eighths of an inch in thickness. These two planks are joined together pretty evenly at the inner edges and held in place by four battens in the upper side, three of them at equal distances along the flat surface, and a double batten holding the two ends together in front. These battens are firmly secured in place by a lashing of rawhide which passes over the batten through the boards. On the under side, the holes through which the rawhide passes are countersunk, so there is no danger of being injured by abrasion. These rawhide lashings are put on with great regularity, showing on the under

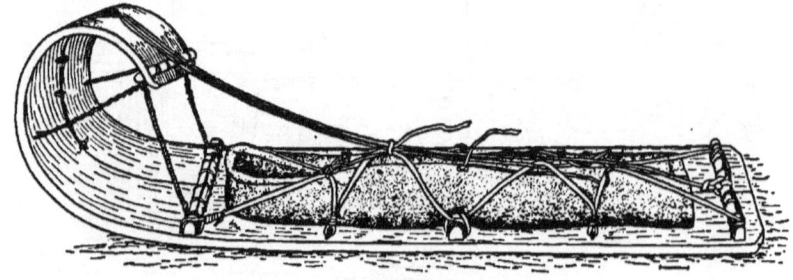

Fig. 254.

CANADIAN TOBOGGAN OR FREIGHT SLED.

Cat. No. 1976, U. S. N. M.   Collected by R. MacFarlane.

side a pair of countersunk cavities on the boards so that every part is securely held in place where the most strength is needed. On the upper side the rawhide line shows an alternation of simple turns and marline hitches. The boards constituting the toboggan are curled up in front after the manner of an elegant sledge and sewed together with rawhide. This sewing is done in a very interesting manner. On the upper surface the holes appear some distance away from where the two margins are joined together, but on the underside they come out very near the margin so that they are bored out and unite along these edges. The front of the sled is braced by means of small cables of rawhide passing from the tip end to the planks below and to the first batten. There is also a strong rawhide line carried from the tip to the end of the last batten in the rear. This gives stability to the vehicle in every direction without increasing its weight.

Upon this model is lashed a long capsule or open bag of tawed reindeer hide bound around the edges and representing the cover or protection in which the pack or load is placed and held securely.

The knots on this model are mostly half or marline hitches alternating with round turns. Here and there, in fastening off the work (among the American aborigines), a square knot is found (which is somewhat unusual in this writer's experience), the Indians of this continent using the plan of merely taking in a loose end and relying upon the shrinkage of the rawhide to hold it in place. Length, 2 feet 4 inches. Collected by B. R. Ross.

Example No. 166974 in the U. S. National Museum (fig. 255) is a traveling sled from Canada. The apparatus is based on a toboggan made of short planks and crossbars. The front is covered with leather for ornamental purposes and the side and back are of moose skin set up on a frame of wood and iron painted red on the outside. The body or riding part extends backward to within 22 inches of the end, which is left free either for luggage or for the driver to stand on when he is riding. Rawhide lines or loops are attached to the side for the purpose of holding baggage or for the convenience of the driver. From the front to the rear extend doubled-braided lines a half inch wide, and the

Fig. 255.
CANADIAN TRAVELING SLED, FULL-RIGGED.
Porcupine River, Alaska.
Cat. No. 166974, U. S. N. M. Collected by J. H. Turner.

interior is provided with a cover or boot of soft moose skin either for protecting the driver against the weather or for covering up the freight. Width, 14 inches; height of body, 18 inches. Collected by J. Henry Turner.

Dr. Rae tells us that the Boothians use sleds of rolled-up sealskin, not from choice but of necessity, because they have little or no wood, and no large bones of the walrus or whale with which to construct them, as the Arctic Highlanders have.[1]

McClintock also says that the runners (or sides) of some old sleds left at Matty Island were very ingeniously formed out of rolls of sealskin, about 3½ feet long, and flattened so as to be 2 or 3 inches wide and 5 inches high. The sealskins appeared to have been well soaked and then rolled up, flattened into the required form, and allowed to freeze. The underneath part was coated with a mixture of moss and ice laid smoothly on by hand before being allowed to freeze, the moss answer-

---

[1] "Eskimo Migration," Journ. Anthrop. Inst., London, 1878, VII, p. 129.

ing the purpose of hair in mortar to make the compound adhere more firmly.[1]

The Pima Indians of Arizona are also said to make a wagon of hide for dragging their crops, and Peary relates that on one occasion he made a sled of musk-ox skin.

"It is easier," he says, "to haul 150 pounds on a sled than to carry 50 pounds on your back, particularly over the snow. The weight on the back sinks one down into the snow, while the sled is a much more easy process. For instance, on one occasion I hauled a sled carrying 60 or 70 pounds for 1,100 miles, and our average day's journey was 24 miles. The snow was in fairly good condition, and we came back well. If I had been carrying that weight, it would have been very difficult."

Petitot says of the Slave Indians about Fort Rae, Hudson Bay territory, that it is a singular spectacle to see a horde of these savages on their march over a frozen lake. As far as the eye could reach could be seen a long file of sleds and dogs, of women loaded with burdens and young children.[2]

The Western Déné travel in winter by means of light toboggans drawn by three or four dogs trotting in Indian file. In summer, when families are en route for their hunting grounds, the dogs are used for pack animals.[3]

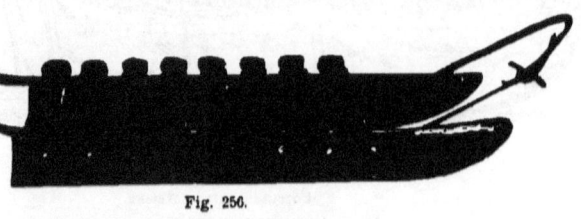

Fig. 256.

ESKIMO SLED (QAMUTING), FROM CUMBERLAND GULF.

From a figure in the Sixth Annual Report of the Bureau of Ethnology.

The sleds of the Chippewayan are formed of thin slips of board, turned up in front, and are highly polished with crooked knives in order that they slide along more smoothly. They are made of the red or swamp spruce-fir tree.[4]

Boas, from whom the following is taken, declares that during the greater part of the year the only passable road for the Central Eskimo is that afforded by the ice and snow; therefore sleds (qamuting) of different constructions are used in traveling.

The best model is made by the tribes of Hudson Strait and Davis Strait, for the driftwood which they can obtain in abundance admits the use of long wooden runners (fig. 256). Their sleds (Boas, fig. 482)

---

[1] McClintock's Narrative, etc., Boston, 1860, p. 233, with figure.

[2] Smithsonian Rep., 1865, p. 135.

[3] Cf. Father Morice, Proc. Can. Inst. (Series 3), VII, p. 131.

[4] Mackenzie, "Voyages, from Montreal through the Continent of North America," Philadelphia, 1802, p. 125.

have two runners, from 5 to 15 feet long and from 20 inches to 2½ feet apart. They are connected by crossbars of wood or bone, and the back is formed by deer's antlers with the skull attached. The bottom of the runners (qamun) is curved at the head (uinirn) and cut off at right angles behind. It is shod with whale's bone, ivory, or the jawbones of a whale. In long sleds the shoeing (pirqang) is broadest near the head and narrowest behind. This device is very well adapted for sledding in soft snow; for, while the weight of the load is distributed over the entire length of the apparatus, the fore part, which is more apt to break through, has a broad face, which presses down the snow and enables the hind part to glide over it without sinking in too deeply.

The shoe (Boas, fig. 483) is either tied or riveted to the runner. If tied, the lashing passes through sunken drill holes to avoid any friction in moving over the snow. The right and left sides of a whale's jaw are frequently used for shoes, as they are of the proper size and permit the shoe to be of a single piece. Ivory is cut into flat pieces and riveted to the runner with long treenails. The points are frequently covered with bone on both the lower and upper sides, as they are easily injured by striking hard against hummocks or snowdrifts.

The crossbars (napun) project over the runners on each side and have notches which form a kind of neck. These necks serve to fasten the thongs when a load is lashed on the sledge. The bars are fastened to the runners by thongs which pass through two pairs of holes in the bars and through corresponding ones in the runners. If these fastenings should become loose they are tightened by winding a small thong around them and thus drawing the opposite parts of the thong tightly together. If this prove insufficient, a small wedge is driven between the thong and the runner.

The antlers attached to the back of the sled have the branches removed and the points slanted so as to fit to the runners. Only the brow antlers are left, the right one being cut down to about 3 inches in length, the left one to 1½ inches. This back forms a very convenient handle for steering the sledge past hummocks or rocks, for drawing it back when the points have struck a snowdrift, etc. Besides, the lashing for holding the load is tied to the right-brow antler, and the snow knife and the harpoon are hung upon it.

Under the foremost crossbar a hole is drilled through each runner. A very stout thong (pitu) consisting of two separate parts passes through the holes and serves to fasten the dogs' traces to the sledge. A button at each end of this thong prevents it from slipping through the hole of the runner. · The thong consists of two parts, the one ending in a loop, the other in a peculiar kind of clasp (partirang). Figure 484 (Boas) represents the form commonly used. The end of one part of the thong is fastened to the hole of the clasp, which, when closed, is stuck through the loop of the opposite end (see Boas, fig. 482). A more artistic design is shown in fig. 485 (Boas). One end of the line is tied to the hole on the underside of this implement. When it is in use the loop of the other end is stuck through another hole in the center and hung over the nozzle. The whole represents the head of an animal with a gaping mouth. The dogs' traces are strung upon this line by means of an uqsirn (fig. 257), an ivory implement with a large and a small eyelet (Boas, fig. 486).

This whole account of the central Eskimo sled should be studied in the original memoir.

Other sleds are made of slabs of fresh-water ice, which are cut and allowed to freeze together, or of a large ice block hollowed out in the center. All these are clumsy and heavy, and much inferior to the large sled just described.[1]

Fig. 257.
ESKIMO DOG HARNESSED FOR SLED.
From a figure in the Sixth Annual Report of the Bureau of Ethnology.

The inhabitants of Hudson Strait leave Tuniqten in the spring, arrive at the head of Frobisher Bay in the fall, and after the formation of the ice reach the Nugumiut settlements by means of sleds.[2]

The Eskimo sleds seen by Parry vary in size, being from 6½ to 9 feet in length, and from 18 inches to 2 feet in breadth. Some of those at Igloolik were of larger dimensions, one being 11 feet in length and weighing 268 pounds, and two or three others above 200 pounds. The runners are sometimes made of the jawbones of a whale, but more

---

[1] Sixth Ann. Rep. Bureau of Ethnology, pp. 529–538, figs. 482–489.
[2] Ibid., p. 423.

commonly of several pieces of wood or bone, scarfed and lashed together, the interstices being filled, to make all smooth and firm, with moss stuffed in tight and then cemented by throwing water to freeze upon it. The lower part of the runner is shod with a plate of harder bone, coated with fresh-water ice to avoid wear and tear and to make it run smoothly. This coating is performed with a mixture of snow and fresh water about a half inch thick rubbed over it until it is smooth and hard upon the surface. When the ice is only in part worn off, it is renewed by taking some water in the mouth and spirting it over the former coating.

He noticed a sled which was curious on account of one of the runners and a part of the other being constructed without wood, iron, or bone of any kind. For this purpose a number of sealskins were rolled up and disposed into the required shape, and an outer coat of the same kind was sewed tightly around them. This formed the upper half of the runner, the lower part consisting entirely of moss, molded, while wet, into the proper form, and being left to freeze, adhering firmly together to the skins. The usual shoeing of smooth ice completed the runner, which for six months of the year is as hard as wood. The cross-pieces which form the bottom of the common sled were made of bone, wood, or anything they could muster. Over these was generally laid a sealskin as a flooring, and in the summer a pair of deer's horns are attached to the sled as a back, which are removed in winter to enable them when stopping to turn the sled up to prevent the dogs running away with it.

The whole is secured by lashings of thong, giving it a degree of strength combined with flexibility which no other mode of fastening could effect.[1]

The sleds of Smith Sound were made up of small fragments of porous bone, admirably knit together by thongs of hide. The runners, which glistened like burnished steel, were of highly polished ivory obtained from the tusks of the walrus.[2]

Nowadays, says Bessels, the sled is the only means of conveyance used by the Eskimo of Smith Sound. Before they came in contact with the white man this was composed of pieces of bone ingeniously fastened together with thongs of rawhide, but now wood is frequently used.[3]

In the U. S. National Museum is a model of a sled from North Greenland, example No. 10418. The parts to be noticed on this sled are the runners, the ivory shoeing of the runners, the crosspieces or flooring, the braces and handles, and the method of lashing the different parts together. Owing to the great scarcity of material in this Eskimo region,

---

[1] William Edward Parry, "Second Voyage for the Discovery of a Northwest Passage," London, 1825, pp. 514–515.

[2] Kane, "Arctic Explorations," Philadelphia, I, 1856, p. 205, with illustrations.

[3] Bessels, Am. Nat., 1884, p. 868, fig. 4. Also "Die Amerikanische Nord-pol Expedition," Leipzig, 1879, p. 359, with two excellent figures of old sleds.

most of their sleds as well as other apparatus are made of oak and other timber gathered from whaleships or wrecks.

The runners are each of a single piece of wood, straight along the top and pointed in front by a long curve. Through the runners holes are bored along the upper margin for the lashing of the crosspieces and the handles, and in the lower margin for lashing of the shoeing. Between these perforations and the part to be lashed the wood is cut away, so that the thong or other seizing is always countersunk and not exposed to be injured by abrasion of ice or snow. The shoeing is made up of pieces of ivory or bone fastened on by treenails at each end of the strips and firmly held to the runner by a series of lashings through counter-sunk holes. To effect this, first, a larger-sized hole is bored in a little way from the bottom; then two holes are bored from this point diagonally, one having an outlet on the inner margin of the runner, and the other just on the outer margin of the runner, to meet the two holes bored for this purpose through the runner itself. A coarse lashing of thong is then sewed through the hole and through the runner around and around until the hole is filled up and well bound together. To hold the floor pieces on top each bit of wood is cut away so as to leave only a narrow end; a hide thong is wrapped around these ends down through the hole in the runner from side to side, in the usual method of the Eskimo. Braces run from the front crosspiece out toward the front of the sled and are held in place by treenails and lashings of hide passing through holes bored in each. The handles are of the typical shape, and they also are sewed to the upper margin of the runner as described. A round piece of wood passes from handle to handle and is slightly let into each and held in place by a lashing of thong.

In a word, the parts of the sled are all sewed together in such manner as to take the strain in every direction, and not to expose the material to abrasion at any point. This model is a fair representation of all the sleds, small and great, from this region. Length of model, 14 inches. Collected by Dr. E. K. Kane.

The parts of sled (No. 2676) to be now studied are the runners, the shoeing, the crossbars, the handle, and the lashing. (Fig. 258.) The runners (as in the case of most from this region) are made of oak planks less than 1 inch thick, 4 inches high, and 2 feet 4 inches long, taken from whaleships. Evidently these runners have formed part of a sled prior to their use in this one, for there are a great many holes bored along the top and bottom which now have no function. Each runner is shod with strips of narwhal ivory. Holes are bored through the runners three-fourths of an inch from the bottom, and the wood is cut away between these holes and the bottom so that the rawhide lashing may be countersunk. The shoeing is fastened to the runners in the following manner: Holes half an inch apart are bored diagonally through the ivory so as to meet in a single countersunk cavity below. At every point of attachment there are two sets of these holes, one near the outer margin

of the shoeing, the other near the inner margin. The rawhide lashing
passes through the runner, then down through one of the diagonal holes
in the shoeing and up through the other, then through the runner to
the inside, and down, and up through the diagonal bores in the shoeing
back to the outside, as indicated in the drawing. The only exception
to this method of attachment is where two ends of the shoeing come
together. In that case the bore passes down through the shoeing a
quarter of an inch from the end, and a slight gutter is cut from
this perforation to the end of the ivory. When two pieces are
bored and guttered in this way, a rawhide line passes down through
one along to the other in the countersink; the lashing then passes up
through the hole in the runner to the inside, and down
through the other two perforations, backward and forward,
until they are firmly sewed on and the rawhide is protected at
every point. When the process is understood, the ingenuity
of the Eskimo will appear, the object being at every step to
secure the shoeing permanently in place and yet to protect
the rawhide line from abrasion by the ice. There
are five crossbars to the sled on which the load
rests. They are made of the roughest kind of pine
and oak from old box covers or barrels, and the

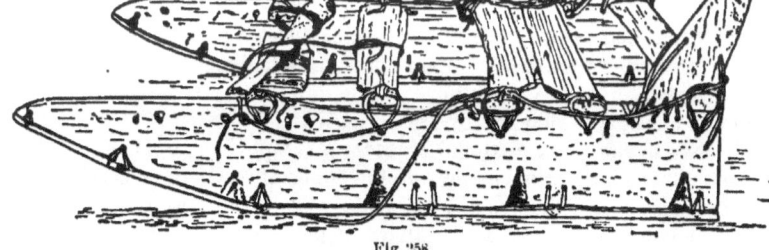

Fig. 258.

EASTERN ESKIMO SLED.

Cat. No. 9676, U. S. N. M. Collected by Dr. E. K. Kane.

front one has been mended by a splicing of bone, as there is no bracing
whatever in the Greenland sled beneath. The lashing of these crossbars is very complete and efficient; holes are bored through the runners
1¼ inches from the top, just below where the crossbar is to be attached.
The crossbars are cut away at the ends, so as to form a notch like a
dovetail. A stout rawhide line passes over this notch and down through
the runner to the inside, up over the notch and down to the hole in the
runner, and back to the outside. These excursions through the runner
and over the end of the crosspiece continue until the holes are filled
up; the strands of the lashing are seized firmly by several turns of the
rawhide line. In this particular case a half turn of the lashing passes
also through old holes that were used when these runners were part of
another sled.

The handles are very much like those of a plow. They fit on the top

of the runner at the hind end, and are held on by a rawhide line passing through a series of holes bored in the runner and in the handle.
In addition to this, a rawhide line passes from a hole in the handle 2
inches above the runner to another hole in the heel of the sled. Two
inches below its upper margin a rawhide line is rove four times through
and fastened off by a half hitch; this part of the work is very neatly
done. The upper part of the handles are joined together by a crosspiece, which is held on by a diagonal lashing.

The knots on this sled are very interesting, consisting of splices or
whip knots (a very common device in all rawhide lines), overhand knots,
and a series of half turns. After all, the most efficient knot is that shown

in the attachment of the crosspieces to the runners, consisting of a seizing
fastened off with a single half hitch; the side strand and fore-and-aft
strand are taken up very effectively by this method of lashing.

In a land where there is no other mode of attachment, of course the
sled maker has to rely upon his rawhide line to hold the parts of the
vehicle together. Collected by Dr. E. K. Kane.

There is in the U. S. National Museum (example No. 10417, fig. 259),
a sled runner made from sections of the bones of a whale, mitered and
fitted together, and then sewed by lashings of rawhide lines.

The shoeing is made of seven strips of ivory and bone sewed on to
the runner by means of a rawhide line passing through the runner and
through the shoeing, the gutters being countersunk, so as to prevent
the abrasion of the united material. Length, 25½ inches.

General Greely figures a modern Greenland low sled with crossbars
and handles of wood, and by the side of it an old specimen with runners
of driftwood shod with bone, three wooden crosspieces and handles of
whale rib lashed on to the runners with thong and having a crossbar at
the top.[1] The specimen is much dilapidated.

Example No. 89941, in the U. S. National Museum (fig. 260) is a sled
from Labrador, consisting of three parts, the runners, the crosspieces,
and the floor or bed. The runners are of wood, bent up slightly at the
front. On the top of the runners, front and rear, jogs have been cut
and perforated. On the top of these rest the crosspieces or sills, and
above this three slats running longitudinally, one in the middle, and
one at each side connected with the runner in front. The parts are

fastened together by lashing. Length, 9½ inches. Collected by Lucien M. Turner.

The komatik, according to W. A. Stearns, is a sort of sled used by Indians of Bonne Esperance Island, and looks very much like a magnified specimen of one of those latter articles. Its dimensions vary from 9 to 13 feet in length, from 2 to 3 feet in width, and it stands about 8 inches from the ground. The wood is wholly pine, and the side bars are cut out of thin deal boards, planed down to about 1 or rarely 2 inches in thickness, with the front ends turned up like the front runner of a modern sled; the sides are often beveled, so that the bottom is one-fourth or one-half an inch wider than the top. The upper part of the sled is made of a number of thin pieces of wood of equal length and about 4 inches in width, with the ends rounded, and then notched— for a purpose that will appear hereafter. The front and rear pieces are similar, but of double the width, while the thickness of all is about the same, generally one-half an inch, though the end pieces are perhaps a little thicker. Each piece has two pairs of holes bored through it on either end, the distance between each pair of holes being that of the width of the top of the runner, and the distance between the holes of each pair being about half an inch. Between each pair the end is then gouged out crosswise about one-fourth of an inch deep, while the inner pair are connected at right angles by another gouge, the purpose of

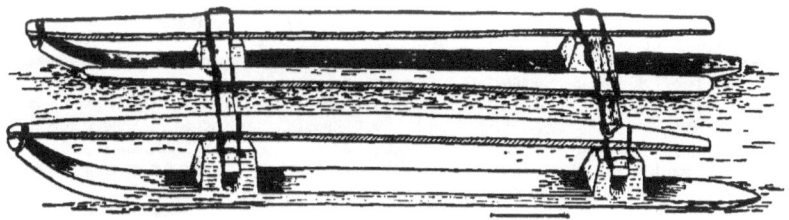

Fig. 260.
BUILT-UP SLED FROM LABRADOR.
Cat. No. 89941, U. S. N. M. Collected by Lucien M. Turner.

which will soon be seen. A curious fact is that all these holes are bored out with a red-hot iron, to make them smooth and even. On the side bars or runners, at a regular and previously measured distance apart, are bored holes to the exact number of the crossbars. The holes are bored one a little above and the next a little below the preceding one, so that when done the whole presents two unequal rows, hence the liability of splitting the soft pine in the sewing process is lessened. The next work is sewing the parts together. For this a coarse salmon net twine is threaded into a needle used for the purpose, and each crossbar is sewed to the corresponding holes in the runner, in and out of the holes on either side of the bar itself, and drawn as tight as possible;

the needle then slips under the twine through the groove across the inner pair of holes, and a loop and a stout pull fasten it; thus each bar is sewed on till all are tight. The forward end of each side bar must be strengthened by a long, thin iron placed lengthwise along the inner side of each bar and sewed tight to the boards.[1]

The sleds of the Iroquois Indians, says Charlevoix, which serve to transport the baggage and in case of necessity the sick and wounded, are two small and very thin boards half a foot broad each and 6 or 7 feet long. The fore part is somewhat raised and the sides bordered with small bands, to which the thongs for binding whatever is laid on the carriage is fastened. Let these carriages be ever so much loaded, an Indian draws them without difficulty, by means of a long thong or strap, which is passed round his breast.

They use them likewise for carrying burdens, and mothers for carrying their children with their cradles; but in this case the thong or collar is placed upon their forehead, and not on the breast.[2]

The line between savagery and barbarism puts the wheel on the side of the latter. Barbarous man in traction should therefore form a later chapter, full of interest and necessary to the whole history of land transportation and travel. As late as 1878 the only railroad in China extended 10 miles from the Kaiping coal mines to the sea. The motive power was men, who worked twelve to fourteen hours and received 10 cents a day.

SLEDS IN THE U. S. NATIONAL MUSEUM.

Museum No.	Specimen.	Locality.	By whom contributed.
14800	Sled, reindeer, and driver	Norway	University of Christiania.
74534	Sled	Lapland	Centennial Commission.
2811	.....do	Kamchatka	Lieut. Wilkes, U. S. N.
73018	Sled, model	.....do	Dr. L. Stejneger.
46261	Sled runner, shoe of	Icy Cape	Dr. T. H. Bean.
63388–63389	Dog sled, model	St. Lawrence Island	E. W. Nelson.
15597	Sled, of whale bone, double	Poonook, Alaska	Henry W. Elliott
15609	Sled, wooden runners shod with whale's bone.	.....do	Do.
48104	Sled, model	Norton Bay, Alaska	E. W. Nelson.
129323	Sled (of wood)	St. Michaels, Alaska	L. M. Turner.
30771	Sled, model	Norton Sound, Alaska	Do.
48147	Sled (Ingalik)	Anvik, Alaska	E. W. Nelson.
168567	.....do	Togiak, Alaska	World's Columbian Exposition.
49111	Sled	Tanana River, Alaska	E. W. Nelson.
166974	.....do	Porcupine River, Alaska	J. H. Turner.
595	Babiche sled line (Dog Rib Indians)	Fort Simpson	R. R. Ross.
2042	Reindeer sled line	.....do	Do.
570	Dog sled (Chippewayan)	Slave Lake, Canada	Do.
1638	Sled (Eskimo)	Mackenzie River	R. MacFarlane.
10268	Sled runners (Eskimo)	Frobisher Bay	Capt. C. F. Hall.
10378	Sled runners and crossbar (Innuit).	Ross's ship, Victory, Repulse Bay.	Do.

[1] Stearns, "Labrador," Boston, 1884, pp. 145–146.

[2] Charlevoix, "Voyages to North America," i, p. 336.

SLEDS IN THE U. S. NATIONAL MUSEUM—Continued.

Museum No.	Specimen.	Locality.	By whom contributed.
10419	Whale jawbone, used in making sleds.	Repulse Bay	Henry Grinnell.
10376	Sled, runner of	do	Capt. C. F. Hall.
12357	Sled runner (Eskimo)	Polaris Bay	Dr. E. Bessels.
12363	....do	do	Do.
89941	Sled (toy)	Labrador	L. M. Turner.
90271	....do	Ungava Bay, Labrador	Do.
153511	Sled (Montagunis Indians)	do	Henry G. Bryant.
531	Sled, reindeer	British Columbia	B. R. Ross.
1639	Sled (dog), Eskimo	Anderson River	R. MacFarlane.
2153	....do	do	Do.
2676	Sled or traineau	do	Do.
7472	....do	Fort Anderson	Do.
7473	Sleds (2)	do	Do.
7474	Sled	do	Do.
532	Sled (dog), model	Fort Resolution	R. Kennicott.
1970	....do	Slave Lake	B. R. Ross.
169044	Sled (Eskimo)	Labrador	Henry G. Bryant.
561	Sled, boys', whalebone runners	Greenland	Dr. J. J. Hayes.
10377	Sled (Dr. Kane's)	do	Henry Grinnell.
10418	Sled model (Dr. Kane's)	do	Do.
127136	Sled, shod with iron	South Greenland	Mrs. Olivia Pavy.
108968	Sled	East Greenland	Dr. Sophus Müller.
127040	Sled, child's (model)	Smith Sound	Dr. E. Bessels.
43920	Sled	Fort Yukon, Alaska	E. W. Nelson.
7970	....do	Nushagag	T. T. Minor.
15593	Sled runners (2 ivory and 2 wood)	Poonook, Bering Sea	Henry W. Elliott.
15613	Sled, shod with whalebone	do	Do.
15597	Double sled, whale rib	do	Do.
55889	Sled, Eskimo	do	Chas. L. McKay.
63387	Sled (dog)	do	E. W. Nelson.
153653	Sled (model)	do	J. H. Turner.
153654-153655	Sled (dog team), model	do	Do.
38793	Sled (model)	St. Michaels, Alaska	E. W. Nelson.

ROADS AND TRAVELERS' CONVENIENCES.

To this vast subject of going about afoot and riding, of carrying singly and cooperatively, and of shifting the burden upon the backs of beasts, there are subsidiary conveniences of great importance, such as the following, including all activities covered by classes 4 and 5, mentioned on page 254.

1. Roads and bridges, involving the entire subject of primitive engineering.

2. Provisions for extending the length of the journey and the time that may be spent away from home.

3. Condensed and special food for long trips, and travelers' drugs.

4. Natural, artificial, and human guides.

5. Provisions for camping, resting, relaying, sleeping, feeding animals, etc.

6. Signaling, postal service, and couriers.

7. Measures of time and distance, clocks, calendars, stations, milestones, length of journey and extent of commerce, etc.

8. Apparatus of trade, money.

9. Markets, bazaars, and fairs.

10. Amnesty and laws of travel and trade. The social organizations, laws, and customs involved in and created by this vast industry.

None of these topics can be fully elaborated here. Some of them will be considered and illustrated from material in the Museum later.

1. *Roads and bridges.*—The U. S. National Museum has among its treasures a collection of primitive bridges, to be used in illustrating the history of that series of inventions which led up to the modern roadbed and railroad. The earliest roadmakers were not engaged in casting up highways, but in keeping them clear. The most primitive bridges were logs or great rocks across streams, and, after that, bridges supported on trees, posts, vines, and braces, anticipating in a rude way the pier bridge, the suspension bridge, and the cantilever. Fords and portages were a part of this activity.

Mankind had walked over every habitable part of the globe before there was a beast of burden. The trails laid down by ruminants were adopted by man until the earth was a network of primitive roads.

"Locomotion among the Western Déné," says Morice, "is ordinarily by walking in very narrow paths, though the Tsil-koh-tin and Southern Carriers now travel on horseback. More commonly the Carriers use as highways the numerous lakes that dot the country in summer and winter."[1]

The obstacles in the way of early travel and the indefatigable energy of men in passing over them are well set forth in Mrs. Bishop's travels among the western Tibetans. The following elements of difficult primitive travel are mentioned about the Shayok River:

Winter traffic along river beds nearly dry.

Summer caravans laboring along difficult tracks at great heights.

Climbing difficult rock ladders and perilous stairways.

Crossing glaciers filled with yawning crevasses.

Riding along precipice ledges on the yak.

Leading baggage horses down precipices, with men holding the head and tail of each.

Travelers and goods making perilous runs in scows, poled and paddled.

Swimming the animals through the cold water.

"We had," writes Mrs. Bishop, "twelve horses, all led. 'Water guides' with 10-foot poles sounded the rivers ahead; one led Mr. Redslob's horse in front of mine with a large rope, and two more led mine, while the gopas of three villages and the zemindár steadied my horse against the stream. * * * All the chupas went up and down sound-

[1] A. G. Morice, Proc. Canadian, Inst. (Series 3), VII, p. 131.

ing long before they found a possible passage. All loads were raised higher, the men roped their soaked clothing on their shoulders, water was dashed at our faces, and then with shouts the whole caravan plunged into deep water, strong and almost ice cold. The traveler from Kashmir to Tibet can not be borne in a carriage or a hill cart. Much of the way he is limited to a foot path, and walks down all rugged and deep descents and dismounts at most bridges. The roads are bridle paths, worn by traffic alone across the gravelly valleys, but elsewhere constructed with great toil and expense, along narrow valleys, ravines, gorges, and chasms. For miles at a time this road has been blasted out of precipices from 1,000 to 3,000 feet in depth, and is merely a ledge above a raging torrent, the worst parts, chiefly those around rocky projections, being scaffolded, i. e., poles are lodged horizontally among the crevices of the cliff, and the roadway of slabs, planks, and brushwood or branches and sods is laid loosely upon them. This track is always wide enough for a loaded beast, but in many places, when two caravans meet, the animals of one must give way and scramble up the mountain side."[1]

In a subsequent paper trails, roads, portages, and bridges, especially of aboriginal America, will be more fully treated.

2. *Increasing the length and the time of journeys.*—There are many regions of the earth that were positively inaccessible to primitive man; but there are also vast tracts that, while they are uninhabitable, are yet accessible and may be crossed. A part of the history of travel relates to invading and traversing these spaces. If there had been no such intervals, there would have been little travel. As we have a modulus of early culture in the depths at which people might operate in the earth or in the sea, so we have another in the length of journeys and the number of months or years that would be devoted to a single round or excursion in walking, packing, boating, sledging, or with flocks and herds. These distances in modern commerce constitute the haul between producer and consumer.

Birds of passage made formerly longer journeys than men, and the length of their migrations in time and distance was equaled, perhaps, by those of fishes and marine mammals. The motives which governed the movements of these creatures were very simple, but these same constituted the incentive to human movements over the earth. The coming and going of birds and marine creatures are likewise the occasion of an enormous amount of human bustle and running about. Most of the domestication of animals is caused by a desire to have them at our doors, and to make us independent of their migrations.

In addition to the great migrations of aerial and marine creatures, many land animals were often obliged by natural conditions to travel great distances; and the inquiry is also concerning the self-imposed

---

[1] Mrs. Bishop, "Among the Tibetans," Chicago, 1894, pp. 36, 76.

loads of men and the distances to which they bore them in order to follow the caribou, the buffalo, the elephant, etc., for the purpose of living
upon them.

All of these combine to give confidence to men, to enlarge their cos-
mogony and to stimulate the cooperative activities which make it possible to go away farther and return.

In every tribe there are stories of travelers who have made long voyages and returned. Dr. Boas says that the myths of the northwest
coast of America point across the Pacific; all of them are Odysseys.
Besides that class of traditions which fix upon the present habitat as
the primal home, there is another class of migration myths. One
school of interpretation may appreciate and another depreciate the
real length of the migration. That is not mooted here. They are
migration myths, and relate to wanderings.

The U. S. National Museum comes in contact with such by its collections of mythological material—carvings, totem posts, paintings, marks
on pottery, masks, dress, figures on boats, paddles, carrying baskets,
and even in the stitch or mesh in weaving. The length of a sled or of
a boat, the number of parts to a dog harness, the existence of certain
kinds of packing cases, the calendar, and many other objects which
the curator has to handle every day, are in fact metric apparatus to
indicate how far away the owners are bold enough to go.

Again, the perfecting of devices prolongs the day's travel. Nansen
tells of a kaiak journey of 80 miles in a single day, and Schwatka said
in a lecture that he had made over a hundred miles in one continuous
excursion with a company of Eskimo.[1]

The East Greenlanders journey around to West Greenland to get
snuff, and will consume four years in a single excursion there and back.
Nansen says that they often remain no longer than an hour at the
trading station and then take up their homeward march.

The Manchu and Manyarg who navigate the Sungari are said to
spend eight days from the mouth of the river to Sansin; and the voyage to Tsitsikar or Mergen requires a month. They either tow their
boats from the land or push them along with long poles.[2]

The Tuski, near East Cape, undertake journeys to Kolima occupying
six months, and to other points requiring four months.[3] Wrangell
supposed that some men passed their lives thus, but Hooper does not
seem to be of this opinion. The journeys are undertaken with reindeer
and large covered sleds. Furs and ivory are taken to be exchanged
for tobacco, beads, knives, prints, sugar, spirits, etc.[4]

Formerly, says Seton-Karr, the different tribes of northwest British
Columbia were afraid to quit their tribal territory, but now Indians

[1] F. Nansen, "The First Crossing of Greenland," London, I, p. 367; II, p. 436.
[2] Ravenstein, "Russians on the Amur," London, 1861, p. 261.
[3] Hooper, "Tents of the Tuski," London, 1853, p. 185.
[4] Ibid., p. 186.

can be found willing to accompany the white man through regions that are as strange and unknown to them as to him. Some, for instance, have accompanied miners as far as the mouth of the Yukon, and returned home by way of San Francisco.[1]

The extent and direction of aboriginal journeys and commerce have been in one place cut off, in another greatly stimulated, by contact with the Caucasian race. Certainly in Canada the fur-bearing animals were soon killed about the trading establishments, and the Indians were stimulated to make greater and greater excursions into the wilderness and from the wilderness to the trading posts.[2]

3. *Travelers' food and drugs.*—Condensed food and stimulants are necessary to a long journey, and the invention of them has incited much ingenuity. So frozen food in the north is succeeded by pemmican and this by meal, cassava, taro, tsamba, or what not, in order that a great deal could be put into a small space.

The U. S. National Museum has made a large collection of this packed and condensed travelers' food, and among the specimens illustrating early medicine are many of the strength-sustaining drugs among savages.[3]

The Indians of southern Yucatan, according to Morelet, never set out on any expedition without a supply of *pozol.* This is maize made into a kind of paste, sweetened with sugar to suit the taste, and when mixed with water serves at once for food and drink. It is at the same time the most economical and portable kind of provision for a journey.[4]

Chocolate, says Humboldt, is easily conveyed and readily employed. As an aliment it contains a large quantity of nutritive and stimulating particles in a small compass. It has been said with truth that, in the East, rice, gum, and ghee (clarified butter) assist man in crossing the deserts; and so, in the New World, chocolate and flour of maize have rendered accessible to the traveler the table-lands of the Andes and vast uninhabited forests.[5]

4. *Guides, natural and human.*—Nowadays the steel rail holds the vehicle smoothly and directly to its course, and on the waters artificial buoys, light-houses, and apparatus for observing the heavenly bodies and for steering do almost as well for the ship.

Primitive men were not without their folk astronomy, instincts, natural pilots, and experiences. They also knew how to keep the traveler or the boat on a direct way. Winds blow, waters run, natural objects animate and inanimate on which man depends move and have their areas of dispersion.

[1] H. W. Seton-Karr, Proc. Roy. Geog. Soc., London, 1891, XIII, p. 73.

[2] Mackenzie, "Voyages from Montreal through the Continent of North America," Philadelphia, 1802, p. i. On lengthening the journey, consult also W. C. Bompas, "Northern Lights on the Bible," London, 1894, pp. 63–68.

[3] Cf. Index-Catalogue Surg. General's Library, Washington, s. v.

[4] Morelet, "Travels in Yucatan," New York, 1871, p. 65.

[5] Bohn, "Travels to the Equinoctial Regions of America," London, 1852, II, p. 59.

It has been said that' the islanders of the Pacific wandered after all automatically about and settled their archipelagos.[1]

Above this unconscious guidance there is an accumulation of folk-lore and folk experiences in all savages that are truly the marvel of all intelligent travelers.

Moreover, there is a sign language of travel. The Africans had one system, the Americans another. It is an interesting group in the U. S. National Museum, merging on one side into music, on the other into the apparatus of war.

Early in September, 1513, says Helps, Vasco Nunez set out on his renowned expedition for finding the "other sea," accompanied by 190 men well armed, and by dogs, which were of more avail than men, and by Indian slaves to carry the burdens. He went by sea to the territory of his father-in-law, King Careta, by whom he was well received, and accompanied by whose Indians he moved on into Poncha's territory. This cacique took flight, as he had done before, seeking refuge among his mountains; but Vasco Nunez, whose first thought in his present undertaking was discovery, not conquest, sent messengers to Poncha, promising not to injure him. The Indian chief listened to these overtures and came to Vasco Nunez with gold in his hands. He did no harm to Poncha, and, on the contrary, secured his friendship by presenting him with looking-glasses, hatchets, and hawks' bells, in return for which he obtained guides and porters from among this cacique's people, and was enabled to prosecute his journey.

Following Poncha's guides, Vasco Nunez and his men commenced the ascent of the mountains until he entered the country of an Indian chief called Quarequa, whom they found fully prepared to resist them.[2]

Balboa on arriving at the coast of the Pacific in 1543 "seems to have heard of a wealthy tribe who lived on the seacoast far to the south and used large sheep as beasts of burden.[3] * * * The supposition that accounts of Peru had reached the Isthmus, notwithstanding the great distance, involves nothing impossible."

Quite as much as shepherds watching their flocks, travelers and carriers have watched the stars, mapped out the heavens, and guided their way on land and water by the celestial lanterns.

The Eskimo in traveling use the north star as a guide. Their knowledge of seasons is also wonderful. The seasons have distinctive names, and these are divided into a great number, of which there are more during the warm weather than during the winter.[4]

Roger Williams says, "The wildernesse being so vast, it is a mercy, that for a hire a Man shall never want guides, who will carry provisious

[1] "Die unfreiwillige Wanderungen im Stillen Ozean," Petermann's Mittheilungen, 1894.

[2] Helps, "The Spanish Conquest in America," New York, 1856, I, p. 340.

[3] Bandelier, "The Gilded Man," New York, 1893, p. 5, quoting Herrera, Dec. I, Lib. x, Cap. III.

[4] Lucien Turner, Eleventh Ann. Rep. Bureau of Ethnology, p. 202.

and such as hire them over Rivers and Brookes, and find out oftentimes hunting houses or other lodgings at night.

"I have heard of many English lost and have oft been lost my selfe,
and my selfe and others have been often found and succoured by the
Indians.[1] * * *

"They are so excellently skilled in all the bowels of the Countrey (by
reason of their hunting) that I have often been guided twentie, thirtie,
yea, sometimes forty miles through the woods a streight course, out of
my path."

5. *Provisions for camping on the road.*—Lengthening a journey
beyond the endurance of a single effort involves the putting down of
the load and resting. The steps in the progress of invention leading
up to the resting and relaying elements of many modern cities seem
to have been—

1. Modifying the packing apparatus so that it could be laid aside
and resumed with least effort.

2. Carrying the means of providing temporary bed, shelter, fire, food,
and defense.

3. On the establishment of regular trails, temporary shelters were
provided, which the traveler might use and proceed. No attendants
were needed.

4. Caravansaries, where for a fee the traveler and porter might sleep
and be fed, and where his commodities could be safely housed from
thieves.

5. Hostelries, villages, repair shops, stores—in short, the setting up
of a travel center.

Aboriginal hospitality had its first motive largely in the traveling
industry, and its abolition was caused by the superabundance of travel
causing the existence of hostelries and guilds relating thereto, creating
a public sentiment against receiving strangers free of charge.

The methods adopted by the Central American Indians when preparing to pass the night upon an open savanna were instructive. In
the first instance they placed upon the ground a quantity of broad dry
leaves to protect them from the damp grass. They then dispersed, and
in a few minutes the adjacent forest resounded with the noise of the
blows made by their machetes. They returned bearing loads of firewood and also several strong forked branches. These they sharpened
at one end and fixed into the earth near the camping place to form
supports to carry the bales of tobacco. In this manner the cargo was
raised about 3 feet, and thus they carried out the invariable rule of the
Indians, who never leave anything upon the ground at night. They
then lighted a large fire.[2] The tambo of Peru was a hut of refuge along
the public trails and highways across the despoblader or desert regions.

[1] Roger Williams, Coll. R. I. Hist. Soc., I, p. 72, with vocabulary for guide, hire, etc.,
with derivatives.

[2] Brine, "The American Indians, Their Earthworks and Temples," London, 1849,
pp. 291-292.

Mr. im Thurn speaks of the Indians who accompanied him in Guiana as lying in hammocks under which fires were lighted. But they also compelled the boys to take lighted palm leaves and singe them as they lay in their hammocks to destroy savage insects.[1]

6. *Signals, couriers, and posts.*—The U. S. National Museum has an interesting collection relating to conveying information for and by travel. The emergencies of the growing state, as in Peru, demanded that the central power should be more rapidly informed. The separate elements in the problem before the early man were the following:

1. To substitute for the long walk a succession of quick runs—couriers.

2. To have trained professionals with road conveniences and guard—posts.

3. To have an esoteric sign language to the eye and to the ear, by which information may be conveyed to the traveler as he goes along, by which one traveler may leave word for another or, finally, to get rid of the traveler altogether by a system of telephoning or of visible speech.

Langsdorff mentions the use of fire signals in Japan. "In defiance of the interdict the fishermen informed us that four days before intelligence was communicated to Nagasaki by fires in the night of a three-masted vessel being off the coast; that at our appearance off the harbor information of it was conveyed by a post of observation upon the nearest hill."[2]

"The Micmacs have a system of communicating while in the woods. Sticks are placed in the ground; a cut on one of them indicates that a message in picture writing on a piece of bark is hidden near by under a stone. The direction in which the stick leans from its base upward indicates that in which the party moved, and thus serves as a convenient hint to those who follow to keep off their hunting ground."[3]

The method of the Karankawa of communicating with each other when parties were at a distance was by smoke. By some means known only to themselves, and carefully kept secret, the smoke of a small fire could be made to ascend in many different ways, as intelligible as spoken language to them. At night the horizon was often dotted in various directions with these little fires, and the messages thus conveyed seemed to govern the movements of the Indians.[4]

Das Ausland for February, 1889, et seq., has a very interesting article by Robert Muller on "Life and Occupation in the Cameroon," in which a curious instrument is thus described: A log is hollowed out and is divided along the transverse diameter by a bridge, upon which a drumstick is beaten to produce sounds of different tones. This rather unpromising instrument becomes of great importance as

---

[1] "Indians of British Guiana," London, 1883, p. 12.
[2] Langsdorff, "Voyages and Travels," London, 1813, I, p. 220.
[3] S. Hager, Am. Anthropologist, Washington, 1895, VIII, p. 31.
[4] Gatschet, "The Karankawa Indians," Cambridge, 1891, p. 19.

a means of communication and may, in fact, be called a "drum tele-graph." The villages are situated comparatively close together, and by means of the drum news is communicated rapidly from one village to another. A regular drum language has been invented, and this can be imitated with the mouth or beaten on the breast, so that conversa-tion can be carried on by the natives in the presence of white men without the latter understanding it, though comprehending the spoken language. The drum also serves the ordinary purpose of an instru-ment to dance by, etc.[1]

The Jivaros practice a system of telephony, which has at all times been very dangerous to their adversaries in war, by giving strokes on the "tunduli," a large drum, which is heard from house to house and passed on from hill to hill. The houses are all over their territories at convenient distance for the purpose; and in this manner very varied information is conveyed in a few moments to all the families of hordes dispersed over a large extent of country. This was the greatest danger the Spaniards had to contend with, and is still a main source of protection to these Indians, as they can rouse a large number at a moment's notice and sound the alarm through entire hordes.[2]

The messenger, mail carrier, dispatch bearer, professional courier, is equipped and exercised after the manner of the traveler. Altogether these men are a device like a machine, transforming numbers of men into velocity.

To develop an extensive system of couriers in ancient times, extended territory and a strong central government were needed. Hence the Greeks, having a small territory and disunited states, were not moved to establish any such institution.

In very early times among the Egyptians there were provisions for the conveyance of letters; but their system of rapid communication, if they had any, is not revealed.

Rome, on the other hand, and especially under the Empire, had, as will be seen, roads through all the territories they conquered. Besides the marching of armies over them and the general traffic, these roads were the means of continuous and rapid intelligence.

Among the Italian allies of Rome, officials on public business imposed any conditions they chose on the people along their way, such as fur-nishing food, lodging, fresh beasts, and even transport. Senators or ministers carried a mandate to subjects and allies to supply them with all necessaries for the journey. For the purposes of dispatches there were a variety of men and methods. These are well worked out in Smith's Dictionary of Greek and Roman Antiquities, third edition, under the phrase *cursus publicus*. Such terms as couriers, messengers, mounted couriers, stations, or relays (*mutationes*), postal stations (*man-siones*), conductors, guards, drivers, beasts of burden or conveyance,

[1] H. W. Henshaw, Am. Anthropologist, III, p. 292.
[2] A. Simson, Journ. Anthrop. Inst., 1880, May, p. 387.

rolling stock, passports, smack of the road and great movements of
people and money and goods. We read that the communities were
bound to furnish and maintain the teams and to keep the stables in
repair. They had further to secure the services of muleteers, mule
doctors, wheelwrights, grooms, and conductors (*vehicularii*). To organ-
ize and to keep moving such complicated machinery required excellent
management and training. From such a well-defined system backward
to more primitive methods constitutes the early history of culture in
this regard.[1]

The Persian Empire under Darius, son of Hystaspes, affords the
earliest instance of a national postal service. Mention is made of a
class called symmaci as existing in the most ancient times among the
Egyptians for the conveyance of letters by land.[2] In Persia horsemen
stationed at intervals, and relieving one another, conveyed the imperial
will in all directions from Susa, Ecbatana, or Babylon.

"The post is carried by Lapps and reindeer overland in Finmarlân
from Alten to Vadsö, Kautokeenö, Karasjok, and other points in the
Arctic, and it rarely fails to arrive on schedule time."[3]

Langsdorff thus speaks of travel in America at the beginning of the
century. In consequence of an entire failure of communication by
water, that by land exceeds what anyone could expect. Posts go regularly from Vera Cruz to all the provinces of North and South America.
A courier comes in about two months from Mexico to San Francisco,
the farthest establishment to the north. It commonly brings the news
from Europe of about six months back. From San Francisco anyone
may travel with the greatest safety, even to Chile; there are stations
all the way kept by soldiers.[4]

On the lofty plateau of Vilque, between Puno and La Paz, says
Wiener, there are regular couriers. The master of the post has in his
stable several mules and in his service chasqui who are accompanied by
their women. This service is well done. At 2 kilometers from the station the courier sounds on his horn, and beasts are put in the post road
to be ready when the chasqui arrives. Only half an hour is lost at the
station.[5]

7. *Metrical appliances.*—In many places and ways transportation has
been a promoter of invention for metrical appliances. The pack load
of a man is a unit of weight in Africa and America. Layard says that
wheat and barley in Armenia are sold by the camel load, nearly 480
pounds. It is said that Charles V amused himself with clocks when

[1] Beare, in Smith's Dictionary of Greek and Roman Antiquities, s. v. *Vehicularii
Cursus Publicus.*

[2] Ibid.

[3] Rasmus B. Anderson, Senate Ex. Doc. No. 73, Fifty-third Congress, second session,
p. 148.

[4] Langsdorff, "Voyages and Travels," London, 1814, II, p. 207.

[5] Wiener, "Pérou et Bolivie," p. 392. On the whole subject of signals, cf. Mallery,
Fourth Ann. Rep. Bureau of Ethnology.

his mind became enfeebled. But some one remarks that his study of clocks was a profound appreciation on his part of the fact that his ships could go no farther until his clocks ran better.

Almanacs or records of the days of the year and clocks or artificial devices for recording time of day must necessarily have occurred to those who had to get about more forcibly than to those who stayed at home. Indeed, antedating the invention of weights and measures was the art of counting, or simple arithmetic. The systems of counting were greatly improved by the art of transportation. The thousands of tally clerks on the docks belong to an old race, older than their demure prototypes on Egyptian monuments keeping the tale of bricks.

Vaca says that the Indians of a tribe he visited gave him "2,000 back loads of corn." The back load was therefore the unit of measure.[1]

"They are punctuall in measuring their Day by the Sunne, and their Night by the Moon and the Starres, and their lying much abroad in the ayre; and so living in the open fields, occasioneth even the youngest among them to be very observant of those heavenly lights."[2]

While exchange and all its mechanism constitute a separate body of industry, it can not be denied that weights and measures set agoing a large fraction of these activities. Before things can be bartered, some one must go and get them for that purpose; he must bear them to and fro or to stated meeting places, and arrive on time. Commerce instigates very largely the ransacking of the earth and the manufacture of her raw materials. All these, as well as barter at every point, regulated most of the travel and carrying, by perfecting clocks and calendars.

The early conquests of the Assyrians in India had enabled the Indians to carry on a great trade in ivory, and from them the Tyrians drew their ivory for the great throne of Solomon. "The men of Dedan were thy merchants, they brought thee for a present horns of ivory and ebony" (Ezekiel, xxviii, 15; Isaiah, xxi, 13).[3]

The inhabitants of the settlements about the mouth of the Anadyr divide their time in summer between fishing and hunting the wild reindeer, which make annual migrations across the river in immense herds. In winter they are generally absent with their sledges, visiting and trading with the wandering Chukchi going with merchandise to the great annual fair at Kolima.[4] The reindeer is their calendar.

The Giliak of the Tymy collect immense stores of frozen fish, not only as food for themselves and their dogs during winter, but also as an object of trade with the Aino, Orochon, and Giliak of the coast and mainland, and the Mangun of the Amur. The Aino bring to the valley of the Tymy at stated seasons Japanese goods, the Orochon furs, the others copper, seals, Russian and Manchu merchandise.[5]

[1] Davis, "Spanish Conquest of New Mexico," p. 105.
[2] Roger Williams, Coll. R. I. Hist. Soc., I, p. 67.
[3] Hart, "Animals of the Bible," London, 1888, p. 91.
[4] Kennan, "Tent Life in Siberia," p. 288.
[5] Ravenstein, "Russians on the Amur," London, 1861, p. 271.

Hooper says that the Tuski exchange skins of the reindeer and a small portion of the meat for sealskins, whale, walrus and seal's flesh, tusks, sinews, etc., all of which are much less valuable than their own commodities. Sealskins they need for marine employments, as those of the reindeer are destroyed by salt water; the aliens require deerskins for hut furniture.[1]

A company of hunters in 1646 sailed down the Kolima River to the Polar Sea. East of the Kolima they fell in with the Chukchi, with whom they dealt in this way: They laid down their goods on the beach and then retired, on which the Chukchi came thither, took the goods, and laid furs, walrus tusks, or carvings in walrus ivory, in their place.

Herodotus already states in Book IV, chapter 196, that the Carthagenians bartered goods in the same way with a tribe living on the coast of Africa, beyond the gates of Hercules. The same mode of barter or commerce by deposit was still in use nearly two thousand years later, when the west coast of Africa was visited by the Venetian, Cadamosto, in 1454.[2]

Hooper saw in the hands of an Eskimo at Barter Island an example of the knife called "dague," obtained from Hudson Bay Company's Indians.[3]

Since the beginning of our century European fleets have visited the west shore of Baffin Bay and Davis Strait, and thus manufactures from that country have found their way to the inhospitable shores of the Arctic Sea. The most valuable articles which were bartered were metals and wood. The value of the former may be seen in its economical application for knives and harpoon heads.[4]

The ordinary trade of the Eskimo is purely primitive, people going to the sources to procure the commodity. But Murdoch tells of a company of more southern natives who brought a boat load of skins of the bearded seal to Point Barrow for sale, to be used to cover Umiaks.[5]

The very simplest form of commerce on the western continent does not seem to have been in the hands of peddlers; but certain necessary articles like salt and other minerals existed in mines or quarries situated inside the boundaries of certain tribes. The owner did not dig the material and carry it about to sell or exchange it, but the people who wanted the article had to go after it and pay some kind of tribute for the privilege. Thus, the Tanos held the veins of turquoise or kalaite at Cerillos. The Teguas, Piros, and Zuñis were settled near salt marshes. The Queres of San Felipe had in front of their village large veins of mineral paint, for adorning pottery.

According to Bandelier, in 1540, the Pecos Indians came to Zuñi

---

[1] Hooper, "Tents of the Tuski;" London, 1853, p. 35.

[2] Ramusio, "Navigationi et Viaggi," I, 1588, leaf 100; Nordenskiöld, "Voyage of the Vega," New York, 1882, p. 453.

[3] "Tents of the Tuski," London, 1853, p. 257.

[4] Sixth Ann. Rep. Bureau of Ethnology, p. 466.

[5] Ninth Ann. Rep. Bureau of Ethnology, pp. 44-55.

with buffalo hides. The people of Acoma exchanged cotton mantles against deerskin with the Navajo; the Utes traded at Taos; the Apaches of the Plains came to Pecos with buffalo robes. The Pecos people did not allow the Apache to enter their village. They even kept a watch with trumpets.[1]

The Wyandots bartered the surplus of their maize fields to surrounding tribes, receiving fish in exchange. The Jesuits styled their country (Lower Canada) the granary of the Algonquian.[2]

As evidence of traffic in the mound-building period, Professor Putnam instances finding obsidian knives. Now this material belongs stratigraphically in the Yellowstone Park or in the Colorado Valley or in Mexico. He found also mica from North Carolina, gold, silver, meteoric iron, alligator's teeth, and shells from the Gulf of Mexico.

The trade between Ottawa River and Hudson Bay is mentioned by the Jesuits.[3]

"Among themselves they trade their Corne, Skins, Coates, Venison, Fish, and sometimes come ten or twenty in a company to trade amongst the English. They have some who follow onely making of Bowes, some Arrowes, some Dishes (the women make all their Earthen vessells) some follow fishing, some hunting, most on the seaside make money and Store up shells in Summer against Winter whereof to make money."[4]

Breckenridge remarks that the Louisiana nations have considerable trade or traffic with each other. The Sioux have for this purpose regular fairs or assemblages at stated periods. The same thing prevails with the nations on the southwest side of the Missouri. Those toward the south have generally vast numbers of horses, mules, and asses, which they obtain in trade, or war, from the Spaniards or nations immediately bordering on New Mexico. These animals are chiefly transferred to the nations northeast of the river by such of the southern tribes as happen to be on good terms with them, who obtain in exchange European articles, procured from the British traders. Their stock of horses requires to be constantly renewed by thefts or purchases. From the severity of the climate and the little care taken of the foals, the animal would otherwise be in danger of becoming extinct. Their mode of trading with each other is perfectly primitive. There is no bargaining or dispute about price. A nation or tribe comes to a village, encamps near it, and, after demonstrations of a thousand barbarous civilities on both sides, as sincere as those which are the result of refinement, one of the parties makes a general present of all such articles as it can con-

---

[1] Archæol. Inst. Am. (Am. Series), III, 1890, p. 164, quoting Espejo and Castañeda.

[2] Parkman, "History of the Conspiracy of Pontiac," etc., Boston, 1891, I, p. 23, referring to Mercier, "Relation des Hurons," 1637, p. 171. Also F. J. Turner, Johns Hopkins University Studies in Historical and Political Science, Series 9, Nos. XI–XII.

[3] "Relations des Jesuites," 1640, Tome I, 34. "Ceux-cy ont au Nord les Timiscimi, les Outimagami, les Onachegami, les Mitchitamou, les Ontnrbi, les Kiristinon qui habitent sur les rinves de la mer du Nord où les Nipisiriniens vont en marchandise."

[4] Roger Williams, Coll. R. I. Hist. Soc., I, p. 133.

veniently spare. The other a short time after makes in return a similar present. The fair is then concluded by a variety of games, sports, and dances. They hold the mode of trading by the whites in great contempt. They say it displays a narrow and contemptible soul to be weighing and counting every trifle. The price is usually fixed by the chief and his council, and the nation as well as traders must submit.[1]

The Crows annually visit the Mandans, Minnetarees, and Ahwahha ways, to whom they barter horses, mules, leather lodges, and many articles of Indian apparel, for which they receive in return guns, ammunition, axes, kettles, awls, and other European manufactures. When they return to their country they are in turn visited by the Paunch and Snake Indians, to whom they barter most of the articles they have obtained from the nations on the Missouri for horses and mules, of which those nations, i. e., the Paunch and Snake, have a greater abundance than themselves. They also obtain of the Snake Indians bridle-bits and blankets and some other articles which those Indians purchase from the Spaniards. The bridle-bits I have seen in the possession of the Mandans and Minnetarees.[2]

In the volumes of Lewis and Clark the Arikaree are described as middle men. Being agriculturists, their corn, beans, and other products enabled them to procure peltry from other tribes and to exchange these with the white traders for goods. The Arikaree are described as willing to give anything they had to spare for the most trifling article. One of the men gave an Indian a hook made out of a pin, and received in return a pair of moccasins.[3]

The buffalo is procured by the Skilloot from the nations higher up the river, who occasionally visit the Missouri; indeed, the greater proportion of their apparel is brought by the nations to the northwest, who come to trade for pounded fish, copper, and beads.[4]

The Chilkats and Chilkoots will not allow the inland tribes to approach the coast with their furs, but insist on acting as middlemen between them and the white traders. For this reason they assure themselves whether or not anyone comes to trade with these inland tribes.[5]

Among the coast Indians north of Puget Sound there are in each tribe officers who keep record of the mutual debts of individuals—a kind of public ledger. The astonishing thing is the fact that these men hold the accounts in their memories. There is also a fixed rule about interest—that is, the amount of property that must be returned for a gift or a loan.

The Makahs, from their peculiar locality, have been for many years

---

[1] Brackenridge, "Views of Louisiana." 1811, p. 71.

[2] "History of the Expedition under the command of Lewis and Clark, 1804-1806," New York, 1893, I, p. 198, quoting from Lewis's "Statistical View," London, 1807, p. 25.

[3] Ibid., I, p. 164.

[4] Ibid., III, p. 957.

[5] H. W. Seton-Karr, Proc. Roy. Geog. Soc., London, 1891, XIII, p. 82.

the medium of conducting the traffic between the Columbia River and coast tribes south of Cape Flattery, and the Indians north as far as Nootka. They are emphatically a trading as well as a producing people; and in these respects are far superior to the Clallams and other tribes on Fuca Strait and Puget Sound. Before the white men came to this part of the country, and when the Indian population on the Pacific Coast had not been reduced in numbers, as it has been of late years, they traded largely with the Chinook at the mouth of the Columbia, making excursions as far as the Kwinaiult tribe at Point Greuville, where they met the Chinook traders, and some of the more venturesome would even continue on to the Columbia, passing through the Chehalis country at Grays Harbor and Shoalwater Bay. The Chinook and Chihalis would in like manner come north as far as Cape Flattery; and these trading excursions were kept up pretty regularly, with only the interruption of occasional feuds.[1]

All the tribes living on Puget Sound sold strings of dried clams and oysters to the interior tribes. The Haida went down to Vancouver Island every winter and dried these mollusks to carry home and use in barter.

It was their custom to catch and dry not only enough for their own use, but also a vast quantity for the purpose of trade with the inland and mountain tribes. Every fall they loaded their canoes with dried salmon and sturgeon and quantities of hiaquas and went to the Cascades (the rapids of the Columbia River, about 150 miles from its mouth), where they met the Indians from the mountains and plains and bartered their dried fish and hiaquas for slaves and for the skins and meat of the buffalo. They used the buffalo skins for making their summer wigwams and their winter clothing and beds. The gray seal, beaver, and otter were abundant in and about the mouth of the Columbia and its tributaries; and bear, panther, elk, and deer roamed the forests at will, but the Chinook were fishermen, not hunters, and killed only enough of the land game to partially supply them with meat and skins.

In olden times the Chinook dealt very largely in slaves. Trading as they did with the inland Indians—who were much of the time at war with each other, and, making slaves of their prisoners, desired a market that would take these slaves as far as possible from their native country—the Chinook had a fine opportunity to purchase and bring these slaves to the coast These they sold to the tribes both north and south, realizing a handsome profit, and becoming the wealthiest nation in all that part of the country.[2]

On account of the demand for animal products, commerce extended in the Southwest over much greater expanses than might be supposed. Iridescent shells from the Gulf of California found their way to Zuñi through Sonora and the Colorado peoples. The Hova, who dwelt in

---

[1] Swan, "Indians of Cape Flattery," Washington, 1869, pp. 30-32.

[2] Strong, "Wah kee nah and Her People," New York, 1893, Putnam, pp. 126-127.

Sonora and Chihuahua, exchanged the feathers of the large green parrot for greenstone. At Casas Grandes, Bandelier saw turquoises, shell beads, and marine snails; among the latter, species found only in the West Indies or in the Gulf of California; among others, *Turritella broderipiana* from the Pacific, *Conus proteus* from the West Indies, and *Conus regularis* from the west coast of Mexico.[1]

"The possession of turquoise in the small range of mountains called Cerillos gave the Tanos Indians, of Galisteo Basin, a prominent position among their neighbors. The Zuñi enjoy similar privileges, which cause their modest relations of commerce to extend as far as the interior of Sonora and the Colorado of the West."[2]

When Marcos de Niza was thirty days' journey from Cibola he talked with Indians who had been there. "Upon being asked why they had traveled so far from home, they answered that they were going in search of turquoises, hides of cattle, and other things; * * * that they were in the habit of going into the first cities of the province and serving the inhabitants by tilling the soil and in other occupations, for which they received in exchange hides and turquoises."[3]

The first President of Mexico had in his employ a Tejos Indian, the son of a merchant engaged in trading, in the interior of the country, bird feathers, to be made into plumes, for gold and silver. This Indian said he had made two trips with his father to Cibola.[4] This connects the city of Mexico with Zuñi.

Bandelier speaks of the civilized tribes of Central Granada, who carried their salt over the beaten mountain paths to the cannibal inhabitants of the Cauca Valley and received gold in exchange for it.[5]

The most precious commodity among the Muysca was salt. In white cakes, like sugar loaves, it was carried over beaten paths from Bogota west to the river Cauca, and north from tribe to tribe down the Magdalena for a distance of 100 leagues. Regular markets were maintained, even in hostile territories, and the Muysca received in exchange for their goods, gold, of which they were destitute and which their neighbors had in abundance.[6]

Each tribe of British Guiana has some manufacture peculiar to itself, and its members constantly visit the other tribes, often hostile, for the purpose of exchanging the products of their own labor for such as are produced only by the other tribes. These trading Indians are allowed to pass unmolested through the enemy's country. When living among the Macusi, I was often amused by a number of those Indians rushing into my house, in the walls of which we had had windows pierced, who, with bated breath, half in joy, half in terror, used to point through the

[1] Bandelier, Archæol. Inst. Am. (Am. Series), III, p. 39.
[2] Ibid., p. 36.
[3] Davis, "Spanish Conquest of New Mexico," p. 123.
[4] Ibid., p. 113.
[5] "The Gilded Man," New York, 1893, p. 6.
[6] Ibid.

window to some party of their enemies, the Arecunas, coming with cotton balls and blow pipes for exchange. It is these traders who carry with them the latest news.[1]

8. *Money and its predecessors.*—The collection of primitive money in the U. S. National Museum includes those objects that among savages are prized not only for their intrinsic qualities, but because they afford fixed standards of wealth and media for the exchange of other commodities as they have been transported from tribe to tribe.

1. Shells, different species in different localities.
2. Disks of shell, that is manufactured money.
3. Feathers, in tufts or made up into standard ornaments.
4. Blankets, skins, and robes.
5. Cut stone.

Long-distance carrying and multiplied handlings, added to the cost of production, created money, and thus the things to be handled and carried were so greatly increased in number by the demand for them that the ultimate price was lowered by the transportation.

The original treasure of the Pueblo Indian consisted of shell beads, green stones, and of objects of worship. Many a good horse is still purchased from the Navajo by means of turquoises alone. Bandelier also refers to the exchange of turquoises for parrots' plumes, quoting Cabeça de Vaca.[2]

The Samoan women manufactured fine mats from "the leaves of a species of hibiscus, scraped clean and thin as writing paper and slit into strips about the sixteenth of an inch wide. When completed they were from 2 to 3 yards square. Few of the women can make them, and many months, yea, years, are sometimes spent over the plaiting of a single mat. These fine mats are considered the most valuable property, and form a sort of currency which they give and receive in exchange. They are preserved with great care. Some of them pass down in a family through several generations, and as their age and historic value increase they are all the more prized."[3]

9. *Markets, bazaars, and fairs.*—In a museum such things exist in pictures, photographs, and descriptions. In reality the market, the bazaar, and the fair are organized and temporary gatherings of merchants and buyers agreed upon for certain hours, months, or years for the purposes of exchange.

They become more and more world embracing. Primitively they are known to have existed on each of the continents and to have furnished temporary political and industrial centers of great stimulus. In all the epochs of culture few stimuli to universal travel have been greater. They are in the same class with convocations, anniversaries, and public fêtes. But they involve carrying no less than travel. In a paper now

---

[1] in Thurn, "Indians of British Guiana," London, 1883, p. 271.
[2] Bandelier, Archæol. Inst. Am. (Am. Series), III, 1890, p. 213.
[3] Turner, "Samoa a Hundred Years ago and Long Before," London, 1884, p. 120.

being prepared on American Aboriginal Industries a list of trade centers on the Western Continent will be given.

10. *Amnesty and laws of travel.*—Finally, there do not seem to have been anywhere in the world tribes of savages living contiguous that did not grant special amnesty to travelers and carriers and traders. From these agreements have sprung international law, the latest word in the comity of nations.

In the development of the rudiments of international law, the establishment of treaties, and agreements concerning amnesty the trader or mercator must have been a largely ruling motive. International law was and is largely evoked by the exigencies of trade movements.

"If any robbery fall out in travell, between persons of diverse States, the offended State sends for Justice. If no Justice be granted and recompence made, they grant out a kind of Letter of Mart to take satisfaction themselves, yet they are carefull not to exceed in taking from others, beyond the proportion of their own losse."[1] There is no doubt of trade amnesty and the law of reprisals, but it is questionable whether the old rule was not interpreted as elsewhere to mean "an eye for an eye," etc., or even more than that.

Cabeça de Vaca remained among the Charruco Indians six years (1528–1533), dressing like a savage. He traveled as a peddler from tribe to tribe over many hundreds of square miles. This was said to be convenient to the Indians because they could not traffic in time of war. Into the interior Cabeça carried sea snails and their corn, medicine, sea beads, etc., and brought back skins, ocher, flint, cement, arrow shafts, tassels of deerskin, ornamented and dyed red. He was treated kindly everywhere, the Indians trading food for wares. He became a person of great importance and was much sought after.[2]

As intimated more than once in this paper, travel and transportation by land pass in their elaboration from man power to the forces of physical nature through the epoch of beast power, and it will be in order, in a subsequent paper, to study out the rude appliances and methods of primitive peoples in their first employment of domestic creatures to carry them on their backs, to haul them in some sort of conveyance, or to draw loads for them.

There are a number of elements which enter into the organization of traveling on foot which pass into more definite forms as soon as beasts take the place of men in the labors here considered, such, for instance, are roads, bridges, harness, and others, which it will be necessary to consider or to investigate with much greater care in the study which follows.

It is also more than once mentioned that the two great phases of carrying were by land and by water. It will be in order, therefore, to follow this paper with a second one, in which should be studied out the

[1] Roger Williams, Coll. R. I. Hist. Soc., I, p. 77.
[2] Davis, "Spanish Conquest of New Mexico," Doylestown, 1869, p. 58.

inventions of the lower races of men pertaining to the use of water as a means of traveling or moving burdens. The first devices of this kind were simply floats for bearing up the human body or some sort of load, in order to move it across still water. Many substances were employed in this capacity, such as very light wood, the hollow stems of plants, the skins of animals inflated, and vessels of pottery. The second step in the elaboration of water conveyance was that in which some kind of displacement took the place of mere flotation. As soon as means were found to direct the course of a floating body, the ship was in progress of invention.

Among primitive forms for navigation the earliest represent the efforts of the human mind to devise the rudder, the fixed keel, the shifting sail, and means for storing up provisions for a long journey. As soon as these were achieved, savagery changed to barbarism or civilization, and the limits of this study were fixed.